JEFFERSON COUNTRY

JEFFERSON COUNTRY

A STORY OF LOVE AND REVOLUTION
IN THE ONCOMING AGE OF AQUARIUS

L. T. KUHLMAN

Commonwealth Books of Virginia, LLC
Boothbay Harbor, Maine
703-307-7715
www.commonwealthbooks.org
e-mail: info@commonwealthbooks.org
www.jeffersoncountry.net

Library of Congress Control Number: 2021948382

ISBN (paperback): 978-1-943642-56-4
ISBN (ebook): 978-1-943642-57-1

Cover and text design and composition
by Mayfly Design

Cover Icon Image
Du Temple de Jupiter Tonant, Rome
Les Edifices Antiques de Rome
Antoine Desgodetz
Printed for I. and J. Taylor
at the Architectural Library
Holborn, London
1795
Vol II. Plate l. 135.

Monticello, Thomas Jefferson's Home
Virginia, Charlottesville
Omniphoto/UIG
Bridgeman Images

ᨈ

A POEM FOR THE ENLIGHTENMENT

Greek logic could never explain
The problem of stasis and change,
So the sage proved the notion
That laws govern motion.
Thus enlightened, the world rearranged.

—William Adcock: *The Bodleian Review*; Oxford, May, 1728
On the occasion of the first anniversary of Isaac Newton's death

ᨈ

A POEM FOR THE ENDARKENMENT

Nature's truths Newton's System reflected.
But in Utopia, his laws are rejected.
For the only rule there
That applies everywhere
Is: society must be perfected.

—Henry Tilghman: *Rapier Magazine*; Charlottesville, May 1970
Woodstock Edition

FOREWORD

Natural Laws govern Man in Nature and Man in Society. In the state of Nature, a man has the natural right to preserve himself by all means. This is the law of self-preservation. In the state of Society, Nature dictates that as the cell grows, it divides. This is the law of perpetual social conflict.

The conflicts generated by these immutable laws are never more intense than during periods of generational change. This is so because, during this recurring process, existing populations are replaced by new ones that have new people with new visions of the common good.

The generational change that began in the third quarter of the 20th century was further disturbed by one of Nature's rarest phenomena, being the transition from one celestial age to another. This was the end time prophesied by the ancients. The transit that began then was the dawning of the Age of Aquarius.

Before this fabled passage can occur, so the ancients said, Gaia, daughter of Chaos, must be cleansed. In these pages, I tell the tale of the Anti-Christ, the instrument of this cleansing, and the devastation he causes fulfilling the prophecy. This cosmic strife will produce, some believe, a perfect world. Tertium Datur!

The impending birth of the new cosmic age is announced in a message sent from the beyond so all will know that its perfections are at hand. This message is contained in the pictogram on the body of the young woman who sits in the vortex of the cataclysm.

The stars bring Claire Fox (beautiful and ambitious reporter at *The Washington Post*) together with Henry Tilghman (bright and handsome secretary to Raymond Paige) to decipher this cosmic message. Claire and Henry find themselves in a deepening personal relationship as they pursue their celestial mission. To accomplish it, they must solve the cultish murder of Roberta Wiley. Wiley is the director of publicity at the Jefferson Academy in Keswick, Virginia. Before her shocking demise, she transformed the Jefferson Academy into a national platform its founder, Mr. Paige, could use to launch his candidacy for the presidency. Paige is the one man in America who can stop the insurgencies that are threatening to destroy the country he loves. But he is surrounded by agents of the Endarkenment who will stop at nothing to reach their celestial destination.

To decipher the pictogram and prevent a cosmic catastrophe, Claire and Henry discover that they must unlock the secret of the frieze on Thomas Jefferson's mantle. Time is running out! Where is Fred Ried?

L.T. Kuhlman
Somewhere Safe
July 2021

PLOT SUMMARIES

A love relationship between Henry and Claire develops through six inter-aggravating conflicts:

I. Roberta Wiley's Murder:

Roberta Wiley, public relations director for the Jefferson Academy, was responsible for arranging travel plans for Nelson Rockefeller, Barbara Tuchman, Barry Commoner, and the other honored guests of the Jefferson Academy's first National Issues Conference.

The morning the conference is to begin, Henry Tilghman finds her meditating on the dock at a lake on the Jefferson's Academy's grounds outside Charlottesville, Virginia. When he attempts to confront her, Henry finds that Roberta is dead. Strangled! Stunned, he copies the strange pictogram on her body—perhaps it will help him determine who murdered her. When he reports his discovery to his boss, Raymond Paige, Mr. Paige persuades him to alter the story. By doing this, he protects the Jefferson Academy and its history-making conference, but he also makes himself the primary suspect in Roberta's bizarre murder.

Henry's situation drastically deteriorates when Claire Fox arrives. Claire's boss (and lover) is left-wing media mogul Martin Ogden, publisher of *The Washington Post*. Ogden has sent his aspiring protégé to determine whether Paige is planning to run for President—and to help him sabotage Paige's prospects. Paige avoids the trap by handing Claire over to his aide. Now it is up to Henry to keep this beautiful enemy agent from discovering the weird circumstances surrounding Roberta's murder.

It takes no time for Claire to discover Henry's secrets, and his doom seems certain. Ironically, it is Martin Ogden who saves him. Ogden does this by proving to Claire what everyone else already knows—he is a manipulative bastard. Cut suddenly adrift, Claire begins working with Henry to determine the significance of the ox skull emblem on Roberta's body. It is the same as the one in the frieze on Thomas Jefferson's mantle! What does *Tertium Datur* mean? And what is the connection between Thomas Jefferson, Tim Hardin, and his Aquarian Revolution? As Claire and Henry pursue the hidden truth, she understands that it is not just Henry Tilghman's life that hangs in the balance. So do the fate of the nation and all social order!

II. Raymond Paige's Undeclared Presidential Campaign:

Raymond Paige is one of the most illustrious graduates of the University of Virginia's prestigious Law School. He completed his degree in time to join Naval Intelligence and serve at the end of World War Two. When the war was over, he moved to Wall Street where he was a partner at Lehman Brothers. After two decades of investment banking, during which he substantially enlarged his family's vast fortune, he retired to an estate near the home of Thomas Jefferson.

For the next seven years, Paige was content breeding prize-winning Angus cattle. But by 1974, he was tired of gentleman farming. That was when he answered an inner call and founded the Jefferson Academy. His planned to reinvigorate the nation his grandfather helped transform into the greatest in the world. Like his grandfather a century before, Paige intended to raise the American flag and lead the charge. The fate of a divided nation again hung in the balance. This time, however, the charge would not be made by the Army of the Potomac against entrenched Confederates. Raymond Paige would deploy the forces of Faith and Reason to defend the Common Good against the Anti-Christ and his fiendish agents.

III. Tim Hardin's Aquarian Revolution:

Tim Hardin, founder and director of the Committee for an Open Society, is the leader of an emerging new society the press calls "Woodstock Nation". Hardin's mission is to abolish the government instituted by America's Founding Fathers and replace it with the egalitarian system Thomas Jefferson framed in his long-lost constitution. The cognoscenti in Hardin's inner circle, know this document as "Burr's Unicorn".

Glib, self-assured, and charismatic, Hardin is the darling of America's media whose far-seeing visionaries are heralds of the time when all will be equal and care for one another. Hardin had prepared himself to create this pleasure garden reading Sociology at Columbia University. His doctoral dissertation, "The Cultural Barriers to an Open Society", allows him to speak persuasively about leveling society through redistribution of the nation's wealth. To accomplish this humanitarian objective, Hardin must retrieve Burr's Unicorn. Before vanishing into thin air, Hardin's mercurial lieutenant, Fred Ried, reportedly sent the document back to Thomas Jefferson!

IV. Frances Rank's Women People's Revolution:

Frances Rank, President the United Women-People of the Earth, is leading the daughters of Gaia to sever all bonds with man-society. Her objective is to establish a new Woman-nation under the constitution written by Jefferson's enslaved mulatto sister-in-law, Sally Hemings. Her senior aide in this crusade is Ashanti Shoate', Professor of Black History at the University of Virginia and the world's foremost authority on Jefferson's enslaved concubine.

Rank has chosen the opening ceremony of the Jefferson Academy's issues conference to declare the independence of women-people from man-society and to demand reparations for the injustice suffered by women-people since Atlantis sank into the sea. Not only will women-people be free from the covenants of man-society, Rank vows they will also cease to obey the Law of the Excluded Middle. Tertium Datur!

V. William O. Douglas's Communitarian Revolution:

William O. Douglas, Associate Justice of the United States Supreme Court, has labored four decades to manufacture a society he prefers. His partner in this murky private utilitarian rebellion is Martin Ogden, hierarch and elitist publisher of *The Washington Post*. Douglas has conducted his revolution from the cloistered chambers of the nation's highest court. Ogden has supported it in the pages of his influential newspaper and in the Georgetown salons where the nation's intelligentsia commune. What is it these two self-sequestering giants are rebelling against? Privilege!

It is now September 1975, and Douglas is preparing to retire. Through the untiring efforts of Ogden and his allies in the press, the American people have been conditioned to reject the predatory property system Alexander Hamilton instituted at the birth of the nation. Douglas will soon present its communitarian replacement, which he has gleaned through years studying the writings of "The Father of Human Rights", Thomas Jefferson. As he prepares for the final victory, Douglas is stunned to learn that his protégé, Tim Hardin, plans to unveil a plan that will destroy everything he has devoted his life to accomplish.

VI. The Battle for Fred Ried's Albemarle Green Marijuana

Fred Ried is an alumnus of the conservation camp William O. Douglas directed in the Cascade Mountains of Washington in the early-1960s. That is where he met Tim Hardin and Bo Bildner. He and Bildner went on to serve with distinction in Vietnam War, where they developed valuable skills destroying things. Since then, Ried has learned how to crossbreed the marijuana plants he brought back from Indochina with coca plants he retrieved from the Andes Mountains of Peru. A crew of entrepreneurial counter-culturals is now harvesting his first full crop. It will be worth a fortune in Woodstock Nation. More valuable still are the Albemarle Green seeds. Paige's son is plotting to get them. Is Aster Paige's weird companion his real competition?

———————

The story in this book and its portrait of Thomas Jefferson rest on information found in two long-lost documents, which the author has taken the liberty to create. The first is the journal of Jefferson's confidant, Baron Frederick de Riedesel, which passed down to his great-great-great-great-grandson, Fred Ried. Through Ried's association with agents of the revolutions described above, Jefferson's radical theories on Property, Natural Right, and the Common Good became important forces of change during the birthing of the Aquarian Age. American history, and our understanding of Jefferson's place in it, are further enriched by Professor Ashanti Shoate's discovery of the diary of Sally Hemings. This long-lost document reveals how, through instructions Jefferson received from his beautiful and brilliant slave, he was able to master the progressive doctrines of the French Revolution and become "the Universal Man" acclaimed by the citizens of the enlightened world.

Disclaimer: Passages in this text reflect material found in William O. Douglas's *Of Men and Mountains*, Archibald Cox's *The Court and the Constitution*, "The Inaugural poem" of Mia Angelou, the Books of *Daniel* and *Revelations* as rendered in the King James version of the *Bible*, and material from the following websites: Astrology in the Age of Aquarius (www.foturnecity.com), AstologyNow – the Dawning of . . . (www.astrologynow.com), Edgar Cayce On . . . (edgarcayce.org), Has the Age of Aquarius Arrived (www.accessnewage.com), How do I interpret a horoscope (www.ephem.net), New Age Spirituality (www.religioustolerance.org), The Coming of the New Age (www.greatdreams.com).

The conflicts that comprise the story told in this book are based on the interpretation of news and events the author encountered while researching and writing this work. Several historical figures are characters in this book. Any resemblance between its other characters and real persons is strictly coincidental.

LEAD CHARACTERS

HENRY TILGHMAN

CLAIRE FOX

RAYMOND PAIGE

MARTIN OGDEN

WILLIAM O. DOUGLAS

WOMEN PEOPLE

ASTER PAIGE

ASHANTI SHOATE

FRANCES RANK

GERTA BIEDERMAN

PICTURE CREDITS

ASTER PAIGE

BY JAMES THOMPSON

ASHANTI SHOATE
FRANCES RANK
GERTA BIEDERMAN
MARJEAN

DRAWN BY ROXANNE TARLOWE

MARJEAN

OTHER NOTABLE CHARACTERS

TIM HARDIN

DELILAH WANAMAKER

BART PAIGE

SUZIE

PICTURE CREDITS

TIM HARDIN
DELILAH WANAMAKER
BART PAIGE

BY JAMES THOMPSON

SUZIE

DRAWN BY ROXANNE TARLOWE

CHARACTERS LIST

MAIN CHARACTERS

Tilghman, Henry — Aide to Mr. Paige at the Jefferson Academy; Protégé of Oscar Denker; Framed in the murder of Roberta Wiley; Lover of Claire Fox; Henry and Claire rescue de Riedesel's journal; They then solve the mystery of the frieze on Jefferson's mantle and save the world.

Fox, Claire — *Washington Post* reporter; Author of its frontpage article about the Jefferson Academy's issues conference; Martin Ogden's lover; Assigned by Ogden to dig up information about Raymond Paige and the Jefferson Academy; Guided by the stars into a love relationship with Henry Tilghman.

Paige, Raymond Wallace, III — Grandson of Sgt. Raymond Paige; Wealthy founder of the Jefferson Academy in Charlottesville, Virginia; Admirer of Thomas Jefferson and individual initiative; Defender of the American way; Presidential candidate; Employer of Henry Tilghman and Roberta Wiley; Parent of Aster and Bart.

Denker, Oscar — Director of the Jefferson Academy; Friend of Mr. Paige; mentor to Henry Tilghman; Formerly Professor of Economics at the University of Virginia.

Somerville, Fenton — Curator of Monticello; Leading white male expert on Thomas Jefferson; Steward of the newly discovered correspondence between Thomas Jefferson and Baron de Riedesel; Recruiter of Henry Tilghman to translate the Jefferson–Reidesel correspondence; Advisor to Mr. Paige.

Hoagland, Ted — District Attorney for Charlottesville, Virginia; Fix-it-man for Raymond Paige

Prout, Jim	PhD in Philosophy; Expert on B.F. Skinner's Linguistic Behaviourism; Fellow at the Hoover Institution; Bartender at the Boar's Head Inn; Ex-Marine; Friend of Henry Tilghman.
Wanamaker, Delilah	Professor of Legal Ethics at the University of Virginia's Law School: Jim Prout's companion.
Dudley, Trip	Friend of Henry Tilghman; Emergency Room physician at the University of Virginia Hospital; Attending physician for Oscar Denker.
Rank, Frances	Leader of the Women People's movement; Commander of the Women People's revolutionary army; Author of the constitution for the new state of Women People; Follower of Gaia; Guest of Aster Paige.
Shoate', Prof. Ashanti	First Professor of Afro-American Studies at the University of Virginia; Foremost black female authority on Thomas Jefferson; Discoverer of Sally Hemings personal diary; Author of the Carquest Award winning book *Sister Slave*; Sister in the communitarian society of Women People; Friend and advisor to Frances Rank.
Marjean, Madam Marja	Companion of Aster Paige; Man-hating feminist; Advocate for a society of "women people'; Versed in the mysteries of the cosmos; Medium for Gaia, protectress of women people.
Paige, Aster	Daughter of Raymond Paige; Poetess; Companion of Marjean; Member of Roberta Rank's political movement; Star child.
Biederman, Gerta	Companion and financial supporter of Tim Hardin; Sister in the community of Women People.
Ogden, Martin	Publisher of *The Washington Post*; Long-time comrade of William O. Douglas; Douglas's comrade in the communitarian social reform movement; Behind-the-scenes supporter of Tim Hardin and his confrontational methods; Secret enemy of Raymond Paige, Claire Fox's boss and lover.
Douglas, William O.	Associate Justice of the United States Supreme Court; Communitarian social engineer; Comrade of Martin Ogden; Partisan.
Hardin, Tim	Founder and Director of the Committee for an Open Society; Radical social activist and urban revolutionary; Bent on dismantling the existing materialist system and implementing the communitarian

	state defined in Thomas Jefferson's long-lost constitution; Mastermind of the bombing of the Rotunda; Rebellious protege of W.O. Douglas.
Ried, Fred	Great-whatever grandson of Baron Frederick de Riedesel; Protege of William O. Douglas; Vietnam veteran; Demolitions expert; Drug impresario; Member of Tim Hardin's Comradeship of Guardians; Considered by some to be the long-awaited anti-Christ.
Bildner, Boswell	William O. Douglas's chauffeur; Member of the Fred Ried's drug ring.
Paige, Bart	Black sheep son of Raymond Paige; Manager of Mr. Paige's cattle breeding business; Caretaker of Aberon of Belmont; Drug entrepreneur; Hated enemy of Marjean and Frances Rank.
Suzie	Bart Paige's girlfriend.

OTHER CHARACTERS

Bailey, Sheriff George	Sheriff of Albemarle County; Red Neck.
Burr, Aaron	Onetime ally of Thomas Jefferson; Chosen by Jefferson to found a republican state in the West; recipient of a constitution written by Jefferson, subsequently known as "Burr's Unicorn," to serve as a plan for the government of this state.
Cabanis, Pierre	Friend of Thomas Jefferson; Member of Madame Helvetius's salon; Admirer of Sally Hemings.
Claude's Grandson	Leroy is Mr. Paige's chauffeur and butler.
Commoner, Barry	Panellist at the Jefferson Academy's issues conference; Spokesman for the environmental movement.
Condorcet, Marquis de	Friend of Thomas Jefferson; French intellectual and social engineer; Mentor to Sally Hemings.
Condorcet, Madame de	Wife of the Marquis de Condorcet; Social reformer and champion of the bonheur general; Admirer of Sally Hemings.
Cosway, Maria	Companion of Thomas Jefferson; Femme dangereuse.
Cox, Archibald	Guest speaker at the Jefferson Academy's Issues Conference; Former Watergate special prosecutor; Apologist for court activism; Friend of William O. Douglas and Martin Ogden.
Custer, Genl. George A.	Division commander US Cavalry under Genl. Phillip Sheridan.

Davis, Susan	Nurse at the University of Virginia Hospital.
Drucker, Peter	Panellist at the Jefferson Academy's Issue Conference; Advocate of economic liberalism.
Edgar, Sgt. Jethro	Aide to Genl. Phillip Sheridan; Mentor to Raymond Wallace Paige.
Edmond, George	Friend of Henry Tilghman; Graduate of the University of Virginia's Law School; Retained by Henry Tilghman after he discovers Roberta's tattooed body.
Epicurus	Classical hedonist; Inspiration to Thomas Jefferson.
Fisher, Huntley	Heiress; Proprietor of Rose Hill Farm; Member of Fred Ried's drug ring; Friend of Aster Paige and T.P. Wells.
Ford, Helen	Doctor at the University of Virginia Hospital; friend of Trip Dudley and Henry Tilghman.
Helvetius, Madame de	Wife of Claude Helvetius; Salon hostess; Advocate of perfecting society with the bonheur general; Friend of Benjamin Franklin and Thomas Jefferson.
Hemings, Sally	Disciple of Jean Jacques Rousseau; Protege of the Marquis de Condorcet; Tutor of Thomas Jefferson on the political philosophy of the French Enlightenment; Slave property of Thomas Jefferson; Half-sister of Jefferson's deceased wife.
Home, Prof. David	Professor of Philosophy at the University of Virginia; Oxford-educated academic tyrant; Henry's former instructor; admirer of Jim Prout.
Homer	Ancient poet and seer of truths.
Jefferson, Thomas	Founding father; Author of the Declaration of Independence; Enlightened sage; Friend and corresponding partner of Baron de Riedesel; Placed the mysterious ox skulls in his mantle frieze; Framer of the bon mot "tertium datur".
Lafayette, Marquis de	Idealist; Member of the duc de la Rochefoucauld's circle of social reformers; Friend of Thomas Jefferson.
Leibniz, Ludwig von	German rationalist philosopher; Source of inspiration for Baron de Riedesel.
McCray, Tad	Local director of Americans for Democratic Action; Member of Fred Ried's drug ring; Comrade of Tim Hardin and Boswell Bildner.
Meany, George	Former employee of Mr. Paige's father; President of the AFL-CIO.

Paige, Sgt. Raymond Wallace	Scotch immigrant; General Phillip Sheridan's batman; Hero of the battle of Five Forks in April 1864; Raymond Paige's grandfather and hero.
Paige, Mrs. Raymond Wallace	Prickly wife of Raymond Paige.
Paine, Tom	Friend of Thomas Jefferson; Disagrees with the Marquis de Condorcet on how to perfect society.
Perrault, Pericles	French tutor and suitor of Sally Hemings; Disciple of Jean Jacques Rousseau; Comrade of Jean-Paul Marat.
Riedesel, Baron Frederick de	Member of the general staff of Frederick the Great of Prussia; Member of the Prussian Commission for Military Preparedness; Pioneer in the use of organic substances to increase performance of military conscripts; Friend and confidante of Thomas Jefferson; Forebear of Baron Frederick de Riedesel and Fred Ried.
Riedesel, Baron Frederick de	Onetime owner of Belmont Farm; Builder of the resort Raymond Paige converted into the Jefferson Academy.
Rockefeller, V. Pres. Nelson	Friend of Mr. Paige; Guest speaker at the Jefferson Academy's issues conference.
Rousseau, Jean Jacques	French philosopher and social reformer; Source of inspiration for Pericles Perrault, Jean-Paul Marat, and other radicals in the Cordeliers District of Paris; Source of inspiration for Cabanis, Condorcet, and their fellow chateau reformers: Source of inspiration for Sally Hemings.
Sheridan, Genl. Phillip	Chosen by Genl. U.S. Grant to command the US Cavalry during the final year of the southern rebellion; Victorious commander of Union forces at the Battles of Cedar Creek and Five Forks; Source of inspiration for Sgt. Raymond Paige.
Skinner, B.F.	Social scientist; Developer and champion of the science of Behaviourism; Refuted by Dr. James Prout.
Thomas, Frank	Panellist at the Jefferson Academy's issues conference; President of the Ford Foundation; Advocate for economic justice for Blacks.
Troupe, Officer Ed	Officer in Albemarle County's Sheriff's Department.
Tuchman, Barbara	Moderator for the panel discussion at the Jefferson Academy's issues conference; Mentor to Claire Fox; Friend of Martin Ogden; Admirer of Thomas Jefferson and Raymond Paige.

JEFFERSON COUNTRY

≋

PART I

Henry knew it was Roberta by the tattoos on her naked back. She was sitting in the lotus position at the far end of the dock, facing east toward the sunrise. The sun had been up for an hour, but that wasn't the point.

She was supposed to be at the airport greeting Mr. Paige's guests. Henry called her name. When she didn't respond, he flushed with anger and stepped out onto the dock. She did not move in spite of the crack of his footsteps coming up behind her. He stood for a moment, waiting, then tapped her roughly on the shoulder. Her body tilted, then slumped forward and splashed into the lake. Henry watched it sink into the green water and, finally, settle among the algae on the bottom. He could still see the sign of Leo between her shoulder blades. Little by little the horror descended upon him. When he could no longer bear it, his knees buckled, and he collapsed onto the dock. For a long time, he lay there, numb, staring at Roberta's lifeless body.

Slowly he became aware of a sound. It was somewhere beyond the cloud that engulfed him. As he listened, it grew louder. Louder. He waited as it drew nearer. Then it was there—with him—the rasping, groaning sound of heavy breathing. He turned his head slowly. The dock was empty! He took another pain-filled breath, lowered his hands into the green water, and splashed his face. What was he going to do? Before the answer came to him, a strange force seized him and carried him to the edge of the dock. It pulled his hands down into the water and stretched his fingers toward the skull. He felt Roberta's cold lifeless flesh. A new tremor shot through him. "No!" He roared fighting to regain control of himself. "Don't touch her." In the next instant he was on his feet racing off the dock.

Henry pushed open his front door and went to the phone in the study. He picked up the receiver, steadied himself, then dialed Raymond Paige's private number. A gruff voice answered on the second ring, "Yea."

"Mr. Paige, this is Henry."

"Yea, Hank."

"Something has happened at the lake."

"What do you mean?" His employer demanded.

"Are you alone?" Henry asked tensely.

There was a pause on the other end followed by the muffled sound of a door shutting. A second later Mr. Paige was back, "What is it?"

"It's Roberta..."

"What about her?"

"She's in the lake."

There was another pause, "What the hell are you talking about?"

"Roberta is dead!"

"Drowned?" Mr. Paige asked, like a man sizing up a substantial wager.

"It's more complicated than that."

"What do you mean?"

"There are tattoos on her body."

There was another long silence. "What kind of tattoos?"

"... like in a Zodiac."

"Jesus!" The voice swore in helpless rage. Then a pensive question. "Have you talked with anybody else?"

"No." Henry sensed Mr. Paige's relief.

"Where are you now?"

"At my cottage."

"Is anybody with you?"

No."

"... Good. Here's what I want you to do. Go back up to the lake—you understand? Don't let anybody get close... I'll get some people up there and take care of it."

"All right."

The line went dead.

Henry hurried back to the lake. This time he did not notice the fragrance of the autumn grass or the color that was coming into the foliage. It felt better to look down. Shit! He chanted the word grimly in the cadence of his march.

When he reached the dock, he made an anxious survey of the surrounding fields. Nothing had changed. He stepped out onto the dock and sat down, careful to avoid the place where Roberta had been. In a moment, his eyes were fixed on the motionless body beneath him in the green water. As he watched it, the sound of Marjean's chanting crept into his brain. Once again, he felt the throbbing of Aster's drum. The strange figures began to appear on the body stretched out before him. What happened next? His mind went blank. The chanting stopped. How much time did he have? Twenty minutes? Thirty max. He would have to work fast.

He jerked to his feet and ripped off his coat. He stood for a moment contemplating his task, then he lowered himself down onto his stomach and sank his arms into the placid water. It was deeper than it looked. He could reach Roberta's arm, but he could not get a strong grip on it. He pinched it as hard as he could and pulled it gingerly toward him. His fingers slipped before the body moved. He tried again. And again. Each time Roberta resisted him. He was sweating now. He remembered the time and began to worry. Roberta's shrill laugh echoed in his ears. It would have amused her—to see him conquered by a corpse. Her corpse! The thought enraged him. "GODDAM YOU," he roared down into the water. The curse unleashed a terrifying power within him. He lunged at her and seized her with violent hands.

This time she submitted, emerging from her watery lair and settling obediently on the edge of the dock. He straightened up and breathed a relieved sigh. The sound of his heart beating knocked loudly in his ears. He noticed that his shirt was soaked with sweat. And that he was exhausted. For a moment he thought he might faint. He gulped down another mouthful of air and steadied himself. How much time did he have? He turned and picked up his jacket. The draft of Mr. Paige's address was in the inside pocket with his pen. He pulled them out. He turned back to the body as he opened the draft to its blank first page. That was when he noticed the lanyard cinched around Roberta's throat. An image of a ghoulish face flashed before him. The medallion! It was gone. He looked down into the murky water. There was no point looking for it in there.

He squinted at the form in front of him and carefully traced its outline on the page. Around it, on the edges of the paper, he reproduced the figures on the body. They were clustered on her breast, her thigh, her arm, her neck, her stomach, and her ankle. He stuffed the paper into his pocket and rolled the body over and resumed his work. When he finished, he checked his drawing. Satisfied that he had captured all the figures, Henry folded the diagram into the draft and slipped it back into his coat pocket. He looked around before lowering the body back into the water. When it was settled again in the algae, he rolled his sleeves down and pulled on his coat.

Henry turned his head in time to see the unmarked patrol car creeping over the crest of the hill. A shiver ran down his spine. There was no sound! He had expected sirens and flashing lights. Henry's muscles tensed and he began to feel queasy again. The cruiser glided to a stop in the hollow a short distance from the dock. Two men got out. One was heavy set and wore a brown uniform. The other wore a grey suit and a pink shirt. Henry recognized the uniformed man from a campaign poster he had seen at the gas station. It was Sheriff Bailey. The other man was Ted Hoagland, Charlottesville's District Attorney. He had finished law school and started a practice in Charlottesville while Henry was still an undergraduate. They had met a few times at Mr. Paige's office.

The sheriff gave Henry a hard look. "We'll take over now." He spoke without introduction. "You go about your business." Ted Hoagland watched Henry but said nothing. Henry stood there for another moment staring at the two men, "We'll handle this. You go on," the Sheriff repeated sharply, Henry turned stiffly and walked off the dock. As he passed in front of the two officials, he looked back at the dock! It was still wet! Bailey wasn't interested. He was waiting for Henry to follow his order. Henry quickened his pace. He looked back again before he descended the hill. It was their turn now. The two men were huddled on the end of the dock where he had been.

"Give 'em hell Roberta," he whispered.

Someone called Henry's name. Turning, he saw Leroy waving to him from the opened gate at the bottom of the hill. Henry moved toward him, reaching the opening a few steps ahead of the cruiser. He stepped aside and watched it float by. It motored silently through the gate and picked up speed as it moved up the gravel driveway. A second later it disappeared over the knoll. A dust cloud lingered in the air. Then it too was gone.

Leroy was Claude's grandson. He did most of the driving now. If he was there, then Mr. Paige was also nearby. Henry looked over Leroy's shoulder and saw Mr. Paige's Mercedes.

Leroy was excited. "Hurry up. He's waitin' for you." Leroy led the way to the car, shuffling a few steps ahead in an attempt to hurry Henry along. Leroy opened the door when Henry reached the car. Henry bent down and looked in. A wall of frigid air hit him in the face. Behind it sat Mr. Paige. His head turned slightly. His expression was blank—the way it would have been if he encountered a stranger in a public place. "Get in Hank." Leroy shut the door behind him. "Did everything go all right?"

"As far as I could tell . . ."

"Good." Paige did not ask so Henry did not elaborate. "I'm going to release a statement after lunch," Paige announced as he pulled a piece of folded paper from his breast pocket. He unfolded it and handed it to Henry. Henry read it.

We are deeply saddened to announce the drowning death of our valued associate, Roberta Wiley, while swimming with a friend yesterday evening in a lake on the Belmont Farm property. Her body was recovered this morning by county authorities. She is survived by her parents who reside in Danville, Virginia. In accordance with their wishes, the body will be cremated and flown to Danville for interment on Wednesday. In lieu of flowers the family requests contributions be sent to the Church of the Brethren's building fund in Danville.

"Who was she swimming with?" Henry asked obtusely.

"There will be an inquiry sometime next week," Mr. Paige said, ignoring the question. "If we handle it properly, there shouldn't be any problems." Mr. Paige looked at him hard. "I'm counting on you, Hank."

Henry stared back at him blankly. "You want me to say I was swimming with her?"

"That's the best way to do it, I think." Mr. Paige's voice was calm and reassuring.

Henry let the idea sink in. What was his alternative? Mr. Paige nodded thoughtfully. Maybe this would take care of everything. The tattoos. The lanyard. Marjean's weird ceremony. Mr. Paige continued to nod. Maybe it didn't matter what really happened to Roberta. Mr. Paige continued to nod. Wouldn't it be nice if it were that simple? Henry looked at Mr. Paige. For him it was. Was that the difference between them? Mr. Paige nodded silently. Henry raised his eyebrows in submission and handed the paper back. Mr. Paige stuffed it into his pocket. "I knew we would see it the same way," he said approvingly. "We can't allow this to interfere with our work." Paige fixed a penetrating look on Henry.

Now it was Henry's turn to nod.

That was the signal Mr. Paige had been waiting for. He motioned to Leroy. "Take the day off, Hank. Get settled. I'll send Leroy over for you tomorrow. We'll get back to work then."

Henry opened the door and climbed out. Mr. Paige called after him as he shut it. "Remember our mission."

Raymond Paige took Henry's call at 7:43AM Monday morning. Guest registration for the Jefferson Academy's inaugural Issues Conference was to begin in 107 minutes.

Nelson Rockefeller, the Vice President of the United States, had been his house guest over the weekend. Mr. Paige was having breakfast with him at 8:30. There was no choice but to proceed, and this he quickly resolved to do. But first he had to get the body off the premises. This would be the easy part. As for the rest, he would have to take his chances. As he dialed Ted Hoagland, he wondered if anything had transpired between Roberta and his guests. He clenched his teeth as if to crush the unsettling thought before it could affect his judgement.

Roberta had been on his staff for a little over a year. Before that she had worked on the Charlottesville newspaper. She'd met Mr. Paige's son Bart one night at a bar. Things went along, and he set her up in one of the tenant cottages on the Belmont estate. Eventually she met Mr. Paige. Her experience as a reporter seemed to be a good qualification for the public relations work he wanted done for the Jefferson Academy. She was aggressive. That seemed like an asset then. Now he wasn't so sure.

Mr. Paige had founded the Jefferson Academy in the summer of 1972. That was the first indication he had succumbed. By then, of course, it was an obsession among white American males of substantial means. Washington's thoroughfares were clogged with them—wealthy men eager to surrender themselves to public service. Once upon a time it had been noblesse oblige. Now the upper class was filled with grasping status seekers. Vulgar egotists. Merely being rich did not satisfy the soulful cravings that haunted these new men. Having everything was not enough. They wanted to be celebrated for it. They wanted to be admired by their peers. Old money was different. It kept its own council. Being admired by common people meant nothing. Old money had no commerce with common people. Old money looked across the past as it waited calmly on the future. Heraclitus knew it at the dawn of civilization. Those who held power coveted something more sublime. They wanted fame!

Mr. Paige was different. He was a man history would remember. The scion of a great industrial fortune amassed over one hundred years by his grandfather and increased by his father after that, he was a hereditary member of the American aristocracy, His life's journey had begun in the cloistered preserves of wealth. He had learned that his place was in front, in the company of society's most privileged. Leadership was neither an effort nor an experiment for him. It was a natural part of life. Like other great men, he had no complicating questions to ask himself, no ambiguous view of the world. He had no philosophical curiosity about life. No self-doubt. Decision making was therefore simple, and he handled the responsibility with ease.

Raymond Wallace Paige had come to Virginia from the Midwest via Exeter and Yale. His first exposure to the Old Dominion and the legacy of Thomas Jefferson had been as a law student at the University of Virginia. Like others from his social class, he had retired early to an estate in Jefferson's country after a successful career on Wall Street. Roberta seemed to understand that the Jefferson Academy was the vehicle the Fates had provided to carry him to his destiny. She had labored with selfish determination to entwine herself within it. The conference had been her idea. Paige liked it. It suited him to have the media transform him into a national figure. That was smart. It was the way he liked to work. It was September 1975. The presidential election was fourteen months away. And the media needed a story.

It was a troubled time. Vietnam had dealt America its first military defeat and caused its most promising generation to feel shame toward its country. Defeat projected boundaries on America's once limitless potential and created a void of national purpose that gave life to the destructive politics of special interests. Public confidence in its political institutions melted in the Watergate furnace. The nation's public servants, battered by public resentment, attacked each other like stray dogs fighting for scraps of respectability. Feelings of bitterness and distrust spread with each assault. It suited newsmen to fill their broadcasts with these character assassinations. Behind the cameras, the nation's industrial infrastructure rusted away, and Arab sheiks fixed a shadowy grip on it sputtering economy.

Mr. Paige often quoted his grandfather. The first Raymond Paige had made himself a national hero leading the charge that breached the Confederate line outside Petersburg that rainy April day in 1865. When the battle is pitched, he would say, rally around the flag. Mr. Paige's grandfather had carried it proudly and bravely into the enemy's withering fire. Now his grandson planned to do it again.

Watergate and Vietnam had changed American politics. The Left had staked its future on pessimism and fear. The Right, having conceded its intellectual bankruptcy, had abandoned the field altogether. Mr. Paige's ignored them both. He was focused on something they did not comprehend—the greatness of the American character. There was no natural place in the American heart for introspection or defeat. Soon the American people would grow tired of doubt and shame. Soon they would be ready to renew their mystical quest for MORE. The day was coming. He knew it.

Mr. Paige had persuaded his friend Oscar Denker to leave the Economics Department at the University and join him as Director of the Jefferson Academy. Dr. Denker's first responsibility was to assemble a scholarly faculty to graft intellectual flesh onto Paige's vision. The academy's professional thinkers agreed that a new economic era was dawning. That it could be a new golden age if Americans were allowed to apply their

special genius. But they had not yet resolved the crucial question about the malaise that gripped the nation. The claim that over regulation was stifling America's entrepreneurial spirit did not seem adequate to explain the uncharacteristic drift. Denker sensed that a new force was at work, an unknown virus sapping the nation's energy. Mr. Paige's plan was, in his opinion, the only way to treat it.

––––––––––

Henry poured two inches of bourbon into a tall glass. He swirled the amber liquid and studied it as the light danced through it. His first taste was a sip. It burned as it went down. He took another sip. "To the dead . . ." he said, lifting his glass toward the heavens beyond his window. He poured the rest of it down his throat before picking up the receiver.

––––––––––

The phone rang on George Edmond's private line. He answered it on the second ring. "Edmond here."

"George, this is Henry."

"Wa'll shit on ma' shit," he drawled as he spun his chair around to view the Atlanta skyline.

"I've come into some serious trouble," Henry announced.

"What have you done now?" Edmond asked. "Knocked up Paige's daughter?"

Henry ignored the joke. "I pulled Roberta Wiley out of the lake about an hour ago."

"Roberta!" Edmond repeated after a hard swallow.

"She was dead . . ."

"Dead?"

"A lanyard was cinched up around her throat. It looked like she'd been choked."

"Were there any marks on her body?" Edmond now sounded like the high-priced litigator he was.

". . . There were several tattoos . . ." Henry answered haltingly.

"What do you mean—tattoos!"

"Marjean and Aster had some kind of initiation rite last night in the barn."

"You were there?"

"Yea.

"And that's where the tattoos came from?"

Henry took a deep breath, "Yea."

"Did you have a hand in it?"

"I don't recall it too clearly—I drank something that must have been laced."

"So you don't remember what happened."

"Not really."

"But Roberta was alive the last time you saw her." Edmond's voice had become hard.

"So far as I know."

"Don't give me that crap, Henry. It's yes or no."

"Yes."

"... and you just happened to find her body this morning?"

"Yes—on my way to the academy."

"There's a pond on your way to the academy?" Edmond sounded skeptical.

"I was cutting through the field behind the house."

"Is that how you normally go to work?"

"No.

"Why did you go that way today?"

"I figured it would be congested because of the conference, so I decided to walk."

"What happened then?"

"I came back to the cottage and called Mr. Paige. There are a lot of big wigs here for the conference. I thought he should know about it first."

"What did he do?"

"He sent the Sheriff and the District Attorney. You know him, Ted Hoagland. They picked up the body."

"Anything else?"

"... Mr. Paige was here when they left. He showed me a statement he was going to release to the press."

"What did it say?"

"It said that Roberta drowned last night in a swimming accident."

"Is that all?"

"It said she was swimming with a friend."

"Who was that?"

"It didn't name the person."

"But you talked with Mr. Paige about it."

"Yes."

"And you agreed to stand in . . ."

It took Henry a while to confirm the lawyer's assertion. "Yea," he said finally.

Edmond let out a low sinking whistle. "Anything else?"

". . . The note said the body was going to be cremated."

"That's interesting, " Edmond said to himself.

"What do you think, George?"

"I think you better retain me so I have an excuse to keep this thing quiet."

"Ok . . . Good."

"I wouldn't say that." There was a pause while the lawyer organized the facts he had just

collected. "You're aware that Paige's statement is false and misleading."

"Yes . . ."

"You have claimed that you were with her when she died."

". . . I guess I did."

"You did. And you lied about how she died."

"I . . ."

"You said she drowned when she was probably strangled."

"What about the tattoos?" Henry protested.

"You're a pervert as well as liar and a murderer." George paused. "A jury would fry you."

"That bad, huh?"

"Maybe they'll destroy the evidence, but my guess is this thing is going to surface again when the conference is over—and Paige has gotten himself out of town."

Henry waited as Edmond's legal brain computed the correct course.

"I want you to write down everything that happened—date it and get it to me as soon as possible."

"Ok."

"Don't talk about it with anyone—you understand. Not Paige. Not

Aster. Not Marjean. Got that?... And don't put my name on it. Send it to... let's see... how about to Caius—who hath the lean and hungry look." George chuckled at his cleverness. "You have my address, don't you?"

"Yes."

"I'll call you once I've seen it."

"Ok."

"One more thing, Henry..."

"Yea..."

"Did you..." Edmond left the question dangling coyly.

"Did I what?"

"Did you screw her?" He smacked the words down like a mackerel onto a gutting board.

Henry didn't answer.

"I didn't hear you," Edmond yelled into his mouthpiece.

"It wasn't like that." Henry's voice quivered despite his effort to sound calm.

"Ok... Ok... take it easy." Edmond was satisfied. "Let's not get all worked up..."

Henry struggled to regain control over his emotions. "I'll get to work."

"Get the information to me as fast as you can."

"Yea..."

Henry laid the receiver down slowly.

Henry took the yellow pad that was lying beside the phone and went out on the porch. He paused before he sat down and pulled the crumpled sketch out of his pocket. A feeling of hopelessness gripped him as he stared at the bizarre collection of figures. He gazed over the railing. The crest of the red barn's roof peeked up at him from behind the ridge line. It was strangely peaceful now.

He remembered the first time he met Roberta.

It was a warm summer evening. He was sitting on the porch as he was now. Swan Lake was playing on his stereo. Its melody drifted past him and dispersed in the fading light. He was drinking a bourbon and waiting for the sun to set. It was the time of day when the light plays tricks on the eye—when the best way to see something is to look past it. That was how he saw her. She was a stirring in the shadows along the fence row. A movement solidified into a form and floated toward him through the tall grass, He watched as it glided toward him—like a vessel drifting on a smooth current. Well now, he thought, a muse of the evening. He took another leisurely drink.

She was dressed in blue jeans and a pressed white cotton shirt. He could see by the counter-beat of her breasts against the fluid motion of her body that she was not wearing a bra. His expectations faded as he watched the two points chafe beneath her blouse. He took another sip from his drink and prepared himself to meet a liberated woman. She opened the gate and entered the yard. She walked in silence across the lawn and up onto the porch. Her dark hair was brushed back off her forehead. A blue ribbon held it in place. Her features were sharp in a pleasing way. But her eyes were what struck him. There was something about them. He would have considered her pretty except for her eyes.

Henry clicked his pen and set it down on the pad in his lap. When he looked at his watch, he was surprised to see that it was after two o'clock.

No wonder his head ached. He had been working for more than three hours. He realized that he had a killing thirst. He set the pad down and went inside. In the kitchen he grabbed a can of beer out of the icebox and popped the top. A chill radiated through is body as he drank it down. When he was done, he tossed the empty can in the trash bin and rubbed some tap water on his eyes.

Back on the porch Henry found his pad filled with pages of scratched out lines. They looked like corpses from a regiment whose attack had failed. He contemplated the complex structure painstakingly assembled over twenty years of formal education. Was there anything left of his mind? The last page contained only a few words like random shots at the end of a battle. Henry scanned the page the way he would read a putt—eyes fixed, mind blank, waiting for the line to reveal itself.

He focused on the name "Fred Ried." Ried was the male presence at Aster's functions. He was a robust theatrical sort, just the way an artist bohemian should be—a man without logical premises who could drift in and out of Aster's fantasy world without shredding its gossamer sets.

Henry wondered why he had not been there. He put the point of his pen on the page and drew a thick dark line under the word "initiation". That's what Marjean had called it. Henry had always dismissed Aster's group as a kinky social club for gay heiresses. How ironic, he thought, to help Marjean induct Roberta into Aster's society of rich flakes. He picked up the diagram and studied the hieroglyphics on Roberta's body. They had been a prominent part of her initiation. It suddenly occurred to him. Maybe they meant something!

––––––––––––––

It was not easy to park at the University, but Henry had a secret place. He turned left off Rugby Road at Beta Bridge and coasted down the hill. At the bottom, he turned right into the alley behind the Beta House.

It ended in a small enclave littered with trash. Henry pulled to a stop next to an over-laden dumpster. He had just enough room to crack his door and squeeze out. He knew the way by heart. Up the hill to the sidewalk. Down Rugby Road past Mad Bowl. He had followed that path every day for three years as an undergraduate. The ginkgo trees that lined the sidewalk in front of Fayerweather Hall had begun to drop their foul fruit. As he stepped through the slippery mess, he remembered how a drunken classmate had chopped one down in a rage after falling. Too bad he didn't get them all, Henry thought as he tiptoed through the drop zone.

The Rotunda loomed before him. How different it looked surrounded by the orange police barricade. Most of the wreckage had been cleared away, but the smoke stains on its towering columns and the blackened holes that had been windows were ghastly testimony to the changing times. Oscar said the damage had been caused by a bomb. There had been dozens of threats to blow up Cabell Hall while Henry was an undergraduate. The times were different then, with the way and all. New people had begun to come out, but Henry and his friends always assumed that the threats were called in by fraternity men who had not prepared for their quizzes. Dean Runk took the calls. Henry had a special fondness for F.D.B. Runk. He was a fixed point. A man you could count on. A gentleman. Not even a bomb threat could draw Dean Runk out of character. Calmly, decently, he would evacuate the building and cancel classes. Never shrill. Never whining. He knew from long experience that he would prevail over these misguided undergraduates. Like a force of gravity. He would draw them back into the fold. Time would work its way. Back then it was not necessary to destroy University property. The University looked after its own.

Henry hurried past the shattered pedestal of Jefferson's statute. It lay on its side on the walk at the bottom of the embankment. What a shame. It has been the sole survivor of the fire of '95. Where would the Sevens take their mail now, Henry wondered. The final event of the conference was to have been a formal dinner in the Rotunda. Henry wondered in passing if this had something to do with the bombing. The desecration of the Rotunda had not changed the pattern of life for the Grounds' crews. They were busy as usual herding leaves into piles beside the chapel. Now they all used gas-powered blowers. Too bad, Henry thought. Nobody would hear Thomas singing his spirituals. It seemed like a waste of time keeping the lawn neat with the Rotunda in ruins.

Pedestrian traffic was heavy on the other side of the chapel. Well-groomed white boys in oxford shirts and Bass Weejuns and girls in miniskirts marched down the sidewalk along the West Range. Henry maneuvered between them, skipped up the granite steps and entered Alderman Library. After a quick stop at the card catalog, he disappeared into the stacks. His destination was the 7th floor, new wing, section 133. It was a dark, joyless place with a low ceiling and a musky, stale smell. He located his shelves and began pulling out books on astrology.

The symbols in his drawing were in these books. He learned that the Zodiac consisted of the twelve constellations the sun traversed during its annual rotation. Each constellation had an identifying sign. The ten planets in earth's solar system were also astrological agents and had their own distinguishing characters. These were in Henry's diagram, as were the characters that fixed the positions of the planets in the Zodiac's twelve Houses. Henry searched in vain for the ox skull in the emblem on Roberta's stomach.

He kept two reference volumes on astrology and a thick tome on witchcraft written decades earlier by a Frenchman whose name he could not pronounce. The others he replaced in the stack.

Having completed his research library Henry returned to the front desk.

Henry needed to clear his head before getting down to work so he went for a run. He returned, as usual, through the back gate.

On his way into the house, he stopped at his garden and pulled up a few weeds. Four more tomatoes had ripened. He picked them and crossed the yard to the back steps. The steps led through a small, screened-in porch to the kitchen. Inside he set the tomatoes on the windowsill and pulled a beer out of the refrigerator. He took it with him to the front porch where he finally settled down to his books. It was five o'clock.

The title of the first book that came into hand was "The Complete Astrologer." It was authored by a pair of Brits, Keron Parks and his wife Cecilia. It was filled with pictures of witches, medieval devils, and things like that. As he thumbed through the illustrations, it occurred to him that most of the books he had seen in the stacks had been written by Brits. *What is it about astrology that attracts these people . . .* He considered the question. *Must have something to do with Celtic blood . . .* Suddenly a new thought seized him. *Only an idiot could believe that God ordered the universe to communicate the secrets of his creation! . . . Or that he would choose to reveal them to witches and devil worshipers . . . the same stone-hut creatures sacrificed their kin to the bogeyman at the dawn of time . . . Man is perfectible! Bull shit . . . reason barely has a toe hold in the human mind . . . These medieval conjurors have no concept of a rational order . . . all they have is a vision of spooks and specters spiraling through the ether . . . the human race hasn't progressed . . . It's the same wild herd it was at the dawn of time . . . still afraid of demons lurking in dark places . . . still squeezing spirits out of the cracks in nature . . . still sacrificing helpless victims to calm its pagan phobias . . . There's no hope . . . Bombing the Rotunda! What better proof is there?*

Henry settled at last into his work. He moved methodically through the texts, jotting notes as he went along. It took several hours to finish the odious task. When he was done, he took the stack of papers into his den and placed them in a manila folder. On its cover, he wrote the word "Caius."

He set the folder on his desk and turned off the light.

At 7:15AM Tuesday, September 10, Mr. Paige's Mercedes rose over the crest of the hill. Henry was waiting on his front porch.

He walked out to the parking area as Leroy pulled to stop in front of him. Leroy was a cheerful young man, good looking with sharp Ethiopian features. He and Henry got along well for no particular reason. Sometimes Henry pondered Leroy's situation. He could never decide whether he was stealing a victory over the system or just one more of its unknowing victims. Mr. Paige made no effort to educate him, but he did provide him all the comforts of life. It was hard for Henry to accept the trade off, but Leroy seemed satisfied. And why wouldn't he be? He was the personal servant to one of the world's richest men.

Leroy stepped on the accelerator and started back up the gravel drive. "Hey boy," he said without lifting his eyes from the road, "you gonna get back to work?"

"Yea. Did they do Ok without me?"

Leroy slipped his hand down and nudged a copy of *The Washington Post* toward him. "See for yourself."

Henry scooped it up and spread it out full-page in front of him. The photograph in the top center had a familiar face. "What's this?" He read the caption out loud, "Raymond Paige welcomes Vice President Rockefeller to the Jefferson Academy in Charlottesville. " He let the paper crumple into his lap and looked at Leroy. "Well shit on mah shit!"

"He'll go into orbit when he sees that," Leroy predicted.

"Yea, he'll go into orbit," Henry repeated, his spirits rising. Jesus Christ! He'd done it. "Is there anything in here about Roberta?" Henry asked, suddenly anxious.

"I don't get paid to read the paper, white boy, that's your job."

Henry's eyes settled back on the paper. The headline beneath the picture was three columns wide. *Jefferson Academy Aims to Preserve Jefferson's Legacy*. Henry looked at the by-line. "Why do you suppose they would run a political essay on the front page that's not written by their Pulitzer Prize winner?" He asked absent-mindedly.

"Gotta be a woman involved . . ."

"Is that all you black dudes ever think about?"

"Better watch your mouth honky. I'll smack you."

"I'm ready . . ."

"You better stay ready is what I'm tellin' to you."

Henry read the name again. Claire Fox. Who is Claire Fox, he wondered as he passed on to the article.

The Jefferson Academy's first annual Colloquium on National Issues opened today at its well-manicured central Virginia campus. The topic of deliberation during the three-day program will be "Human Capital in the Age of Technology."

The Post was Henry's paper. He loved to hate it. Its rumor mongers. Its self-righteous snoops. What an extraordinary pack of knaves. He marveled at the way they could present themselves as dedicated defenders of people whose company they avoided and whose cultures they privately mocked. He often wondered what Thomas Jefferson, champion of the free press, would think now that it had gained the deciding voice. Henry raised his guard as he started to read Claire Fox's article:

Raymond Paige intends to save Thomas Jefferson's legacy. Who is Raymond Paige and why does he care about Jefferson?

Paige founded the Jefferson Academy three years ago. Now he is worried that the technological revolution will undermine our Jeffersonian society... Paige is an unlikely champion for Jefferson populism. Educated at Exeter, Yale, and the University of Virginia's School of Law, he settled in the Old Dominion after a successful investment banking career with Lehman Brothers in New York... Sounding more like an anti-establishment radical, Paige wants America to reaffirm the social principles that Jefferson framed in the nation's founding covenant. These principles, Paige claims, reflect Jefferson's belief in the Creator and the rights of individuals to pursue their private interests. 'If we are to preserve the blessings of political freedom for America's future generations,' he told his audience, 'then we must teach them what political freedom is'... mmm... mmm... Paige pointed out that Jefferson framed his masterpiece around two fundamental principles... mmm... Page invoked Alexis de Tocqueville... mmm... Paige cited the late Joseph Schumpeter who argued in "Capitalism Socialism and Democracy" that creative destruction is an inevitable... mmm... a society managed by 'cybercrats'... is the future predicted by Alexis De Tocqueville in which 'Extremes are softened or blurred, and all that was most prominent is superseded by some middle term ... mmm ... To prevent this, Paige proposed a three-part program ... mmm ... Paige wants to update Schumpeter's free-market manifesto ... mmm ... by connecting his ideas on capitalism with Thorstein Veblen's ideas on the value of labor. He cited "The Engineer and The Price System" where Veblen wrote, 'the foundation and driving force of the industrial system, is a massive body of technical knowledge' that resides in the minds of 'gifted, trained and experienced technicians ... mmm ... Knowledge will be the essential asset in a technology economy ... mmm ... In closing, Paige called the country to move beyond what he characterized as 'old orthodoxies' ... mmm ... Following his address Paige descended from the stage to greet an old friend in the audience. George Meany, the conference's senior participant, once worked in Paige's father's automobile plant ... mmm ... When asked to comment on the speech the crusty labor leader answered, 'A free country is essential to the American worker and we're going to see that it stays that way—we always have and always will ... But I don't just want a government of citizen-legislators. I'm looking for a government that helps me solve my problems ... I've never read those books and I don't know whether I've ever met a cybercrat, but I think Ray has a point and I'm going to start watching for them.'

"Here you go, bro'—even you will get this! Here's how Claire Fox ends her piece: *"When asked what he would do if he found one, Meany replied, 'It all depends on who buys the beer.'"*

Henry closed the newspaper.

"So, what'd she say?" Leroy asked with a sideways glance.

Henry considered it for a minute. "You want the long answer or the short answer."

"Gotta be the short one. I'm runnin' late."

"She says we're going to be part of the policy making machinery."

"That's what you want ain't it?"

"Yea.

"Then you're in bidness."

Henry rolled the pager into a cudgel and slapped Leroy on the shoulder. "Godammit Leroy, I'm putting you up for a promotion."

"Don't need no promotion, white boy," he shot back. "I already got it made. And don't mess up the paper. He's waitin' ta see it."

Leroy guided the car through the farm's entrance and up the gravel road to the residence. Henry noticed for the first time that there was a car ahead of them—a green MG. The two cars crossed the cattle grate at the compound gate in close file. The MG pulled to a stop in Mr. Paige's vacant space. Leroy pulled up beside it. Henry glanced over at the driver. She was an aristocratic blond. They opened their doors simultaneously and climbed out together. Henry nodded a cautious greeting. She looked toward him without looking at him.

"Could you tell me where I might find Raymond Paige?"

Henry knew she was not part of the conference—not coming up the back way in an MG. As Henry considered the matter, it occurred to him that she was beautiful.

Her blue eyes were the last thing he noticed. Henry breathed a silent oath. "I'm on my way to see him," he answered. "You can follow me," Henry turned without waiting for her response and started toward the stairs. Her blue eyes lingered in his mind as he climbed the steps to the mansion's lawn. *There's a dame who could tear your guts up.*

A brick walk led from the landing at the top of the steps across a manicured lawn. It ended in a towering boxwood hedge that enclosed the house. Henry had traveled a few paces up the walk when the woman behind him called his name.

"Henry Tilghman? Are you Henry Tilghman?"

He stopped and turned toward the voice. "Yes... I'm Henry Tilghman."

"Hi! I'm Claire Fox. Mr. Paige said you would be meeting with us this morning,"

She spoke in a cheerful voice and flashed a first-rate pretend smile,

The smile unhinged him. Claire Fox? He tried to place the name. "He did? I'm... I mean... I haven't talked with him since..." The unfinished sentence hung awkwardly between them.

"Since?" she said cordially, nudging him back into the conversation.

"Since... huh, Saturday," Henry stammered.

She smiled encouragingly. "I guess you're wondering who I am."

It was a line. He grabbed it, "Yes . . . I don't believe we've met."

"Hank, bring Miss Fox up here."

Mr. Paige had stepped through an opening in the hedge and was waiting for them. He was a solidly built man carrying about two hundred and ten pounds on his six-foot two-inch frame. He stood ramrod straight in the pose of the Naval Commander he had once been. Paige's massive head sat confidently on broad, square shoulders that still showed the power that carried Yale's eleven to three Ivy League titles. His old coach was now the President of the United States. They were still close friends.

Henry stepped aside. "Please," he said, gesturing to his companion. Smiling again, Claire Fox glided past him and proceeded up the walk.

"How nice to see you, Miss Fox." Paige said in a sonorous voice. He extended his hand with the greeting. He turned then to Henry, "How do you feel, Hank?"

Henry felt as though their eyes were burning holes into his soul. "Fine" he said, hoping to sound off-handed, "I'm feeling fine." To prove it, he handed Paige the paper he was holding. "Congratulations. You're front-page news."

Paige studied the picture and grunted his approval. The two visitors waited as he scanned the article. He looked up when he was finished. "Looks like Denker was right about you, Miss Fox," he nodded.

"You like it?"

"Not many journalists are disciplined enough to simply report the news—I think we're going to be able to do business."

She responded with a professional smile.

"Hank wrote the speech," he added, winking at Henry.

Claire fixed her blue eyes on Henry and smiled again.

"You two have met, I see."

"Informally," Claire replied.

"*The Post* has decided it's time for the world to know about us, Hank. I've got to meet Rockefeller, so I want you to look after Miss Fox. Show her around. Answer her questions. Get her whatever she needs—you understand?" Henry understood. "That's all right with you isn't it, Miss Fox?" Paige pretended to ask. "Hank is my right-hand man. He's in on everything that goes on here."

"That will be fine," she said with practiced smoothness.

"Good." Mr. Paige turned and started toward the lodge. After two steps, he turned back "Hank, check with Oscar before you go out. I think he has something for you." He nodded to Claire and stepped into the passageway in the hedge.

Before he disappeared, he paused again. "Hank, " he motioned to Henry. Henry hastened up to him. "The grand jury will sit next Wednesday," he said quietly. "It's going to decide whether there are grounds for a formal investigation into your accident. I've asked Barton DeForrest to be present with you when you give your testimony. Expect a call from him." Paige glanced back toward the young woman. "Better keep her on a tight leash."

Henry glanced at the package Paige had just placed in his care. It seemed to be ticking. Just then a shrill voice pierced the quiet morning. "Ray, who in the world are you talking to?"

Paige wheeled around without saying another word and disappeared through the hedge.

"What was that?" Claire asked, when Henry returned.

"Mrs. Paige."

Claire made a mental note before changing the subject. "I'm starved," she announced. "Can we start with some breakfast?"

"Sure," Henry agreed. "Let me check with Dr. Denker, then we'll go over to the dining room."

Henry's mind raced as they walked along the path to the Jefferson Academy's main hall. He needed a plan.

"It was a good article," he said along the way.

"I was happy with it," she agreed.

"Did you talk with Mr. Paige before you wrote it?" Henry inquired offhandedly.

"Actually, no," Claire confessed, "I spoke with Dr. Denker, and he sent me a copy of your speech."

"Huh . . ." Henry nodded trying to bring a picture into focus.

"I thought the insights on Jefferson were particularly interesting," she volunteered. "You won't believe this, but when I was in college, I wrote a paper on *Thoughts on English Prosody*."

"No kidding. I didn't know a normal person could survive that kind of torture."

"I've never considered myself to be a 'normal person,'" she answered crisply,

"I'm sure you're not," Henry agreed.

"Sorry to bother you, Oscar," Henry whispered through the opened door of his office. "Mr. Paige thought you had something for me."

Dr. Denker looked up from behind his desk. Seated in front of him was a man in a saffron robe. Henry stared at the long dark hair that hung down over his shoulders in two tight Indian braids. "Yes Henry!" The scholar called back warmly. There was a momentary pause. "Is Miss Fox with you?" Claire peeked over Henry's shoulder and greeted him with a fluttering wave.

Denker's face brightened into a smile. "Ahh . . . there you are Miss Fox."

The robed figure turned to see what had animated his host. "I'm sorry," Denker said, scolding himself. "Let me introduce Tim Hardin. Mr. Hardin is the founder and director of the Coalition for an Open Society."

Henry extended his hand. "Welcome to the Jefferson Academy."

Hardin took it with his left hand. His eyes remained fixed on Claire. "Claire Fox from *The Washington Post*?" He asked.

"The same."

They gazed at each other for a moment in approving silence. "You have a following at *The Post*, Mr. Hardin," she added coyly.

"Yes, I know," he replied offhandedly. "Call me and I'll do an interview for you."

"I will."

Denker picked up the conversation. "I wanted to suggest that you take Miss Fox to Monticello a little early this evening. My friend Fenton Somerville has offered to give you a private tour."

"Who is Fenton Somerville?" she asked.

"Fenton is the curator of Monticello and an old friend of mine."

"I think we'd like to take you up on that," Henry said with a confirming nod from Claire.

————————

Claire filled her plate with toast, yogurt, and fruit. Henry poured a cup of black coffee.

"You're awfully quiet," she observed as she ate.

An image formed in his mind of a Mayan priestess preparing her patient for a trepanning.

"Let me tell you what I want," she said, getting down to business.

"Ok."

"First, I want background information about the academy. You know, the usual reporter stuff. Why was it formed? What are its principles? Who is it speaking to? What is it trying to accomplish?"

"Ok."

"Then I want to get into Mr. Paige. You know—the man behind the hedge. What makes him tick? Who does he talk too? What does he think? Where does he get his ideas? What is his connection to the academy?"

"Ok," he repeated.

"After I get the background together, I want to interview the staff and collect some anecdotal material—you know, human reactions to victories and defeats so our readers can relate to what's going on here." She watched the expression on Henry's face darken. "Is something wrong?"

Henry tried to come up with a glib answer but couldn't.

"Do I make you nervous?" She asked with a sudden laugh.

"Yes," Henry confessed. "I'm a little nervous . . . "

"Why?" She waited, studying him. "Well? Come on . . ."

"I guess I'm not used to talking with reporters," he said at last.

"Is it such a big deal?"

"It's just that . . ."

Claire laughed out loud. "You think I'm dangerous!"

Henry frowned. "You know what I mean. Your business is dissecting live specimens . . . ideas get distorted . . . people become targets." Henry twirled his spoon as he faced his beautiful adversary.

Claire weighed his response. "Your boss liked my article . . . You liked my article."

Henry didn't answer.

"All right—what do you propose?"

Henry paused to consider his options. "Maybe we could begin with a tour. A historical perspective might help you to understand the Jefferson Academy."

"If you say so," she said gamely. "Where do we start?"

"Well, I could take you up to the Bird Field—and give you the big picture."

"Would it help you to relax?" she asked with an encouraging smile.

Henry shrugged, "It wouldn't hurt . . ."

Henry climbed into the passenger seat. "Where to?" Claire snapped like a New York cabbie. Henry pointed to the entrance gate. Claire backed the car out onto the service road and started forward. The car rolled uncertainly across the cattle guard and picked up speed. The mansion and the academy disappeared behind them in a cloud of dust. Up ahead the sky was blue.

"Keep to the left at the fork," Henry said as they approached the turn-off to the shed.

The landscape before them glistened in the clear white light that comes to Virginia's Piedmont after the summer heat breaks. Fall colors had begun to replace the summer greens. The air carried the scent of dry grass mingled with nature's vague hummings. Henry was attached to these Virginia days by the same mysterious force that bound him to the traditions of Mr. Jefferson's University.

"Why would a nice girl like you become a journalist?" he heard himself ask. He watched the reporter stiffen. "It's just a line," he added with a placating gesture.

"Actually," Claire said, deciding to play along, "my father was an editor at *The Post*."

"Does that make you part of *The Washington Post's* old boy network?"

"It could," Claire replied crisply, "but I also happen to be a Phi Beta Kappa from Radcliffe."

"Pull up over there," Henry said, abandoning the conversation. He pointed to a spot beside the shed.

Claire stopped the car where Henry said. She followed him into the shed where she saw a collection of mysterious farm implements, three tractors, and a bulky, boxlike machine that almost touched the rafters.

"What is that?" Claire asked, staring at the ungainly contraption.

"It's called a Unimog,* Henry replied. "It's a 4-wheel drive all-terrain vehicle—Mercedes' version of a tractor. Say, if you have any play clothes, I suggest you put them on,"

Claire turned and disappeared through the shed's door. Henry heard the trunk open. A moment later Claire returned wearing a pair of blue jeans.

"That's more like it," Henry said as he lifted a key out of the lock box on the wall.

"What are we going to do?" Claire asked.

"We're going to take a ride up the hill," Henry said, gesturing toward the ridge that defined the valley's western perimeter.

Henry guided the ungainly vehicle along a rutted path that led toward the tree line. "Interesting isn't it," Henry shouted over the drone of the engine. "We are riding a jet age buckboard up an Indian trail that was old before the first white man ever saw it."

"Is that right?" Claire tightened her grip on the frame of her seat.

"It's kind of a sad story, don't you think?"

"In what respect?"

"The noble savage driven from his paradise home by the march of an alien civilization—that's how *The Post* would write it, isn't it?"

"I suppose we have written stories like that," she conceded blandly.

"The first white men came here in the early 1700's," Henry said shifting back to his subject. "By 1725 a few settlers had put up cabins in the area, but the history of this tract didn't begin until the mid-1730's when William Randolph came exploring with his friend Peter Jefferson. William was the son of a wealthy planter named Thomas Randolph of Tuckahoe, which was on the James River about ten miles north of Richmond. Thomas was one of the James River grandees. Evidently, he was also a loving husband—he and his wife are known today as the Adam and Eve of Virginia. Thomas's cousin Isham Randolph was the father of Peter Jefferson's wife—if you follow that."

Claire stared out the cab window. She was thinking about her failed interview with Raymond Paige. She remembered her conversation with Martin Ogden the previous morning. Who are these people? And what are they up to? That's all *The Post's* Managing Editor wanted to know.

"Do you know anything about tobacco?" Henry asked suddenly.

"It causes cancer," Claire answered, attempting to dismiss the question.

"Tobacco destroys soil fertility," he said, correcting her. "Three crops were all that most fields could support in those days. It was tobacco that brought William Randolph out here. He needed fresh land. Peter Jefferson was a surveyor who had visions of making a fortune speculating in western land. Unfortunately for him it was Randolph who knew about land. They started at the Rivanna—somewhere down there," Henry pointed off to his left, "Jefferson set off on the south side, and William came up this way. The land he inspected was relatively flat and fertile enough to grow four crops of tobacco. While Jefferson was busy measuring off the hillside on the far side of the river, Randolph was hiking up this trail. When they got back to Williamsburg, Randolph went over to the Governor's office and filed a petition for 2400 acres that extended from the river at Shadwell along the eastern slope of the ridge up to about this trail."

"Interesting!"

"Yea. A few days later Jefferson filed his claim for about 1000 acres. Most of the land he wanted was on the other side of the Rivanna, but a two-hundred-acre parcel was on this side—Jefferson wanted to build his house on its hill because it overlooked the river. Unfortunately, it was part of his friend's claim." Henry glanced at Claire. "It worked out all right, though. Randolph swapped him the two-hundred acres for a bowl of punch."

"How kind."

"Well not exactly. Shortly after that Jefferson married Randolph's cousin Jane. Jane lived at Dungeness in Goochland County—about ten miles further up the James from Tuckahoe. Her father, Isham, was born there. He was an interesting guy. He attended William and Mary. After graduating, he married and started a family. His wife died shortly afterwards. Then he went to England where he served as Virginia's colonial agent. In England, he married again and had several more children. One of them was a daughter named Jane who was born in London's Shadwell Parish in 1720. Somewhere along the way Isham went to sea and made a fortune in the slave trade. Eventually he brought his family and one hundred slaves to the new world and settled down at Dungeness."

"You think they were connected?"

"Sure. Randolph got his cousin a husband and brought his friend and new neighbor into the family."

Claire's thoughts wandered back to Raymond Paige. What did she expect? A lapdog? Another image burst into her mind. She gritted her teeth as she contemplated Martin Ogden's chiseled face. I don't have to apologize for that, she swore silently. *They would all do it—if they could. That's the difference,* she reasoned coldly. *I made it happen with Martin. Now I'm going to make it happen here!*

"There were three kinds of plantations," Henry said, continuing his narrative. "There was rice in the coastal swamps of South Carolina and Georgia. Cotton was grown across the western frontier. Tobacco was grown in Virginia and North Carolina.

"Growing rice in those swamps was hard work, and the mortality rate among the field hands was high. Rice planters had to use brute force to keep their slaves under control. Conditions on the cotton plantations were slightly better. The work wasn't as hard. The planters sometimes even worked the fields with their slaves—they were used to field work having raised food crops and cattle before cotton became the staple. That work had made them hard, and they could be as ruthless as their rice-growing cousins when their authority was questioned. They resolved their conflicts with appropriate violence. If a peer offended them, they challenged him to a duel. If an offense was committed by an inferior, they caned him or gave him a horse whipping. If a slave transgressed, he was flogged. If that didn't solve the problem, he was sold."

They were halfway up the mountain now. Claire was looking out the window as they came out from behind a grove of trees. "Wow! What a beautiful view!" She exclaimed.

"It was only on the tobacco plantations in Virginia and North Carolina that the social pyramid was sustained without physical violence." Henry said, ignoring the view. "They functioned more like patriarchal families. It could operate that way because the tobacco society was mature enough to have a set pattern. The master's authority over his black children rested on the strange intangible—things had always been that way. Slaves came to their understanding of society over changeless generations during which any concept they might once have had a life in another position was totally obliterated."

"Of course, relations among whites were based on the same perceptions of inevitability. During Jefferson's adult life, only about half of Virginia's 100,000 white males were eligible to vote. Less than half of them actually did. The power was monopolized by an oligarchy of 300 or 400 broadly extended families that constituted the gentry. They supplied all the candidates for the popularly elected offices. These men stood at the top of the pyramid."

Claire watched Henry as he worked through his narrative.

"Tobacco planters saw themselves as cultured gentlemen. They viewed violence as a vulgar trait that belonged to the classes beneath them. Even in the face of adversity, they seldom resorted to force. They preferred to use reason to settle their disputes. When that failed, they would retreat to politics. That's why they were so good at it."

She was surprised to find his analysis interesting.

"The best of them read deeply in the classics and took pains to master political theories dating back to ancient times. They perceived this as part of their duty as disinterested servants of the people. Of course, in their view the 'people' consisted only of themselves and the yeomanry who lived within their jurisdictions." Henry stopped the Unimog in front of the upper gate. "The other defining characteristic of the class was the habit of command. The gentry deferred to their peers and gave orders to everybody else." He stared at the obstruction in front of him. "Would you mind opening that gate?"

Claire opened the cab door and swung down. She fumbled with the latch for a moment, then walked the gate back and held it open as Henry passed through. He revved the engine a couple times as he waited for her to get back into the cab. When she was seated, he started off again. The Unimog wheezed as he steered it off the trail into the tall grass. A couple minutes later they were perched in a higher corner of a large field. The crest of the ridge was two hundred feet above them.

"This is called the Bird Field," he said, shutting off the engine. "I'm not sure why." Henry opened his door and took a deep cleansing breath. It was peaceful the way big empty spaces are. The distant sounds of civilization, muffled by miles of empty air, somehow added to its serenity. The panorama stretched to the horizon 50 miles away. Henry's mind drifted as he gazed off into eternity. That's when he felt it. That bad feeling was coming back—like Roberta's ghost was lurking in the corner of his mind, goading him to self-destruct. *Admit it. Go ahead. Confess!* He felt a sudden strong impulse to scream it out. *I killed her! That's why you're here. That's what you want to know. Isn't it?* Instead, he snorted in another deep breath. *Whoa! Get a grip on yourself.*

He turned reluctantly to Claire. It was unnerving to see her penetrating blue eyes fixed on him. "How do you like the view?" He finally managed to say.

"It's beautiful."

Henry swung out of the seat and landed on the ground. Claire kept her seat as he walked around to her door. He pulled the handle and opened it. "Come on," he said holding up his arms. Claire sat there for a long moment, then leaned out and slid her hands over his shoulders. He inhaled her scent as he lifted her down. Nice . . .

Henry guided her a few paces up the ridge for a better view of the panorama. Below them to the right was the Belmont mansion. Behind it was the Academy with its green and white tents. Henry motioned across the landscape in the direction of a small round hill toward the head of the valley thirty degrees further to the right.

"This is Jefferson country," he announced. "It has always attracted strong-willed independent men. That's the first thing you have to understand."

———————

"Thomas Jefferson is the paradigm for American individualism," Henry said, introducing the Jefferson Academy's namesake.

"See that hill?" Henry pointed to the small cone-shaped mountain at the head of the valley. "That's Monticello Mountain. Jefferson defied conventional wisdom by building his home on top of it. It was the consuming passion of his life."

"I've always admired Jefferson," Claire volunteered.

"Is that right?"

Claire smiled. "He was a revolutionary. "

"Well, you can't get much closer to him than this. Jefferson loved this land—I think his spirit still haunts these hills." Henry gazed across the landscape toward Monticello. "Actually, it was his father's empire. Thomas inherited it when his father died in 1757. He was fourteen."

"How did that work?"

"His mother managed it for him until he turned twenty-one. That was in 1764."

"When did he build his house?"

"He started leveling the top of the mountain there in 1768."

"That would have made him twenty-four years old."

"Good math," Henry nodded approvingly.

"He had a habitable dwelling on the site in the fall of 1770."

"Where did he live prior to that?"

"At Shadwell—with his mother."

Claire did another quick tabulation. "He lived with his mother until he was twenty-seven years old? Was that normal?"

"I've wondered about that myself," Henry confessed. "Shadwell burned to the ground on February 1, 1770. That's what prompted him to put up the cottage on the mountain. It remained his residence until after he married the widow Skelton on January 1, 1772."

"I suppose it took a while to build the main house..."

"Altogether, it took him about forty years to finish it."

"Forty years!"

"Think of it this way," Henry explained. "Jefferson was not building a house. He was creating a private universe."

"What do you mean?"

"Jefferson needed a special environment to nurture his enlightened intellect. It was his shelter from the imperfections of Everyman's world. Ironic isn't it. A contemporary of his once called Monticello 'the chateau high above contact with man.' For all his brilliance, he never understood common people or the forces that shaped their lives."

"But surely he was concerned with the public's interest. He couldn't have understood political democracy otherwise?"

Henry shrugged. "You assume that he was motivated by concern for others."

"You don't agree?" Claire sounded surprised.

"No. Jefferson was a well-entrenched member of Virginia's aristocracy. When his mother died in 1776, he had an income from his law practice and his farming of about $5,000 per annum. He was fabulously rich by the standards of his day. The only thing he may have shared with common people was their determination to be free of oppressive authority. Fortunately for us, he thought the best way to achieve it was to dilute power of the governing plutocracy. To the extent this improved the lot of the common man it was fortuitous. But the well-being of the common man wasn't an issue that particularly interested Jefferson."

"That's hardly the assessment I would have expected to hear at the Jefferson Academy," Claire advised him.

"We're not trying to peddle a cult hero," Henry replied. "We're concerned with the social, political, and economic traditions that have enabled our country to flourish. Jefferson had a strong self-interest. The fact that he did demonstrates how important self-interest is to the success of political democracy."

"Mr. Paige made that point in his address," Claire observed, unconvinced of its merit.

"It's not easy to find the reality behind the rhetoric today," Henry observed. "Jefferson believed that truth could defend itself. But what is it? You tell me. Do human rights derive from Divine Law? Is majority rule tyranny? It depends on your point of view—doesn't it? Look—you're surprised I would even bring it up!"

"I just . . ." Claire seemed confused. "I just don't think a complex figure like Thomas Jefferson can be cast in such simple terms."

"You shouldn't be afraid of the truth." Henry smiled sarcastically.

"You have it all figured out, don't you," Claire answered. Her mounting irritation was audible in her voice.

"Jefferson casts a big shadow around here. He gives our reality its shape, if you see what I mean." He knew she didn't.

"I think you're talking about things that are a little too abstract for the man on the street," Claire said, finishing the conversation.

Henry gazed out across the vista. "In one sense, Jefferson was a victim of his times."

"Oh?"

"He came of age just as the tobacco market was collapsing."

"How did that affect him?"

"Jefferson's wealth and social position were built on tobacco, and there was too much of it. Among other things, that meant there were too many mouths to feed down on the old plantation. Jefferson reacted like other members of his class—he called for the abolishment of slavery. Of course, he was no more willing than his unenlightened peers were to emancipate his own slaves—he was right in the sense that there was no place for them in the clannish, laissez faire European society that existed in British America."

"Anyway, as Jefferson and his neighbors debated the problem, their debts mounted. Eventually paternalism gave way to the pragmatic realization that if money could not be made growing tobacco, it could be made raising and selling labor to cotton planters. To succeed, however, it was necessary to clear Georgia's cotton land of its Indians and Spaniards and to shut off the slave trade with Africa."

"Are you saying that Jefferson opposed slavery on economic grounds, not because he believed the rights of man?"

"Jefferson spoke out against slavery but remained one of Virginia's largest slave owners. He considered Blacks inferior to Whites, and he sold them when he needed money or if they caused trouble. You tell me. How does that square with the idea of human rights?"

"I don't know . . ."

"Neither do I. The point I am making is that declining tobacco prices had a significant financial impact on Jefferson and certainly affected his view of the world. First and foremost, it transformed him into a debtor. He made an earnest attempt to deal with his financial problems when he returned from France in 1789. Washington had asked him to become the United States' first Secretary of State, and his daughter was about to be married, so he had compelling reasons to put his financial house in order."

"How did he do it?"

"He sold 6,000 of the 11,000 acres he had inherited from his wife's father. He took a note for the land. He tried to pass the note to his British creditors, but this was against the law—which he certainly knew. They refused to accept it."

"So he was out the land and still had his debt?"

"Yep . . . and he had to service his debt with a smaller base of production. You can imagine the impact that had on his opinion of the creditor class."

"Is the Jefferson Academy really concerned with Thomas Jefferson's debts?" Claire asked hoping to turn the conversation in a more useful direction.

"Well of course!"

"Why?"

"Because Jefferson's mounting personal debt shaped the political philosophy that carried him to the presidency."

"How?" she asked, bewildered.

"By transforming Jefferson's rivalry with Hamilton into an ideological war."

"You've really lost me now," Claire admitted with a frustrated laugh.

"Jefferson perceived debt as a device that allowed speculators to accumulate wealth dishonestly—that is, without land or labor. Hamilton was their leader."

"I knew that!" Claire announced defensively.

"Their first clash was over chartering the Bank of the United States which happened during Washington's first term. Hamilton supported it arguing, correctly, that good credit was necessary for the new nation to develop economically. Jefferson, the man who had long since lost control of his own finances, objected. Some have claimed that he was expressing the utopian thesis of a British Whig named Henry St. John, Viscount Bolingbroke. Bolingbroke had argued that mankind could be uplifted by education and self-discipline, but only if society is firmly rooted in the land. In Bolingbroke's estimation, only land gave people the environment and the wherewithal to improve themselves. Whether or not Jefferson took this idea from Bolingbroke, he was well-equipped to defend it and proved it by advancing several famous constitutional arguments. But the heart of his position was his personal resentment toward the creditor class—and Hamilton. Hamilton, of course, was no fading rose. He met Jefferson's attacks with equal vigor. And he enjoyed an important advantage."

"What was that?"

"He had earned Washington's confidence on the battlefield while Jefferson had been cloistered up there on Monticello Mountain revising Virginia's colonial code. When Washington sided with Hamilton on the bank issue, he handed Jefferson a political defeat from which he never fully recovered. The rest is history—200 years of American political factionalism."

"Is this Mr. Paige's assessment or yours?" Claire wondered out loud.

The question seemed to catch Henry off guard. "Mr. Paige pays me to research his positions," he replied.

"Look, you wanted to show me something," Claire said. "Why don't you do that. Then let's go back to the 20th Century."

Henry laughed for the first time. "Ok." He pointed to a green pasture in front of Monticello Mountain. "See that little rise there? That's where Peter Jefferson built his house. He named it after his wife's birthplace. Go another 20 degrees to the right and you're at Pantops Mountain. Jefferson concocted the name himself. It has a Greek meaning, something like having-a-view-all-around. Today we drive across Jefferson's Pantops farm to get to Charlottesville. Jefferson gave his younger daughter Maria 900 acres on Pantops as a dowry when she married Jack Eppes in 1797. It was an attempt to persuade her husband to settle in the area, but he had an estate on the west bank of the James and settled his bride there. That always bothered Jefferson. He never gave up trying to lure them back."

Henry pointed to a chimney visible in a grove beyond Belmont, "That's Edgehill. It was the main part of William Randolph's original patent. Its history is as much a part of Jefferson's life as Monticello itself."

"What makes you say that?"

"Shortly before his death in 1745 William Randolph asked Peter Jefferson to assume personal charge of his estate and his only son, Thomas Mann Randolph. Jefferson agreed to his friend's deathbed request, and when he died, Jefferson moved his household to Randolph's plantation on the James River. He remained there seven years. Thomas Jefferson claimed his earliest memory was as a two-year old boy making the trip to Tuckahoe on a pillow hand carried by a slave. Thomas Mann Randolph and Thomas Jefferson grew up together and became close friends. It was Randolph's first son, Thomas Mann Jr., who married Jefferson's oldest daughter Martha.

"Naturally, Jefferson was pleased by the match. In his preparations for the wedding, he suggested to his friend that Edgehill would be a suitable endowment for the groom. Randolph, however, had recently married a young bride and preferred to keep the unencumbered farm for himself. Instead, he dowered his son with a mortgaged farm south of Richmond in Varina, Virginia. That had a very bad effect on Jefferson who had no intention of allowing his eldest daughter to be taken from him. He responded by concocting a plan for his compliant son-in-law to buy Edgehill. The elder Randolph expressed the depth of his objection by dying, but not, fortunately, before he sold the property to his son. That was in 1792. Until he finally built his home there ten years later, Thomas Mann and his family spent a good part of every year living with Jefferson at Monticello.

"Thomas Mann Randolph, Jr. was also burdened by debt. In 1793 he was unable to pay the mortgage on his Varina farm—Jefferson loaned him $1,000 to cover it. Three years later, he and his brother lost a suit brought by British creditors to his father's estate. Randolph's personal liability was fixed at the staggering sum of $43,000. To help resolve the crisis, Randolph sold 400 acres of his Edgehill farm. The parcel consisted of this field," he raised his arm in a broad sweeping gesture, "the land around the house, the ground the academy sits on, the field over there to our left, and the pass.

"That sale was intensely painful to Jefferson. That it was purchased by John Walker, the owner of Belmont Farm, probably made it worse. Walker was the son Jefferson's childhood guardian. They had been close friends, but their friendship had ended many years before when Walker learned that Jefferson had tried to seduce his wife."

"Between that time and his death in 1826, Thomas Jefferson fought a nonstop battle to preserve what remained of Edgehill as an estate for his daughter. He spent more time fighting for those 2000 acres than he did for the thirteen colonies. It was only saved because Thomas Randolph signed the deed over to his son, Thomas Jefferson Randolph. In exchange for Edgehill, Jeff Randolph assumed his father's debts. The transaction finished Thomas Mann Randolph. He died a homeless pauper soon afterwards. Jefferson followed suit a short time later."

"That's an awfully sad story," Claire volunteered.

"Sometime before he gained ownership to Edgehill, Jeff Randolph began building the manor house at Edgehill. Jefferson designed it for him. You can see its chimneys there," Henry said, pointing toward them.

"The Edgehill tract was the only piece of Albemarle land that slipped out of Jefferson's grip during his lifetime. He preferred to struggle under massive debt than to sell his land. It was like fate conspiring against her own progeny," Henry mused. "As rapidly as he mortgaged his property to get the money he needed to maintain his household, the value of his land declined."

"Why would it decline in value?" Claire sounded surprised.

"The promise of a better life in the west lured away the skilled labor needed to run the large plantations. Slave labor was cheaper, but it was also mostly unskilled, which made it marginally productive. Jefferson hardly ever earned a profit. You have to respect him though. He never faltered. He continued to tend his land like a parent would a wayward child. He experimented throughout his life hoping to find a way to free it from the stranglehold of tobacco and slavery."

"What do you suppose carried him on?" Claire asked, probing to find the point of Henry's interest in Thomas Jefferson.

"He was driven by a vision." Henry spoke into the distance. "Jefferson was the child of the Enlightenment. As a young man at William & Mary, he was captured by the idea that man could create order out of nature's chaos through the power of his mind. He convinced himself that he could make nature conform to his own rational design. That idea was as tangible to him as God's salvation was for his pious neighbors."

Claire began to comprehend how vast the distance was between them. He was out there somewhere in Jefferson's country, scavenging in a dim world of lost ideas. She was impatient to reach tomorrow.

"He never doubted he could do it." Claire listened to his voice from the far side of a metaphysical void. "He helped to create a new social order. But even his intellect wasn't powerful enough to tame nature's brutal processes." Henry's voice now sounded less remote. "The fortune and the effort he spent all would have been wasted if it weren't for the mansion he built on the top of that mountain." They were together now. "Jefferson lived the last three years of his life in bankruptcy. Did you know that?"

"No." She stared into his eyes, trying to see who he really was.

"Yea . . . by the time his estate was settled five years after his death everything he owned had been auctioned off. Monticello, his most prized possession, was the last to go. It was sold to a local pharmacist for $9,000. The new owner plowed up his gardens and planted mulberry trees."

"Interesting," she said, satisfied that she had found the door into his private world.

"We come up here today and see the same stunning sights that put his mind to flight two hundred years ago. Standing here we get a glimpse of the dreams that drew men like Peter Jefferson and William Randolph and kept Thomas Jefferson working forty years at his kilns. But for all that," he added soberly, "when you live here, you also come to know the destructive forces of nature. In the end, it defeated all of them, you know." Henry looked at Claire. "They say over at the University that Charlottesville is good to you, but not good for you."

"I didn't realize they got so heavy down here," she pretended to joke. "Tell me again, Henry, how does this relate to the Jefferson Academy?"

"It's the vision, I guess. People come here because they want to share his vision."

"Do you?"

"Do I? I don't know. I guess I'm just trying to figure out who Jefferson really was . . ."

"Why?"

The question seemed to annoy him. "It's my job," he replied after a brief pause.

"That's not why," Claire said, challenging him.

Henry eyed her cautiously. "Because he claimed the right to change the world. Does that make sense to you?"

"I don't know," Claire answered honestly.

"This is Belmont in front of us," Henry told her.

He pointed to the roof and chimneys poking out of the grove of trees where they met with Raymond Paige. "That's the main house. There's not much historically interesting about it. It was built by a German Baron who bought the property a few years before the First World War. I've been told that he wanted to turn the estate into a retreat for his wealthy countrymen. He built a hotel and made other improvements to accommodate them, but the war put an end to the enterprise. He went back to Germany and, so far as I know, never returned. That's the hotel," he said pointing toward the academy. "Today it's the Jefferson Academy's main hall. You see the road winding down from the compound," he said, pointing to the pale gray ribbon winding through the shallow valley below them. "It leads to the tractor shed. Now keep going. You can see the top of the barn that we passed on the way up. If you look on beyond the barn—you see that silvery reflection?" Claire caught the glint of the sun on a distant tin roof and nodded. "That's my cottage. That's about the edge of the parcel that Thomas Randolph sold in 1797. I guess you could say that was the northern boundary of Jefferson Country. The Belmont property stopped at that line before Thomas Walker added the Edgehill tract. His land stretched on past the lake for another half mile or so on the other side of that knoll. See the roof there in those trees? That's where the original Belmont mansion stood. It burned down around 1800. Surviving sketches suggest that Jefferson may have designed it, but no formal link has ever been established. The architectural historians at the University think the work was done by Jefferson's craftsmen during interruptions in the building of Monticello—construction typically slowed or stopped while Jefferson's was away, which was most of the time between 1785 and 1809. That's when he finally retired from public life and settled for good at Monticello."

"Henry, what is that to the right of the barn?" She was pointing toward the geodesic dome Buckminster Fuller had built for Aster Paige.

Henry scrutinized the peculiar-looking structure. "Mr. Paige's daughter lives there," he said. What could he tell her about Aster?

Henry met Aster—and Marjean—shortly after he moved into his cottage. The occasion was fixed forever in his memory. They appeared apparition-like in his living room one evening while he was wiring his stereo. He looked up and found two strange creatures dressed in black standing in front of him. Their eyes were painted with purple mascara. Their faces were caked with thick orange make-up. His first impulse was to laugh, but the look in their eyes told him that would be a mistake.

Aster had silken hair cut to the shoulder. It was a shimmering chestnut color and quite beautiful. She was thin, almost emaciated. Henry assumed she had done too many drugs. She looked older than her 30 years. Her sunken cheeks resembled glacial ravines separated by the craggy esker, which was her nose. Her mouth was small and shapeless. Her lips were pressed together in an expression of perpetual tenseness. They were painted in a dark color that emphasized a cadaverous quality in her being. Her eyes, close-set like a rodent's, darted nervously about as though she knew instinctively that she was prey.

Marjean made an interesting contrast. Her face was broad and round with plain, nomadic features like a tribal woman from the steppe. It was dominated by a pair of large black, joyless eyes that sat without expression in an inhospitable wilderness. She was slender though and moved with the gracefulness of a dancer. Her long black hair hung down her back in wild neglect.

"I am Marjean. This is Aster. We have come because we sensed your vibrations," she told him. "What is your birth sign?"

Henry had heard about Aster. He was not surprised that she was peculiar. The idle rich were peculiar. It was a burden imposed on them by the masses. Peculiarity was the imperial symbol of privilege. It gave wealth a savory mystique that enthralled ordinary people. It was the spice. The bonding agent. The indispensable preservative. In the horse country of central Virginia, eccentricity was the mark of good breeding. The queer traits of the truly rich were of such exquisiteness that the parvenu class gathering on hilltops around the old estates could only gasp in admiration. How disgusting. How vulgar they were. What a breach of public trust to resemble them in any way. Aster's life was successful in this regard at least.

Henry first encountered the leisure class as an undergraduate at the University. It was a great irony that this pretension would be a characteristic of Thomas Jefferson's academic village. But at his University, it had become a respected skill. For some it would become a life's occupation—attending the rich, drinking with their children without becoming sick, and amusing them with polished sarcasm. It was a misguided notion, the idea that common people might someday dwell like Dionysus among these living gods. The University seemed to gain prestige from it. Unfortunately, the idea did not hold up well outside the laboratories of daydreamers. In the real world, the rich were like Aster. How could ordinary people possibly bridge such a chasm? Henry reflected on the question as he watched the strange pair astralizing before him. Was it worth an effort?

"Vegetarius," Henry said finally, in a similarly solemn tone.

"You must not joke about the celestial powers," Marjean snapped back at him.

"Ok. I'm a Libra," Henry said, retreating to politeness.

"The date?" Marjean commanded fiercely.

"Say, how about a beer? Or would you prefer a glass of wine?"

Marjean cut him off. "We know who you are, Henry Tilghman. You were born on October 10, 1948."

"Now how do you know that?" Henry was genuinely surprised.

"Your stars are interesting to Aster," Marjean continued, ignoring his question.

Astrology was the perfect navigation system for Aster. Hard living on a carte blanche expense account had purged her mind of its power to reason. In the absence of this essential rudder, it had been easy for her to descend into the web of the indefinite, interpretive science of the stars. Marjean was her companion and guide, dominating in the way new people with single names are. She molded Aster's tattered mind around the notion of the macrocosm. The doctrine that stars hold dominion over the human body and all beings in general now ruled Aster's life. Marjean was careful to keep these precious revelations fixed in her mind. Aster was a Pisces linked to Henry, Marjean explained, by astral polarity. His natal chart revealed that he was to be a vessel in her cosmic voyage. Aster accepted this without questioning why Marjean had plundered her father's office to read Henry's file.

"Henry!" Claire nudged him impatiently.

"I'm sorry, I was . . ."

"I know—you were digging up another relic. It's a good thing you don't have to deal with traffic out here. You'd have a short life. You're supposed to be telling me about Mr. Paige's daughter."

"There's not much to tell," Henry dissembled. "She's not involved with the academy."

"I suppose Mr. Paige is just trying to be like Thomas Jefferson."

"In what respect?"

"Keeping his daughter near him."

"Yea. Kind of. See that house on the ridge?" Henry changed the subject without elaborating. "Dr. Denker lives there." He didn't see any reason to tell her about Bart Paige. The less said about him the better.

"What did Mr. Paige do before he founded the academy?"

"One of his great successes to revolutionize the cattle industry by re-configuring the confirmation standards for Black Angus cattle. Belmont was home to an internationally famous herd."

"What happened to it?"

"Somewhere along the way the Angus Association decided it wanted to change things. When he heard about that, Mr. Paige liquidated the herd. But he couldn't bring himself to sell his prize bull, Aberon of Belmont so he set up his son to run a breeding station over there on Fox Den Farm." Henry pointed beyond the trees on his right. "Selling sperm costs a lot less than keeping cattle," Henry added. "People used to fly in from all over the world to attend the sales. That's why we have a show barn and fancy board fences. Field green was Belmont's trademark color.

"I'm going to take you down the back way," Henry told her, as they walked back to the Unimog, "so you can see our most famous historical landmark."

"It seems that you don't like Thomas Jefferson," Claire observed, when they were seated again in the tractor cab.

Henry considered the question as he started the engine. "I don't dislike him. I just don't gloss over his faults."

"What were they, in your opinion?"

"He was self-serving and inconsistent."

"Consistency—you put a lot of stock in that don't you."

"In Logic," Henry replied stiffly, "a proposition is invalid if it holds both A and not-A."

"Juries consider the circumstances before fixing guilt," Claire observed.

"Circumstances? The circumstances were that Jefferson intended to create a social system that violated the economic laws governing human nature."

"You mean democracy?" Claire responded incredulously.

"Democracy was a device for Jefferson."

Claire frowned. "Device?"

"Look," Henry continued, "he squandered a fortune in pursuit of his own happiness, but still could not bring himself to admit the essential relationship between happiness and property."

"You can't be serious! Jefferson invented political democracy!"

"He despised the British monarchy and being subject to the English King. That's how he became a patriot. The independence movement was a way to get rid of the monarchy and the king, so he joined it. It was that simple."

Henry revved the engine and let out the clutch. The Unimog lurched forward toward the tree line at the west side of the pasture. On their right was a curtain of trees that rose abruptly to the peak of the ridge. Ahead of them was a gate. Claire opened it and closed it again when Henry had passed through. They continued down a canopied trail, which opened after a while into a wooded glen. In its center was a small lake spotted with flowering lilies. The place was enchanting.

"This is deceptive terrain," Henry explained. "There are a lot of hidden valleys along the ridge that make it difficult to keep your bearings. The first time I hiked on this trail I got lost. I thought I was heading south toward Shadwell until I discovered I was on Pantops Mountain. It's kind of interesting though. The Pantops trail ties into another one that leads to Monticello. Halfway between the two it crosses the Rivanna River. Thomas Randolph made a name for himself by fording it on horseback at high water in the dead of winter. I don't know whether that drove him mad, or whether he was already mad."

"I suppose life was pretty rough back then," Claire volunteered.

"This lake is said to have been Thomas Jefferson's favorite fishing hole." Henry announced, turning the engine off.

Claire studied the setting quietly. "I can understand why."

"The Baron claimed that it was fed by a mineral spring—that was supposed to lure globetrotting German health fanatics."

"What's that up there?" Claire asked, pointing to the frame of an abandoned building on the hill overlooking the lake.

"That was the Baron's arboretum."

"That's an odd place to build a greenhouse," Claire observed.

"Yea . . . maybe he thought mineral water would promote plant growth too. Claude, Mr. Paige's chauffeur, was a little boy when it was built. He told me once that he put it there to capture the eastern light."

Henry restarted the engine and drove around the edge of the lake. On the far side, he turned onto a path that traversed a gently sloping pasture. From the crest of the hill, they could see the back of the academy.

"What happened to the hotel after the Baron disappeared?" Claire asked.

"It moldered for a couple of decades. Shortly before the start of the Second World War it came into the hands of the spooks at the OSS. You know about the old boy network. Some of them had been down here in school and viewed it as the right kind of place for their bump-in-the-night stuff. Mr. Paige did a tour here," he added. "They fixed it up and added a few essentials, like the pool and tennis courts, so the chaps could let off some steam. Sometime after the war, Mr. Paige purchased the property. The CIA continued to lease the facilities until about fifteen years ago. That's when he closed up his investment banking practice in New York and started the herd."

Claire parked her MG beside Mr. Paige's limousine. Leroy was wiping off its windshield. That meant Mr. Paige had also just arrived. Henry spotted him on the landing at the top of the steps and called his name. Paige turned stiffly and looked down at them.

"Oh, it's you Hank . . . and Miss Fox!" He started down the stairs and walked across the blacktop. "Did it go all right?" He asked, looking at Claire.

"Yes," she answered with a cheerful smile.

"Good. I knew you two would get along."

"I've been showing her the local sights," Henry added. "I wonder, Mr. Page, would you have time to give Claire your perspective on the Jefferson Academy?"

"Sure . . ."

Claire felt her nerves tighten as he settled his gaze on her.

"I'm giving away my age," he observed without inflection. "During the Depression, I was in law school with a young man whose father happened to be the President of the United States." He reflected on the experience for a moment. "Those were hard times Miss Fox. You can't really understand what I mean because you did not live through them."

Claire nodded dutifully.

"There is no doubt about it. Franklin Roosevelt was the greatest man I ever met. He wasn't smarter than other men, but he was courageous and confident in ways other men weren't. He understood the American people. He told me once that it was their faith in the future that made America great. They would follow a leader anywhere, he said, so long as he had courage and vision. I learned from him the importance of good leadership." He watched closely to see whether she grasped his point.

Claire's image of Franklin Roosevelt merged comfortably into the persona of Raymond Paige. She sensed that she was on a wave rolling down the stream of time. The past she had come to admire drifted reassuringly into the present. She felt a warm emotional bond forming with her host.

"But there is a limit to what government can do in a free society Miss Fox. Our society is becoming more complex, and pressure is increasing for government to expand. Technology is creating opportunities for it to intrude where it performs no legitimate function. I read Alexis de Tocqueville as an undergraduate at Yale. I can still remember what he wrote in his conclusion to *Democracy in America*." Paige paused to remember the passage. "Above this race of men," he recited, "stands an immense and tutelary power, which takes upon itself alone to secure their gratifications, and to watch over their fate. That power is absolute, minute, regular, provident, and mild. It would be the authority of a parent, if, like that authority, its object was to prepare men for manhood; but it seeks instead to keep them in perpetual childhood; it is well content that people should rejoice, provided they think of nothing but rejoicing. For their happiness such a government willingly labors, but it chooses to be the sole agent and the only arbiter of that happiness; it provides for their security, foresees and supplies their necessities, facilitates their pleasures, manages their principal concerns, directs their industry, regulates the descent of property, and subdivides their inheritances: what remains, but to spare them all the care of thinking and all the trouble of living. The will of a man is not shattered, but softened and bent, and guided; men are seldom forced by it to act, but they are constantly restrained from acting: such a power does not destroy, but it prevents existence; it does not tyrannize, but It compresses, enervates, extinguishes, and stupefies a people, until the people are reduced to a flock of timid and industrious animals, of which the government is the shepherd."

Paige focused again on Claire. "Today we are unsure of what is good and what is bad, unable to distinguish right from wrong! We're paralyzed, Miss Fox. We have become the timid animals Tocqueville described."

Claire churned furiously through her mental notes. This ties into Veblen and his experienced technicians. Doesn't it? That is his message. Isn't it? The people are going to get control of the system. Aren't they?

"We're at a crossroad, Miss Fox. We need new leadership," Paige intoned. "The decisions we make today will determine whether we survive as a nation. The Jefferson Academy is going to play a leading part in this deliberation. We're going to focus the nation's attention on these fundamental issues. We have to start at the beginning and reintroduce our citizenry to American democracy." He raised his hands as if to fend off an objection. "I know everybody talks about democracy. But few among us today understand the link between the freedoms we enjoy as a society and the creative energy we contribute to it as individuals. That's why we have to sound Tocqueville's warning again. When was it Hank? One hundred and fifty years ago?"

"Just about."

"The conference is the first step . . . an important first step," he added. "We've brought the nation's most respected social thinkers together to take part in this forum. You have been a great help, Miss Fox. Thanks to you we're getting our message out to the American people."

It was beginning to sink in. Claire's mind began to spin. "You're launching a political campaign!"

Paige considered the comment. "American history is the story of political campaigns, Miss Fox. It started with the American Revolution and has continued through the Watergate trial. America is propelled by social impulses. They erupt like geysers among people obsessed with exercising their God-given right to pursue happiness. The power of this natural drive is the one American quality that Tocqueville failed to fully comprehend."

Claire listened without responding.

"Vietnam inflicted a serious wound on the American spirit," he continued. "It isn't clear yet, but it will be very soon."

"What's not clear?" Claire demanded, revealing her anger.

"Their asphyxiating new orthodoxy."

"Orthodoxy?"

"Well-being!" Page fired back. "They want to replace Jefferson's society, and the chance it offers individuals to find individual happiness, with a cabal of Orwellian shepherds to tend us once we've become a properly compliant flock. Karl Marx had a similar idea, but his prescription for well-being proved to be a poor substitute for personal happiness. We believe individuals have a right to life, liberty, and property. This is not just another enlightened theory, Miss Fox! It's a God-given right. The law of nature! Mark my words. If we don't defend it, there will be no freedom, no happiness, and no well-being."

Claire thought she knew all the angles in the property debate. She kicked herself for not catching on when Henry brought it up in the Bird Field. "What about equal protection?" She threw her heaviest punch first. "Isn't fairness important?"

"It's a minefield." Paige said, dismissing the idea. "We'd be crazy to get into it. We'd have an endless stream of pleaders marching on the Capital. No Miss Fox, America would be finished. Our mission is to help the American people understand. We have to replace a system that accumulates power to regulate change with a system that disburses power so that talented people can excel. To preserve freedom in the post-industrial age, people have to become self-sufficient. They have to become builders like their forefathers."

"How do you expect to do that?" Claire objected.

"We are going to put Thorstein Veblen and Joseph Schumpeter in harness together." The idea clearly pleased him. "We are going to tear away what is old and unproductive and make way for the new and vital. That's going to be the operative principle in the post-industrial age. We're going to move Keynes out of the economic spotlight and put fresh ideas to work. They're a good match," he added, referring again to Veblen and Schumpeter, "not because they overlap on a central point but because they have disciples at both ends of the political spectrum." He paused and fixed an expectant gaze on Claire. "You see?"

Claire shook her head defiantly.

"Realignment! It's the basis for a major political realignment. We need new coalitions. That's the only way we're going to get a leash on these damned utopians. We're going to rally 'round the flag." He struck his hand with his fist to emphasize his point. "We're going to rally around the flag!"

Before Claire could challenge it, Oscar Denker called down from the wall at the edge of the lawn. "Ray . . ." he hurried down the steps toward him.

"Excuse me." Paige stepped back to meet him.

Henry could tell it was important from Denker's demeanor. He strained to make out what they were saying, but the only word he was able to make out was "Hardin."

Paige stepped back toward Claire. "I apologize again, but there is something I have to tend to. Let's continue this conversation later." He looked across to Henry. "Will Miss Fox be joining us for dinner?"

Henry looked over at Claire who nodded back firmly. "Yes."

"Good." With that, Paige turned and marched off with Denker.

After they had made their sandwiches at the buffet, Henry led Claire to a table by the window. Claire took the seat facing into the room. Henry took the seat across from her with the view of the valley.

Claire lifted her sandwich, then set it down again.

"Is something wrong?" Henry asked reluctantly.

"Mr. Paige's comments . . ."

"What about them?"

"I can't believe . . ." she left the sentence dangling.

Henry braced himself. "What?"

"Does he really think Communists are taking over the country? Is that the political vision of the Jefferson Academy?"

"Your picture is not quite in focus . . ."

"No?"

"Put it this way. Mr. Paige sees modern American politics as an ideological war. In his opinion, liberals and conservatives are like two competing armies fighting a winner-take-all battle for the mind of the American people. What they're really doing is killing the idea that Americans share a common heritage. The society is breaking into incompatible factions. As it does, the people are abandoning the political process. That's why Mr. Paige created the Jefferson Academy. He wants to reacquaint the American people with the principles of political democracy and restore the 'American vision.'"

"I don't see the value, frankly," she said, rejecting Henry's explanation.

"We don't understand what they are anymore."

"Who are the utopians?" Claire asked, changing the subject.

"Well . . ." Henry searched for an answer. "Are you familiar with the original criticisms leveled against political democracy?"

"No," Claire conceded.

"One was that it would deteriorate into anarchy as the mob gained control of the apparatus of government. Another was that it would lead to a tyranny of the majority—that was Madison's primary concern. Mr. Paige touched on another in his address. Tocqueville characterized it as the "great leveling process" that would destroy the individual genius which propels social progress. Gladstone merged these last two when he described our political process as all sail and no anchor. Nobody believed that democracy would produce wise leaders or responsible citizens. It was supposed to collapse under its own weight."

"Ok. So where do the utopians fit in?"

"The utopians are the social levelers who frightened Tocqueville."

Martin suddenly appeared in her mind's eye. She could see his rage behind his blank expression. His paper had just endorsed the political agenda of a rich, right-wing reactionary. She wrote the article. Now what? she wondered.

"Madison is an interesting case," Henry said, oblivious of her trauma.

"Who?" Claire asked, returning reluctantly to her companion.

"James Madison. He was a real oddball," Henry repeated.

"Was he?"

"Yea. He was a social democrat like Jefferson and an economic liberal like Hamilton. He may have been the only Founding Father who understood the American people."

Claire sat quietly, pondering at her situation.

"He designed a system of government to prevent legislative majorities from entrenching themselves. In Madison's view, that was how the tyranny of the majority manifested itself. Tocqueville, on the other hand, was concerned with social dynamics. He expected social pressures from a bland, overbearing orthodoxy to destroy the initiative of society's exceptional members and undermine the progressive forces that would otherwise propel society in America. That's what Mr. Paige is talking about."

"I don't think the American people will understand what you are talking about."

"They will," Henry assured her.

"What makes you so sure?" She asked skeptically.

"Because they are motivated by self-interest—just like you," he added as a matter of fact.

Claire shrugged. "Can I ask another silly question?"

"Sure.

"Is Mr. Paige running for President?"

Before Henry could respond, someone called his name.

Claire looked up to see Dr. Denker leading a tall, stately woman across the room. "That's Barbara Tuchman," Henry whispered. "She's going to host our panel discussion this afternoon."

Denker looked unsettled. "Henry, Mrs. Tuchman's plane was delayed, and she is running a bit late. Could you see that she gets some lunch. But be sure she is at the auditorium by 1:15."

Henry looked at his watch. It was 12:50. "No problem."

Denker turned to his guest. "I'm going to have to leave you in the care of Henry Tilghman. He'll escort you to the auditorium after you've eaten." He gave her hand a vigorous shake, then hurried off.

"It's a great honor to meet you, Mrs. Tuchman. I've read all your books."

"Why thank you Henry—is it Tilghman?"

"Yes . . . and this is Claire Fox of *The Washington Post*."

"Why, Claire! What a pleasant surprise. So nice to find you here!"

"Hello Barbara." Henry watched as the two women embraced. "Henry told me that you are leading a discussion this afternoon."

"I am! I think it's so kind of Raymond to ask me." She turned back to Henry. "Henry, you could do me a great service by giving me directions to the powder room."

"It's out the door and to the right. And if you trust me to make a sandwich for you, I'll have it ready when you get back."

"That would be very nice. See if they have sliced turkey. And hold the mayonnaise." A moment later she disappeared through the dining room door.

"How do you know Barbara Tuchman?" Henry asked when she was gone.

"She's a fellow Radcliffe alumna—we've served together on a couple of committees . . ."

"Small world!"

"Not to change the subject," Claire continued, "but what is the discussion Barbara is leading this afternoon?"

"You haven't seen the program?"

"No."

There was a pamphlet on the table beside them. Henry picked it up and handed it to her. "Read this. I'll go make Mrs. Tuchman's sandwich."

Claire scanned the room for familiar faces. Seeing none she looked down at the pamphlet.

The conference schedule started on page two. Monday was gone so she turned to page three. The first event on Tuesday was Rockefeller's address, *Three Challenges for Post-Industrial Society*.

Washington was full of losers, the sort of people one found in every capital around the world—arrogant, ambitious, self-envisioning men. Men with aristocratic tastes and temperaments. Men in single-minded pursuit of their own interests. Once they had been the people's servants. Doers of the public's good. Getters. Givers. Spenders. They had been the deal makers, the manipulators, the facilitators—whatever promoted their careers. Now, somehow, they were ex officio. Political non-entities. Dead. They were vagrants in the public thoroughfare. Beggars. Panhandlers scrounging for lost power. They needed to be acknowledged. They needed to be thanked for their generosity. They needed to be praised for their vision. They were potentates. They needed to rule.

Claire learned about these men at *The Post*. She learned that they were fillers. That they were footnotes. They were takers who had nothing valuable to give. She saw them now as time wasters. Space wasters. Name users. Influence borrowers. She had learned to avoid them. And now, she realized, she hated them. Not because they were self-serving. They were insignificant. That's why she hated them. Yet here was Nelson Rockefeller, at the head of a new campaign—the new man of the hour.

The sound of a chair moving nearby caused her to look up. Barbara Tuchman was taking her seat. Henry was behind her carrying a lunch tray.

"How am I doing for time Henry?" Mrs. Tuchman asked as she settled into the chair beside Claire.

"You're in good shape." Henry replied, setting a tray down in front of her.

"Henry," she continued, "I want you to be sure to introduce me to Roberta Wiley. She'll be amused when I tell her about my trip. She warned me against flying on Albemarle Airways, but I was not wise enough to listen to her."

Claire could tell something was wrong by the look on Henry's face. He looked like he was being overwhelmed by some massive internal trauma. She watched him turn stiffly and move away from the table. He crossed the room to the service table. When he reached it, he gripped it to steady himself and bowed his head.

"Is he all right?" The older woman asked in quiet alarm.

"I don't know!"

"I hope he's not sick," Mrs. Tuchman added, giving a name to her concern.

"Who is Roberta Wiley?" Claire asked abruptly. The question caught her companion by surprise.

"She's Raymond's assistant—she helped me with my travel arrangements. Is she . . ."

"I think something has happened to her."

"Oh my!"

When he looked up, the barn was in front of him. He remembered that before he stepped inside, he had glanced back across the valley at the moon's ghostly shadows, which dappled the peaceful landscape.

It was dark inside, and the air was musty. He heard the drum begin to beat in the chamber above. Next, he heard the voice chanting and the footfalls of the dancer swirling and leaping. He remembered groping through the darkness toward the stairway on the barn's back wall. As he mounted the steps, the drum beat quickened, and the chanting grew frenzied. A partition on the upper landing separated the stairs from the loft. A thin ribbon of light rimmed the door. Henry remembered the strange sensation that swept over him as he pushed it open and stepped in. The stifling vapor. The difficulty catching his breath. And how the chanting had stopped, and everything became still.

A black canvas covered the floor of the chamber. In the center of the canvas was a red circle divided into twelve sections. Each was marked with a symbol. Henry recognized them as signs of the Zodiac. At the center, he saws the motionless form of a woman. Her back was arched, and her head was thrust back so that her face pointed upward toward an object hovering above the cone of light that illuminated her body. Her hands strained upward toward it in tortured supplication. Henry's gaze shifted to the object. As he watched, it began to glow. Little by little a form settled around the eerie light. First an elongated, hoary face. Then thick pointed horns protruding from its crown. Then a garland dangling down either side of the skeletal face. An anxious chill crept down his spine.

Behind the dancer, on the far side of the circle, Henry saw the altar with its silver candelabra. To its left, Henry saw the silver cup. To its right, he saw a collection of instruments.

A light flickered in the darkness behind the altar. It was the reflection from a golden disk that wavered gently in a silent rhythm. As he watched, another form emerged. It resembled a shield with a crest. The ornament was . . . Roberta! Her body stretched across the space within the circular frame with her hands and feet touching its rim. Henry recognized the symbols on the rim. They were astrological signs. Roberta's face was expressionless, but the medallion on her breast sparkled again with each listless breath.

The drumming resumed. Henry located the drummer crouching at the edge of the dancer's circle. It was Aster. Her eyes were fixed on the figure before her. It was Marjean. The pulsing sound of Aster's drum brought her out of her trance. She turned toward him. Henry felt her eyes upon him.

"Prince of Darkness," she said, in a cold, carnal voice, as she floated toward him. As she approached, she lowered her arms in a sweeping arch. Her hands met at his groin. She sank to her knees before him and bowed her head. He watched as she raised up again and began circling around him. Her steps were punctuated with the harsh guttural chant he heard from below. Her movement quickened with each circuit. Round she went. Round and round. His mind blurred as he watched her.

At last, she swirled to a halt before him, her hot breath searing his face. She wrapped her arms around him and kissed his lips. In the next instant, she sprang away like a frightened deer, flying through the halo light to the altar. The silver cup was in her hands. She passed it across the flame. And again. Then she turned and extended the cup to him. Henry felt himself drawing toward her, closer, until he was beside her. He shuddered at the taste of the bittersweet liquid. Her dark eyes remained riveted upon him as he consumed it.

A narcotic tingle spread through him. His mind dimmed as he slipped deeper into a paralyzing cocoon. His eyes remained fixed on the gold medallion on Roberta's breast. It rose and fell in the cycle of her breathing. As he watched, it changed. A face appeared; eyes burning with a malignant luster; mouth glowering in a ghoulish smile. He was afraid, but he was powerless to move. Then there was a voice. "Come Master . . . all is ready . . ."

There was no longer structure in his reality, only disconnected fragments whirling about. The voice, droning. An implement in his hand. A figure appearing on the pale surface before him. Then another. And another. The space around him continued to shrink with each new form. At last, there was nothing but the voice. On and on it droned until his brain could take no more. Then it too faded and was gone. Then only darkness remained.

Henry shook himself and straightened up. When he was sure of his balance, he picked up a glass. He filled it with water and took a long, careful drink. The cool liquid sent a welcome chill through his steaming body. He would have to tell that Roberta was dead. Did he remember the official version? He took another drink. Mrs. Tuchman wouldn't ask him any questions. He glanced back at the table. She wasn't the problem.

"Are you all right Henry?" Mrs. Tuchman asked. Her face bore an expression of deep concern.

"I'm sorry about the interruption," he said timidly. "I wasn't ready for your question. They made the announcement before you arrived. Roberta Wiley drowned Sunday afternoon in a swimming accident."

"Oh! What a tragedy! I'm so sorry." The older woman's face was a portrait of care and sorrow.

"Thank you," Henry said, shielding his eyes. "We're all in a state of shock." He glanced at his watch. "We should head on over to the auditorium." He stood up and walked toward the door. Mrs. Tuchman and Claire followed him out of the dining room and across the lawn.

Mrs. Tuchman spoke quietly with Claire as they walked. "When one spends one's time reading history, it is impossible not to become a student of human tragedy," she observed. "In a way it's a blessing, I suppose—to understand the failings of the past. What I regret is that we seem to learn so little from them. If I could do one thing, it would be to change that.

"This gathering is an opportunity to turn on a light," she continued. "I'm particularly glad that it is being held here in Thomas Jefferson's own community. It was his profound knowledge of Greek and Roman history that enabled him to shape not only a view of man's potential, but of society and government as well. He used his knowledge for the good of humanity. We will always be indebted to him.

"We must try to be like him, Claire. He did not just take from the past. He gave to the future. The issues confronting us today are no more complex than the ones he faced. If they seem harder to understand it's because we don't look to the past the way he did to find wisdom. Sometimes it's frustrating," she laughed self-consciously, "Anyway, those are the reasons I wanted to participate in this program."

She fell silent as they reached the stage door. Henry held it open for the two women, then followed them inside. Mr. Paige appeared as if on cue. He nodded to Henry, "Thank you, Hank. I'll take over now." He welcomed Mrs. Tuchman with a friendly exchange, then led her off through a door on the far side of the room.

"Thank you, Henry," Mrs. Tuchman called back before she slipped out of sight.

"We'll be out front," Claire called after her.

"Good luck!" Henry added in a muted postscript.

———————————

When they were seated, Claire leaned toward Henry. "What was the Vice President's speech about?"

"The speech?"

"*Three Challenges* . . ."

"That's right," Henry nodded, straining to remember. "I didn't actually hear it," he confessed. "I read an advance copy. He made some good points. Did you know that it's the topic for this afternoon's discussion?"

"No . . . What were the three challenges?"

"Let me see. The first is to create a firm capital foundation. I doubt anyone will argue with that under the current circumstances. Do you think?"

"I suppose not," she said without interest. "What was his second point?"

"His second point was . . . we have to create a modern workforce. That's the education issue—modernizing curricula, more funding for hard sciences, developing better job training programs, etc. He also touched on the need for new management techniques—kind of an interesting idea for a man who has never worked for a living."

"Hmmm . . . What was his last point?"

"Minorities and women. We have to bring them into the economic mainstream. You know, spread the wealth."

"How did he propose to do that?"

"Didn't say. The speech was more symbolic. Like reciting the Mayflower Compact on Thanksgiving Day."

Their conversation was interrupted by a sudden burst of applause. They looked up together to see Mrs. Tuchman striding across the stage toward the podium. The lights dimmed and the audience quieted. When she reached the stand, she looked out across the audience to signal the program had begun.

"Good afternoon ladies and gentlemen. Welcome to the Jefferson Academy's first annual "issues" conference. I am Barbara Tuchman. I will be your host today. Like most of you I am a guest here. I hope you feel as much at home as I do. It is a great honor for me to be a part of the program. Those of you who attended Vice President Rockefeller's address this morning are familiar with the issues we will be discussing. They are central to our evolving society: equal opportunity, skilled labor, and capital. We have with us a distinguished panel who will share their thoughts with us as we proceed. I encourage all of you to join us as we exercise the rights Mr. Jefferson fought so fiercely to create.

"Let me introduce the panel, then we will begin . . ."

"Some of you may not know our first panelist. *Time Magazine* has called him 'a professor with a class of millions.' Many consider him the father of environmental movement. He is the author of two best-selling books, including *The Closing Circle* which Newsweek called 'the best book on ecology ever written'. Currently he is Director of the Center for the Biology of Natural Systems, a private biology and energy research institute in New York. Ladies and gentlemen, please welcome Barry Commoner." The audience responded with enthusiastic applaud.

"Thank you. Thank you . . . Our next panelist is, in my opinion, one of America's most remarkable men. His law degree is from Columbia University, where he also earned renown as a basketball player. He has served as Deputy Police Commissioner and President of the Bedford Stuyvesant Restoration Corporation. He is the recipient of many public service awards as well as Honorary degrees from Yale, Fordham, and the Pratt Institute. Currently he serves as President of the Ford Foundation, the first Afro-American to hold this position. Ladies and gentlemen, would you welcome please Mr. Franklin A. Thomas." More vigorous applause.

"Our final panelist has distinguished himself in many fields. He earned his doctorate in public and international law while working as a newspaper man in Frankfort, Germany. He has taught economics and statistics at Sarah Lawrence College. At Bennington, he taught politics, history, and philosophy. For twenty years he taught management in the Graduate Business School of New York University. Currently he is the Clarke Professor of Social Science at Claremont Graduate School in Claremont, California. He is a regular contributor to *The Wall Street Journal*, and his latest book, *The Unseen Revolution: How Pension Fund Socialism came to America*, will be released early next year. Ladies and gentlemen please welcome Professor Peter Drucker."

Mrs. Tuchman continued when the applause subsided. "I'm going to take advantage of my position as moderator to ask the first question. I'll direct it to the panel. Then I will open it to the floor.

"Panel, we are just beginning to understand the extent of the damage our industrial society is causing to the life support systems of our planet. The air is no longer safe to breathe, nor the water safe to drink. Plants and wildlife are being indiscriminately destroyed. Short sighted land use practices are causing our soil and forests to be poisoned. Chronic shortages now seem to exist for many essential natural resources. And, here on the eve of a technical revolution, policy makers are studying plans for rationing the most basic staples of life—food, shelter, and medicine. In light of these ominous developments, one wonders whether we are presuming too much? My question, panel, is this. Do we really have a future? Mr. Commoner, would you start please."

"Thank you, Mrs. Tuchman. You are asking a very profound question. Let me start by restating what I call the First Law of Ecology: Everything is connected to everything else."

What the hell was she doing? The question burst in Henry's mind like a grenade. *Did she think she was going to change who she was by joining Aster's weird circle?*

"The essential aspect of the First law of Ecology is the tight interconnectedness between the Environment, the Economy, and Energy. This is easily confirmed by observing how our environment is being destroyed by our system of throw away capitalism. We have devised a process in which we use technology to make products that do not last and garbage that does not disappear. We have transformed a natural cycle into a linear progression. We have reached the point now where we are choking on our own refuse.

"And that brings us to what I call the Second Law of Ecology: Everything has to go somewhere. As we accumulate virtual mountains of garbage, we are not only displacing nature, we are poisoning our environment and impeding nature's regenerative processes. The man-made technosphere is on the verge of becoming sufficiently large to alter the natural processes of the ecosphere. These human attacks on the ecosphere have instigated an ecological counterattack. The two worlds are now at war. If we allow the technosphere to prevail, we are going to destroy our own habitat.

"As Mrs. Tuchman just noted, the news is not good. But it's not all bad either. For one thing, we are becoming more knowledgeable about the state of the environment—what needs to be done to protect it and what kinds of technologies are safe. This is guiding us in making changes in the major components of the technosphere—automobiles, power plants, and petrochemical factories.

"To win this war, we are going to have to take radical steps. First, we have to change the way we think of ourselves in the world. Up to now we have been able to separate our creations in the world from the natural world. We must come to grips with the fact that this division is on the verge of being eliminated. Events in the natural world that we think of as 'acts of God' may actually be unintended consequences of technospheric encroachment. This will help us appreciate the scope of the changes we have to make in the way we operate in the technosphere. But if recent history is any indication, we're going to encounter heavy opposition. The moguls of industry are going to fight us every step of the way."

. . . What a life . . . running away from home at sixteen . . . with a rock band . . . what was it called . . . Street Noise . . . and the guy . . . Arty Lincoln, that's it . . . being his grunt . . . like it was cool. Lucky she knew how to hustle . . . she said she got them the gig at the Phillie Spectrum . . . backing up the Stones on their '67 tour . . . That must have been a trick . . . and their manager

liked her tits! Had her doing go-go numbers topless for 20,000 screaming pot-heads. Jumpin' Jack Flash is a gas, gas, gas. That was before Arty got tied up with the New York pusher . . . they were all potheads . . . how else could they stand that music? That was the only money he made—dealing! When was he busted? . . . In the spring of '68 . . . in Boston . . .

"In your opinion, Mr. Commoner, can we solve these problems?"

"There is a growing movement in that direction, but we have to overcome a great deal of negative inertia. Ignorance is the first obstacle. Many people are content to think of the Earth as an orbiting pile of raw materials. They'll say it's still here after five billion years so why worry about it now? We have to educate these people. At the same time, it's easy to be overwhelmed by the magnitude of the problem. People who allow themselves to be discouraged are apt to throw up their hands and give up. We have to encourage them and keep them in the process. But the greatest problem is the lack of political commitment to implement effective policies. To get them we have to increase the pressure on our elected officials."

"We're dealing with a greed-based economic system that values profits over a clean environment. To overcome it, we must pull together at the grass roots and purge the system of the capitalists who control it. At this point it's by no means sure that the right side is going to win."

"What needs to be done?"

"We have to make major, collective changes in the way we do things. The needs of the community have to be recognized as the highest priority. This means changing our views on private enterprise, private property, and what we consider to be our rights as individuals."

"Thank you, Mr. Commoner," Mrs. Tuchman called out above an avalanche of enthusiastic applause.

. . . The narcs promise not to prosecute her if she leaves town . . . no problem there . . . being hip is hard work—even for someone like Roberta. She needs a place to lay low . . . She hears that summer money is good on Nantucket, so she hitches a ride to the Cape and hops the ferry. That's where she meets prince charming . . . good ol' George . . . He's not like the bums she's met on the road. He's on track . . . he has a plan . . . he's going to change the world from the inside . . . Jesus . . . Only Edmond could make that line work . . . He's out there on Nantucket building his portfolio of life experiences . . . doing the Nantucket thing will put him higher on the food chain with the swells

at Virginia's law school. I bet George had never met a chick like Roberta . . . What a match . . . the blue blood Yalie and the hustler with the cute tits . . . They even had things in common . . . like sounds . . . getting high . . . and photography. That clinched it . . . Roberta is an artist. George has all the gear. In a delirious moment, he asks her to come with him to Charlottesville . . . God . . . that must have been something to see. And she agrees . . . Off they go. At the law school, everybody's smart. Everybody's polished. Everybody is self-assured. Roberta realizes that George is going somewhere . . . she kind of digs it . . . She meets the Dean at a lawn party . . . After a few cocktails, he gives her the name of the editor of the Daily Progress. "Call him," he says . . . "Tell him I told you to."

Claire clapped loudly into his ear. "I interviewed him after *The Closing Circle* was published," she gushed. "If you haven't read it, you should. He's brilliant!"

Henry nodded.

"Thank you, Mr. Commoner. I'm sure our audience will have questions for you, but before we open the floor, let us hear from the other panelists. Mr. Thomas—would you continue please?"

"Thank you, Mrs. Tuchman," he said after the applause subsided. "Those of you who do not come from New York may not know that Bedford Stuyvesant is a ghetto on the lower east side of Manhattan. The people who live in it are poor, isolated, and black." He paused to let the audience form a picture. "I don't disagree with what Mr. Commoner has just said about the environment, but let's not kid ourselves into thinking the environment is our only problem. This country has millions of people whose lives are being destroyed day by day in the pollution of poverty."

The audience responded with a supportive burst of applause.

"The future Mr. Commoner points to is where these people live right now. How can a man worry about the destruction of a rain forest or an arctic wilderness when he is fighting every day for his own survival? Think about it—are human lives any less important than plants and animals?" The question triggered another burst of applause. "Conditions in minority communities, especially those in the inner cities are rapidly deteriorating. We have to stop this slide." Again the audience applauded. "To do it we have to substantially increase the resources we put into them." Another burst of applause.

"But we have to be careful how we do this," he continued. "Welfare is undermining the infrastructure of our black communities. The foundations they rest on are crumbling. It's going to take more than bricks and mortar to put things right. No amount of money will be enough unless we also take care to rebuild their cultural infrastructure. Without this, our minorities are going to remain forever in a state of economic slavery."

This seemed to confuse the audience.

"Folks living in ghettos have come to depend on social programs run by white people who teach them that the way to get out of poverty is to act like white people." The white audience listened quietly. "How are black folks supposed to build self-respect when they're taught that they're in the ghetto because they don't behave like white people?

"We like to talk about America as the world's melting pot. That's nonsense. It's the most predatory society on earth. America is a cultural battlefield. European cultures dominate the rest of us by terrorizing us. The real social problem is cultural genocide! Poverty and minority disenfranchisement are just aspects of this larger problem.

"Look at American history. White Europeans have nurtured their cultural roots for two centuries in the nation's richest economic soil. They have built their wealth on the backs of blacks and other minorities whom they have excluded from the benefits of capital. After laboring on the land for generations, blacks have been herded into ghettos and made to live where there is no good soil. They get leftovers—enough to keep them alive, but not enough to keep their dignity from withering away. This is how white society controls minorities and keeps them down."

The audience, overwhelmingly white, stared back self-consciously.

"Everyone here understands the relationship between community health and money. I'm here to tell you that minorities can't achieve equality without their fair share of the nation's financial resources. But if I had to identify the single greatest obstacle to racial equality, I would say it is the idea that black folks have to be like white people. It conditions black people to think they are inferior... that is destroying our communities from within.

"We are not going to achieve equality while our communities lie in ruins. We're not going to achieve equality while rich white suburbanites create social programs that humiliate poor black ghetto-dwellers. America's minorities need to be given the means to prosper like the rest of society. They have a right to prosper in their own communities, like the rest of society. On their own terms! Like the rest of society!

"The nation owes compensation to the people it has oppressed. This debt isn't going to be settled by moving a few grateful Uncle Toms into white neighborhoods.

"The trend is going in the wrong direction," Thomas announced to the sea of white faces. "Instead of promoting economic and cultural parity, we have chosen to create a patchwork of laws that punish people for obstructing cultural genocide. We have institutionalized the problem, not the solution. The effect will be to destroy all non-white cultures in America."

A few sympathetic white people applauded. Then a few more. Slowly the applause grew until it was as loud as thunder. It was an incredible outpouring. Henry watched the communal purging. This is going to change some plans, he thought. He could almost hear the calculators whizzing. How can we use this guy?

Barbara Tuchman spoke into her mike as the applause began to die down, "As far as I am aware, Mr. Thomas, the accepted view is that cultural repression is the result of racism. You seem to think it's the cause."

"I'm saying that acts of racism are expressions of disrespect for another man's culture. I am saying that I do not think minorities can achieve social equality unless they first come to respect themselves within their own communities. Without this there is not going to be any respect from the outside. But a community has to be economically viable for its culture to thrive. As long as we force our minorities to live in poverty, there is going to be no culture and no self-respect. Does anyone really think we will achieve equality because we have laws that forbid discrimination?"

Claire leaned over and whispered a question into Henry's ear. "Is Franklin Thomas one of your Utopians?"

"I don't know," Henry whispered back. "I don't think he knows which side he's on yet."

"I mean his ideas of social justice—aren't they utopian?"

"You're asking the wrong question."

"I am?"

"The Constitution enumerates the responsibilities of government and defines rights reserved to individuals. The idea that individuals should be deprived of their constitutional rights so cultural minorities can receive special benefits violates the natural law that we claim is the cornerstone of our society."

Claire's frown irritated Henry. "That's what Jefferson said, 'Government derives its just power from the consent of the governed.' It's right there in the Declaration of Independence. If you haven't read it, you should. He's brilliant!"

"Our final panelist is Peter Drucker. Professor Drucker would you . . ."

A sudden crash at the rear of the auditorium caused Mrs. Tuchman to stop in mid-sentence. Henry turned with the others and watched as a short, stocky woman with close-cropped gray hair stormed into the hall. She was followed by a procession of a placard-waving women.

"Oh God!" He blurted it out before he could stop himself.

"What?" Claire asked turning toward him.

"Nothing," he snapped, with a quick headshake. If she didn't already know, he wasn't going to point it out—Marjean and Aster were carrying one of the banners. MEN ARE PIGS it said.

When their pinch-faced leader raised her clenched fist over her head, the procession behind her began to chant. FREEDOM . . . FREEDOM . . . FREEDOM . . . still chanting, the protestors marched down the aisle to the stage. When they reached the pit, their commander lowered her fist, and the chanting stopped.

She turned and faced the audience. "By the power vested in me as the duly elected President of the Congress of Women-Peoples of the Earth," she announced solemnly to the bewildered assembly, "I hereby dissolve all political bands with Man-Society. Be it known that from this day forward, Women-Peoples of the Earth are fully and totally independent and are no longer bound by the covenants of Man-Society. Being free and independent, women people of New America herewith assert our right to join together in a new order according to the way of Gaia our Mother."

"Order! Order!" Mrs. Tuchman cracked her gavel down in an angry barrage. "Ms. Rank, if you wish to declare independence, you will have to rent your own hall. This one is occupied. I must insist that you and your colleagues remove yourselves immediately."

With that Frances Rank, founder, and self-appointed Chair of the

Women People's Committee of Well-being, sank down onto the floor in front of the stage. Her colleagues quickly followed. A few women from the audience rose and joined them. Henry glanced over at Claire. To his relief, she remained seated.

"We do not recognize the authority of traitors to our cause," Rank intoned without looking at Mrs. Tuchman. As she spoke, she raised her fist. Her accomplices resumed their chanting. "FREEDOM... FREEDOM... FREEDOM..."

"You will remove yourselves from this hall immediately, or I will have no choice but to have you forcibly evicted."

The protestors responded by locking arms. "We hold these truths to be self-evident according to the way of Gaia," Rank sang out over the continuing chant. "All Women-People are equal... FREEDOM... and are entitled to safety of body and peace of mind... FREEDOM... to self-determination... FREEDOM... to an environment that is not detrimental to their health... FREEDOM... to assemble and demonstrate... FREEDOM... to be free from sexism... FREEDOM... to live in the way of Gaia..."

Mrs. Tuchman hammered the declaration to a close. "I DECLARE THIS MEETING ADJOURNED! CLEAR THE HALL."

Barry Commoner appeared out of the mounting confusion and stepped to the edge of the stage. "Ladies and gentlemen! Could I have your attention. Could I have your attention PLEASE..." Frances Rank stopped chanting and a tense hush settled across the auditorium. "If I may make a suggestion," he turned to Barbara Tuchman, who nodded cautiously. "To avoid unnecessary conflict, may I suggest that we invite Ms. Rank and her associates to participate in this forum."

Mrs. Tuchman flashed a look of angry disapproval but seeing that the idea held a solution to a complex problem, she pounded down her gavel again. "Can you be orderly, Ms. Rank?"

Rank rose steadfastly and faced the audience again. "We agree to participate in an orderly manner on the condition that we be allowed to make a statement."

"For God's sake, Frances!" Mrs. Tuchman bellowed in frustration, "Can't you just go along?... Oh! All right. Go ahead—I'll give you exactly two minutes."

"Be it known that for the uncounted ages of tyranny and suffering inflicted upon us by Man-Society, Women-People have an inalienable right to reparations. We hereby demand settlement for this accumulated damage, which shall be the full and complete sovereignty of the Order of the Women-People over the geographical territory of North America and all property therein contained."

"Is that it?" Mrs. Tuchman asked incredulously.

"Yes..."

"Hmm... Ok..." Having restored the peace, Mrs. Tuchman turned back to her third panelist. "Now Mr. Drucker, if you are able, it is your turn to respond to my question."

"Thank you, Mrs. Tuchman." He gazed introspectively at the silent figures huddled in front of the stage. "There is need for change. To that extent, I agree with Mr. Commoner and Mr. Thomas and, I suppose, with the "women-people" before me. I also agree that the problems they have identified are valid and serious. But purging society of capitalists, to say nothing of men in general, will not make America successful in tomorrow's economy—or benefit women or minorities.

"Society needs risk takers who are willing to invest in the future," Drucker explained. "Without them, we are going to lose control of our economy <u>and</u> our freedom. It's as simple as that."

Henry's eyes remained fixed on Frances Rank, but his thoughts drifted back to Roberta.

... The Daily Progress ... she liked it there ... it suited her better than George's law school circle ... where they traded on degrees and pedigrees that she didn't have. Being tough and streetwise didn't cut it at the law school. She knew she didn't belong there ...

"Let's consider what the economic future holds." Drucker said.

... He needed a facilitator ... someone who could open doors ... she saw it coming ... she didn't fit the bill ... she even told him she didn't mind ... They split up after six months ... She was ready to get on with her life ...

"To begin with, we have a generation of baby-boomers entering an essentially full job pipeline. They are facing a vacuum in management positions. Because of this, most baby-boomers are going to reach plateaus relatively early in their careers. That will create a mismatch between reality and expectations."

. . . She persuaded her editor to give her a new assignment . . . writing a column on rock music . . . she told her friends he was paying her to hang out . . . One night she went over to the Albemarle Lounge . . . Arty's band was there . . . he was out of the slammer and 'touring' . . . you'll see everybody you've ever known in Charlottesville . . .

"This gap widens in inverse proportion to one's level of education and training, which means that minorities are going to have an even tougher time ahead."

This blunt assessment sent a chill through the hall and jarred Henry out of his reflection.

"This logjam exists because we are substituting knowledge and capital for manual labor in our manufacturing economy. Mr. Commoner is no doubt aware that as we automate, we are shifting from industries that are primarily labor intensive to industries that are primarily knowledge intensive. We are, in short moving away from materials-based manufacturing to information and knowledge-based manufacturing. Take for example the communications industry. One hundred pounds of fiberglass cable transmits as many telephone messages as one ton of copper wire. Yet to produce one hundred pounds of fiberglass cable requires no more than 1/20 the energy needed to mine, smelt, and draw copper into wire. In the auto industry, plastics, which are replacing steel in automobile bodies, represent a raw material cost, including energy, of less than half of that of steel.

"To remain competitive nations must automate. If, in the next quarter century, they do not sharply increase their manufacturing production while sharply reducing their blue-collar workforces, they will not be able to compete—or even remain 'developed'."

Drucker's analysis was unarguably correct. Henry glanced over at Claire to see her reaction. She was sitting stiffly in her seat, her face frozen in a grim stare. Henry noticed her hands. They were clasping each other like two frightened children.

"We are struggling now between polices that emphasize industrial production and policies that emphasize industrial employment and other social issues. If we promote social policy over international competitiveness, we will actually increase unemployment and social dislocation. Countries, industries, and companies that downgrade the urgency to be internationally competitive will soon have neither production nor steady jobs."

Henry felt dead air spreading around him. He wondered whether he would have the guts to talk about economics to this crowd.

"As employment opportunities in the raw materials economy shrink, we are going to become increasingly dependent upon the entrepreneurial economy to create jobs. Fortunately, we have a large number of well-educated baby-boomers who will, as opportunities for jobs in big corporations and government become scarce, find career paths among small businesses and new ventures. But the idea that high technology will lead the economy is mostly wishful thinking.

"The world's computer industry, for example, has run losses for over two decades. It has been profits flowing from no-tech, low-tech, and mid-tech industries that have financed high technology during this period. Without these profits, there would not have been enough capital to start our budding high technology revolution. Worthy as they may be, encumbering the economy with costly transfer programs that do not increase our productivity will deprive us of capital we need to maintain competitiveness in the world economy of the post-industrial age."

A long low boo rolled up from somewhere in the audience. It was soon joined by another. The pair with the banner behind Frances Rank took this as a signal and resumed their chant. Mrs. Tuchman pounded her gavel twice to restore order.

"Make no mistake about it," Drucker repeated bravely, "profits are the cost of the future—profits pay for staying competitive and staying in business."

Someone suddenly cut loose a raucous cheer. "SHIT YEA BABY . . ."

The outburst was followed by two shrill whistles. Claire tilted her head toward Henry to get a better view of the whistler. He was in the second row on the far side of the hall. He wore a calico shirt. His black hair swept down over its loose collar. He was rocking back and forth and clapping. The kewpie doll blond next to him was doing the same. Claire caught a glimpse of his face when he looked around. He wore a clipped black beard and a pair of reflector shades. His broad grin suggested that he was having fun.

"Who is that?" Claire asked.

"Bart Paige," Henry answered dryly.

"Mr. Paige's son?"

"Yea . . ."

"What is he doing?"

"Making an ass of himself, I'd say." Henry's answer was drowned out by the hammering of Mrs. Tuchman's gavel. Paige and his companion quit rocking, but Paige kept on grinning and looking around.

Drucker was unfazed by his uncouth supporter. "That concept was framed by Joseph Schumpeter. With it he refuted the Marxist claim that profits are surplus value stolen from workers. The fact is profits are the ONLY source of jobs."

"Yea!!!" Paige bellowed, starting again to rock and clap.

Mrs. Tuchman cracked her hammer again, "Sir, you must be quiet!" Her icy tone settled him once more in his seat.

"Intellectuals and bureaucrats have always been uncomfortable with Schumpeter's idea because it requires them to abandon their claim that it is society's right to redistribute profits generated by private enterprise."

"He is going to ruin your conference," Claire warned Henry.

"Bart?"

"Drucker!"

"Why? He's right!" Henry whispered back.

"We face a serious problem in this respect," Drucker went on. "As labor and material costs decline and become less important in the total cost of a product, the cost of capital will become the major factor in international competitiveness. The wrong policies will raise capital costs. If our actions cause foreign investors to lose confidence in our dollars and stop lending to us, dollar exchange rates will crash. An extreme credit crunch, if not a liquidity crisis will ensue. What we don't know is whether this will trigger a deflationary depression or severe inflation. The worst scenario, of course, would be where we have both at the same time.

"We are relying on Keynes to defend us against these contingencies. Keynes prophesied some time ago that the emergence of the symbol economy of money and credit would transform economists into pseudo-scientists whose job would be to manipulate a few basic monetary keys—government spending, interest rates, the volume of credit, the amount of money in circulation—to maintain equilibrium at full employment. Schumpeter said it would open the door to tyranny. He saw that economists would never get to exercise this power, because bureaucrats would horde it for themselves."

The booing started again. Henry noticed that Frances Rank had turned red. Her clenched fists hovered ominously beneath her chin. Mrs. Tuchman, flushed with anger, smashed the podium with the hammer. "ORDER! I DEMAND ORDER!" When at last the disturbance subsided, she turned to Drucker, "I apologize, Professor Drucker, for the rudeness of some members of our audience. If this happens again," she warned the audience, "I will close the meeting. Is that clear!" No one spoke. "Now, Mr. Drucker…"

"I came prepared for disagreement," he responded with a resolute smile. "I think it is ironic," he added, "that when Peter Schumpeter published his *Capitalism, Socialism and Democracy* in 1942 he argued that capitalism would be destroyed by its own success. He predicted it would breed a parasite class that would live off its economic fruits, while opposing the ethos of wealth production, of savings and of allocating resources to economic production. That prophecy, I have to say, is being fulfilled."

Those words triggered another angry protest that quickly gained in intensity. Catcalls and loud booing poured out from every corner of the room. Frances Rank jumped to her feet yelling and screaming, followed by the rest of the enraged women people. Several of their placards flew at the speaker. Members of the audience waved their clenched fists in the air to show they were joining Frances Rank's protest. Henry's eyes happened to fall on Bart Paige. As he watched, Paige grabbed the collar of a man in front of him who was on his feet shouting at Drucker. Paige yanked him back down into his seat. At the same instant, he delivered a thudding blow to his head. The kewpie doll blond with him followed suit, smacking the pant-suited female who was protesting beside her. The percussion from these assaults pulsed through the audience telepathically. In that moment, the last vestige of order dissolved. Mrs. Tuchman rushed forward to shore up a sagging line. But it was no use. What had been an audience had dissolved into a mob.

Shouting and scuffling spread through the room. Henry watched Marjean and Aster, with a cohort of women-people, converge on Paige. He and the blond stood their ground gamely trading blow for blow until Marjean's banner pole landed on his head. Paige sagged down onto the floor and lay motionless beneath a shroud, which said MEN ARE PIGS. The blond was too busy kicking and biting her assailants to notice.

Out of the chaos… *Om*… mysteriously… *Om*… *Om*… a strange force seemed to manifest itself. Gently, relentlessly it enveloped the fury.

Om ... Om ... Om ... Henry strained to see what was happening. Between the weaving bodies he caught a glimpse of a yellow-robed figure with Indian brains. He stood meekly yet unconquered by the violence around him ... *Om ... Om ...* The sound moved through the theater with the power of a seed splitting a boulder. *Om ... Om ...* Human rage was impotent in its presence. *OM ... OM ...* Hate had no power to resist it. *Om ... Om ...* The crowd quieted as Tim Hardin cast his spell. Frances Rank unclenched her fist, and the Congress of Women-Peoples returned to their places in the pit. When it was quiet again, Hardin sat down.

Mrs. Tuchman had advanced to the front of the stage. Now she addressed the audience in a weary, but firm voice. "We are going to talk now about the First Amendment. Ladies and gentlemen, we are meeting today in the name of Thomas Jefferson. That great American helped forge a society where citizens have the right of FREE SPEECH. Disagreement with another's opinion can NEVER be justification for infringing on this sacred right. It is intolerable that members of this audience should abuse it. Those of you who are not willing to advance your views in open debate can leave the hall now!"

No one moved. No one spoke. "Professor Drucker," she seemed to be considering an approach that would nurture the fragile calm, "are you saying that we cannot launch a new technical age because it costs too much?"

"That was not my point, but it's an interesting idea," he conceded. "The fact is that popular support for high-tech entrepreneurial economy is relatively weak. Mid-tech, low-tech, and no-tech entrepreneurship are likelier avenues for growth over the next quarter century. Gearing government policies toward hi-tech entrepreneurship would be as counterproductive as trying to preserve blue collar jobs. Sooner or later, we would have to abandon support for hi-tech to bail out uncompetitive smokestack industries, which is where the great majority of jobs are.

"Of course, this analysis does not alter the need to replace labor and raw materials for knowledge and capital. In this respect, we are certainly moving forward in a new technical era."

The sullen audience allowed him to finish, then clapped briefly to celebrate its own deliverance. Henry hurried Claire out of the hall, determined to avoid any unwelcome encounters.

"Where are you staying?" Henry asked as they emerged from the auditorium.

"What's convenient"

Henry stared at her blankly. "You don't have a room?"

"I was going to check into a motel after our meeting this morning." Claire lied innocently.

"This is Openings Weekend at the University. I can tell you now that you're not going to find anything between Gordonsville and Crozet."

"Oh really!" Claire settled an uncertain expression on her face and waited for Henry to propose a solution. He considered the alternatives. They were all bad.

"I've got a couch in my living room," he said finally. "You're welcome to use it—it will be easier than commuting to Gordonsville."

Claire's face lightened. "That would be great! Are you sure it wouldn't inconvenience you?"

"No," Henry answered flatly. "I guess we're finished here. We don't need to be at Monticello until about 5:00. Let's go on over to the house . . . I'd like to get a little exercise. You can get settled or work on your story if you need to."

"That's perfect," Claire beamed.

Claire drove back down the farm road past the turn off to the shed.

"Turn left at the farm entrance," Henry told her.

She pulled out onto the blacktop and headed north. "It gets hot down here doesn't it . . ."

"Yea, 'bout the same as Washington, isn't it?" Henry agreed.

Claire nodded.

Henry's driveway was exactly half a mile long. It ran up on a low grade from the state road over a pair of ridges, then down to the house. The house itself was small and trim like the other tenant cottages on the estate. It sat in a grove of shade trees. The wire fence which separated it from the pasture marked the boundary of a neatly mowed yard. Like all the other buildings on the estate it was field green. Its tin roof, painted silver, shown brilliantly in the afternoon sun. One apparent concession to leisure was the spacious porch that overlooked the valley below Monticello Mountain. Claire noticed a small garden at the far end of the yard. She would never admit it, but she hated gardening. It was hot, dirty work and took too much time. She thought it was odd, therefore that Henry would have a garden. The pasture stretched on beyond the compound, past the barn in the hollow to the left, and halfway up the ridge that formed the western perimeter of the valley. There were no other houses in sight.

Claire pulled her car to a stop beside Henry's copper Falcon. "It's peaceful here," Claire said as she gazed out across the valley.

Henry watched uncertainly as Claire prepared to enter his sanctuary. He stepped in front of her and opened the gate then followed her across the lawn and up onto the porch. His eyes remained fixed on her satchel—his father had had one like it. He wondered what was in this one. Claire waited as Henry opened the screen and turned the front doorknob. "Come on in," he said as he stepped inside. The room she entered was light and airy. Its walls were covered with landscapes of the valley she had just admired. The strong scent of oil paint suggested that the artist lived there.

"There's the couch," Henry said, pointing at a nondescript sofa.

"Great!" Claire dropped her satchel down beside it.

To the left of the front door was the doorway to the next room. Henry slipped through it. Claire followed. It was obviously his studio. The floor along its outer walls were lined with canvasses. Ignoring them, he pointed up the stairs on the inner wall behind the front room. "The bathroom is at the top on the left."

Claire followed him back into the first room. "Why don't you take a seat on the porch while I clear out these fumes. It'll just take a minute . . ."

"All right." Claire turned and disappeared through the screen door.

Henry stepped quickly through the door at the back of the room. The fan was there, in his study. So were the books on astrology and the folder with his notes. Henry stacked the astrology books and set them in the corner next to his shot gun and waste basket. He grabbed the copy of Thorstein Veblen's *Theory of the Leisure Class* out of his bookcase and set it on top of the stack. That should be enough to discourage a roving eye. Now . . . where to put the folder. Just then he heard the screen door open. He lifted the desk blotter and shoved the folder under it. In the same motion, he picked up the fan and started back into the living room. He stopped suddenly and turned back toward the bookshelf behind him. A second later he found the item he was looking for—*The Paige Family: An American Adventure.*

Claire was bending over her satchel but straightened up when Henry entered the room. "Here's something you might find interesting," he said, handing her the book.

"What is it?"

"It's the Paige family history."

"That would be interesting!" She took the book and set it on her satchel.

Henry stuffed the fan into the window and plugged it in. "There," he said, turning it on. "Just give it a minute and you won't notice the fumes." With that he headed through the studio door.

"Thank you," Claire called toward the footsteps on the stairs.

Henry stepped out onto the porch. Claire was coming in across the lawn with a stylish clothes bag on her shoulder.

"I won't be gone long," he told her. "There are cold drinks in the icebox. Clean towels are in the closet beside the shower. Dinner is formal so wear a dress—if you happen to have one with you."

"Where are you going?"

"Up there." Henry pointed across the valley.

"Wow!" Claire followed his finger with her eyes. "That's a long way."

"Four miles 'round trip."

"But the heat . . ."

"You get used to it . . ."

". . . If you say so . . ."

Henry bounded off the porch and started across the lawn.

"Enjoy yourself!" she called after him

Henry held up his hand but did not look back. A moment later he disappeared into the hollow behind the house.

Claire went inside and fetched the book Henry had given her. The fan was spinning away, but the room still smelled of turpentine, so she returned to the porch. There was an old rocker in the corner. Claire seated herself in it and began to thumb through the book. It might be useful she decided, setting it down. Leaning forward she unfastened her satchel and pulled out a tape recorder. She was used to working on the fly. Without thinking she pressed the record button and lifted the device toward her mouth. Nothing happened. It almost surprised her that her mind was blank. She lowered her hand back into her lap and let her eyes drift slowly across the landscape. A movement on the far slope attracted her attention. It was Henry. He was advancing spryly up the hill. In the next moment, he disappeared behind a hedgerow. Claire set the tape recorder down and got up. The refrigerator was in the kitchen behind the studio. She opened the door and looked inside. There was a case of beer, a large bottle of white wine and a pitcher of lemonade. Claire took a glass from the rack beside the sink and poured some lemonade. She sipped it as she inspected the paintings in Henry's studio. They were all landscapes. Not bad, she decided.

She wandered into the living room and then into Henry's study. It was already dark in the afternoon light. Its interior walls were lined with books. In front of them, in the center of the room, was a writing table that looked out the window on the east wall. A framed copy of Raphael's *School of Athens* hung beside it. The window in the north wall looked out over the garden. A set of diplomas formed a casement around it. The corner between the windows was filled with a well-worn easy chair. Opposite the chair was the door that led into the kitchen.

Claire stepped over and inspected Henry's degrees. One was a BA. The other was a Doctorate in Economics. Both were from Mr. Jefferson's University. An engraving, in red, of Houdon's famous bust of Thomas Jefferson partially filled the space above Henry's name.

She turned back to the bookshelves. Claire liked to browse through other people's libraries. This is business, she told herself—basic research.

The shelves nearest her were filled with books on economics. Her gaze came to rest on Joseph Schumpeter's *Capital, Socialism, and Democracy*, the book that caused the riot in the auditorium an hour earlier. Henry had also mentioned it at lunch. She had a sudden impulse to see if he had actually read it. She set her glass down on the corner of the table and pulled it from the shelf. It was dog-eared from use. Inside she found page after page of underlined text. Many pages had extensive margin notes. There was no question that he had read it. It looked like he had memorized it. That's enough economic theory, she decided, stuffing the book back into its slot.

She pulled out *The Odyssey of Homer* by Richard Lattimore. It was one of her favorite works—she loved the way Lattimore made the language flow. She allowed the book to open to its own page then settled her eyes on its passage:

There I saw Minos, the glorious son of Zeus, seated,
holding a golden scepter and issuing judgments among
the dead, who all around the great lord argued their cases
some sitting and some standing, by the wide-gated house of Hades.

She closed the book and slid it back into its place on the shelf. As she did, she noticed Plato's *Republic*. A Pavlovian hiss escaped her parted lips as she remembered reading it for an introductory class in Political Philosophy. Way back then she thought she should know something about Political Philosophy. Her interest in Philosophy died when she discovered that Plato thought that while women can, in theory, perform all the tasks men do, men do them all better. She wondered again how anyone could consider the prating of a misogynist worth studying.

She shifted her gaze to the next shelf. This one contained books on the Civil War. Why are all men in Virginia hung up on that stupid slave war? she asked herself. Can't they just admit that the Confederacy is dead? Well at least he has a balance, she thought, pulling out the first volume of Carl Sandberg's *Lincoln: The War Years*. Next to it was Douglas Southall Freeman's *Lee's Lieutenants*. She was impressed to see an ancient copy of Grant's *Memoirs*. Beside it was a familiar tome: Edmund Fuller's *Patriotic Gore*. This was the book that decided her on becoming a critic. She took it out and began thumbing through it. As she did, she sagged absent-mindedly against the table behind her. That was when she tipped her glass. Her lemonade spilled across the table and onto the floor.

"Damn it!" She grabbed the empty glass and set it upright. Her lemonade was dripping from a pool on the tabletop into another pool on the floor below. Claire scanned the room for something to mop it. Seeing nothing, she raced into the kitchen. A moments later she was back with a fist full of paper towels. After covering the pool with a blanket of towels, she wiped off the table. Then she returned to the kitchen for a new supply of towels.

Back again, she spent several more minutes wiping and polishing. When she finished, she collected the spent mops and transported them gingerly to the waste basket that sat beside a shot gun in the corner of the room. As she deposited the soggy paper towels in the waste basket, she noticed the book on the top of the stack next to it. Thorstein Veblin! Par for the course, she thought. Before setting it back on the stack, she read the title of the next book. *The Complete Astrologer*? She read it again. Why would an analytical person like Henry Tilghman have a book about astrology? Lifting the book to inspect it, she saw that the one beneath it was also about astrology. And the one beneath this one was about witchcraft.

She set the books down in their stack and turned back to her task. A sweep across the table removed the last traces of the spill. Finally, she lifted the blotter and ran her hand beneath it. Thank goodness it was dry. She was about to pull her hand back went the tip of her finger brushed against something loose. Cocking her head, she peered beneath the mat. It was a manila folder. She pulled it out and turned it around. The cover had the word "Caius" printed on it. Inside she found a sheaf of loose papers. The top page carried a list of abbreviated questions in a scribbling hand:

> *Sequence of sun signs?*
> *Rulership over what parts of body?*
> *Activities governed by each House?*
> *Characteristics of planets?*
> *Significance of planetary relationships?*
> *Planets' influence on each other?*
> *Roberta's ascending sign?*

Roberta! This is it! She turned hurriedly to the next page. What in the world? In the center, was an outline of a female form. Around were clusters of astrological characters. She counted twelve sets in all. Each group was connected by a line to a location on the figure. As she studied the diagram, she noticed that the sun signs were attached to the areas of the body they governed. That's odd, Claire thought. She flipped back to the previous page and reread the second question: Rulership over what parts of body? How could he have made these connections if he didn't know the sun signs' governance?

On the reverse side of the page, she found another figure—an ox skull in a circle. A note referenced the figure's stomach. She fixed the image in her mind and set the page down. The next page contained a short list of names and a few random notes. Claire read each name: *Roberta, Aster, Marjean, Fred Ried*. She didn't recognize the last one. The accompanying notes were hard to read. One word she could decipher was "initiation." She shuffled through the rest of the pages to see if there was anything else, but the script was indecipherable. Claire put the papers back in their folder and slid it under the blotter. She had enough to keep her busy.

She pondered her discovery as she climbed the stairs to the shower. A PhD in Economics had drawn an astrological chart that somehow connected to a drowning victim. How odd . . .

———————

Henry came in the back gate as he always did and went over to his garden. A few more tomatoes were ripe, so he stopped to pick them.

When he turned again toward the house, he noticed her. She was standing in front of the window in his study. It looked like she was drying her hair. Her back was toward him, but as he watched, she tucked her towel into a neat turban and turned toward the window. He stared helplessly at the alluring curves of her body. Her skin shown like polished marble in the afternoon light. In the next frightening moment, their eyes met. She held his gaze without flinching, as if she were daring him to behold her.

Henry stumbled up the back steps and into the kitchen, his mind in an uproar. Why didn't he just laugh it off? It was funny wasn't it, like coming into a room with your fly down. This wasn't funny though. It felt like a lineman had driven a heavy shoulder into his rib cage and crushed the air out of his lungs. Like he had stepped in front of a truck. He could feel a fire burning deep within him. That was a bad sign. He had to put it out fast. Now he was angry. Why not just go in there and take her—that would set things straight enough.

As he entered the kitchen, he glanced toward the door to his study. It was closed. Thank God! She was still in there. He could see her in his mind's eye clutching her towel around her, quivering in fear. A helpless victim, waiting to be sacrificed to brutish lust. Bullshit! Henry snorted. I'm the one trapped in the labyrinth. I'm the one about to be devoured by the monster. He grabbed a beer out of the icebox and stalked out onto the porch. Before he opened his beer, he took a deep breath.

He was standing with his foot on the railing and his beer in his hand when the screen door opened behind him. He didn't want to look, but he turned anyway. It was worse that he expected. She was stunning in a sleek black cocktail dress. Her blonde hair was pinned back with gold combs. A dazzling gold necklace lay on her throat. It was matched by a pair of gold disc earrings. Another fiery flash shot through his veins. Was this Ariadne, come to deliver Theseus from his prison? Not this time pal, Henry thought. This time it was the monster! He felt the pressure building inside him. His heart was pounding so hard he was sure she could hear it across the porch. Unable to speak, he just nodded and took a sip of beer. "Can I get you a glass of wine?" he said at last in a tight voice.

Claire's smile filled with pleasure. He cringed to see it. "I would love a glass of wine," she crooned. "White?"

Henry nodded. "I'll be right back." A moment later he returned with two glasses of wine on his only tray. She stepped forward and lifted one in a toast. "To Jefferson Country..." Henry set the tray down and took the second glass. Turning toward her, he raised his glass to hers, "To Jefferson Country," he repeated as their glasses touched.

Claire came to the rail and stood beside him. "What a lovely view," she said, gazing out over the valley.

"Yes it is," Henry agreed. Then he set his glass down. "I'd better shower and change if we're going to get up to Monticello on time." Before she could respond, he turned from the rail and stepped back into the cottage.

———————————

Henry took the back way up the mountain. His eyes remained locked on the curving road as though he had never traveled it before.

Claire finally broke the silence. "You asked me earlier what I know about Thomas Jefferson. How's this: Author of the Declaration of Independence. Third President of the United States. Advocate for an agrarian democracy. Founder of the University of Virginia. What have I left out?"

Henry was still too tense to talk freely. The smile she flashed on the porch—he knew what it meant. She thought she had hooked him. Now she expected him to sit there like an idiot babbling about Thomas Jefferson while she reeled him in. He cursed to himself.

She thinks that all she has to do is show her tits and smile . . . You're just going to plop into her silky web . . . but instead of laying down for you, she's going to suck the blood out of your veins. That's the way they do it . . . they lure you in, get you under control, then squeeze out the logic that orders your life . . . and if you don't play ball . . . you're a menace . . . a sociopath . . . a PIG. It's brilliant! What a scam . . . women are victims of male aggression . . . and men are too pussy whipped to deny it. Woodstock Nation . . . those pitiful bastards. They did it . . . they made peace with feminism . . . pleaded guilty and handed over their balls . . . acknowledged bitching as a mode of enlightened discourse. Now she's working it on you . . . women get what they want . . . men get it for them . . . or the sirens sound. She was probably there when they figured it out . . . another sister in the Mother Jones movement . . . another liberated coed who decided to show her boyfriend how he could have his cake and eat it too . . . if you will wash the dishes, Sweetie, I will cook it and take you to bed. That was when it was a sexual revolution. Now it's a women's movement . . . an economic rights movement . . . A GIMME POWER MOVEMENT. . .

The spirit of martyrdom swelled in Henry's breast. It was exhilarating—the vision of himself rising up and severing the endarkenment's blanketing vine. He would answer the animal call of Maleness. He would be a REAL MAN. He would force her to hear the Truth: WOMEN ARE NOT VICTIMS! You know it, and so does everybody else. There is no new order. There is no new society. There are only old order harpies grabbing more power, scheming to get it on their own terms. God in his wisdom revealed the truth—whatever it is. Man's best hope is to live virtuously. To be generous and kind. It's older than the written word. Jesus Christ died and rose again to prove it. Aristotle . . . Hume . . . Kant . . . John Stuart Mill . . . they all recorded parts of it. Does anyone really believe what they said can be improved by a cult of man-hating women?

You're crazy . . .

The words ricocheted through his mind like a sniper's bullet. Doubt spread quickly in its wake.

They'll destroy you. You'll be thrown into the outer darkness . . . and she'll be there to torment you . . . with her exquisite body and irresistible smile.

Why are you sulking? she'll ask. *Everything will be Ok. Just cooperate . . . be a good boy . . . like everybody else . . .*

It unfolded before him—the vision of her patient, helpful smile. Like an impenetrable fortress begging to be attacked. Waiting ominously to destroy him. No man could endure that specter. To be pummeled by a silken hand. To be humiliated by a woman who dismisses nature's imperatives as passive aggressions. To be humiliated by a creature with no principles beyond expediency. No man could tolerate that . . . having to submit to a devious woman.

Then he heard another voice. *What's the point?* it asked. *Why make a scene?* As he groped for an answer, his Male Spirit faded back into the darkness.

"Let me put it this way," Henry said when the fire was out. "A few years ago, one of the University's literary magazines published a poem that went like this:

> *An artist and philosopher sat down to have a chat.*
> *Truth is beauty the artist said.*
> *Well, what you mean by that?*
> *Knowledge is salvation the sage returned in kind.*
> *What a pity, the artist shrugged, to find a man so blind.*
> *Then each arose and walked away thinking as he went,*
> *What an unenlightened fellow.*
> *I wonder what he meant?*

For the first time, Henry heard Claire laugh honestly. "That's very amusing. Tell me the truth, Henry. You wrote that didn't you. "

"What makes you ask?"

"Because the only poetry I remember is my own," she said, laughing again, this time at herself.

"Mr. Paige was right about you," Henry said with an exasperated grin.

"I like it. Do you have any others?"

"A few."

"I'd like to hear them sometime," Claire said gaily.

Henry looked at her. He knew it then. She was going to suck him in.

Like a black hole absorbing light. It didn't matter whether he liked it or not. Nature was going to have its way. It was just going to happen.

"That's my point of entry to Thomas Jefferson," he said.

"Jefferson was the artist and philosopher dwelling in one lanky, disheveled frame. We're not given much of a chance to see him that way today. He's been taken over by propagandists who have reduced him to a cliché— CHAMPION OF THE COMMON MAN." Henry trumpeted the words like a Barnum & Baily's ringmaster.

"Is he treated any different than Washington in that respect?" Claire asked, trying to join the conversation.

"Only to the extent that it's not true."

"He wasn't the Champion of the Common Man?" She sounded surprised.

"No."

"Where does the idea come from then?"

"From Hamilton."

Claire gave him an uncertain look.

"Alexander Hamilton viewed the British parliamentary system as the perfect form of government. Jefferson therefore accused him of being a monarchist and a threat to the republic. The battle lines they formed have defined every American political debate since. It's all there. Rich versus Poor. Urban versus Rural. North versus South. Industrial versus Agricultural. Federal versus State. Liberal versus Conservative. *DEMOCRAT* versus *REPUBLICAN*. Thanks to Hamilton and Jefferson, Americans can pick their side in any dispute and pass it off as though they are informed on the issue. Jefferson has become the head of a people's party. Hamilton has become the spokesman for the insiders' party. When it started though, it was pretty mundane. Jefferson, the debt-ridden aristocrat from plantation society, resented the money class. He looked upon financiers as parasites who profited from his labor. We've transformed a man who opposed the interests of capitalists for his own sake into the defender of the common man."

"You don't agree . . ."

"I think Jefferson intended for us to form that image of him," he said, glancing at Claire.

"What do you mean?"

"He was no different than other men in his position—he wanted history to remember him on his own terms." Henry looked again at Claire. "I would. Wouldn't you?"

"I suppose so. "

"He was luckier than most other men though."

"How so?"

"He lived long enough to edit his dairy so posterity would read the history he wanted. He sculpted his positions in ways that eliminated pettiness and conflict. He hid himself behind words like 'self evident' and 'inherent' so what was on his mind, however parochial or self-serving, would appear universal, appropriate for all thinking men. Beyond the need for proof! His biographers have generally cooperated with him. They're content to evaluate his public documents and works as though self-interest did not bear on his views or influence the causes he supported."

"You think they did . . ."

"Of course they did!" Henry snapped. "The guy was a human being! And he was weaker than almost everybody. Every aspect of his life, each cause he championed large or small, was born out of a system that served himself. It was Thomas Jefferson who dwelled at the center of his universe. Hamilton understood that and hounded him mercilessly. We'll be there in a minute. See for yourself. Try to find a place for the common man— he even buried his slaves' quarters so they wouldn't obstruct his view. It wasn't love for his fellow man or his conviction about human rights that motivated him!"

"What was it then?"

"PLEASURE!" Henry announced. "His own damned pleasure!"

"If you're right, why don't we know this?"

"How closely have we looked? Remember. This man possessed one of the most extraordinary minds, not just in American history, but in History—period! Does it make any difference if he was horny or pinched when he wrote the Declaration of Independence? No! The fact is, in a few brilliant lines he changed the world. Here was a man with an insatiable curiosity. He jotted notes about everything that crossed his mind. Scholars have had their hands full just getting his papers organized! But for all his genius, he was still just a man . . . and he was obviously concerned about that."

"Why do you say that?"

"Because he took such pains to hide the fact."

"For example?"

"He destroyed all the letters between himself and his wife. Imagine what they revealed? Here was a woman left alone for extended periods of time in a dwelling that was barely habitable. She was educated and artistic. He left her to run a sprawling household that included scores of slaves. Most of the time he had her pregnant in spite of her frail health. After ten hard years, she wore out and died. Have you seen Fawn Brody's new book? She called him a 'transparent shadow' She's right. He wanted to be invisible."

"But you've found him out . . ."

"I'm closing in . . . Did you know that with the exception for George Washington, there are more things named in honor of Thomas Jefferson than any other figure in American history?"

"No."

"Jefferson was not like Washington though. The American people loved Washington. "Do you know why?"

"Why?"

"Because he loved them! Simple, huh? There is a painting by N. C. Wyeth called *General Washington's Entrance into Trenton*. Are you familiar with it?"

"No."

"Wyeth was an illustrator from the Brandywine School in Wilmington, Delaware—it was founded by Howard Pyle around the turn of the century."

"I've been to the Museum at Chadd's Ford."

"That's the place. Pyle taught his students to be accurate portrayers of the events they painted. When the Trenton National Bank commissioned Wyeth to paint a picture of Washington's visit to Trenton on his way to his first inauguration in New York, Wyeth started by finding out what happened. Washington arrived on the western bank of the Delaware River on the afternoon of April 21, 1789 and was ferried across the river with his companions. A committee of leading citizens greeted him on the other side with a great ceremony. They gave him a milk white stallion to ride and escorted him on to the town. At the bridge over the Assunpink

Creek the ladies of the town had constructed an arch. The picture Wyeth painted shows Washington on his charger passing beneath their arch. He is graciously receiving the welcome of the village maids who are spreading bouquets of flowers in his path. On the arch above his head, in a haze of dazzling sunlight, there is a plaque with the words "The Defender of The Mothers Will Also Protect the Daughters." You see? The people wrote that. It was an expression of their love and admiration. They had written the simple truth with their own hands. He had done these things!"

Claire pondered the story.

"You said you admire Jefferson." Henry continued, I bet if I asked you why, you would have a hard time telling me." Claire did not object. "If I asked you about the man himself you probably won't know what to say. He's a mystery—a virtual black hole . . . Ah . . . here we are."

Claire looked out at the sign beside the road on their right. MONTI-CELLO.

Henry turned into the entrance and proceeded to the right. Ahead of them was a closed gate. Henry pulled up to it and stopped. Rolling down his window, he reached out to the gray speaker box and pushed a button below its vent.

"Can I help you?" a crackling voice asked.

"This is Henry Tilghman and my companion from the Jefferson Academy. We're here to see Fenton Somerville."

"He is expecting you," the voice in the box replied. "Drive up the hill and come to the front of the mansion. Leave the car with the attendant and come up to the house."

"Thank you," Henry answered, settling himself back in his seat.

The gate opened, and Henry drove through. The driveway wound around the mountain through a dense wood. After a hundred yards, the car emerged into an orchard. "The house is up there," Henry said, gesturing toward the sky above the orchard.

Henry drove past a parking lot that served the bookstore on Mulberry Row. Proceeding around the corner, he reached the crest of the mountain. A valet parking station had been placed on the drive beside the mansion's front walk. Henry stopped in front of it and waited as an attendant stepped forward to greet him. He was dressed in an 18th century costume—knee britches, white stockings, a ruffled blouse, and scarlet waistcoat. The walkie-talkie antenna that stuck out from under his tunic looked like an unruly tail.

"Good evening," he said, peering into Henry's window and inspecting the evening's first guests. Seeing Henry's companion was a trophy, he stepped around the front of the car and opened her door. "Go on up to the house," he said, as Claire extracted herself from the car. "The footman will show you where to go," he added, staring at Claire as she straightened her dress. Henry pulled out a fiver and handed it to the attendant.

"Thank you," he said. After stuffing it into his vest, he handed Henry a ticket with a number.

"Do you think I need this?" Claire asking, holding up her purse.

"Not unless you plan to lift something small," Henry joked.

Claire gave him a pained look.

"Here," she said, pulling out a few necessities. "Put these in your pocket."

Henry did as he was told. He gazed at her as he stowed the gear. "I'll put this in the car," he said, taking her purse. The attendant waited then climbed into the driver's seat. "The clutch is a little tricky," he added, handing the valet his keys.

"Right," the driver said, turning the ignition and revving the engine.

Claire watched Henry as the car pulled away. He was looking out across the valley. "Some view huh?" he said, turning to Claire.

"I'll say . . ."

"That field—there behind the row of pine trees—is where Shadwell stood," he said. Claire looked in that direction. "In the grove on the knoll behind it is Edgehill . . . Behind Edgehill, you can see the tops of the tents at Belmont."

"Shall we," she said, taking his arm.

"If Jefferson was just a scholarly dabbler," Claire wondered as they started up the walk, "why didn't he just stay home and dabble?"

"He did!" Henry replied. "But don't forget. A big part of Jefferson's dabbling had to do with creating a world he considered suitable for himself. To do that, he had to be active in government. Of course, it was natural for a man in Jefferson's position—being a member of Virginia's governing class—to sit in the legislature. He was expected to govern! But unlike his unenlightened peers, Jefferson intended to shape the government around his ideas. That was his passion, and it guided his course through life. Besides," Henry added, "he liked being a philosopher-king."

"I suppose that's possible," Claire allowed, studying the mansion that loomed in front of them.

"Jefferson's law tutor was a man named George Wythe. Wythe was a renown classical scholar. Taking on Wythe's mantle, Jefferson found reading the law intellectually stimulating. Parts of it then were based on ancient Roman codes that he would read in their original text. Because he excelled in his training, he was able to begin his practice presenting cases before the colony's Superior Court. That was a privilege reserved for the brightest and the most ambitious men. Yet, despite his success, Jefferson quit practicing law as soon as he was elected to the House of Representatives in 1769—you know the old saying, 'gentlemen don't work for wages' . . ."

"That's a new one," Claire sighed.

"Jefferson learned why practicing law."

"What do you mean?"

"It was hard to collect fees from his cash-strapped and neglectful social peers. Not only was it embarrassing for him to dun them for the money they owed him, it compromised his social standing."

"What did he do?"

"He quit practicing law and devoted himself to 'public service.' You know how he won his seat to the House of Burgesses?" Henry asked, changing the subject.

"How?"

"By putting a pot of rum at the polling station—it may have been degrading to work for wages, but there was nothing in the gentleman's code about pandering for the votes of one's social inferiors!"

"That doesn't sound right," Claire conceded.

"He was just playing the game."

"Shame on him . . ."

"Yea. When he arrived in the legislature, his cousin set about raising him up. Of course, that wasn't hard to do in Jefferson's case. His knowledge of the law was among the most profound in the new world. His writing skills were superior. And he had meticulous work habits. What would you do," Henry asked as mounted the steps of the east portico, "if the leaders of the government handed you the gavel and asked you to take charge?" The question floated unanswered out across the lawn.

The massive pillars of the east portico stood like sentries on perpetual vigil. Engineering triumphs in their own right, they illustrated the grandeur of their master's vision. Two towering glass doors opened as they crossed the portico. A black attendant, also dressed in period attire, stepped forward to greet them.

"Mister Somerville will be with you presently," he told them before withdrawing.

They stood in the center of a spacious, high-ceiling room. The drab copper-green hue of its walls cast an air of gloom in the day's fading light. Claire's eyes settled on the smiling bust by the window of the south wall.

"That's Alexander Hamilton," Henry said, inspecting the plaster bust. "See," he said, pointing to the bust of Jefferson on the opposite wall, "Jefferson placed them in opposition to remind him of their philosophical differences." He turned to his left and gestured to the laughing face to the right of entry. "I'm sure you recognize Voltaire", he said, glancing at Claire for confirmation. "It's interesting, isn't it, that Jefferson would give him a place of honor in his home?"

"What is so interesting about that?" Claire wondered.

"He never mentioned his name in public."

"How do you know that?"

"I read a lot!" Henry snapped. "What I mean is that Jefferson was a staunch supporter of the French Revolution."

"Is that remarkable?"

"It wasn't popular in those days."

"No?"

"Americans didn't like heads being cut off—even if they belonged to kings."

"Didn't Voltaire die before the French Revolution began?"

"Voltaire loathed the French Monarchy and blamed it for the poverty and suffering of the French people. Jefferson saw how awful it was during his service as Ambassador to France—it transformed him into a political activist *ala* Voltaire."

"The author of the Declaration of Independence wasn't an activist until then?" Claire was obviously skeptical.

"Well . . ." Henry reflected for a moment. ". . . What I mean is, he wasn't close to the bomb throwers like Richard Henry Lee. Before he went to France, he just hated being a subject of the King of England. His mature political views formed as he digested the abominable conditions in which the French people lived. Their suffering was his rationalization for opposing Hamilton's plan for a powerful federal government. In a letter he wrote to a friend while he was in Paris, Jefferson quoted Voltaire who said once that in France men were either hammers or anvils. It wasn't like that in America, but Jefferson assumed it would become that way if a powerful central government took control of the country—so he dedicated himself to preventing it."

"Who is this man," Claire said, stepping toward the heavily curled bust to the right of the door.

"That's Turgot."

"Turgot?"

"Turgot was a friend of Pierre Samuel du Pont—both men were economists!" Henry announced beaming. "Jefferson admired his plan to tax landowners to create a fund to pay urban laborers who had been dispossessed of their 'common stock' of land."

Henry turned to face the interior of the room. It had five doors. Two doors in the south wall led into Jefferson's apartment. The double glass doors beneath the balcony on the west wall led to the parlor. The far door in the north wall entered the dining room. The near door opened into the north passage, which led past Madison's bedroom onto the north terrace. Only the first door into Jefferson's quarters was open. Somewhere beyond it, they heard muffled singing.

"Let's go see," Claire commanded, setting off. Through the hall door, she entered the room on the left, which was dominated by a massive fireplace.

"This is where Jefferson gave his grandchildren their lessons," Henry volunteered, assuming the role of a tour guide. "The picture over the mantle is his daughter, Martha Jefferson Randolph. It was painted by Thomas Scully in 1836. That was the year of her death—ten years after her father's," he added. "She obviously charmed the artist. She would have been sixty-four when she sat for the painting but look how youthful he made her! "

Just then a man appeared in the doorway beside the hearth. Like the doorman and the attendant, he was dressed in a period costume. This one didn't quite fit. His ruffled blouse bulged through the seams of his under-sized waist coat. His britches strained to cover his thick hocks. One of his stockings sagged from the knee revealing a milk white shin. The flush in his smiling face suggested to Henry that his collar was also a size too small.

"I thought I heard someone," the man said in a cheerful voice. "You're looking for Master Jefferson, no doubt." He looked around the room. "He is here, of course." His smile broadened as his eyes settled back on Claire. "I suppose I'll have to do the talking though. I'm Fenton Somerville. I'm Master Jefferson's, shall we say, valet."

Somerville was a man unsullied by the hurly-burly of mercantile society. That was not surprising. He hailed from an old Tidewater family and had spent his entire adult life caring or Jefferson's artifacts. His agreeable disposition confirmed that his work suited him.

"How do you do," Henry said, offering his hand, "I am Henry Tilghman from the Jefferson Academy, and this is Claire Fox from *The Washington Post*."

"Nice to meet you," Claire said, squeezing his soft hand.

"Oscar told me you were coming," Somerville said, after the greetings. "I was just touching up a few things in the library. Oscar said that you wanted a tour of the house."

". . . if that would be possible," Henry added with a hopeful nod.

"Yes, of course," Somerville responded. "Mr. Jefferson loves for cognoscenti to see how brilliant he was." He crossed the room as he spoke and stepped back into the south passage.

———————

"Now let's see," the curator said, organizing his tour. "Jefferson was twenty-four when he drew the original blueprint for his home. A couple years after that he acquired a copy of Leoni's *Architecture of Palladio,* which changed his ideas about the kind of dwelling he should build. He abandoned the Georgian style that was popular with Virginia's gentry and designed a structure based on Palladio's principles. Jefferson wanted to avoid the architectural commonplace," his valet explained.

Somerville continued to talk as he led them back to the center of the foyer. "Even in its first Palladian form, the house was an expression of the originality that characterized Jefferson's way of thinking. It consisted of this two-storied 'middle building,'" he said, gesturing to the part of the structure in which they were standing. "This structure was flanked by two two-story wings." He pointed to the inner doors on the north and south walls. "The first room in the south wing was to be a drawing room. Jefferson added the octagon-bay beyond the drawing room after he determined that his initial plan did not provide enough living space. This south bay was to be the bedroom he would share with his wife. Because it received the sunlight throughout the day," Somerville explained, "it tended to be the warmest room in the house on cold winter days. The inner room on the north wing was to be the dining room. The north bay, which Jefferson attached to preserve the structure's symmetry, was apparently to serve as another bedroom. Jefferson added the half-octagon to the parlor after deciding it too was inadequately sized. His drawing of the house shows its east facing adorned with a double portico. The lower portico was supported by four Doric columns. The upper portico was supported by four expensive Ionic columns. There is no record of it, but according to Palladian rules, he would have constructed a similar portico on the west facing.

"Jefferson's original foyer contained two alcoves," the curator continued, "one on either side of the entry." Somerville gestured to the places where the partitions had once been. "He referred to the center alcove into which the front door opened, as the 'lodge'. As we face the door, the alcove to our left would have housed a full single staircase to the building's second floor. The alcove to our right contained a small closet with cropped steps that led into the cellar. The front wall of this section of the house would have been about there," he said, pointing toward Claire's feet.

"That's awfully small," she observed, envisioning herself inside the imaginary room.

"Yes, but remember," Somerville agreed. "He was designing a dwelling for himself—he was thinking about his needs as a bachelor, which were modest. He hadn't reached the point then where his day-to-day activities extended beyond the interests he pursued in his library. That appears to have been the functioning principle underlying his plan, which was to support his library. In his revised plans, the library was the mansion's most spectacular room. It filled the back half of the middle building where it overlooked his gardens and received afternoon light. That was significant," the curator explained, "because Jefferson only read in the day's light. After he met the requirements for his library at the top of his mansion, he set about allocating space for the work rooms necessary to sustain the household. These were in the subterranean corridors beneath the north and south wings. He did all this with painstaking care to follow Palladio's rules."

Somerville focused his guest's attention on the imaginary north alcove. "The stairs would have been there," he said gesturing across the middle of the room. "They ascended to a landing on the second floor, which traversed the middle of the building. The door to the library would have been in the center of the landing. At its extremities, there would have been doors to 'attics' that formed the upper rooms of the house's two wings. Jefferson lowered the height of these rooms to keep the roofline in proper Palladian proportion. Consequently, they had only six-foot ceilings. It seems they were also used as bedrooms since the house had storage capacity in its cellar. Both these attics opened onto balconies, which filled the open areas above the polygonal bays.

"This confirms Jefferson's architectural conviction," the curator observed. "He was bold enough surrender the functionality of these upper rooms so the house would have the proper exterior form.

"He settled his new wife and her son in the house even though it was hardly more than a shell," Somerville continued. In fact, construction continued through the entire ten years his wife resided in it. Shortly after her death," the curator added, "Jefferson went to France."

"You can understand that her death opened a void in his psyche, which may explain why French architecture had such a powerful effect on him," the scholar speculated. "Overwhelmed by the beauty of its buildings, he began an intense program of study to master it. Of particular interest to him was the way the French applied rules of Roman architecture. One aspect of this was to hide their second-floor apartments above the high-ceiling rooms on their main floors. By doing this, they gave their hotels the appearance of single-storied structures." Somerville paused and settled a perplexed look on Claire. "Does that strike you as odd?"

"I hardly know," she smiled.

Somerville shrugged and resumed his narrative. "His most important reference was Antoine Desgodet's *Edifices Antique de Rome*." He directed his companions' attention to the crown molding at the edge of the ceiling.

"This is one of three friezes he borrowed from the engravings he found in Desgodet's remarkable book.

"Jefferson returned from France in 1789 with bold ideas for remodeling his home. He was slow implementing them, however, because he was absent almost continuously for the next four years—serving in President Washington's first cabinet as Secretary of State. Not until he resigned this post in 1793 could he devote his attention to his construct project. First, he removed the unfinished portico on the east front, the alcoves, and staircases they held, which occupied his narrow entrance hall. There were two staircases," Somerville added. "The one on the left reversed with a landing and descended to the lower level. The one on the right was L-shaped and ascended to his library, which, as I say, occupied the second floor.

"You can see here how much grander his architectural vision was after he studied the great houses of France," Somerville observed. "Jefferson intended to virtually double the size of the original structure. He intended to do this by adding rooms along the exterior wall of its eastern front. He became master of space and light by studying European architecture. In place of the original utilitarian entry, he constructed this magnificent hall. Beside it on the north and south wings, he added new sets of rooms. Of course," Somerville acknowledged, "his ingenious design created some problems. The first was the matter of access to the upper floors? The second was the problem of moving from one wing to the other on the mezzanine level.

"He solved the first by installing two "private" stairwells, one in the north passage and the other in the south passage. Unlike the original stairways, both these extended from the cellar to the third floor. This provided access to the mansion's upper rooms. To allow access to the wings on the second level, Jefferson installed this cantilevered gallery." He gestured toward the balcony along the foyer's interior wall.

"He went on to alter the windows in the two wings by bringing the upper casements down onto the tops of the lower casements. This followed the French way of disguising the second story."

Somerville strode over to the towering glass-paneled doors in the center of the west wall. Before opening them, he tapped the plaster wall. "These walls are sixteen inches thick. Jefferson set the thickness of the structural walls himself based on his calculations of the strength that was needed to carry the weight they would bear. "And, of course," Somerville said, pushing gently on the door in front of him, "these are his famous mechanical doors." Both panels opened in a synchronous arc. "As you can see, they still work perfectly. They have never needed repair!" Somerville marched through the open doorway and looked up at the ceiling. Jefferson enlarged this room by removing his library. By doing that, he created a room with the same eighteen-foot ceiling as his foyer." He looked up approvingly. "The last major structural change to the original building was the dome, which sits on the frame of the parlor's semi-octagon exterior wall. He professed distaste for English houses," the curator confided, "but his fabled 'sky room' bears a distinct resemblance to one on Lord Burlington's Chiswick House, which was inspired by Palladio's famous Villa Rotunda. By the way, this room has the first parquet floor installed in North America. Much of it is original wood."

Somerville crossed the parlor and opened the door on the parlor's north wall. "The rooms in the house are as interesting for their architectural details and their decorations as the mansion is for its classical conception," he said, passing through it. Claire and Henry followed him into the dining room. "This room makes the point far better than I can. It has always been special for me. During his retirement, Jefferson would spend several hours each day here. He and his guests often remained in conversation late into the night—consuming several bottles Madeira in the process," he added. "Jefferson therefore took great care to create an inviting atmosphere.

"The blue and white color scheme you see is not Jefferson's," the curator informed his companions. "It was installed during a general renovation in the 1930's. We're still analyzing paint samples collected at that time," he added, "to determine how Jefferson did decorate the room. In the meantime, I suppose we will keep it the way it is. The logic behind the Wedgewood motif is that Jefferson visited Josiah Wedgewood's showroom during his tour of London and the English countryside in the spring of 1786—he went there, as you know, to assist John Adams in negotiating a commercial treaty. Of course, the treaty came to naught, but during his visit, Jefferson had the opportunity to see several of Britain's most celebrated homes, including a few like Chiswick that applied Palladio's architectural rules. We also know that Jefferson was impressed by Wedgewood's craftsmanship because in addition to several pieces of china and porcelain, he purchased the plaques on the mantle."

Somerville stepped over to the mantle and inspected them. "These are Muses that Wedgewood copied from an ancient sarcophagus. They have greater significant than other decorations in this room because Desgodet pictured them in his reference text, *Edifices antique de Rome*. Whether Jefferson knew the history of the original works, I do not know, but in other cases he did . . ."

The curator moved to the side of the mantle and opened its panel. "Here is another example of his cleverness," Somerville said, focusing Claire and Henry's attention on the miniature dumbwaiter tucked behind it. "He built these into both ends of his mantel—one delivered full bottles of wine, the other to remove the 'dead' ones." Their host then turned toward the table and its chairs. "These Hepplewhite chairs are original Jefferson pieces," he boasted. "The Waterford epergne, the French bisque figurines, the ormolu clock, and the bust of Anne Cary Randolph, Jefferson's granddaughter, were all owned by Jefferson.

"We cannot be sure that Jefferson met Wedgewood," Somerville continued, "but he did socialize with Houdon, with whom he negotiated a contract for the monument of Washington in the Virginia statehouse. He also purchased a dozen of Houdon's busts, some of which you can see in the tearoom there," the curator gestured toward the sunny room beyond the opened doors in the north wall. "He also met young David, who became a member of the dreaded Committee of General Security during the Reign Terror. (Jefferson claimed David's 'pencil' was the only one that truly interested him.)

"Then there was John Trumbull, whose works you may have noticed on the interior wall of the foyer. That heroic American artist stayed with him for some time in Paris. Well-known connoisseurs of the classical arts like Baron Grimm also called on him in Paris."

Somerville moved around the dining room table to the sliding doors on the north wall. "Jefferson was also a conservationist!" He pulled a sliding glass door out of the wall. "This was his solution for conserving heat in the winter. Jefferson called this alcove his 'most honorable suit'. It was where had breakfast in the morning and tea in the afternoon. Here again we have the monumental scale. The massive arch, the frieze, and the entablature. The three sash windows were his own design. They became his architectural signature. The pavilions he designed for the Lawn at the University all have them. And see how he disguised the heavy brackets supporting the marble busts of America's patriots to look natural in their airy setting."

The curator pulled a watch from his pocket and checked the time. "We still have enough time to see Jefferson's apartment," he said as he stepped through the opening into the serving station. On its left end was a door into the mansion's north passage. Somerville passed through it and crossed the hall. "Just a peek," Somerville said, gesturing for Claire and Henry to come through the door he had pushed open. "This is Madison's bedroom. As you see, he cordoned off the interior wall to form a closet, and in doing so he created another octagon." The curator focused on the chambered bed. "The idea for putting the bed in an alcove was another of the things he picked up in France—it appealed to him because he disliked furniture cluttering his rooms." That was all he had to say about Madison's bedroom. Claire and Henry followed him back into the north hall and past its stairwell. At the hall's end was another door. Somerville opened it and led his guests into a square room. "This is where Citizen Genêt slept when came to visit during his famous invasion," Somerville informed them. Having said that, he reentered the hall and passed back into the foyer.

Crossing it without speaking, he opened the door to the right of the fireplace on its south wall. "This is Jefferson's bedroom," Somerville said, as his guests entered the chamber. "It was his dressing room in the original dwelling. The ceiling would have been about eight feet. Another bedroom would have occupied the attic above it. The roof of the original house would have fit comfortably under the current skylight," the curator added, gazing at it. "This was another idea Jefferson brought back from France. You see how successfully he used it to enhance the room's space."

Somerville focused on Jefferson's bed. "In his original design, this was the opening to a small bay room. When he remodeled the house, he converted that room into his 'cabinet', or as we would say today, his study. He placed his bed in the doorway so he could rise into his study or into his dressing room according to his mood. Above the bed is his closet—he stored his winter clothes there during the summer and his summer clothes there during the winter, much as we might do today. He loved these little nuances," Somerville confided. "Anything he could do to remove clutter . . ." Somerville gestured to the door to the right of the bed. "The stairway to his storage closet is in there."

"The closet wall was the interior wall of the original south attic bedroom?" Henry wondered.

"That's right," Somerville confirmed.

"Is the doorway to the balcony still there?" Henry asked.

"Yes, well no," the curator corrected himself. "The door is still there. But the balcony was converted into a bedroom during the second construction. Since the door no longer had a function, Jefferson sealed it with plaster. Today it is an inconspicuous indent in the north wall of my office." Somerville stepped into the passage at the foot of Jefferson's bed. He turned there and addressed his guests. "What I'm about to show you is one of the most interesting features of the house." To his right was a small open closet. To his left was a narrow door. "Jefferson hung the clothes he wore here," he said, gesturing to the bar that ran across the alcove. "As you might gather, he did not maintain a large wardrobe. Now," he said, pushing on the door with his right hand. "This is the greatest concession he made to his person." He stepped back and invited Henry and Claire to look in.

A door about two feet wide opened inward into a space about the same width and depth. The chamber beyond was three feet deep and four feet across. The wall behind the door crossed to the back wall at a forty-five-degree angle so the space looked as though it had been fitted into the hull of a ship. In the recessed area to the left was a plain board with an oval hole in the center. Beneath it was a chamber pot.

"It's a privy!" Claire exclaimed.

"Exactly," Somerville laughed. "When Jefferson saw these in France, he decided that he had to have one. It's something of an architectural wonder," he continued. "In the first place, he enclosed it in so much brick that it could probably withstand a nuclear explosion. In the second, he went to great pains to ventilate it so it would not foul the atmosphere in his apartment. An air duct enters from below and," he directed their attention to the ceiling, "as you can see, it opens to the roof to form an air shaft. Wasn't he clever . . ."

"Very," Claire agreed, taking a seat. "It could use a back support though," she added.

"Well, he was something of a Spartan," Somerville smiled.

Claire followed Henry back into the passage at the foot of Jefferson's bed. Somerville led them on into Jefferson's study. "Jefferson would rise before dawn," the curator said, stepping over to the octagonal table. "If he were at home, he would take a seat here and write a dozen letters before breakfast. Breakfast was usefully served around 8:00 AM. After breakfast, he would return here and work on other matters of business, such as his drawings for his academic village. He also invented things here, like his curve-bladed plow and his duplicating machine." Somerville pointed toward a wooden construction sitting on the desk with an armature that connected two quill pens. "He also kept extensive records. His *Garden Book*, for example, contains a log of everything that he grew in his garden. Daily temperatures. Rainfall. When the lettuce sprouted. When the peas bloomed. He was man of extraordinary energy," Somerville added.

"I've saved the best for last," he told them, crossing through the arched portal into Jefferson's library. "This was his sanctuary." Somerville obviously shared Jefferson's love of books. For a moment, he remained motionless basking in the sight of the leather-bound volumes that lined its walls. "These rooms held Thomas Jefferson's famous library. Actually, during his lifetime, he accumulated three. The first perished in the fire that destroyed his boyhood home. He sold the second, about six thousand volumes, to the Federal government to start a new Library of Congress after the British burned Washington in 1814. He assembled the third during his retirement. That one was auctioned off at his death to pay his debts." He walked over to a small glass case with shelves. "These were actually Jefferson's. The others, I regret, are mere staging." He smiled wanly.

"This was Thomas Jefferson's heart and soul. It was the cement that held the towering edifice erect. It was the fuel that gave the filament its brilliant light. Jefferson never ceased to draw inspiration from his books and never tired in his quest to expand his knowledge. 'Knowledge is power, knowledge is safety. Knowledge is happiness . . .' Those were his words. Nowhere does his meaning come across more clearly than here in his own library." The curator patted his brow absent-mindedly with a dust clothe he lifted from a nearby bookshelf.

"Jefferson believed that dialogue with the ancient world in thought and in art was the natural means for personal development. His grandchildren recalled him saying in his later years that if he had to decide between the pleasure derived from the classical education which his father had given him and the estate left to him, he would have chosen the former."

"A bold claim," Henry whispered, "for a man who squandered his estate in pursuit of pleasure!

"It has always fascinated me that Jefferson could live on the edge of the civilized world and still receive a classical education better than most of Europe's royalty," Somerville observed.

"The credit goes to William Small of Scotland, Professor of Mathematics at William & Mary College when Jefferson arrived there in the spring of 1760. Jefferson described him as 'a man profound in most useful branches of science, with a happy talent of communications, correct and gentlemanly manners, and an enlarged and liberal mind.' It was Small who made Jefferson appreciate the principles of the Enlightenment. That's what Jefferson meant when he said that Small 'fixed the destinies of his life.' To do that, he went far beyond mere instruction. Small has never been given his due," the curator added sympathetically. "He did more than plant a seed in a fertile mind. He nurtured it in his own garden. He brought his young friend with him on his own intellectual travels. Small included him in his scholarly circle and introduced him to men like George Wythe—who Jefferson called the best Latin and Greek scholar in the state, and Francis Fauquier, the acting governor of the colony.

"Small was well acquainted with the best thinkers of his own age. Of course, they were revolutionaries in their own right—men like Isaac Newton, John Locke, and Francis Bacon. Jefferson once identified these three as the greatest men the world ever produced. Small was familiar with Newton's work," Somerville observed. "But more than that, he perceived it to be the crowning achievement in the development of western civilization. You have to understand," Somerville continued with growing enthusiasm. "Newton's discovery was the single greatest influence on human thought for the next hundred years. It's astonishing when you consider it—he made it possible with a few fundamental laws to determine the properties and behavior of every particle of every material body in the entire universe. He transformed the material world in the mind of Man. Our knowledge of the world around us advanced to such a degree that the accomplishments of his predecessors seem trivial by comparison! Bacon, Descartes, Spinoza, Leibniz, Hobbes... all of them used quasi-mathematical terms in their efforts to eliminate the superstition and prejudice of Medieval Theology. But the order and clarity of Newton's physics made them seem... well... superficial. His methods set a new standard for all scientific examination—even those that related to the social life of man.

"Of course, the objective was always the same. Formulate general laws based on observation and prove them through experimentation. Find the truth by applying the Newtonian canons of science. The notions of substance compounded from irreducibly different qualities and categories disappeared. The Aristotelian concept of final cause and the explanation of phenomena in terms of the natural tendencies of objects to fulfill their own inner purposes. They were abandoned for lack of observational evidence. They were not only unscientific. Newton made them... irrelevant!

"You've no doubt heard the famous limerick that John Adcock composed on the first anniversary of his death:

Greek logic could never explain
The problem of stasis and change,
So the sage proved the notion
That laws govern motion.
Thus enlightened, the world rearranged.

"This was literally true," Somerville added emphatically. "The world re-organized to fit Newton's system." Somerville naturally assumed that Claire and Henry shared his pleasure exploring the history of knowledge. "The terms of mechanics—force, momentum, rest, time—gradually took the place of the classical metaphysical notions that defined the world before Newton. Final cause... substantial form... divine purpose. The entire apparatus of scholastic ontology and theology was abandoned and replaced by symbolism referring to measurable aspects of the universe— and by 'sense perceptions.' Locke, for example, defined knowledge as 'the perception of the connection and agreement or disagreement and repugnance of any of our ideas.' Perception being that which examines simple ideas to determine whether or not they agree.

"I have a theory about this," he whispered. "Someday I'm going to publish it—if I can ever get it put down on paper."

"What would that be?" Henry wondered.

"You know, of course, that Locke was a physician by training," the scholar began. "Voltaire praised him as an anatomist who could explain human reason as easily as he could explain the mechanics of the human body. This is my point." Somerville's voice rose with excitement. "He was the real source of Jefferson's opinion of Locke. It didn't come from reading the *Second Treatise* during the Revolution! It came from reading about Voltaire while he was in France!" Somerville announced.

"It's no coincidence that his only public expression of admiration for Locke came after he returned from France! He was putting his political rivals on notice. That was his way of throwing down the gauntlet. Of course, only three men in the New World understood his meaning..."

"Who were they?" Claire asked dutifully.

"John Adams, Alexander Hamilton, and Aaron Burr," Somerville said, rattling off their names. "Apart from the analysis he performed while drafting his bill to disestablish the Church of England in the fall of 1776 and the memorable lines in the *Declaration of Independence*," he continued, "there is no good evidence that Jefferson paid any attention to Locke. He said nothing at all, for example, about Locke's *Essay Concerning the Human Understanding*. That was Locke's greatest work!" "Somerville exclaimed, his face reddening. "Small probably made him aware of the main points in the *Two Treatises*, but there is no convincing evidence that Jefferson studied then further on his own.

"Small would also have acquainted him with Locke's intellectual contributions to the advancement of western civilization and his general method of investigation, which was based on empirical observation and common-sense judgements. I agree that Locke's preference to examine present beliefs and states of mind by tracing them to their psychological origins would have interested Jefferson. After all, Locke's account of the 'natural' growth of ideas re-enforced Jefferson's system of values with its premium on personal independence. This justified Jefferson's inclination to treat man as an object that could be explained by the generic methods of the natural sciences. But this was an orientation he had already taken from Newton—he did not need Locke! No... the evidence all points in one direction—Jefferson apotheosized Locke because it pleased him to hold the same view as Voltaire. Remember. Voltaire was the implacable enemy of the Roman Catholic Church!"

Somerville paused to take a breath. "Voltaire was opposed to all institutionalized Christianity. It was quite a strong endorsement for Jefferson that Voltaire credited Locke for putting an end to Theology and Metaphysics. That alone would have been enough. It would have been like a declaration of independence for his own mind. Other than that, he had no need for Locke. The ultimate proof of this is . . ." Somerville let the sentence dangle for a second as if to heighten the suspense, ". . . his reformulation of Locke's position in the *Declaration of Independence*! Instead of Life, Liberty, and ESTATE, he chose Life, Liberty, and THE PURSUIT OF HAPPINESS. For Jefferson that was an acceptable substitution because, as you know, for him, happiness was rooted in the intellect. And finally," he pronounced in triumph, "who's bust did he place on display in his great hall?"

"Voltaire's," Henry answered.

"Precisely!"

"Fascinating," Henry said in admiration.

"Thank you," the curator replied proudly. "With encouragement like that, I may just write it out. Why don't you come over some afternoon, and we'll talk about it further."

"I'd like to," Henry replied.

"Jefferson deserves his title of 'Philosopher' in recognition of his ongoing search for knowledge," Somerville explained.

"He mingled his studies of ancient history with daily experience to develop his own unique outlook on the course of human affairs. But he was not a philosopher in the 18th century sense that he offered a comprehensive theory of knowledge. In fact, he loathed all doctrinal theories. His aversion to systems was so intense that it must have been deeply rooted in his psyche." Somerville looked perplexed. "I'm not entirely certain what to attribute it to."

"I guess it would be hard to pin that on Newton," Henry said, nudging him back onto his track.

"You are quite right, Mr. Tilghman," Somerville agreed. "It must have come from somewhere else. Perhaps it derived from his life on the frontier where self-reliance and individual ingenuity were the qualities most highly prized. But I suspect another force was also at work. Jefferson admired the Greek and Roman nations, despite their faults, because he considered them to be civilized and learned. His admiration for their antique civilizations made him a true descendent of the Humanistic tradition of the Renaissance in which Man was the measure of all things. This idea was brought into the world by the Greeks—Jefferson granted the cultured Romans the Humanist label because they made the Greek sense of civilized personality their own.

"This idea of Humanism appealed to Jefferson as someone who was naturally disposed to view individuals as free, self-reliant intellects. After all," Somerville observed, raising his eyebrows, "that's how he perceived himself. Jefferson adhered to the Greek view of the individual as an independent entity whose character was formed through the free development of his own natural gifts. Isn't this the light that guided the author of the *Declaration of Independence*?" Somerville smiled at Claire as though he was addressing one of her deepest interests.

"Man must be free to pursue his personal development. That's the key! Jefferson accepted it as a prerequisite for personal happiness. 'It is neither wealth nor splendor, but tranquility and occupation that gives happiness,'" Somerville recited triumphantly. "That's how he phrased it. And if you asked him who was free, he would have quoted Horace. 'The wise man, who is lord over himself, whom neither poverty nor death nor bonds affright, who bravely defies his passions and scorns ambition, who in himself is a whole, smoothed and rounded, so that nothing from outside can rest on the polished surface and against whom Fortune in her onset is defeated.' He copied that passage from Horace's 'Satires' into his Literary Commonplace Book when he was in his twenties."

"The Greeks shaped Jefferson's view of individual happiness," Claire repeated.

"Very definitely. In his later years, he recognized this ideal in the philosophy of Epicurus. Of course, the ancient philosophies mostly aimed at aloofness and detachment from the natural impulses and passions of man. The Epicureans offered what was for Jefferson a more congenial analysis. They sought serenity and tranquility of the human mind, which they shared with other philosophies of antiquity, but they also aimed at bodily ease, which for them meant healthy and enjoyable but not extravagant living. That was how tranquility of mind, the *summum bonum* of the Epicureans, was achieved."

"How does that relate to pleasure?" Claire asked, casting a challenging glance at Henry.

"You are thinking about the Epicureans the way their Spartan detractors did, Miss Fox. We are certainly talking about pleasure, but the Epicureans were not hedonists as we understand the concept today. What is the current phrase?" Somerville's expression darkened as he labored to retrieve the Aquarian motto. "If it feels good, do it!" he beamed at Claire. "That's not quite what the Epicureans had in mind. They acknowledged human passions and desires as the source of life in man's body and mind. The Epicureans sought to teach how to govern them by reason and by correct appraisal of consequences. They sought to keep human passions alive in an equilibrium by means of natural checks. In this way, they endeavored to make them positive tools for the happiness of man and the richness of life. Pleasure in that sense."

"Interesting..." she said, smiling a satisfied smile at Henry.

"But I should add," Somerville cautioned, "that Jefferson was not merely an Epicurean. He was an eclectic who, as you can see, gathered ideas from a wide range of heterogeneous sources." He gestured toward the bookshelves.

"His broad statements about nature and man in general are consistent with the views of Bacon, Locke, and the other predecessors of positivistic empiricism. Lord Kames, the Scotch realist, was someone he read as a student. As time went on, he added the works of French encyclopedists, ideologues, and physiocrats to his library."

"Do you think he actually absorb their theories?" Henry inquired, looking back at Claire.

"Well..." Somerville searched for the right words. "He was probably more comfortable with the ancient texts he read as boy," he replied with an evasive smile.

The questions brought the scholar back into the material world. "He arranged his library according to Bacon's three faculties of the human mind—Memory, Reason, and Imagination. For Jefferson, conversing with the Greeks and Romans strengthened and enriched each category.

Memory, the recorder of history, warned humanity of the dangers inherent in social life. Reason and imagination forcefully expressed in the works of the ancients, books, and buildings alike, gave enjoyment and hope.

"Jefferson held that enjoyment of beauty was interwoven with—and inseparable from—the exercise of all the faculties of the body and mind within the microcosm of the individual's life. Poetry was his abiding pleasure and refuge. It served to counterbalance the sense of darkness that sprang continually from his reading of history," Somerville considered the burdens his master carried. "Jefferson's constant examination of history, of course, sharpened his awareness of evil and gave birth to a deep-rooted pessimism and skepticism about the course of human events. Perhaps because he was often alone with his thoughts, he emphasized the power of evil to undermine the good in man's nature. Once when he was traveling in the south of France, he joked half-heartedly that along with the other citizens of that province of the Roman Empire, he feared a return of barbarism which might destroy civilization. At other times, he worried that the enlightenment might give up morals for mysteries and Jesus for his arch-nemesis, Plato."

"You think Jefferson preferred Jesus to Plato?" Henry asked skeptically.

"Absolutely!" the scholar answered decisively. "Jefferson acknowledged the morality of Jesus Christ while he condemned the *Republic* for depriving the individual of his natural right to liberty."

"Jefferson learned from his extensive readings that lust for wealth and power had fueled destructive ambitions among men throughout the ages. He blamed it for undermining man's natural morality. To buoy himself in these dark moments he would retire here and read poetry. Homer and Virgil were his favorites. He quoted Homer at length in his so-called 'Literary Bible.'"

"His literary what?" Claire interrupted.

"I am referring to a literary scrapbook published under that title by Professor Chinard in 1928. It contained numerous passages that Jefferson deemed important enough for whatever reason to record. Most of the entries were made while he was a college student in the early-1760's and while he was studying law in the mid-1760's. It's interesting, now that you mention it—the last entries were excerpts from Homer's Odysseus that he made in 1800 and 1801." Somerville finished his tour as the first limousines were arriving from the academy.

"Thank you so much, Dr. Somerville. You've made Thomas Jefferson a living person for me," Claire said in parting.

"You're most welcome, Miss Fox. Thank you for coming! Mr. Jefferson is a companion of whom I never tire."

"We'll see you at dinner, won't we?" Henry asked.

"Oh, yes," Somerville assured them. "But if you will excuse me now, I must tend to a few final chores."

"How about some fresh air," Henry suggested as they reentered the foyer.

"That sounds good. Isn't Jefferson buried here?" Claire asked, as they stepped onto the portico.

———————

They stood together silently before Jefferson's grave. Henry remembered the first time he had visited the site—the strange, haunting sadness he felt to see the final, quiet resting place of a man so much larger than life.

He remembered Odysseus among the shades. How he had wept to hear his fallen comrades express their longing for life and the company of their loved ones. There too was Jefferson, doomed to lie for eternity beneath his drab granite obelisk. Henry stared impassively at the monument, observing how it rose from the platform of decaying stones that marked the graves of his family. What kind of man would design a monument for himself? Henry wondered.

"'Nay, if even in the house of Hades men forget their dead, yet will I even there remember my dear comrade.' That was the epitaph Jefferson selected for his wife," Henry observed, thinking of Martha. "He took it from *The Iliad*. I think she would have chosen something warm, something that spoke of her love–something about life. You poor woman! There's nothing left of you but a few meager entries in your lofty husband's journal . . . and this crumbling stone!"

"Are you ready to head back?" Claire asked, ending his meditation.

"Yes . . ."

They strolled up Mulberry Row, stopping now and then to read the plaques. It was a welcome interlude that they both needed. When they reached the stone wall that enclosed Jefferson Levy's grave, Henry led her off the pebble track and up the gentle slope to the west lawn. Ahead to their left was the spacious tent where they would gather later for supper.

As they emerged from behind the South Pavilion—Jefferson's Honeymoon Cottage—they saw three men standing together on the grassy apron of the west portico. Henry recognized the lanky form on the right as Dr. Denker. The stocky figure on the left appeared to be Nelson Rockefeller. He did not know the man standing between them, but even from a distance Henry sensed that he was a prickly character. He stood stiffly with his head high in a haughty pose—like a debutante's escort, Henry decided. The way he dressed reinforced Henry's impression. His shirt was bold red and white striped. As Henry and Claire got closer, Henry could see the sparkling gold cuff links and the collar pin that kept his paisley tie perfectly mounted under the board-hard fabric of his collar. The oversized handkerchief spilling out of the breast pocket of his blazer matched his tie. A thick gold bracelet sparked on the wrist of his drink hand. The drink it held was full. His face was tanned and chiseled and radiated the cold, hard determination of an athlete who knew how to win.

"Who do you suppose that is?" Henry said, mostly to himself.

"That's Martin Ogden," Claire answered.

"Who?" Henry repeated.

"He's my boss."

"He looks like a tough son of bitch . . ."

"He is."

The three men continued to talk as Henry and Claire mounted the portico steps to their right. Henry came up beside his mentor and touched his arm. Ogden was about to speak but stopped when he saw the professor turning away.

"Why Henry! You're here." His voice was warm and friendly. "And Miss Fox is with you. Good! Did you get to see the mansion?"

"Yes. Thank you for arranging it," Claire replied, smiling. "Dr. Somerville is a wonderful host."

"Henry, have you met the Vice President and Mr. Ogden?"

"I have not."

"In that case, allow me to introduce Henry Tilghman from our staff," he motioned to Claire, "and Claire Fox from *The* Washington *Post*. His Honor the Vice President, Nelson Rockefeller." They shook hands, "And, of course, Mr. Martin Ogden, Managing Editor of *The Post*."

Ogden gave Henry a firm handshake, but kept his eyes fixed on Claire. Claire shook the Vice President's hand and smiled at Ogden.

"If I may say, Mr. Vice President," Henry said, "I thought your assessment of the economy was first rate."

"Thank you, Henry." Rockefeller rested his hand on Henry's shoulder while he shared his signature grin with Dr. Denker. "He's sharp, Oscar . . . should be in politics."

Ogden interrupted him there. "All you're doing, Denker, is putting up another damned conspiracy theory." The tone of his voice sent a chill through the group. "I've heard lots of people talk about how rich, powerful whites plot against poor downtrodden blacks, but you're the first I've ever heard claim it's the other way around!"

"Now Marty," the Vice President interrupted good-naturedly, "you don't have to give the good professor a hard time. He's not running for public office."

Ogden gave the Vice President a searing look. "You better wake up Nelson. Denker's boss is launching a presidential bid right under your nose, and Denker is out here trying to make him into a folk hero. I'd be worried if I were you!"

"That's the first time anybody has accused me of that." The professor winked at the Vice President. "Sounds like he would make a formidable candidate."

"I'd appreciate it if you would stick to the point," Ogden added humorlessly.

Dr. Denker stiffened. "What is the point, Mr. Ogden?"

"You're glorifying a corrupt status quo."

"Nonsense! Where did you get such a foolish idea?"

Ogden reddened at the upbraiding.

"The fact is, we're shining a light on the principles that make political democracy possible. As the editor of a great metropolitan newspaper, I should think that you, above all others, would appreciate that, Mr. Ogden."

"I object to self-promoting hustlers using the national media to pros-elytize the American public."

Rockefeller watched warily as the confrontation sharpened.

"So far as I am aware," Denker said with quiet conviction, "the press is here because it considers this gathering to be newsworthy. You heard Frank Thomas, did you not?"

"Thomas said that blacks are victims of racism," Ogden answered de-cisively. "And that is precisely my point."

"I'm not trying to take issue with Mr. Thomas, but I think if you looked around you would see that all segments of our society are facing the same problems."

"I beg your pardon?"

"We are all being disconnected from our cultural roots. Our younger generations are growing up in a cultural waste land."

"We are all victims of racism—is that it?" Ogden added sarcastically.

"Well, to the extent that we are all subject to hostile social forces—all our cultures are being attacked . . ."

"What does that mean, for crying out loud?"

"Social anthropologists call it 'cultural collapse.' The black commu-nity is a conspicuous example."

"Maybe you think it's collapsing. I say it's being crushed!" Ogden objected.

"That's a poor rationale for shredding the fabric of our society."

"This society is sick," Ogden intoned. "Isn't that clear to you, Denker?"

"It is what it is, Mr. Ogden. It gets sick when you try to make it into something that it is not. Let me ask you. Who has benefitted from the leveling process you seem to espouse?"

"You are missing the point. White society has consciously excluded these people. Don't you understand that? It won't take them!"

"Our society is not perfect. I'll grant you that. But it is the best the world has ever produced. For all its flaws, we have accomplished more than any other people in history! We have become the greatest nation on earth because we demand that our citizens accept responsibility for them-selves. We prosper as a nation because we are free as individuals to make our futures better. There is no precedent for thinking that government can manufacture anything remotely near as goods."

Ogden took a sip from his drink. "You're content to sustain the current status quo. I cannot accept that."

"To whom do you propose to give our sovereignty—the new Utopians?"

Ogden snorted into his drink, "Utopians?" He looked at the Vice President, "Really, you should stop him before it's too late."

Rockefeller shrugged. "It's a free country—I'm told."

Just then a waiter appeared. Ogden set his drink down on the tray and looked at Claire. "I want to see you."

"Are you leaving?" She sounded surprised.

"Yes." Ogden turned back to the two men and gave them a curt nod. "Gentlemen. It has been a pleasure."

Ogden paid no attention to the Corinthian entablature as he strode through the parlor. He passed quickly through the mechanical doors and entered the mansion's darkening foyer. His eyes fixed on the attendant who stood at attention beside the tall glass-paneled entrance door. As he crossed the green linoleum floor, the attendant drew the door back and made a courteous bow. Before he could pass through, a yellow-robed figure stepped into the passage.

"Well! Look who's here," Tim Hardin announced gaily. "You forgot to tell me you were coming..."

"Er... it turned out that this was a good place to meet with Bill," the newspaper man stammered.

Hardin took Ogden's hand and drew him out onto the porch. "You won't forget to give him my message..."

Ogden nodded perfunctorily. "When are you going to show me the document?" He asked, changing the subject.

"I'll call you in the morning," Hardin replied. "Where are you staying?"

"At the Boar's Head, room 501," Ogden answered quickly. "You haven't shown it to *The Times*..." he added in an urgent whisper.

Hardin laughed again and patted the older man's shoulder. "You know that I wouldn't do that to my favorite publisher."

Ogden blinked his response and continued on his way.

"Are you coming, Henry?"

Henry turned to see Dr. Denker leading the Vice President onto the lawn. Claire was already halfway down the steps. "Yes," he answered.

The sun had settled behind the distant mountains, and evening was coming on. Guests were beginning to drift across the grass toward the pavilion that had been erected for the occasion. Dr. Denker guided the Vice President to the head table where he joined Mr. Paige and Barbara Tuchman. The others he led to the table a few yards away. There were six places at the table. Henry could see that three seats were already occupied.

Dr. Somerville greeted them with a warm smile and a wave. "I'll bet he's glad to see us," Henry whispered to Claire.

Somerville was seated between Tim Hardin and a somber woman Henry did not know. He recognized her face, though. She was one of Frances Rank's demonstrators. Her hair was long and straight and hung down over her shoulders in the American Madonna style that was now becoming vintage. It was streaked with grey and insinuated accumulating decay rather than the youth and freedom the style once symbolized. They made an odd combination, Somerville in his ill-fitting 18th century tunic and ruffles, Hardin in his saffron robe, and the colorless woman in a denim skirt and tie-dyed t-shirt.

Henry stared at Tim Hardin. He was a perversely fascinating character. Glib, self-assured, charismatic. The model of a New Man. A Media Man. He was the self-appointed spokesman for the New People. He had become a herald for the New Age. The Aquarian Age. And its vision? The world is imperfect—someone's gotta to pay.

Hardin would have made a formidable capitalist had his inclinations run in that direction. But he had come of age in the antiwar movement of the late 60's. Activism was relevant. It was the way to get power. Hardin had a knack for that. He had led a regiment of hippies into battle with mayor Daily's bodyguard at the Democratic Convention in Chicago in the summer of '68. In the spring of 1970, he became chairman of the central strike committee at Berkeley—he liked to say that the position had been created for him by Richard Nixon. He hated Nixon with a mindless, animal hatred. He shut down American higher education and led half a million chanting, ranting college students to Washington so Nixon would understand the power of the adversary that was pursuing him. From there, he went to Woodstock and spent three days on the platform smoking dope and communing with pilgrims from the new America.

New opportunities opened to him after Columbia University awarded *him a* Doctorate in Sociology for a Dissertation titled *The Cultural Barriers to an Open Society*. With it, he became a prominent advocate for the new social order. Leonard Bernstein invited him to a cocktail party at his New York City apartment. The famous composer introduced him to his close friend William O. Douglas and to Gerta Biederman.

Biederman was the daughter of Adolph Biederman, jazz-age tycoon. Adolph had built a fortune selling tabloids to the immigrants who were flooding into lower Manhattan. He left everything to Gerta when he died. Hardin used her money to create his not-for-profit foundation. The Committee for an Open Society had the right credentials to speak on social issues. And Hardin's timing was perfect. The government had lost its war in Vietnam and was anxious to redeem itself. Finding and saving victims of American capitalism was a mission that suited the benefactors of America's rapidly expanding welfare state. They listened sympathetically to Hardin's demands for an equitable distribution of national resources. Soon government money was pouring into his coffers. The technocracy officially welcomed him into its brotherhood with an invitation to testify before the Watergate Commission.

Dr. Denker greeted them in a friendly way. He offered the seat beside Hardin's wife to Henry and the one beside Tim to Claire, then settled himself safely between them. Hardin noticed Claire but did not interrupt his conversation with Fenton Somerville. "We reject historical practices as a basis for society's institutions," Hardin announced. "Willingness to accept the way things have always been done is what keeps us from perfecting our social institutions. It's our moral duty to fix this broken society."

Fenton Somerville nodded absent-mindedly.

"As social scientists," Hardin continued, "we are not interested in the origins of society's institutions or their sociology, per se. We are concerned only with whether they are properly designed and organized to meet the needs of the people, visa viz., the promotion of economic justice. Our methodology is no different from scientists in other fields. We judge institutions in terms of their ability to achieve these objectives."

It seemed to Henry that Hardin was making the same correlation self-styled scientists had made at the dawn of the Enlightenment when they promoted metaphysics as a branch of Newtonian mechanics. He wondered what Dr. Somerville thought hearing a post-enlightened so-ciologist make an argument Immanuel Kant had refuted 200 years before.

A wave of attendants in period costumes carrying covered platters swept into the tent. Somerville's attention immediately rivetted on them. "You may be interested to know," he announced, bringing Hardin's lecture to a sudden end, "that this evening's menu includes some of Jefferson's favorite recipes! He was very particular about his menu, you know. Most of the dishes served here he brought back from France." Henry watched Hardin's eyes as they shifted around the tent.

"Jefferson's appetite for the finer things in life made him an easy target for his opponents," Somerville observed. "Hamilton, for instance, accused him of being a 'voluptuous Epicurean opposed to Stoic virtue.' But as I was telling Miss Fox and Mr. Tilghman earlier, Jefferson indulged himself with bodily comforts not because he valued them as ends in themselves but because they provided a means to unite the spirit and the flesh. For Jef-ferson, there was no distinction between his ideas and the world he lived in. Man was a biological unit encompassing body and mind in an insepa-rable whole. He searched for vital increase—for enrichment–through life experience. Beauty and comfort strengthened his imaginative powers and stimulated his intellect.

"His admiration for cultural expressions of perfection, whether in lit-erature, architecture, or food, was the natural offspring of his training as a classicist."

Somerville followed the waiters as they delivered their toothsome cargoes. "Our main dish this evening is veal with olives in a breaded crust sautéed in butter," he informed his tablemate. "We debated whether to serve boned and stuffed rabbit, but alas, our wild stock was insufficient." His perfunctory smile betrayed his relief that the evening's honored guests had been spared eating game. "Perhaps you are not aware that several of the recipes Jefferson brought back have become American standards." Hardin's vague response did not discourage him. "*Pommes de tere frits*?" Somerville called out like a travel guide seeking a misplaced tourist. "And, of course, vanilla ice cream! Did you know that the first written recipe for it is in his hand?" Somerville conjured an image of the original document. "He made it much the same way we make homemade ice cream today," he added, reading the recipe in his mind's eye. "He started with a custard made from two bottles of good cream, six egg yolks and a half a pound of sugar." Somerville squinted as he imaged the faded script. "The cream was placed in a skillet with a stick of vanilla and heated to a near-boil. It was then stirred into the mixture of egg yolks and sugar." He stopped abruptly when a waiter set a plate down in front of him. His eyelids closed as he inhaled the delicious aroma, and his hand drifted to his fork. He opened his eyes just enough to see whether anyone else had picked a utensil. Seeing that the others had been served, he stabbed a corner of his veal and darted it into his mouth. Then suddenly he stopped and craned about. He settled back when he saw a waiter approaching with a silver pitcher. Somerville watched the pitcher bearer fill his cup with an amber fluid. "This cider was pressed here at Monticello specially for this evening's dinner," he announced proudly. "The apples are from our own orchard."

Claire lifted her cup and took a sip. "Oh!" she scowled, pursing her lips. "That has quite a kick. What did you call it?"

"Fermented cider," Somerville answered. "Jefferson frequently served it with dinner."

Denker interrupted him. "I thought he favored wine."

"Yes—Jefferson considered wine a 'necessity of life,' but he only served wine after the dinner cloth had been removed. We will be serving a white Bordeaux this evening," he added. "And, of course, Madeira."

"Jefferson was quite an expert on wines. In fact, he advised three presidents, Washington, Madison, and Monroe—on their selections. During his own presidency," Somerville informed the table, "he purchased immense quantities of wine his with his own money. In his first year alone, his wine bill was nearly $2,800."

"Are you insinuating, Fenton," Denker spoke with feigned indignity, "that Jefferson drank too much?"

"Certainly not!" Somerville flushed. "It was his congressional colleagues—they were the drunks. He hosted weekly dinners for them. That was where he did his politicking. He used the wine to soften them up."

"Wasn't that his strategy to win his first election?" Claire asked, blinking at Henry.

"Very good, Miss Fox," Somerville replied. "Jefferson was smart enough to stick with his winning strategies. He made a special point to cultivate his knowledge of wine while he was in France. He always bought the best—whatever the cost—so of course it was helpful to know what the best wines were. That was the way a proper gentleman approached life.

"Jefferson preferred to deal with the producers themselves. He bought his Bordeaux from such famous vineyards as Chateaux Margaux, Lafite, Latour and Haute-Brion. He also enjoyed French sauternes and champagne. He distinguished himself from his countrymen though because he did not enjoy sweet, fortified wines. He liked unfortified wines with a taste he described as 'silky'. That was a compound of dryness with a dash of sweetness." Somerville took another bite of his veal.

"His drinking habits also changed in France. During his retirement, he typically drank three glasses of wine a day. When he had dinner guests, which was regularly, he would drink four or five glasses." Somerville smiled. "You can imagine how, in the course of an evening, the conversation might become animated."

"It sounds like he went to France to become cultured," Henry observed.

"That's an interesting idea," Somerville said. He pondered it as he savored a plum olive. "France was a very important interlude in Jefferson's life. I think he was fated to be there when he was," he observed, taking a sip of cider ". . . because he had such a difficult time getting there."

"What do you mean?" Claire asked.

"He was called to go to France in the fall of 1776 but chose to stay in Virginia where he was recasting the law of his new state. In June of 1781, the Congress appointed him Minister Plenipotentiary to negotiate peace with Great Britain with an American delegation consisting of Adams, Franklin, Jay, and John Laurens. He recorded in his autobiography that the Empress of Russia was expected to mediate it. Jefferson declined that appointment due to his wife's illness. In any case, the peace process did not begin then. "The Congress renewed his appointment in November of 1782 because the negotiations were then resuming. His wife had died nine weeks before, and Jefferson was anxious to leave the gloom of his empty house, so he immediately accepted this offer. He departed from Monticello three weeks later, leaving unsettled such urgent matters as the management of his estate and the heavy burden of the supervision of his three motherless daughters."

"Are you saying that he accepted the offer because he was depressed? " Dr. Denker wondered.

"He wanted to escape the gloom," Claire answered decisively.

Somerville hurried another mouthful of veal before responding. "Well, of course, he was overwhelmed by the death of his wife. And the atmosphere at Monticello must have been dark. But remember, this mountain was the spiritual center of his life. That did not change."

"Why did he leave then?" Claire objected.

"He was . . . lured away."

"Lured away?" Claire asked skeptically.

"The Marquis de Chastellux . . ." Somerville raised his eyebrows in a way that invited question. "Actually," the scholar continued, "Jefferson had fallen into his thrall during a week-long visit he paid to Monticello in the spring of 1782. Jefferson and Martha were preparing for the delivery their sixth child. Imagine how tense he must have been! Jefferson's biographers have made a mistake by ignoring Chastellux. In many respects, he exerted one of the most important influences on Jefferson. Today, Chastellux is little more than a footnote, which shares little about the qualities that attracted Jefferson to him.

"The fact is, however, that Chastellux was a man of rare accomplishment. Beyond his success as a soldier, he was a famous author and a laureate of the l'Académie française. His knowledge was profound, encompassing the arts and science. He wielded it brilliantly in conversation and was great enough in character to be able to communicate across the social strata. In addition to his great social skills, he was a perceptive judge of character. 'It seemed as if from youth he had placed his mind, as he had done his home, in an elevated situation from which he might contemplate the universe.' That was how Chastellux described Jefferson. Jefferson, anguishing at the loss of his life's companion, stumbled by accident into a soul mate. That was what drew him to France—the hope that he might polish himself in the image of Chastellux.

"Jefferson was in a rush to leave his mountain top because he had been invited to sail with Chastellux back to France. The ship was scheduled to leave in mid-December so there was no time to lose."

"But Jefferson didn't go to France until the fall of 1784," Henry interjected.

"Very good, Mr. Tilghman," Somerville nodded. "Before the ship sailed, word came that a provisional treaty had been signed in Paris on the 3rd of September. Finding himself with no business to conduct, Jefferson returned home."

"Finally, in May of the following year, he had his fourth chance. Congress appointed him Minister of France and asked him to help negotiate commercial treaties with European nations. This time there was no last-minute snag. He set sail from Boston on the Ceres on July 5th, after depositing Maria, and his youngest daughter Jane Randolph, with their aunt, Elizabeth Eppes."

"Of all the thoughts streaming through his mind as he watched the shoreline recede, the expectation of seeing Chastellux and immersing himself in the French laureate's culture, no doubt, gave him the most satisfaction. It's just as you alluded to it earlier, Mr. Tilghman. Jefferson went to France with a private plan to complete his own transformation into a Renaissance Man. He intended to embroider the furnishings of his encyclopedic mind with the refinements of society's most perfect culture.

"Only in this context can we understand his peculiar enterprises. The revision of his *Notes on the State of Virginia,* for example, which he published for private distribution in February of 1787. And, of course, his most unusual work, *Thoughts on English Prosody,* which he finished in October 1786 after months of intense labor.

"I personally think that it should be described as a final examination that he assigned to himself to prove his fitness to enter the salon. He chose a subject utterly impenetrable to the common intellect to show the literati that he was indeed worthy."

"How can you be so sure about his motives," Claire wondered.

"Because we have ultimate proof!"

"What is it?" Henry asked.

Somerville's eyes grew wide. "Jefferson dedicated his master's thesis to . . . the Marquis de Chastellux!"

———————————

"Most people don't pick fights with Martin," Claire whispered.

"I handled that badly," Denker conceded.

"You and Henry seem to have the same problem when it comes to the press," she observed.

"You have to understand, Miss Fox. The Jefferson Academy is a living memorial to the democratic principles of Thomas Jefferson. Our 'weltanschauung', if I may use that word, is built upon them. Jefferson's concept of natural rights gives our government its legitimacy. The social problems we have today must be approached in that context."

Claire nodded politely.

"Have you read Plato, Miss Fox?" Denker asked suddenly.

"A little . . ."

"What have you read?"

"I read the *Symposium* once in a comparative literature class and part of *The Republic* in a political philosophy course, which I dropped when I discovered that he considered women inferior to men."

The answer startled the professor. "You'll be pleased to know that Jefferson was a severe critic of Plato. People today aren't generally familiar with the anti-Platonic themes in Jefferson's political philosophy."

"I suppose not . . . what are they?"

Denker nodded. "Jefferson rejected the autocratic management system that Plato recommended. We talk about that today in terms of his opposition to "monocrats," meaning Alexander Hamilton. But remember, Jefferson did not encounter Hamilton's federalist concepts until the late 1780's—well after he had fixed his views on the rights of man and majoritarian government."

"I'm not following you," Claire confessed.

"The point, Miss Fox, is that Hamilton's were not the only politics Jefferson opposed. He was a determined opponent of Plato long before he began to fear that Hamilton would persuade Adams and his Federalist party to set up a monarchy. Mr. Ogden and his sort want to see every issue in terms of 20th century Hamilton-Jefferson dichotomies. And that has blinded them to what Jefferson feared most."

"What was that?"

"Government run by *sophocrats*."

"I'm sorry to be so dense, Dr. Denker, but what is a sophocrat?"

"A sophocrat is an individual who advocates government by the wise."

"Jefferson opposed that?" Claire sounded shocked.

"Well of course he did!" Denker expressed his surprise. "He believed in government by consent of the people! He believed that the law rests on the rights of individuals, not the other way around. I'm sure you would see that if you reread *The Republic*."

"I would?"

"In Plato's ideal state, the philosopher-king ruled with absolute power. His authority did not rest on the consent of the people. It rested on force. Plato created a warrior class to 'protect the flock' and enforce the law. Together with the philosopher-king, they formed a governing class Plato called..."

"Guardians!" Henry interjected over Dr. Denker's shoulder.

The professor leaned back.

"Sorry, I couldn't resist," Henry apologized.

"...That's all right, Henry. Come and join us."

"Am I following you, Dr. Denker?" Claire continued. "Are you making a connection between Plato's ruling class and today's utopians?"

"Yes! Precisely. The connection, Miss Fox is the proposition that the wise should rule. Jefferson, as I was saying, disagreed. He thought society should be guided by the collective wisdom of the people. And that puts him at odds with modern utopians who hold the collective wisdom of the people in contempt."

"Really, Dr. Denker..."

"How else would you describe it, Miss Fox? They reject the judgment of the majority."

"You're making me wonder whether Martin was right..." Claire replied sheepishly.

"You would think better of that if you were aware of the facts," the professor answered gravely.

"What facts?"

Denker leaned forward. "They blew up the..." There was a sudden loud hum of a microphone. Denker turned to see Raymond Paige standing at the podium at the head table.

"Blew up what?" Claire whispered urgently.

"Shhh!" Denker signaled, turning toward Paige.

"Honored Guests, Ladies and Gentlemen. Could I have your attention please." Mr. Paige spoke in a firm, friendly voice.

"On behalf of the Jefferson Academy I want to thank all of you for joining us this evening. I would also like to thank the members of the press who are here on behalf of the general public. It seems hard to believe, but there are 150 representatives from the media here tonight... He swung around and winked at Nelson Rockefeller, "that's a better turn out than Ford had at his first news conference." There was a ripple of knowing laughter. "I want to give special thanks to the Trustees of the Thomas Jefferson Foundation for making it possible for us to incorporate this historic property into our program this evening. It has been in their care since 1922, and they have done a magnificent job refurbishing it. (Applause)

"I'm told Thomas Jefferson was the nation's first native born architect. This house—with the possible exception of that place down on Pennsylvania Avenue—is probably the best-known residence in America. It is surely one of our greatest national treasures. We are all indebted to the Thomas Jefferson Foundation for its fine work." (More applause)

Paige stepped back then and joined the audience in thanking the stewards of the mansion museum.

"I also want to recognize the special contributions that Dr. Fenton Somerville has made to our program this evening. Fenton would you please stand." The audience responded with another round of applause. "Dr. Somerville is the curator of Monticello and is widely recognized as the foremost living authority on Thomas Jefferson. He tells me that Jefferson did not actually settle into his house until he retired from public life in 1809. It was during those final years that he came to be known as the 'Sage of Monticello.' Dr. Somerville has assisted us in preparing this next part of our program... Fenton would you come up here and introduce it for me."

The shy scholar shuffled to the podium.

"Thank you, Raymond," he said as he adjusted the microphone. "Ladies and gentlemen, Mr. Paige is referring to the arrangement we made for Thomas Jefferson to speak to us this evening. This is a rare treat, for as you may know, he does not consider himself a natural orator and seldom speaks publicly. Nevertheless, his words have come to be an important part of our national heritage, and he has kindly consented to share a few of them with us tonight. Bear with me, if you will, while I make this brief introduction." So saying, he opened a folded paper and began to read.

"Jefferson was a man of tremendous intellect and power and unbounded energy, a man whose curiosity was exceeded only by his vision. This becomes clear when we remember that his ideas are as current today as they were when he formed them nearly two centuries ago."

"We are accustomed to praising Jefferson as a visionary. But his words remain vital today because he was also a realist. It was his greatest fear that the society he labored to form would be destroyed by the corrupting forces of human nature. Tonight, we will hear him express his visions and his fears. They reveal the special qualities of the man who gave life to political democracy in America and around the world." He stopped momentarily, then leaned back to the microphone, "If you detect a physical resemblance between our Mr. Jefferson and the Sage himself, it is because they are related. Our Thomas Jefferson is the great-great-great-grandson of the architect of our political freedom—and of this fine house."

With that, Dr. Somerville stepped away from the microphone and looked to his right. A faint light appeared in the south piazza. The assembly watched as the light moved out onto the terrace and down the steps to the lawn. It advanced cautiously through the darkness toward the pavilion. With each passing moment, another decade vanished from the calendar.

When the tall lean figure finally emerged from the darkness it was late summer, 1812. His hair flowed casually over his ears in comfortable dishevelment. It was a pale color. No longer red. Not yet white. He held his chin high. Not in defiance, rather as a man might stand as he searched for comrades in a crowded room. He had a fine straight Virginia nose. His mouth was set in an aristocratic expression, lips sealed, in a faint smile as if prepared to offer a greeting or an encouraging word. When his eyes adjusted to this light, he turned to Raymond Paige and extended his hand.

Then, he stepped to the podium.

"I am pleased you have made the journey safely," he said without introduction. Because his voice was soft, he shaped his sounds with care so that his listeners would hear him and gather his sentiments. *"The children are finally abed so we are free to pursue to our own pleasures . . . I've asked*

Wormley to bring up more Madeira," he added, lifting a glass from a stand beside him and taking a sip. *"Mr. Somerville advises me that you do not play an instrument. That is a pity for I would have asked you to join me in playing the new melodies Lafayette has sent me. But I know what interests you, so let us proceed on to that . . ."*

He closed his eyes and stroked his forehead with his long delicate fingers.

"It's hard to believe that 25 years have passed since the Constitution was ratified . . . and that so many of those who carried it into being are gone." He paused and reflected for a melancholy moment. *"Those were glorious and hopeful days,"* he continued. *"But Madison still lives and Adams."* His voice grew firmer. *"And long live the Republic!"*

"My friends, the revolution of 1800 was as real a revolution in the principle of our government as that of 1776 was in its form; not affected indeed by the sword, as that one, but by the natural and peaceful instrument of reform, being the suffrage of people. The nation declared its intention to institute this reform by dismissing the functionaries of one principle and replacing them with those of another in the two of the three branches of their government, being the executive and legislative. I am sorry to say that the Constitution deprived them of similar control over the third department, to which I say, we must live within the law.

"The same day we learned the vote, I called on Mr. Adams on some official business. He was very sensibly affected and accosted me with words I still clearly remember. 'Well,' he said, 'I understand that you are to beat me in this contest. Of this I will only say that I will be as faithful a subject as any you will have.' Mr. Adams, I replied, this is no personal contest between you and me. Competing principles of government have divided the people into two parties. One of these parties has placed your name at its head, the other mine. Were we both to die tomorrow, two other names would be entered in place of ours without any change in the motion of the machinery. 'I believe you are right,' he replied, 'we are nothing more than instruments of a machine that is driven by the will of the people. That is what we both labored to accomplish in the war, and I am prepared to live with it in the peace.' He ended the interview taking my hand and saying this. 'Sir, may God help you preserve it for the sake of all, and God bless the republic.'"

"He's referring to his own election," Denker whispered into Claire's ear. "He saw it as the triumph of Republicanism over Hamilton's Monarchism. For Jefferson, it was America's Second Revolution . . ."

"I suppose the reservations I expressed about of the present federal Constitution will lead some of you to wonder how strongly I support it. I will say here that I wish an inviolable preservation of our Constitution, but it must be according to the true sense in which it was adopted by the states. What do I mean by that? I consider the true foundation of the Constitution is that all powers not delegated to the United States by the Constitution, nor prohibited by it to the states, are reserved to the states or the people. To take a single step beyond the boundaries thus specially drawn around the power of Congress is to take possession of a boundless field of power no longer susceptible of any definition. This is the path to the tyranny we rebelled against in in the early 1770s and defeated in the war.

"I made my objections to the plan known at the outset. First among them was that the plan had no bill of rights. A bill of rights was needed, I argued, to guard the inherent liberties of the people against usurpations by branches of the government, which history showed us would, in due course, fill with wolves. What liberties are these, you wish to know? They are the things which make a people free: freedom in religion, freedom of the press, freedom from monopolies, freedom from unlawful imprisonment, freedom from a permanent military, and trail by jury in all cases determinable by the laws of the land.

"Equally great among my fears was the Federal Judiciary. That body, like gravity, ever acting with noiseless foot and unalarming advance, gains ground step by step, and holds what it gains to the detriment of political liberty. The intention of the founders was for coordinate branches to be checks on each other. But opinions which have given unelected judges the right to decide what laws are constitutional and what are not—not only for themselves in their own sphere of action, but for the Legislature and Executive also, in their spheres—makes the Judiciary a despotic branch.

"A fraudulent use of the Constitution made judges irremovable. Since then, they have multiplied themselves, not in pursuit of better justice, but rather to strengthen their phalanx. To prevent this cunning encroachment on the liberty of the people, I say, we must keep the people fully informed as to the activities of the Judiciary. If the people become complacent about the activism

of this inconspicuous department of their government, they will lose their re-
public. We need only read history to know that the law of human nature is
for men to devour each other. In Europe, the rich have always preyed on the
poor! We must not allow ourselves to become like them! And how are we to
preserve the Republic, Liberty, and Equality? Let there be now and then a
revolution! In the political world, these storms are the medicine necessary for
sound health of government!"

"That was Jefferson's warning to Madison, which he sent from France
in 1787," Denker whispered.

"To be clear, let me repeat what I hold to be the essential principles of
our government: First, equal and exact justice for all men, whatever their
state or persuasion, religion or political affiliation; Second, peaceful commerce
and honest friendship with all nations, but entangling alliances with none
of them; Third, support for the state governments in all their rights as the
best defense against anti-republican tendencies; Fourth, the preservation of
the general government in its whole constitutional vigor as the anchor of our
peace pursuits at home and abroad; Fifth, the zealous protection of the peo-
ple's right to elect their representatives; Sixth, the acquiescence to the decisions
of the majority, above whose authority stand only our good will and moral
sense; Seventh, the sacred preservation of the public faith in the government
through its honest administration; Eighth, economy in the public expense;
Ninth, encouragement of agriculture and commerce.
"And here is the tenth: the sacred principle of our government and polit-
ical society, that the will of the majority is in all cases to prevail, must be in-
terpreted in terms of the good of all the people, being their <u>common</u> good. Let
us understand, that the political principles that guide the nation are rightful
insofar as they are reasonable and protect the rights of everyone equally, in-
cluding those who constitute the minorities in political matters. Those who
violate this principle are oppressors who have no place among a free people.
In this spirit of good will, let the people be united with one heart and mind.
Let this harmony and affection guide them as they conduct their social in-
tercourses for without it there will be neither liberty nor happiness. Let us
also remember that although we have banished cults and superstitions that in
ages past divided one man against another, we have gained little if we allow

ourselves to be lured from our founding social and political principles by the promise of something better . . ."

Mr. Paige appeared suddenly at Claire's shoulder. "Are you enjoying your evening, Miss Fox?" he asked in a gravelly whisper.

"Yes! Immensely . . ."

"Good. I want to visit with you before you leave. Will you be available tomorrow?"

"When would be a good time?" Claire answered eagerly.

"Why don't you join me for lunch at the house . . . Henry can show you the way."

"I'd love to."

"I will see you then." He touched her gently on the arm to confirm the appointment. He turned then to Henry. "I need you for a few minutes," he said, gesturing.

Henry rose and followed Paige to the edge of the tent. Claire watched him whisper something into Henry's ear. Having said whatever was on his mind, he stepped out of the tent and marched off toward the mansion. Henry disappeared into the darkness.

"This is my vision, and I believe that all men would benefit from its actualization. This conviction notwithstanding, I am sensible how far short I would fall if I were to undertake to impose its particulars on the people. History shows us, does it not, how difficult it is to move the machinery of society and to advance the notions of a whole people. Therefore, in spite my impatience to achieve what I have no doubt would be better, I remember the wisdom of Solon who observed that no more good must be attempted than a nation can bear.

"But patience does not make me complacent in respect to the positive evil I have witnessed with the passage of time. I close this evening by repeating my objection in the strongest of terms to the strides the federal branch of our government is making in consolidating all power within itself. Remember friends that when we confronted a similar tyranny, we stood to arms! Good evening and safe journeying . . ."

Jefferson then relit his taper, stepped off the dais, and stepped back into the darkness. As the dim light floated back toward the mansion, Denker again leaned toward Claire. "He wrote that just six months before he died," the Professor said. "That gives you an idea of how his expectations changed with time."

"What did they blow up?" Claire whispered through the applause.

"This is strictly confidential. Do you understand, Miss Fox?" Denker glanced about then focused again on Claire who nodded gravely. "A group calling itself the Guardians of Open Society," he whispered behind his cupped hand, "has claimed responsibility for blowing up the R-o-t-u-n-d-a! They sent a letter to Dr. Shannon at the University a few days after the explosion."

"I never saw anything in the paper about it," Claire informed him skeptically.

"The FBI wants it kept out of the papers while the investigation is going on."

"How convenient," she scoffed.

"There's more to it," Denker continued, ignoring her response.

"Oh?"

"The letter warned of further reprisals—against 'the enemies of the people.' That was the phrase in the letter."

"How do you know so much about it?" Claire asked in a skeptical tone.

The Professor considered her question for a long moment. "The FBI thinks the Jefferson Academy may be the next target."

"Do you agree?"

"These are dangerous people, Miss Fox."

"Why would they target the Jefferson Academy?"

"They see us as a threat."

"The Jefferson Academy? How could it be a threat?"

"Because we think, Miss Fox!"

"What do you think?"

"In January we are going to start a year-long program commemorating the 200th anniversary of the Declaration of Independence."

"I guess I knew that," she nodded.

"Mr. Paige will be discussing it at the dinner tomorrow night."

"Why would they care about that? I mean . . ."

"We intend to teach the American people about the system of values that guided Jefferson in shaping his great American doctrine."

"I'm sure it will be very interesting," Claire observed without enthusiasm.

"If we are going to meet the challenges of the technical age, we need to restore the values that vitalized Jefferson's republic."

"I mentioned that in my article . . ."

"The problem we have to resolve," Denker explained, "is one Tocqueville identified one-hundred and thirty-five years ago . . ."

"The one Mr. Paige mentioned yesterday," Claire injected, trying to recall the quote.

"Exactly, "Denker nodded. "The government has become a caretaker that provides for the well-being of its citizens rather than the guarantor of their right to pursue happiness."

"Dr. Somerville said Jefferson developed his concept of happiness studying the Greeks. Did he know anything about the happiness ordinary people pursue?" Claire wondered.

Denker seemed confused. "I suppose one could argue that happiness is not an enlightened concept." He paused for a moment. "But, of course, thinkers like Bentham and Mill equated it with the good and used as it the cornerstone of their utilitarian theories of morality. Newton, as a fanatical Christian, could not have accepted such humanist reductions of God's moral law. But God bless him, he died before Hume formulated the concept in 1752. Jefferson criticized Hume's history of England for defending the Monarchy, but there is no indication that he ever read Hume's *Ethics*.

"In any event, Jefferson was more in phase with Newton's empirical method of science than he was with Hume's empirical verification of utilitarianism. As to the Greeks . . ."

"Forgive me, Dr. Denker," Claire interrupted, placing her hand on his arm. "I was just . . . I mean . . . It's been a long day."

Denker was too engaged in his thought to catch her drift. "I think you've missed his point. I can't see how Fenton could have connected Newtonian mechanics with classical ethics. They're quite different disciplines. So far as enlightened moral theory, it is necessary to distinguish between Morality as it was conceived by Hume and his followers, and Ethics as it was treated by classical thinkers. Moral theories promulgated during the early Enlightenment addressed man's treatment of his fellow man . . . Of course, since the Utilitarians purged God from the moral dialectic, it has become increasingly a matter of defining the common good. Classical ethics, on the other hand, looked inward and instructed man on how to achieve excellence of character.

"Newton was not quite on either side of this distinction. He saw Nature as 'God's sensorium.' By verifying the laws of mechanics, Newton supposed he was revealing the true order of God's universe. The laws he formulated made sense because they followed the order in creation according to his faith. The same might be said of Jefferson."

"I see," Claire said patiently.

"Are you familiar with the concept of Due Process?" Denker asked suddenly.

"In a general way." Claire answered with a sigh. "It's the constitutional right of the individual to equal protection under the law as specified in the 5th Amendment of the Bill of Rights?"

"You're partially right," he said graciously. "The 5th Amendment guarantees individuals 'due process' of law in federal jurisdictions. The Equal Protection clause is part of the 14th Amendment which established similar guarantees in areas of state authority. Jefferson knew 'due process' as the common limitation to the Law of the Land. It was a shield to protect the private rights of the individual against encroachment by the police powers of the state. Its specific intent was to prevent government actions that unjustifiably restricted personal liberty."

"Ok . . ."

"Jefferson was following Locke. A century earlier, Locke had argued that private rights have their basis in reason. Laws are needed to protect and develop them, not to create them. The only limit Jefferson applied to the natural rights of the individual was the common law concept of 'sic to et alienem non laedas.' Roughly translated that means a man has a right to swing his fist as far as the end of his neighbor's nose."

"Ok . . ." Claire repeated cautiously.

"Due process is the core concept of our law, the cornerstone of American society. In Jefferson's estimation, it has the power of a Natural Law whose authority derives from the will of God. Do you follow that?" She nodded again. "It was more than a social convention. It was a categorical imperative by which I mean it was inviolable. Now look what has happened," he continued. "Due process has been superseded as the operative principle of our law with something called 'equal protection.' We're replacing an ancient, essentially qualitative principle with a hastily-manufactured quantitative one."

Claire looked perplexed. "Is that supposed to be a problem?"

"Yes!" Denker replied gravely. "Quantities have no natural value—they are whatever it pleases us to call them. There is no established path to guide our steps—no sure foundation on which to build our society. That is why 'comparable standing among groups' cannot be a substitute for 'due process of law' as a foundation for a democratic society."

Claire stared at him blankly.

Denker massaged his temple with the tips of his fingers. "The 'group' is not a political unit in a democracy," he explained hopefully.

"Oh come on, Dr. Denker," she said with a faint smile. "We're finally working together to achieve social equality!"

"I wish it were true. But don't you see? Beneath your cheery headline, we're undermining our political system."

"You don't really believe that!" Claire exclaimed.

"We like to think we're enlightened," the professor continued. "But we have forgotten a key point. Being enlightened is not being tolerant. Being enlightened is to examine ideas in the light of reason."

"Hasn't it occurred to you that we might make the system work better?"

"You must remember, Miss Fox! God endowed *human beings* with natural rights. That's why Jefferson said that the power to govern comes from the people. Their will can only be expressed by the voice of the majority. Government has no other legitimate source of authority. That's why it has no authority to limit the natural rights of individuals—even to equalize the standing of groups. Mr. Jefferson made that very point this evening."

"The people are making democracy work," Claire protested.

"They are being hoodwinked—as Mr. Jefferson would say," Denker responded pessimistically. "That's why our program is so important."

Claire sat there silently. "You think you're a target for a group of terrorists," she said, finally abandoning the debate.

"They're afraid they will lose if we tell the public what they're doing!"

"I'd be surprised if anyone takes you seriously," Claire admitted accidently.

"The American people are not stupid, Miss Fox. They are just poorly informed about their political system and the concepts that underpin it."

"People look to the government to solve their problems," Claire pleaded.

"You have to understand something. Miss Fox. These people don't believe in promoting the greatest happiness for the greatest number or solving their problems. They believe in promoting their ideology. That's how they understand the common good. Government is the ultimate source of power. If they can get control of it, they'll transform the world according to their ideology. That's their definition of perfection. For them, people are merely objects to move around. What happens to them is irrelevant!"

Claire strained to produce a smile. "It sounds like you're the ones who want to start the next revolution."

"The revolution has begun, Miss Fox. We're going to make sure that the people understand what it's about . . ." Dr. Denker looked weary.

"Who are these people anyway?" Claire asked, diverting the subject.

"Who are they?" Denker shook his head, "I guess we'll just have to wait and see. I can tell you one thing though. They're wrong if they think that we can be intimidated!"

"And Mr. Paige?"

"He's ready to face them . . ."

"Do you think you can just dump the poor into the ocean and forget about them?" she asked, trying one more time to move him.

"We're not going to lift up the downtrodden by undermining the platform of their freedom. Montesquieu said it best 200 years ago. Governments are doomed when they abandon the principles on which they are founded."

"How can you square all this with the idea that all men are created equal?"

"I don't understand your question."

"Men who are created equal are unequal in this system."

"Now, there's an interesting inversion," Denker replied. "You understand don't you that our Constitution makes no philosophical assertions. It simply states the fundamental law of the land and guarantees equal justice—Justice in the universal sense."

"What sense is that?"

"We could say in the Biblical sense! Let's define it as the Will of God as revealed in the Old and New Testaments. Isn't this reinforced by our application of reason, which we learned from the Greeks? If you take a closer look at the ideas Jefferson shared with us this evening, you will see that his views were quite consistent with this. Do you remember what he said in the Declaration? "We hold these truths to be self-evident; that all men ARE CREATED EQUAL that they are endowed by their creator with inherent and inalienable rights; that among these are life, liberty, and the pursuit of happiness.

"You see—that is the political expression of Good Will. Jefferson understood that the exercise of these inalienable rights by the individuals who possess them is what makes society democratic. This becomes quite clear in his concluding phrase: "whenever any form of government becomes destructive of these ends . . ."

"You're living too far in the past, Dr. Denker. The majority of people I know want to change the system. Isn't that their Jeffersonian right?"

"They cannot alienate their natural rights," Denker replied. "Nor can they establish a government that violates the inalienable rights of others. Do you and your friends ever consider that?"

"What about people who are being deprived of their rights?"

"First of all, I reject the rhetoric of your statement. No system of government is better suited for social evolution than political democracy. Do you disagree with that? Or are you saying that change should occur outside our system? In which case, who should decide the particulars? You?"

"Well, I . . ."

"Look . . . American society—like every other society—is full of imperfect human beings! But does it make sense to pretend that we will change human nature by overturning man's most virtuous political achievement?"

Claire considered the question. "I think the problem is that you don't know what to do now that the Enlightenment you all talk so much about down here has finally reached the people."

"I don't mean this as a personal criticism, Miss Fox, but it is the nature of youth to attack the status quo. Every rising generation has a new perspective. But it is also prone to misconstrue the facts. Youth is idealistic, but that does not make it wise, or its principles virtuous—and without them, the systems they espouse are *degenerations* not *improvements*."

Claire noticed Tim Hardin as he slipped into the tent behind Dr. Denker.

"We can invent hundreds of well-meaning rules to improve society, but we will accomplish just the opposite if these rules do not conform to the concept of individual right that underlies our Constitution. Our law is not a tool to enforce a synthetic system of values. If we allow it to be used that way, we will end up in Plato's *Republic*. I wish you had read it. Sophocrats are not concerned with individual freedom—or happiness." He shook his head in dismay.

"So!" A voice announced. "It was the Sophocrats who invented social reform . . ." Denker turned to see Tim Harden smiling mischievously at Claire. "If you'll show me one, I'd like to shake his hand." Then, addressing Denker, he added, "Oscar, I need to talk with you in private."

"By all means Tim. Can it wait until tomorrow morning?"

His tone changed abruptly. "No!"

"Very well." He looked back at Claire. "Would you excuse me."

Claire realized that she was shaking. This cursed place, she thought.

"Mind if I sit down?"

Claire looked up into the smiling face of Fenton Somerville. "Oh Dr. Somerville! Please do." She had a sudden impulse to throw her arms around his neck.

"What did you think of our Mr. Jefferson?" he asked as he seated himself.

"He was good." She was glad to be able to say something positive. "Was he really that somber?" she wondered.

"Yes, he had many cares," Somerville acknowledged.

"Did he actually say those things?"

"We did some rearranging," he conceded, "but they were his thoughts."

"Did you put them together yourself?"

"I was the junior partner in the enterprise. The real work was done by a young woman from the Jefferson Academy. Perhaps you have met her—Miss Wiley?"

"Roberta Wiley?"

"Yes, she's the one. I've been looking for her . . ."

"Haven't you heard?"

"Heard what?" he said, his smile dimming as he looked at the expression on Claire's face.

"Roberta Wiley drowned in a swimming accident two days ago."

"Oh! My . . ." The curator's smile disappeared. "How unfortunate. We were together just Saturday putting the finishing touches on the script."

"So you knew Roberta Wiley . . ." Claire probed gently.

"Yes, of course. We worked closely on this program. We were also working together on the Academy's bicentennial program. Several months . . ."

"Is Henry working on that too?"

"I think he is working with Oscar on the economic and social aspects of colonial life."

"That would explain why he knows so much about Thomas Jefferson," she thought out loud.

"Yes—I suppose it would," Somerville agreed.

As Claire weighed the information, she felt herself being lifted by a surge of new energy.

"Are you familiar with the Due Process issue Dr. Denker was talking about?"

"Yes," he said, his own spirits raising slightly. "It's important if you want to understand the politics of the American Revolution. We have done some interesting work on it—quite original I'd say."

"Really?"

"For some reason the subject hasn't interested historians. We seem to be the first," he announced proudly, "to trace the development of Due Process from English Common Law as it existed at the time Jefferson wrote the Declaration of Independence back to its seeds in the Roman codes."

"Can I ask you a question, Dr. Somerville?"

"Certainly."

"Are you familiar with Plato?"

"I think so—that would be fair to say," he answered with a scholar's modesty.

"Dr. Denker tried to explain the anti-Platonic themes in Jefferson's thinking, but he lost me somewhere between Platonic sophocrats and Hamiltonian monarchists."

"Dear me!" The scholar sympathized. "I know the problem exactly. Economist!" He cursed in sudden disgust. "They treat everything as a regression analysis."

"So you understand the point he was making?"

"Oh yes. Absolutely."

"Could you explain it to me?"

"I'll try," he said, squaring himself to the task. "Plato was the first utopian. That is the essential point. In the *Republic,* he lays out his idea of utopia. He tells us there that in its original form, society was a kingship of the wisest and most godlike men. That was the ideal Form of a state—you understand all that of course." He said this in passing as though it was common knowledge. "This ideal city-state was so near perfection that it is hard to imagine it that would ever change. Plato said it did because of strife, which he considered, so to speak, the driving force for all movement. Social strife, which he understood to be class warfare, was fomented by self-interest, especially economic self-interest. Plato saw that as the main force of social dynamics. Am I sounding a familiar theme, Miss Fox?"

"I guess so," she answered self-consciously.

"Yes, of course I am!" he agreed enthusiastically. "This idea is closely paralleled in the writings of Karl Marx who argued that the history of all hitherto existing societies is a history of class struggle. But I think you might agree that it is also quite contemporary."

"Yes, I suppose so," she allowed.

"It's the point Dr. Denker just made about modern society. You understand about Platonic Ideas don't you, Miss Fox?" She was relieved that he did not wait for her to answer his question. "Plato held that a thing becomes real by participating in its Form. It decays by diverging from its Form. His Theory of Forms and Ideas also applies to the evolution of the world. We can summarize it by saying that corruptibility of all things in the world continually increases."

Claire found herself struggling to keep up with Somerville's narrative.

"The *Republic* was his attempt to define what has since been referred to as the 'royal knowledge' of politics—the art of ruling men. In the beginning, when Cronos himself ruled the world, men sprang from the earth. That golden age was followed by the age of Zeus. During the age of Zeus, the gods abandoned the world and left it to fend for itself. That was the beginning of corruption. In the *Statesman* there is a suggestion that when complete corruption has been reached, the gods will return and restore the world to its original purity."

Somerville sensed that he was losing her. "Let me put it in a historical setting."

"Could you?" Claire asked hopefully.

"Plato lived not long after Pericles. Some argue that Pericles' generation of Athenians was the most gifted in the history of civilization. Actually," he said, correcting those unnamed misguideds, "Jefferson's was . . ."

"Pericles guided Athens into its great experiment with democracy," he said, resuming his narrative. "Plato was a member of the patrician class. It was his uncle Critias who ended the experiment after Pericles death by conspiring with Sparta to defeat Athens in the Peloponnesian War. That was an extended period of political strife and violence, which explains why Plato was so concerned with establishing political stability. Remember! For Plato, the state was perfect to the degree it resembled its form during the Golden Age of Cosmos. To preserve it, Plato argued that it was necessary to suspend change—that was how he proposed to eliminate corruption. Do you see what that is, Miss Fox?"

"No," she said with a hint of irritation.

"It's the first back-to-nature theme in man's long romance with utopianism!" He smiled with their shared satisfaction. "How charming it appears in the soft light of two-and-a-half millennia," he mused, "dwelling in the welcome stability of nature. The hook had a barb though."

"What was that?" Claire wondered.

"Social order in Plato's perfect state was enforced by a para-military ruling class."

"You're saying that Plato's utopian state was a dictatorship," Claire observed.

"Precisely! It was a rigidly structured sophocracy whose first principle was political stability—the antithesis of Jefferson's republic. For Jefferson, government by the consent of the governed was the essential characteristic of the ideal state. Plato perceived this sort of public involvement in the government as an advanced state of political decay."

"Decay?"

"There were essentially four stages of degeneration in Plato's concept of political evolution," Somerville continued. "Sophocracy, which is the rule of the wise, gives way to Timocracy, which is the rule of nobles seeking honor and fame. Timocracy gives way to Oligarchy, which is the rule of rich families. Oligarchy gives way to Democracy, which Plato equated it to lawlessness. And finally, there is the rule of tyrants—Tyranny. According to Plato, the degeneration begins when sophocrats start to show off and spend money. This creates rivalries and efforts to twist the law to gain personal advantage. This produces class conflict. At first it is between the established feudal order and the new order of wealth—a conflict between virtue and money if you will. The transition to oligarchy is completed when the rich establish laws that disqualify those whose means are below a stipulated amount from holding public office. Establishment of the oligarchy sets the stage for civil war in which the poorer classes align against the rich. War begins when one party or the other becomes strong enough to wage it.

"Democracy is born when the poor win the day. The victors celebrate their victory by killing off a few of their vanquished foes. They banish a few more. But with the rest they share the rights of citizenship and public office on equal terms.

"Jefferson saw Democracy as the supreme political achievement. It was the ultimate fulfillment of the Enlightenment! But Plato, who had lived through a different life experience, condemned democrats in every imaginable way. He called them profligate and niggardly, insolent, lawless and shameless, beasts of prey seeking to gratify every whim, living solely for pleasure, and for unnecessary and unclean desires."

"No wonder Jefferson disliked Plato," she agreed.

"Plato is quite unenlightened in terms of Jefferson's frame of reference. Being an advocate, if not a strict practitioner of Newton's scientific methods, Jefferson was bound to reject Platonism and its Socratic method. But he was sensitive to one of Plato's key tenets."

"What was that?"

"Plato said that the transition from democracy to tyranny begins when politicians begin to exploit class antagonisms to solidify their power."

———————

Henry mounted the stairs slowly, taking care to plant his feet firmly on each tread. As he climbed upward in this careful way, he remembered the story he had once read about how Jefferson had to lower his wife's body from the window of second-floor room where she had died.

He breathed a sigh of relief upon reaching the top step safely. Mr. Paige said he would be in the staff library to the right of the stairs. Henry turned and entered the narrow passage that led to the library's door. As he prepared to open it, the quiet was broken by an angry voice. "Let me make this perfectly clear, Paige. I'm offering you a fair trade. If I were you, I'd take it because I'm going to get it anyway."

Henry waited for Mr. Paige to respond. "You haven't been listening to me, young man."

"Oh, I've been listening... I just don't like what I'm hearing," Tim Hardin snorted. "And neither will my associates."

"Who are your associates, Hardin?" Mr. Paige demanded.

"You really disappoint me, Paige. I thought you were smart guy. I see I was wrong." The door opened suddenly, and Hardin charged out. In his haste, he was hardly able to avoid trampling Henry who was waiting in the shadow a step back from the door.

"What the hell..." Hardin swore at the sight of the unexpected obstacle. "Where did you come from?"

"Sorry," Henry said, raising the object in his right hand. "Is Mr. Paige in there? I've got Dr. Somerville's plaque?"

Hardin glared at him another second then stormed on and disappeared around the corner. Henry listened for the sound of a body crashing down the steep staircase but heard only the thudding of feet on the creaky steps.

———————

Fenton Somerville was leading a group of out of Jefferson's bedroom as Henry stepped into the foyer. The last person in his line was Claire.

"Learn anything new?" he called out as she passed by.

Claire swerved out of line and latched her hand under Henry's arm. With a gentle tug, she pulled him into the procession beside her.

The curator led his company through Jefferson's celebrated mechanical doors and into the parlor. Claire and Henry were the last ones to enter the room. Somerville had stationed himself to the left of the fireplace on its west wall. He waited for his guests to get settled then began. "Jefferson purchased most of the paintings in the house on two shopping trips in Paris while he was Ambassador to France. As you can see, the ones on display in the parlor here are not of the first rank artistically. But they all had special significance to Jefferson." He was about to explain what he meant when the man at Henry's elbow interrupted him.

"Excuse me, Dr. Somerville, could you tell us about the carving on the mantle?"

The curator smiled. "As a matter of fact, that is not a carving. If you look closely, you will see that it's a plaster frieze. It was created for installation in the mantle by craftsmen in Alexandria."

Henry was standing in front of the hearth and leaned forward to inspect the ornament. "The skull . . ." he exclaimed. The shock carried him backwards into the man at his shoulder. Claire's deft hand saved the man's drink from crashing to the floor, but not before its contents splashed out. Henry's eyes remained fixed on the skull. Claire guided him gently back to his starting point and steadied him there as he absorbed his strange discovery.

"Jefferson certainly admired the piece," Somerville observed, oblivious of the disturbance. "You will notice that he incorporated variations of it in the entablatures of this room and the dining room." His gaze shifted to the frieze at the top of the wall. "We have here an excellent illustration of the complexity behind the simple forms with which Jefferson chose to surround himself . . ."

As Somerville directed the attention of his guests toward the edge of the ceiling, Claire leaned forward to see what caused Henry's convulsion. She recognized it immediately. It was the figure in Henry's diagram. She glanced back at Henry, who was still staring at it.

". . . Jefferson felt that he needed to prepare his home to entertain men and women whose cultural attainments were comparable to his own.

He therefore devoted a great deal of attention to the decorative details in his public rooms. Somerville paused to study the figures in the frieze that ringed the ceiling. The entablatures, for example. You can imagine how difficult they were to create and install. They had to be correct in the Palladian sense, which meant they had to conform to precise mathematical rules in respect to their dimensions. The ceiling in this room is eighteen-feet high, which is also the height of the foyer and dining room! Therefore, the entablatures had to be quite large! That was not all—Jefferson required that they speak to him. Look at the figures in these moldings—the ox skull and the instruments of ritual sacrifice. They were not just bits of artistry! They also meant something . . ."

"Many of you know that Jefferson was a devoted disciple of Roman architecture," he observed. "He supported his study of the subject with an extensive collection of books having illustrations of Roman buildings and sculpture. This frieze, like the one in the hall, was copied from an engraving Jefferson found in Desgodet's *Edifices antique de Rome*. We believe he referred to the same source for the details of his famous 'copy' of the Pantheon at the University of Virginia.

"As for this frieze, the original is in the Temple of Vespasian in Rome, which was also known as the Temple of Jupiter the Thunderer. For those of you who are rusty on your first century Roman history, Vespasian was the founder of the Flavian Dynasty and Emperor of the Roman Empire between 69 to 80 AD. Jefferson knew a great deal about Vespasian from his frequent reading of Tacitus who recorded the events of his reign in his *Histories*. As a boy, Jefferson read the *Histories* in its original Latin. He transcribed many of its passages in his Literary Bible, which served him as a kind of a rule book in his youthful efforts to form a view of society and government.

"A few facts about Vespasian will help to give meaning to the characters in the frieze. First, he rose to a position of prominence as a general in the Roman army during the reign of Nero. He distinguished himself by pacifying the Germanic tribes and adding Briton to the Roman empire. Later he became the conqueror of Judea with the valuable assistance of his son and successor, Titus.

"Vespasian came to power at the end of what we know today as the 'Year of the Four Caesars.' It began with the suicide of Nero whose thirteen-year reign left the empire in shambles. Galba, one of his generals, was chosen by the Senate to be his successor, but was assassinated seven months later in the Forum of Rome by the praetorian guard, which had been incited by his rival, Otho. Otho's rule ended just three months later, when his army was defeated by Vitellius at the battle of Cremona. Otho committed suicide a day after hearing the news. His death ended the brief civil war and secured the crown for Vitellius.

"Unfortunately for Vitellius, the treasure that awaited him in Rome was too much for his battle-hardened troops. Idle and undisciplined, his army soon disintegrated into a mob and began plundering the city.

"Vespasian's troops were enraged when they learned that Vitellius had been crowned Emperor and demanded their commander to claim the throne for himself. He deferred long enough to fix firm alliances with the armies in the east. Then he began his advance on Rome. When his troops arrived, they encountered the remnants of Vitellius's army and cut them to pieces. Vitellius suffered a similar fate being butchered by the enraged citizens of Rome. Vespasian's troops proclaimed him Emperor in absentia. His rule ended with his death in 80 AD. Titus rededicated this temple as a memorial to his father shortly after his father's death.

"On the face of it," Somerville continued, "it's an illustration of ritual sacrifice." He paused so his audience could confirm it. "In my opinion, it was also meaningful to Jefferson because it illustrated the year of the Four Ceasars! The skull symbolizes the degenerate condition of the empire at the time of Nero's death. Notice the braided ribbon draped over its horns and dangling languidly beside death's mask—that represents the veil of luxury Nero used to mask the decay that was consuming his empire. The skull, which was a pagan emblem, reminds us that the empire crumbled during the reign of Nero.

"The spilling urn represents the fall of Nero. Notice that the stream emanating from the vessel is separated into three distinct segments, being the three ill-fated claimants to Nero's throne: Galba, Otho, and Vitellius. The butcher knife below it signifies their bloody demise.

"Beside the cascade of succession is a medallion. One like it would have adorned Vespasian's battle standard. The emblem selected for Vespasian's memorial was the one his legions carried in their march on Rome. Vespasian chose a symbol that would inspire his troops as they marched homeward to destroy a tyrant. The symbol he chose to lead his army was the face of Ulysses. The choice reveals his shrewdness. Marching home under Ulysses' banner would have reminded his troops that their odyssey would soon be over and that they were an army of deliverance.

"Notice that Vespasian's medallion is supported by the Roman battle axe. Its power served as the base for the rising scepter of Vespasian's government. Finally, to the right we see Vespasian's laureled helmet of victory and triumph.

"Jefferson was well-versed in the tragic story of the Trojan War and the sad fate of its famous combatant. He might have selected this piece of art simply because it paid homage to the hero of Homer's epic poem, which he identified as one of his greatest sources of pleasure and release, but I believe Jefferson saw it in terms of his own successful struggle to save the new American republic from the monarchists. Think about it. Isn't it also an illustration of his own personal victory? And where better to celebrate it than here—where appreciative citizens came to pay him homage.

"Consider the irony. All who entered this room admired the craftsmanship of the frieze. Yet it was for Jefferson alone to know its true meaning. As Vespasian had saved Rome from tyranny, so had Jefferson saved the American republic!"

Claire leaned forward and examined the mantle frieze a second time. "There's no face on this medallion," she said.

"Very observant, Miss Fox," Somerville said, commending her for drawing attention to the detail. "The medallion in this particular set has been altered. As you can see, it contains a floral design."

"What is it?" Claire asked leaning back down for another look as the others in the group crowded forward to see.

"We think it is the blossom of the betel nut."

"The betel nut . . ," Claire said, filing the information for further investigation.

"Why would he have changed it," Henry inquired finally emerging from his trance. "It doesn't fit the classical parallel."

"Well of course, Jefferson was not above tinkering with antiquity when it suited his purpose," the curator explained. "In this case the original frieze probably did include Ulysses' likeness. We know from an entry in Jefferson's Memorandum Book that he paid George Andrews, his Richmond plasterer, for an ornamental composition in the parlor in June 1801. That suggests the frieze was installed shortly after his election as President. He finished the interior of his public rooms about that time. There is a second entry in his *Memorandum Book* from September 1801, which specified another payment to Andrews for modifications to a "parlor ornament". We don't really know why he altered the frieze," Somerville continued. "All we have are a few murky clues."

"What are they?" Henry asked.

Somerville reflected for a moment. "In our archives, there is a letter from Baron de Riedesel, which Jefferson received sometime after he returned from France. The letter refers to a bag of seeds he sent to Jefferson following a meeting they had while Jefferson was touring the Rhine River Valley in the spring of 1788. The Baron asked Jefferson about the climate in central Virginia and asked him if he had been able to germinate the seeds."

"Seeds?" Claire repeated.

"We know from entries Jefferson made in his *Garden Book* about that time that he succeeded in cultivating seeds from the areca palm it in his arboretum

"How does that relate to the frieze?" a woman next to the curator asked.

"The betel nut is the fruit of the areca palm," Somerville answered.

The candles in the parlor cast a dim light across the stone floor of the west portico. "Your dress is wet," Henry said, noticing it for the first time. "Did I do that?"

Claire's silence answered his question.

"Why didn't you say something?" Henry didn't wait for her to answer. "Here, let me get a napkin ..." He turned resolutely and started for back into the house. Claire caught his arm before he could leave.

"It's all right, Henry," she said, letting her hand slip away.

"Are you sure?"

"Let's just go."

Henry stood motionless trying to decide what to do. Claire forced the issue by stepping past him back into the parlor. He followed her through the house and out onto the East Portico. It was quiet there. The great stone sentinels maintained a silent vigil in the flickering candlelight. Henry escorted Claire between them and down the worn steps. "Who is Baron de Riedesel?" she asked, when they were halfway down the walk.

"I don't know much about him," Henry replied.

She could tell he was still upset. "Doesn't that strike you as strange?"

Henry did not answer.

The attendant at the foot of the walk took Henry's ticket and disappeared. Claire waited until he was gone. "Henry, what happened in the parlor?"

Henry tensed when he heard the question. "What do you mean?" he pretended not to understand.

"The skull startled you."

Henry could feel the terror coming over him again. "It . . . It just surprised me." He could tell by the way she looked at him that she knew he was holding something back.

"Are you sure you're Ok to drive?" she asked, changing the subject.

"Yea, I'm fine."

A pair of headlights swung into view. A second later Henry's car pulled to a stop in front of them. Henry gave the valet a couple of dollars as Claire got in.

"Would you mind if we stop by Tim's for a few minutes?" Claire asked, as they started down the winding driveway.

"What's that?"

"Tim asked me to come by after the program."

"Why don't you do it in the morning?"

"That's all right," Claire answered agreeably. "Just give me a lift to my car, and I'll drive over by myself."

Henry swore a silent oath, ". . . where's he staying?"

"At the Holiday Inn off Route 64."

Henry gritted his teeth and gripped the wheel more tightly.

"You know what I think was really weird?" Claire continued unfazed.

"No." Henry snapped.

"That medallion."

Henry guided the car down the west side of the mountain and into the woods below the first round-about. There was something about the stillness of the forest that made Claire uneasy. "Do you feel that?" She asked, looking over at Henry.

"No. What?" He answered without taking his eyes off the narrow road.

"Oh, nothing I guess." As she stared out the window into the darkness, she suddenly noticed a blinking light below them off to her right. A moment later the car emerged from the woods and came to a stop at the front gate. A state trooper stepped forward to meet them. Henry rolled down his window and leaned out. "Good evening Officer. Is everything all right?"

"Just checking to see everybody makes it back to town," he said

"Thank you, sir, I believe we're all set," Henry replied.

Another trooper was positioned in the road outside the gate. He flashed his light at Henry and signaled for him to proceed. Henry waved as he passed by and drove on slowly down the mountain toward Route 20.

Claire waited a few miles for Henry to get over what had bothered him. When he seemed himself again, she resumed her investigation. "What do you know about betel nuts?" she asked innocently.

"One fell on Siddhartha's head while he was waiting for enlightenment," Henry answered without interest.

"He was sitting under a baobab tree," Claire corrected him.

"What's the difference?"

"You might enlighten yourself if you chewed on a betel nut leaf."

"What are you talking about?" he asked with a darting glance.

"I did research for an article last year on drug use on Capitol Hill."

"What kind of research?"

"On social drugs ... You know—cocaine, mescaline, pot, ..."

"What about them?"

"When I started," Claire confessed, "I thought cocaine came from cocoa..."

"You don't have to play that game with me," Henry said dryly. "I'm not going to tell on you."

"No. Seriously!"

"Where does it come from?"

"It's made from coca plants."

"What's that got to do with betel nuts?"

"If you'll listen," she objected, "I'll tell you."

"Ok . . ." Henry slouched down behind the steering wheel and waited.

"Cocoa is a tropical plant," Claire noted by way of introduction. "Coca is a sub-tropical plant. It grows in misty climates at elevations between 1500-1600 feet. The first Europeans to encounter it were the Spanish conquistadors who penetrated the border of the Inca Empire in about 1525. This size of the empire had vastly expanded during the century before the arrival of the conquistadors and was then at its peak, extending southward from what is now southern Columbia to Chile and eastward from the Pacific Ocean to the edge of the Amazonian jungle.

"The Spaniards were searching for gold. When they discovered the Incas had lots of it, they launched what is called today the Conquest of Peru. It continued for four decades, but by 1580, the Incas had been subdued and their empire ceased to exist. The Spaniards devoted themselves then to enslaving the people and stealing their treasure.

"The Incas were mountain people who lived in an extremely difficult environment. They were able to overcome it in large part because they harnessed the power of the coca plant. Coca contains a narcotic that lessened fatigue while stimulating strength . . . It also elevates the spirit and promotes potency and sexual drive . . . By wrapping its leaves around pellets of limestone or plant ash and sucking it, the Incas ingested this narcotic, and this allowed them to labor at high altitudes and endure long periods with little food. These strengths helped them to subdue their neighbors, but they were not enough to withstand the technologies of the invading Spanish. Once the Spaniards completed their conquest, they launched a campaign to stamp out the use of coca so the conquered people would be easier to manage—in place of coca, they promoted Catholicism!" Claire looked at Henry to see if he was listening.

"Ok," he said, nodding for her to continue.

"That was about as far as official interest in the drug went," she observed. "But at some point along the way, a pair of Spanish missionaries documented the effects the plant had on its users. The journal with their notes surfaced a couple centuries later in the library of a German baron named de Riedesel. No one knows how he acquired it, but he had some kind of interest in the plant's narcotic and discussed it with a few professorial sorts in his circle. They considered it important enough to study it 'scientifically.'"

"What do you mean?" Henry asked.

"The Spanish missionaries recorded their observations and anecdotes they gathered from others. But the Germans cultivated the plant and conducted reproducible tests on its roots, branches, and leaves. They also experimented with substances they extracted from their plants to confirm the characteristics of the narcotics they contained and the effects they produced in humans.

"The Germans unlocked the secrets of the coca plant," Henry summarized.

"Yes. They determined its drug was an alkaloid—they named it 'cocaine.'"

"Alkaloid . . ." Henry repeated. "I've heard the word but have no idea what it is."

"An Alkaloid contains carbon, hydrogen, nitrogen and oxygen," Claire explained. "There are hundreds of them. They have pronounced physiological effects on animal organisms, and many of them also have pronounced psychological effects. Caffeine, mescaline, and morphine are all members of this group.

"Cocaine soon attracted the attention of the European medical community. Freud was instrumental in its acceptance as an anesthetic in the late-1800's. He also dabbled with it as a stimulant to overcome his own depression. He found it so beneficial that he prescribed it to his patients and recommended it to his friends. It also attracted the attention of the German military. The German high command saw that, in the event of war—which they were then planning—it might be used as a weapon. For the record, it was used in mustard gas during World War I."

"Ok . . ." Henry was impressed by Claire's knowledge. "But what about the betel nut?"

"I'm coming to that," Claire replied. "There are two other plants that have similar characteristics in terms of these narcotic effects. One is the cola plant of West Africa. The other is the areca palm of India. The Indians made a substance called 'pan' by shredding the fruit of the areca palm and mixing the pulp with powered lime and spices. They would then wrap the mixture in the betel leaf."

"The betel nut is the fruit of the areca palm . . ."

"Yes."

"The effect of 'pan' is similar to the effect of coca . . . huh! Do you suppose Jefferson knew about any of this?" Henry asked.

"It would have been unlikely," Claire replied. "Very little of this had been discovered in Thomas Jefferson's time."

"But if Somerville is right, the betel nut figured into his victory over the tyrannical Federalists," Henry observed. "Maybe he just liked the appearance of its blossom. That would be a more collegial explanation."

"The coca plant has a small yellow blossom—nothing remarkable. I've never read anything about the areca palm."

"Doesn't sound too plausible, does it . . ."

"We do know one thing," Claire observed.

"What's that?"

"Betel nuts made some kind of impression on him . . ."

"What are you going to get her do for you?" Gerta asked.

Hardin was stripping stems off the marijuana leaves he had picked in Ried's greenhouse. He answered without looking up. "I'm going to get her to find the journal."

"How are you going to do that?"

"I'm going to tell her that Paige stole it." He smiled at the thought. "She'll be all over him like a cheap suit!"

"What makes you so sure she'll believe you?"

"You saw her," he answered with a sarcastic laugh. "She'd sell her mother for a frontpage story. Besides," he added dryly, "Ogden's pissed."

"What makes you say that?"

"She was supposed to write about how the Sheriff of Nottingham is f–king the poor. Instead, she wrote about how Robin Hood is going to make them rich." Hardin snorted and shook his head. "Ogden can't stand suckers, but it's worse than that. He's set to promote our Aquarian revolution. Paige is supposed to be the model of the bad guy in this revolution, but she's made him out to be the hope of the future. If Ogden lets her off the hook, she'll cost him a fortune"

"You think Paige has the journal?" Gerta asked, changing the subject.

"I know Paige has the journal!"

"How can you be so sure?"

"I have a reliable source—let's just leave it at that." Hardin chuckled quietly.

"Why is the journal so important?" Gerta asked after a brief silence.

"What the f—k is this?" He said, looking up. "Some kind of quiz show? My f—king name's in it. Is that what you want to know?"

"How did it get there?"

"The asshole put it there."

"You mean Fred? Why would he have done that?"

"Because his brains 're fried. I bet he was using it as a book marker!" Hardin said to himself. "Can you believe that? All those months he spent up there studying his fascist ancestor's journal . . . as if it contained the secret of life! Here we are, all set to lead humanity forward into the promised land, and we have to wait for a guy with the brain of a medieval peasant to lower the drawbridge."

"He was close to Douglas, wasn't he?"

"Naa . . . well yea! Douglas gave him that trip to his leadership program in the Cascades. That made Douglas a big deal for Fred—like he was the Messiah," Hardin shook his head. "Douglas—the vainest, most pompous son of a bitch that ever lived. Can you image taking a guy like Ried seriously? That shows you where he was coming from."

"You shouldn't be so hard on him, Tim. He's done a lot to help us."

"That was before he realized he was Jesus Christ's father!" Hardin snorted. "Now he's only concerned with being worshiped. He can't face the fact that real revolutions need powder and shot not a moldy figurehead." Hardin muttered a curse. "He's an artifact! He belongs in a museum . . . I'm through pandering to him."

Gerta did not argue with him. She never did. "What happened to the journal? I thought Fred always kept it with him."

"That squirrelly bastard! Shows you how unstable he is. Paige's son said he sent it to Thomas Jefferson! Right? THE THOMAS JEFFERSON ACADEMY!"

"How did he know?"

"He said Ried told him . . . he's a child moron! No adult could be that stupid . . ." Hardin cursed but continued cleaning Ried's leaves.

"Why would he have done that?"

"How the hell should I know!" He paused and looked up. "I bet the angel Gabriel came to him! Yea! He heard Gabriel blowing his horn!" Hardin's face contorted into a demented grimace. "While he was stoned, he saw a vision . . ." Hardin suddenly stopped his work. "Of course! That's exactly what happened—Douglas said something that scared him . . . Douglas threatened him . . . Shit! That would scare anybody—opening the door and finding yourself face to face with a shriveled up, mop-headed maniac in a long black robe." Hardin cackled as he resumed his work.

"What did Douglas say in the letter?"

"Same old crap. He disavowed acts of violence and warned us not to compromise his sacred principles."

"He didn't contact you directly?"

"He knows better than to waste my time."

―――――――――――――

They could feel the vibrations at the bottom of the stairwell. Henry recognized Jimmi Hendrix's Fender guitar as they stepped into the upper corridor.

The chords rippled back and forth between his ears as he walked with Claire down the hall. A door at the far end was ajar. The music got louder as they approached it. When they reached it, Henry gave it a rap, and the door opened far enough to reveal a man seated at a table beside the bed. He froze when he heard the knock. His fingers spread over the cellophane bag in front of him, and he squinted toward the door to see who was there.

"Come on in," Tim Hardin called out when he saw Claire. She pushed forward into the room, leaving Henry standing alone in the hall. Hardin leaned over and turned down the volume on his stereo then stood up. He was wearing cut-off blue jeans and a pair of orange plastic beach sandals. He had no shirt on. Henry noticed the medallion around Hardin's neck as he stepped forward to welcome his guest. He followed the new age ritual of hugging and body rubbing. It ended with Hardin's hands cupped intimately on Claire's buttocks. When the ceremony was over, Hardin flopped back down into his chair and began rolling joints.

In Hardin's culture, sharing a joint was a condition for friendship. Getting high together completed a shared Aquarian journey to a better place. In the acrid haze of burning hemp, new people found insights into a reality that swirled beyond the bounds of reason.

Henry preferred bourbon—it helped him appreciate the irony of the human condition. Hardin sensed his hostility. "Get yourself a drink Amigo—there's bourbon and scotch on the counter by the sink." He nodded toward the alcove at the back of the long narrow room as he rolled a second joint.

Henry drifted back to the bar. There was a small bottle of Johnny Walker Black Label scotch and a half gallon of Jack Daniels Tennessee sour mash sippin' whiskey. He picked it up and reached for a glass. As he did, the bathroom door opened, and Gerta stepped into his shoulder.

"Uhhh!"

"Are you alright?" Henry asked, setting down the bottle and taking her arm.

"Yes," she said, pulling away.

"Can I get you something?

At first, she hesitated, but she changed her mind when she saw her husband huddled at the front of the room with Claire. "Jack Daniels and coke," she said.

Henry made it double strength to help her mellow out. After handing it to her, he poured two fingers for himself. "Did you enjoy the evening at Monticello?" he asked, looking up. By then, she had gone to the front of the room to be with her own kind of people. Henry suddenly remembered the night he met the Traveler.

A traveler was the highest rank in Aquarian heraldry. Like Samurai and Knights-errant of ages past, travelers were cult heroes for the new people. Promulgators of the faith. Storytellers. Shamans with special insights into the mysteries of life and the world beyond. The Traveler was a beacon for Charlottesville's Aquarians. Henry met him at a gathering of Aquarian whisperers at Duncan White's.

Duncan had set the stage. The Traveler worked on a trawler in the

Straits of Alaska during the summer. When the fishing season there was over, he traveled to places where he would commune with kindred spirits. Charlottesville was a waystation in his transcendental odyssey. Duncan told Henry about the Traveler's wager . . . how he and a shipmate accepted a challenge from two heavies they encountered in a waterfront bar. Out they went into the street, the Traveler and his companion and the two brawlers. Henry imagined hairy brutes in dirty flannel shirts with arms like tree limbs. But according to Duncan, the Traveler and his partner beat them to a pulp. Henry had never heard of a new age wayfarer starting a fight. Still, Duncan's strange tale could have been true. Aquarian travelers did unlikely things . . . and there was a message in the story. It wasn't a new age revelation. It was the age-old fact that the world is a dangerous place.

When Henry entered Duncan's cottage that night, the air in Duncan's cottage was already thick with marijuana smoke. The Grateful Dead were playing traveling music, and small clusters of quiet people were talking quietly as they waited for the Traveler. Suddenly, for no apparent reason a wave of excitement rippled into the room, and the room filled with awareness. Yes! The Traveler had come! There were expressions of new age emotion. Wow! Awesome! Heavy! The quiet people thronged around the Traveler, greeting him in the new age away. It was good to be with him. Good to hear him speak. Good to share his energy. Wow! Once they had shared his peace, the gatherers drifted back into quietness.

Henry got his first glimpse of the Traveler after that. He was in the kitchen—a short, stocky man with a red beard—smoking a joint with an aging American Madonna in a batik smock. Aside from his broad shoulders, his physique was not remarkable. But he had a strange power. Henry could feel it.

Henry introduced himself. "I'm Henry Tilghman," he said. The Traveler nodded. "Tell me something, would you," he continued deferentially. "Did that fight really happen?" The Traveler gazed at him from across a great metaphysical void. It seemed like a long time before he spoke. "Hey man . . ." The Traveler said at last, ". . . you gotta travel more . . ."

That was it. A riddle. The Traveler and the woman in the batik smock melted away, leaving Henry to unravel it on his own. Woodstock Nation in a breath. Without beginning. Without end. Without rhyme. Without reason. The cornerstone of new age knowledge. He could find the answer smoking dope. Dropping acid. Screaming down Highway 66 with Bob Dylan. Zapping past blurred yellow lines. Hair whipping in the wind. Out of his f—king gourd.

Henry went over to Trip's after that. They drank some red wine and played chess. Henry knew he would never understand the Traveler. He felt the same way about Tim Hardin.

He glanced back toward the front of the room. Claire was sitting next to Hardin in a cloud of marijuana smoke. She seemed pleased by the attention he was showering on her. A pang of jealously stabbed Henry's breast.

Hardin looked around just then—as if he felt Henry's revelation. "Hey Amigo, come up here and join the party."

Henry walked back and sat down on the low bureau across from the foot of the bed.

"Claire tells me you've been giving her the low down on the Jefferson Academy." He made it sound like a waste of time.

"Yep. I've been delegated that responsibility." Again, Henry noticed Hardin's medallion. It was like Roberta's! And the figure in the frieze in Jefferson's parlor. He took a swallow of Jack Daniels.

Three fat joints lay on the table. Hardin picked up the one in the center and calibrated its diameter between his thumb and forefinger. Satisfied, he laid it in the trough of his coiled tongue and rolled it gently back and forth until it was soaked with saliva. Placing it in his puckered lips, he struck a match and held it under the twisted tip. The burning ember crackled and danced like a Chinese firecracker as he pulled its smoke deep into his lungs. When they were full, he closed his eyes and passed the joint to Claire. Hardin waited for Claire to finish her hit before releasing his smoke. It hissed out of his mouth like a slow leak. His eyes settled then on Henry. "Hey Amigo, did you share your secret with your guest?"

Henry stiffened.

"I didn't think so," Hardin smirked as he took the joint back from Claire. "How 'bout it, Amigo?" Hardin raised his eyebrows and pointed the joint at Henry.

"What are you talking about," Henry snapped, rising to his feet.

Hardin took another leisurely toke. "De Riedesel's Journal." He exhaled the words through his smoke. "Ever heard of it?"

"De Riedesel's Journal?" Henry's face filled with a strange look of relief. Then it darkened. "What the hell are you talking about, Hardin."

"You know damned well what I'm talking about, Tilghman." Hardin's eyes flashed. "I want it back!"

Henry took another sip from his glass. "Why don't you tell us what you are talking about it—Amigo."

Hardin studied his guest for a moment. "Sure . . . why not," he smiled. "I'll tell you all about it . . ."

"Baron de Riedesel?" Claire asked while Hardin inhaled the last quarter of his joint.

"Jefferson's alter ego . . ." he answered, without exhaling.

"They were friends?"

"Soul mates!" Hardin whispered. "Jefferson shared all his secrets with him."

"How do you know that?" Henry demanded.

"I've read their correspondence . . . Jefferson told him everything . . . what he thought about his political rivals . . . why he hated capitalism . . . why he needed to be President. He even sent his buddy a copy of his *communitarian* Constitution."

"Burr's Unicorn!" Henry exclaimed.

"You know about that . . ."

"I know it's a bunch of bullshit!"

"What are you talking about, Tim?" Claire asked, setting her hand on his knee.

"You tell her, Big Shot. You seem to know it all."

Henry gave the other man a cold look but did as he said. "Burr claimed that Jefferson opposed the Constitution the convention approved in his absence. According to Burr, Jefferson drew up a replacement while he was still in France. When he reached home in 1789, he had this plan but no prospects for ratifying it. In 1791, he and Madison made a trip to New York—Madison had just broken with Hamilton over the issue of the bank. Publicly, the purpose of the trip was to inspect the flora and fauna of the Hudson River. Privately, it was to build political alliances with northern republicans. Burr was the leader of this faction, so they were anxious to connect with him. Burr subsequently claimed that during their meetings, Jefferson tried to recruit him to create a new state in the west based on Jefferson's orphan constitution. Burr declined on the grounds that his sights were already set on winning a seat in the Senate.

"In 1795, Jefferson invited Burr to visit him at Monticello. By then, of course, Burr was in the Senate, and Jefferson was on track to become Vice President. Jefferson told Burr that he was going to run for president in the election of 1800 and that when he became President, he would correct the errors the framers had incorporated into the original constitution. Jefferson then offered Burr a deal. In return for delivering New York in the election of 1800, Jefferson would support Burr as his successor. Burr accepted, and Jefferson spent the next day instructing Burr on the flaws of the existing government. As a parting gift, and to cement the deal, Jefferson gave Burr a copy of his constitution. There is no indication, however, that it was any different from the constitution he wrote for the state of Virginia."

"Not bad," Hardin nodded.

"The story about Burr's Unicorn didn't surface until after Jefferson had ruined Burr," Henry continued. Jefferson's enemies claimed that the document Jefferson had given Burr in 1795 proved that it was Jefferson rather than Burr who planned to create the new state in the west. Of course, Jefferson's supporters denied it. Unfortunately for history, before the truth could be ascertained, Burr put a bullet into Hamilton at Weehawken, New Jersey. When Hamilton died, Burr fled from New York, and in his flight, he lost the constitution Jefferson had given him!"

"Abbie Hoffman snitched it from his New York apartment," Hardin suggested through a plume of marijuana smoke.

"Jefferson called it Burr's Unicorn," Henry added in closing.

"He was making a joke." Hardin cackled. "Get it? He was rubbing Burr's face in it. The President of the United States! The guy in the White House... WAS RIDING BURR'S F—KIN' UNICORN." Hardin dissolved into a fit of wild laughter. "I've seen it," he announced, suddenly composing himself. "He was so proud of it he sent a copy to his German buddy."

"Yea," Henry said, "and I bet you've seen the fairies who dance around the moon."

"You ought to listen when somebody tells you something important, Amigo." He looked at Claire. "You see how they act when they know their ship's going down."

"Whose ship is going down?" Claire asked innocently.

155

"Paige and his fascist buddies . . ." Hardin smiled unctuously at Henry. "I'm turning you guys into history before you make it to current affairs." He laughed again.

"What is it, Tim?"

"Paige stole the journal from a friend of mine . . ."

"You're a damned liar," Henry snapped, taking a threatening step forward.

Hardin winked at Claire. "There's your story, Sweetheart."

"I'm leaving," Henry announced, stepping to the door. "Are you coming, Claire?"

"Now there's a first-rate idea! Go ahead and shove off, Amigo. The lady and I have some things to discuss—in private."

"If I were you, Hardin," Henry said, squaring himself, "I'd keep my mouth shut."

His eyes fixed suddenly on the medallion hanging from Hardin's neck. He was staring into the same face that terrorized him in the loft. He heard Marjean's weird chanting. Once more he saw Roberta's tattooed body sinking into the green water.

"Tell your boss that we're not going to let him get away with it," Hardin answered defiantly. "I'll help you," he said, looking at Claire. "It's going to be the biggest story of the century—how the power-hungry capitalist robbed his country of its political heritage! You'll be more famous than Woodward and Bernstein."

Henry studied Claire's expression.

"There's no journal and no constitution," Henry said again. "He's making the whole thing up." He scrutinized the white man with the Indian braids. "The question is, why?"

Claire seemed less certain.

"It's disgusting how ambition corrupts people," Hardin said, shaking his head. Then, looking languidly at Henry he added, "Isn't it . . . a-s-s-h-o-l-e!"

Henry lunged before the word was out of Hardin's mouth. The full weight of his body caught Hardin in the chest and sent him crashing into the lamp on the table behind him. An explosion was followed by a shower of glass. Henry rode Hardin's crumpling body to the floor. A violent rage consumed him as his fists pounded Hardin's face. Darkness made the chaos more terrifying.

"DON'T!" Claire shrieked. "OH GOD! HENRY! STOP IT!" The terror in Claire's voice held him for the split-second Henry needed to re-gain control of himself. He released the body and stood up. As he did, Hardin's wife turned on a light in the back of the room. Henry's eyes fixed on the pathetic figure at his feet. When the ringing in his ears subsided, he reached down and took hold of Hardin's arm. With a harsh jerk, he pulled the battered figure up.

Hardin wavered for a second before gaining his balance. Then he turned toward Henry. On his swollen face was the sickening smile of a man who took pleasure in provoking hatred.

"I told you," Hardin hissed as he lifted the last joint from the floor beside the bed. "You see what these people really are ..." He licked it carefully and lit it. "Get me a coke will you baby ..." He blew a spout of gray smoke into the air as he gingerly wiped his face with a handkerchief he'd pulled from his back pocket. Gerta marched glumly passed Henry and disappeared out into the hall.

When she was gone, Hardin seated himself on the bed beside Claire. She was still trembling. "Easy baby." He slipped his hand around her waist. "Why don't you stay here with me tonight?" His eyes locked her in a searching gaze. Without releasing her, he took the joint and placed it between her lips. Claire inhaled the listless fume. "We have a lot of work to do ..."

Henry watched Hardin's hand rise slowly from her waist. As it reached the curve of her breast, the door opened, and Gerta appeared with her husband's soda. Claire pulled away; her eyes fixed on the sullen figure in the door. Henry watched as an expression of horror and shame appeared on Claire's face.

"We can talk tomorrow," she stammered, struggling to her feet. Henry guided her past Gerta into the hall. The night air was cool and refreshing. He filled his lungs and breathed out the poison. Claire walked a few steps in front of him. Henry watched her shuffle anxiously down the empty corridor. Neither of them spoke until they were back on the highway.

"I don't understand," Claire said in a trembling voice.

"What don't you understand," Henry asked reluctantly.

"Anything..."

Don't do it, a little voice warned him. *If you become her confessor, you'll have to absolve her of all her sins.* "Hardin hit on something back there," Henry said, changing the subject. "The Burr conspiracy is the most incredible political potboiler in American history—bigger than Watergate!" He welcomed Claire's silence.

"Jefferson hated Burr more than Nixon hates Kennedy. He pursued him, literally, to the end of the earth. It wasn't enough for Jefferson to destroy his political career. He wanted to ruin his reputation for posterity. What I find most amazing is that he did it without guilt or regret. I think it reflects a serious character flaw.

"Bear in mind that it was Jefferson who violated the pact! Burr delivered New York for Jefferson in the election of 1800 just as he promised so he had every right to expect Jefferson to uphold his side of the bargain. But Jefferson wanted to be President. When the balloting was finished, Jefferson and Burr had the same number of electoral votes. It took the House thirty-six ballots to break the tie. Jefferson grew more anxious with each ballot. By the time the matter was resolved—in his favor, his deal with Burr was dead...

"Burr was acquitted of all the charges Jefferson later brought against him, but Jefferson accomplished what he set out to do. All we know about Burr today is that he was a scoundrel. By some accounts, Burr was raising an army to invade Mexico. Others accuse him of plotting to overthrow the government of the United States. The grand juries that heard the charges dismissed them all. But that didn't dissuade Jefferson. He brought Burr to Richmond in irons and put him on trial. He would have hanged him if John Marshall had not interceded. Marshall was the presiding judge at Burr's trial. How's that for irony—Jefferson's own cousin saved Burr from the gallows. Marshall was a staunch Federalist and a fierce political opponent of Jefferson.

"The not guilty verdict handed down in Marshall's court was entirely consistent with the findings of earlier grand juries.

"In view of the record, it's not surprising Burr would want to avenge himself. We'll probably never know what really happened," Henry added.

"Not only were Jefferson and Burr two of the cleverest men in American history they were also among the most secretive."

"I don't understand why historians today aren't interested in unraveling the mystery. After all, their rivalry turned on issues that are central to the political conflicts we have today. Burr was a capitalist like Hamilton, and he perceived commerce and economic growth as the best means to promote the general well-being. But he separated from Hamilton in his conception of republicanism—Burr thought every man should have the opportunity to advance. That also distinguished him from Jefferson whose republicanism was a rebellion against Hamiltonian monocrats.

"Burr supported abolition of slavery, universal suffrage, and the education of women as proper means to achieve the common good. Jefferson had no clear understanding or interest in the common good. He was inspired instead by a utopian vision that came to him on his mountaintop. Citizens in Jefferson's republic were faceless entities that would work with their hands, eat what they produced themselves, and be healthy. Funny isn't it—the devout anti-Platonist promoted the society that Plato invented in the *Republic*. Yet all today's historians are interested in is whether he screwed one of his slaves!"

Henry glanced over at Claire. Her head was tilted against the window. He knew she was asleep.

Henry coasted down the hill into the parking area in front of his house. "Claire," he whispered. He reached over and touched her gently on the shoulder. She opened her eyes. "Think you can make it inside?"

"Where are we?" she asked, pulling herself up.

"My place."

She opened her door slowly. Henry met her as she climbed out. "Come on," he said, putting his arm around her waist. He guided her across the yard and into the house. She sat down heavily on the couch. Henry turned on the lamp. He could see her now. See was deathly pale.

"Could I have something cold to drink?"

"A glass of ice water?"

She nodded.

Henry disappeared through the studio door. A moment later he was back with a glass of water. "Would you like to sit on the porch? Fresh air might make you feel better.

"What time is it?" she asked.

"10:30."

"Is that all?"

"You're not used to Hardin's dope. It was probably laced with acid."

She stood up and walked uncertainly out to the porch. Henry went to his stereo and put on a record. The overture to *Swan Lake* began to play. A second later Henry appeared with her drink in his hand. Claire was sitting in the rocker, looking toward Monticello.

"How're you doing?" he said, pulling a chair up beside her.

"Not good." Her voice quivered.

"Can I get you something?" He asked anxiously.

Claire slowly buried her hands in her face and began to sob.

"It's Ok, Claire." He hesitated then put his arm around her. "It's Ok . . ."

"Ohhhh . . ."

"Take a deep breath," Henry said, tightening his hold on her. "Everything is going to be all right."

Her body shook, and she released another wrenching moan. Henry watched helplessly as she fought to stay sane. What a small space sanity occupies in the continuum, he thought as he waited for her to find it.

She groaned again and clutched his hand. "I'm here Claire," he assured her.

"It's tearing at me," she panted, gripping his hand fiercely.

"What is it, Claire? Can you tell me?"

"Like a bomb exploding inside me," she wailed. Then she began to pant nervously and rock back and forth in her chair. "I'm filling up with blackness," she gasped, fighting to catch her breath. "Oh God! I'm splitting apart! Ohhh! . . . It's coming toward me . . . Burning eyes! . . . It's mouth . . . ohhh . . . its foaming . . . it's going to break loose! . . . Noooo!" Her head suddenly shot back as though she had been struck by a projectile.

"Listen to me, Claire . . . you're imagining these things. It's just a hallucination . . ."

Claire looked up at him. Her face was white. "Don't leave me, Martin." Her eyes were red, and tears were streaming down her cheeks.

"I'm not going to leave you, Claire. Come on, let's go inside. It's light there. Can you come with me?" She nodded. Henry guided her into the living room and settled her back on the couch. Her face was drawn and haggard. Henry was appalled to see how her ordeal had changed her appearance.

"It's too bright," she told him. "It's hurting my eyes."

Henry reached over and turned off the lamp beside the couch. The music had ended. It was quiet now except for the crickets. Henry listened to them. He found their trill comforting but wondered how it would affect her.

She took a deep breath. "I'll be all right here," she said hopefully.

They sat together quietly. Every now and then she took another deep breath.

"Would you like a blanket?" he asked.

"No." she whispered, "Just stay with me. I don't want to be..." her voice was suddenly frightened. "I'm going to fall! Don't let me fall!"

"You're not going to fall. We're in the middle of a huge field covered with thick green grass that you can roll in and sleep in. Can you smell it?"

"No...don't talk to me about that! Don't say anything—I don't want to..." her voice died. Henry could see that she was growing uneasy. She took another fierce breath.

"Do you have any coke?"

"Ginger ale?"

"Yes."

"Will you be Ok if I leave you here for a moment?"

"Yes...I'll be all right."

Henry returned a moment later with a glass of ginger ale. She took a sip. "Are you feeling better?"

"A little."

Henry sat down beside her and waited. Time passed. Her breathing gradually became easier. The struggle seemed to have ended.

"Henry..." she said at last.

"Yes..."

"Thanks..."

"You don't need to thank me...anybody would have done it."

"Thanks anyway," she repeated. As she did, she reached over and took his hand. Henry held it and looked into her eyes.

" I'd like some fresh air now."

"Go on out on the porch. I'm going to get some coffee."

———————

Henry came through the screen door backwards. He turned and walked forward with a mug in each hand. "I forgot to ask if you take anything in your coffee."

"No."

"Good." He set a cup on the railing in front of her and sat down.

"Drink that. You'll feel better." Henry sat down next to her and gazed out into the peaceful night. "You have to hear *Swan Lake*," he said suddenly. "It does magical things to summer nights."

"I guess it would be Ok." She took a sip from her cup and looked out into the darkness.

Henry jumped up and went inside. A second later the orchestra began to play. As it did, Claire noticed the night change. The landscape before her stirred from its repose and followed the movement of the music. Gently at first, like the dawning of a day. She could feel the excitement growing, filling the valley. Then it leaped into the sky. Claire did not witness the spectacle. She was part of it. A chord dancing with the sprites across the face of the moon. Dispersing through the universe. Out of space and time. A thrill streaked through the core of her soul, radiating with brilliance beyond the calculus of thought. It was wholeness. Unity. TRUTH! The music consumed her with pleasure as it whirled her around the cosmos. The notes were like colors from an artist's pallet, drenching her with waves of inspirational light. "It's beautiful," Claire murmured.

"I think so too," she heard Henry say somewhere in the distance.

"Yes," she called back from the other side of the universe.

"You had me worried there," Henry said, taking her hand gently. "What happened?"

Claire sighed and took another sip of coffee. "I was listening to Tim's voice. How strong it was. How smooth. Then I began to feel something growing inside me. As he spoke, it grew larger. I realized I was choking. I tried to drive the voice out . . . then everything was dark." She shivered. "The darkness . . . the violence . . ."

"Why don't we talk about something else . . ."

162

"It was like I was riding on a wild creature—racing through a maze. If I let go, I would pitch off into an abyss and be lost forever. As it raced forward, I could feel my strength fading. Just as I was about to let go it stopped." She sounded more surprised than relieved. "That's when I saw its face. I thought it would be terrifying, but it wasn't. I knew it in a way I can't explain." She reached over and took Henry's hand in hers.

"I didn't know it could be like that. I could have . . ."

"You had a bad trip, that's all. You've faced it. Now let it go. It's over."

They drank the rest of their coffee without talking. When they were done, Henry stood up. "You must be tired."

"I don't think I can sleep."

"I know what you mean . . ." He noticed the bourbon on the rail by the roof post. He picked it up and took a sip.

Neither spoke for a while. Then Claire began to speak. "I've always known pretty much what I wanted."

"Did you always want to be a journalist?"

"I love literature. Journalism is a way to apply a literary skill in an occupation with social relevance."

"I guess that's the difference between going to school in the north and the south," Henry observed. "We never thought in terms of social relevance."

"My family has always been involved . . . my father is a Horace Greeley Yankee—you know, someone who thinks he has a responsibility to make the world a better place."

"Huh . . . How long have you been at *The Post*?"

"Two years in June."

"So you're a veteran . . ."

"Does that make me a veteran?"

"Was that your first front page story?"

"Yes."

"You must be proud."

"It's a great honor. Not many make it."

"How do you get a story on the front page?"

Claire stared off into the night. "I'm not sure there's any one way," she answered vaguely. "You write and write. Eventually you find your voice . . . and maybe you find that you have something to say."

"You enjoy your work then."

Claire nodded. "It's very . . ." she broke off suddenly.

Henry waited for her to finish, but the words never came.

"You called me Martin," he told her. "Did you realize that?"

"No."

"Martin Ogden?"

"That's none of your business," she snapped.

"It might be good for you to talk about it . . ."

"I don't want to talk about it!"

The telephone rang beside Henry's bed. He opened an eye and squinted at his clock. It was 2:30. He picked up the receiver as it rang the third time. "Yea."

"Hank . . ."

Henry recognized Mr. Paige's voice. "Yes Mr. Paige." He was awake now.

"Ted Hoagland called a few minutes ago. He said that Oscar lost control of his car on his way down the mountain."

"An accident?"

"Yes."

"Is he . . ." Henry paused to consider his question, ". . . alive?"

"Yes. But I'd like you to go over to the hospital and find out how he's doing. Call me when you have something concrete."

"Where will you be?"

"At the residence."

"Ok."

"Hoagland said something else," Paige continued before Henry could hang up. "It sounds like somebody tinkered with his brakes."

"It wasn't an accident!"

"No," Paige answered matter-of-factly. "Hoagland was going over to keep an eye on things. Go over and give him a hand."

"I'm on my way."

Henry dressed quickly and went downstairs. Clair was asleep on the couch. He listened for a moment to her breathing then proceeded through the room and entered his study. He went to his desk and lifted the pad. He slid his free hand beneath it in search of the envelope. When he found it, he drew it out and tucked it under his arm. A moment later he was on the porch. Before setting out across the yard, he turned back and tested the door to be sure it was locked.

The black shape of his car was visible in the darkness. Henry passed through the gate and went over to it. The key was in the ignition. He turned it and pumped the accelerator. The engine coughed once then started. Henry guided the vehicle forward in a slow loping arc that intersected the driveway halfway up the hill. He waited until he was on the main road before turning on the headlamps. They cast an eerie light on the empty road. He passed the farm entrance and continued on to 250. There were no cars coming so he pressed the accelerator to the floor and merged onto the highway at full speed. The car raced by the quarry at Shadwell and up Pantops Mountain to the 64 Overpass. Henry's eyes remained fixed on the center line. It flashed at him like a strobe. Rapidly. Rhythmically. As he settled into a trance, he noticed the image that was forming in his mind's eye. There were rows of cars parked in a dark field. Someone was running through them, a shadowy form in yellow robes. His hair was tied in Indian braids. Henry noticed the object in his hand. He strained to see what it was. Suddenly the figure wheeled around. As he did, he raised a pair of wire cutters and shook them at Henry. A hateful smile spread across Tim Hardin's face. "How 'bout it, Asshole!" he shrieked with a burst wild laughter. Then the image vanished. Henry contemplated the grinding, burning hatred that replaced it.

Tim Hardin was capable of murder. Henry had no doubt about that. He thought of Oscar. Mr. Paige had asked him to check on him, but there was more to it than that.

Henry descended Pantops Mountain and crossed the bridge over the Rivanna River. At the first stoplight, he turned onto High Street and drove up the hill to the center of town. Tarleton's Oak was at the top of the hill. Henry turned there onto Court Street. Court street ran past the Court House and the memorials to Robert E. Lee and the Confederate veterans. It continued on to the bottom of Vinegar Hill. Henry turned there and drove up the hill to the Lewis and Clarke Memorial. He turned right there onto Main Street. Like the other streets, it was deserted. Henry passed the Albemarle Hotel and on to the railroad station. The dome of the Rotunda would have been in view then, but the University had turned its lights off after the bombing. Before he reached the Corner, he turned left onto Jefferson Park Avenue. The University Hospital was ahead of him on the right. Henry found a parking place a block away. Before climbing out, he gathered his papers.

The University Hospital was sprawling architectural horror. What started as a simple stately structure on the edge of Mr. Jefferson's academic village had long since disappeared within the fluid perimeter of the University's Medical Center. It had taken generations to transform it into the shapeless, proletarian maze that stood before him now. Henry had been in it a couple of times during his first year–before he understood how unhealthy it was. Since then, he had avoided the place.

Henry entered the building through an access door beside the emergency entrance. The waiting room was filled with the usual assortment of drunken fraternity men and wounded red necks. Ahead of him sat a stern-faced nurse who eyed him suspiciously as he approached her desk. He cleared his throat before speaking. "Is Dr. Dudley on duty?"

The nurse looked at a list of names on the clipboard at her elbow. "Yes," she replied.

"Could I speak with him?"

Before she could respond, a door flew open, and a wheeled stretcher flew out guided front and back by orderlies in green hospital scrubs. It was followed by a throng of medical specialists dressed in green caps and pajamas. When the procession was abreast of the receptionist's desk, she called Dudley's name.

A tall figure stepped out of the line and approached the desk.

"Dr. Dudley, this gentleman . . ."

"It's Ok," he said, interrupting her. "He's my chess partner . . . Kind of late for you to be out, isn't it Henry?" he observed, lowering his mask. Before Henry could answer, he started off down the hall. "Follow me," he called over his shoulder.

Henry raced to catch up. "I'm trying to find Oscar Denker. He was in an automobile accident coming down Monticello Mountain a couple hours ago."

The surgeon pressed ahead without speaking. Henry followed him through a pair of swinging doors, around a corner, and into a room with an assortment of lounge chairs. Dudley proceeded to the far side of the room and lowered himself into one of the chairs. In the same motion, he settled his feet on the hassock in front of it, laid his head back, and closed his eyes.

Henry waited.

After a few minutes, the surgeon turned his head slightly and squinted at him. "My feet are killing me."

"Your feet! To hell with your feet! What about Denker? Did you treat him or not?"

Dudley exhaled slowly. "Denker's Ok."

"Do you know where he is?"

"He's in recovery up on the fifth floor."

"What's wrong with him?"

"Broken ribs. Fractured jaw. Severe scalp lacerations. Looked like he went through his windshield. He was probably thrown from his car judging from the debris we dredged out of him before sewing him up. Brain damage is always possible with head injuries like that, but he did all right," the surgeon added, closing his eyes again.

"What do you mean?" Henry asked.

"You can't sedate head injuries."

"You mean you stitched him up cold turkey?" Henry was horrified.

"Had to."

"How many?"

"I don't know—over a hundred."

"Jesus Christ . . ." Henry's voice trailed off.

"He won't remember a thing," Dudley responded. "He's a lot better off than I am in that respect." He pushed his slippers off and began massaging his feet. "Have you ever tried standing up for thirty-six hours . . ."

"Are you done?"

"Yep." He stretched out again and closed his eyes. "Sounded like somebody ran him off the road," Dudley said when he was settled.

"What makes you say that?"

"He kept repeating the words 'back off.'"

"Do you know if there is a guard on his room?"

"No."

"I'd like to go up there?"

There was a pad of paper on the table beside the chair. The doctor fumbled with his fingers until he found it. "Gotta pen?" Henry pulled one out of his pocket and handed it to him. Dudley scribbled something on the pad and tore it off. "Give this to the nurse at the desk. She'll take care of you."

Henry rose with the note in his hand. "Get some sleep—you've earned it."

"I'm riding with the Keswick Hunt this afternoon—out your way."

"Don't tell me," Henry objected.

Dudley was asleep before Henry finished speaking.

"Thanks Doc," Henry said as he leaned over to turn off the light.

———————

Henry handed the note to the nurse at the front desk.

"Just a minute", she said at last looking at Henry with a faint smile. She picked up her phone. "Albert—would you come to the front desk, please." A moment later a heavy-set black man dressed in hospital clothes stepped through the door next to the operating room.

"Yas ma'am."

"Albert, would you take Mr. Tilghman up to the recovery area on the fifth floor. He has a note from Dr. Dudley. Susan Davis is up there. Give this to her." She handed him the note."

"Cert'nly," Albert said. "B' glad to." He looked at Henry. "Cum on wif' me and ah'll fix ya' raht up." He turned and stepped over to the elevator.

"Thank you, Albert." The desk nurse called after him.

Henry followed the orderly to the elevator. "Nurse Davis's a fahn nurse," Albert added as the elevator door opened. "Ah'm onna tak' yo' raht to her." He stepped into the car and turned to the control panel beside the door. Henry stepped in and took his position behind Albert. The door shut and the car began to rise. Henry watched the numbers light up...2...3...4. "Dat Nurse Davis runs thin's raht... mmm hmm. She sho' duz," Albert repeated as the door opened. The nurse seated at the nurse's station watched him guide Henry to her. Albert handed her the note. "Dis genneman's godda a note fom Dr. Dudley," he announced.

"Thank you, Albert." Nurse Davis took the note.

Albert turned to Henry. "Jez' do wha' da lady sez."

"Thank you, Albert," Henry replied.

"Yassir." Albert returned to the elevator. "Ga' naht." He raised his hand.

"Good night," Henry answered as the door closed.

"What does this say?" Nurse Davis asked, looking up at Henry.

Henry shook his head. "I don't know—I haven't read it."

She set the note aside. "Tell me then, why did he send you up here?"

"I'm here to keep an eye on Dr. Denker—he's one of Dr. Dudley patients."

She gave him a funny look. "How many watchmen does he need?

Henry stiffened.

"A Mr. Hoagland arrived about fifteen minutes ago." She gestured toward a dark form halfway down the hall to Henry's right.

"Do you mind if I speak with him?"

"Is that what Dr. Dudley's note says?"

"Yes . . . I think it does!" Henry nodded.

"You understand that our patients are sleeping," she cautioned.

"Yes. Thank you, Nurse Davis."

"Shhhh . . ." She held her finger to her lips.

Henry's eyes remained fixed on the shadowy figure standing in the center of the hall. He could feel Hoagland's stare as he approached the District Attorney and stopped. They continued to eye each other without speaking.

"Paige sent you," Hoagland said, breaking the silence.

"He's concerned . . ."

"Yea . . ."

"Mr. Paige told me . . ."

"About the breaks." Hoagland cut him off.

"Is he safe here?" Henry asked.

"I suppose so," Hoagland said, glancing around. "But there's no point in taking a chance."

"Have you spoken with him?"

"No. The nurse said he was not to be disturbed. We're going to have to wait until morning."

"I spoke with the emergency room surgeon," Henry volunteered.

"What?" Hoagland sounded annoyed.

"He's a friend of mine," Henry explained.

"What'd he say?"

"While he was surgery, he kept repeating the words 'back off.'"

"So somebody was pushing him . . ."

"Sounds like it."

"You were at the dinner, weren't you?" Hoagland asked.

"Yes—I was at Dr. Denker's table."

"Did anything happen?"

Henry studied the DA without answering

"Listen Tilghman," Hoagland growled, "I pulled your chestnut out of one fire the other day. I can put it back in. You understand."

"There was an incident," Henry continued, without acknowledging the DA's threat.

"That's more like it," Hoagland said.

"Tim Hardin threatened Mr. Paige."

"Hardin?"

"He's the . . ."

"I know who Tim Hardin is," the District Attorney snapped. "Why would he threaten Paige?"

"I didn't hear that part of their conversation," Henry lied.

Hoagland gave him a hard look, then moved on. "So Hardin has some kind of ax to grind with Paige." His voice trailed off in thought. "Maybe he decided to take it out on Denker."

"He's capable of it," Henry agreed.

Hoagland gave him a dark look. "How did you come to hear this threat?"

"Mr. Paige prepared a plaque for the curator of Monticello—you know, in consideration for his help. I took it up to him. He was in the staff library on the second floor of the mansion. When I reached the top of the stairs, I heard voices. I didn't want to interrupt a private meeting, so I waited in the hall. I couldn't help hearing part of the conversation."

"What did you hear?"

"Hardin told Mr. Paige that he knew he had the manuscript and that if Mr. Paige was smart, he'd hand it over."

"Mr. Paige has a manuscript that belongs to Hardin?" The prosecutor sounded genuinely puzzled.

"Of course not . . ."

"Mr. Paige told him that?"

"Yes."

"What happened then?"

"Hardin dismissed Mr. Paige's answer. That was when he threatened him."

"What did he say?"

"He sounded very angry. He said something to the effect that his friends would take whatever steps were necessary to get it. "

"What did Paige say?"

"I didn't hear . . ."

"Then what happened?"

"The door flew open, and Hardin came charging out. I was standing a couple steps back from the door, but he was coming so fast that he almost knocked me down. I suppose I surprised him. He cursed and raised his hand as if he meant to strike me. I held up the plague, partly in self-defense and partly to show him why I was there. He stared at it for a second then disappeared into the stairwell."

"At which point you went into the office and saw Paige."

"Yes."

"Did he say anything to you about the exchange."

"No."

"Hmmm . . ." Hoagland tried to picture of the event. "What would make Hardin get into an argument with Mr. Paige about a manuscript he didn't have?" He wondered, thinking out loud. His gaze settled back on Henry. "You think Hardin was agitated enough to cut Denker's break lines?"

"What do you know about Hardin," Henry asked, deflecting Hoagland's question.

"He's a nut," Hoagland answered candidly, ". . . with connections to left wing establishment sorts. He uses them to legitimize his ties with various radical underground groups."

". . . the kind of people who espouse violence as a means for social 're-form'?" Henry interjected.

Hoagland's eyebrows raised. "Yea—those kinds."

"Are they the kind of people who might blow up the Rotunda?"

Hoagland laughed and shook his head. "If I don't keep my eye on you, Tilghman, you're gonna take my job."

Henry nodded. "Tell me, will you Ted, who is Gerta Hardin?"

"Gerta Biederman?"

"Is that her name?"

"Yea. She's the bank . . . has connections down here too—or did you know that?"

"No!"

Hoagland smiled again. "Paige's daughter."

"You're kidding!" The news stunned Henry. "She knows Aster?"

"They were roommates in New York."

"That must have been when she was busted . . ." Henry had heard the story. She had been caught carrying dope through customs at Kennedy Airport. She should have had the book thrown at her but ended up on Belmont Farm instead. Everybody assumed her father had pulled strings. Henry had made it his business not to know anything more than that. Suddenly it dawned on him. "That's your connection to Mr. Paige!" The words slipped out before he could stop them.

Hoagland stiffened and a dark expression appeared on his face. "I'm going to tell you this just once, Tilghman, and you had better heed me. If you don't keep your nose out of things that don't concern you, you're going to find yourself in a very unfortunate situa . . ."

A noise caused Hoagland to stop in mid-sentence. Both men turned in time to see a medicine cart wheel around the corner. A woman in a nurse's uniform pushed it to Denker's door and stopped. She went about her business without acknowledging them. She pulled a clipboard from a shelf beneath the medicine tray and studied it for a moment. Then she lifted a plastic container filled with clear liquid from the tray and pushed through the door into Denker's room. Henry watched Hoagland watch the nurse disappear. Before the door closed the District Attorney slipped through it. Henry followed him.

The nurse was at the head of the bed replacing an empty container with the one she had brought in with her. When this was done, she took his pulse and felt his forehead. Then she turned to her two observers. "I must insist that you wait outside," she said firmly.

"Would you mind showing me your identification," Hoagland replied.

The nurse stepped over to the intercom on the wall beside the door. "Nurse Davis, would you send an orderly to room 513. There are two unauthorized visitors in the room." She turned back to the two men. "If you do not leave immediately, you will be forcibly removed."

"I don't think so," Hoagland replied as he pulled out his ID. "I am Ted Hoagland, District Attorney for the County of Albemarle. As an officer of the court with power to exercise legal authority in this jurisdiction I am going to place you under arrest unless you provide me with satisfactory identification—immediately."

Tension filled the room as the two authorities faced each other. Henry remained frozen in his place, afraid that his slightest move would detonate an explosion. Suddenly the door opened, and Nurse Davis appeared. "Oh My!" she said with an uncomfortable frown. "I think we've got a failure to communicate going on here." All eyes fixed on the sprightly nurse. "Let's all just take a deep breath and step out into the hall." She pulled the door back and held it open. Hoagland went through it. "Come along Alice, everything is all right." The scowling night nurse followed Hoagland through the door. Nurse Davis gestured to Henry to join the others. "I'm sorry, Alice. I should have told you that these men would be watching Dr. Denker's room. They're authorized to be here and are just doing their duty. Can you just go on with the round?"

"I've never seen anything like this," the nurse huffed. "But if you say it's all right, that's all I need to know." She slipped the clipboard back into its rack below the medicine tray and moved on down the hall. Before entering the next room, she looked back at the group and shook her head.

Hoagland was the first to speak. "Will there be any more hospital personnel stopping in to see Dr. Denker before dawn?"

"No. And I'm sorry for the confusion."

"That's all right. Everything seems to be in order. We'll just carry on as we were—if you don't mind."

"That will be fine. I'll be up front until 6:30. Just let me know if you need anything." She smiled sympathetically and started back up the hall.

Hoagland looked at his watch. "It's 4:00. I'll stay here. Go catch a few winks and come back at 5:15. Officer Mackie from the State Police will relieve you at 6:30. Think you can handle that?"

Henry nodded. "See you in an hour." He turned and followed Nurse Davis up the hall. A few minutes later he returned pushing a swivel chair. "Nurse David thought you might like to sit down," Henry said, sliding the chair over to Hoagland.

He pulled it around so he could sit with his back to Denker's door, then sat down. "Thank her for me . . ."

"Will do. . ."

At the desk, he conveyed the DA's thanks to Nurse Davis. "Say," he added, looking at the empty workspace in front of him, "would you mind if I sit here for a few minutes?"

"Not at all," she said, pointing to the chair beside her. She watched as Henry came around behind the counter and settled into the chair. Henry laid his manila folder on the desk. "I'm sorry to keep bothering you, but would you happen to have some paper?"

"As a matter of fact, I do." She opened a drawer and took out a sheaf of lined paper and handed it to Henry. ". . . and here's a pen. How's that?"

"That's great. Thanks."

"It's none of my business," she said, breaking a brief silence, "but why all the cloak and dagger stuff?"

Henry considered her question. "Dr. Denker's accident occurred under questionable circumstances. We're just taking appropriate precautions."

"What is he? A spy or something?"

"No. It's nothing like that. He's the director of the Jefferson Academy in Keswick."

"Aren't they having a conference out there this weekend?"

"That's right. Do you know about that?"

"Not really . . . I mean . . . there was a guy in here yesterday afternoon who needed a couple stitches to close a scalp wound. He was a case! And so was his girlfriend. They were a real pair," she added after a moment's reflection. "I think he had been struck in the head with a pole or something during a demonstration. Does that sound right?"

"Do you happen to remember his name?"

"Oh yes! I won't forget that name any time soon."

"Was it Bart Paige?"

"How did you know?"

"I witnessed the assault."

"Gosh! What a small world." She sounded truly amazed. "He claimed his father founded the Jefferson Academy. Is that right?"

"That's right . . . but what about Bart? Was he all right?"

"Yes. He seemed to take pride in his injury—I guess I should call it a wound, shouldn't I." She looked at Henry uncertainly. "Anyway, he laughed and carried on about it. Does the term 'women people' mean anything to you?" She asked out of the blue.

"I may have heard it somewhere," Henry said, suppressing a sudden urge to laugh. "Did he use it?"

She rolled her eyes. "He went on and on about the 'women people'— apparently he doesn't get on with them very well, whoever they are."

"No?"

"He'd rant for a while then he would let loose a roar of laughter and tell everyone that he had them in his hip pocket."

"His hip pocket?" Henry frowned. "I wonder what he meant by that?"

"He was probably just babbling," she answered, shaking her head. "I just hope that the Jefferson Academy doesn't have too many people like that at its conference."

"They're special cases," Henry re-assured her. "What are Dr. Denker's prospects?" he added, changing the subject.

"He has extensive lacerations of the scalp, but the preliminary indications are that he has no brain damage. We'll know more about that when he wakes up. It looks like he was extremely lucky," she added.

"Has he said anything?"

"Not to my knowledge." Just then something beeped. "You'll have to excuse me," Nurse Davis said, rising out of her chair."

"You go right ahead. I've got some work to take care of."

She stepped out from behind the desk and headed toward a light that was blinking at the far end of the hall. Henry set the pad of paper down in front of him and began to write.

George: To the best of my knowledge, this is the way it happened . . .

The sun cleared the knoll above Henry's cottage at about 6:45. Its rays flooded Henry's living room with a bright, pure light that roused Claire out of her slumber. She was awake now, but she did not open her eyes. Instead, she watched her thoughts as they streamed across the screen of her mind. They were shaded in strange, distorting colors. She tried to understand them, but the images shattered as she tried to see them clearly. Then it came to her, the scene in Tim Hardin's motel room. She felt his hands on her, touching her. Her humiliation transformed quickly into anger. What are you doing? she demanded. She opened her eyes. For a moment, she did not know where she was. Then she remembered.

She sat up and placed her feet on the floor. That's when she realized that she was still wearing her dress. She stood up gingerly and smoothed out the wrinkles. She listened to the field sounds for a moment, then stepped over to the door. It was locked. She turned the lock and pulled the door open and looked out. It was going to be a beautiful day. As she gazed across the panorama, she realized that Henry's car was gone. The cattle were grazing their way down the pasture, and she watched as they moved through the tall grass. A cow bellowed three times from somewhere in the herd. Claire saw a calf dart forward. Its tail stood straight-up, so she was able to follow it as it navigated its way back to its mother. The herd grazed on without noticing and slowly passed out of sight into the hollow at the bottom of the pasture. She focused on the trail the herd had plowed through the tall grass. It occurred to her that the cows were following their regular pattern. It was part of their natural cycle. Unhurried. Predictable. Secure. How nice, she thought looking at the hill at the head of the valley. Maybe Jefferson had the same experience here once upon a time. The thought reassured her. She began to feel at home.

Back in the living room, Claire went to her bag. She lifted the book Henry had given her and rummaged for her smock. She pulled the straps of her dress off her shoulders and let it fall to her feet. Standing in front of the window, she remembered the trick she played on Henry. She slipped out of her panties and stretched her arms, daring Henry to look at her naked body. Men are such saps, she giggled, sliding her hands across her body. She imaged that Martin was with her. Her body responded with a tingle. "Naughty Claire," she laughed again. "Waste not. Want not."

The phone was in the study. Before she lifted the receiver, she went to Henry's desk and lifted the blotter. The folder was gone. He took it with him, she quickly concluded. She wondered where he was—not that it mattered. Then she lifted the telephone and dialed 0.

An operator answered. "Yes operator. Could you connect me to the Boar's Head Inn. Thank you." A second later Claire heard the phone ring.

"Boar's Head Inn."

"Martin Ogden's room please."

"Do you know the number?"

"I'm sorry. I don't."

There was a pause. "Mr. Ogden is in room 501. I will connect you now."

The phone rang twice. "Yes." Ogden's voice was careful and alert.

"Martin darling."

"Is that you Claire?"

"Yes. Did I wake you?" She asked sweetly.

"No." A touch of warmth came into his voice. "Are you downstairs?" He asked suddenly.

"No. I'm in Keswick—I'm staying in one of the tenants' cottages on Belmont Farm."

"I see..." Ogden did not ask which one.

"I'm meeting Paige for lunch," Claire announced proudly. "Can I see you after that?"

"That's fine," Ogden answered abstractly. "Justice Douglas will be here with me at midday—we'll be dining here. We should be finished by 2:30."

"Darling. You're going to be so proud of me."

"I'm sure I will be," Ogden answered in a measured voice. "Let's talk when you get here."

"Ok... Good-by darling—I love you."

"Good-by dear. I love you too."

Claire pulled on her smock and lifted the book before strolling out onto the porch. The day was new and sparkling and made her tingle again.

She set the book down on the porch rail. Before stepping down into the dewy grass she slid out of her shirt and let it fall onto the deck. She felt her body floating downward and into the cool, refreshing bedding. She imagined a wind-blown seed. She stretched her sinewy limbs under the watchful eye of the sun and began to breathe slowly. In. Out. Breath... Deep... Breath... Deeper... Her mind drifted with the rhythm of her body. Breathe... She stretched her frame. Breathe... Her limbs. Deep. Release the tension. Breathe in... Breathe out... Purge... the darkness... Ahhh. Her body called to her. She touched it, gently. Breath in... Stroked it. Breathing out... Follow its rhythm. Slowly. Breathe... in...

Her bare breasts . . . touch them. The call became more urgent. Breathe. Breathe. Her fingers glided over her ribs and across her stomach. Her eyes closed. Breathe. Oh! There . . . Breathe . . . Ahhh . . . She lay quietly in the grass. Bathing in the sun's cleansing light. Her body was wet. A moment longer to savor . . . Then she rose.

Back on the porch she gathered up her smock and took it inside. The shower was on the stairs to the left. Before she returned to the porch, she stopped in the kitchen. She wanted tea. She found it in the cupboard beside the sink. When the water was hot, she brewed a cup and returned to the porch. She settled herself in Henry's chair and cracked the book. It opened to a photograph of three men on horseback. The figure on the left was a youth with a gravely formal expression. In his hand was a lance with a pennant. The man on the right was leaning on his saddle bow as if he were bored or tired. Claire counted three stripes on his tunic. He was a sergeant! Between these two was sour-faced man in a hat that resembled an upside-down soup tureen. She assumed from the brevets on his shoulders and the double row of brass buttons down the front of his coat, that he was a general or something. The caption beneath the picture read: *Corporal Raymond Wallace Paige and Sergeant Jethro Edgar, winners of the Congressional Medal of Honor for gallantry at Five Forks, with General Phillip Sheridan. This picture was taken on October 23, 1864, at Belle Grove Plantation in the Shenandoah Valley of Virginia, three days after his great victory at Cedar Creek by Matthew Brady.* Printed in large letters on the following page were the words *How I Became an American.*

The first chapter was titled *Trial by Fire.* A sub-title read "*Rally Round the Flag, Boys.*" Paige had used these same words during their conversation the day before. She took a sip of tea and gazed across the peaceful valley. She then turned to the opened page and started to read.

TRIAL BY FIRE
(Rally Round the Flag, Boys!)

I have been involved in many enterprises and accomplished many things in the course of my life, but nothing I have done has been more personally rewarding than becoming an American. Americans have a unique frame of mind. They cherish personal liberty. They seek opportunity. They dare to try. They strive to succeed. Americans are self-interested, but seldom are they selfish because their actions are governed by civic mindedness. Their view of the common good is illuminated by their faith in God. The same faith gives them hope and allows them to believe that all things are possible. Thus, Americans are optimistic, and their lives are purposeful and rich. I have learned these things by living in America. As I came to understand its ways, I became an American myself. The following story is for those who follow me to these foreign shores that they might better understand America and succeed in their own quests to become Americans.

My story begins on April 12, 1864, the day I disembarked the schooner Iberia in the port of New York, having sailed from Glasgow, Scotland fifteen days before.

Since my funds were insufficient for a berth, I spent the voyage on the ship's forward deck facing the harsh spring gales of the North Atlantic. Despite my hardship, I did not regret my decision to emigrate from the land of my birth. Indeed, I had no prospects there, for I was but a poor orphan. My mother had died when I was a small boy. My father, who served the 12th Earl of Moray as a stableman, had been killed in a fall that winter. We had often spoken of coming to America and of the life we would live here, but my father never possessed the money for our passage. When he died, he left me just enough for my own fare. When I reached the new world, I had nothing more than the clothes on my back and the knowledge of horses that my dear departed father had imparted to me.

I was greeted in New York by agents of the United States government who extended to me an invitation to enlist in the armed services of my new country. This I elected to do being that I had no other offers and no other means for providing for myself. So it was that I spent the first three weeks of my life in America training to become a soldier in the Union Army. At the end of this time, my comrades and I were loaded onto a troop transport and sent to Virginia to take our places in the ranks. I learned in transit that our destination was the river city of Fredericksburg, the port nearest to the winter encampment of the Army of the Potomac.

Some short time prior to my arrival on American soil, President Lincoln had made Ulysses S. Grant a Lieutenant General. General Grant's appointment was the first to this rank since 1779 and made him the highest-ranking military officer in the United States. Only the Commander-in-Chief himself had a higher military authority. It was rumored that upon receiving this appointment General Grant had solicited the advice of his chief lieutenant in his western army. According to this rumor, General Sherman instructed General Grant not to remain in Washington as it was a crucible of political intrigue. I cannot vouch for the truthfulness of this rumor, but I do know that General Grant followed its council for he established his headquarters in Culpeper, Virginia where he shared the company of the Army of the Potomac and its commanding officer, General George Meade.

Mr. Lincoln perceived in General Grant a man of action. This was a fair assessment based on his success in the suppression of the rebellion in the west. It was well understood that Mr. Lincoln intended for General Grant to finish the job in the east. To help him accomplish this objective, General Grant enlisted the services of one of his high-strung subordinates from the western army. General Philip Sheridan was to have command of the Union cavalry. The General had demonstrated his ability to defeat Confederates in countless engagements along the Mississippi, and in this respect, the two men were well-matched.

General Grant intended for General Sheridan's cavalry to lead the Army of the Potomac south toward Richmond as soon as the roads were dry enough to march.

General Meade was to have command of the army during this campaign, but the authority to initiate its actions was to be with General Grant alone. Indeed, I heard from a reliable source, that General Grant told General Meade, "Wherever Lee goes, there you will go also." It bears repeating for the benefit of my younger readers, that although General Meade had defeated General Lee at Gettysburg, he had also allowed Lee's rebel army to escape. This breach had caused Mr. Lincoln to lose confidence in General Meade. Therefore, he was to have no role in planning the army's campaign. Under these circumstances it is not surprising that the poor man cracked up.

General Grant aimed the army toward the Confederate capitol, but capturing it was never his objective. His true goal was to destroy the power of the Confederacy to wage war. He intended to do this by attacking General Lee at every opportunity. By keeping the two armies locked in combat, General Grant expected to consume his enemy's manpower and thereby make prolonged southern resistance impossible. This strategy was practical for the northern party as General Grant had a large reserve in manpower where General Lee had none. The plan was commended by the General's lieutenants, but let me assure you that it levied a great hardship on the rank and file. Still, the troops were willing to carry their burden so long as they were following a strong leader.

General Sheridan was such a man. The first mark he made on the cavalry was to re-organize it into three divisions. The first division remained under the command of General Alfred Torbert until the cavalry left the Shenandoah Valley late in the winter of 1865. The second was commanded by General David Gregg who continued in that position until resigning his commission shortly before we made our final assault on General Lee's flank in April of 1865. The third was commanded by General James Wilson. General Wilson did not get along with General Sheridan for a variety of reasons and was transferred to service in the western army before six months had passed. Taken together, General Sheridan's legion exceeded 13,000 men. In the brief time that he had before the commencement of its southward march, the General succeeded in sharpening them into the most lethal weapon ever crafted for warfare.

No man was better suited than he to guide it. During his service in the west, General Sheridan had come into possession of a powerful black gelding which he named Rienzi in honor of his victory over Col. William Faulkner at a village in Mississippi bearing that name. He had ridden Rienzi into every battle he fought after that. I was to learn in due course that the man and the horse shared the same temper. Like his master, Rienzi was always impatient to meet the enemy and was not happy unless they were running before him.

The Union army began its campaign in the pre-dawn darkness on May 4th, three days before our transport steamed into the mouth of the Rappahannock River. The Confederate capital lay less than sixty miles to the south. Though the distance was not great, no Union army had traversed it in four bloody years of warfare. When a reporter asked General Grant how long it would take him to get there, he said, "Four days, if General Lee becomes party to the agreement." The Confederate general was not party to the agreement, however.

General Lee and his vaunted Army of Northern Virginia stood on guard between General Grant and Richmond. Even with the return of Longstreet's

1st Corp from East Tennessee, General Lee had scarcely more than 60,000 men in his command. General Grant was bringing against him an army nearly twice that size. But despite its superior numbers, there was a disquieting uncertainty in the ranks. The battle-tested veterans who formed the core of the northern army did not know General Grant, but they did know that they had never beaten General Lee. Nor did they think they could.

On the morning of the 4th, General Sheridan's legion led the army eastward along the north bank of the Rapidan River. Crossing at Germanna Ford and Ely's Ford, it proceeded south into a dense jungle of underbrush and second growth trees known to the local inhabitants as "The Wilderness". General Grant understood that his army would be in danger as it passed through this maze, but it was a risk he was prepared to take. If he managed to outsmart his wily adversary, he would have a clear march to the Confederate capital.

General Lee, however, was not to be outmaneuvered. He responded quickly when he received word of the Union march and summoned his army from its defensive positions south of the Rapidan. The Confederates marched in several columns along interior lines keeping between the enemy and their capital. A. P. Hill's Third Corp led the procession, hewing its way through the Wilderness from the west as Meade's men marched southward. As events soon proved, General Hill was advancing on a course that intersected the Union column.

At mid-morning on the 5th, skirmishers from Charles Griffin's Brigade, moving west on the Old Stone Road, ran head-long into John Jones' Brigade of Johnson's Division. This was the vanguard of Lee's army. What started as a skirmish between these two units developed quickly into a full-scale engagement as the opposing armies converged. The contest continued to expand through the day in a forest so thick that its progress was hidden even from its participants. The first day ended inconclusively with General Lee's Confederates in position behind a complex of earthworks that spread rapidly across the forest's floor.

At dawn on the morning of the 6th, General Grant sent Major General D.B. Birney's 3rd Division against the right side of the Confederate line. His attack was supported by Brigadier General Gershom Mott's 4th Division of Hancock's powerful II Corp. The Federals crashed into the depleted ranks of Generals Heth and Wilcox and quickly put them to flight. This opened a gaping hole in the Confederate line through which the blue tide surged. Divided, General Lee's army was now in imminent danger of destruction. Barely moments before this was accomplished, General Longstreet's First

Corp arrived at the front. General Longstreet grasped the situation immediately and unleashed John Gregg's Texans in a precipitous charge that stalled the northern advance. The fate of the South hung in the balance as Kershaw's Alabamans joined the Texans in a violent counterattack. Now besieged, the Federals fought bravely, but finally yielded. Thus was the breech sealed in the Confederate line and General Lee's army saved.

Now General Lee took the offensive. Massing quickly on the right, three of General Longstreet's fresh brigades attacked Hancock's exposed left flank. As the din of the attack rumbled through the smoke-filled underbrush, General Longstreet hurled the remainder of his Corp against the Union center. The Yankee line crumbled beneath the double blow. For a moment, it seemed as if General "Stonewall" Jackson was leading the rebels through the woods where he had won his greatest victory. But Providence chose not to bless the South this day. Before the Confederates could exploit their advantage, shots rang out from a thicket and General Longstreet fell stricken, pierced in the throat by a ball fired by one of his own advancing troops. In the ensuing confusion, the initiative passed from the grays. That day, the 6th of May, ended in a blood-soaked stalemate with both armies now entrenched in the defoliated and burning forest.

I disembarked with my regiment several miles below Fredericksburg late in the afternoon of May 7th. We marched first to the town, then on to the battlefield by way of the Orange-Fredericksburg turnpike. In two days of fighting, General Grant had lost nearly one seventh of his command, more than seventeen thousand men. They filled the open spaces for miles around. Along the roadsides lay the dead and dying. The groans of the wounded filled the air with an anguished chorus of human suffering. The devastation grew still more awful the closer we came to the front. I beheld the ghastly wreckage and wondered if General Grant still had an army in the field.

At sunset, we fell out beside the road to eat our supper. The thought was common among us that it would be our last. As I sat in the gathering gloom contemplating my death, something in the shadows along the tree line caught my eye. In the next instant, I saw a riderless horse burst out of the darkness and gallop toward me. As it came nearer, I could see its reins whipping the ground in violent strokes. The creature would certainly catch one of these strands under its crashing hooves and that would be the end of it. But still, it was such a fine-looking animal! I rose instinctively and prepared to intercept *it, measuring its course as it closed ominously upon me. At the last second, I leaped forward. By the grace of God, it veered off, but not before I caught its saddle bow and pulled myself up onto its back.*

I was swept away in an apocalyptic tide. Yet, despite the prospect of momentary doom, my mind was fixed, and my eyes never shifted from the strands that danced in the terrifying cadence of the creature's mad gallop. Clinging to its neck with one arm, I strained to reach them, but all my efforts were in vain. Surely the end was near at hand for horse and rider! Then suddenly, as often happens when all hope is lost, Fortune interceded. Perhaps it was a loose pebble in the road. Or perhaps it was a ridge created by a wagon wheel. I believe it was the will of our merciful Lord that caused one of the reins to fly into the air, just high enough to graze my fingers. I seized it and pulled it fiercely to the side. That was enough to break the animal's stride. Its pace immediately moderated. As it was then practical, I slid from my precarious perch on its neck and settled back into the saddle, master as last of the whirlwind.

It was then that I noticed horsemen closing on my flank, one closing on either side. A moment later they were beside me and my death-defying adventure was over. Grateful I was to have survived. And grateful too for the deliverance of that magnificent steed!

I could see by their uniforms that one of the men was a general officer and that the other was a Sergeant. The officer's expression was one that I shall not forget. His clenched jaw conveyed grim determination. His eyes flashed with fiery light. When he fixed them upon me, I discovered that for the first time I was afraid. The officer studied me for a moment. Then he said, "You saved my horse." He spoke as though he were noting the fact in some mental journal. When he was finished, he wheeled his mount and gave it the spur. "Bring him back," he shouted over his shoulder as he galloped off. The Sergeant followed him without uttering a sound.

I pursued them along the course we had just come down, finally catching them near where my regiment was at ease. The general officer reined in long enough to address my captain who had apparently witnessed the cavalcade. "Sir," he thundered, "I require the service of your private." This was the first time I had seen my captain at a loss. "Sir!" He responded with a confused salute. "Whom is it that I have the honor to address?" The officer tore off his cap. "It's General Sheridan!" someone cried. A spontaneous cheer went up through the ranks. General Sheridan responded with a pugnacious wave of his cap. Before the cheer died away, he was off again—and I was with him. We raced on-ward to the woods. Before entering them, I stole a glance back at my comrades. They were standing there in the twilight, still cheering. Somehow, I knew they were cheering for me—in the hope that I had been delivered. And so I had!

Back at headquarters, the General left me with his sergeant and went on with his duties. Sergeant Edgar saw to it that I got a hot supper and a new uniform—one with two stripes on its sleeve. From that point on I was Corpo-ral Paige of General Sheridan's staff.

Like General Sheridan, Sergeant Edgar was from the west. He had earned his stripes helping the General chase Confederates out of Mississippi. He was not an educated man, but he had learned well enough how the Gen-eral operated. That first night he took me aside and explained it to me. "Son," he said in his rough western dialect. "Ain't many men could do what you done back there. That's somethin' the Gen'ral ain't never gonna fergit. You can count on that. So if you keep on his good side, you're fixed." He spat out a stream of brown tobacco juice and wiped his chip with his sleeve. "Now pay at-tention, boy, 'cause I'm only gonna tell you this once." He spat another stream of tobacco juice into the dirt between us and once again wiped his chin on his sleeve. "There's just two things impor'an 'round here. The first is gettin' done what the Gen'ral wants. The second is gittin' it done the fastest way that flesh an' bones can do it." He pointed to the stripes on his sleeve. "See these here? I got 'em 'cause I know what the Gen'ral wants and how to git it done. That means when I tell ya ta do somethin' you're gonna git at it like the Devil's on yer heals. Got that?" "Aye, Sir," I said. "An' by the All Mighty, don't waste no time on stuff that ain't impor'an." I nodded gravely to show that I understood. "Good lad!" he said with an encouraging pat on my shoulder. "The Gen'ral wants his horse groomed and ready to ride in front of his tent at daybreak. That's your job. Now git to it."

Any success I had in the army—and much of the success that I have en-joyed since then—I attribute to the instructions I received from Sergeant Ed-gar. They remain my guiding principles to this day.

As we were to march at dawn, there was no time for sleep that night. The entire camp was a buzz with activity. The tension in the air was sharpened by the dark mood of our commander. It seems that he had clashed with General Meade the day before and was still smarting over the exchange. Relations between the two men had deteriorated as the battle had progressed. In fairness to General Meade, he was in a bad situation, being responsible for an army whose movements were being directed by his superior. The carnage of General Grant's offensive had unhinged him. Under the circumstances, it is not surprising that he would have sharp words with General Sheridan. General Sheridan had been equally blunt with General Meade. He was angry because General Meade had used his finely-honed war machine to guard supplies in the rear of the army. If General Meade would leave him alone, General Sheridan snapped, he would go whip Jeb Stuart. General Meade scoffed at the boast. In an attempt to embarrass his brash cavalry commander, he went so far as to relate it to General Grant. General Meade was surprised when General Grant told him that General Sheridan usually knew what he was talking and that he should let him go out and do it. That suited General Meade. Nothing could please him more than to send his nettlesome lieutenant off to fend for himself.

Before dawn on May 8th, I brought Rienzi to General Sheridan's tent. The air cracked with excitement in anticipation of the adventure that was about to begin. I held his horse as the General barked out his final instructions. Then he climbed into his saddle and reached down for his reins. He was going off with his thirteen thousand men to force the gates of hell. In that moment, while his great war machine waited, poised for his order to march, he said to me, "You ride, don't you Corporal?"

"Aye Sir," I said. "I do."

"Then get a horse and come along because..." he turned as if he were looking for someone. "Sergeant Edgar!" he roared. "Where the hell is Edgar?" He cursed hotly into the face of thirteen thousand hardened warriors. "Here, Sir," came a reply from somewhere back in the ranks." "Well get the hell up here! By God! I'll wager that you're the only man in this whole goddam army that isn't ready to march. By God..." The General reddened into a deep flush and primed himself to explode. Just then Sergeant Edgar appeared, carrying a red and white banner. "By God, Edgar, you're clairvoyant!" He exclaimed with ferocious delight. The Sergeant trotted forward and handed the banner to the General. "I thought you would be wanting this, General," he said offhandedly. "Good... Excellent!" The General roared. "By God! This is exactly what I want!" He snatched it from the Sergeant. "Corporal," he said, thrusting the banner into my hand, "this is the most important piece of equipment in the whole damned army. From now on, it's your responsibility. Keep it clean. And whenever I take the field, I want you to have it here at my side."

I took the lance and raised it up. "You can count on me, Sir."

"I believe I can," he said. With that, he gave the signal and the column set off to war.

To carry his personal emblem was the greatest honor that General Sheridan could bestow on any soldier. I was sure of that. But I did not understand what he meant about it being the army's most important piece of equipment. That came later.

We started our raid on Richmond with a countermarch through the Wilderness. We turned east off the Plank Road in the direction of Fredericksburg. This thoroughfare was heavily rutted, having borne the supply trains that supported the army as it fought its way out of that lethal maze. The returning wagons carried an endless line of wounded to the rear. Since few of them had springs, evacuation was a new torture for their passengers. Their cries filled the air as the wagons rumbled along. Grim though this testimony was, it had no effect General Sheridan. His plans were set, and nothing could shake his resolve. I vaguely understood that this was the source of his strength as a leader. His unwavering determination proved to be our inspiration in the difficult months ahead.

At Aldrich's Station, we left the train of wounded and turned south on Telegraph Road. Being that this was the main highway to Richmond, the General's intentions were at last clear. The column responded with a cheer that shook the ground beneath us. We understood that we would be the first to reach the Confederate capital and the knowledge filled us with new pride.

Our column stretched thirteen miles across the Virginia countryside in defiance of General Stuart and his heralded cavalry. Measuring our strength and finding his unequal, he could do little more than nip at our heals. General Sheridan ignored these triflings and marched boldly onward toward Richmond. Three days later we were on the outskirts of the Confederate capital.

Not until May 11th, by which time we had destroyed several large stockpiles of Confederate supplies, was General Stuart able to throw a line in our path. This was the opportunity for which General Sheridan had been waiting. He relished smashing things, and nothing was more suitable than enemy cavalry on the steps of his capital.

He was boiling with excitement when he handed me his orders for General Merritt who commanded General Torbert's forward brigade. Upon receiving

General Sheridan's instructions, General Merritt sent Colonel Alfred Gibbs down the Brook Turnpike toward Yellow Tavern, which despite its name, was nothing more than an abandoned building six miles north of Richmond's outer line of defense. Just to the north of it, General Stuart had deployed two brigades of Virginia cavalry. They were in position on the north side of the Turnpike along ridges that ran to the east side of the Mountain Road when Colonel Gibb's arrived on the scene at about 11:00 AM. The engagement soon became hot with both sides demonstrating a firm resolve. Sporadically heavy fighting continued through the afternoon during which time neither side gained ground. At 4:00 PM, General Sheridan sent General Custer's Michigan brigade around General Stuart's left while sending the rest of his dismounted troopers in an assaulting against Stuart's center and right. A countercharge by the First Virginia checked General Custer's attack and sent him into a disorganized retreat. During this melee, a number of unhorsed Federals came running through a grove where General Stuart had engaged himself in the battle. Among these fleeing troopers was a 48-year-old Union private who turned in his flight and fired a shot at the General. The ball struck the Confederate leader in his side below his rib cage and penetrated his spleen. General Stuart, who claimed that he would rather die than be whipped, expired the following evening in the Richmond home of his brother-in-law.

The battle over, we proceeded eastward past the outer defenses of Richmond to Meadow Bridge. There we fought a sharp skirmish with a hastily assembled force of home guard before entering the sanctuary of General Butler to end our raid. Thus, did General Sheridan defeat the heralded southern cavalry commander and make good on his boast to General Meade.

Owing to the speed of our advance and the skirmishing pattern of our engagements, the occasion did not arise for General Sheridan to personally lead an attack. Consequently, there was no call for me to carry his standard. Instead, I earned my keep as a courier and by bringing prisoners to the rear.

We remained in the Federal enclave east of Richmond while General Grant fought General Lee at Spotsylvania and Cold Harbor. Cold Harbor was a neglected crossroad on the peninsula formed by the parallel courses of the Pamunkey and the Chickahominy Rivers. The bloody defeat suffered there on June 3rd marked General Grant's final attempt to conquer General Lee in open combat. Both Generals knew that battlefield tactics would be useless in the siege conflict that was now opening. General Lee was now essentially trapped inside the defenses of Richmond. Since General Grant was not strong enough to crack them, he began to look for strategic diversions that would weaken his opponent.

In early June, General Grant ordered General Sheridan to cross to Charlottesville and make a link there with General Hunter. General Hunter's army had recently defeated a small force of Confederates and regained control of the Shenandoah Valley. He had then entered the town of Lexington where he inflamed Southern sentiments by burning the Virginia Military Institute, the alma mater of many of the Confederacy's officers. We broke camp on June 7th and crossed the Pamunkey at New Castle Ferry with a force of eight thousand men. Riding northwest, we kept on the north side of the North Anna River moving in the direction of Gordonsville. Wade Hampton's and Fitz Lee's divisions, about five thousand men combined, set out in pursuit the following day, shadowing us on the river's south side.

As we rode along, I fell into conversation with Sergeant Edgar. At one point, I remember asking him what the war was about. "It's about e pluribus unum, son," he said. "Everybody in America's part of the same thing—like it er not. In case you don't know it, America ain't just a place. It's a country! These here rebs has started a rebellion 'cause they figure it's up ta them ta do things whatever way they want. Since that ain't the way countries work, we're down here putting it right." When I asked him why it mattered, he said, "If we leave it be, we'll end up in a place where every man's fer himself and agin his neighbor." When I told him that I didn't understand why America needed the South to begin with, he looked at me with a puzzled look. "Son," he said, "I'm a sergeant in the US Army. All I gotta know is what the Gen'ral wants me to do. If he tells me to jump of a cliff, all I got ta worry about is finding the cliff. The rest don't make no difference. Soon as you learn that you'll be fixed."

On the night of the 10th, General Hampton made his camp in a grassy meadow in Green Springs Valley near the Trevilian Station on the Virginia Central Railroad. General Lee camped eight miles to the east at Louisa Court House. In these positions the Southerners stood between our force and the railroad which linked Richmond to the Shenandoah Valley. The Confederates correctly understood that the objective of our raid was to cut the rail line.

Early the following morning General Sheridan sent General Torbert's division south from Brock's Bridge on the Marquis Road with instructions to find an access to the railroad. General Sheridan gave General Torbert *additional instructions to accept a fight if the opportunity should present itself. General Torbert was moving south looking for the rail head as General Calbraith Butler and his brigade were coming north on the same road looking for our column. We met at Clayton's Store. This chance encounter quickly grew into a pitched battle as reinforcements came up on both sides. As the battle was unfolding, General Lee continue northward from Louisa Court House on the Marquis Road, expecting to join with General Hampton at Clayton's Store. General Lee's column was advancing toward this junction when he heard the gunfire from General Butler's fight with General Torbert. Responding to the danger, General Lee re-called General Wickham's brigade, which was at the head of his column. General Wickham's countermarch widened the space between General Lee and General Hampton, who had dismounted his men and sent them on foot to support General Butler. In the confusion, General Custer found the opening and raced through it. The covered road on which he advanced led him to the Gordonsville Turnpike about one quarter mile northeast of Trevilian Station. From there he moved without obstruction to the rail junction where he found General Hampton's lightly guarded baggage train and the horses of his dismounted troopers. General Custer quickly overran the thin line of defenders commanded by General Rosser. Having gathered up what could be taken, he started up the highway in the direction of Gordonsville. Before General Custer could complete his withdrawal, he was assailed by units that General Hampton had disengaged from his attack on General Torbert. This allowed General Torbert to concentrate on General Lee who was showing strength on General Torbert's left.*

When General Lee fell back, General Torbert assumed he was driving the Rebels off. In reality, General Lee was redirecting his attack westward into the right flank of the line General Custer had formed to meet General Hampton's attack. This created an opportunity the Confederates were quick to exploit. Dismounted troopers from both General Lee's and General Hampton's divisions fanned out as though their objective was to encircle General Custer's isolated command.

About this time, General Sheridan summoned me. "I want you to take a message to Custer," he said. "He's in a fix across the way so you're going to have to go around some rebels to reach him. You think you can do that?" I had no way of knowing, but remembering the Sergeant's counsel, I said I could. "Good lad! Good lad" The General said, patting me on the shoulder. "I knew

I could count on you." With that he handed me an envelope and sent me to his adjutant to see his maps.

Lt. Col. James Forsythe briefed me on the situation. My route to General Custer was to be around General Hampton's left flank. Colonel Forsythe supposed the Gordonsville-Trevilian Road was still open and advised me to approach General Custer from that direction. I understood from the Colonel that General Sheridan wanted General Custer to join him at Gordonsville so he could resume his advance to Charlottesville and connect with General Hunter. Any attempt by General Hampton to interpose himself in that line would place him between the two Union armies, which would assist us in our effort to destroy him. Having received this intelligence, I was confident that we were on the verge of another great victory. I selected a fast horse, stuffed a second pistol into my belt, and set out cross country to find General Custer.

I circled General Hampton's position and arrived at the Gordonsville-Trevilian Road about three miles up from Trevilian Station. Colonel Forsythe told me that I could follow it down to General Custer, but as I proceeded southeastward toward his position, I could hear an ever-increasing volume of gun fire. About a mile down the highway, I entered a wooded area. As I passed through it, it became evident that the armies were engaged on the other side of these woods. I crept out from my shelter to ascertain the situation before proceeding on. To my right, I could see cannon shot churning through lines of gray clad men. I deduced from this that General Lee was assailing General Custer's position which apparently was behind the woods up ahead. As I marveled at the sight, I happened to glance to my left. There, about three hundred yards off the road, was a line of rebel skirmishers coming toward me. These, I assumed, were General Hampton's men. If this was so, the Confederates were on the verge of completing their encirclement of General Custer. My time for figuring ended abruptly as bullets began to whistle about my ears. I spurred my horse into a gallop and raced across the open space and into the next line of trees. There was a bend in the road about one hundred yards into these woods. Turning through it at a gallop, I came charging head long into a phalanx of raised carbines. Fortunately, they belonged to a squadron of Union cavalry. More fortunate still, the men who held them had enough discipline to hold their fire as I careened into their midst. As it was, they recognized my blue tunic and gave out with a cheer. Having welcomed me into their line, they sealed the path behind me, and I was safe. Quickly confirming the nature of my mission, the leader of the patrol, Lt. Stewart Bishop, led me straight on to General Custer.

General Custer was about twenty-five years old, but under attack, he appeared much older. Like many of General Sheridan's officers, he was a westerner by birth and a West Pointer by training. And like the General, he had finished near the bottom of his class. Nevertheless, he was a tenacious fighter and for that reason, the two generals got along well despite General Custer's rashness. When I reached him, the General was in a state of high excitement. He managed to calm himself long enough to read the message I handed him, but immediately upon finishing it, he returned to his former state of agitation. "Be so kind as to convey my compliments to the General," General Custer bellowed through the din. "But you can inform General Sheridan that I have no intention of leaving this place without _all_ the baggage currently in my possession." He glowered at me for a moment to confirm that I comprehended his message. "And furthermore," he continued, "since the whole damned Confederate Cavalry is within a rifle shot of where we are at this moment conversing, please tell him that the pleasure will be mine if he will join me here at his earliest possible convenience!" With that he commenced pacing back and forth in front of me as though he were waiting for General Sheridan to arrive.

I might have been overwhelmed by the situation except that I was accustomed to General Sheridan's brusque manner. I therefore snapped to attention. "Begging the General's pardon, Sir," I said. "But could the General put his response in writing lest I mis-communicate the General's sentiments." He pulled up suddenly and stared at me with a wild, impatient expression. A tense moment followed at which point he grunted and went to his desk where he proceeded to write out his reply. He then sealed it in an envelope and handed it to me. Having done that, he summoned Lt. Bishop. When Lt. Bishop arrived, General Custer instructed him to select two good men to accompany me back to General Sheridan's headquarters. In consideration of the circumstances, he advised me to wait until twilight before setting out. In the meantime, he said, he would push up the highway and clear the road so far as he was able.

All the while this meeting was in progress, General Lee had continued his assault south of the Gordonsville highway. General Custer troopers finally succeeded in repulsing it, and the front was now quieting. I and my escort slipped out at dusk as General Custer had advised. The road was clear as we dashed through the opening between the two woods. Off to either side we could see campfires burning, but we passed on without incident and completed our escape. Sometime before midnight, we arrived back at General Sheridan's headquarters. Of course, the General stirring. When he saw me, he saluted. "Good man!" he roared as I handed him General Custer's note. He took the envelope, tore it open and commenced to read its contents. When he was finished, he crumpled it in his fist and shouted for his staff to prepare for a dawn attack. "Corporal," he said looking at me. "I'm going to need your flag tomorrow!"

The regiments formed their lines in the pre-dawn light. The General seized the opportunity to cross in front of his men to give them encouragement. I was at his shoulder with his pennant, keeping it always in clear view. As the men saw the flag, they would begin to cheer. The General responded by exhorting them to follow their own flags. Soon after the initial assault, we were able to open a passage to General Custer and the army was again united. General Custer's only embarrassment seemed to derive from the loss of his prizes—we discovered later that he had also lost his own wagon.

Having extricated General Custer, we were ready to resume our advance. Our path, however, was now blocked by the combined forces of General Hampton and General Lee which were by this time entrenched in a strong defensive position in anticipation of our attack. At midday on the 12th, we renewed the assault, but this attack failed with heavy casualties. Weakened and low on ammunition, and having received no word from General Hunter, General Sheridan decided to abandon his effort to join with him. Instead, we gathered up the wounded and re-crossed the North Anna at Carpenter's Mills. From there we marched back to safety in the Union Lines.

The dust had hardly settled at Trevilian Station when General Jubal Early, commanding Jackson's Third Corp, marched past our battlefield on his way to Lynchburg. General Lee had sent him west to deal with General Hunter who was still in the Piedmont. Weighing his prospects against General Early and finding them uncertain without General Sheridan's cavalry, General Hunter turned around and marched back into the Valley. General Early followed close on his heals but could not catch General Hunter's caravan before it cleared the Valley and disappeared into the mountains of West Virginia.

General Hunter's hasty departure left the Confederates in sole possession of the vital Shenandoah Valley. This created an opportunity which General

Early quickly seized upon. Gathering strength and confidence as he went, General Early marched down the Valley. On July 2, the first anniversary of the Battle of Gettysburg, he met and defeated General Sigel's advance guard. On the 6th, he crossed the Potomac and entered Maryland. General Early delayed his advance until a shipment of shoes could be distributed to his barefoot troops. Then he marched east toward Frederick. The capital lay two days' march to the southeast.

The city of Washington had been heavily fortified by General McClellan early in the war, but because of the heavy demand for manpower to support the siege in Richmond, most of its defenders had been sent there by General Grant. The Union capital was therefore, to some extent, vulnerable. Major General Lew Wallace led a patchwork force to obstruct the advancing Confederates, but his make-shift command was no match for General Early's battle-hardened veterans and on July 9th, General Early overwhelmed it at Monacacy Creek outside Fredericksburg. General Early pressed his advantage in spite of stifling heat and dust. Fortunately for Washington, after marching 50 miles in two days, the Confederates were too exhausted to assault the capital's massive fortifications. The Confederate General rested his men at Silver Spring the evening of the 12th, intending to attack the following morning. During the night, he received word that Wright's powerful VI Corp had arrived. The Confederate General therefore waited for the sun to rise to see for himself whether his intelligence was correct. At daybreak, he inspected the Union parapets and found them thick with defenders. Unable to see from his vantage point that the lines of riflemen in the trenches at Fort Stevens were clerks from General Mieg's Quartermaster Corp, General Early delayed his attack 24 hours. This was the time General Wright needed to reach the front. His men moved into position on the 13th and closed the door of the capital to the Confederate's daring adventure. General Early remained in front of the Union position one more day, then, heavily disappointed, collected his army and marched back into Virginia.

Although the panic was over, the Confederate withdrawal did not solve the problem for the Federals in the capital. So long as General Early was loose in the Valley, he would be free to renew his aggression whenever the Northerners lowered their guard. And so long as the Shenandoah Valley remained in Confederate hands, it would remain a source of food and manpower for Lee's besieged army. This was something General Grant was not prepared to tolerate. The time had come, he decided, to eliminate this Confederate resource once and for all. He passed word to President Lincoln announcing his intention to send General Sheridan to the valley with a strong force and for the General to "put himself south of the enemy and follow him to the death." "Take your men," he told General Sheridan, and "eat out Virginia clear and clean as far as they go so that crows flying over it for the balance of the season will have to carry their provender with them." The General received these orders with remorseless enthusiasm. To implement them, he would have an army of 40,000 men, triple the number of General Early's brash Confederates.

By mid-August, General Sheridan had advanced more than a third of the way up the Valley. General Early, aware of the Federal's superior numbers, played a deft game of cat and mouse. Finding no opportunity to strike a decisive blow, General Sheridan withdrew from Harrisonburg and marched back down the Valley, burning crops and barns and driving off livestock as he went. Behind him he left a charred and smoldering wasteland. In mid-September, General Grant came out from Point City to see what the General had accomplished. It was not enough. General Grant told his lieutenant to catch General Early and defeat him.

Within the week, General Sheridan was moving again. At 2:00 AM on September 19, General Wilson's cavalry splashed across the Opequon Creek at the Berryville crossing. He would make the first assault on General Early's divided army, which held a line two miles to the east of Winchester. General Sheridan planned to follow General Wilson's strike at daybreak with a full-scale attack by the VI and XIX Corps, which were under General Wright's command. In view of his superior numbers, the prospects were good that we would overwhelm the rebels before General Early could gather his scattered forces. If he succeeded, there would be little left to do aside from mopping up the remnants of General Early's army. The success of his plan depended on the army crossing the Opequon quickly and getting into its battle line before sunrise. But this it did not do. In the confusion of the pre-dawn movement, General Sheridan's ammunition train found its way into the center of his infantry column. The road to the west of the creek traversed a narrow valley which made it impossible to extract the non-belligerents from the assault force. The resulting delays gave the Confederates six precious hours to form their regiments for battle.

By 12:00, General Wright's Corp was in position on the left and center of

195

the planned line of attack. Beside him on the right was General Emory's first division under General Dwight. Behind General Dwight, in reserve, was General Grover with Emory's second division. Determined to strike before General Early could concentrate his forces, General Sheridan sent General Wright's first two divisions forward, holding General Russell in reserve pending developments. The advancing Federals met resistance immediately. General Ramseur's division, holding the Confederate left, took the weight of the Union blow. Beside him on the right was General Rodes' division, standing athwart the Berryville Pike. In the tumult of the battle, General Wright's left flank separated from General Dwight. Seeing the opportunity, General Rodes sent Colonel Battle's brigade charging into the opening in the Union line. Colonel Battle's sharp counterattack sent General Dwight's men flying in confusion into General Grover. This entirely uprooted the Union left. General Sheridan responded to the impending disaster with an order to General Russell to advance his reserve. Against this fresh force, the budding Confederate offensive stalled.

While the Confederates were falling back, General Upton's brigade from General Crook's VIII Corp came up and went into position in the contested space between General Wright and General Emory. Now General Sheridan was ready to envelop his foe. His attack would carry across a five-mile front. With two strong divisions of cavalry under General Torbert overlapping the Confederate left at the Valley Pike, the victory was assured. The General was bursting with excitement. Together we rode down the line, I holding his pennant and he exhorting the troops and priming them for victory. As we passed from one group to the next, the same scene repeated itself again and again. The troops would see the flag and rise. Then they would recognize the General and cheer. He would respond with a wave of his hat, saluting them for their impending success. As we crossed the face of the army, I began to understand his method. He loved his men almost as much as he loved his horse. He demanded a lot from them, but when they delivered, he saw to it they were rewarded. They were the best and they got the best. When he was ready to strike a blow, they were ready to deliver it. Obstructions that he encountered were merely opportunities to strike again. It dawned on me that I should apply the General's method in my own undertakings. He had started with nothing and was now in command of a great army. What great things might I accomplish if I would but approach my own life the same way the General did?

In the ensuing attack, General Torbert quickly turned the Confederate's *left flank. Soon after that, the center gave way. Our infantry pressed its attack all along the crumbling front, forcing the grays into an anxious withdrawal. General Early formed a new position five miles south of Winchester at Fisher's Hill. General Sheridan attacked him there on September 22nd with similar results. General Early lost 12 guns and more than 1000 men.*

General Grant proposed that General Sheridan follow up his victory by driving the battered Confederates out of the Valley and thus close their access to Maryland. But General Sheridan was not warm to the suggestion. It would over-extend his supply line, he argued, and expose his force to general attack from the main Confederate army at Richmond. He preferred instead to complete the destruction of the Valley's agricultural resources and close the door to for good on General Lee's granary. When this was accomplished, he proposed to send the VI Corp back to General Grant. General Grant consented to this.

The morning of October 17th, our army was camped across the Valley Pike behind Cedar Creek, twenty miles south of Strasburg. General Early's Confederates had returned to Fisher's Hill where they were apparently content to stand a watchful guard. Before the sun rose, General Sheridan, in the company of his staff crossed the Blue Ridge Mountains and boarded a train in Rectortown. His destination was Washington where he was to give General Halleck his assessment of General Early's offensive capabilities, then confer with the President.

At noon, the General departed Washington on a special train bound for Martinsburg. With him were two engineers sent by General Halleck to survey the terrain outside Winchester. General Sheridan concurred with General Halleck's plan to build a line of fortifications across the Valley at this point and had therefore consented to escort the overweight, overheated staff officers into the heart of his military district.

The company passed a quiet night in Martinsburg. The following morning, the General and his guests were joined by 300 mounted troopers from the 17th Pennsylvania who had come down from Maryland to escort the General's party back to Winchester. Because General Halleck's engineers were not unaccustomed to their saddles the procession advanced at a walk. At 4:00 we finally completed our twenty-eight-mile trek. General Sheridan retired to the headquarters of Colonel Edwards, the commander of our Winchester garrison, to review reports from the front. He discovered to his satisfaction that General Early was still at Fisher's Hill. This pleased him because it provided him with an opportunity to deal him a final, crushing blow. He proceeded to order General Grover to undertake a reconnaissance in force the next morning to feel out the Confederate position. Having issued these orders, the General turned his attention to entertaining his guests.

At 6:00 O'clock on the morning of the 19th, I awakened the General to tell him that Captain Levi Old, the officer of the picket was waiting to deliver a report. The General arranged himself, then ordered me to show Captain Old in. Captain Old's manners suggested that he was ill at ease. "What is it, Captain," the General demanded impatiently. "Sir," the captain responded with a crisp salute, "There is artillery fire at the front." "Indeed," said the General, showing no alarm. "And is it desultory, or steady?" "It is occasionally heavy," the captain replied. "Then it is Grover doing his work down at Fisher's Hill," the General concluded. He thanked Captain Old for his observations and dismissed him. Though sure in his opinion, the General could not remain in bed. Dressing quickly, he went down to breakfast.

The army was posted in three camps that formed a line running roughly north to south, about two miles end to end. General Wright's VI Corp was on the northern extremity, about one half mile up from General Emory whose XIX Corp was in the center on the higher ground just to the west of the Valley Pike. General Crook's VIII Corp, which was camped on the eastern side of the pike, held the southernmost position in the line. Below him was flat bottom land which stretched another two miles to the Shenandoah River. To the east of this meandering stream, Massanutten Mountain rose in a scarp the Union commanders assumed made their position unassailable from that side.

This assumption soon proved to be false for during the night of the 18th, General John B. Gordon led the three divisions of his Second Corp in Indian file along the base of Massanutten Mountain. In the pre-dawn hours of the 19th, he formed a battle line in a clearing beside the Manassas Gap Railroad just in front of Bowman's Ford. Across the ford, not four-hundred-yard distance, were the Federal vedettes. Through the busy night, the Confederates did not raise a sound loud enough to disturb their watch.

A mile west of General Gordon, at Cedar Creek, General Early had joined General Kershaw's Division. He intended to watch its attack on General Crook's front once General Gordon had made the initial assault on

General Crook's left flank. Left of General Kershaw, at Hupp's Hill, was General Breckenridge's old division, now commanded by General Gabriel Wharton. General Wharton's men were to move up the Valley Pike and carry the attack through General Emory's Camp and into General Wright's once the battle had been joined. General Rosser's cavalry was stationed on the left end of the Confederate line. He would begin the assault at 5:00 AM with a feint against General Wright. From that point, his job would be to draw off the powerful Federal cavalry and keep it from passing into the Confederates' rear.

At the center of the Union camp, about a quarter mile back from the front, was Belle Grove Plantation. This was General Sheridan's headquarters. It was also the objective of Colonel W.H. Payne who was posted with General Gordon across Bowman's Ford. With his three hundred horsemen, Colonel Payne's mission was to cordon off the manor and seize the Union commander.

General Rosser's guns sounded at the appointed hour. The fire on the Confederate's left was soon echoed on the right as General Gordon's pickets drove the Union sentries off the ford. General Gordon's brigades pressed forward as confused defenders grabbed their weapons and raced for the trenches on the perimeter of General Crook's camp. Unable to hold themselves back in the face of the thickening fire, the Confederates broke into a charge that carried them over the breastworks, through the Union bivouac, and into General Emory's compound on the west side of the Valley Pike.

Owing to the order of the battle, no significant pressure had been brought to bear on the strongest element of the Union army. General Wright's VI Corp had been roused by General Rosser's demonstration, but had not been struck directly. But the disorder spilling over from General Emory's and General Crook's camps kept it from forming a battle line. Led by General Wright, his chin bloodied by a Confederate bullet, the Sixth withdrew a mile to the north. Then, before the clock struck 9:00, it turned and counterattacked. This proved to be hard work for the Confederates had seized their abandoned artillery and, wheeling the guns round, poured a dense fire of shot and shell into the advancing blue line. This broke their charge. Having failed in this initial assault, the Sixth resumed its withdrawal, but unlike the VIII and XIX Corps, the men did not run. Two miles further back, they re-formed their line. There they waited as General Early and his brigadiers rode forward to survey the situation.

"It's very well so far, General," General Gordon announced, "but we have one more blow to strike and then there will not be left an organized company of infantry in Sheridan's army." General Early listened as General Gordon presented his plan of attack on the waiting Sixth. "No use in that," he replied contentedly. "They will all go directly." General Gordon could see units of cavalry forming on the ends of the Union line. "This is the VI Corp," he protested. "It will not go unless we drive it from the field." But General Early was satisfied that the Yankees had been beaten. "Yes, it will go directly," he repeated calmly, assuming he had defeated General Sheridan. But it was foolhardy of him to think that General Sheridan would quit without a fight.

Back in Winchester, I brought General Sheridan's his horse at 8:45. A little after that the General stepped out onto the porch. His face darkened the moment he laid eyes on the animal. "What is it, Corporal? He demanded without taking his eyes off his mount. "The guns have been firing since before daybreak, Sir." I said, "It's brought up his battle blood."

The General glanced off into the distance and listened. Without saying another word, he mounted Rienzi and set off down the Valley Pike. I seized his pennant and rode off behind him accompanied by Sergeant Edgar. As we passed through the town, we noticed the women—smiling and shaking their skirts. At once we were on guard. They had not shown this defiance the day before when we entered their town. Outside the town the General's escort joined us. They would accompany us the final fifteen miles back to field headquarters. Looking grave, General Sheridan greeted Major Shera with a few brisk words. Then suddenly he handed me his reins and dismounted. The surprised horsemen watched as the General put his ear to the ground and listened. Without speaking, he re-mounted and led the company on in silence. All ears were now trained on the steady rumble of the distant gunfire.

As we came up over the rise at Mill Creek, which was less than a mile from town, we encountered an appalling spectacle—the road stretching out before us was clogged with wagons heading north. "Get up there, Sergeant, and find out what the hell those people think they are doing," the General ordered in a chilling tone. I could not resist joining him.

Galloping forward, we encountered a disheveled old teamster who was sitting on an unhitched mule that had stopped in the middle of the road. The wagoner was kicking and cursing a blue cloud, but the mule would not budge. "What the hell do ya' think you're doin', old man?" Sergeant Edgar demanded. "I'm trying to git this dammed critter moving, sonny. And when

I do, you kin fall in line 'cause your mule-headed army's on its way back to Maryland." The mule suddenly lurched forward and the two of them resumed their flight. A sutler's wagon came clattering past us a moment later. "We bin whupped bad," the fat, red-faced driver yelled as he passed by. "You better git movin' 'cause Johnny's comin' up righ' behine me." That was all Sergeant Edgar needed to hear.

When we reached the General, he was already issuing orders. "Major," he said, "I want your twenty best men. Take the rest and clear this mess off the road. When you're done, post a guard across the creek. Let no one pass except the wagons. You two come with me," he said to me and Sergeant Edgar. "You know what we have to do." He then set off in the direction of the gunfire. Sergeant Edgar and I followed him on either flank. Behind us were the twenty troopers from the 17th. We had not advanced far before signs of the catastrophe began to fill the landscape. Wagons heading north paced by panic-stricken camp followers. Artillerymen without their caissons. Deserters and walking wounded wandering along and in small groups. The fields were covered with the remnants of the Union army. Hovering ominously above the calamity was the sound of gunfire which grew steadily louder.

General Sheridan pressed onward through the confusion, leaving the road, and leading us cross country when the roads were impassable. As we rode on, we passed soldiers sitting around campfires boiling coffee. "Turn back men," the General would shout, waving his soup tureen hat. "Face the other way," he would roar to another cluster as he rode by. The men would see the flag and rise to their feet, many cheering as we passed. Word somehow spread—Sheridan was coming! "Rally 'round the flag," he would yell. "Get up men, and rally round the flag!" I held it high so that it was plain to see. Transformed by the sight, men began picking up their rifles and following us toward the front. "Sheridan! Sheridan!" They cheered as we rode through them. The sound of his name echoed across the valley.

Just south of Newtown, about three quarters of a mile west of the Valley Pike, we came upon General Rickett's and General Wheaton's divisions of the Sixth Corp. To their right and rear was the Nineteenth. The General dispatched Sergeant Edgar to find their commanders. We pressed on without stopping. At last, about a mile north of Middletown we reached the front. General Getty's division, supported by General Torbert's cavalry, had taken a position on the reverse slope on some slightly rising ground behind a barricade of fence rails.

Seeing the General's banner, General Torbert rode up to greet us. "By God! I'm glad you've come," he exclaimed breathlessly. The situation was daunting. A Confederate battle line was formed a few hundred yards across the way and an attack appeared imminent. It took only a moment for the General to assess the situation. "Come with me, Corporal," he ordered. Spurring Rienzi onward, he jumped the barricade and rode to the crest of the hill. I followed him waving the army's most valuable possession. Then, in a defining act of leadership and defiance, the General turned and faced his men. It was the most awesome spectacle. As I watched, he raised his cap and saluted them. They responded by rising up from behind their shelter and giving him a cheer. In this exchange the compact was made. The beleaguered remnant of his army had now become the center of a new battle line.

There was no time to lose. The General retraced his course to the rear of Getty's division where Sergeant Edgar had assembled the army's brigadiers. Behind them I could see a row of new battle flags. These were from General Crook's division which had been dispersed in the first shock of the battle. Establishing his command post on the crest behind General Getty, General Sheridan commenced to deploy his massing troops. Not before midday had General Wright's two divisions and General Emory's Nineteenth taken up their positions to the right of General Getty. As this re-alignment was being completed, General Gordon's Confederates moved forward to renew their attack. Time and events, however, had dissipated the power of the grays and their assault failed without seriously testing our line.

Through the afternoon the two armies continued to face each other. But as the Confederates pulled men away to withdraw their captured stores, more and more of our scattered army re-entered the line. Satisfied that the situation was stable on his left, The General at last sent General Custer to join General Torbert on our right. His orders to the cavalry were to press the Confederate flank. At 4:00 O'clock, we rode out again and the General addressed the army. Once again, hat in hand, waving and cheering, we rode down the line. "Follow your flags boys," he yelled. "We'll whip 'em for good this time!" His words ignited their spirits. Every man there was eager to join him. Together they would soon erase the shame of the morning's defeat.

Shortly after that, a chorus of two hundred bugles sounded the advance. General Getty's division from General Wright's VI Corp opened the *attack on the Confederate's left. Their objective was a pair of knolls about three-hundred-yards distance from our line and about the same distance from the Confederate line. This ground was defended by General Gordon's men. General Gordon had withdrawn only this far after probing the right side of our line earlier in the afternoon, evidently expecting General Early to follow through with a full-scale attack. Had General Early done so, General Gordon's troops would have been in an advantageous position as they would have had two hundred yards less lead to dodge coming at us.*

Now that the shoe had been moved to the other foot, however, they were the more vulnerable to our assault. Worse for them, their line was too thin to withstand a serious challenge. Worse still, the cavalry General Rosser had to shield General Gordon's exposed left flank was far below the strength he needed to deal with the force General Sheridan was about to send against him. The situation was therefore grave for the Confederates. Indeed, it was comparable to Winchester and Fisher's Hill where General Sheridan had routed them by engaging their center, then flanking them on the left with his powerful cavalry. The parallel was clear enough to the troops who advanced to the sound of the 4:00 O'clock bugles. The men seemed to hear their notes as the beginning of a foot race back to the camps from which they had been driven so ignominiously at the break of day.

Our artillery covered General Getty's advance with shot and shell. In spite of a spirited resistance by the rebels, General Getty's men quickly reached the enemy's line and poured through a gap between General Evans and General York's brigades. Soon blue-clad soldiers were massing on the crest of the hill. Seeing their position was lost and recognizing their peril, General Gordon's men abandoned their line and raced for safety on the far side of Cedar Creek. General Sheridan, who was eager to follow the events at the front, accompanied the third wave of General Getty's attack. I, of course, accompanied him with his flag. We proceeded to the crest where General Getty was reorganizing his line for another attack. From there we could see the assault by General Emory's XIX Corp on the center of the Confederate line. General Kershaw's and General Ramseur's brigades were dealing General Emory's men a killing fire from behind an improvised stone wall. Unable to dislodge them, General Emory's assault was in danger of failing.

General Sheridan bristled at the set back and unleashed a string of colorful oaths. Having blunted the edge on his anger, he sent Sergeant Edgar over to General Getty with orders to suspend his attack until General Custer had dispersed the Confederate cavalry on our right. The General then sent me out to find General Custer. Before I could leave, he grabbed the pennant out of my hand and planted it in the center of the new line.

General Custer had already formed his division when I reached him. He was bursting with excitement, which I assumed derived from the prospect of having another shot at General Rosser, who had been his classmate at West Point. I soon learned that there was more to it than that. It seems that General Custer, having tasted the fruit at Trevilian Station, was anxious to resume foraging in the Confederates' rear. So eager was he to have his way on this that he meant to plead his case personally to General Sheridan. He accompanied me back to the General. As we proceeded, he rehearsed his speech. When he saw General Sheridan's standard, he left me and galloped on to where the General stood. Being entirely consumed with the glory that he was about to garner for himself, his brain was too full for such triflings as military protocol. Reining his horse at the General's feet, he leaped from his saddle. General Sheridan turned in time to see his lieutenant hit the ground beside him. Instead of offering a proper salute, General Custer threw his arms around the General's neck as if he meant to kiss him. The sight was mortifying to behold!

General Sheridan was a good deal smaller than General Custer, but he possessed strength far in excess of his size. Outraged by the affront, he struck a blow that sent his subordinate sprawling. "By God Custer, if you lay your hands on me again, I'll have you guarding baggage until your precious hair falls out." The rebuke made no impression on General Custer. Instead, he gathered himself up and commenced with his speech promoting the expedition he envisioned behind the enemy's line. "You clear out Early's cavalry," General Sheridan snapped. "After that, I suppose you can find something else to do." General Custer gave out with an Indian whoop and, leaping on his horse, galloped off in search of his glory. In the ensuing attack, General Custer dispersed General Rosser's over-matched guard. At this point he moved to the enemy's rear. This marked the beginning of another Confederate rout.

The men holding the center of the Confederate line could see the hill on their flank filling with soldiers in blue uniforms. This caused the gray line to waver. When General Custer's cavalry suddenly appeared in their rear, panic set in. *This was the moment General Sheridan had been waiting for. I was standing beside him with his second horse—Breckenridge—at the ready. He snatched the reins out of my hands, leaped into his saddle, and charged off at a gallop down the front of the hill toward General Emory's division. I grabbed his standard and followed him into the center of the battle. He was like a dervish spinning about madly waving his hat and calling for the troops to move forward. Responding eagerly, they were soon over the stone wall and snapping at the heels of the scattering rebels. Had not some stout-hearted units of Confederate artillery obstructed us, we would have finished off General Early's army then and there. As it was, the chaos which overwhelmed the Confederate ranks soon communicated into our own. Darkness fell with our exhausted men stumbling back into the camps they had so deserted at daybreak.*

General Sheridan returned to his Belle Grove headquarters shortly after dark. Taking up a position on the mansion's porch, he paced back and forth like a caged tiger as he listened to reports from his field commanders. He continued in this way for several hours, during which time stretcher bearers continued to bring in the wounded. Indeed, our victory was costly. We had suffered twice as many casualties as our defeated opponents with our killed and wounded exceeding fifty-three hundred men. Despite this staggering toll, the mood at headquarters was distinctly festive. Some officers—I believe they were from General Crook's command as they had seen little action during the bloody afternoon—built a bonfire and commenced a celebration. They were dancing and cavorting like aborigines in the crackling light of their bonfire when General Custer arrived.

He was leading a great caravan of wagons and guns that he had taken behind the enemy's line. They rolled into the camp in an endless procession. General Custer directed that they be parked around the mansion where they would not escape the General's notice. Spying him there on the porch, he sprang off his horse and bounded up the steps. "By God, Phil," he shouted, wrapping his arms around the General's waist and lifting him into the air like his beloved sweetheart, "I've cleaned them out, haven't I!" So brazen was he in his self-promotion that the General was mute in stupefaction. Sergeant Edgar and I were standing near General Emory and heard him say to an aide. "That young man is going to make a name for himself—if we don't watch out." The Sergeant leaned over and whispered in my ear, "That son of a bitch 'ud be a memory now if we hadn't saved him at Trevilian Station." Time proved him right about General Custer was right. He was too selfish to be great.

Four days after the battle, Assistant Secretary of War Dana arrived with a prize from President Lincoln. It was well after midnight when I roused the General from his sleep. After a handsome speech that General Sheridan mostly slept through, Secretary Dana presented him with a paper signed by President Lincoln announcing his promotion to the rank of Major General in the regular army. This was indeed to be coveted as it assured the General's place in the army for as long as he cared to serve. The General shook hands with the Secretary then returned to bed. Sergeant Edgar was more excited about the promotion than the General himself, as he was the General's most loyal supporter.

Having defeated his enemy, General Grant wanted General Sheridan to move east of the Blue Ridge and to apply himself disrupting transportation on the Virginia Central Railroad. The General had little enthusiasm for this as there was slight prospect for success and a strong likelihood of failure conducting a winter campaign deep in enemy territory. Instead, he responded to General Halleck's request to break up Colonel Mosby's band of partisans who had continued to menace Union supply lines since the beginning of General Grant's southern offensive. He sent General Merritt with the First Division across the Blue Ridge to Loudoun County were his "Burning Raid" destroyed a million dollars of property, most belonging to non-belligerent Quakers. Having made this gesture, General Sheridan announced that the problem was solved and re-called his men. From that point, his attention was fixed on preparing his army for winter.

As if to confirm his intention to remain in camp until spring, the General sent General Wright's VI Corp back to General Grant at the end of November. This did not placate General Grant, who continued to prod General Sheridan to do something about the Virginia Central Railroad. Finally, on December 19th, the General responded with a plan to sweep through the central Virginia countryside in a two-pronged operation to destroy tracks and bridges. General Torbert was to lead the First and Second Divisions of his cavalry across the Blue Ridge Mountains at Chester Gap and proceed down the eastern side of the mountains through Gordonsville and Charlottesville. From there he was to proceed to Lynchburg where he would make a link with General Custer. General Custer was to take the Third Division up the Valley to Staunton and Waynesboro, then cross the Blue Ridge at Rockfish Gap.

From there he was to follow a parallel course with General Torbert before meeting him in Lynchburg.

No sooner had the men gone off than the weather turned bad. General Torbert got through Gordonsville but bogged down when the local militia burned the bridge over the Rapidan at Liberty Mills. Concluding that fording the river was impractical due to the bad weather and the presence of the enemy, General Torbert resolved to turn back. His retreat was complicated by the arrival of two brigades of infantry sent up by General Lee to re-enforce the militia. When he finally reached camp, he had with him two pieces of Confederate artillery. Acquiring them had cost him one hundred and two casualties and two hundred and fifty-eight horses lost.

General Custer boasted before setting off on his part of the expedition that he would spend Christmas eve in Lynchburg. As it turned out, he failed to reach Harrisonburg. On his second day out, as reveille sounded in his Lacey Springs camp, General Rosser led a fiery charge of rebel cavalry through his classmate's camp. The startled Federals scattered long enough for the revenge-seeking Confederates to escape with a bounty of horses and supplies. Finding prospects of this sort of guerilla warfare unpalatable as winter fare, General Custer abandoned the mission and marched back to camp. Since General Sheridan had not championed the operation, he said little about its failure.

I had little to do until the army broke camp on February 27th. I spent a lot of time talking with Sergeant Edgar. He told me that I was lucky to be with General Sheridan as it was safer in the Valley than fighting in the trenches with General Grant. He said that more men were dying from diseases in the trenches around Richmond than were being killed by Confederates. When his time came, he said he would be happy to go leading a charge. He seemed to see that as a suitable end for a Westerner.

The Sergeant expected the war to end soon. When I asked him what made him thinks so, he said that the Confederates were out of men. Of course, that had been General Grant's plan from the beginning, so he looked pretty smart. The Sergeant expected General Sheridan to join back up with General Grant when the weather cleared. That way he would be there to share the victory when the rebellion went down. That was important to Sergeant Edgar, too. He had been fighting for four years and said that he had earned the privilege.

I asked him why it mattered, seeing that he might still be killed. He said, "Son, a man ain't nothin' if he ain't got a cause." The General's was good with

Sergeant Edgar. For some reason that set me to thinking about General Custer and how different he was from the General Sheridan and Sergeant Edgar. The thing about General Custer that stood out most clearly to me was his concern for himself. That's how I understood what the Sergeant meant. Men of worth see a broader horizon and take on causes larger than themselves.

The Sergeant was not like the men I came down with from the north. He was not fixed on conquering the South or reconstructing rebels. He was focused on some bigger idea, and he was certain that the General was going to help him find it. Doing his soldierly duty was his way of keeping the road clear. "I can git it done, whatever it is," he announced proudly. He called it his "natural cussedness" and said that it was just the way folks were in the West.

I knew he meant to go back there after the war. "America's future is waitin' ta be found out thar, boy." That was the way he put it. That's why he expected the General to go west after the war. Listening to Sergeant Edgar, I knew that nothing compared to it. It had plains that reached to the horizon and buffalo herds that were too large to count. It had sparkling rivers filled with gold and mountains that touched the sky. It was an empire waiting to be claimed. "If ya' b'have yourself, boy, you can come along," he said. I couldn't wait to get started.

General Sheridan had grown wholesomely sick of the Shenandoah Valley. When General Grant called him to back come to Richmond, he was ready to go. We broke camp at dawn on February 27th. By this time, our force had been reduced to about ten thousand men. These included our three cavalry divisions and some units of artillery. General Torbert's failure at Liberty Mills had finished him as one of General Sheridan's brigadier. The General left him in the Valley with a broken-down regiment of cavalry, having given his division to General Devin. The Second Division, which was given to General Merritt, would lead the column. The Third Division was led by General Custer.

We marched up the Valley in pelting rain. On our second day out, we crossed the north fork of the Shenandoah River at Mt. Jackson. General Rosser tried to slow us down by burning the covered bridge across the river's south fork, but General Sheridan flanked him by fording a regiment across the swollen river. Nine men drowned in the crossing, but we drove the rebels off and repaired the bridge without significant delay. Two days later we reached Staunton.

General Sheridan intended to cross the Blue Ridge at Rockfish Gap. General Early indicated that he would oppose this crossing by deploying his

army—now only about two thousand men—in our path outside of Waynes-
boro. The position he selected proved to be a bad one as the Shenandoah River
was close behind his line. General Sheridan was eager to fight and dispatched
General Custer's division to attack him. As it turned out, we had assistance
from three rebel deserters who knew the area. They guided General Custer to a
path that led through the woods behind the Confederate line. General Custer
dismounted three of his regiments and sent them on this path. These troops
uprooted the left end of the Confederate line just as General Custer attacked
across its front with the rest of his division. The Confederates broke and scat-
tered, but being hemmed in by the river, found themselves trapped.

General Early had ridden up the mountain to the east of Waynesboro to
get a better view of the terrain. When he looked down from his perch, he saw
his army marching off into captivity. It was a sad end for such brave men.

About this time, I went out on a mission with Colonel Forsythe. He
wanted to pay his respects to a woman who lived in the city. He referred to
her as Mrs. Gallaher. She had been kind to him and his men during their
imprisonment in the area after Battle of Cross Keys in 1862. Now events had
come around to where he could repay her kindnesses.

We were coming up to a crossroad not far from her house when a rider
galloped across our path with such reckless abandon it appeared he was trying
to outrun the Devil himself. No sooner had he passed by than a squadron of
our cavalry came on shooting and shouting like a mob of banshees. We spurred
our horses and set out after them. About a mile on we found them. The fugi-
tive's horse had tripped jumping a fence to the side of the road, and he was on
the ground peering up at his captors. It looked like the end had come for the
poor fellow, but as the Colonel came forward, he flashed him a hand signal,
which Colonel Forsythe later explained was a secret sign of the Order of Ma-
sons. As luck would have it, the Colonel was a Mason himself. When he saw
this sign, he went up beside the man and took charge of him. "Put your guns
up soldiers," he ordered. "This man is my prisoner." The men weren't happy to
hear this, but nothing came of their grumbling. We got the fugitive back on his
horse and were soon on our way once more to Mrs. Gallaher's.

That was not the end of the adventure though. Our prisoner was dressed
in civilian clothes and by his manner was plainly a gentleman. As we road
along, he introduced himself as Doctor Hunter Maguire, formerly surgeon
on General Thomas Jackson's staff. He was now supervising treatment for the

Confederate soldiers who were convalescing in the vicinity of Waynesboro. I learned during supper that Dr. Maguire had attended General Jackson at the time of his fatal wounding and had performed the amputation on his shattered right arm.

It so happened that he had been at the home of Mrs. Gallaher when the patrol appeared. Circumstances being as they were, he became alarmed and had taken flight. As the battle was now over and his services were required, he asked Colonel Forsythe for a parole so that he might resume his humanitarian duties. Colonel Forsythe readily consented and scribbled his parole as we rode along. At that point, the question arose, into whose custody he was to be released. Since we were on the way to Mrs. Gallaher's, and being that, by the hand of Providence, she was well-known to both men, Dr. Maguire suggested that he be paroled to her household. This was done as we proceeded on to that very place.

The timing of our arrival was indeed fortuitous as a band of scavengers was swarming about the poor woman's house and barns. She was standing on her porch watching them helplessly when we appeared in her yard. The spectacle so outraged the Colonel that he drew his pistol and fired off several shots. "Onward men," he shouted in a stentorian voice. "Show them no mercy!" I took that as an order, and drawing my pistol, commenced to race about the enclave whooping and shooting as if I were an entire company. That was more than enough for those cowardly scoundrels. They set off in a panic and disappeared without looking back.

Of course, this happened all at once. Being overwhelmed by the sequence of events, Mrs. Gallaher broke down in a fit of tears. Her effusions were so great that it was heart-wrenching to behold. After a bit, Doctor Maguire was able to comfort her, and she regained her composure. It was a relief for her then to describe her ordeal. During the battle, which took place not far from her house, she and her cook, who she called Mammy Sally, hid in her cellar. As the firing subsided, they crept out in time to witness the capture of fourteen Confederate soldiers who had sought refuge on the porch where she now stood. Doctor Maguire arrived soon after that trying to find General Rosser, who's troops had not been present at the battle. No sooner had he appeared than the patrol came into view. As they raced off to some unknown fate, the scavengers descended upon her. Being alone and defenseless, all seemed lost. Then she straightened up and announced in a resolute voice, "But all things conspire to the good for those who love God. For look, we have been delivered and Doctor Maguire is alive and well here with us."

Doctor Maguire described the circumstances of our meeting and, as the Colonel had acquainted him with the nature of our visit, he took this as an opportunity to re-introduce the Colonel to his former benefactress. Recognizing the gallant Union officer for first time, she burst again into tears and threw her arms around his neck. For a long moment, she held him in a grateful embrace. Then she released him and, stepping away, dried her eyes with her apron. "Please excuse my lapse," she said with the dignity of the Queen's Lady in Waiting.

Colonel Forsythe ordered me to stand guard with the horses, then joined Doctor Maguire in the parlor. Shortly after that, Mrs. Gallaher retired to the cookhouse, which was in a building directly behind the residence. I stationed myself outside the kitchen window where I could enjoy the fragrances as they emanated forth. I could imagine the feast that would soon be served. As it was now towards evening and I had not eaten since before dawn, I was nearly starved. However, before the call to supper came, Colonel Forsythe stepped out onto the porch. "Corporal," he said, handing me an envelope, "take this to the duty officer at headquarters. I want you to bring a squad of troopers back here on the double." My heart sank at the prospect of leaving without so much as tasting Mrs. Gallaher's home cooked meal. I mounted sullenly and was about to depart when she appeared in the cookhouse door. "Now Colonel," she scolded in a sweet but firm voice, "it will do no harm for that young man to have his supper before going on. Have you forgotten how hungry you were the last time I fed you?" He reddened slightly and bowed. "You're perfectly right, Madam. He shall have his supper." The meal I had that night was as fine as any I ever ate.

During supper, Mrs. Gallaher remarked how much I resembled her son Clinton, who was serving in the Confederate cavalry as a courier to General Rosser. She was very concerned about him, having heard nothing from him in the past several days. The Colonel was able to provide her some small comfort in the intelligence that General Rosser's regiment had been south of Staunton during the day's battle and had played no part in it. Then changing the subject with diplomatic skill, the Colonel asked his hostess about the certificate in the parlor. Mrs. Gallaher told him that it belonged to her husband who was a Knight Templars. The Colonel then astonished us all when he explained that *he was a Knight Templars in the same order as Mrs. Gallaher's husband. Mr. Gallaher was in Richmond at the time supervising the distribution of goods he had managed to bring through the blockage. This news did not phase the Colonel, who accepted it as his sacred obligation to protect the family and the property of his fraternal brother. Understanding the situation, I finished my dinner and set out on my mission.*

When I returned later that night, I found the Colonel engrossed in conversation with Doctor Maguire and Mrs. Gallaher as though there had never been a war. The kindness and consideration these Americans showed each another, even though they were on opposing sides of a cruel and bloody conflict, made an indelible impression on me. I shall always revere that great and noble woman, whose faith allowed her to extend the hand of friendship and good will, even to her enemies.

The next day we marched over the mountains and entered Charlottesville. This lovely town, the home of Thomas Jefferson and the University of Virginia, which he had founded forty years before the rebellion, had been spared the ravages of war. The mayor of the city and the President of the University led a delegation of citizens to meet us outside the town. There they surrendered the city—keys and all—to General Sheridan. Being that his primary objective was to disrupt rail traffic into Richmond, General Sheridan did not disturb the city. Indeed, we spent a peaceful night in the dormitories of the university before pushing south toward Lynchburg the next day.

Earlier in the war Charlottesville had been an important railroad junction as two rail lines crossed there. The Virginia Central Railroad was the primary link between Richmond and the Shenandoah Valley. It extended from Covington, which lay at the western extremity of the Valley through Charlottesville and Gordonsville then over to Hanover Junction and down to its terminus in Richmond. The Orange and Alexandria, which originated in Alexandria, ran south through Orange and Charlottesville, and terminated in Lynchburg. As we now controlled the Valley and all regions of the state north of Orange, and as we also held the area north and east of Richmond, there was scant opportunity for the Virginia Central to provide much support to the army in Richmond. However, the situation was different in Lynchburg. The Virginia and Tennessee Railroad ran from Tennessee across the southwest part of the state and terminated there. The Southside Railroad met it in Lynchburg and continued on to Petersburg. Provisions were therefore being gathered in the central and southwestern parts of the state and shipped to General Lee through Lynchburg. As it was the more important target, General Sheridan was determined to capture it and severe Richmond's rail link to the west. Once he had accomplished this the General planned to march east along the railroad line and link General Grant outside Petersburg.

As we prepared to leave Charlottesville, the General received word that the garrison at Lynchburg was being re-enforced. This was troubling news as it meant that our cavalry would have to attack entrenched infantry deep in the enemy's heartland. Despite this information, the General divided his force into two columns to increase the destruction of tracks and bridges on the Orange and Alexandria as the army marched south. Two days later we arrived in Amherst, a small hamlet about fifteen miles north of our destination. General Sheridan halted us there to evaluate the situation. Reports he received confirmed that General Lee had sent several regiments of infantry to support the local militia and that they had burned the bridges across the James to the north of the city. In addition to that, as there had been a week of heavy rain, it appeared that the river at Lynchburg was too high to ford. General Sheridan therefore decided to abandon his attack on Lynchburg and move directly to his juncture with General Grant.

It took us about two weeks to cross the center of the state. Skirting Richmond to the north, we followed the Pamunkey River down to White House which we finally reached on March 19th. Despite the absence of Confederate opposition, the expedition had been an extremely hard one. Fortunately, General Grant anticipated our needs and had a healthy store of food and forage, and blacksmiths waiting for us. We spent the next ten days resting and refitting.

General Grant's greatest concern at this time was that General Lee would evacuate the capital and complete a link with General Johnston who was retreating northward ahead of General Sherman's Army of the Cumberland. He was therefore anxious for our cavalry to get back in the saddle and move to the right of the Confederate line where he would be in position to strike either the enemy's exposed flank or the Southside Railroad. As this was the only rail link that remained between the Confederate army and the world beyond Petersburg, if General Lee was to make good his escape, it would have to be down these lonely tracks.

We set out for Dinwiddie Court House on the morning of the 29th. Torrential rains had turned the thoroughfares into rivers of mud, but we managed to reach our destination in the afternoon of the 30th. The Din-widdie Court House Road ran from this dilapidated collection of buildings northwest through Five Forks and on up to the Southside Railroad. As soon as we reached Dinwiddie Court House, General Sheridan ordered General Devin to determine if the enemy had taken up a position at Five Forks. At the same time, he ordered General Crook to move up the Boydton Plank Road which ran from Dinwiddie Court House northeast into Petersburg.

The General received word at his headquarters at Dinwiddie Court House that General Pickett had been dispatched to defend the railroad. Reports from General Crook confirmed that there was a gap to the left of the Confederate fortifications at Dabney's Mill and General Pickett, wherever he might be. This intelligence settled the General on establishing himself in the gap to isolate General Pickett's force from the rest of the General Lee's army. As General Sheridan developed his plan, General Grant watched the sea of mud rising about his headquarters and concluded that General Sheridan could accomplish nothing of value until the roads dried. He therefore sent an order to General Sheridan, instructing him to secure his position with what troops he needed and to send the rest of his force back to General Grant. When General Sheridan received this communication, he flew into a rage and ordered me to saddle Breckinridge. Then, together, we set off for General Grant's headquarters at Gravelly Run where the General intended to appraise the commander of the army as to the seriousness of the "mistake" in his recall order.

In our haste, we sped by one of our infantry pickets without saluting. They responded by opening fire on us. Fortunately, they missed—though not by much. We finally reached the mud-clogged compound that was General Grant's headquarters. General Sheridan charged into his commander's tent and began at once to set matters straight. During the entirety of his speech, no one uttered a word. He finished his peroration by assuring General Grant and his staff that if he were given infantry, he would either crush Lee's right flank or force him to weaken his line enough for General Grant to break into Petersburg. Then, as if to suppress quibbling objections, he smacked his fist into his palm and growled, "I'm ready to strike out tomorrow and go smashing things!" None of the officers who heard his speech raised any objections. General Grant conferred privately with him for a few minutes then said, "We will go on."

The General said very little during our return trip, but I could tell by *the set of his jaw that he was pleased. On our way back to Dinwiddie Court House, we passed through the camp of the Fifth Corp which was under the command of General Warren. As this was the infantry nearest to us, General Sheridan stopped to pay his respects to its commander. Although it was the middle of the afternoon, we learned that General Warren was asleep. This astonished and dismayed General Sheridan who seemed to gain strength the more sleep he lost. As it turned out, this midday nap was a foreshadowing of the General's lethargic performance on the battlefield.*

We arrived back in camp late in the afternoon. A report was waiting from General Merritt, which informed the General that General Pickett had been re-enforced with five brigades taken from the defensive line south of Petersburg. This increased the uncertainty about our attack on the morrow but did not dissuade the General from setting his plan motion.

At dawn on the 31st, General Devin led his division about five miles up the Dinwiddie Court House Road to Five Forks. He reached the crossroads without incident but found upon his arrival that his rapid advance had separated him from the rest of our force. General Pickett, who had formed a battle line among the trees west of the crossroads, struck General Devin at mid-afternoon. As General Pickett's infantry attacked the center of General Devin's division, General Fitzhugh Lee's cavalry moved south across Chamberlain's Creek and went into position to cut off General Devin's path of escape. General Sheridan responded to this crisis by ordering General Crook, whose division straddled the Boydton Plank Road north of the Dinwiddie Court House, to shift to the west where he could meet any advance made by Fitzhugh Lee's cavalry. With this assistance, General Devin managed to withdraw from his exposed position and form on the left of General Crook's line. General Pickett then wheeled right and attacked them.

At this point, General Custer, who had been bringing up the supply trains, reached the front and struck the Confederate left. This sudden development caused General Pickett to halt his assault to re-assess the situation. General Sheridan, who had been watching developments from a position on the right side of our line, saw the Confederate line waver under General Custer's attack. Interpreting this as an opportunity, he took off across the front urging General's Crook's troops to join General Custer's attack. I followed him with his flag, dodging bullets and mud holes. For all his fire and brimstone, the General's efforts proved in vain. The Confederate center was strong, and as the ground was soaking, the footing was treacherous. And so, night fell with the two sides facing each other in close quarters.

General Lee had sent General Pickett out from behind the Confederate defenses to defend the Southside Railroad. This was, as I say, the only remaining escape route available to the Confederate army so it was imperative they keep it open. Five Forks was about two miles from the rail junction and in the direct path of General Sheridan's line of march. General Lee therefore had no doubt where the Federals intended to strike. General Pickett had a force of about ten thousand men to deal with General Sheridan's thirteen thousand mounted infantry. General Pickett's force might have been sufficient had he been able to remain on the defensive but fighting as he was in open country against a highly mobile foe, he could not simply wait to be attacked. The offensive maneuvering he undertook therefore made sense—accept for two things. First, he had no prospects for reinforcements from the main Confederate army. And second, General Warren was marching his seventeen thousand man Fifth Corp into the gap at the extreme right of the Petersburg line and would soon be in position to strike.

General Pickett realized the danger he faced in the position he held at the end of the day on the 31st. During the pre-dawn hours of the 1st, he therefore drew his men back from their exposed position outside Dinwiddie Court House to the vicinity of his original position at Five Forks. His new position was an earthwork that stretched along the White Oak Road about mile on the west side of the intersection with the Dinwiddie Road and another half mile on the east side of the intersection. General Sheridan responded with his own realignment. He brought General Custer's division around behind General Crook and General Devin and formed it on the left so that it overlapped the Confederate right. In this formation, the hostilities resumed when the sun rose on April 1st. General Custer opened the engagement with a demonstration on the Confederate's right. They were in a strong position and easily resisted this assault. However, the Fifth Corp was coming up and would soon strike them on their left, which was the weakest part of their line.

The problem facing the grays was magnified by one of those chance happenings that so often decides the course of events. Having successfully withdrawn his forces into a strong defensive position, General Pickett accepted an invitation from General Rosser to attend a shad bake at Hatcher's Run about a mile behind the Confederate line. During his absence, General Sheridan sent General Merritt's dismounted division into position opposite General Pickett's left with orders to hold it until General Warren's Fifth Corp arrived. General Pickett's absence from the front kept his brigadiers from responding to the changing situation, which continued to deteriorate through the morning.

At daybreak, the first of General Warren's units arrived at Dinwiddie Court House. General Sheridan waited impatiently for the General himself to arrive and was about wrung out when he finally appeared at midday. In the meantime, his men continued to form behind General Merritt. Having finally found his man, General Sheridan took him aside and, with all the passion he could harness, explained the urgency of the situation. The problem was, in the General's estimation, that unless General Pickett could be defeated before darkness set in, he might move his army out of harm's way. Now that his battle blood was up, the General viewed this as a looming disaster. The only way to avoid it, in the General's estimation, was for General Warren to strike the Confederates and overrun their positions before darkness set in.

General Sheridan had reached the end of his tether when General Warren finally ordered the Fifth Corp to attack at 4:00 O'clock. In its first phase, the attack was a disaster. General Crawford and General Griffin marched north beyond the enemy's position and took themselves out of the battle entirely. This left General Ayres, who led the left wing of General Warren's line, without support. As the Confederates could concentrate their fire on these men, the assault soon stalled. Seeing this, the General's frustration got the best of him. "By God!" He raged. "Where's my battle flag?" Reading the mind of his commander and fearing the consequences of a rash act, Sergeant Edgar snatched the banner out of my hand and charged forward into the eye of the battle. "Edgar!" The General roared to no avail. "Where the hell does he think he's going?" This was the only time I ever saw the General appear unsure about what to do.

We all watched the banner as it advanced through the lines. We saw the momentum begin to swing forward as the men of the Fifth Corp followed General Griffin's men toward the Confederate trenches. Then suddenly the flag disappeared, and the advance once again stalled. That was when I heard Sergeant Edgar's call. I spurred my horse and shot forward across the littered field toward the point where the flag had fallen. Men swirled past me like leaves in a windstorm. The cloud of discharged gun powder thickened as I advance into the maelstrom until it seemed that I was enshrouded in darkness.

Onward I charged, trusting in Providence to protect and guide me on my way. Then suddenly, I saw a dim light shining through the darkness. There was General's red and white pennant—and Sergeant Edgar! He was lying on his side, his tunic soaked in blood, struggling with the last ounces of his strength to keep the flag aloft. I leaped from my horse and knelt down beside him. With a great effort, he focused on my face. His eyes seemed to brighten for a moment. "Tell me, boy, are they over the top?" Before I could answer, he coughed up a mouthful of blood and slumped over. I grabbed the flag from his hand and leaped back on my horse. It was up to me now. I was determined to finish the job.

"Rally 'round the flag boys." I heard the words echoing across the narrow seam that separated me from the enemy. I could see them behind their earthworks, their faces blackened and taut with the strain of battle. Without hope or fear, they raged against the oncoming tide of death. I leaped the barrier and descended amongst them like a dark angel, come to carry them off. The confusion surrounding me was overwhelming. Bodies and objects and noises crushed together into a frenzy of violence that is impossible to describe. Then, suddenly, it was quiet.

The next thing I saw was the General's face. His expression was different from our first encounter. It was tense and full of care. As I looked more closely at him, he smiled. "Well then Paige, you're with us after all!" His comment seemed odd until I realized that we were no longer on the field. Indeed, I was in a bed—with white sheets! "Did they make it over the top?" I asked. "Yes," he answered proudly. "They followed the flag and carried the day." "And Sergeant Edgar?" "Sergeant Edgar has been called to his reward, God bless him," he answered fiercely. I felt tears welling up in my eyes. "Now wait a minute son." The General protested, "There's no reason to begrudge him his glory! He answered his call. By God! He's a hero—as are you, my brave lad. It was your incomparable display of courage that turned the tide." He took my hand and stroked it gently. "America will be great as long as men like you and Sergeant Edgar have the courage to face down death for the good their country." The delegation behind him murmured an affirmation. "When you're ready to leave this place," he continued, "we have work to do." "We do?" I asked hopefully. "Yes. We're going West, Sergeant. That's where America's future lies!"

A tall man in a black suit stepped forward. General Sheridan snapped to attention and gave a crisp salute. I knew from his chin whiskers that it was

President Lincoln. "Sergeant Paige," the President began in a quiet, reassuring voice. "I have come here today on behalf of a grateful nation to thank you for acts of bravery above and beyond the call of duty. Your self-sacrificing leadership in the face of enemy fire was instrumental in accomplishing his final military defeat. In recognition of your unselfish love of country it is my privilege to ward to you the highest honor this nation can bestow." With that he handed me the Congressional Medal of Honor. As the observers applauded and a band played the National Anthem, President Lincoln placed his hand on my shoulder and closed his eyes as if in prayer. "With peace now at hand," he continued, "it is my fervent prayer that you fully recover from your wounds. More than that, I pray that you will find ways to apply your bountiful gifts in helping your wounded country to overcome the divisions that have caused such great suffering for all its citizens."

Sergeant," he said, "our most difficult battles will always lie ahead. Our future will always depend on the men who carry our flag. May they always be men like you." He turned to General Sheridan, who handed him a small package. President Lincoln turned back and handed me the red and white banner I had taken from Sergeant Edgar. "God Bless you, Sergeant Paige, and God Bless America." He then stepped back. The ceremony was over, and I was an American!

Claire put the book down and looked out across the valley. *Rally 'round the flag boys.* The words echoed in her mind.

She tried to envision Raymond Paige in this context, but her concentration was broken by the sound of tires crushing gravel behind the crest of the hill. A moment later a car rolled into view. She watched it coast down the hill and stop in front of the gate. The driver's door opened, and Tim Hardin climbed out.

"Hey baby, looks like you hit the jackpot." He sidled up to the gate and eased the latch. His eyes remained fixed on Claire as he crossed the yard. She started to get up, but he was already mounting the porch steps.

"What do you mean?" She answered defiantly, settling back in her chair.

Hardin walked over to the porch rail next to Claire and surveyed the view. "Mmm Mmm . . . so this is where Tilghman gets all those big ideas."

"Tim . . ." Claire said, cutting him off.

"Yea." He turned casually and faced her.

"Don't ever touch me again."

"Hey . . ." He raised his hand and shook his head. "You don't have to say it. I came to apologize." His became serious. His eyes filled with something that might have been guilt. "I made a mistake. I'm sorry." He waited as Claire weighed his apology. "Please," he continued, "don't judge me on one mistake."

Claire stared at him fiercely without answering.

"Claire," he said again, appealing to her, "our work is too important to let a regrettable accident come between us."

She continued to stare at him, watching his eyes.

"Let me explain . . ."

She realized to her horror that she was becoming confused. She looked away. "Ok," she said at last.

"Thank you." It sounded as though a great burden had lifted from his shoulders. Claire looked back at him. He was smiling—like nothing had happened. "Got any more of that tea?" he inquired cheerfully.

Tea! What's going on, she wondered, looking once more to see the message in his eyes. She was too late. Hardin had already turned and stepped to the door. "In the kitchen, right?" he said as he disappeared inside.

"Beside the sink," she added, letting the issue die. She tugged her shirt down over her knees and slid deeper into the chair. A moment later Hardin reappeared with a cup in his hand.

"Did Henry tell you I was here?" Claire asked pointedly.

"That wild man?" Hardin touched his swollen eye. "He'd rather slit my throat."

"Who told you, then?" Claire demanded.

"Gerta told me," he answered absent-mindedly.

"How did she know?"

Hardin sipped his tea. "Gerta and Aster Paige are old friends—didn't Tilghman tell you that either?" He sounded disgusted.

"How would he know that?" Claire demanded, still not satisfied.

"Forget about Tilghman!" The cheerfulness was gone from his voice. "We're talking about something way out of his league."

"You've done all the talking so far," Claire answered. "What are *we* supposed to be talking about?"

Hardin treated the question as an invitation and sat down. He became very serious. "Paige has gotten hold of an important collection of papers."

"De Riedesel's Journal . . ."

"Yes."

"What makes you so interested in it?"

"It contains the only existing copy of Jefferson's lost constitution.'

"Henry said it doesn't exist."

"I know for a fact that Paige has it."

"Why would Henry lie about it?"

"Because he's Paige's lackey, and Paige doesn't want the public to know it exists."

"It seems like the Jefferson Academy would want to publicize it."

Hardin shook his head impatiently. "You gotta get past the facade and see what's really going on. Jefferson's constitution is a threat to these people. You see? Paige is afraid of what it stands for."

"What does it stand for?"

Hardin leaned forward as if to tell her his inner-most secret. As he did, she saw the medallion on the chain around his neck.

"It stands for the victory of the common man over the moneyed grabbers," he said. "This document defines the government we would have had if Jefferson had been here in 1787."

"What's wrong with the one we have?" she asked skeptically.

"It's an insult to the American people!" Hardin's eyes flashed in sudden rage. "It's a property system invented by Hamilton and Madison. They pushed us into an unending competition for material possessions—and guess who gets them all?" Hardin sneered. "The men with the dough—guys like Paige! They like to quote Jefferson because they want the public to think that we've realized his vision. They don't mention that Jefferson rejected the entire market concept because it was exploitative. He intended for society to be free from this insidious form of oppression. He wasn't like the others. He cared about the health and well-being of the people . . . ."

"That was two hundred years ago," Claire protested. "You can't just . . ."

"That's where you're wrong, Claire. It's not just our right. It's our *duty* to make this country a fit place for human beings to live." He took a deep breath. "They can't articulate their feelings about this in so many words, but the vast majority of Americans share Jefferson's vision. They know the system we have is a piece of shit. They know that it's ruining their lives and their environment. They know they haven't got any say in how decisions are made. They know they have no control over the decision-making process. They know they're nothing but pawns for men like Paige. The only reason they haven't junked it is because they don't know what to replace it with." He looked into her eyes, searching for a reflected light. "Now do you see? Jefferson's constitution is the missing piece! It's the spark that's going to detonate the *Aquarian* revolution." The words lingered in her ears.

"You think the American people will accept it?" Claire asked, unable to extract herself from his web.

"All we need to do is explain it to them," he said reassuringly. "Every time they turn on their televisions. Every time they pick up their newspapers, you'll be there telling them about it. They'll understand. They know their rights. They deserve to have a government that cares about them and solves their problems. Look, they trust me, Claire. And you trust you! They know we're on their side. If we tell them that we've found Thomas Jefferson's plan for a society that honors the common man, they'll believe us."

"Then what?" Claire asked pensively.

He stood up and began to pace along the rail. "We'll form a citizens' committee... We'll demand the resignations of the President and the Congress... We'll organize a march on Washington ... We'll shut the place down ... I'll lead a million citizens up Pennsylvania Avenue to the Capital." He was lost in his vision. "Clear 'em out ... Clear 'em out ... Clear 'em out," he chanted, pumping his fist into the air with each refrain. "I'll run up the steps of the Capital and try to reason with them. Clear 'em out, they'll roar. No ... Wait, I'll say. This is America." He giggled at the joke. "Clear 'em out ... Clear 'em out ... Clear 'em out ... Ok! I'll say, placating them ... I understand. What do you want me to tell them?" One Hour ... One Hour ... One Hour." He looked down at Claire. "I'll tell them they have one hour to get the hell out of town. They'll be in their limo's heading to National Airport before I finish the sentence." His eyes brightened with anticipation. "I'll be like Gandhi! The power will be with the people and the people will be with me.

"When the government collapses, I'll arrange for a plebiscite to ratify

Jefferson's constitution." He stopped suddenly and looked at Claire. "I've dedicated my life to this. It's my destiny." He turned and faced Jefferson's mountain. "I'M GOING TO FINISH YOUR REVOLUTION, MOTHER F—KER!" He spun around, breathless. "I'm going to rip this society out of the hip pockets of these greedy, exploitative capitalist bastards. Nothing will stop me." He resumed his pacing. "Paige thinks he can stop me . . . with his greed-based, planet-poisoning, hate-filled ideology." He stopped again and sat down beside Claire. "But I need your help."

The words startled her. "What can I do?" she protested.

"You can find the manuscript."

"How am I supposed to do that?" she exclaimed.

"Dammit Claire!" Hardin snapped, "You're the snoop . . . you tell me . . ."

Claire recoiled at the thought. "Where did you get the idea that I'm here to do your 'snooping'?"

Hardin flushed and gritted his teeth. Then something came over him. Claire watched as he closed his eyes and placed his fingers on his temples. He continued to massage them for several long moments without speaking. She felt the calmness radiating from him. When at last he looked up, he was a different person. The center of peace. The source of authority. *Master of the Universe.*

"Claire," he said in a mesmerizing voice. "A principle is involved here that transcends our personal interests. It is bigger than you. It is bigger than me." Somehow, she knew it was true. "Many people have given their lives to preserve it. They have come from all walks of life. But they have been united in one shared conviction. *All men are equal!*

"I know you share my conviction about this. If you didn't, Martin wouldn't have sent you down here. There's a man here who I have known for many years. His name is William O Douglas. He is second only to Thomas Jefferson as a champion for the common man. Last night I heard you speaking with Dr. Somerville about Jefferson and Plato. Bill has spoken to me many times about the vision these two men shared—both men recognized what society could become if it is allowed to follow this fundamental truth. And that wise government can make it a reality—by eliminating the pseudo-aristocracy so government can serve the common people. Above all, both men understood the destructive power of private property. Plato prohibited his guardians from possessing private wealth. Jefferson planned to return it to the state at the end of each generation. Bill has toiled for forty years to make their ideas the law of the law. Because of his accomplishments, it's in our power to eliminate social inequality forever.

"This is what we've all been waiting for, Claire. It's the dawning of the Age of Aquarius! We're going to make the world new again. We're going to tear it down and rebuild it on a sure foundation. I call it 'the Covenant of the New Millennium.' The government will care for its people! It's up to us, Claire. The future depends on you and me!"

Claire stared out into the valley. Finally, she looked at him. "Don't ask me to do this, Tim."

"It's your duty." He answered solemnly.

Claire watched the dust billow into the clear morning air. A moment later Tim Hardin's car vanished over the hill. The drone of his engine gradually faded away, and the dust cloud dissipated. As it did, nature's formless peace began to flow back into the void that surrounded her. She sat quietly in Henry's chair waiting for it to reach her.

"He is a violator!" Claire turned with a start to see two strange creatures looking at her from the opposite side of the porch rail. "And he has violated you!"

Claire opened her mouth to scream, but no sound emerged. All she could do was stare at the unnatural figures looming before her. They were clothed entirely in black. Their faces were painted in a thick, disturbing orange hue. Their eyes and lips were shadowed in purple. They were the undead from a Hollywood horror film Claire had seen as a child. She groped anxiously to understand how they had found her.

"Gerta told us," the taller one announced.

"Gerta?" Claire repeated in confusion.

"I am Marjean. This is my companion, Aster."

"Gerta!" It suddenly dawned on Claire. "You are Marjean and Aster!"

Marjean responded to Claire's revelation with a cosmic smile.

"You live over there," Claire blurted out, pointing in the direction of Buckminster Fuller's geodesic dome.

"We reside there." Marjean said, correcting her. "We live in our mother's cosmos."

Marjean led Aster up the steps and onto the porch. Claire followed them warily. When they were in position beside her, Marjean spoke again. "Woman Spirit has called you to be with us," she announced. "Welcome." Having said that, she wrapped her arms around Claire and, locking her in a liturgical embrace, kissed her full on the lips. "The stars are in alignment," she continued, her arms raising in supplication. "It is the time to ingather their cosmic powers." Looking toward the sky, she made a sun sign. As she did, she cried out. "TERTIUM DATUR!"

"Tertium Datur," Aster repeated in a frail, mechanical wail.

"Women people unite!" Marjean continued, still addressing the universe. "We are ready for our deliverance. Tertium Datur! Woman Spirit I conjure you. Be among us. Guide us to do thy will." With that she took a great breath. "DEATH TO THE VIOLATORS!" she bellowed across the valley.

"Tertium Datur," Aster sputtered again.

The invocation over, Marjean turned back to Claire. Claire's eyes settle on the medallion hanging on her breast. On it was the familiar ox skull with the laurel braids woven through its horns. Something prompted her to touch it. Marjean slapped her hand away. "Never touch my person," she hissed.

Claire continued to stare at the disk as she tried to decide what to do. "What happened to Roberta?" she said at last, deciding to begin with her missing person question.

"Roberta?" Marjean sounded amused.

"Do you know her?" Claire continued.

"You are asking about her because you know that she is dead . . ."

"Yes."

"Do you also know that Henry Tilghman killed her?" Marjean's face brightened with a malevolent smile.

As Claire struggled to digest her words, Marjean held an object up in front of face. It was another medallion with another braided skull. Claire took it into her hands and studied it. On its reverse side, she found the letters RW.

"It was Roberta Wiley's," Marjean announced. "We found it at the lake after Henry Tilghman raped and strangled her." She turned to Aster who handed her a pair of white tennis shorts. "These were beside her body."

Claire looked from the medallion to the shorts, then back at Marjean. "You are to be the instrument of Roberta's retribution." Marjean informed her. Having said that, she raised a clenched fist over her head and bellowed out to a point somewhere above Wolfpit Mountain. "TERTIUM DATUR!"

"SISTER!" Aster screamed. Marjean wheeled around and looked at her companion. Claire saw it in the same moment. A polished black pickup truck was parked on the crest of the hill. It may as well have been the black plague. Marjean sprang like a deer across the porch and through the gate. Aster raced after her. Claire followed them with her eyes as they careened across the pasture and disappeared into the overgrowth along the fence line. When she looked back at the crest of the hill, the pickup truck had also disappeared.

Claire realized she was exhausted. She tried to meditate. After some time breathing quietly, she regained her composure.

That was when the silver Mercedes appeared on the crest of the hill. It was too much. Claire fled into the house and locked the door. Peering through the window, she watched the vehicle coast down the hill and pull to a stop in the same place Tim Hardin's car had been. Clare waited anxiously as the driver's door opened. Gerta Biederman climbed out. As she did, the passenger door opened, and another woman appeared. Claire recognized Frances Rank. A gigantic black woman in a leopard dashiki and matching turban extricated herself from the back seat and joined the other two by the yard's gate. They stood for a moment, staring at the cottage. Finally, Gerta called out in a tentative voice. "Marjean! Are you there?" When Marjean failed to answer, she called again "Aster? Is there anyone there?"

Claire was stricken with indecision. At last, she unlocked the door and stepped out onto the porch. She raised her hand in a silent greeting. "They just left," she called back.

Gerta stared blankly at Claire, but her barrel-shaped companion had seen enough. "What the f–k is going on here!" She roared, charging through the gate like a boatload of marines coming ashore. "First two as-sholes in a pick-up nearly kill us getting up here. Now, the two assholes we're supposed to meet have disappeared!" She marched up onto the porch and stopped in front of Claire. "Where did they go?"

Claire pointed toward the fence line on the far side of the pasture.

"Jesus Christ!" the heavy-set woman swore. Gerta Hardin and the black woman in the leopard wrap arrived on the porch and came up be-hind her. Rank turned to them. "What kind of people are we dealing with anyway?"

"Very reliable," Gerta nodded gravely.

Rank bowed her grey-thatched head and pinched the bridge of her nose.

"You saw the pick-up truck?" Claire asked hesitantly.

"Damn straight," Rank roared. "It almost rammed us coming out of your driveway."

"And the driver?"

"I won't forget him—white male, black beard, dark glasses, and a red bandanna tied over his head . . . the little blond bimbo with him gave me the finger as they went by!"

"Do you know Bart Paige?" Claire inquired.

Frances Rank stared at Gerta in disbelief. "The f–ker driving that truck was Aster's brother?"

"Sounds like it," Claire said, looking at Gerta for confirmation.

Gerta suddenly lost control. "He's a product of this violent phallic culture! His truck is just an extension of his penis. No woman is safe in a country run by penis-worshiping males. We're nothing but slaves in their dictatorship, victims of sexual intimidation . . . coercive marital unions . . . legalized rape . . . economic servitude." She became more agitated with each indictment. "American men are the new Nazis!" She shrieked. "Down with monogamous marriage! Down with the nuclear family! DOWN WITH PENISES!" She stabbed her fist into the air. "TER-TIUM DATUR!"

"Oh! For God's sake!" Frances Rank bellowed. "Will you shut up! All I ever hear from you is penis, penis, penis! Why don't you try using your f–king brains occasionally!" Rank gave Claire a tired, frustrated look. "She hasn't been the same since she met Kate Millett during the Columbia riots in '68." Rank cast a disparaging look at Gerta. "Now you're an expert on penises. Hell," she added, looking back at Claire. "She's probably never even seen one."

"I have too—hundreds of them," Gerta protested lamely.

"I'm going to tell you this one more time," Rank said, her lips pursing together in grim determination. "We're <u>not</u> a therapy group for dykes with penis envy. You got that? We're a sovereign people! We have just declared political independence. Remember? Thomas Jefferson managed to do it without ever mentioning penises. If you've got a penis problem, go take care of it on your own time. DO YOU UNDERSTAND?"

Gerta blanched. "Kate says..."

"F–k Kate! That... farthead!" Frances Rank expelled a purging grunt and looked at the black woman in the leopard robe. "This is what we are going to do. We're going to go over to Aster's and wait for her there until she gets back from her visit with Castor and Pollux." Then she turned to Claire. "Marjean says you're in on this..."

"What?" Claire recoiled. "How could she say that? I have never spoken with her."

"She knows these things—it's uncanny," Rank replied with genuine admiration. "She studies the stars."

"It's not that I..."

"Never mind that," Rank said, waving her off. "You're in! Come on." With that, she turned and marched off the porch. Her two companions followed her back across the lawn.

Claire struggled to resolve the conflict raging within her. "I have to get dressed," she called out at the last second. "I'll meet you there."

≋

PART II

B ehind the hedgerow ahead on the left, Claire could see the top of Buckminster Fuller's geodesic dome.

As she came nearer, she saw Gerta's silver Mercedes parked beside the walk that led up to the front door. Claire pulled up behind it and turned off her engine. She had been conditioned to think of Fuller as the foremost genius of her time. But here in the countryside of Virginia, his dome was merely an eyesore.

The quiet was suddenly shattered by loud cursing inside the dome. Claire hurried up the flagstone path to the dome's door. It was ajar so she pushed it open and stepped in.

"Oh for Christ's sake!" Frances Rank bellowed after a tense silence. "Go ahead!"

Rank and her companions were sitting on a padded bench seat that ringed a sunken council circle floor before the dome's stone hearth. Rank's back was toward Claire. Her three counsellors were facing her—Gerta, Marjean, and Aster. The massive black woman in the leopard dashiki was Professor Ashanti Shoate', the recently appointed Chair of the African Studies Department at the University of Virginia. *The Post* had featured her in its *Style* section after her appointment the previous spring. Professor Shoate' was, it reported, the foremost black authority on Thomas Jefferson.

Her appointment had caused a flap at the University because of the leadership position she held the Black Panthers. Until she joined the Black Panthers, she was Alice Coleman sharecropper's daughter from Greenville, North Carolina. Alice changed her name to one culturally appropriate when she joined the group in the spring of 1970. Ashanti Shoate' became a national figure in the winter of '71 when she and Angela Davis were arrested for their roles in a botched San Quentin jail break. The charge was smuggling the guns the inmates used to kill their four white hostages.

By the time of her acquittal seventeen months later, Ashanti Shoate' had become a national celebrity and media darling. She made this astonishing transition during her incarceration in the Soledad Women's Correctional Institution by writing a PhD dissertation for UCLA. Published in 1973 under the title *Sister Slave,* it won the prestigious Carquest Book Award for the best historical work by an African American female.

Shoate's research dealt with Sally Hemings's long lost diary, which she tracked down with help from her Black Panther network. Shoate's revelationary investigation confirmed that Hemings' influence on Jefferson extended beyond his communitarian philosophy. Shoate' found that the two also shared a strangely inverted master/slave sexual relationship that began shortly after she arrived in Paris in the summer of 1787 and continued until his death thirty-nine years later. Dr. Shoate' discovered that during these years, Sally gave birth to and raised six of Jefferson's children.

Shoate' had become a disciple of W.E.B. DuBois' during her brief tenure as chief information officer for the Black Panthers. A dedicated DuBoisian, she assumed the role of spokesperson for people of color everywhere on earth. At the same time, she embraced Patrice Lumumba's liberation philosophy and made it her operating methodology for the "rainbow" nation she had decided to establish. The best way to advance this cause, she soon determined, was with the militancy espoused by Malcolm X. Following the light of these guiding beacons, she teamed up with UCLA's outspoken black Philosophy Professor in support of social justice. While incarcerated with Davis, she studied Sally Heming's writings and wrote her bloc-buster dissertation on the many ways Sally educated Thomas Jefferson.

Her meteoric rise as a public intellectual occurred at an opportune time because the administrators of Mr. Jefferson's picturesque University were then seeking a way to enhance their standing among the cognoscenti who were taking control of the nation's most prestigious colleges and universities. The best way to do this, they decided, would be to make a full professor of someone opposed to the University's heritage in southern elitism and debauchery. This proved to be a brilliant move, and it accomplished more even than Dumas Malone had imagined. Shortly after the deal was made, Ashanti Shoate' moved to Charlottesville and brought her social justice revolution to the University of Virginia.

Claire had not read her book, but she was familiar with Professor Shoate's condemnation of the Founding Fathers and of Jefferson in particular, whom she claimed led the effort to deprive African Americans of their natural rights. As Claire was remembering this, she heard someone called her name.

"Claire . . . beautiful Claire . . ." It was Frances Rank. "Come join us. Aster is about to consecrate our gathering with a recital of her new poem." Claire descended the stairs and crossed to the council circle. Settling in the space beside Gerta, she gazed around the spacious dome. That was when she noticed the ox skull hanging from the crown of the dome.

Aster rose like a kindergartner selected to lead the pledge of allegiance. The name of my poem is "Oh Rock, Oh River, Oh Tree," she announced. She took a deep breath, looked inward, and began to recite it:

"Oh Rock! Oh River! Oh Tree!
You are the hosts to species destroyed long ago,
The mastodon and dinosaur
Left dried tokens upon your nurturing carpet
But the alarming message of their doom
Is now lost in the dust of ages past.

Today the Rock cries out to us. Clearly. Forcefully.
Come, stand upon my back, and face your destiny.
Let not the desolators seek haven in my shadow,
For I will give them no hiding place.

You, violated ones, as glorious as the angels,
Have been forced to crouch down in
The bruising darkness which they have made.
You have lain too long
Face down in their imposed ignorance
Your mouths spilling their words
As they arm themselves to slaughter you.

233

The Rock cries out to us today.
Stand up proudly upon my back.
Hide your rage no longer.

We hear the Tree.
It speaks to us:
    Come to me,
    Here, beside the River
    Plant yourselves under my outstretched arms.

As is passes by the Rock and the Tree,
The River sings its beautiful song, saying
Come, rest here on my rich banks.

Each of you, forced to be an island in the land,
is worthy and strangely proud.
You are forced to struggle under perpetual siege
Against their lust for your labor and profit.
They have left collars of waste upon my shores,
and laid currents of debris upon my breast,
In their quest for lucre.
Now, I call you to covenant with one another:
Rise up and take from them their tools of war.

Come, clad in green garments,
And sing with me songs of praise to Gaia,
Who gave birth to the Rock and the Tree and Me,
Before their greed inflicted bloody scars upon our brow
And persuaded you that you are nothing.

We have felt the true yearning and respond to
The singing River, the wise Rock, the gentle Tree.
So say those who have been drowned and crushed
Asian, Hispanic, Jew
African, Native American
Catholic, Muslim, Irish,

Women-people and their peers
Hear!

Each of you, descended from some passed-on traveler,
Has been paid for.

"Thank you, Aster," Frances said with a strained smile. "How moving . . ."
"I'm not finished," Aster replied pointedly.
"Oh! . . . I beg your pardon," Rank stammered, her face reddening.
Aster squared herself and resumed her recitation:

"Let them beware, for their time is passed.
Those who violated my verdant heritage
And the sacred places of those who knew me.
Pawnee, Apache, Seneca, you,
Cherokee Nation, who rested with me, then
Forced on bloody feet,
Left me to the takers–desperate for gain,
Starving for my gold.

You African, you Arab, you Asian, you Slav
With your many tongues,
All of you innocent victims,
Arriving in a nightmare
Praying for a dream.
Rise up united against them.

Root yourselves within me.
I planted the Tree in the Rock by the River,
And I will not let them be taken from you.
You are mine and I have paid your passage.
My fruits belong to you.

A bright morning is dawning.
Lift up your eyes and your hands.
Take hold of me.

I, Woman Spirit, shall give birth again
To the dream.

I have a place for everyone:
Women-people and their children.
I will take you up in my arms,
And mold you with my bountiful blessing.
I will sculpt you in the image of my cosmic oneness.
Lift up your hearts.
Each hour a new promise unfurls.

I have prepared a new beginning for you.
Free of fear. Free from greed.
From paternalism – free at last!
Welcome new day!

The muse departed from her as she breathed the last word. She stood frozen in a motionless trance for another moment then collapsed onto the floor. "Aster darling!" Gerta exclaimed, rushing to her side. "You brave soul," she cooed, gathering her former lover in her arms and rocking her gently, "taking this fight on your frail shoulders. We all feel your pain . . ." she sobbed, ". . . your humiliation . . . your rage . . ."

Out of the corner of her eye, Claire saw Marjean rise.

Marjean's eyes were fixed on a point beyond the skull that hovered ominously above the council. "Gaia, Eternal Mother," she cried, raising her hands in supplication. "I conjure you in the name of your children. Come among us and make your will known." She waited in statuesque silence. A moment passed. Then a strange stirring came into the air. A straining, painful expression appeared on Marjean's face, and her body began to stiffen. Little by little she transformed into a new being.

Then she turned. "I am Nut," she announced in a rasping voice. "I am the beginning and the source. I am Isis, the sustaining essence. I am Isthra. Life springs from me. I am Hera, Mother of the Earth. I am Metis, Mother of the Gods. I am Athena, defender of the sacred city. I am WOMAN SPIRIT! The cosmos lives through me.

"Man was born of my body. I preserved him from his cradle. I protected him from Nature's untamed processes. I saved him from his own insatiable brutishness. I bore the burdens of his desolation.

"Now I tell you the time has come to restore the cosmic harmony. Let the earth be delivered. TERTIUM DATUR!" she cried.

"Hear me, sisters, my children. Be not deceived. The power of man does not reside in the strength of his arm. It is in his ability to apply three simple words. *Tertium Non Datur*–the third element does not exist. For philosophers, this is the Law of the Excluded Middle–propositions are true or false. Reason is built on this foundation. It is power in Aristotle's logic. It gives meaning to Descartes' geometry. It is the ordering force in Newtonian space.

"Until Man saw Nature in this light, he was in my thrall. For a thousand and a thousand and a thousand years, he remained huddled in the darkness of my womb, pleading for my mercy. The light of reason ended my timeless peace, and Man became free to create his own world!"

She gathered over them like a storm. "Tertium Datur . . ." she intoned. "The third element exists. Follow the way of women people! CONFUSE AND CONQUER!" She cried out in a wild, wrenching voice. "We shall rule again! We shall dwell again in the comforting darkness of Gaia's womb. Priestesses will again teach Gaia's ways. The unity of the cosmos will again be manifest. Oneness and harmony will again be venerated. HAIL GAIA!"

"Amen and Hallelujah," Frances concluded, reining the curtain down on Woman Spirit's prophesy. "Honestly Comrade Sister, you are the most animated woman person I've ever known. Your visions never cease to astonish me. Now," she said, turning to Gerta, "on to business."

Gerta, looked up into the granite face of her leader and saw that the moment had passed. Separating herself from the arms of her lover, she crawled back to her place and resettled herself.

Frances Rank waited patiently. "Now Sister Gerta," she said in a business-like voice, "why don't you can tell us what Tonto is up to."

Claire watched Gerta's face contort.

"He raped Claire Fox," Marjean screamed above the silent torrent of Gerta's despair. ". . . last night—right in front of her." Marjean glared contemptuously at Claire. "And he was with her again this morning!"

Rank looked at Claire. "Is that right! He raped you?"

Before Claire could respond, Marjean leaped to her feet and raised supplicant hands to the skull above them. "Spirit of the Void, bring down your retribution on the worthless carcass of our sister's violator!!"

"Oh for Christ's sake, Marjean," Rank cursed. "Sit down. We'll get to that in due course." Marjean assumed a defiant pose then returned to her place. "All right Claire, what happened?"

"He raped her," Gerta cried out. "He used her body as an instrument to satisfy his own disgusting pleasure." Her anguish gave way to rage. "Women are just objects for his self-gratification," she cursed. "I hate him!"

"Did he . . . do it again this morning?" Frances asked Claire, probing deeper into the matter.

Claire realized that she was ashamed. Not because of the incident, but because she was the object of this queer interrogation. "He made a mistake. He came over to apologize. That's all. It's over. Ok?"

"No!" Marjean screamed, challenging Claire with an expression of warlike hostility. "It's <u>not</u> Ok! It's *not* Ok for men to violate women. And it's *not* Ok for women to excuse them!" She turned to Frances. "He asked her to help him, and she agreed."

"Oh?" The grey-haired revolutionary raised an eyebrow and looked again at Claire.

"He wants me to find Jefferson's constitution," Claire answered sheepishly.

"He wants you to find Jefferson's constitution . . ." Rank repeated thoughtfully. "Did you agree?"

"I may have given him that impression," Claire conceded. "It was a little confusing. You know how he comes over you . . . "

"Then we've got him. BY GOD!" Rank swore, punching her fist into the air above her head in a salute to Gaia.

"You want this sister to do Tim Hardin's bidding?" Marjean's voice crackled with suspicion.

"Godammit!" Rank shouted, shaking her clenched fist at Marjean. The other woman settled back but continued to leer at her comrade. ". . . It so happens . . . " Frances Rank continued, pulling a scroll from the bag at her feet, ". . . it just so happens that I have Jefferson's constitution right here." She opened the scroll and showed it to her astonished companions.

"Where did you get that?" Gerta gasped.

"To hell with Jefferson's constitution," Marjean interrupted angrily. "He's just another violator of women. Or haven't you read her book?" Marjean pointed toward Professor Shoate'. "Or have you forgotten that the purpose of this movement is to eradicate male tyranny."

Rank ignored the challenge to her authority. "Claire," she said in a measured voice, "tell the council, will you please. Why does Tim Hardin want Jefferson's constitution?"

Claire glanced at Marjean, then back at Frances Rank. "He sees it as a blueprint for a new utopian society. He thinks it will be the spark that sets off the Aquarian revolution."

Rank's smile broadened. "The catalyst for an Aquarian revolution!" As she spoke these words, she raised the document in her hand and waived it at her audience. "Sisters, I have it in my hand—the catalyst for the Aquarian revolution."

"Nobody cares about your dumb constitution," Gerta screeched defiantly.

"How will they know it's mine?" Rank responded placidly.

"Don't be ridiculous," Gerta sneered. "Universities are full of people who know those things. You won't fool a single one of them."

"To hell with them," Rank snapped. "We don't have to trust the opinions of self-interested paternalists! We have our own expert—don't we Professor."

Dr. Shoate' nodded. "Tha's right—Sally Hemin's wrote it, and Tom got it fom her."

"There you have it," Rank said, stowing her charter. "The foremost living authority on Jefferson says that Sally Hemings wrote this seminal document. Explain it to the sisters, will you Professor . . . "

Professor Shoate' hoisted her massive frame off the council bench and stepped to the center of the circle. "Listen up," she barked with drill-sergeant toughness. "In case you ain't figgered it out, we're in na same war Sally wuz in! An' we're gonna fight tha same way she done. So keep yer moufs shut an' pay 'ttention."

The scholar began to pace around the perimeter of the circle. "Whadda fokes think when ney hear tha name Thom's Jefferson?" No one spoke, "They think about tha *Decleration uv Innapendence*. Right! An' wha da dey know 'bout tha *Decleration uv Innapendence*?" She stopped and looked

239

down at the council. "Nuffin! Hear whut ahm sayin'? Fokes don't know shit 'bout it! They gotta be tole. Ya wif me? That's tha firs' sing you gal's godda know." The Professor rested her dark eyes on the counsellors. Nobody moved. "Good!" She resumed her march round the ring. "In na *Decleration uv Innapennance,* Tom Jefferson put out a buncha shit 'e didn't even hol' wif. Why? Cuz 'e figger'd it'd git tha revolution goin'. Ain't nobody tellin' fokes 'bout dat cuz tha guys tellin' um got thar own fish ta fry. See whut ahm sayin'? They jes' make up whut suit's 'em ta keep umselves on top. Right? It's like tha Good Book sez, we gotta figh' fahr wif fahr. Ya wif me?" No one moved.

"Soonaz Tom finish'd wif the *Decleration uv Innapennence,* he went down ta Williamsburg an' took a seat in na new 'sembly. He sat thar fer two monfs then 'e went on back ta Monticello whar 'e spent two-and-a-half years writin' a new setta laws fer 'is new state . . . Soon ez he wuz done wif dat, his pals 'lected him governor, an' 'e spent tha res o' tha war bein' chased 'roun' Virginnie by Cornwallis. When nis term wuz up, he went back ta Monticello an' starred workin' up ansers fer a lis' o' questions fom a French guy named Barbé-Marbois.

"Stay wif me now . . . In na spring uv 1782, da marquis de Chastellux come up ta tha house fer a visit wif him an' Marfa. She died in na fall, bless her heart, so Tom d'cided ta go ta France an' be a man o' tha worl' like tha marquis. Off he goes in July ov 1784—got 'is notes fer Barbé-Marbois in one han' an' nis daughter Patsy in n'ther. Ya followin' whut ahm tellin' ya? He wuz goin' ta France ta be a 'Ren'sance Man' like tha marquis de Chastellux!

"Now here's whut ahm sayin'—Tom aimed ta get in wif tha marquis' crowd cuz zese fokes war on na top o' tha French heap, an' that's whar Tom figgered he b'longed. But it warnt simple cuz tha French highbrows warnt lookin' fer walk-ons fom na backwoods of Virginnie. Ya wif me? People in na top spots thar wuz all good at sompin! See whut ahm sayin'? So Tom hadda be good at sompin too. Course he hadda plan! He took tha notes he wuz makin' fer Barbé-Marbois an' printed 'em up in a book. When he got 'is books fom na printer, he starred passin' um out ta tha mose spech'l fokes in Paris. Ya wif me? He figgered they'd read 'is book, see 'e wuz a big thinker like tha marquis, an' 'vite 'im ta join thur crowd.

"Ol' Tom had it figger 'bout right! Turns out ever'body in na marquis' crowd wann'd ta know whut wuz happenin' in Am'rica. How come? Cuz zey waz sick o' tha king an' tha church ownin' ever'thing an' tellin' um whut ta do. Right! They wann'd ta know 'bout tha Am'rican Rev'lution an' ef tha time wuz right ta git one goin' fer umselves. Tha marquis knew sompin 'bout this an' figgered 'e'd cash in wif 'is own tellin' 'bout da time he spent wif George Washington an' Tom Jefferson. Ya wif me? He cum home one night, an' nar's Tom's book on nis front stoop. Tha marquis give it to 'is pal Abbe Morellet an' tole 'im ta fine some stuff 'e kin use. Ya wif me? See whut ahm sayin'? Tom's plan's startin' ta work!

"All lis's goin' on whal Tom's givin' out 'is book ta 'stablish 'imsef wif tha bes' people in France. One ov um is 'is boss, Ben Franklin. Tom gives Ben a copy ov 'is book, an' tha nex' sing he knows, Ben wants ta innerduce 'im to 'is girlfrien'. Ya wif me? This gal's name's Madame Helvetius, an' she's sompin spech'l. Hear whut ahm tellin' ya? She got 'er own set out at tha chateau, and Ben's been hangin' out wif 'er so long it's OK fer 'im ta bring 'is new guy ta dinner. Ya gettin' na pitshure? Tom primps up wif 'is wig, an' ruffles, an' nis perfume so he can impress 'er an' ner friends.

"He comes in na firs' room an' thars Abbe Morellet translatin' nis book fer da marquis. Tha Abbe stars talkin' wif 'im 'bout it. Tom's keepin' up wif 'im 'til tha Abbe gets ta tha part 'bout tha church an' religion. Prob'em is, ain't no part in Tom's book 'bout tha church er religion cuz he kep' that kina stuff to 'imself. Ya wif me? Ya see whut ahm sayin'? Tha Abbe sez that might work in tha new worl' whar fokes ain't got no sufissication, but it ain't goin' nowhar wif Madame er 'er crowd. Right? He's godda talk 'bout tha high stuff ef 'e want's ta git on wif them.

"Tom 'llows that makes sense. So tha Abbe takes 'im ta tha library an' pulls a book down. When Tom sees it, his eyes bug out cuz it's 'bout a guy 'e read in college! 'Read dis an' you'll be OK,' Abbe Morellet tells 'im. Ya wif me? Tom knows all 'bout Lor' Bolin'broke an' he remembers whut 'e said 'bout religion screwin' up the worl'. That's tha kina thin' this crowd goes fer, Abbe Morellet tells 'im. An' John Locke too, cuz he sed we know tha truf 'bout things from esperience 'sted o' rev'lation. Course that wuz right up Tom's alley. See whut ahm sayin'? He pulls up a chair an' stars readin' Madame's book.

"Nex' sing, Madame blows in wif 'er crowd o' dainties. 'T'night,' she tells um, we eez going to talk a'bout peerfecting s'ciety.' They're all keen on nis cuz they's all *philosophes* like 'er dead husban' Claude. Madame stars thumpin sompin called *la bonheur general*, which 'er husban' cum up wif b'fore 'e died. All ov um er noddin' an' smilin' while she's showin' ol' Ben how it's done. Cordin' ta Madame, this's tha bes' sing ta cum along. Ya wif me? Fac' diz, allov um er tryin' ta git rid o' tha church an' religion cuz iss keepin' um fom usin' ner reason ta perfec' s'ciety. Allov um know this cuz France's bes' philosophe said so. Madame turns roun' ta git tha book whar 'e sez it, but lo an' b'hold, iss missin'! 'Merd', she sez. 'Whar eze zee book ov Missur Voltaire?' Tha's when she sees Tom settin' nar wif it in nis han'. Ya got tha pitshure? Tom ain't never heard o' Voltaire, but tha stuff he's got in nis book 'bout Bolin'broke soun's jes' right. 'Commau!' sez Madame Helvetius, swellin' up wif pride. 'Ze great American sinker eez reading ze boook by ze great French writer!' Wif dat, she raises 'er glass an' sez, 'Écrasez l'infâme!' Ever'body repeats 'er toas' an' swallows zur wine.

"Stay wif me now," the Professor ordered. "Perfectin' s'ciety wuz za main thin' tha salon crowd talked 'bout. See whut ahm sayin'? Like ol' Claude Helvetius—he had 'is ahdea 'bout tha *bonheur general*—Right! That means tha *gen'ral good*. Soun's Ok. Right? But lissen ta me now. He figgered he'd make fokes perfec' by gettin' 'um goin' wif kinky sex. That's tha gospel truf!" the Professor swore, looking around with big eyes. "I spect he come up wif it out at tha mansion whal foolin' wif 'imself! Ya wif me? Ain't got nuffin ta do wif reason. He jes' d'cided tha way ta make fokes better wuz by manipulatin' um tha way he liked ta do. Hear whut ahm tellin' ya? Perfesser Helvetius figgered that ef ya say grace wif da king, you kin go on upstairs an' diddle wif da princess. That's how it wuz—jes' like t'day, ever'body screwin' eve'body else. See whar ahm goin'? That's how da French upper crus' spected ta perfect s'ciety.

"Tha bes' o' tha bunch wuz tha marqis de Condorcet. He wuz zar when Jefferson wuz makin' nis move. In fact, Tom give 'im a copy ov 'is book. That tells ya how impor'ant 'e wuz. Stay wif me now! Turns out Condorcet wuz a frien' o' Sally's so Jefferson got ta know 'im. Condorcet wuz a cut above tha res' o' tha doodlers cuz he wuz a math'matician, which is a kina scientis'. Ya hear whut ahm sayin'? He ac'shally knew sompin! Numbers gotta add up. Right? It ain't jes' hot air like da *bonheur gen'ral*. Anyway, Condorcet's out thar on na same track. But e's got 'is own noshons 'bout perfectin' s'ciety. Tha way ta do it, 'e sez, is wif Science. How's zat work?

He's gonna get all tha judgemen's t'gether an' calca'late the math'matical prob'bility ov 'um bein' right. Ya wif me? Am ah makin' sense?

"Tom's lissenin' hard ez 'e can. By an' by 'e sez ta imsef, 'this is a bunch o' shit! Why don't these jaspers jes' git on wif a rev'lution like we done?' Ya see whut ahm gettin' at? If ya wanna make s'ciety perfec', head's gotta roll! Tom learned nat firs' han'. Right! So he's watchin' tha dainties struttin' 'roun' in nur ruffles an' stockin's an' talkin' 'bout how they're gonna make s'ciety perfec'. It don't take long b'fore 'e's headed ta tha door. But when 'e leaves, 'e's got tha cards ov all la guys that 're inta politics, which er tha best an' na brightes' fokes in France. Right! La Rochefoucauld, Lafayette, Condorcet, Cabanis, de Stutts de Tracy, Volney, De Corney—guys like that. These guys 're all utopians, an' ney all got tha same slant. They got thur stuff fom Voltaire, Locke, an' Newton so they spect ta make s'ciety perfec' by usin' nur reasonin'. See whut um sayin? That's how they plan ta git up wif tha higher good.

"Tom packs 'is bags an' takes um back ta his place an' sets up 'is own salon. Makin' rev'lution's his sing. Right? That's whut 'e knows 'bout. So 'e figgers he'll git these jaspers over an' start um movin' in na right d'rection. When na king an' nis crowd run outta gas, he'll be wif tha crowd dat's comin' in. Tha prob'em is these French guys ain't buyin' Tom's plan. An' he's got some baggage slowin' 'im down. Right? These guys 're talkin 'bout tha rights o' man'. Ya wif me? An' ney're aksin' 'im this an' that 'bout Natur'l Rights. But Tom's got a couple pieces ov 'is prop'ty peelin' p'taters down in nis basemen'. Ya see whut ahm sayin'? Whut kin ya' tell a crowd o' ruffle-bloused utopians 'bout tha rights o' man when ya' own a bunch uv um? Ya wif me? Tom's startin' ta git edgy. He ain't no Horatio on na bridge, an' na govermen' he's crowin' 'bout ain' no utopia cuz is's sittin' on na backs ov a mill'on African slaves.

"'Course tha Frenchies warnt no choir boys neither. The peasants workin' out in ner gardens had bin nar since Willum tha Norman lef' ta conquer Inglin'. See whut ahm sayin'? Ever'body at tha table's paddlin' in na same canoe. Tha thin' they liked 'bout Tom Jefferson wuz zat he wuz an Amer'can. Right? Amer'ca'd already had its rev'lution. Tom wuz part o' da brave new worl', an' nat's whar they wanted ta be. Right? That's whut 'ttracted these barnburners to 'im. So Tom's got plenty o' comp'ny. They're all sittin' 'roun' watchin' King Louie creepin' out on nis limb an' lickin' ner

243

chops whal their waitin' fer 'im ta fall off. This's tha mos' 'mazin' part—ain't none ov um figgered out wha's comin' nex'! "See whut ahm sayin'?

"None ov 'um's lookin' in na right d'rection. How come? Cuz all they done wuz talk wif 'umselves. They wuz so wrapped up wif thur own no-shons they don't know wha's happenin' pas' tha garden gate. Ya wif me? It ain't never 'curred to 'um that poor fokes got thur own noshons! Fac diz, tha fokes down in na ghetto 're workin' on nur own scheme. Am ah makin' sense?" No one moved.

"Anyway, Tom's havin' nis breakfas' one mornin' when ne hears a knock on nis door. 'Jimmie,' he sez, 'go fine out whoze zar.' A few minutes later Jimmie's back wif a package. Tom tears it open, an' lo' an' b'hol', it's za book by Voltaire. Right! This's tha guy who wrote tha one Tom wuz readin' 'bout religion an' Lor' Bolin'broke at Madame Heltevius's chateau. Tom looks at tha note an' sees its fom her. Since he's sech a big thinker, she sez, an' cuz 'e's perfectin' s'ciety jes' like tha philosophes in ner crowd, he needs ta read this book. She an' them 're fixin' to talk 'bout where Voltaire sez it's tha bes' ov all poss'ble worls. Come over ta tha house, she sez, when you got it straight. Tom looks at tha title—*Candide*.

"He ain't got no time ta read *Candide* jes' zen cuz he's goin 'roun wif a little pink gum drop called Maria Cosway. She's runnin' 'im 'roun' an' 'roun' like a cat's mouse. Ya see whut um sayin'? He don't know wha she's up to an' she ain't lettin' on. Soun' familiar? Anyway, that's how it wuz when Miss Sally Hemings 'rrived.

"That wuz sure a sad tale," Shoate's said with a sigh. "One day a let-ter rived fom 'is wife's sister tellin' 'im that 'is littlest girl had died ov tha whoopin' cough. He sent a letter back ta Ant Betsy tellin' 'er ta pack up 'is nex' daughter an' sen' 'er over on na nex' boat so he kin take care ov 'er 'imself. Ant Betsy ain't keen on na plan, but she does whut 'e sez 'cep' she sen's 'er slave gal Sally 'long as 'er chap'rone. That tell's ya' sompin don't it? Tha white fokes knew this gal wuz spech'l. Ya wif me? She warnt jes some stupid chile. See whut ahm sayin'? Fac diz, she wuz Marfa's half-sister, an' she's wuz smart nuf ta steer Polly clear 'roun' na worl'.

"Soonas they git ta France Tom puts Polly in na convent whar 'e had 'er sister. After Polly went inta tha convent, Sally dint have nuffin ta do 'cep hang 'roun' wif 'er haf-bro' Jimmie. Stay wif me now. Jes' like Sally, Jimmie wuz a slave back in Virginnie. But jes like Sally, he wuz sharp ez a tack, an'

244

it dint take no time fer 'im to fin' out that slaves warnt 'llowed in France. Ya wif me? He knew Tom couldn't keep 'im as a slave in France so he tole 'im he was frew wif tha slave shit. He dint look like no slave, ner ac' like one, ner wuz he gonna be one. Whut's Massa gonna do 'bout that in Paris, France? Right? Whip 'im an' sen' 'im down ta hoe tobacca? Ya got tha pitshure?

"Ain't nuffin Tom kin do 'cep' work up a new plan, an' nat's jes' whut 'e done. He starred payin' Jimmie wages. An' 'e 'greed ta sen' 'im ta cookin' school an' get 'im some French lessons so he kin buy da groceries. Course, Sally's takin' all this in. Ya wif me? She's Marfa's youngest sister! She's Tom's sister-in-law! Ya got that! An' she's jes' es good lookin'!

"Fac diz, ever'body's no'cin' 'er, spech'ly Pericles Perrault whose teachin' Jimmie 'is French. Sally's daddy's tha same ez Marfa's an' Jimmie's. Ya un-nerstan' whut ahm tellin' ya? An' ner mama's ol' man—he's a white man too. This gal's jes' 'bout thar 'ersef. She's bright e'nuf ta be Tom's cuzzin'. That's how Pericles Perrault's got it figgered. So 'e starts gettin' friendly wif 'er. Ya gettin' na pitshure? Tom don't know nuffin 'bout it cuz 'e's out get-tin' run 'roun by da gum drop. He ain't payin' no 'ttention ta whut's goin' on down in na kitchen!

"Course ol' Pericles Perrault's travelin' wif a dif'rent set den Tom Jef-ferson. Ya wif me? Tha crowd Pericles Perrault hangs wif ain't got no wigs ner ruffles like tha crowd at Madame Helvetius's chateau. They ain't blue blood utopians, an' they ain't thinkin' 'bout whut's wrong wif poor fokes cuz zey are poor fokes! Right! An' ney're readin' a paper wrote by a guy name' Marat. This guy's 'n *AN'RCHIS*! Ya wif me? Whut's tha dif'rence 'tween a Utopian an' 'n An'rchis? Utopians 're rich guys who figger they kin make tha worl' perfec' by improvin' poor fokes. An'rchiss 're poor fokes who figger they kin fix umselves by gitten ridda rich guys. See tha prob'em? We got conflict! Right!

"So Sally's goin' 'roun wif Pericles Perrault, an' one day 'e takes 'er down ta tha Cordelier ta see Marat. He's zar on nis soap box in na middle o' da street lecturin' 'bout a guy name' Rousseau. Cordin' ta Marat, Rousseau's got tha pitshure in focus. Course Perrault's thinkin' na same way, so 'e gives Sally 'is copy o' Rousseau's book—*The Social Contract*—an' tells 'er ta read it. This's tha new deal. Fom now on, Rousseau's book's gonna be 'er tex' book. Ya gittin' na pitshure? He's gonna make 'er into an an'rchis jes' like him an' Marat! Course it don't make no dif'rence ta Sally cuz nobody's never tole 'er nuffin 'bout nuffin 'cep' bein' na slave. Nex' day she opens tha book an' boom. Tha firs' sing she reads is whar Rousseau sez, 'Man is born free; and everywhere he is in chains.' Whoa! She sez to 'ersef. This guy's got sompin ta say—the pitshure's comin' in loud an' clear. Right!

"All this's happenin' while Tom's out sightseein' wif tha gum drop. In na meantime, tha flu shows up in town. Soonas Tom hears 'bout it, 'e's ready ta move. Right? One ov 'is salon pals is a doct'r so Tom tells 'im ta come over an' innoc'late ever'body in nis house. Nex' day, Pierre Cabanis shows up wif 'is bag. He's gittin' set ta take care o' Sally when he noc'ces tha gal's got sompin spech'l. Right? Now he's scratchin' nis head. Who's zis gal? See whut ahm sayin'? Tom ain't never sed nuffin 'bout 'er cuz 'is utopian friends don't need ta know 'bout 'im ownin' people—that might screw up 'is plan. See whut ahm sayin'? Bes' sing's ta keep um in na dark.

"When Cabanis fines Sally's in Tom's house, he comes up wif tha no-shon that she's tha chile o' Tom's girlfrien'. You wif me? That kina stuff's ez common ez house flies whar Pierre Cabanis' fom. He's goin' on wif 'is usual pleasantries when lo' an' behol', Tom's secret daughter stars talkin' wif 'im in French. This's tha cat's meow. Right? They go on a li'l bit an' Cabanis hears zat she's readin' tha same book ez him! When Cabanis hears zat Sally's studyin' Rousseau, tha pitshure comes inta focus—Tom's arranged fer 'is secret daughter ta have private lessons so she kin be a utopian jes' like him an' 'is new friends!

"Cabanis's fillin' up wif a'miration fer tha famous Amer'can rev'lution-ary. Course, fer Cabanis, teachin' nis beau'ful young gal 'bout perfectin' s'coiety's jes' ez natur'l ez tha spring rain. See whut ahm sayin'? He's talkin' wif 'er 'bout Rousseau an' Sally's tellin' 'im tha part whar fokes 're sposed ta be free but 're sittin' 'roun' in chains. She knows sompin 'bout that. Right! Cabanis' noddin' an' strokin' nis chin. Ya gettin' na pitshure? He's begin-nin' to see that tha chick's got a future in na moo'ment.

"Now here's tha thin'. Cabanis an' nis buddies been readin' tha same book ez Marat an' Perrault, but they're lookin' atta dif'rent part ov it. Ya followin' whut ahm sayin'? That stuff 'bout bein' a slave don't mean nuffin to French utopians cuz they're mos'ly sippin' Chablis an' eatin' keesh down nat tha chateau. Right? It ain't a 'chain' thing fer Cabanis er tha dainties 'e's hangin' 'roun' wif. It's 'bout gittin' thur han's on na wheel an' steerin' na ship o' state. Ya wif me? They warnt like fokes t'day who're tryin' ta tear tha place down. No sir! They wuz aimin' ta re'rrange tha furniture. Ya see whut ahm sayin'? When ney got ta steerin' na bus, they wuz gonna drive it straight up ta tha higher good, an' Rousseau wuz tellin' um how ta git thar. Right?

"Cordin' ta Rousseau, tha train'd run off tha track cuz fokes warnt equal, an' fokes warnt equal cuz prop'ty got spread 'roun' na wrong way. Ya wif me? Fokes wuz equal, he sed, back when ney wuz livin' in na state o' nature cuz didn't none of um have prop'ty back then. That made fokes free. Right? When ney starred 'cumulatin' prop'ty, tha curt'in come tumblin' down cuz zey had ta pertect whut they had fom tha ones that wanted it. Right? This's whar tha chains come in. Ya wif me? Ya caint leave stuff layin' 'roun' cuz tha neighbors got thur eyes on it. This wuz whar Cabanis an' nis buddies pick'd it up. They figgered tha way ta git up wif tha higher good wuz ta spread tha welf 'roun' so ever'body had puddy much tha same stuff. When ney got that done, tha worl ud be perfec'. See whut ahm sayin'? That's whut utopians 're all 'bout—helpin' poor folks by givin' 'em stuff.

"Cabanis an' nis crowd war pullin' nis outta Rousseau whar 'e sed, *'the frui' o' tha earf b'longs ta all uv us, but tha earf itsef don't b'long ta nobody.'* Ya see tha pos'bilities! Cabanis an' nis crowd figgered they should have whut tha French call *carte blanche* cuz that 'llowed 'em ta do whutever they wanted. Tha's tha way it works in utopia. You wif me? They wuz headed ta tha higher good, an' anythin' that got um thar wuz Ok. An' ney war gonna hep ever'body else git up thar too.

"Cabanis' layin' all this out fer Sally, which she's ain't heard fom Marat er Perrault. She figgers Cabanis' onta sompin so she stars workin' on it fom bofe sides, being tha slave side, an' na 'quality side, an' na prop'rty side. She's bringin' um all t'gether. Right? Miss Sally's bringin' na whole pitshure inta focus.

"'Bout this time, Tom calls it quits wif 'is gum drop. He figgers tha bes' way ta clear 'is head's ta git outta town fer a whal. Right? So 'e packs 's bags an' heads souf. Course, 'e's lookin' fer sompin ta read on niz trip so 'e takes tha book Madame Helvetius sen' 'im. One day, after 'e's finished lookin' at some ruins b'side tha road, he picks up tha book an' starts thummin' fru it. Course he don't know nuffin 'bout it so 'e d'cides ta read tha innerduction. Lo an' b'hole, its by Perfesser Helvetius! 'In zeze pages,' tha Perfesser sez,

'Voltaire wages ze war of ideas between ze two great philosophical princee-ples. On ze one hand eez ze rational principle zat knowledge of ze world zat eez deduced from ze ideas zat are inate in ze rational mind. On ze other han' eez ze princeeple zat knowledge eez constructed from ze esperience srough ze natural processes of combination an' abstraction.' Cordin' ta Perfesser Helvetius, tha firs' principle boils down ta sompin called 'meta-physics' tha way Herr Leibniz sed. Tha secon' bolls down ta tha natur'l philosophy 'spoused by Isaac Newton an' John Locke. 'Let ze reader judge for heemself ze merits based on ze eveedence,' Helvetius tells 'is readers.

"Stay wif me now," Shoate' commanded, "Tom Jefferson dint hole nuffin wif no metaphysics cuz 'e didn't b'lieve nuffin 'less 'e kin count it er weight it. Right! If an apple hit 'im on na head, he'd count tha res' ov um so 'e'd know how many more apples war gonna lan' on nis head. See whut ahm sayin'? He could see tha 'effect', but 'e wudn't innerested in na 'cause'. That made 'im dif'rent fom Isaac Newton. Ya follow whut ahm sayin'? It didn't 'cur ta Tom Jefferson ta aks <u>why</u> da apple hit 'is head. That kina phil'sophical shit wuz clean ov'r 'is head. Right! Tha's why he wen' wif Voltaire—Voltiare don't hole nuffin wif metaphysics neither. Nor wif tha church er religion. See whut ahm sayin'? Tom didn't hafta read Leibniz's book ta see fru him. He jes' had ta look 'roun' an' seen that it warnt tha bes' ov all poss'ble worls. An' he 'greed wif Voltaire when 'e sed fokes autta cultivate thur own gardens cuz Tom liked ta do that 'imself. Right!

"Tom's travelin' fru tha souf o' France sinkin 'bout cultivatin' nis own garden. Back in Paris, Sally an' Jimmie d'cide ta go shoppin' at a place called tha Halle aux Bleds. Fokes liked ta go thar cuz it had a roof over tha middle ov it. Right? So Sally's thar wif tha kitchen hep pickin' out greens fer supper an' boom! She walks smack inta Pierre Cabanis an' nis pal, tha marquis de Condorcet. Cabanis makes a big bow cuz 'e knows 'es sayin' hello ta Tom's secret daughter. Then 'e innerduces 'er ta tha marquis. Nex' sing ya know, their talkin' 'bout da frui' b'longin' ta ever'body.

"Turns out Condorcet spen's a lot o' time thinkin' 'bout this 'imsef, an' tha only thin' 'e likes more 'n thinkin' 'bout is's talkin' 'bout it. So thar they are in na middle o' tha collard greens an' cabbages talkin' politics. Sally's tellin' 'um 'bout how prop'ty's spread 'roun' wrong an' that poor fokes got rights by tha law o' nature an' how good it wuz b'fore fokes 'cumulated prop'ty. Condorcet's splainin' right back how they godda git rid o' tha dead han' o' tha pas' an' shit like that. They're havin' a fine time 'til Jimmie stars gettin' itchy cuz 'e's gotta git back ta tha house an' cook supper.

"Well yo' go on back ta tha kitchen an' mine yer bidness, Sally tell's 'im in no uncertain terms. So happens my bidness's here talkin' wif dese gennemen. So Jimmie marches off inna huff an' that's zat. Meantime, good lookin' Sally spens tha res' o' tha afternoon sippin' tea an' talkin' 'bout Rousseau an' tha good ol' days when fokes lived in Nature an' 'bout gettin' utopia goin' wif tha marquis an' Pierre Cabanis.

"She's puttin' this stuff out, an' thur shakin' ner heads. This gal's got sompin ta say, they 'gree, winkin' back an' forth. How 'bout we take 'er over ta tha club an' have 'er talk wif tha bros? She sez that's fine wif her. So off they go over ta Adrian DuPort's place. Right? That's whar tha club wuz meetin' that day. Nex' sing ya know, Sally's in nar laughin' an' jivin' wif tha brightes' lights in na moo'ment, ya know—Tallyrand, Mirabeau, Abbe Morellet, Abbe Sieyes, Rabaut Saint-Etienne, Lois-Sebastian Mercier, an' ol' DuPont de Nemours. All ov um 're lissenin' ta 'er splain 'bout equal'ty an' gittin' utopia goin'. An' ner all admirin' tha gal Cabanis sez ez tha secret daughter o' tha famous Amer'can rev'olutionary. Whut a great guy 'e mus' be teachin' 'is chile tha new ahdeas. An' ain't Amer'ca sum special kina place!

"Ain't too long b'fore Cabanis comes up wif tha ahdea ta play a li'l sprize on Tom Jefferson when 'e get's back ta town. Why don't dey git La-fayette ta bring 'im over ta tha club fer dinner an' have 'is secret daughter thar ta meet 'im. Won't he be plezed! Ever'body 'grees, so Cabanis makes tha 'rangements.

"Tha night comes 'roun' an' Lafayette brings Tom wif 'im ta tha club. Ya followin' me? Tom 'rrives an's bein' innerduced ta all tha big dogs in na moo'ment. Nex' sing 'e knows 'e's shakin' han's wif 'is slave gal fom na kitchen. Holy shit! 'e sez to 'imsef on na inside. On tha ou'side 'e's turnin' red's a t'mata. Ya wif me? Nuffin like this ever happin back in ol' Virginnie. See whut ahm sayin'? But whut's 'e gonna do—make a scene in fron' o' tha bes' people in Paris? They're smilin' an' pattin' umselves on na back fer pullin' off thur sprize. Ya wif me? They ain't got no ahdea that Tom Jefferson's turnin' red cuz 'e's soc'lizin' wif a piece ov 'is prop'ty. Anyway, he ain't got no choice but ta play 'long wif tha game. Cabanis's so happy that 'e offers a toas'. 'Ta tha new worl', he sez. 'Ta tha new worl', ever'body 'grees clinkin' ner glasses. Ya wif me? Here they're fixin' ta buil' utopia on Tom's big fat lie an' they ain't smart nuf ta figger it out.

"All these calc'latin' rad'cals 're out in na dark, but tha light's comin' on fer Miss Sally. Ya wif me? Now she sees how tha game's played. Right! She's got Massa by 'is balls. He caint give out wif tha truf cuz it'd be tha en' of 'im at tha club. An' he can't push 'er 'roun' cuz she's in na club 'erself. Right? Sompin's gotta give. See whut ahm sayin? Did ah say 'e'd finished wif da gum drop? Dat flame'd burned out, an' whut'd ya know. Tha sun ain't gone down b'fore Tom noc'ces zat Miss Sally looks jes' like 'er sister. Whoa! Ya followin' me here? This's whar nature takes iss course. Right? Tom stars seein' sompin new. Tha gal 'e's lookin' at's smart ez a whip, knows all 'bout Rousseau, an' utopians, an' an'rchiss, an' prop'rty. Ya wif me? Get outta tha way cuz here comes tha brave new worl!

"Tha guys in na club 're fed up wif tha ol' ways. Right? Whut's tha prob'em? Tha King's bin makin' all tha rules since all uv um kin r'member. Tha King's fat, dumb, an' happy, but tha mob 'cross tha mote's wearin' rags an' starvin' ta deaf. Ya got tha pitshure? So tha guys in na club er itchin' ta git sompin new goin'. Tha firs' sing dey got on ner list is fixin' it so tha king ain't callin' na shots. They're sittin' 'roun' readin' Rousseau who's tellin' um that tha King's bin foolin' wif sompin dat ain't his to fool wif. See whut ahm sayin'? Tha common good b'longs ta ever'body, an' ney aim ta fix it so tha King caint mess wif it.

"Jes' so happins that tha marquis's been bringin' Rousseau up wif tha times. Cordin' ta Condorcet, tha Almighty don't mean fer tha earf ta b'long ta dead fokes cuz zat don't make no sense—might ez well give it ta tha cats an' dogs! See whut ahm gettin' at? Thin's gotta add up. That's how a scientis' tells ef iss right. Ya wif me? Condorcet's comin' up wif a plan, but iss gotta add up. Tha way 'e sees it, tha prob'em's 'bout gittin' power outta da hands of the fog-boun' King an' his crowd. He figgers tha bes' way ta do it's by sayin' tha King's workin' on da wrong side o' tha Law o' Nature. Right? Cordin' ta Condorcet, kings ain't got no right hangin' 'roun' fom one gen'ration ta tha nex' doin' whutever plezes um. An' tha same goes fer Dukes, an' Barons, an' na res' o' tha h'reditaries. Ya still wif me? Condorcet's gonna get rid o' tha lan' laws zat's bin keepin' 'em all on na top o' tha heap.

The scholar stopped there and focused on Claire. "Lemme aks you sompin Honey. Zis sound fermilier?" Claire stared back in silence. "It should cuz iss za same drum wuz Tom 'uz thumpin' ta git tha Amer'can Rev'lution goin'. Right? Lissen ta me now—this's tha essent'al point. Jefferson wuz pushin' it fom tha common law side. But tha Frenchies ain't got no common law! Ya wif me? Ever hear anybody talkin' 'bout tha rights o' Frenchmen? Ya ain't cuz thar ain't no sech sing'. See whut ahm sayin'? So Connie come up wif a new ahdea. Whut's lef'? Natur'l Law! That's whut's lef'. Ya see whut ahm sayin'? This fits jes' right cuz natur'l law's whutever ya say it is. See whut ahm gettin at? Who's gonna argue wif tha marquis de Condorcet? He's a scientis'! Right!

"Course zis iz za kina thin' that put Tom on edge cuz 'e never stopped thinkin' like a lawyer. He figgered fer sompin ta add up, ya had ta have a prec'dent. He didn't much like tha way Condorcet wuz doin' it, but he kep' 'is mouf shut cuz tha guys in na moo'ment 'greed wif tha marquis.

"Meanwhile, Sally wuz on ta tha nex' sing. See whut ahm sayin'? She'd bin readin' in Tom's *Decleration* whar fokes kin change thur govermen' whenever it suits um. Right? An' she'd also been lissenin' ta tha marquis whur he sed that new gen'rations have tha right ta come up wif thur own plans fer thur governmen'. Right? Tha way she figgered it, these wuz two side o' tha same page. She wuz usin' reason like Connie ta see tha big pitshure, while Tom 'uz wanderin' 'roun' in na fog searchin' fer legal prec'dents ta make 'is case stan' up. See whut ahm sayin'?

"An'way, one day Tom comes by all frien'ly an' stars chattin'. 'Sally, honey,' 'e sez, 'how ya feelin'? Ever'thin' Ok? You sure lookin' good.' Ya know whut ah mean. Sally's workin' on na paper she's readin' at tha club that night, an' she ain't got no time fer 'is so'shalizin' so she ain't payin' no 'ttention. Right? Nex' sing ya know, Tom's huggin' an' kissin' on 'er!

"Tha's it! She prise 'ersef loose 'nuf ta smack 'im 'cross 'is chops. 'Yo' keep yo' han's t' yo'sef buster,' she sez, cuz ah ain't got time ta fool wif ya.' That's whut her chulren she sed she tole em 'bout tha fam'us Amer'can rev'lutionary. Hear whut ahm sayin'? She tole 'im, you're so far down nar in na fog ah caint even see ya.'

"'Huh?' Tom's so flummoxed tha's all 'e kin say. He ain't never heard a piece ov 'is prop'ty say sompin like that b'fore. Right?

"'Yo' ain't never gonna git that stuff 'bout whar tha earf b'longs ta tha livin'.' That's the nex' sing Sally tells 'im. 'All you kin do's copy whut other fokes say.'

"'Sally honey,' he sez back, nice ez 'e kin be, 'Ah know that stuff 'bout tha bes' ov all poss'ble worlz cuz ah bin readin' *Candide*. How 'bout we git t'gether an' share.'

"'Well,' she sez, 'ef ya wanna know 'bout tha way ahm seein' it, yo' kin bring your white ass over ta tha meetin' an' hear whut ah got ta say thar. Now git on cuz ah got work ta do.' Dat's all she got time ta say.

"Ol' Tom walks off shakin' nis head. One thin' 'e's got figgered out is that this gal ain't like tha gum drop 'e jes' finished wif. See whut ahm sayin'?

"Evenin' comes 'roun' an' Sally's givin' 'er speech 'bout how tha earf b'longs' ta tha livin'. Only she's addin' sompin new. Ya wif me? When na gener'tions change, it ain't like tha ol' crowds' checkin' out in na mornin' an' tha new crowds' checkin' in af'er lunch. Right? Fokes 're checkin' out an' checkin' in all la time. Sally's gotta prob'em wif dis cuz she's sinkin' like Connie. See whut ahm sayin'? She's approachin' tha prob'em like a scien-tis'. So she aks 'ersef, if tha new crowd's comin' in whal tha ol' crowd's still checkin' out, when ya sposed ta start tha new plan? See tha comp'ication? Whut's lef' ov tha ol' crowd's gonna say hol' on nar! Don't be screwin' 'roun' wif da plan cuz its gittin' us to tha higher good jes' tha way we wan' it. But tha new crowd's gonna say, shit on nat! We're sick o' waitin' 'roun' fer ya'll ta leave cuz we're ready ta git up wif da higher good da way we wan' it.

"Sally's splainin' tha prob'em. Tom's zar waitin' fer tha part 'bout cul-tivatin' nis garden. Right! Sally's goin' on an' on 'til 'is head stars bobbin'. Nex' sing ya know, Tom's soun' asleep. 'Cross tha aisle, tha marquis's wide awake an' eatin' it up like a hungry horse. Ya wif me? By an' by, 'e stan's up an' sez, 'Madmosel, si vous plaî. How eze we going to fix ze crowd problame?'

"'Ahm glad yo' aks me that, marquis,' she sez. 'Tha way ta fix it is ta 'llow each crowd ta be tha boss fer nineteen poin' sev'n years. Ain't that fair?'

"While tha marqus's mullin' it over, this woolly guy in na back jumps up an' stars wavin' nis han's an' makin' a fuss. 'Iss gotta be thirty years,' 'e yells, 'tha's tha right nummer. Take it er leave it!'

"Turns out this guy's Tom's pal fom na Amer'can Rev'lution—ol' Tom Paine. He jes' arrived fom Inglin' wif 'n iron bridge he's spects ta sell ta tha King o' France. Course tha ruckus wakes up Tom Jefferson. 'Bout tha same time, tha marquis finishes 'is calc'lation, an' ne yells out over tha commotion that tha right nummer's twenty-one. Well, Tom Paine don't take kinely ta fokes messin' wif 'is nummer so 'e storms out. Jefferson's got twenty-one ringin' in nis ears an' 'e's watchin' 'is pal runnin' out o' tha hall. So 'e' wan's ta know wha's goin' on. Ya still wif me? Tha marquis ain't got time ta git Tom Jefferson up wif 'is calc'lation cuz 'e an' Sally's jes' figgered out how ta keep tha dead han' o' tha pas' fom chokin' na fokes that ain't checked in yet. See whut ahm sayin'? 'e's too busy plannin' 'is nex' move wif Sally ta splain 'is calc'lations ta Tom.

"Lafayette's sittin' nex' ta Tom. He bin followin' ez bes' 'e can so 'e sez, 'cordin' ta Connie, Sally's got it 'bout right an' Tom Paine's got it mos'ly wrong.'

"'Holy shit!' sez Tom to 'imsef. He's tha smartes' guy in na club an' 'e's puttin' Sally ahead ol' Tom Paine! That's all Tom's gotta hear. Right! He gits on up wif tha marquis an's shakin nis han'. 'This's tha bes' news ah've heard since tha Virginnie 'sembly give up tha Western R'serve.' That's whut Tom Jefferson tells za marquis de Condorcet. Course he ain't got no ahdea whut tha marquis' talkin' 'bout, an' na marquis ain't got no ahdea whut Tom's talkin' 'bout. Ya wif me? Anyway, Tom's still tryin' ta make tha connection so 'e keeps goin'. 'An' ahm moddy proud o' Miss Sally heah cuz she bin learnin' right 'long jes' tha way ah plann'd it, spesh'ly tha stuff she's gettin' from esperience.'

"Tha marquis smiles when ne hears zis. See whut ahm sayin'? He don't know nuffin 'bout Tom Paine er tha Western R'serve, but 'e figgers Sally's gonna hep 'im finish tha plan ne's workin' up. Right? 'Si vous plaî,' he sez ta Sally. 'Zer eze somezing else zat I weesh to speech wees you. Ze pleasure eze mine wees your company for ze supper.' That's fine wif Sally cuz she likes tha way tha marquis goes 'bout thin's. Nex' zing ya know she's walkin' out tha door right pas' Tom Jefferson.

"The marquis takes 'er in nis gold carriage back ta chez moi. He takes 'er out ta 'is gard'n whar a bunch o' white-stockin' servants 're layin' out a table wif pate' an' truffles an' tha kina food rich people in France eat. Right? Tha marquis takes 'er to a chair. B'fore he sits down, 'e pours two glasses o' champagne—one fer Sally an' one fer 'imself. Sally's lookin' jes' ez sweet ez a sugar plumb as za marquis sits down b'side 'er. He smiles an' makes a toas'. 'To our plan!' he sez, clinkin' 'er glass. He swallows 'is champagne an' hums a few bars o' Yankee Doodle while 'is white-stockin' servants finish settin' na table. By an' by they got thin's jes' right an' march back fru da hedge. Now tha two ov um 're a'lone. Right? Tha marquis' lookin' at Sally wif zat certain look. An' Sally's lookin' back jes' ez pert ez she kin be. Ya gettin' na pitshure? Nex' sing, 'e pulls off 'is wig an' tosses it over tha hedge. Ya wif me? 'Zare eze no need for ze formality. Nez pa?' he sez. 'Let us be naturelle like ze birds.' That's Ok wif Sally cuz she's tha natur'l kine. See whut ahm sayin'? Nex' sing, he unbuttons 'is ves'. Right? Course Sally figgers zat's tha way it works in na marquis' neck o' tha woods so she goes 'head an' unbottons 'er dress. She ain't finished wif tha las' button when na marquis reaches into 'is shirt pocket an' pulls out a big white env'lope. Course Sally ain't got nuffin in 'er dress cep' 'ersef so she jes' sets zar waitin' fer tha nex' sing ta happen. Tha marquis ain't payin' no 'ttention ta 'er now cuz 'e's buzy openin' tha env'lope. 'You eer ze wise one, Madmosel,' 'e sez when 'e's done. 'Ze time eze run srough for ze ol' plan. Nez pa?' Sally 'llows zat she's thinkin' 'long tha same line. 'So let us make ze new one togezzer?' That's ok wif Sally. So 'e unfolds za paper an' han's it to 'er. 'What you sink ov zees one?' On tha top o' tha page, it sez *The Constitution of the United States.*

"She's readin' tha marquis' plan an' noddin'. Mmmm . . . mmmm . . . He's hummin' Yankee Doodle an' sippin' nis champage. Ever'things goin' 'long Ok 'til she gits ta tha part whar it sez zat repr'sentation's gonna be calc'lated based on na hole number of free fokes an' indentured servants, an' three fiss o' tha res' ov um. 'Whut's zis here, marquis?' That's whut Sally wan's ta know. He takes up tha paper an' reads it 'imsef. 'Ze part people ere ze slaves,' he sez an' han's it back to 'er as if it don't make no dif'rence. 'If all men er tha same by tha law o' nature, what's zis stuff 'bout part people?' That's whut Sally aks 'im. He stops hummin'. 'Que?' 'Tha part people?' She sez again. 'Madmosel, zis eze an anzer zat I do not have! What does ze beel of rights say on ze matter?' She skims down fru tha res' o' tha paper right ta tha bottom. 'Ain't got no bill o' rights,' she sez, tossin' tha paper on na table. 'Sacre bleu!' tha marquis sez, settin' down nis glass. 'Zis eze no plan wees ze part people an' weesout ze beel of rights?' He's strokin' 'is chin. 'Zen we take ze nozzer course.'

"Tha marquis picks up tha silver bell nex' to 'is glass an' rings it jes' ez neat ez ya pleze. B'fore you kin say 'all men er created equal,' 'is butler's standin' nex' to 'im. Tha marquis gestures an' tha butler leans down. Sally watches az za marquis whispers sompin in nis ear. Nex' zing, tha butler's gone. Tha marquis fills up thur glasses wif more champagn an' makes a new toas'. 'To ze great Amer'can rev'lutionary,' he sez. Course Sally don't know nuffin 'bout no great Amer'can rev'lutionary cuz ain't n'body never sed nuffin to 'er 'bout it. So she jes' smiles like she knows all 'bout it. Soonas tha marquis' finished drinkin' nis toas', tha butler's back. This time 'e's gotta silver tray wif a li'l red book in na middle ov it.

"Tha marquis picks it up, an' tha butler's gone again. He thumbs fru it ta tha right place an' puts 'is toothpick thar ta mark tha page, then ne han's tha book ta Sally. 'Zis eze ze key to ze problame.' 'Zat Right!' she sez, takin' tha book. On tha cover it sez, *Notes on the State of Virginia by Thomas Jefferson.* She looks over at tha marquis. He's smilin' back at 'er like da cat dat ate tha cheese. Ya wif me? Zis eze ze plan of ze famous Amer'can rev'lutionary heemself! Nez pa? Ete eze weesout doubt heze greatace masteerpeeze.' Sally opens tha book ta the page wif tha marquis's toothpick an' reads tha words at tha top: *The Constitution of The State of Virginia.*

"This's tricky ladies," tha scholar announces, "cuz it ain't ac'shally tha cons'tution fer tha State o' Virginnie. Ya followin' me? Ol' Tom hated tha real un more'n he hated tha King o' Inglin' so 'e kep' it out ov 'is book. Tha cons'tution 'e put in 'is book wuz tha one 'e wrote 'imself. He wuz parsh'l to it caze it had 'is stuff fer layin' tha ax ta tha root ov Virginnie's aristocursy. That wuz 'is big thin'," Professor Shoate explained. "Don't never ferget it! Tom stuck it in nis book cuz 'e sposed n'body in France'd know tha dif'rence. See whut ahm sayin'. That's how inlightened 'e wuz. He pulled one ov 'is fas' ones on um by sneakin' nis own plan inta 'is book like it wuz tha real thin'! That's tha kina thin' 'e did when na coas' wuz clear. Lissen ta me now—this's tha way lawyers op'rate, switchin' papers 'roun' right in fron' o' tha bes' an' brightes'. See whut ahm sayin'? He wuz fiddlin' wif da fruit! Lawyers call it settin' a *prec'dent.* Got dat?

"Tom's prec'dent dint make no dif'rence ta tha marquis cuz 'e an' Sally wuz workin' on nir own plan. Right? He jes' wanned Sally ta see how Tom wuz movin' na fruit 'roun'. Course, Sally had tha chain stuff all figgered out an' he'd figgered out how ta change tha plan ever' twenty-one years. See whut ahm sayin'? Tween um, they had tha whole scene covered. 'By ze way,' sez za marquis, 'has you ze copy of ze *Virginnie Decleration of Rights?'* 'I ain't got dat wif me,' Sally sez. Nex' sing he's ringin' nis bell an' whisperin' in nis butler's ear. His butler disappears, but in tha blink of Sally's eye 'es back an' handin' 'er a copy ov tha *Virginia Decleration of Rights.*

"'Si vous plaî,' sez Connie. 'Ze constitution of Meesure Jefferson eze not like ze constitution of ze Oonited States. Zer ere no part peuple and zer eze ze beel of rights.' He smiles zat certain smile.

"Course Sally's gettin' na pitshure loud an' clear. She's goin' fru Tom's plan an' sho' nuf ain't no part people in it. By 'n by, she comes ta Section Four an' dars a bunch o' rights set out in black an' white. She's readin' fru um ... mmmmm ... mmmmm ... Then she gits ta tha part whar fokes ol' nuf 're gonna git fifty acres o' lan'. That soun's ok. On she goes ta tha nex' part ... mmmmm ... mmmmm ... That's whar it sez lan'hol'ers ain't gonna have n'body 'bove um. That soun's ok so on she goes ta tha nex' part ... mmmmm ... mmmmm ... Tha's whar it sez tha gals 're gonna have tha same rights ez tha guys. That's it. She shuts tha book. "This one's got tha frui' prob'em fixed!" she sez.

"'Très bien!' he sez.

"B'fore 'e kin say 'is nex' word, sompin comes whirlin' fru tha hedge an' plops down b'side 'er. 'Yoohoo! Ete eze ze time for ze bonheur general,' sez a lady wearin' flowers in 'er hair an' nuffin else. She takes a big-eye look at Sally wif 'er dress open. 'Oo la la!' she sez. 'Ze young fruit!' She fro's 'er arms 'roun' Sally an' stars kissin' 'er.

"'Pardon mon sheri,' tha marquis sez, 'ze bonheur general eze aiftair ze suppere—remember?'

"'Merd!' sez tha lady slumpin' back in 'er chair dark an' grumpy.

"'Madmosel,' sez da marquis. 'Eet eze ze pleasure for you to meet Madame Condorcet who eze peerfecting ze societie in ze messod of Meesure Helvetius.'

"'Tha pleasure's mine, yer highness,' Sally sez ez sweet ez she can.

"'Bon!' tha naked lady sez back wif 'er big eyes an' stars feelin' 'roun' fer tha frui' in Miss Sally's dress. 'Oooo! Ze pleasure eze also wees me.'

"Tha marquis' smilin' cuz 'e's in na bidness 'bout perfectin' s'ciety jes' like 'is wife. An' 'e figgers'e's jes' 'bout thar. Ya wif me?

'We have now only to pour ze nectair into ze vessel,' tha marquis sez.

"'How ya spect ta do that,' Sally aks 'im once she's clear ov 'is wife.

"'We must have ze fruit move in ze way of Meesure Rousseau so ze erse eze wees ze living peuple. Zen weel ze societie be peerfet.'

"'I spose ya got that worked out?' Sally sez, buttonin' up 'er dress.

"'Exactamon!' sez za marquis. 'Eet eze nossing but ze trifle. Meesure Jefferson takes ze power from ze rich and geeves eet to ze not so rich. We

256

poot ze power wees ze people. N'est-ce pas? Meesure Jefferson geeves ze vote to ze men wees ze land. We geeve ze land to all ze men and ze all women so all ze peuple has ze vote. N'est-ce pas? Zen we clean ze slate every twenty-one yeers wees ze new *contrat social* and ze strong weel no more tred oopon ze weak! Eze zis ze utopia or what eze it?' Tha marquis refills 'is glass, 'is wife's glass, an' Sally's glass wif more champagne, then 'e stans up. 'To ze leeberty, eequality, and fraterneety!' he sez. 'An' to ze bonheur general!' His wife sez, standin' up wif 'im.

"'Hol' on nar, marquis,' sez Sally. 'We gotta prob'em.'

"'Pardon?' the marquis sez wif a dark look.

'How fokes gonna own lan' wif no super'or ef you spread tha frui' 'roun' one way an' roll heads 'roun' an'ther?' 'That don't square wif tha rights Tom sez they got.'

"'Qu'est-ce que c'est!' sez tha marquis, grabbin' na book outta Sally's han'. He shuffles fru 'til 'e gits ta tha place.' Mmmm . . . mmmm. Then 'e stops dead. 'Sac'ray blu!' 'e sez. 'Zis eze not ze way for ze rights of ze man in ze peerfect societie!'

"'That's whut ahm tellin' ya,' Sally sez. 'Tom Jefferson's ahdea's 'bout tha rights o' man 're ez stale ez a Chris'mas frui'cake!' That's whut she tells tha marquis.

"'Stale frui'cake?' he sez back. 'How can ete be?'

"'Iss simple es A-B-C,' Sally tells 'im. 'Tom Jefferson's a lawyer. His ahdea 'bout rights comes fom tha common law tha Saxons put out when Harol' wuz runnin' Inglin.''

"'Mon dieu!' sez tha marquis, 'Zat eze not ze way for ze utopia. Ze law in ze peerfec' societie eze like ze bread. Eet must avery day be fraish! Ef eet eze stale like ze fruitcake, we cannot move ze fruit an' we cannot have ze utopia. N'est-ce pas? We must keep ze oven hot!'

"'That's 'bout tha only way ta solve tha chain prob'em an na frui' prob'em,' Sally 'grees. 'But lemme aks you sompin else, Connie.'

"'Certainemau, Madmosel.'

"'How ya gonna keep tha new fokes fom eatin' up all la frui' fer umselves?'

"'Ah!' tha marquis sez smilin' nat certain smile. 'Zat eze ze beeziness of ze rolling heads. Zis eze how we fertilize for ze higher good. N'est-ce pas? We keep ze peuple all ze same lengse!'

"'Then we gotta git tha rights o' man fom tha law o' nature, not fom prec'dent like Tom done,' sez Sally. 'Iss zat simple, ain't it?'

"'Cum see, cum sa,' tha marquis 'grees.

"Tha's how thins got starred 'tween na marquis an' Miss Sally. She's puttin' in her stuff an' 'e's fixin' it. An' 'e's givin' 'er his stuff an' she's gittin' nit straight. This'd been goin' on fer a whal when Tom no'ces zat Miss Sally's spendin' a lotta time wif tha marquis. Yo' wif me? So 'e comes by one day. 'Honey chile,' 'e sez. 'Yo' sho is tight wif tha marquis de Condorcet.'

"'Whut you spect?' she sez. 'Me an' him's got a new French Cons'tution jes' 'bout done. How yo' like dat?'

"'Wull dip me in shit,' sez he all s'prised. 'I been writin' cons'tutions ma'sef tha pas' twelve years. Ain't thar sompin ah kin do ta help?'

"'Ta tell ya' tha truf,' Sally tells 'im, 'yo' ain't got tha pitshure in focus.'

"'That's da mose shit ah've heard!' Tom sez wif 'is dander goin' up. 'Mah stuff's all over tha place back in Virginny.'

"'Tha prob'em,' Sally tells 'im, is zat you got stale frui'cake in na pantry.'

"'Oh yea!' Tom sez, standin' tall es 'e can.

"'Tha's right!' Sally tells 'im, raisin' up 'er chin so he knows she ain't foolin' 'roun'. "Yu' got tha frui' movin 'roun', but you ain't got nuffin in none o' yer plans 'bout gittin up wif da higher good, er perfectin' s'ciety.'

"'Huh?' Tha's all Tom's got ta say cuz he don't know nuffin 'bout perfectin s'ciety.

"'Lemme tell ya sompin else,' Sally sez. 'Ain't none o' this new stuff in na Amer'can Cons'tution neither. All it got's whut it don't need an' it ain't got none o' whut it do need. An' ah might jes' wanna do sompin 'bout that when me an' na marquis' done wif tha French one.'

"'Ah s'pose yo' got sompin ta figger on nar,' Tom sez. 'Les' git t'gether on nat cuz ah wanna be up wif tha new stuff.'

"'Lemme git back ta ya cuz ahm full up jes' now wif tha French bidness,' she sez.

"'Now ya menshon it,' Tom tells 'er, 'Me an' na marquis de Lafayette's writin' a decleration on na rights o' man.'

"'You say!' sez Sally.

"'Tha's right,' 'e sez, proud ez 'e kin be. 'It's jes' 'bout like tha one George Mason put out fer tha state o' Virginny back in '76 cep' is's got summa tha gardenin' stuff like Rousseau said.'

"'Zat right!" Sally sez. "Ah jes' might like ta take a look at it.'

"'Yo' wait here an' ahl go fetch it,' Tom sez an' runs off.

"Sally's settin' nar hummin' na tune that jes' come up fom na country. B'fore she's haf way fru, Tom's back. 'Ahm moddy proud o' this,' 'e tells 'er. 'Iss gonna put tha French people jes' ez good ez tha fokes back in Virginny ownin' lan' an' all.'

"'Shutcher mouf an' lemme read it,' Sally sez, cuz she ain't gonna lissen ta no truck fom Tom Jefferson 'bout da fokes back in ol' Virginnie.' Ya wif me? She's readin' mmmmm ... mmmmm. An' readin' sommo' mmmmm ... mmmmm. All ov a sudden, she fro's tha thin' down. 'Lemme tell yu' sompin,' Sally sez. 'You got ol' frui'cake in na pantry, but this here part 'bout da men bein' born free an' equal in rights ez tha same's whut Rousseau put out. Zat whar ya got it?'

"'Ta tell ya' tha truf,' Tom sez, 'Lafayette wrote that stuff.'

"'Well then,' Sally sez, 'whut 'bout this here part wif da prop'ty bein' 'a natur'l an' imperscrip'ble right'? That come fom Lafayette too?'

"'Now that ya menshon it, it wuz kina his ahdea,' Tom sez. 'He tole me that ever'body's fer it 'roun' here cuz John Locke said 'bout tha same thing one time. Truf is zoh, ah ain't fer it ma'sef so much ez ahm against tha ol' mules havin' na hol' patshure fer umselves—see whut ahm sayin'?'

"'Mebbe ah do an' mebbe ah don't,' Sally tells 'im, keepin' 'er cards close in 'er han. 'Whut ahm tellin' ya is heads gotta roll. Ain't no way 'roun' nat cuz that's how ya keep tha frui' movin' so yo' kin get up wif tha higher good.'

"'Ah s'pose that makes sense,' sez Tom.

"'Certainemau!' Sally tells 'im, slappin' nis shouder. 'Ef yo' wanna git dis sing workin' yo' need ta put sompin in it 'bout tha bonur gen'ral. Got that? Once tha fokes kin 'spress thur a'pinions on ever' fool thin' that comes inta thur heads, yo' jes' 'bout at tha higher good.'

"'Zat how iss done?' Tom sez, scratchin' nis head. 'Whut 'bout tha church?'

"'Fergit 'bout tha church,' Sally tells 'im. 'Ya' gotta move tha goal pos' ta whar ya need um. Ain't that plain? Fokes don't know nuffin—mos' all they think ain't nuffin but shit n' nonsense. Right! So ya' jes' run um 'roun' 'til ya' got um whar ya need um. That's how Marat's bin doin' it. See whut ahm sayin'?'

"'This's startin' ta make sense,' Tom sez.

"'Now yer gettin' it,' Sally tells 'im. 'That's tha rollin' heads salution, Ya wif me? That's how ya perfec' s'ciety. Connie's got it all figgered out. In na perfec' s'ciety it don't mean nuffin ta say that prop'ty's 'involuable and sacred' cuz tha frui's gotta move ta keep up wif tha higher good. Got that?'

"'Ah hafta sleep on nit 'b'fore ah kin say fer sure,' Tom tells 'er. 'Ta tell ya tha truf, ah thoug' tha part 'bout ownin' tha lan' wuz moddy strong.'

"'Well ef yo' wanna be up wif tha new crowd yo' bes' git tha new frui'cake,' Sally sez. 'Elsewise I reckon ain't nobody in na club gonna have nuffin ta do wif ya.'

"'Hallaluya!' ol' Tom sings out allov a sudden. 'I jes' seen na light. But jes' en case they aks me 'bout it, gimme that part on na dead han' o' tha pas' one more time.'

"Sally splains it ta 'im again an' how it jives wif tha chain stuff an' na frui' stuff an' perfectin' s'ceity.

"'Well fritter mah wig,' Tom tells 'er when she's splained it to 'im. 'That's tha same stuff ol' Doc Gem's bin tellin' me 'bout, cep' I ain't bin able ta keep it straight.'

"'Zat right?' sez Sally.

"'Now that ah got it clear, ah reckon ah'll sen' a letter ta Jimmie Madison 'n splain it ta him,' Tom sez, beamin'.'

"'Tha's ok,' sez Sally, 'jes' be sure yer clear 'bout tha heads rollin' cuz that's how ya perfec' s'ciety. Ef yo' ain't got that, yo' ain't goin' nowhar. Yo' jes' gonna have tha big mules lordin' wif tha dead han' ov tha pas' an' all tha res' ov um sittin' 'roun' 'n chains.'

"'Tell me 'gain honey chile, whut's zis higher good stuff?' Tom wan's ta know. "That's tha kina quession Jimmie Madison'll aks me.'

"'Tha higher good's whut's in na law o' nature,' Sally tells 'im.

"'Ah never did know whut that wuz,' Tom tells 'er.

"'Iss whutever ya say it is,' Sally tells 'im wif a smack upside 'is head. 'Caint yo' keep nuffin straight?'

Claire glanced at her watch. "Oh!" She exclaims, jumping to her feet. "I'm late for my lunch with Raymond Paige!" Before anyone could say a word, she was at the door.

"Hole on nar, Cinnerella," Professor Shoate' shouted after her. "Yo' ain't hear'd tha part whar Sally shows Tom 'bout da boner genr'l . . ."

"Let her go, Professor," Frances Rank said in a calming voice. "We'll catch up with her after she finds Tim's papers."

"Yes?" The voice answering the phone was cold and impatient.

"Martin?"

"Who is this please?" He demanded.

"Martin, you've got to learn how to relax," Tim Hardin advised sarcastically. "You know what I'm gonna do—I'm gonna send you an ounce of Fred's special Albemarle Green hash as soon as I get off the phone"

"Ok, Tim." Ogden pretended to laugh. Then he became serious. "Do you have the document?"

"I've run into a snag," Hardin answered.

"What kind of a snag?" Ogden asked tensely.

"Paige's son told me that Fred sent it to his father."

"Whose father?" Ogden snapped.

"Paige's."

"That stupid imbecile!" Ogden cursed. "I told you to get rid of him." The edge on his voice was threatening.

"I know what you said . . . "

"Well, what have you done besides . . . "

"I'll take care of it," Hardin shouted into the phone. "You understand?"

"What's this about Paige's son?" Ogden demanded, changing the subject. "Why is he suddenly part of our discussion?"

"Forget about Paige's son. That doesn't concern you."

"Is he another operator in your drug ring?" Ogden's voice was cold as ice.

"By the way," Hardin added, ignoring the taunt, "guess where I found your kitten reporter this morning."

"I have no idea," Ogden snapped.

"Over on Belmont Farm shacked up with Paige's gofer."

"She's here on assignment," Ogden announced with cold patrician superiority.

"Don't bullshit me, Martin. I read her goddam piece. It sucked. She needs a baby-sitter, not an 'assignment.'"

Ogden did not respond.

"Well . . ." Hardin prodded sarcastically.

"We were looking for something different," Ogden conceded.

"Something different!" Hardin sneered. "That's good. That's really good." His voice became menacing. "You better get a harness on your little playmate or you're going to get something different. Have you forgotten about our deal?"

"Ok, Tim, you've made your point," Ogden said curtly as though he was terminating the conversation. But then he added, "These people are damned cunning, Tim. What they've done, if you look at it closely, is to invent a whole new mumbo-jumbo. Claire was taken in by it. We mustn't crucify her for one mistake . . ."

"I don't want to hear that shit, Martin. I wasn't born yesterday—and neither were you. You better decide right now which game you're playing. If you want to play her game, then I'm gone. If you want to be in my game, then you're going to have to play by my rules.

"I'm looking into it, Tim" Ogden replied. "That's all I'm prepared to say at this point."

"Good! Say . . ." Hardin was again cheerful, "have you met with Douglas yet?"

"He's joining me for lunch."

"Oh! Isn't that nice," Hardin chirped. "I hope you'll remind him to keep his ugly old puss out of the news."

Ogden laughed perfunctorily. "Ok, Tim." He swore as he hung up the phone. "Oh, God!"

———————————

Henry was not there to take her in the back way, so Claire decided to go in the main entrance.

Passing through the Shadwell intersection, she proceeded up 250 East to the Belmont sign and turned in. Ahead of her was a sparkling lake. The field green sign in front of it said *Belmont*. Its arrow pointed to the right. Claire followed the lane up a gently rise. A herd of Black Angus was grazing in the pasture beside her. Behind them she could see the towering poplar trees that sheltered the residence. At the corner of the pasture was another sign. One of its arrows pointed straight ahead to the academy. Another pointed right toward the residence. She turned there and drove two hundred yards along an ancient boxwood hedge. It opened there for a circle that turned in front of the mansion's portico. There were no other cars in the circle so Claire pulled to a stop directly in front of the front door.

She studied the structure before getting out. The door was at the back of an imposing four-columned portico decorated with a Tuscan entablature. There was an arched transom above the door and a sidelite panel on each side of it. The Chinese lattice railing that rimmed the portico's flat roof reminded Claire of Monticello. The impression was reinforced by the triple sash windows on either side of the portico—Jefferson had installed windows like these at Monticello and in the pavilions on the Lawn. The portico's entablature extended above these windows to the sides of the house. There were three windows on the second floor. Like the triple windows below them, each was flanked by a pair of dark green shutters. The facia panel that filled the space between these windows and the roof had the same form as the entablature that adorned the lower level. The mansion's roof was slate and rose in a low pyramid. Four chimneys stood near its peak, each about four feet tall. Two of them were situated on the roof's front slope. The building faced southwest toward Shadwell. Behind it in the distance was Monticello Mountain.

The grounds on the left side of the house were enclosed by another ancient boxwood hedge. To the right of the house, the ground receded in tiered gardens. Taken together, the estate was just as it should be for a member of Virginia's 20th century gentry.

Claire mounted the portico's three stone steps and crossed its flagstone paving. Squaring herself and smoothing her clothes, she reached toward the brass knocker. Before she could lift it, the door opened. A young black man in a white waste coat and a black bow tie greeted her. "Come in, Miss Fox," he said, stepping to one side and gesturing with a sweep of his arm. "Mr. Paige is expecting you." Claire entered a wide central hall that continued past a stairway to the mansion's upper floor. "If you will follow me . . ." He turned and walked toward an archway at the far end of the hall.

Claire paused to look through the door on her left. It opened into a spacious living room that Claire guessed was at least thirty feet long. It had a ten-foot ceiling and three floor-to-ceiling windows that looked out over the boxwood enclosure and across the valley that formed below Wolfpit Mountain. Her guide conducted her through the archway to an exterior door, which he opened for her. Claire stepped out onto a broad balcony that overlooked the terrace. The lawn on the far side of the terrace extended through a colorful fall garden to a fountain. Beyond the fountain was a swimming pool. Branches of giant poplar trees spread over the compound and covered it in pale shade.

Mr. Paige was sitting in a chair at the edge of the terrace. He was talking to someone on a telephone that sat on the patio table beside him. As Claire surveyed the scene, he looked up. Without interrupting his conversation, he signaled for her to join him. As she descended the stairway, he replaced the receiver in its cradle and rose to meet her. "Welcome, Miss Fox," he said. "What a pleasure to see you." He extended his hand and gave hers a firm shake. "That was Hank," he continued. "He's running a little late."

"Where is he?" Claire wondered.

"He's over at the hospital with Dr. Denker," Paige replied off-handedly.

"The hospital?" She repeated, her voice filled with alarm.

"Yes. Denker had an accident on his way home last night."

"Oh! No!" Claire exclaimed. "Is he alright?"

"Yes. The doctors say that he's going to pull through it."

"Thank goodness!" She sighed.

"Well thank you for your sentiments," Paige said. "I appreciate your concern."

"If he's receiving visitors, I'll go see him," Claire said, deflecting the compliment.

"I'm sure he would like that," Paige observed. "I'll let Hank arrange that when he gets here." He gestured toward the linen covered table at the center of the terrace. "Here—have a seat?" Claire followed him to the table and seated herself in the chair he held for her. He took the one next to hers. "Will you have something to drink?" He continued, "A Bloody Mary? A glass of wine?"

"Do you have . . . iced tea?" Claire asked.

"Yes, of course." Paige picked up a bell from the table and rang it. A moment later Leroy appeared. "Could you bring Miss Fox an iced tea . . . and I'll have the same." Leroy withdrew. "Now tell me, Miss Fox, how are you getting on? Are you getting everything you need?"

"Well, yes . . ." she paused, ". . . but I keep finding things that I . . . don't understand."

"Really!" Paige sounded surprised. "Such as?"

"One of your staff members drowned a few days ago. There's ... "

"Roberta Wiley," Paige confirmed, shaking his head reflectively. "What a tragedy. This conference was her idea! Did you know that?" He raised his eyebrows to emphasize her significance. Then he leaned toward Claire as if to share a confidence. "A grand jury is going to meet on Tuesday to investigate the matter. I think it best if we leave it there until they issue their findings."

"Have you spoken with Henry about it?" Claire asked, trying to pinpoint his place in the business.

"He's given me a full accounting," Paige answered firmly. "I feel badly for him. He tried, but apparently was unable to save her. It's a testimony to the quality of our staff that we've been able to pull this meeting off without her."

Claire compared his response with her own information. There was probably truth in it somewhere, she decided. "Then there's Dr. Denker's comment about the group that blew up the Rotunda," Claire went on. "He insinuated that it may be targeting the Jefferson Academy. None of this is in the published reports I have seen ... "

"Dr. Denker is a very reliable source, Miss Fox. It is entirely possible—I presume you know what happened to the Rotunda ..." Paige took a deep, settling breath. "But even if we are a target, we're not going to alter our course! I'm sure you understand that." He fixed his eyes on her so that she had no choice but to agree. "There's a growing void in the public's understanding of American history, Miss Fox. Fewer and fewer Americans have any idea what underpins our republic or what makes our society *civil*. E pluribus unum, Miss Fox. My grandfather learned what that meant at the peril of his life. If we allow our citizens to forget it, our society will shatter into a thousand pieces. That's our mission!" he continued. "We're going to see it through. Americans need to rally 'round their flag.'"

Claire had prepared herself for this speech. "It sounds like you're launching a political campaign, Mr. Paige. Could you confirm that for me?" She asked boldly.

"You're in Jefferson Country now Miss Fox, not Washington, DC. We're not caught up in politics down here. We don't think in cliches. We don't speak in sound bites." She could feel the heat radiating through his words. "Am I making myself clear?" He said pointedly. She did not respond. "Frankly, Miss Fox, it's in my power to light a light for the good of our country. If it turns out that I can use this light to lead, I am prepared to do that. But I am not a politician, and it would be difficult for me to be a figurehead in a political campaign—not that I wouldn't consider if it's the right thing to do! But at this point, it's more important to organize the people who share our vision. If I succeed in doing that," he continued, "there's no limit to what we can accomplish. Does that answer your question?" The look he gave her told her that it did.

"I've read your grandfather's account of how he became an American," Claire volunteered on the chance it would relieve the mounting tension.

"Really!" Paige said, brightening up. "He was quite a guy—don't you think?"

"Yes. His story is fascinating," she said, avoiding his question. "I suppose he's your inspiration?"

"Now that you mention it, Miss Fox, I'd like to know if he is an inspiration for you. America is your future. What do you expect to make of it?"

"Well . . ." she felt suddenly trapped. "That's not really relevant. Is it?"

"It is and for this reason," her host replied. "I am looking for a dynamic individual with strong media credentials to handle the academy's public relations work." Claire stiffened. "I've talked it over with Dr. Denker, and we both agree you're that person." She stared at him blankly. "I want you to help me save America," he said, looking calmly into her glazing eyes.

She felt suddenly dizzy and confused. This was worse than a nightmare—being pressed into service by an establishment tycoon whose self-appointed mission was to make America safe for rich male capitalists!

———————

The sleek black limousine pulled to a stop beneath the entrance canopy of the Boar's Head Inn. A bellhop stepped forward and opened its right rear door and looked down onto the craggy face of William O. Douglas. The old man grasped his outstretched hand and allowed himself to be pulled out.

"Meet me here in two hours Bo," he said to his chauffeur, after finding his footing on the sidewalk.

Boswell Bildner had been one of Bill Douglas's rangers. That's where he met Fred Ried and Tim Hardin. They had all been Bill's "boys". Bildner and Ried had gone on to serve in Vietnam. During their tour, they had acquired extensive knowledge about explosives and how to blow things up. Douglas had taken "Bo" under his wing after his tour ended. When he was incapacitated, Bildner became his full time attendant.

Bildner responded with a nod and stepped on the accelerator. The Supreme Court Justice watched his limousine pull around the circle and onto the access road. He turned then and hobbled into the hotel. The foyer opened into an elegantly decorated lobby. Its walls were paneled. Vases with bouquets of fall flowers adorned the tables under the room's two wall mirrors. Douglas found the atmosphere calming. He advanced slowly to the front desk where a clerk in a dark suit was waiting to greet him.

"I'm here to see Martin Ogden," he said.

The clerk referred to the hotel's registry. "That would be the Jefferson Suite on the fifth floor." Then he looked up. "Are you Justice Douglas?"

"Yes," the shaggy visitor replied proudly.

The clerk hit a bell on the counter beside him. A moment later, another dark-suited staff member appeared. "Roger, would you escort Justice Douglas to the Jefferson Suite."

Justice Douglas's escort withdrew as the door opened. Martin Ogden nodded a silent greeting and beckoned his ancient friend to enter. The aged jurist shuffled past him. Ogden followed him into the sitting room.

"You're right on time," he said in a business voice. "Are you ready to eat, or can I entice you into a refreshment?"

Douglas surveyed the room and, finding a chair that suited him, took a seat. He sat there for a moment without responding. "Perhaps I will have something," he sighed. "I've been growing more depressed ever since I arrived in town . . ."

Ogden stepped to the bar and lifted a tall bottle of amber liquid. He pulled the cork and filled two six-ounce Jefferson cups. "I thought people came down here to escape their cares," he opined, handing his guest a libation.

Douglas took a careful sip. "Tim has defied me," he announced, wiping his lips with the back of his hand. "I have to do something about that. I've already terminated Fred Ried."

"For the Rotunda thing?" Ogden wondered.

"That's part of it," Douglas acknowledged grimly.

"What's the rest of it?" Ogden asked.

"Tim told me that Fred mislaid one of my letters," Douglas answered.

"Is he going to blackmail you?" Ogden asked.

"He's no longer in a position to do that," Douglas answered vaguely.

"I see," Ogden said without inquiring as to his meaning. "Was there only one letter?"

"There were several . . ."

"That's a problem . . ." Ogden acknowledged, taking a sip of Lillet.

"Thank God for Bo!" The jurist brooded. "He's the only one I can count on . . ."

"I don't know him," Ogden observed, "but Tim's certainly a hand full."

"He has so many gifts," Douglas said, shaking his head. "But he lacks . . ."

"He called me this morning," Ogden interrupted.

"Oh?"

"Yes. He complained about Claire's article and made a few of his characteristic threats . . ." Ogden paused there and took another sip of his aperitif, ". . . and he told me to remind you to 'keep your ugly puss out of the news.' I believe those were his exact words."

Douglas sighed and shook his head. "This isn't a good time for a mutiny," he said, study8ng the silver cup in his hand. "He's one of these new men, you know. Everything has to be his way."

"Yes," Ogden nodded. "I see that."

"He's pathologically incapable of listening to advice," Douglas continued, his features darkening. "Now they're blowing things up! Something has to be done . . . ." He swallowed the rest of his drink. "What's happening, Martin? Where do these young people get their ideas?"

The newspaperman studied his colleague, recalling the risks they had taken in launching their revolution. "I suppose you're right, Bill," he said at last. "I'll have them serve lunch. We can talk while we eat."

Douglas sat quietly as his host dialed room service.

When he had finished giving his instructions, Ogden rose and went to the sliding glass partition that separated the sitting room from the suite's canopied balcony. He slid the door back and stepped out. The porch looked over a lake. "It is lovely down here, don't you think?" He filled his lungs with fresh fall air and gazed at the Blue Ridge Mountains, which loomed in the distance.

The table on the balcony had already been set. Douglas took the seat with the better view. "Martin," he said, gazing at the mountains, "you've been a good friend . . . "

His friend took the place beside him. "Now don't make me sound like a . . . "

Douglas waved him off. "I may not have another opportunity to say these things so let me speak."

"As you wish," Ogden responded patiently.

"You've done your share—and more. I want you to know how much I appreciate it."

Ogden smiled. "Was it Voltaire who said that revolutions succeed when they're led by unreasonable men?"

"I don't know," he answered, scowling. Then he sighed. "I haven't been the same since my stroke, Martin. My mind isn't sharp anymore. I'm losing it. I can feel it slipping away."

"Nonsense!" Ogden bristled. "You'll be as good as new in a couple of months."

"I'm resigning my seat on the Court, Martin. I wanted you to be the first to know."

Ogden bowed his head. "When?"

"In November."

The newspaperman raised his eyes and looked at his companion. "The country owes you a great debt, Bill. No one has been a more faithful friend to the common man than you. I'll see to it that message gets out."

"Thank you. And take some credit for yourself. It's taken a lot of courage to stay in this fight. You could have sat by—no one would have faulted you . . . "

"I did what was right . . ." Ogden answered defiantly, ". . . the same as you. I'm proud to have stood with you, Bill. And I'm proud of what we've done for the men and women who make this country work. If it weren't for us, they'd have been trampled by people like Paige."

The other man agreed. "It's been a productive relationship . . ."

There was a knock on the door. "Come in," Ogden answered, holding a finger up to silence his companion.

The door opened, and a young man in a waiter's uniform backed in pulling a cart. He guided it through the partition and parked it beside the host. Douglas watched as the waiter raised a bottle out of its cooler and present it to Ogden. After inspecting the label, Ogden nodded his approval. The server then set the bottle on the carriage and, with a skillful flourish, sliced off its seal. Peeling it away, he polished the exposed neck. An implement appeared in his hand as if by magic. In one seamless motion, he pierced the cork and sank the screw. In another, he freed the cork and placed it on the table beside Ogden's plate.

Ogden pinched it reverently between his first two fingers and his thumb. He pressed it thoughtfully before raising it to his nostrils. Perceiving the meaning of his patron's glance, the serveur poured half an inch of pale liquid into Ogden's glass. Ogden lifted it solemnly by its stem and studied its color against the midday sky. He brought it to his lips, but before tasting it, he swirled it and inhaled its bouquet. Next, he tilted the vessel and took an aliquant of the liquid into his mouth. The steward listened attentively as Ogden clicked his lips. The ritual completed, he set the glass down and nodded for it to be filled. Ogden continued to analyze the wine as he poured.

"'67 was an exceptional year for the Montrachet," he said, finally returning to his guest. "It's just now reaching its peak.... Dry," he mused, "yet luscious—just what you would expect of a great wine!" He took another introspective sip. "Try it and see if you don't agree."

As Douglas lifted his glass, the waiter set a plate down before him.

"It's pumpkin soup," Ogden announced. "Your favorite!"

"It's quite nice," Douglas agreed, referring to the wine. "You're wasting it on me, though Martin. I'm just a hayseed from the Cascade Mountains." Douglas's gaze drifted back across the lake to the spine of the Blue Ridge. "You know Martin, we're just a step or two away from finishing Jefferson's revolution!" He set his glass down and focused on his host. "And I have an idea that I think might take us the rest of the way."

"Oh really," Ogden said, focusing on his honored guest. "And what might that be?"

"I call it ... *diversity.*"

"Diversity?" Ogden repeated. "What is Diversity?"

"Divide and conquer," Douglas responded obliquely. "We'll apply Jefferson's techniques and finish dismantling the old-boy establishment!"

"I'm afraid you've lost me," Ogden said with a polite frown.

"You're going to seed the news with stories about how all cultures and peoples need to be treated with equal respect."

"Ok . . ." Ogden agreed tepidly.

"It isn't enough that we tolerate minorities—or dump them into the melting pot. We need to *celebrate* them . . . you follow what I'm saying? Make it a litmus test for moral rectitude. Insinuate that people who obstruct diversity are . . ." Douglas searched for a label, ". . . against equality. Don't say it in so many words but make them out to be . . . extremists. You know what I mean."

"No Bill," Ogden sighed, shaking his head. "We'd never be able to sell something that transparent."

"Why not?" Douglas objected. "You sold Johnson's economic justice thing didn't you?"

"Well . . . yes . . ." Ogden conceded.

"So do it the same way. Give it to the groups you're already bankrolling—they're always looking for a new bone to gnaw on. Keep repeating it until the public is accustomed to hearing it. That will give it credibility."

"You know," Ogden said, warming to the idea, "You might just be on to something." He stroked his chin thoughtfully. "Our existing system stifles diversity . . . minority cultures are being deprived of . . . "

". . . their civil rights!" Douglas chimed in. "Who's going to argue against civil rights?"

"Bigots and racists!" Ogden responded with a confirming smile. He shifted his focus and began framing the first article. "We'll have a picture of a gap-toothed redneck in a pickup truck with a rifle rack and a Confederate decal in the window. Beside it we'll have a black choir in their robes singing 'we shall o-o-v-v-e-r-r-r-c-o-mmmm . . .'" Ogden crooned it as if he were in a freedom march.

"That's it!" Douglas cried, slapping the table. "Make it a moral imperative.

"We'll call it . . . let's see . . . ," Ogden began to play with the idea. "'multi-culturalism'—how's that sound?"

"Perfect!"

Ogden moved further into the idea. "I'll have my staff cook up some mumbo-jumbo. We'll squeeze an endorsement out of some publicity-starved academic—I bet there's at least one tenure-track assistant professor at Georgetown who'd sell his mother to get his name in *The Washington Post*." He paused. "How about 'pluralism'? Does that have the right ring? 'Mono-cultural hegemony'! Say," he laughed, "this is going to be fun."

"Well, that's my idea," Douglas said with a self-deprecating smile.

"I like it," Ogden agreed. "It's good." Having passed his judgement, he turned back to his guest. "So why all the gloom, Bill?"

Douglas became serious. "I'm sick, Martin. Sick and worried!" He spoke with growing emotion. "I've poured my life into this cause. You know that better than anyone. I've fought off the fascists, I've re-invented the constitution, and I've gotten rid of Nixon. Now I'm an old man looking across the Jordan into the Promised Land—like Moses. And what do I see? Wet-behind-the-ear kids blowing it to kingdom come . . ."

"Whoa! Don't get yourself so worked up that you can't eat," Ogden chided. "I've gone to a lot of trouble to create a meal you'll enjoy."

Douglas responded with a feeble smile. "You're right, Martin. Your friendship is a great comfort to me." He picked up his spoon and dipped it into his soup.

"So, Tim's causing trouble again," Ogden observed after a period of silence. "What else is new?" Ogden skimmed a spoonful of soup. "Look," he said, dabbing the corner of his mouth with a starched napkin. "I remember when you introduced him to me at the *Pacem in Terris* Conference in '65."

"You have a good memory," Douglas replied.

"You said he would attract young people into the movement. Do you remember that?"

"That's right. I said that . . ." the old man remembered.

"He did it too—didn't he? What did we have—four hundred thousand at the anti-war protester filling the Mall in 1970? He inserted himself into Nixon's impeachment hearings—that was a nice piece of work. And since then, he's created a national following. He's in the news every day. Why, you can't pick up a paper without seeing his face. And the shows are lined up to have him on! He's a huge profit center!" Ogden observed reverently. "Did you know he raised a million dollars at Leonard Bernstein's Black Panther fund raiser last month? He's got charisma, Bill." Ogden fixed understanding eyes on the ancient rebel. "The fact is, without Tim, our movement could stall out."

"You're missing the point," Douglas answered stubbornly.

"I'm not missing the point." Ogden objected. "We have to do what it takes to prevail."

"I told him about our deal with Nixon," Douglas announced.

Ogden seemed stunned. "You did what?"

"I told him about our deal with Nixon," Douglas repeated.

"But . . . why?"

"It was going to come out sooner or later," Douglas said off-handedly.

"Something like that doesn't just 'come out,'" Ogden shot back.

"You know how Tim is—always pushing. Always looking for an angle. He started complimenting the way Nixon manipulated public opinion." Douglas set a trembling fist on the table. "Maybe he was just trying to get my goat, but I wasn't going to sit by and listen to that. Nixon's the most corrupt man I've ever known. He made his career selling out to fat cats and baiting reds. You know how I feel about that. But Tim just brushed me off. He said that success is an end that justifies its means and that Nixon had succeeded. He made Nixon sound like a hero."

"Bill! Bill . . ." Ogden reached across the table and placed a consoling hand on Douglas' clenched fist. "Tim's a professional. He's looking at it as a practitioner. You've got to separate your idealism from the practical necessities of winning a modern political revolution. It takes money. It takes influence. And you have to have media support . . ."

"Nixon didn't succeed," the unrelenting Justice fumed. "He would never have become President without us. That son of a bitch was willing to sell out to us because he thought it would help him get the Presidency! The scumbag!" Douglas swore angrily.

"What exactly did you tell Hardin?" Ogden asked warily.

"I laid the whole thing out—how we agreed to keep quiet if the bastard would keep funding Johnson's Great Society. That was no hardship for him," the old man fumed. "He had the same craving to be loved that Johnson had. I told him the part about the funding—how much more important that was than who was sitting behind the big desk."

"What did he say to that?" Ogden asked cautiously.

"He wanted to know why we dumped Johnson."

Ogden waited to hear Douglas's answer.

"Everybody knew Johnson was through. I told him that it wasn't just the war. He wouldn't support us in the peace conference and his policies were poisoning the environment. Tim knew he was a dead duck, but that didn't stop him from arguing with me about your plan. I guess it's all right for new men like Tim Hardin to act like fascists," Douglas sneered, "but the rest of us are supposed to be pure . . ."

"Wait a minute!" Ogden cut him off. "You told him it was *my* plan!"

"Well of course!" Douglas snapped.

"And you mentioned my name . . ."

"What kind of plan would it have been without you?" Douglas answered in a strained voice.

Ogden weighed the information. "What happened then?"

"He accused me of being a collaborator," Douglas snorted. "I tried to reason with him. I explained your rationale—what we were going to accomplish. How that money would allow us to expand our organization and build our network. I even explained that it would allow me to increase the size of my youth leadership program! Tim, Fred and Bo were all rangers in my first class—I bet you didn't know that," he observed with a fleeting smile. "You'd think that would mean something to him, wouldn't you?" The old man seemed hurt. "But he just laughed at me and called me an old fool. The world has changed since this new generation has come of age, Martin. These people measure things by Nixon's standards—in terms of money and who they can buy." Douglas stopped there. "He wants to set up a new government with a new constitution. Has he told you about that?"

"All right. All right!" Ogden said, raising his hand. "I've got the picture. I agree something needs to be done, but you're going to have to climb down off your soapbox, Bill. We're not writing a Court opinion, for Christ's sake! We're fighting a political war. Winning it is everything! That takes brains, and it takes *power*. You've spent forty years in the trenches prying Joe Lunchbox out from under the thumb of men like Raymond Paige. You know how the game works. We step back so we can leap forward. While you're re-painting the scenery behind the curtain, somebody's got to be out front diverting the crowd!"

Douglas stared at his host without expression.

"We need him, Bill . . . "

"I went along with you on your Nixon scheme," the old man said solemnly, "but you're pushing me to my limit on this one, Martin. It's not just about power. There's a principle involved here," the Supreme Court Justice observed, admonishing his host. "I'm beginning to wonder whether you understand that."

Ogden stared back uneasily.

"I have a vision, Martin. I see the society Jefferson wanted finally becoming a reality after two hundred years of establishment repression."

"So do I, Bill." Ogden protested. "So do I!"

"Then how can you let Tim Hardin destroy everything I've been working to accomplish for the last forty years?"

"No Bill!" The publisher protested. "Nothing could be farther from the truth. It's just that we can't do all the work behind the bench. We've got to force the issues. Tim's right. We've got to be in the streets."

"Has he told you about Jefferson's Constitution?"

The question caught the publisher off guard. "What about it?" He protested without answering the jurist's question.

"Did he tell you about the rally he's organizing?"

"That's exactly my point, Bill. We want him to be in the streets. We want him to fill the capital with protesters demanding economic justice and reparations from Paige and the other profit-hounds."

"He wants to call a plebiscite and force the Congress to resign," Douglas announced in exasperation. "Then he intends to have a 'people's Congress' ratify Jefferson's Constitution and form a new government—run by his gang of adolescent pranksters!"

"They're our foot soldiers, Bill," Ogden objected. "They agree with us!"

"He's rousing the rabble—just like Nixon did. He's going to keep stirring things up until everybody's angry. Then he's going to move in and take over! When that happens, we're finished. Our hopes and dreams will go right down the drain."

"Ok . . ." Ogden said, shifting quickly onto another tack, ". . . you have a point . . ."

"Look, Martin," the old jurist pleaded. "Thomas Jefferson wanted to eliminate the hegemony of the rich just like we do. He tried to do it the

275

same way that we are—by re-distributing their property. But he never intended for the mob to run things. He always planned to do that himself."

"Maybe you're right," Ogden allowed, searching for a way to placate his companion. "There's a limit to how much power we should entrust to Tim."

"Of course there is!" Douglas answered forcefully. "Part of the reason that Jefferson didn't win his revolution was that he fouled himself up with Natural Rights. You see what I'm saying? He put himself up against a wall. We've finally knocked that wall down, Martin. We can succeed where Jefferson failed because we've weaned the system of that silly notion. And we've done that by burying the idea of *natural* rights under an avalanche of *civil* rights actions." The Supreme Court's longest-serving Justice leaned forward to press his point. "We've made social equality a *moral imperative*! That's the key to our success! That's what allows us to use the Fourteenth Amendment the way we do. John Locke told us three-hundred years ago that government has a moral obligation to promote the *common good*. It's only been in the last twenty years that we've been able to convince people that the 'common good' means economic equality and social justice. That's what <u>we</u> have accomplished Martin!" Douglas's voice trembled with emotion. "We didn't do it by blowing up the system up, for crying out loud. We did it by outmaneuvering our enemies! That's the source of our power—brains. Do you see what I'm saying, Martin? This is not the time to allow Tim Hardin to tip the apple cart over!"

Before Ogden could respond, there was a knock and the door opened. Both men turned to see their waiter carrying a tray toward them. He set it down on a stand in the corner and snapped to attention. "Are you gentlemen finished with your soup?" He asked.

"Yes," Douglas said with a friendly smile. "My compliments to the chef."

"I'm sure he'll be pleased."

"We're having eastern brook trout this afternoon," Ogden announced proudly. "I had it flown in this morning from Lake Wallowa."

"No!" Douglas stared at him in amazement. "Let's see it." The waiter pulled the cover from a plate and set it down before him.

"We followed an old recipe," Ogden informed his guest. "*Dress and boil for exactly three minutes. Skin, de-bone and remove the head. Dust with salt and pepper. Brush with butter. Then brown under the flame of a hard-wood fire.* Does that sound familiar?"

"Sure does. That's the only way to cook trout," Douglas confirmed, lifting his knife and fork.

"That's not all." Ogden nodded to the waiter who turned to the tray and pulled the cover off a serving dish. "How does sourdough bread sound? Barney McPhillips' own recipe."

"Oh! Lord," the Justice exclaimed. "I've died and gone to heaven."

"Well not quite yet, I hope," Ogden said, smiling broadly.

Douglas signaled to the waiter to refill his glass. "Nearly perfect," he said after a full swallow. "All that's missing is branch water from Elk Creek."

"We do what we can," Ogden said, still smiling.

"You know, Martin," Douglas said after the waiter had removed the plates, "this meal really takes me back."

"I'm glad, Bill. You've earned a rest," Ogden replied, looking fondly at his comrade. "What was it like?" He asked.

Douglas settled back into a comfortable position. "Things were different then," he remembered. "When I was growing up in the foothills of the Cascade Mountains, Indians still lived in the area. There were trails that no white man had trod. In fact, the mountains hadn't changed much since Lewis and Clark explored them in the early eighteen-hundreds. Can you imagine that?"

"That's hard to believe," Ogden agreed.

"Yep . . . It was a new land," the old man remembered. "We were close to nature . . . it was a good place to be. I started out hiking in the foothills. As I got older and stronger, I'd go up in the mountains fishing and exploring."

"You must have had some wonderful adventures," Ogden interjected.

"Yes. I did," Douglas said nostalgically. "About my favorite place to go was a place called the Klickitat Meadows. They were perfect for a boy like me. You can reach them now by car, but when I first camped there, they were about sixteen miles into the Cascades by trail. They were in a basin 4600 feet above sea level. The view from the edge of the timber where the trail emerged was in reminiscent of New England. You looked out over a basin that might have been in western Connecticut or Massachusetts or even in Vermont or New Hampshire. The hills that rimmed it were soft and low lying . . .

"The meadows were about a mile long and a half mile wide. They were so lush it looked as though they had been cleared and planted with grass. The Little Klickitat River meandered through them. It wasn't really a river," Douglas remembered. "I don't think it was ever wider than a dozen feet—even downstream after the Diamond Fork and Coyote Creek had merged into it. But still, there were plenty of pools in it, and none of them was too deep for my brother and me to explore. That's just what we did— each one of them. There was not a better place in the mountains . . . ."

The old man had his knapsack on his back and was heading up his favorite trail. "I fished there for rainbow and cutthroat trout—Montana black-spotted cutthroat to be precise," he added. "Seldom did you find one over six or eight inches, which was just the right size for my brother and me. That's where I caught my first trout," he confessed. "On fly—a coachman, I believe it was. I was thirteen years old," he said proudly. "It was a rainbow, about eight inches long. I remember it as clearly as if it were yesterday." He looked inward through his mind's eye. "I held it in my left hand, but it was fighting so hard that I could feel it all the way down to my toes. Here was a champion, I thought, a true heart if there ever was one. He was clean and sleek and committed to life. That made a real impression on me. Seeing that he was not badly hooked, I cut the barb and turned him back into the water. That was the day that I learned to respect all of God's creatures." He was silent for a moment. "You learn what is important traveling on the mountains and fishing their streams. "

"That's a beautiful picture, Bill," Ogden said. "I feel like I was there with you."

"Infantile paralysis was what drove me outdoors," the old man continued. "Did you know that?"

"Really?" Ogden expressed surprise.

"That's right. As a small child, I ran a high fever for several weeks. Everybody thought I was going to die except my old country doctor, and he had only a slightly more optimistic view. He told my mother that there was a good chance I was going to lose the use of my legs. And even if I didn't, he doubted that I would live beyond forty—shows you what he knew." Both men laughed. "He didn't have a cure for a short life but thank God he had a prescription for my legs: saltwater baths and a fifteen-minute massage—every two hours! My Mother, bless her heart, soaked them in warm saltwater and rubbed it into my pores, massaging each leg muscle every two hours, day after day, night after night. The fever eventually passed, but she kept going with those massages.

"She must have been a remarkable woman," Ogden observed.

"She was indeed," Douglas nodded reverently. "I vaguely recall the ordeal, lying in bed too weak to move. My legs seemed like they belonged to someone else. They were so thin that Mother's hands could go clear around them! She kneaded them like bread, pushing her hands up and down, up and down, until my skin was red and raw. That didn't stop her though. She wanted me to be strong, to be able to run like she did when she was a girl. She told me once that she could run like the wind and that no one could catch her. I knew that she could. She was something special . . . "

"I'll bet . . . "

"Finally, one day I was able to walk a bit. My feet went flop. The muscles of my knees twitched. Numb sensations came and went, but I persevered, and the frailty caused by the disease gradually passed.

"I remember walking to school one day when a group of older boys came up behind me. I heard one say, 'Look at that kid's skinny legs. Aren't they something? Did you ever see anything as funny?' I wanted to answer him, but instead, I burst into tears. I figured that proved I was a weakling. That fixed a depression on me that changed my life. I became self-conscious and shy. I imagined everyone who looked at me was thinking, 'Look at that weakling.' It turned me into a rebel," the aged Justice announced. "I was going to show them that I wasn't inferior! I had no one to confide in to relieve my inner turmoil, so my little rebellion just kept on growing in my heart.

"I figured to prove myself by being the best student in school. I poured every ounce of energy into my studies to meet my goal. But despite my success in the classroom, I still couldn't compete in the physical world. That never stopped gnawing at me. As I pursued my studies, I learned what happened to weaklings in nature. How they were cast aside in favor of hardier stock. Coyotes got the deer that were too weak to keep up with the herd. Crippled birds were easy prey for the cats and hawks that prowled the countryside. One day I came across a passage in Plato's *Republic* where he talked about the danger to society in propagating "inferior" types of people. Of course, I figured he meant physical weaklings like me!" Douglas laughed combatively. "When I read what he said to do with them, my depression got even worse.

"Then one crisp fall day I ran into a husky long-legged boy I knew from Sunday school. He was coming down from the foothills on a fast walk. When I asked him where he'd been, he told me that he had been climbing the foothills north of town. I asked him why he'd done that, and he told me that he was following his doctor's advice. His doctor said that climbing the foothills was a good way to develop his lungs and legs.

"I resolved then and there to do the same. I figured that I would use the foothills as other boys might use weights or bars in a gymnasium. Sure enough, over the coming months the foothills began to work a transformation in me. By spring, I could go the two miles to Selah Gap at a fast pace and often reach the top of the ridge without losing a step or reducing my speed."

"That's quite an accomplishment Bill," Ogden said admiringly. "Especially considering where you started."

"Well . . . you're right," Douglas agreed. "I'd be dead tired, but I ached so much that I couldn't sleep. Still, I was growing stronger. More important than that, I knew that I'd found my place!"

"Bravo!" Ogden cheered.

"Yep," the old man nodded. "Those experiences prepared me to carry this torch for the common man. Being out on the land, working hard and breathing clean air made me healthy and strong. And by the way," the old naturalist added with a faint grin, "that was my first point of connection with Mr. Jefferson. In fact, that was all I knew about him until I got to law school—fifty-three years ago! Can you believe it?"

"No! It can't be!"

Douglas smiled. "That was a time too . . . I set out on a freight train from Wenatchee, Washington with two thousand sheep."

"Oh God!" Ogden roared. "All the other students at Columbia Law School arrive in wool suits. But you arrive in a sheep train! Get it–sheep train?"

Douglas smiled at his host's joke. "That wasn't the half of it. We got as far as Idaho when a railroad strike stopped the train. Of course, that kept us from reaching our scheduled feeding points. But we still had to feed the critters. So we unloaded them and started herding them while we waited for another train to come. After two weeks of grazing the herd across Montana and North Dakota, we got a wire from the owner telling us to turn them over to a buyer in western Minnesota. And glad we were to do that! When the sheep were gone, my partner headed back to Yakima while I caught a freight to Chicago.

"I knew a little bit about freight trains by that time because I used to 'ride the rods' up and down the Yakima Valley to jobs in the hayfields and wheat fields and in the orchards—depending on the season. I'll bet you don't know about riding the rods," Douglas said, chiding his host.

"Not a thing," Ogden admitted cheerfully. "I'm an effete eastern snob—remember?"

"It means riding on a small platform of boards laid across the rods that run lengthwise beneath the cars. It was a cramped space, and dusty as hell because the motion of the train whirled up a thick cloud of dirt and cinders. You'd lie on your stomach with your eyes closed, getting more grimy and miserable each mile."

"At least it was free?" Ogden joked.

"Yep. That was its virtue," Douglas agreed. "Open boxcars were much more comfortable," he continued. "The problem with them was that you were liable to meet somebody who would take your money and toss you off the train. The other place to ride was up on top of the cars. The problem with that was you were likely to be discovered by the freight yard police. We called them yard bulls. They were as mean a bunch as you'd ever hope to meet. If they caught you, they'd beat you up, then arrest you. The train crew could also be a problem. More often than not they were friendly, but occasionally a brakeman would try to shake you down for a fare."

"Shocking!" Ogden said in mock indignation. "They expected you to pay?"

"Can you believe it?" The old hobo complained. "Anyway, on this particular trip, I paid a toll to the crew—fifty cents apiece, as I recall. That worked for a while, but then we came to a division plant, and a new crew got on. I was easy prey because I was on a flatter, which was the only available space except the rods and the top of the boxcars. When the new brakeman came along, he asked me for a dollar, and I paid him. Nothing more happened for a long time. Then along came the conductor. By this time, we were on the outskirts of Chicago. It was three or four o'clock in the morning on a clear, cold night. The conductor asked for another dollar. He said there were yard bulls ahead, and that he didn't want me to get into trouble. If I paid him, he said that he would see that they didn't arrest me.

"I was silent for a while, trying to figure out how I could afford to part with another dollar since I only had a few left. I hadn't had a hot meal in a week. I hadn't seen a bed in more than a fortnight. I was filthy and without a change of clothes. I needed a bath, a shave, and food. But above all that I needed sleep. Even flop houses cost money. And the oatmeal, hot cakes, ham and eggs and coffee, which I wanted desperately, would cost fifty or seventy-five cents.

"Why should I pay this guy and become a panhandler in Chicago? I asked myself.

"He shook me by the shoulder. 'Come on buddy,' he said. 'Do you want to get tossed off the train?'

"I'm broke, I answered.

"'Broke?' He retorted. 'You paid the brakeman! You can pay me.'

"Have a heart, I said. I bet you were broke some time. Give a guy a break.'

"He roared at me to get off or he would turn me over to the bulls. I was silent.

"'Well, jump off or I'll run you in,' he threatened.

"I watched the lights of Chicago come nearer. We were entering a maze of tracks. There were switches and sidetracks, boxcars on sidings, occasional loading platforms. And once in a while, we roared over a short highway bridge. It was dark and the train was going about thirty miles an hour. The terrain looked treacherous. Jumping could be disastrous. Even so, I decided to husband my two or three remaining dollars. I stood poised on the edge of the flatcar, searching the area immediately ahead for a place to jump.

"Suddenly the conductor yelled in my ear, 'Jump!' So I did. Something brushed my sleeve. It was the arm of a switch. I lost my footing and skidded on my hands and knees a dozen feet down a cinder bank. Fortunately, I wasn't hurt! I climbed to my feet in time to see the last cars of the freight disappear into the east. My palms were bleeding and full of cinders. My knees were skinned. I was dirty and hungry and aching, so I sat down on a pile of ties by the track and started nursing my wounds. As I sat there, a form came toward me out of the darkness. Turns out it was an old 'bo. He put his hand on my shoulder and said, 'I saw you jump, buddy. Are you hurt?'

"No, I replied. Just a little scratched up.

"'Ever been to Chicago?' He asked.

"No, I said.

"'Well, don't stay here 'cause it's hard on fellars like us.'

"You mean the bulls? I asked.

"'Yes, they're tough,' he said. 'But it's not only that. Do you smell the stockyards?'

"I had been smelling the stench for some time, but I hadn't figured out what it was. Is that the stockyards? I asked.'

"'Yeah,' he said taking a whiff. 'That's where I've been working. The pay ain't so bad. But you go home at night to a room on an alley. There ain't no trees. There ain't no grass, er birds, er mountains.'

"That was a magic word. What do you know about mountains? I asked, thinking of home. That set him off on an odyssey. I listened for about an hour as he praised the glories of the mountains of the West and related his experiences in them. The longer he talked, the more homesick I got. Dawn was coming, and I began to see the squalor my friend had just described.

"When I asked him what brought him to the freight yards at this hour of the morning, he said he had come to catch a west-bound freight–back to the mountains. Lonesomeness swept over me. The old man and I sat just there for a few minutes. 'Do you know your Bible, son?' He asked suddenly.

"Pretty well, I said.

"'Do you remember what the psalmist said about the mountains?'

"I racked my brains. No. I don't recall, I said.

"'I will lift up mine eyes unto the hills from whence cometh my help. My help cometh from the Lord who made heaven and earth.' As he finished reciting his verse, we heard a whistle blow somewhere down the track.

"'That's my train,' he said, shaking my hand. 'Good luck, son.' Then he smiled and added, 'Stay clear of the flop houses. They'll roll you when you're asleep. Go to the YMCA. It's cheap and clean and they're on the level.' The train came up, gaining speed as it passed by. The old man trotted along the track, then grabbed a handhold and stepped abroad the bottom rung of a ladder. Climbing to the top of a boxcar, he took off his hat, and waved it until he was out of sight.

"I sat there, watching the sun rise through the smoke and haze. There was a smell in the air that not even the touch of the sun could cleanse. There was not a tree or shrub or blade of grass in view. The Chicago I saw that morning was a place of unredeemable desolation. The more I studied it, the stronger my impulse was to follow that old hobo back to the mountains. I could settle down in the valley below Mount Adams and live happily ever after. I'd have a job and a home. There would be fishing trips, and mountains to climb, and nights under the stars. But it was too late to go back, and I knew it. Instead, I found the YMCA the old man told me about and slept the clock around. Then I returned to the freight yard and caught a ride to New York City. A few days later I began my classes at Columbia. And I've been working ever since straightening out this crooked society."

"What a story," Ogden exclaimed through his admiration. "You should write a book, Bill. You really should."

"I just might," Douglas answered, savoring the compliment. "You know," he continued, "I never found out what happened to that old hobo, but I always knew the kindness he showed me that night came out of the mountains. I've thought about it many times in the years since and there's no doubt about it—mountains have a decent influence on men." He reflected on the idea again. "I don't remember ever meeting a mean or dishonest man on the trail. Things are different in the woods, Martin. There's a kind of music in the pines at night when the wind blows. It just puts a man right.

"During the Depression," he continued, speaking from his heart. "A lot of men came to work in the mountains from big cities. They had chips on their shoulders and were ready to fight anybody who so much as looked at them the wrong way. After serving a year in the CCC, one such man said to me, 'there ain't no use getting soar at a tree.' Now that struck me as a real insight! Here was a tough customer, but his experience in the mountains transformed him into a thinker. The government had treated him right, and he appreciated it. That's what he meant you know. We can thank FDR for that Martin. He taught the working man that the government is . . ." a twinkle came into Douglas's eye, "the good shepherd?"

"Amen, Brother!" Ogden intoned.

Ogden shifted forward slightly. "Bill . . . you mentioned a 'Jefferson Constitution'. Where it is? Do you know?"

284

"All I know is that Tim was in a fury because Fred sent it off to somebody."

"Why would he have had it at all?" Ogden wondered coyly.

"I got the impression that he found it among the papers of one of his forebears."

A puzzled look appeared on Ogden's face. "Fred Ried had an ancestor that was close to Thomas Jefferson? Is that the picture?"

"I guess so," Douglas shrugged.

"Any idea who that might be?"

"None whatsoever," Douglas answered. "But if what Tim says in true, then this Jefferson Constitution might just be Burr's Unicorn."

"Burr's Unicorn?" Ogden repeated skeptically. "What the devil is Burr's Unicorn?"

"During his impeachment trial," Douglas explained, "Aaron Burr tried to turn the tables on Jefferson by claiming that Jefferson recruited him to set up a new state in the western lands. According to Burr, Jefferson concocted this scheme about the time he realized that the monarchists were going to win the presidential election in 1796. Burr claimed that Jefferson came to him because he was a republican ally who could lead the operation in the field. To seal the deal, Jefferson supposedly gave Burr a copy of the constitution he had drafted for the new state. Of course, everyone who heard the story assumed Burr was smearing Jefferson to save his own hide. When asked to produce the document, Burr claimed that he had lost it escaping from New York after shooting Hamilton. That's how it got the name 'Burr's Unicorn.'"

Ogden compared Douglas's report to the way Hardin had described it. "I'm thinking Bill, . . . this story could be bigger than Nixon's impeachment!" He glanced at the retiring Justice. "We could make it into a political potboiler," he continued, studying his companion's reaction. "We could make it a parable about good versus evil." He began to detect signs of interest in Douglas's wrinkled face. "We could draw a parallel between the crisis then and the crisis now." He smiled inwardly when Douglas nodded. "We could use it to build support for the program. We'd give it an unimpeachable pedigree," he predicted as Douglas contemplated the opportunity. "And we'd blow the *Times* clear out of the water!" he mused out loud.

"Don't go getting your hopes up," Douglas warned with a laugh. "Tim Hardin isn't famous for telling the truth."

Ogden ignored his companion's admonition. "You're a Jefferson scholar. What kind of things would we expect to find in 'Burr's Unicorn'?"

"Now that's an interesting question," Douglas allowed. He raised his eyebrows and collected his thoughts. "Jefferson drafted a number of constitutions around the time the colonies declared independence. I can tell you what he put in them. But this one would have been different."

"Why do you say that?" Ogden asked, suddenly anxious.

"Because his political objectives were different in 1796."

"Is that important?" Ogden asked.

"I think so," Douglas replied. "When he was writing his first constitutions, his primary concern was to get power away from the Tidewater land barons who controlled Virginia's colonial society."

"That's what his early constitutions were about?" Ogden sounded surprised.

"Yes. One of the distinguishing features of these documents was that each of them had a bill of rights and each of these had a provision establishing the right of settlers to hold full title to the land they claimed."

"What purpose did that serve?"

"Jefferson was among the first to understand the relationship between property and political power," Douglas answered. "He figured that if he could break up the large estates, he could move the power to run the government where he wanted it. To do that, he made a few strategic changes in the land laws—like ending primogeniture and allowing women to own landed property. You have to appreciate how clever he was," Douglas added admiringly, "These changes made it just about impossible for a patriarch to maintain a large estate through more than one generation."

"Why was that?" Ogden wondered.

"Because it would be divided between siblings and splintered off to sons-in-law," Douglas explained. "And that was not all Jefferson had up his sleeve! His constitutional right honoring the land claims of squatters would have, in effect, prevented the eastern land barons from setting up new fiefdoms in the western lands."

"Oh my," Ogden observed blandly, "he thought of everything, didn't he!"

"That was just part of it," Douglas said, continuing his discourse. "To support his plan, Jefferson designed a system of proportional representation based on population density. Then he proposed to attract settlers to the sparsely populated western districts by granting every landless male citizen over the age of twenty-five fifty acres of new land."

Ogden interrupted. "Are you saying that his early constitutions were legal schemes to dismantle the colony's hierarchical system?"

"Basically," Douglas agreed. "Jefferson wanted to replace it with a political society in which new social and economic interests would consolidate into voting blocks. He intended to do this by building a class of yeoman farmers who shared his anti-aristocratical views. Their numbers were going to increase while the constituencies of the Tidewater Tuckahoes were going to shrink, so it was just a matter of time until they would take over the government. It becomes even more clear what Jefferson was up to when you understand how his government worked," Douglas explained.

"How was that?"

"All the power was in the legislature!"

Ogden seemed surprised. "Was that unusual?"

Douglas nodded. "Back in 1776, Jefferson didn't know about Madison's idea of checks and balances. He needed the legislature to dominate the government so he could set up a new power base. He intended for it to appoint the governor, the upper house, and the members of the judiciary. In addition to that, he planned for it to appoint a privy council from among its members to keep an eye on the governor. Meanwhile, he limited the governor to a single one-year term!"

"Ok," Ogden said, cutting him off. "The legislature had a lot of power—why did his focus change?"

"There were two reasons," Douglas responded. "In the first place, the political society he was trying to create had come into existence."

"And the second?"

"A new problem arose."

"And what was that?" Ogden wondered.

"A powerful faction developed with an opposing political point view!"

"Whoa!" Ogden snorted. "Are you saying that surprised him?"

"Right! He was so anxious to get rid of civil society run by Tuckahoes that he didn't think much about the problems he would encounter in political society."

"My goodness. We certainly don't hear much about that, do we?"

"There aren't many of us who've figured out what he was really up to," Douglas confided. "Bear in mind that when Jefferson went off to France in 1784 his newly-formed country was still marching in step behind George Washington. It wasn't until Jefferson was in France that politics started to undermine the sense of unity. The issue that fueled the division was the economic depression that set in during the decade after the war. This aggravated the natural differences between the merchants and manufacturers in New England and planters in the South. The first group followed Alexander Hamilton. The second contained men in Jefferson's social class. Washington kept the peace between them as their political differences sharpened.

"In France, Jefferson spent his days observing the horrendous injustices that the French monarchy was inflicting on the common people. Then he would go to the salons and listen to France's most brilliant philosophers debate ideas coined by Scottish Enlightenment thinkers like Adam Smith on how to end feudalism and convert tenured land into usable economic resources. When he was finished in the salons, he would retire to late night suppers with the *Americanistes* in the National Assembly and debate the rights of man.

"Not surprisingly, when he returned home, he was on high alert against any attempt to undermine America's new republican government, which he saw as the last barrier of protection against the kinds of hierarchical tyranny that existed in England and France. But who did he encounter on the steps of the President's house? Hamilton—America's most outspoken admirer of England's commercial and political systems! Of course, by this time, Hamilton was also the most influential man in Washington's cabinet."

"He set up an organization to counteract Hamilton..." Ogden observed, anticipating Douglas's point.

"That's right," Douglas nodded, commending his pupil, "He'd already settled on his ideological foundation, which he found in the salons of Paris and in those seething political clubs that were sprouting up across France before the revolution. In 1789 he wrote a letter to Madison in which he laid out his core idea. Much of it was a paraphrasing from a letter he received from his doctor—an enlightened Englishman by the name of Richard Gem. In this letter, Jefferson asserted that the *earth belongs to the living*. I was in law school when I read it for the first time. It struck a chord then and has never stopped resonating with me. I've had many occasions to reference it during my time on the Court and I'm completely convinced that it is the only workable principle for a modern society." Douglas pounded the table to underscore his conviction. "The better I understand what he meant, the more respect I have for the man. Here's the thing," Douglas announced solemnly, "Jefferson thought that property ownership was a civil right that should be regulated according to the *common good*." The jurist took care to emphasize each word.

"Is that so!" Ogden responded with renewed interest.

"Absolutely!" Douglas declared. "When Jefferson returned from France, he discovered that America's new political society was electing people with *wrong* ideas! So he began to formulate a plan to deal with them."

"Which was..."

"He was going to re-constitute the law."

"Like he did in 1776..." Ogden inferred.

"Exactly. Only this time, he needed to model it so the state would have ultimate control over private property—that way he could prevent Hamilton from setting up a monarchy while at the same time keeping power out of the hands of a new gentry class. Do you see?" Douglas asked hopefully.

"What?"

"It wasn't any longer a matter of re-distributing power in the government. It was a matter of keeping the power to govern in the right hands."

Ogden took a sip of wine. "Some things don't change, do they Bill..."

"No," Douglas replied grimly.

"We're in the same boat as Jefferson..." Ogden observed, looking expectantly at Douglas.

"That's about the size of it..."

"...what would he have put in his constitution?" Ogden wondered, returning to the question.

"All right... Let's see...," Douglas began, scanning his knowledge bank. "He would have talked about the earth as the common stock of man... He would have provided means to protects the will—and voice— of the majority... He would have talked about how it was the obligation of government to promote the common good... He would have described the common good as that which best serves the interests of the people— taken together."

"And what would that have been?"

"A healthy, clean, environment where the needs of the people take precedence over private interests."

"In other words," Ogden announced with a surprised look, "Jefferson's lost constitution would have established *our* communitarian state!"

"Exactly!" Douglas answered decisively.

"Well, now," Ogden smiled. "Isn't that a stroke of luck!"

"Not luck," Douglas corrected. "Wisdom gained through experience!"

"I bet you could write the thing yourself," Ogden speculated with an insider's smile.

"I expect that I could," Douglas replied philosophically.

Ogden stopped smiling. "Then do it."

"You know what!" Douglas's gaze shifted to the mountains. "I think I should!"

"Then we're in business—partner!" Ogden lifted his glass and drank a thirsty toast to Thomas Jefferson's newest re-incarnation. "Now," he said, setting his empty glass down on the table, "let's solve *your* Tim Hardin problem . . ."

———————

"Comrade Sister," Frances Rank said, looking at Marjean, "tell the council where we are in the great cycle."

Marjean acknowledged Frances Rank's invitation and stepped into the center of the council circle. "Sisters," she began, "since the age of Gaia, the stars have never been in such favorable alignment. The time is ripe for woman people to re-establish their ancient dynasty." As she spoke, she began to swirl like the primordial ether and before their eyes transformed into Woman Spirit.

"Hear me!" Woman Spirit commanded, settling in their midst. "To know the secrets of the present we must understand the three cycles of Gaia.

"The first is that which moves the Sun through the constellations of the Zodiac." Woman Spirit swept around the council circle in the way of Gaia. "The second is her daily rotation which makes the Sun rise and set." She spun on her axis to illustrate Gaia's second cycle. "As Gaia proceeds through these two cycles, she wobbles and her axis shifts." Woman Spirit wobbled through a final rotation. "This is known as the Great Transit. Some call it the Precession of the Equinoxes.

"It takes Gaia twenty-six thousand years to complete this transit. When it begins, as when it ends, Gaia's pole points to Polaris, the north star." Woman Spirit formed an axis aimed in the direction of Wolfpit Mountain. "As Gaia moves through this transit, her pole shifts toward other stars in the heaven." She mimed the shift until she had completed half her transit. "Thirteen thousand years ago, Gaia's axis pointed toward Vega, the brightest star in the summer sky." Woman Spirit resumed her circuit. "In the twenty-six-thousandth year," she continued, having completed her rotation, "the Anti-Christ will appear. Then shall there be the great battle between the Anti-Christ and his devils and Gaia and her angels. Gaia will defeat him to end the great cycle. The new cycle will then begin.

"The Precession of the Equinoxes spans 360°," Woman Spirit said, continuing her course. "This circle divides into twelve arcs," she explained. "Each bears the name of a constellation in the Zodiac and extends approximately 30° across the heaven. Gaia therefore crosses each span in approximately 2160 years. Each of these ages divides into two halves. The first half has the traits of the constellation at the vernal equinox." Woman Spirit leapt to the left side of the council circle. "The second half has the traits of the constellation at the autumn equinox." Woman Spirit bounded across to the opposite side of the council circle. "These traits are at their peaks half-way through each sub-age.

"The Great Transit began as Gaia raised Atlantis from the bed of the sea," Woman Spirit informed the council. "Atlantis was a paradise where women people lived in harmony as in their mother's womb. Their civilization flourished in the spirit of oneness. Their priestesses nurtured and cultivated their loving communities and brought forth Gaia's fruit in abundance. Over time, however, male seeders who shared their habitation grew callous and turned away from Gaia, choosing instead to follow malcontents who promised to make them rulers that they might enrich themselves and sate their vulgar appetites. As these troublemakers divided the men people from the women people, the spirit of oneness withered away.

"In its place there were abominations of decadence and corruption. And so, Gaia grew wroth and sent a cataclysm to chasten the violators. Yet they did not return to the way of Gaia. Gaia therefore sent a second cataclysm and shattered their water-bound continent into three fragile islands. Still, the penis-followers rejected Gaia's nurturing spirit. Gaia therefore sent a third cataclysm. The Greek philosopher Plato described how the islands were swallowed up by the sea and how the Atlantean civilization was destroyed.

"What he failed to notice was the band of women voyagers who departed their doomed island home and sailed westward in search of a new paradise. I Woman Spirit was their guide and protector of the precious knowledge of Gaia's way. I led them across the empty continent to the islands of the western ocean. We sailed on beyond the edge of the world and wandered through every recess of Gaia's sacred body. We mated with primitive tribes and shared our knowledge of Gaia's way that civilization might be born among them.

"At last, we reached the Fertile Crescent. There I made a cradle, and the women people of Atlantis dwelled among worshipers of the Sun and bestowed upon the Sun people of the Fertile Crescent a golden age.

"This transpired in the Age of Taurus proper. You know how Taurean traits displayed themselves during this period because the women people of Atlantis taught the Sun people the art of writing so there would be a written history of what they accomplished. Feminine Venus ruled in this Taurean Age, and so, it was an age of fertility worship. The Bull was held sacred among the Sun people and there was much copulation with the women people of Atlantis mating with the Sun people of the Fertile Crescent. Thus, the new civilization became abundant. As they flourished, the power and influence of women people of Atlantis swelled like the womb at birth. And so, they instructed the Sun people to build palaces and libraries and other structures fitting for the Age of Taurus. In this way they advanced civilization and increased their well-being.

"The second half of the Age of Taurus was under the sub-rulership of Scorpio, the sign of death and rebirth. Therefore, the Sun people created ornate and complex funeral monuments and invented elaborate death cults. They chose as their symbols the Scarab and the Hawk, kindred spirits to the Scorpion and the Eagle. During this rulership of Scorpio there occurred a creative transformation where the Sun people applied the knowledge they received from the women people of Atlantis to develop astronomy and astrology so all might know the way of Gaia.

"The Age of Taurus was followed by the Age of Aries proper which was in the rulership of Mars. This was a time of warfare and aggression. Aryan invaders roamed across Gaia's face and males seized control of the nations that formed when the Women People of Atlantis bestowed their knowledge on the primitive tribes. The peaceful empire the women people of Atlantis had created in the Fertile Crescent could not stand against this barbaric onslaught, and it was conquered and the descendants of the women people of Atlantis were led away into slavery and concubinage as the prurient impulses of Mars overwhelmed the sensitizing spirit of feminine Venus. Patriarchalism appeared at this time and women peoples became servants to male rulers who kept them for their sexual gratification and for childbearing. Thus was established the Tyranny of Man.

"The Tyranny of Man continued during the second half of the Age of Aries under the rulership of feminine Libra. Libra's influence caused the male-dominated city states of Greece to evolve. And when they were established, their ideals were manly virtue and the Golden Mean as they were in India where the Buddha taught the Middle Way. Though now merely slaves, women people slowed the decline of civilization by showing their crude masters how to strengthen their lowly intellects. The science of reason was thus created by the philosopher Aristotle. And before he was slain by Spartan invaders, the Syracusan Archimedes invented mathematics and the science of nature to secure male rulership for the coming age.

"After the Age of Aries came the Age of Pisces proper. This was an age of growing darkness as the male overlords ravaged Gaia and flaunted her ways. The defining qualities of Pisces, being faith and religion, helped the captive women people to persevere through this time of dissolution and collapse. Christianity—whose symbol is the fish—therefore took root at this time.

"The second period of the Age of Pisces was under the influence of Virgo. Aggression was therefore mediated by pursuit of scientific knowledge as male underlings searched for ways to uplift themselves and enrich their rapacious masters. In this way, the sovereign state formed, and the growing legion of supernumerary male drones needed to sustain it formed in its wake.

Woman Spirit spread herself like a sheltering canopy over the council circle. "Now hear the good news, Sisters!" Her words filled the space like the rushing wind. "Gaia has completed her twenty-six-thousand-year transit! The age before us marks a new beginning. We are entering the Age of Aquarius!" Women Spirit swept about the council circle in an act of consecration. "The stars no longer favor the man people," she called out as she completed her circuit. "The Tyranny of Man shall soon be over!" Having delivered the glorious news, Woman Spirit swooned and collapsed.

A pregnant moment passed. Then her body began to pulsate with the birthing of the new age. In the next moment she rose fresh and new.

"The Age of Aquarius will be a time of healing and sensitivity," Woman Spirit trilled. "I, Woman Spirit, will guide women people back to Gaia and the ways of Gaia will flourish again!" Woman Spirit began a joyful dance accompanied now by the chanting of Aster.

"Aquarius represents water," Woman Spirit announced. "Its image reflects the destruction of Atlantis and the hegira of its faithful remnant. The hieroglyphs the Sun people inscribed during the Second Dynasty of Women illuminate these legends. There, Aquarius is portrayed a servant who pours out the water of knowledge to quench the thirst of women people. Its Zodiac symbol also reflects the outpouring of Gaia's truths by the women people of Atlantis to the primitives. In that Dynasty of Women People water was the key to life. Every year during the month of Aquarius the rains came and nourished the land. It therefore marked the beginning of the new life cycle. The region of the night sky in which Aquarius resides is populated by water signs—Capricornus, the water goat and Pisces, the fish. In Babylonia, this region of the zodiac was known as the Sea.

"The Sun people of the Fertile Crescent associated this time of year with the goddess Hapi. They believed that she caused the River Nile to flood by passing her water. Peni-centric Greeks personified Aquarius as Ganymede, the son of Tros, King of Phrygia. According to Greek mythology, the god Zeus so admired the boy's beauty that he abducted him to serve as cup bearer on Mount Olympus. It is said that his desire to possess the young prince inspired Zeus to cast his image eternally in the night sky."

Woman Spirit swirled to the center of the council circle and stopped below the skull. "And when will the new age begin?" She wondered. "No one knows," she answered coyly. "But I will tell *you* . . . " She laughed and began to gambol about in the ring. Then, suddenly, she halted in front of Ashanti Shoate' and began to speak as if there were something special about the black scholar. "In 1893 Gabriel Jogand deciphered the Cabbala. There he discovered that the coming of the Anti-Christ would mark the beginning of the new age. According to his calculations, this would occur in ..." a tense silence settled over the council, "... 1975." The council members gasped.

"Jeanne Dixon had a vision seventy years later. It was of a child being born in a middle eastern city. In her vision, this child will become a teacher and lead humanity away from Christianity."

"Tha's whut an'rchise do ain't it," Shoate' inquired.

"There's more," Woman Spirit continued. "In 1911, Madame Blavatsky predicted that a shaman would appear before the end of the century and form a religion for the Universal Way of Women People. She prophesied that this would be the vehicle to carry women people out of their bondage back to paradise. She calculated the dawn of the Age of Aquarius based on the channeling of the Lord Maitreya by Krishnamurti. And the year it is to begin is ... 1975!"

The council members nodded excitedly.

"Then, in 1936, Edgar Cayce announced that the shifting of the terrestrial axis—which activates the transition between the celestial ages—had begun. The following year, while excavating the tomb of the High Priestess La La in the Valley of the Dolls, Professor Indianapolis Jones confirmed that this had indeed begun in the techtonic plates below the Earth's crust. And on February 28th of this year Rudhyar announced that the time had come for the Avatar of the New Age to appear!" The council members looked at each other in awe.

"What about the Anti-Christ?" Rank wondered impatiently.

"Silence!" Woman Spirit commanded. She purified her yang with a moment of meditation. "We know the secrets of the present. But to know the secrets of the future we must study the cycles of Gaia's siblings."

The council sighed collectively in disappointment.

"The convergences of the outer planets reveal Gaia's will," Woman Spirit continued. "Uranus is the maverick. It represents revolution, invention, progress, liberalism, enlightenment, electricity, magic, radical change, and dictators. Uranus rules Aquarius.

"Neptune is the mystic. It represents spirituality, imagination, dissolution, chaos, delusion, deception, scandal, drugs, compassion, collectivism, and peoples. Neptune rules Pisces.

"Pluto is the Lord of the Underworld. It represents death, rebirth, polarity, transformation, plutocracy, energy, and occult knowledge. Pluto rules Scorpio and Aries.

"The ordering of things changes when these planets conjunct," Woman Spirit observed. "Their conjunctions follow cycles like that of the Moon." Woman Spirit drifted around the council circle as though she were a planet coming into phase.

"The Neptune-Pluto cycle is the cycle of civilization. It governs the rise and fall of empires and dynasties. When Neptune and Pluto conjunct the ordering of empires and dynasties changes. These conjunctions occur every four-hundred-and-ninety-four years. Opposition occurs every 246 years. Civilizations peak at these moments, then give way to dissolution and decay.

"The Uranus-Neptune cycle is the cycle of culture. It governs relations between peoples and cultures. The Uranus-Neptune cycle repeats every one-hundred and seventy-one years. Artistic creativity peaks during these conjunctions. Religious upheavals occur. Paradigms change and new social movements begin. The planets move to opposition eight five years later. Important innovations occur at these times.

"The Uranus-Pluto cycle the is cycle of revolution and is one-hundred-and-twenty-seven years long. It coincides with the rise of political movements. These conjunctions have the power to cause unstable social structures to collapse. Virtually all revolutions in modern history correspond with the aspects of the Uranus-Pluto cycle. In 1711 during conjunction freemasonry appeared. In 1759-60 while Uranus and Pluto were in square the Seven Years War began. The American Revolution began while the pair were in sesqui-square in 1776. In 1793 while they were in opposition the French Revolution entered its Reign of Terror. And in 1808 when they were again in sesqui-square Haiti rose against France.

"The pattern has continued into the current century. In 1901 during opposition the Boxer Rebellion was launched, and the Philippines rebelled against Spain. During the sesqui-square of 1917 the Bolsheviks launched the Russian Revolution and Arabia rebelled against the Turks. During the square of 1933 the Fascists took over Germany. The sextile of 1943 marked the turning point of the Second World War. In 1949 during semi-square the People's revolution began in China. And during conjunction in 1966, China began its great Cultural Revolution while the Black Liberation and peace movements began in America

"When Uranus, Neptune and Pluto are together in the higher signs of the Zodiac, their stimulative power substantially increases. Indeed, the Law of High Signs states that the greater the number of planets clustered together in the signs above the autumnal equinox, the greater will be the level of human cultural attainment.

"In 577 BC the Neptune-Pluto conjunction was joined by Uranus, which is the planet of enlightenment. Soon after that the Greek and the Persian Empires were born. One hundred years later, Athens emerged to lead Greece to its golden age and inaugurated the greatest period of intellectual growth and discovery in human history. Socrates, Pythagoras, Buddha, Lao Tze, Confucius, Zoroaster, and La La established schools of knowledge and religion that still influence human thought. The Jews emerged from their Babylonian captivity with their Holy Bible written down for the first time, and their 'God' transformed from a tribal deity into a universal spirit.

"The triple conjunction of 83 BC brought forward the Caesars who transformed the Roman Republic into an Empire and brought civilization to Europe. One hundred years later Christ's mission began on Earth, as did the golden age of Rome under Augustus. The three planets conjuncted again in 411. This coincided with the fall of the Roman Empire and the beginning of the Dark Ages. But a great new civilization emerged 100 years later in Byzantium, and in the Americas, the Mayan civilization entered its golden age.

"In 905, the Vikings were threatening to destroy the social ordering of Europe, and the powerful Tang dynasty was collapsing in China. But even as these catastrophes were unfolding, the peoples of Europe were coalescing into new structures, and reforms in the Church gave rise to the ages of chivalry and cathedral building. A century later the Vikings, having become civilized, sat on thrones across Europe. In China, the new Sung dynasty carried China into its golden age.

"The last conjunction occurred in 1399-1400. Medieval society was in a state of disintegration after the Black Plague killed half the population of Europe. But one hundred years later, the Renaissance had begun in Florence, and Michelangelo was re-defining civilization with his art."

Woman Spirit fulminated with a burst of energy. "This record confirms that the transition which began between the World Wars is the precursor of another epic re-ordering. HALLELUIAH!" she screamed "It has already begun. It has been one hundred years since the last conjunction. The temporal signs confirm what the celestial signs predict: woman peoples everywhere are throwing off their chains and filling the ranks of the movement. In China, India, and Israel sisters are already leaders of their governments.

"The three outer planets are now in communion around the Winter Solstice. This is unprecedented! This convergence is occurring as the Great Transit begins its new cycle. The Age of Aquarius under the rulership of Uranus is beginning. The significance of these celestial signs is unmistakable." Woman Spirit shivered with excitement. "The beginning of the Third Women People's Dynasty is at hand! The birthing process has already begun. We shall return to the way of Gaia and will live again in the security of the womb!"

Woman Spirit paused to catch her breath. "Neptune is the most vital of the planets in this triplicity. It controls the collective mood which is an expression of the feminine person. Its inspirational power will dominate as it transits through the socially conscious signs from Scorpio through Aquarius. All periods of renaissance and renewal in human history have occurred with Neptune in these houses. Neptune passed through Scorpio in the 1960s and is now in Capricorn." Her voice softened as her strength began to fade. "When it enters Aquarius, our golden age will reach full flood!

"Pluto will enter Scorpio in 1984. This will be the first time that the three outer planets are together in the high signs since European males conquered the New World. This condition will prevail until Uranus leaves Aquarius in 2003." Woman Spirit's strength continued to fade. "This is the longest such period in recorded history, and it foretells an even greater accomplishment." Woman Spirit released a final reserve of energy. "One condition only must now be met . . ." she whispered, sagging to the floor.

"...The Unicorn must be destroyed.... *Tertium datur*..." She settled then into a death-like stillness.

"The unicorn must be destroyed?" Rank look at Ashanti Shoate. "Did you hear her say anything about a unicorn?"

"This gal knows some shit!" the UVA scholar observed, as she pulled Marjean to the side of the council ring. She straightened to her full height. "Now we got all tha fac's," she said, looking down on Frances Rank, "le's git on wif da plan."

Rank nodded.

Professor Shoate clapped her hands loudly to command everyone's attention. "We're gettin' on wif da plan," she announced. "Jes' r'member tha way Miss Sally dun it!" She looked again at Rank.

"Exactly!" Frances Rank snorted. "If we do what Sally Hemings did to Tom Jefferson, everything'll be peachy. Now, let's review the Manifesto of Women People's Everywhere one more time." She reached into her bag, pulled out the scroll, and unrolled it. But instead of reading it, she lowered it into her lap. "Remember what Sister Broomstick told us, she glanced over at Marjean who was still huddled in a senseless heap on the side of the council circle. "We're in a cosmic struggle for power! The penis-heads have it, and we're going to get it." She gritted her teeth. "Some of those assholes think the way to get power is by blowing things up—that's the way they operate! Women People aren't like penis-heads," she repeated, nodding confidently. "We use our brains! We're going to get what we want the way Women People always have..."

The panel waited for their leader to tell them again.

"We're going to bitch about every goddam thing until we grind this penis-head system to a halt!" The sisters trilled their approval. "We'll fog the place up so the assholes won't be able to see where they're going—just like Woman Spirit said." Rank smiled approvingly at Marjean, who had finally come to her senses. "What did you call it, deary?"

"Tertium datur?"

"Exactly!" Rank barked. "We'll *tersh* 'em into puddles. First the know-it-alls who think they can manage the sisterhood; then the bossies up there on the high plateau; then the grunts who write their speeches and clean up after 'em. When we're done, the pigs will be back in their sties . . ." Rank cackled, ". . . and <u>we'll</u> be pouring in the slop!"

"Jes' tha way Miss Sally done it wif Tom Jefferson," Ashanti Shoate' bellowed.

"Damn straight!" Rank snapped. "We're going to cut their balls off in a communal castration! Now back to the script."

Marjean staggered to her feet. "We must have the blessing of Woman Spirit," she moaned as she steadied herself.

"Absolutely," Rank agreed. "We need Woman Spirit right up front proselytizing the women men!"

"Hear me great and all-powerful Mother!" Marjean croaked. "Bring us together in the quiet darkness of your womb. Fill us with oneness and harmony. Give us the power of your life-bearing spirit that we might restore your ways and rule again in your name. TERTIUM DATUR!" she cried out fiercely.

"TERTIU DATUR," the leader of the Women People everywhere roared like cannon fire. "Now over the top!" she shouted with all the stony emotion she could muster. The Women's People action committee did not budge.

"Git on wif readin' na plan," the black centurion called out impatiently.

Rank waited a second then raised the scroll over her head like Raymond Paige's grandfather at Five forks. "*The Manifesto of the Women People of Everywhere*," she proclaimed. This statement, as you all know, has been created by the executive committee of the Women People of Everywhere, of which I am Chairperson, Professor Shoate' is deputy Chair, and the rest of you are junior members. You therefore know that the Manifesto of the Women People of Everywhere declares under four headers. The first pertains to Gaia, the World, and the Natural Order. The second pertains to Gaia and the Women People of Everywhere. The third pertains to the rights of Women People of Everywhere. The fourth pertains to protecting Gaia's way and Gaia's temple and perpetuating the blessings Gaia bestows on her children.

Lowering it to the level of her eyes, the Chair of the Women People's executive committee began to read its manifesto. "Header First: *About Gaia, the World, and the Natural Order*. Now remember, she said, looking up, "we've already agreed on all these points, so I don't want any interruptions as a read them. Is that understood?" She held her fierce eyes on the committee's members for a chilling moment then returned to the scroll.

"Proposition 1-A: Gaia is the creator and foundation of the world.

"Proposition 1-B: The ways of Gaia are the ways of Nature and its natural order.

"Proposition 1-C: Nature is Gaia's womb.

"Proposition 1-D: The ways of Gaia are the right ways.

"Proposition 1-E: To follow Gaia's ways is to be fulfilled and perpetually happy.

"These propositions confirm that We the Women People of Everywhere are going back to the beginning of things and starting over. Right!" She looked at the black centurion, who had herself started over, for confirmation.

"Is's tha only way ta pertec' tha flars in na gard'n," Ashanti Shoate' agreed solemnly. She clenched her fist in front of her face and held it there threateningly as she scanned the other members of the executive committee.

"Good," the chairperson grunted and resumed her task. "Header Second: *About Gaia and the Women People of Everywhere.* Rank looked up again. "This is where we affirm the sisterhood and confirm its special place in the natural order. Right!" She looked again at the scholar from the University of Virginia. "This brave warrior got this ball rolling by publishing her award-winning text on Sally Hemings."

"She wuz Gaia's mess'nger," the revolutionary black leader observed, fighting back tears.

"There now, sister," Rank said stroking her shoulder sympathetically. "Now that the world knows her, she will never be forgotten." So saying, she focused again on her own text.

"Proposition 2-A: Gaia is Mother of the Women People of Everywhere.

"Proposition 2-B: All Women Persons, being Gaia's children, are sisters.

"Proposition 2-C: All Women Person are sisters who dwell in their Mother's Womb.

"Proposition 2-D: Gaia is the protectress of all Women Person sisters.

"These propositions confirm that we, the Women People of everywhere, dwell and operate on a higher plain than the penis-heads who have for centuries made the rules. We are better than they are, and the time is now at hand where we take control of our lives and our communities. Right!"

"We have no choice," Aster whimpered.

"Amen," the UVA scholar added, raising her fist again.

"That's the spirit," Rank cheered before returning to her task. "Header Third: *About the Rights of the Women People of Everywhere.*

"Proposition 3-A: It is the right of Gaia's children to be one with their Mother.

"Proposition 3-B: It is the right of Gaia's children to be safe in their bodies.

"Proposition 3-C: It is the right of Gaia's children to be at peace in their Minds.

"Proposition 3-D: It is the right of Gaia's children to be fulfilled and happy.

"Notice how different these rights are from the ones the penis-heads cooked up," Rank observed, looking again at her black deputy.

"Well-bein' ain't got nuffin ta do wif prop-rty," the black activist intoned. "But like Sally sez," she continued, "tha frui'cake's gotta be spread 'roun' in na righ' way."

"No question about that," Rank agreed. "We'll create a committee, and you can be its chairperson." Having approved her ad hoc proviso, she returned to her task. "Header Fourth: *About protecting Gaia's Ways and Gaia's Temple, and perpetuating the blessings Gaia Bestows on her Children.*

"Proposition 4-A: Gaia's Womb is a temple that shall not be defiled.

"Proposition 4-B: The Women People of Everywhere have the right to make any law they deem necessary to preserve the purity and sanctity of Gaia's temple.

"Proposition 4-C: The Women People of Everywhere have the right to make any law they deem necessary to assure their safety and well-being.

"Proposition 4-D: Women People shall establish a Committee of Well-being which shall be empowered to create and enforce their rules.

"Proposition 4-E: A Committee of Well-being shall appoint a sister who shall have authority to enforce its rules as she shall see fit.

"Proposition 4-F: All who dwell in Gaia's womb shall be under the authority of Gaia's Committee of Well-being.

"This's mighty nigh how Sally an' na marquis dun it in France," the black scholar nodded.

"You and Ashanti want to run everything just like Tim does!" Gerta exclaimed.

"Absolutely!" Rank snapped impatiently. "We're giving ourselves the power to do whatever we think is necessary to protect Women People from the aggressions of penisheads like Tim Hardin,"

"Da's da way rev'lutions werk!" the black historian added. "Whut you thin's goin' on here?"

"We're taking over," Rank continued, "just like the Women People of Atlantis did. And when we have the power, we're going to get rid of shitheads who cause problems." She paused a moment, then laid out the plan. "We'll tersh the reactionaries. Then we'll take over the churches and the schools—sisters already run them," she added. "And when we control them, we'll train the penisheads to be gentle and sensitive . . . and submissive. By Gaia!" She snorted. "When we're done, the bozos'll do whatever we tell 'em."

Marjean raised her hand. "What about violators. How are we going to deal with them?"

Rank looked at Sister Ashanti. "What about that, Sister?"

"We're gonna cut off thur balls," she answered, her eyes flashing.

Rank looked back at Sister Marjean. "Ok?"

"If we're going to form a Punishment Committee," Marjean replied, "I want to be on it."

"Perfect!" Rank thrilled. "You can be its Chair." She looked at the black theorist. Professor Shoate' nodded.

"Is there any further discussion on this point?" Rank asked, looking around. "Ok … " Rank continued after a brief pause. "Violating the harmony of Gaia… a-n-d o-t-h-e-r-w-i-s-e b-o-t-h-e-r-i-n-g W-o-m-e-n P-e-o-p-l-e … will be a castrating offense." She scribbled the words in the margin of her document. "All… persons… shall… follow… the… way… of… Gaia. Violators… shall… be… judged and punished… by… the Punishment Committee. How's that?" The commandeer of the order of Women People asked, looking at Marjean.

"Gaia's will be done!" Marjean answered, settling back.

"The Punishment Committee shall consist of Sisters Marjean, Aster, and Gerta. Rank glanced at Marjean who nodded her approval.

"Excuse me," Gerta Biederman peeped. "Kate says that all heterosexual sex is rape."

Rank snorted at the sound of the name. "Ok, … let's see … ," she said gruffly, "We have that here somewhere … mmmm … mmmm … Yes, here it is … Sub-paragraph 1: Unauthorized heterosexual intercourse is a threat to the security of Woman People. First time offenders shall have their sex license suspended. Repeat offenders will be subject to such punishment as the Committee of Well-being shall deem appropriate." Rank looked at Ashanti Shoate'. "Is that what we said?"

"Tha's tha way Miss Sally took it fom Maddum Condorcet," Professor Shoate' informed the gathering. "This's tha mos' crucial piece," she added, "cuz iss a pow'rful tool fer keepin' na bro's in line. See whut ahm sayin'? Less they tow tha line, they don't git no pussy! And tha same goes fer sisters tha's givin' it away."

"That raises another question," Rank observed, sitting back. "How are we going to deal with Tonto?" She rubbed her forehead thoughtfully and focused on Marjean. "How about we leave that to Woman Spirit?"

Marjean nodded solemnly.

Rank resumed reading. " Sub-paragraph 2: "In order to maintain the oneness and harmony of Gaia, there will be no private ownership of property by penisheads. We all agree on this. Right?" she asked scanning the panel. No one moved. "Good! This is going really well . . . "

"Sub-paragraph three: The Committee of Well-being shall protect the environment." The sisters all agreed. "Third sentence: No activities shall be tolerated that in the judgement of the Committee of Well-being harm the environment."

"Sub-paragraph Four, Sentence One: Residents of the realm of Women People shall worship Gaia in the way prescribed by the Women People's Committee of Religion. Any and all violations of this directive shall be reported to the Punishment Committee, which shall take whatever actions it considers fitting." Rank paused. "That reminds me," she said looking again at Marjean. "What about the Anti-Christ?"

Marjean slowly transformed into Woman Spirit. When the deity had fully formed, it began to float about the room. As she did, she spoke.

"The Prophetess La La has said that it shall be as when a he-goat comes upon a ewe standing peacefully beside the river, and runs unto her in the fury of his power and smites her and casts her down and tramples upon her. And he shall wax great even to the host of heaven; and he shall cast down some of the host and some of the stars upon the ground, and trample even upon them." Woman Spirit took a cleansing breath. "How long shall be the desolation of the sanctuary and its hostess trodden under foot? The Prophetess La La has said that that which is shall be undone when the time comes, and the new shall rise to take its place, but Gaia shall continue age after age."

"What about the Anti-Christ?" Frances Rank snapped. "Tell us about the anti-Christ."

Woman Spirit continued. "The Prophet Daniel lived in the Age of Aries under the rulership of Libra. He warned the men people that the judgement would be upon them. And he told of a great evil that would be brought upon them, and upon their judges that judged them. Then he prophesied that their temple would be destroyed, and their holy city would be razed. And when this was done, God turned his anger away from them, and the ages passed."

"And then?" Rank demanded reddening.

"Gaia shall send her angel, which shall confirm to the people that the end is drawing nigh. And a beast shall come who is the false Messiah and the Anti-Christ. And he shall break the covenant and make the temple's sanctuary unclean. Then shall the tribulation be upon men, who shall wail and gnash their teeth. And the earth shall be rent, and the temple shall be torn down unto the end. And fire shall consume the desolation even until the sanctuary is purified, and righteousness is rooted again in their wicked hearts. But first, the false Messiah shall appear as the angel of Gaia and the covenant shall be broken. The Holy City shall be set upon by an army from the west and the army shall be destroyed. And the sacred temple shall be razed, and a great fire shall spread and quench itself upon the desolation."

"I'm not getting the picture," Rank announced, her frustration growing. "How's the Anti-Christ supposed to bring on the new Age of the Aquarius? And for Christ sake, speak English!"

"At the end of the Great Cycle, Gaia will be cleansed of the iniquity of the ages and shall glisten again like pure water in sunlight. And the Anti-Christ is the instrument of her cleansing."

"Ok!" Rank nodded. "Now we're getting somewhere."

"The Anti-Christ shall manifest himself to the masses. And they will anoint him and worship him as their Savior. And he shall reign over them and in his reign shall day be night. And wrong shall be right. And all things shall be thrown together into chaos according to Gaia's will. And in the chaos shall come the grinding of the earth's mantle as Gaia turns onward to the new age. And the Prince of Disorder shall harken to the grinding of the earth's mantle and rebel against Gaia for he covets her crown for himself. And he shall call those who feast with him in the desolation and gather them to battle against her on that great day.

"Then shall Gaia's angel open the bottomless pit. And there shall arise smoke from it as from a great furnace. And the sun and the air will be made dark. And there shall come out of the smoke locusts upon the earth: and with them shall be the power, as the scorpions of the earth have power. And they shall not hurt the grass of the earth, or any green thing, or creature, neither the faithful women people; but only men people and those who have turned their faces against Gaia. And the King they shall have over them, who is the Anti-Christ, shall appear clothed in darkness and bearing the mark of the beast, and they shall know him for his name shall be Armageddon.

"And so his kingdom shall be filled with darkness. And all those who abide with him shall gnaw their tongues for pain. Then shall unclean spirits come out of their mouths. For they are the spirits of men, which shall go forth unto the corners of the earth to gather the iniquitous to do battle on that great day. And on that day shall there be thunder and lightning; and there shall be a great earthquake, such as was not since Gaia drove Atlantis under the sea.

"And when the day has come a woman shall come forth in the raiment of the sun, and she shall be gilded with the silver of the moon, and upon her head shall be a crown of twelve stars: And she shall stand before the sea of glass and receive the blessing of Gaia. Then shall the he-dragon, who is the Anti-Christ in his wrath, appear. And the dragon shall gather before the woman for to devour her. For when her time has come, she shall bring forth a woman child who will rule all nations in the way of Gaia, which is against the will of him who would keep the scepter for himself. So shall the woman flee unto the mountain. Then shall Gaia strike the temple and it shall be purged with fire and flame. And Gaia and her angels shall fight against the dragon and his armies. And they shall fight against each other, Gaia and her angels and the beast and his armies. And the grinding of the earth's mantle shall mark the ending of the old age even in the midst of the battle. And the beast shall take flight and shall flee into the wilderness. Then shall a loud voice cry in heaven, saying: *Now has the new age dawned! And the scroll shall be opened and the new law shall be revealed.*

"Then shall an angel come down from heaven, having the key to the bottomless pit and a great chain in her hand. And she shall lay hold on the he-dragon, which is Man Spirit, and bind him another age. But the time shall come, and he shall be loosed again from his prison. And he shall go out again to deceive the nations, which shall again be ruled of men. And he shall lead them again into desolation. And it shall be as it was again. And an angel shall come out of the temple, crying with a loud voice, saying: Thrust in your sickle, and reap; for the season is come again, and the harvest of the earth is ripe. And she that sits on the cloudy throne shall take her sickle upon the earth, and the earth will be reaped again. And she shall say: I am Alpha and Omega, the beginning and the end. Behold, I have made all things new again."

"Now I see!" Rank exclaimed, leaping up in excitement. "We are the angels of Gaia! And when we defeat the Anti-Christ and put him away, women will rule the world. It all fits together!" Suddenly she stopped, "Who is the Anti-Christ . . . and who the devil is this woman in the raiment of the sun?"

There was a gate in the hedgerow on the far side of the field. Bart Paige's glistening black pick-up truck was parked inconspicuously behind it. Paige was seated behind its steering wheel, as he had been for two hours, staring through a pair of binoculars at the door to Aster's geodesic dome. "What are they saying now," he asked.

Suzie readjusted the headset she was wearing. "The squat one with the gray hair wants to know who the Anti-Christ is," she answered, popping her gum.

"Ah kin tell 'er all 'bout that," Paige said, absent-mindedly stroking the bandage that swaddled his head. "That's all Ried talked about while we were workin' out our deal."

"Shhh . . . Hardin's old lady's saying something," Suzie said, squinting inward into her earphones. "She's telling everybody that she knows who it is."

"Yea? Who?"

Suzie popped her gum again. "Tim Hardin!"

"Shit!" Paige snorted without moving his binoculars from the door of the dome.

"Hold on!" Suzie giggled. "You're going to love this."

"What?"

"Your flaky sister says it's you." She jabbed his ribs with her elbow. "Maybe she's right—you were sure a devil last night!"

"Yea," Paige grunted, reaching over and squeezing her crotch, "an' ahm comin' back fer some more soon ez it's dark!"

"O-o-o-o," she squealed, squirming into his hand. "Wait a minute," she said, focusing back on the headset. "Now the black gal's talking. She says . . . it's your old man!"

"She's smarter than ah thought," Paige quipped, raising his binoculars back to his eyes.

"Yea," she agreed, popping her gum again. "You don't need him anymore now that you got Ried's seeds."

"I'll show that som-bitch who's smart," Paige muttered under his binoculars.

"Yea . . . that was smart to hide the microphone in the skull," she added. "I can hear everything they're saying." She readjusted her earphones. "The ugly old witch's talking again."

"What's she sayin' now?"

"She says they're all wrong . . . somethin' about William O. Douglas." Her face darkened with confusion. "I've never heard o' him—is he Aster's boyfriend?"

"Thomas Jefferson thought it wuz Aaron Burr," Paige said, ignoring the question.

"How do you know that mister smarty pants?" Suzie asked, popping her gum again.

"He said so in one o' tha letters Ried showed me."

"Holy ta Moly! He has a letter from Thomas Jefferson!"

"He had a whole book full of 'em," Paige continued, lowering his glasses. "An' they wuz all wrote in German!"

"He was weird wasn't he . . . " she said. "Why would he do that?"

"'Cause Ried's people wuz German," Paige replied, training his glasses back on the dome.

"Did he speak German too?"

"Yea."

"And Thomas Jefferson wrote German. Wow! A bunch of Germans talking to each other about the Anti-Christ? Is that what Germans talk about, honey?"

Paige shrugged. "It's complicated . . . I guess I could tell ya 'bout it . . . we got plenty o' time."

"Go ahead . . . " she replied without thinking. "It's not like I'm not already bored."

"Yea," Paige agreed. "Anyhow, Jefferson got into it while 'e wuz buildin' 'is house."

"Wow," Suzie said, popping her gum again. "You sure have a knack for rememberin' stuff."

"Yea. Ah didn't pay much 'ttention when Ried firs' started tellin' me 'bout it, but it got kina intristin' after that. Anyhow, he had all these ahdeas 'bout what 'e wuz gonna do, ya know, like what color wallpaper 'e should have, an' what kina moldin' ta put in tha livin' room—stuff like that. But 'e kep' changin' tha plan so 'e never got ta whar 'e wuz ready ta decorate tha place."

"That must have pissed off his old lady," Suzie observed, fixing her hair in the mirror on the sun visor.

"Yea. She died—that's when 'e went off ta France."

"If I was her," Suzie said, patting one final curl into place, "I'd o' gone to France and let him hang his own wallpaper ... and when I got there," she added, with a haughty look, "I'd o' hooked up with a rich, handsome prince!"

"Shut up, will ya. Ahm sick o' listenin' ta that shit."

"Aw," she cooed. "You know I'm just kiddin'. Anyway—you're gonna be rich soon. Right?"

"Yea. An' don't you forget it."

"So tell me about Thomas Jefferson," she added contentedly. "I've always been curious about him. He was smart too. Wasn't he?"

Paige cooled for another minute.

"Come on honey," she said, giving him an encouraging pat. "Tell me ... "

"He had all these high falutin' ahdeas 'bout how 'is house oughta be," Paige said finally. "Ya know what ah mean? He wuz stuck on thangs Ried called Roman orders. When 'e put t'gether tha firs' plan fer 'is house, it all fit accordin' ta one of these orders. That wuz tha way tha Romans built thur houses, ah guess. Ried said thar wuz a bunch of 'em, but that tha ones Jefferson liked wuz invented by a guy named Andrea Palladio. He had this book by another guy named Giacomo Leoni called *Architecture of A. Palladio*. That's whar 'e figgered out how ta calculate stuff tha way Palladio done."

"See—I was right," Suzie said popping here gum. "He was smart."

"Yea," Paige conceded. "The ground floor wuz sposed ta have a big salon decorated in tha Corinthian order. He wuz gonna have niches b'side tha door inta tha entrance hall with copies o' Medici's Venus an' Farnese's Hercules. An' 'e wanted it ta have blue wallpaper. He wanted tha ceiling in tha dining room ta be papier-mache' molded with a pattern from a book 'e had from some guy named Gibbs. Tha moldin' in tha dinin' room wuz sposed ta be in tha Doric order. He wuz gonna paint that white an' put green paper on tha walls. Tha room next ta tha dinin' room wuz fer tea in tha afternoon. It wuz sposed ta be Ionic—same ez 'is bedroom, which wuz gonna have pink wallpaper."

"That sounds cute," Suzie said, reexamining her face in the visor mirror.

"Yea . . . Tha study wuz gonna be Doric with blue wallpaper. Tha attic over 'is bedroom wuz also gonna have pink wallpaper with stuff from tha temple o' Fortuna Virilis in Rome which 'e got from 'is book on Palladio. He wuz gonna put red paper in tha other attic along with moldin's from tha temple o' Nerva Trajan.

"You sound like you got a P-H-D or something from UVA," she said, unwrapping a new stick of gum. "That's the way the smarties over at U-V-A talk."

"Yea. Ahm gonna go over an' pick up mah sheepskin soon's ah git mah money back from that f—king bitch. What're they sayin' now?" He asked, refocusing his binoculars on the dome.

"They're arguing about who's right."

"F–k 'em. Is she still in nar?"

"Yea. She's being Woman Spirit again."

"That f–kin' fraud. Ahl tell ya about her," Paige said, lowering his glasses. "She's tha biggest money-grubbin' whore down here."

"Gosh! That big?"

"She grew up in Hoboken, New Jersey. Did ya know that?"

"Hoboken, New Jersey is that a real place? I thought it was just a joke that Johnny Carson made up!"

"No! It's real—it's right across the river from New York. It's whar all tha oil tanks are. That's whar she come from–crawled raght out o' one of them stinkin' tins like a worm."

"How do you know that?"

"Ried tol' me."

"Yea?"

"He know'd all kinds o' weird shit. He got ta know Douglas some-how–somethin' ta do with bein' a ranger out thar in Washington state. That's whar 'e met Hardin an' Bildner. Tha ol' fart thought he'd get 'em off in na woods an' convert 'em inta communists, but all they done wuz grow dope an' peddle it ta tha rest o' tha campers."

"That's the way Americans are supposed to be, isn't it honey?" Suzie said, popping her gum.

"That's right—Americans're capitalists," he agreed. "Anyhow, Ried and Bildner got drafted an' sent off ta Vietnam. Stupid f__kers—they should o' gone ta Canada like Hardin. Anyhow, they got inta this demolition stuff over thar, ya know, blowin' up bridges an' villages . . . shit like that. Ried'd git high. Then he'd pack up his chopper an' start lightin' thangs off. He said tha most fun 'e had wuz watchin' tha shit fly.

"Tha witch thar," he pointed toward the dome, "started out tellin' fortunes in Hoboken. She called hersef Madam Marja."

"Oooh! I like that," Suzie giggled. "Maybe I'll get her to tell my fortune."

A pained look spread across Paige's bearded face. "She don't know nuffin 'bout fortune tellin'."

"She doesn't?" Suzie was suddenly bewildered. "Then how can she tell fortunes?"

"If you had a brain in that cute little head o' yers," Paige responded, "you'd know that it's jes' another f–kin' scam."

"My old boyfriend used to . . . "

Paige slapped his hand across her mouth and held it there until she was quiet. "We're done talkin' 'bout fortune tellin'. You got that? It's bullshit. Tha's all you gotta know."

"Ok!" she said prying his hand away. "You don't need to get all bent out of shape. It's not like it's a big deal or anything." She straightened her earphones and pretended to ignore him.

"Where was I?"

"Fortune telling's bullshit . . . " she huffed.

"Oh . . . yea . . . Anyhow, Hardin's ol' lady figgered she b'longed in tha women's movement."

"Yea—'cause she's ugly," Suzie observed.

"Yea. She's tha kine o' ugly who hasta pay fer tha party ta get invited."

"Is she rich too?"

"Yea. She's got tons o' dough–from her ol' man. He owned a string o' newspapers up in New York."

"She's got that on you," Suzie said with a mischievous smirk.

"She wuz jes' lucky 'er ol' man died b'fore 'e figgered out how she wuz gonna waste 'is money. Mine din't," he added philosophically.

"Better bein' lucky than smart!" Suzie chirped happily.

"We'll see 'bout that, won't we," Paige said, gingerly stroking his bandaged head.

"So she's got big bucks," Suzie repeated.

"Yea. An' it din't take no time fer Madam Marja ta sniff it out. Next thang ya know, she'd turned hersef inta a lesbo parasite an' wuz livin' with sister ugly in tha *tony* avant garde section of lower Manhattan," he lisped the words to sound like a garden party gay. "Ried's tour in Nam run out 'bout that time an' <u>he</u> goes ta New York . . . The f–kin' chameleon got himsef a lof' down in Soho an' started makin' out like 'e wuz an artis'. O' course tha f__kers down nare din't know tha difference," Paige said. "Ya ever seen tha shit for art they put out?"

"I've only been to Culpeper," she said, popping her gum absent-mindedly.

"Well, he's up 'ere actin' like an artis' an' peddlin' dope. 'Course 'e had all them contacts from Nam so 'e wuz dealin' hot stuff. An' 'e's peddlin' it ta tha assholes hangin' 'round with sister ugly."

"Sounds like he had it made in the shade . . . " Suzie said, checking to see if her nose was still powdered. "That's what the way you're gonna be, isn't it honey?"

"Yea. Now that Ried's gone ahm 'onna take over."

"And you're gonna be RICH!" She snuggled against him. "That's the part I like . . . "

"So 'e's makin' a fortune puttin' out this shit fer art an' peddlin' dope to all the dikes an' fags an' creeps in New York. Meanwhile ol' Madam Marja thar's f__kin' tha uglies fer nothin' an' livin' on handouts."

"And she thinks she's so smart!" Suzie sneered.

"Yea. Anyhow, she <u>wuz</u> smart 'nough ta start peddlin' Ried's dope ta my f–kin' sister after she showed up with 'er shit fer poetry. Madam Marja glommed onto her jes' like that Rasputin guy." Bart Paige stopped suddenly. "Wait a minute! I fergot tha part 'bout how Ried got 'is book."

"Is that the one Hardin's after?"

"Yea. One day while 'e wuz in still Nam, 'e got this package–like from 'is grandfather er somebody. Anyhow, 'e got this package an' 'e opens it up an' thar's this book an' ever'thin' in it's handwrote in German. An' on na cover's this ox skull with a bunch o' flowers in its horns. Course, 'e wuz stoned out o' 'is gourd 'cause 'e wuz gettin' ready ta go blow somethin' up so 'e din't have time ta fool with it jes' then. But while 'e's out demolishin' tha nex' village er whatever was on nis list, 'e hears this voice—like tha angel Gabriel. Ya know what ah mean?"

"Whoa! That's weird," Suzie said, cringing. "It's weird how weird things are, don't you think?"

"Yea, an' this voice tells 'im that God's gonna reveal tha secret o' tha universe to him. Course 'e figures it's in tha book."

"Holy Moly! I'da been peeing in my pants."

"Yea? That's probably why God don't talk ta you," Paige grunted. "Anyhow, Ried starts readin' tha book. It's got all this weird shit—like whar's tha best place ta grow dope, an' how ta make tha German army better, an' how come tha Temple o' Jupiter tha Thunderer got called tha Temple o' Vespasian. Shit like that."

"Wow. That's *heavy*! And it's all in German. And what about the letters from Thomas Jefferson?"

"They wuz in thar too. They wuz writin' letters ta each other."

"God and Thomas Jefferson?"

"Not God! Baron de Riedesel. He wuz tha one writin' Thomas Jefferson."

"Now you really got me confused. Where'd this Baron guy come from?"

"He lived up 'ere on tha mountain next ta Thomas Jefferson."

"Even I'm not dumb enough to believe that Thomas Jefferson lived next to a German Baron," she announced defiantly.

"No! seriously! He wuz captured durin' tha American Revolution an' they sent 'im an' 'is army ta Charlottesville."

"What was he supposed to do down there?"

"Ah don't know—grow dope ah guess."

"You're funny," she said with a nervous laugh.

"Yea . . . it runs in na family."

"Tell me something, will you? Why would Ried have a book with letters by Thomas Jefferson and this Baron guy?"

"Because tha Baron wuz Ried's kin."

"Ried was kin to someone who knew Thomas Jefferson?"

"You got it . . . "

"And they wrote each in German about growing dope and naming temples."

"Yea . . . "

"And they talked about architecture and the Anti-Christ?"

"Yea–an' Leibniz an' Herrschaft an' a bunch o' other weird shit."

"You know what I think?" Suzie said, looking out the window and popping her gum.

"What?"

"The secrets of the universe *are* in that book."

"Shit . . . "

"No seriously—there's stuff we don't understand."

"The problem with you, Baby," Paige explained, "is thar ain't nothin' you do unnerstand."

"Ok smarty. What's in the book then?"

"*Their* secrets," Paige whispered. "It's got all tha stuff they couldn't tell ta nobody else."

"Oh my Gosh!" Suzie gasped, staring into the beyond. "I bet that's worth a million bucks!" She turned toward Paige with fiery urgency. "Ried didn't blow it up did he?

"No."

"Thank God!" She gulped, clutching his arm. "Let's go get it right now." She ripped her headset off and fastened her seatbelt.

"Hol' on," Paige said with a discouraging hand gesture.

"What do you mean 'hold on'? There's a million bucks waiting to be picked up!"

"I'm not goin' nowhar 'til ah git my hunnerd gran' back from that f__kin' bitch in nar."

"Forget about that," Suzie snapped. "That's chump change."

"It's tha princ'ple o' tha thang," Paige explained, suddenly defensive.

Her eyes narrowed into a suspicious squint, "There's something you're not telling me."

"Whaddaya mean?"

"Where did you get that hundred gran'?" She demanded.

Paige swallowed hard. "I pawned Daddy's bull."

"Oh shit!"

"If 'e finds out, ahm toast . . ."

She contemplated the situation. "How are you going to get it back?"

"Ahm onna use some o' tha money ah git sellin' tha crop."

"Wait a minute," Suzie commanded. "How did Madam Marja get your hundred gran' in the first place?"

"She stole it from Ried . . ."

"Then it's Ried's problem . . ."

"Whall . . . kina . . ."

"Kina what," Suzie demanded.

"He wuz gonna lend me enough money ta pay off Bildner—that wuz tha deal."

Suzie considered the matter. "So he's dead . . . and she's got the money . . . and this guy Bildner has the crop. Is that it?"

"That's about it," Paige answered in a deflated voice.

"Where's the bull?"

Paige shrugged.

Suzie spit her gum out the window and opened the glove compartment. Inside was a bottle of Schenley's Red Satin. She pulled it out, twisted off the top and poured a slug down her throat. Then she handed the bottle to Paige. "What're you gonna do?" She asked, staring out the window in a trance.

Paige took a long pull from the bottle. "Ah figger ahl trap 'er an' torture 'er 'til she hands it over," he said, wiping his mouth with his hand.

"Ohhh . . ." Suzie moaned as she envisioned a pile of money evaporating. "When's the crop coming in," she asked suddenly.

"Ahm sposed ta meet that Bildner guy t'night at tha Albemarle Lounge," he said.

"Does he think you have the money?"

"That's kina what he thinks," Paige agreed.

"What if you don't have it?"

"Ah expect he'll sell tha crop to . . ."

"Madam Marja!" Suzie announced.

"Yea . . ."

Suzie slumped in her seat. "What about the book?" She glanced at her companion out of the corner of her eye. "Any chance of getting that before tonight?"

Paige shook his head. "Tha las' sang Ried tol' me wuz that 'e sent it ta Thomas Jefferson . . . "

"Thomas Jefferson's dead!" She exclaimed. "Even I know that."

Paige took another swallow from the Schenley's bottle. "That din't make no difference 'cause Ried wuz stoned," he said. "Ried wuz lookin' fer a smart lawyer ta fix a land deed an' Jefferson come inta 'is head. Hardin figgered 'e sent it ta my ol' man," he added hopefully.

"Why would he think that?"

"He wuz extrapolatin'. Ya know, like Ried wuz confusin' Thomas Jefferson with tha Jefferson Academy. His brain wuz so fried thar weren't no tellin' what 'e wuz doin'."

"You think your old man's got it?"

"Naa . . . if 'e did, 'e woulda said so. He's honest—that's 'is problem."

"Shit!" Suzie cursed, taking the bottle back from Paige. She took another swig. "How about letting her buy the crop," she suggested, "then stealing it back? That would be a lot easier than torturing her . . . and that way you'd get the dope."

Paige slapped the steering wheel. "That's jes' tha way ta do it. You're brilliant Baby Doll!" He laughed and slapped the wheel again. "Gimme a kiss," he said, pulling her toward him. He finished his celebration with another swig of whiskey. "An' she won't make no noise neither," he said, thinking out loud, "not after what she done in New York."

"What did she do in New York?" Suzie wondered.

"She had Aster bringin' dope in through LaGuardia an' they foun' it in 'er bags. Daddy pulled some strangs an' got 'er out o' thar b'fore they could ask who she wuz workin' fer—but Daddy know'd all 'long. That's how come Daddy don't like Madam Marja much."

"Is that when Aster came back to the farm?"

"Yea—an' the witch come with 'er."

"Did Ried come down then too?"

"Yea—he had some crazy notion that 'e owns tha place! See what ah mean. He wuz nuts."

"Why would he think that?"

"It wuz somethin' ta do with 'is grandfather buildin' a resort fer Germans."

"Down here?"

"He din't say... but 'e did tell me once that 'is grandfather wuz tha Baron's kin an' that tha Baron had sent Jefferson some seeds an' that Jefferson planted 'em in 'is greenhouse!"

"Holy Moly! I bet it's the same stuff Ried's got growing today!" Suzie exclaimed.

"Listen ta this," Paige continued. "Ried said 'is grandfather grew some really hot dope right here on Belmont Farm an' sent it to Sigmund Freud!"

"He's another one of those spooky Germans, isn't he" Suzie asked wide-eyed.

"Ried wuz allez tryin' ta figure out whar tha Baron grew it cause tha quality o' dope depends on whar ya' grow it—like wine and tabacca..."

"Hey... I just had a weird thought—is 'Ried' short for 'de Riedesel'?"

"Yea, 'is father changed tha family name 'cause after tha war, Americans din't like Germans much."

"Thomas Jefferson and the Baron's great grandson were growing dope right here!" Suzie said looking around in silent awe. "Holy Moly!"

"Ain't that some shit..." Paige laughed, taking another pull on his bottle. "We're doin' jes' like them famous people!"

"Honey," she said, "if you don't find your bull, you better find that book..."

———————

Henry stepped through the hedge and advanced across the patio toward Mr. Paige. "Sorry I'm late."

"Hank! How's the patient doing?"

"He's pretty banged up, but there is no indication of brain damage. Based on the early indications, it appears that he will make a full-recovery."

"Good!" Paige said.

"Where's Claire?" Henry asked looking around. "I thought she was joining us for lunch."

"You missed her," Paige replied. "We dined without you, then she had to leave for another appointment."

"How did it go?"

"Fine. She impresses me. In fact, I offered a job."

"No kidding!"

"Yes," Paige confirmed. "I think she's the right person to handle our public relations. And that brings up an issue." Paige picked up an envelope that was lying on the table and handed it to Henry. "Can you deliver this to Martin Ogden at the Boars Head Inn. I want him to know that we are in discussions with his employee."

"Sure, be glad to. I'll take it over there now."

"Good." Paige responded.

Claire walked past a black Limousine parked in the entrance portico and into the lobby of the Boar's Head Inn. Beside the door, was a stocky man with trim dark hair and a square jaw. His sunglasses masked his eyes. He might have been an Oscar Hanson statue, but he was spinning a ring keys on his forefinger.

As Claire reached the elevator, the door opened and there was William O. Douglas. His face brightened when he recognized her. "Why Claire!"

"Justice Douglas!" she beamed back. "Martin told me you were joining him for lunch. Did you have a nice visit?"

"Yes," he said. "We always have a lot to talk about. And by the way," he added, stepping from the elevator into the lobby, "your article was very . . . interesting—especially the connections between the academy and Jefferson.

Claire smiled. "Will you be at the Colonnade Club for the Academy's dinner tonight?"

"I will," he said.

"Then I'll see you this evening." She entered the elevator and pressed the button for the fifth floor.

The door to Ogden's suite was unlocked so Claire opened it. "Martin?" She called. There was no response. She walked cautiously through the foyer and entered the apartment's main room.

That's when she saw him. He was sitting on the balcony. He seemed to be contemplating the mountains, which she could see in the distance. She was about to call again but changed her mind. Instead, she allowed herself to be drawn into the comfortable scene. It was a moment worth savoring. Everything she wanted from life was within her grasp. It was just the way she expected things to turn out. She felt a warm rush of satisfaction.

She had prepared herself. She had what it takes, and she knew it. She deserved to be recognized . . . She deserved to be heard . . . What she thought should count . . . She belonged on the inside . . . At the enlightened center . . . Communing with the cognoscenti . . . Quoting them and being quoted . . . Endorsing their books . . . Sitting on their self-congratulating panels . . . A member in good standing of Washington's most exclusive club . . . The men and women who filled its ranks were gifted . . . talented . . . They should sit in judgement—they were *intellectuals.*

Her attention shifted to the man seated on the balcony. It was appropriate that she have this relationship. There was so much he could do for her. And she was doing her part—being smart. looking sharp, and the rest . . .

She knew he was upset with her, but she knew how to handle him. She'd let him rant for a while. Then she'd tell him her news. His cold blue eyes would warm, and he would smile that smile he wore when he knew he was going to win. It was a man's smile. Muscular. Arrogant. Sexy. When he smiled that smile—that's when she would seduce him. They would make love. She would do it for him in a way that he would want her more than anything else in the world.

She tiptoed noiselessly across the room to balcony. Creeping forward with pantomime steps, she came up directly behind him. He showed no awareness of her presence as she bent over and put her lips to his ear. "Hello darling," she whispered, sliding her hands over his shoulders. "I love you."

"Ho!" Ogden gasped, lurching forward in alarm. "What the . . . " he craned around anxiously to see who was there. "My God, Claire! Never do that to a person."

"Martin, darling," she cooed, "did I startle you? Ooh . . . I'm sorry. But I'm so excited," she announced, redirecting the conversation. "Everything is coming together so well."

Ogden settled back stiffly into his seat. "Sit down, Claire," he said finally. "I want to talk with you."

Claire took the seat next to him and waited obediently as her lover contemplated her.

"I'm taking you off the story," he said at last.

"What!" She must have misunderstood him.

"It's about politics," Ogden said bluntly, "so it's in Rhoade's beat."

"You can't mean it," she protested, fighting to maintain her composure. "I've found a gold mine. It's a sure Pulitzer Prize. I've got the whole thing..."

"I've made up my mind," Ogden interrupted.

"But why?"

"You're making too many mistakes," he answered crisply. "It's hurting the paper's credibility..."

Claire stared into his steely blue eyes, searching for the soft edge that had always been there before. This time, however, there was nothing. The light had gone out. She felt a sudden stab of fear. "Please Martin. I've found something really important. If you explain it to Jack, I'm sure he'll understand."

Ogden listened impassively. It really was sad, he thought, the way people degraded themselves. Why don't they just accept that they we're not up to standard and have done. "There's really no point in continuing this," he said. "The story you wrote compromised the paper. And I found it personally embarrassing. You should have checked with me before submitting it." Ogden rose to his feet, ending the interview.

"But I..."

"That's enough..."

Claire stood before him. "You told me..."

"How dare you tell me what I said! Do you think that I'm a child? You've been wandering around down here like a silly coquette at her coming out party. Instead of getting into the story, you've shacked up with one of Paige's underlings. Now you expect me to bite my lip and ignore it!" He raised his hand and slapped her face. "You're through. Do you hear me?"

Claire clutched her burning cheek. "Please Martin," she sobbed, "I love you..."

He looked at her with cold disdain. "You're nothing but a whore," he answered. "Get out."

Henry stopped at the front desk. "I'd like to deliver a letter to Martin Ogden."

"Mr. Ogden has a guest," the clerk confirmed, checking his list. "If you care to leave it with me, I'll be glad to see that he gets it."

Henry handed the envelope to the desk clerk, then proceeded to the club room to find Prout.

Jim Prout was Henry's most reliable drinking companion. The many enjoyable evenings they had spent together at the bar had helped them both get through graduate school. Prout was a philosopher. In his dissertation, he had examined the emerging "science" of verbal behavior. Applying Wittgensteinian techniques in linguistic analysis, he had exposed the conceptual confusions in B. F. Skinner's oxymoronic concept. Henry considered it first rate since the pseudo-sciences were becoming breeding grounds for utopian social engineers.

"Henry," Prout laughed. "It's a little early even for you, isn't it buddy?"

"I was dropping off a letter for one of your illustrious guests," Henry explained as he stepped up to the bar.

"Yea? Who would that be?" Prout asked, polishing the boards.

"Martin Ogden."

"Really!" Prout grunted. "William O. Douglas came through here a few minutes ago. Maybe they were up there plotting how to squash Paige's counter-revolution?"

"That wouldn't surprise me," Henry agreed, settling himself on a stool.

"By the way," Prout said. "I have something for you."

"What might that be?"

"I have it in my car. Hold on a minute . . . I'll go get it." With that, Prout slipped out from behind the bar and disappeared through a door beside it.

While he was gone, Henry visited the men's room.

———————

Claire peered into the bar empty. It was kind of place she needed to catch her breath and regroup. She hurried past the maitre de's station to the far-most corner and slipped into a booth.

Prout ducked back under the counter and resumed his place behind the bar. In his hand was a book. A moment later Henry re-appeared and seated himself on his barstool.

"This is for you–*Verbal Behavior* by B. F. Skinner," Prout said, handing the book to Henry. "I knew you wouldn't buy your own copy, so I bought one for you."

"You're too kind," Henry said, taking the book and leafing through it.

"The best way to find the weaknesses in scribble like this is to read it yourself..."

"You were going to tell me how Skinner responded to Whitehead's challenge," Henry remembered.

Prout set two glasses on the bar then lifted the Old Fitz bottle off the shelf. "Behavioral psychologists don't understand linguistic analysis," he explained, pouring one inch of old bourbon into each glass.

"In other words," Henry concluded, "he couldn't answer Whitehead's question."

"Skinner collected 'data', but he didn't understand much about how language works," Prout answered.

"Does that mean what he says in this book is meaningless?"

"Wittgenstein would have thought so," Prout confirmed.

"Then he's through," Henry laughed. "And you're a genius!"

Henry had taken David Home's Wittgenstein class on the suggestion of Oscar Denker, who was a close friend of the irascible Philosophy professor. That's where he met Prout. They had gotten to know each other working together on Home's Scottsville farm. That had created opportunities for many conversations at the professor's kitchen table. Henry learned during these conversations that Prout had been a marine and served two tours of duty in Vietnam before beginning his graduate philosophy program.

Home had the distinction of being the University's most dreaded academic tyrant. During years at Cambridge, he had taken classes with Bertrand Russell and his famous protégé, Ludwig Wittgenstein. These were the sources of his analytical systems and teaching methods. Not surprisingly, he adhered to a standard unfamiliar to UVA's undergraduates in respect to scholarship. He even ruffled his graduate students with his demands for precision. They had to use the language correctly. They had to speak clearly and say exactly what they meant. If they performed beneath his grade, he let them know. Even so, Prout was a man Home held in high regard. During one of their kitchen conversations, he stunned Henry by complimented Prout's interpretation of Wittgenstein. On another occasion, after a couple glasses of sherry, he admired Prout for being the strongest man in the University.

"Speaking of good-looking blonds," Prout said, interrupting Henry's reverie, "there's one sitting in the corner booth—and she's looking at you!"

Henry turned around. "Claire!" He exclaimed, rising from his stool.

She was looking directly at him, but she did not answer.

"Have you been here long?" Henry asked, walking over to her. As he approached, he could see that she had been crying. "Is everything all right?" Then he noticed the mark on her check. "What happened?"

She answered by lowering her eyes.

"Wait here . . ." Henry instructed.

He returned a moment later with a snifter of brandy. "Take a sip of this . . . it'll make you feel better."

She did.

"Are you Ok?"

"Yes," she said haltingly.

"Did Ogden . . ."

She waved him off. "You and your friend are talking about B. F. Skinner . . ."

"We are," Henry acknowledged, taking her meaning. "Jim—come over here and finish telling us about Wittgenstein and B. F. Skinner."

Prout stepped out from behind the bar and joined them. "Claire Fox," Henry said, "I'd like you to meet Jim Prout. Jim, I'd like you to meet Claire Fox, feature reporter for *The Washington Post*. Jim is a Wittgensteinian," Henry continued. "That means he has particular views about language use and meaning. Tell Claire why you're interested in B. F. Skinner . . ."

Prout looked doubtfully at Claire.

"Please do . . ." She said with a frail smile.

"Ok," he said. "If you think you are up to it . . ." He took a seat, thought a moment, then began. "By the 1930s, Wittgenstein had come to see meanings of words as the ways they are used in language—as opposed to names for physical and mental things. His views, or at least the passionate way he expressed them, produced conflicts between Wittgenstein and his colleagues. The problem reached a crescendo during a famous confrontation between Wittgenstein had with Karl Popper in 1946. The issue was whether philosophical problems are real, which Popper believed, or merely linguistic puzzles as Wittgenstein thought. During their ten-minute exchange, Wittgenstein became so agitated that he grabbed a poker from the hearth and began waving it at Popper. Ever after that, the debate about the nature of philosophical problems has been known as 'Wittgenstein's Poker.' I am using a variation of it to challenge Skinner's theory of Verbal Behavior."

"He was thinking about this as he was slogging through the jungles in Vietnam," Henry interjected. "That's where he developed his aversion to autocratic social engineers who manage society with Skinner's behavior conditioning techniques. The Hoover Institute thinks so much of his idea," Henry added, "that it's given him a grant to write a book!"

"At least somebody understands what you're talking about . . ." Claire observed as she prepared to become lost.

"George Berkeley once complained that philosophers raise dust so no one can see," Prout continued, overlooking Claire's comment. "In terms of my work, Wittgenstein was showing ordinary people why they should stay clear of philosophical dust . . ."

"What are you protecting them from?" Claire wondered.

"Ideological tyranny," Prout replied.

"Ideological tyranny?" Claire wondered.

"Ideologies are systems of ideas that underpin public policy. Ideologues have learned to use them to shape public opinion and manage people."

"I suppose there is some of that," Claire conceded. Martin Ogden's image formed in Claire's mind. "You're doing something about it?"

"I'm reconstituting ideologies the way Wittgenstein reconstituted philosophical problems . . . so ordinary people will recognize their contradictions and resist them."

"Hmmm . . ."

"There are strong parallels," Prout continued. "They're both what Wittgenstein called 'language games.'"

"I see." Claire misspoke with a smile.

"The situation we have today traces back mid-18th century France— that was when it occurred to Turgot that scientific reason could be used to solve the problems of Man in Society."

"Turgot invented the modern concept of *Progress*," Henry interjected.

"That's the hub concept," Prout agreed. "Over the past hundred years, progressive reformers have used Turgot's enlightened concept. But they have used it to develop machinery to manage society, not to solve its problems or improve the well-being of its members."

"Oscar was telling me about sophocrats last night,' Claire remembered, taking a sip of her brandy. "Are these the baddies you are resisting?'

"When social theorists gain enough power to become hierarchical autocrats," Prout observed, "they become 'baddies'. These are the people I'm talking about."

"Jim," Henry nudged his philosophical friend, "We're short on time . . . can you give Claire the abridged version?"

"Ok . . ." Prout nodded. "From the time of Frances Bacon to the time of Newton, the best thinkers in England and Western Europe occupied themselves developing quantitative methods to measure the processes of nature."

"Ok . . ." Claire nodded.

"Francis Bacon got the ball rolling early in the 17th century by rebelling against Aristotelianism. Until then, the study of Nature was conducted deductively by defining the essences and attributes of physical objects and determining their entailments. Bacon wanted to study Nature in terms of the changes objects in Nature experienced—in terms of cause and effect."

"Ok . . ." Claire nodded again.

"Bacon won his debate with the Aristotelians. Between the publication of his *Novum Organum* in 1620 and Newton's publication of the *Philosophiæ Naturalis Principia Mathematica* in 1687, Natural *Science* completely replaced Aristotelian Natural *Philosophy*. Newton completed this process by proving that events in Nature obey general 'laws' that are stated in terms of their mathematical characteristics.

"This Newtonian revolution in science provided the impetus for a *political* revolution that was led by John Locke in England and somewhat later in France by Montesquieu. Both men considered themselves Newtonians in the sense that they were seeking general laws to describe the processes of Men in Society. Locke had two primary interests. The first concerned how the Human Mind accumulates and processes knowledge. The second concerned the sovereign power individuals have in Nature, which he called their Natural Rights, and what happens to these rights when they joined together in communities. This led him to investigate forms of government and to conclude that political majoritarianism is the only legitimate form of government for individuals living together in society. Montesquieu was concerned with the general laws that govern societies. Their analyses of individual rights and societal rules provided the logic for the political revolutions have been going on since the late-18th century."

"... and you think these revolutions have been led by ideologues intent on managing people," Claire summarized.

"Before we get into that," Prout cautioned, "let me mention that Newton's *scientific* revolution fueled an *industrial/economic* revolution. This unprecedented economic upheaval began in the 18th century and gained momentum through the 19th century. One of its important consequences was the destruction feudalism, being the lord/vassal social system that formed in western Europe in the dangerous Middle Ages and continued to order society through the 18th century. During the 18th and 19th centuries, automation of repetitive tasks allowed the mechanical age to accelerate, and as it did, certain work done by society's lowest members disappeared. Peasants and small farmers were forced to move off the land into villages and towns. By the middle of the 19th century, these wayfarers were operating machines in England's first factories ..."

Claire listened without comment.

"During the 19th century, they had become a new social class—the urban poor. As this bottom rung of industrial society grew, it became the center of entirely new sorts of social problems that the political systems Locke and Montesquieu imagined a century before were not equipped to handle. Something new was needed. Right?

"I see that ..." Claire agreed.

"Men like Locke had Montesquieu saw themselves as scientists in the line of Isaac Newton. The men who replaced them in the late-18th and 19th centuries were not Newtonians—let's call them 'social theorists.' Some of them, men like Jeremy Bentham and John Stuart Mill, conceptualized society as a whole and treated its problems as equally detrimental to all its members. Others, men like Jean-Jacques Rousseau and Karl Marx, saw society as a collection of classes and viewed its problems in terms of the conflicting interests of these classes. In 1762, Rousseau unveiled the idea that *class* was based on property. Eighty years later, Marx made *class conflict*, which he based on the inequitable distribution of property, the center of a new social theory.

"In Marx's theory, the unpropertied underclass—the *Proletariat*—are victims of the propertied overclass——the *Bourgeoisie*. Marx then authorized the Proletariat to use every means available to achieve *social justice* ... By the way," Prout added, interrupting himself. "The most interesting work in this field is being done right here! Do you know Delilah Wanamaker?"

Claire glanced at Henry, who shook his head. "No," Claire answered.

"She joined the Law School faculty last year," Prout said. "She's its first female tenure-track faculty member. She's a Legal Ethicist," he added. "I made a point of meeting her after reading her paper on the history of Justice—she supports my use of Wittgenstein's poker to disarm predatory ideologues like Karl Marx and the destructive social schemes of his followers."

"Give me her top line," Claire said, picking up her glass.

"She recognizes four historical models of Justice," Prout explained. "The first is the Ethical Model of Plato and Aristotle. The second is the Legal Model of Aquinas, Hobbes, and Locke. The third is the Economic Model of Parrington and other 20th century progressives. The fourth is the System Management Model of John Rawls. I connect with her on her assessment of what has happened since progressive reformers have transformed themselves into social justice warriors, which they did in the 1950s and '60s."

"Come again?" Claire exclaimed in bewilderment.

"For the past twenty-five years," Prout explained, "partisan activists have used 'Justice' to incite social conflicts that have undermined the unity of the people and destroyed their willingness to pursue common goods. This anti-social behavior leads ultimately to anarchy and societal collapse. But in the meantime, it is transferring the 'power of the people' to autocratic ideologues."

"So Justice is a political weapon ... in the hands of ideologues," Claire summarized. "And they're using it manage public opinion and destroy society ... No wonder you appreciate Professor Wanamaker."

"You've omitted something," Prout corrected her. "When social theorists become partisan activists, they become advocates for themselves! As class warriors following Karl Marx, they endeavor to sabotage socio-economic systems they accuse of being corrupt, and as they do this, they create a hierarchy in which they control everything and everybody.

"By the third decade of the 20th century, progressive theorists had become public benefactors and were using their authority to organize themselves into a permanent technocracy. After that, acquiring political wherewithal to expand their system of benefits became their objective ... and as they acquired it—using justice rhetoric—they transformed themselves from helpers into overlords ... Does this ring any bells for you?" Prout wondered.

Claire bit her lip instead of conceding the point.

"Marxism is the keystone of this process," Prout continued. "It uses social justice rhetoric to portray communist hierarchs as utilitarian protectors of society's underclasses. But they only exist in totalitarian regimes that are violently repressive! In these systems, behaviorism is a tool to simplify the management of drones."

"Are you an ideologue?" Claire wondered, shifting her inquiry.

"There's a difference," Prout objected. "Let's take a closer look at Utilitarianism," he said, returning to his point. "Hume, Bentham, and John Stuart Mill assumed that all members of a society would benefit if right and wrong actions were based on a standard that promotes the greatest good for the greatest number—rather than on Divine Law. So they invented a rational system for defining right behavior according to whether, or how well, actions promoted the common good ... British Whigs used this idea to vitalize their social reform movement during the 19th century. As they were improving society on this line, Marx unveiled a theory that effectively inverted their analysis.

"How did he do that?" Claire asked skeptically, taking another calming sip of brandy.

"Marx had a different view the common good," Prout answered. "Hume, Bentham, and Mill treated it as an end that could be approached by improving the performance of society's institutions. Marx treated it as a standard for judging the structure of society. In Marx's view, individuals did not share equally in the common good because society's institutions were flawed. Because they were inherently flawed, they needed to be replaced. Social "reformers" earlier in this century began using this Marxian social logic to launch *people's* revolutions. During these revolutions, imperfect societies have been destroyed, but instead of equalizing the distribution of well-being, they have produced an overclass of corrupt, self-serving bureaucrats."

Martin Ogden passed again through Claire's mind.

"Here's the point," Prout said. "Whatever philosophers—or social justice warriors—may claim, societies can only exist if their members pursue shared interests. They don't when ideological hierarchs intentionally divide them."

"You plan to use Wittgenstein's poker to make this plain to ordinary people!"

"That's the general idea," Prout nodded.

"Well thank you," Claire said, sinking back into her private misery. "Your ideas are very . . . interesting . . ."

"Why don't you bring Professor Wanamaker to the reception this evening at the Colonnade Club," Henry suggested. "Mr. Paige will be there, and I am sure he will want to meet her."

"I'll see what she's doing," Prout replied. "She might enjoy it . . ."

"I'll see you back at the cottage," Henry said Claire, stepping to the bar and retrieving his book." On his way out, he called to the bartender. "Bill the brandy to Ogden's room . . . "

———————————

Bart Paige pulled up to the gate behind his breeding barn. "Get it, will you Baby."

"Are you sure we can get up there this way," she asked, staring skeptically into the tangled path.

"Yep," Paige assured her. "I been up this way a bunch o' times."

Suzie hopped out and pulled the gate back.

"Latch it," Paige said as he passed by. "We don't want Daddy's precious guests gettin' lost on Hanson Mountain."

When she was seated again, Paige set off into the woods.

"You think we'll find it?" Suzie asked, as they mowed through the underbrush.

"Maybe," he said. "He leveled 'is studio an' broke some windows in tha greenhouse, but tha rest o' tha place is Ok. If he lef' anythin' lyin' 'round— ya know, like an address on a letter—then it's prob'ly still thar."

"O-o-o-h! I hope we get lucky and find it," Suzie fizzed. "You know where I'm going to look first?"

"Whar?"

"By the telephone. He had one, didn't he?"

"Tha frieze on na mantle's tha center o' ever'thin'," Paige announced suddenly.

"What's that honey?"

"Ried used ta say that while 'e wuz figgerin' out tha secret o' tha universe."

"The frieze on the mantle... " Suzie repeated blankly. "Whose mantle?"

"Jefferson's."

"Maybe that means he sent the journal to Monticello,... " Suzie observed hopefully.

"Yea! I s'pose it could," Paige said, considering the idea for the first time.

"All we have to do now is figure out which mantle it's on!" Suzie exclaimed. "How many are there?

Paige was traveling on a different path. "Ried showed me all them letters. Course I couldn't unnerstand a word in any o' 'em. But 'cordin' to him, they proved that tha secret o' tha universe wuz in tha frieze on na mantle—it had somethin' ta do with fulfillin' prophesies 'bout tha Anny-Christ... "

"Is that what you were talking about earlier, honey?" Suzie asked, unwrapping a new stick of gum.

"Yea."

"And it has to do with the frieze on the mantle," she repeated, struggling to see how that might be.

"Yea."

"He must have been a genius to figure that out reading German," she said, popping her gum.

"Jefferson started writin' tha Baron sometime after 'e got ta France," Paige remembered. "He picked up whar 'e lef' off talkin' 'bout what 'e should do with 'is house. They'd already been through that shit a hunnerd times when tha Baron wuz livin' nex' door to him. But Jefferson hadn't done nothin' with it since tha Baron moved out, an' 'e'd been down ta tha south o' France whar 'e seen this place called Maison Carree. So 'e wrote tha Baron 'bout makin' 'is place look thataway."

"You want to know what I think," Suzie announced. "He was a fag."

"That's jus' tha way rich guys did back then," Paige explained. "Anyhow, by tha time 'e got back ta Paris 'e wuz used ta sittin' 'round lookin' at buildin's. Then 'e come 'cross tha manshin they wuz puttin' up on na lef' bank o' tha Seine—tha Hotel De Sam, er sompin like that. Jefferson liked it 'cause it wuz two stories high, but tha way they done it, it looked like et wuz only one. Then 'e found this shrine whar tha vestal virgins kep' tha sacred fahr fer tha hearth an' got tha ahdea ta put a dome onna top of 'is house.

"The Baron was tard o' hearin' 'bout this shit so 'e sent Jefferson a book with engravings by a guy named Desgodetz an' tole 'im ta pick sompin an' get on with 'is life. Tha one tha Baron liked wuz tha Temple o' Jupiter tha Thunderer—it wuz really tha Temple o' Vespasian who wuz tha Baron's favorite gener'l. Turned out that it wuz in tha Corinthian form same as tha Maison Carree. Soon ez Jefferson heard that, 'e started back in 'bout how 'e'd always wanted Corinthian moldin' in nis parlor. That done it fer tha Baron. He tole 'im ta stow tha shit 'bout tha house 'cause 'e wanted ta know 'bout what wuz goin' on with tha King o' France. Turns out that Frederick tha Great had put 'im on 'is General Staff an' tole him ta git tha army ready fer war. Since Jefferson was a diplomat, 'e know'd ever'thing that wuz goin' on. So 'e got started tellin' tha Baron 'bout how tha French King wuz broke an' ever'body wuz itchin' ta get rid ov 'im. An' 'e said how 'e knew a bunch o' radicals who wuz workin' up a plan ta git tha job done an' that 'im an' Lafayette was writin' a declaration o' rights ta put in soon's they got tha new regime runnin'.

"Tha Baron tole Jefferson that if tha Krauts started fightin' tha Frogs, it'd be tough 'cause the Frogs'd have a million men. That's when tha Baron tole Jefferson 'bout tha experiment he wuz doin.'"

"What was that, Honey?" Suzie asked, touching up her nails with a file from her purse.

"He'd been readin' 'bout tha power tha Indians in Peru got suckin' on leaves that growed up in thar hills an' he wanted ta see if they'd have tha same effect on Germans. He tole Jefferson that he'd been tryin' ta grow tha stuff in nis garden, but that tha climate 'er somethin' wudn't right in Germany an' that he wudn't gettin' nowhar. Jefferson heard that an' got all stirred up 'cause 'e figgered 'e could grow it on nis mountain since the weather up thar wuz 'bout tha same ez Peru. He figgered that if tha Germans wanted it an' couldn't grow it umselves, he could sell it to um fer a lot more 'n 'e wuz gettin' fer 'is tobacca."

"He was thinking smart—just like you," Suzie said, patting his knee. "Honey," she continued, staring apprehensively at the cab-high curtain of weeds Paige was plowing through, "are you sure we're going in the right way?"

"Thar's jes' one way," Paige answered, settling back with his arm hung slung sausage out the window. "And it's tha way ahm goin'. Anyhow, Jefferson tole tha Baron ta send 'im some seeds an' 'e'd see what 'e could do back at tha home place. Tha Baron went an' sent 'im a pack ov seeds an' Jefferson got um jes' ez 'e's walkin' out tha door ta catch 'is boat back state-side—he wuz in a hurry to git outta thar 'cause tha mob'd already blowed up tha Bastille an' now it wuz settin' up ta chop tha King's head off an' Jefferson didn't want ta be 'round with that kina shit goin' on."

"That's because he was a wimp," Suzie observed. "Did he ever get the seeds to grow?"

"Yea. When 'e got back home, he planted 'em in nis greenhouse an' tha stuff come right up. Soon's it got up ta size, Jefferson started foolin' with tha leaves tha way tha Baron tole 'im tha Incas did. Next thing ya know, 'e's writin' tha Baron all this weird shit..."

"I bet he was stoned," Suzie announced.

"He wuz high on 'is mountain!" Paige confirmed with a laugh. "It got 'im in this mood whar, ya know..."

"Yea!" Suzie interrupted. "He was seeing things like Timothy Leary..."

"That's it," Paige snorted. "Thangs wuz shootin' off in 'is belfry like Roman candles on tha 4th o' July. Like fer example, 'e started rememberin' this stuff he'd got from a guy named Richard Price when 'e wuz still in France. Jefferson had got friendly with this Price guy—who wuz a parson somewhars in England—'cause even though 'e wuz a Brit, 'e wrote 'bout how great tha American Revolution wuz. He'd sent Jefferson 'is book 'bout what tha New Testament meant. Jefferson hadn't taken to it back then 'cause 'e wuz inta somethin' called *natur'l religion*..."

"You mean, like, if it feels good do it?" Suzie asked.

"Yea. That's what 'e wuz doin'. But onct 'e got ta suckin' on them leaves, 'e remembered that Price said somethin' 'bout how people could be taught ta do things tha right way instead o' tha way they did umselves. That started Jefferson thinkin' that if 'e got ever'body trippin', then mebbe 'e could get 'em doin' nis natur'l religion."

"Everybody starts thinking that way when they do dope," Suzie observed sourly as she studied her nails. "That's why I stick with the Schenley's—there's no religion in it."

"Tha Baron was like that too," Paige said. "Bein' a German an' all, 'e wudn't buyin' into no flower power natur'l religion bullshit. He tole Jefferson that 'e wuz a follower of Vespasian an' 'e know'd what ta do 'cause it wuz all laid out in Vespasian's frieze. Thar wuz tha part 'bout ritual sacrifice which 'e said wuz tha way tha German's started out b'fore Vespasian civilized um. An' thar wuz tha part 'bout cleanin' up tha mess Nero made in Rome an' thangs like that. An' tha rest of it wuz about tha big picture whar tha Good Lord fulfilled tha prophecy Daniel made 'bout tha temple bein' destroyed ta punish tha Jews. Then 'e wants ta know what Jefferson has ta say 'bout that. Jefferson tole 'im 'e dint pay no 'tention ta what's in na Bible 'cause in his religion ever'thing gets took care of natur'lly. B'sides, 'e says, thar ain't no big picture 'cause ever'thing bein' natural, stuff jes' comes an' goes. Tha Baron didn't have no time ta git inta that shit 'cause Frederick had gone an' died an' tha revolution wuz heatin' up an' it looked like tha Frogs wuz gettin' ready ta invade Germany. All 'e wanted ta know wuz when 'e wuz gonna git 'is shipment o' leaves so tha German army'd be ready to whup tha sans culettes who wuz fillin' up tha army in France."

"What's a sands coollot?" Suzie asked, popping her gum.

"They wuz tha poor, filthy, starvin' scum that wanted ta kill tha King an' ever'body else who wuz better'n 'em."

"Yuck!" Suzie said, shaking her hand as if she were trying to get rid of something icky.

"That's tha way tha Baron seen it," Paige said. "He wudn't gonna put up with that kina shit bein' a Baron. So 'e teed off, tellin' Jefferson 'bout how 'e was gonna crush tha rabble an' restore thangs tha way Vespasian done in tha Year o' tha Four Ceasars. That's when 'e said that 'e put tha symbols from 'is frieze on tha cover of 'is journal 'cause Vespasian wuz tha greatest military genius since Frederick tha Great."

"And that's why Ried thought it was special!"

"Yea. That's whar 'e got tha ahdea ta make them medals'—he figgered that since tha secret o' tha universe wuz hid somewhar in that skull, it wuz tha right kind o' symbol fer tha secret society Hardin an' 'im wuz cookin' up. An' b'sides, tha Bible said tha temple wuz gonna be destroyed. An' it wuz!"

"There's stuff we don't understand," Suzie nodded solemnly.

"Anyhow, Jefferson had all these weird religious noshons floatin' 'round upstairs an' one day while 'e wuz out in na greenhouse pickin' a fresh batch o' leaves 'e hears this voice comin' outta nowhar."

"Oh Shit!" Suzie wailed, covering her eyes. "Was it you know who?"

"Naa." Paige shrugged. "He didn't hear shit like 'at. It wuz jes' his own natur'l sef tellin' 'im ta run fer President o' tha United States so he ken git ever'body doin' his natur'l religion. This thang drops down on 'im so sudden that it blows 'im clean away."

"Was it like a revelation or something?"

"Yea—it wuz jes' like that . . . when 'e finally gits himsef back t'gether, he gits 'is friend Aaron Burr ta come down fer a visit an' Burr agrees ta run 'is campaign in New York whar Jefferson ain't got no connections."

"I thought you said that he was the Anti-Christ," Suzie said, challenging him.

"That wuz later. B'fore that, he wuz OK 'cause 'e got enough votes fer Jefferson ta win tha election in New York. Anyhow, onct they got tha ball rollin', all these freaks started comin' out the woodwork 'cause zey liked tha ahdea o' gettin' ever'body back ta bein' natur'l. That's when this guy Benjamin Rush shows up. Rush wuz one o' them Philadelphia radicals who got started durin' tha revolution. Now 'e wuz a member o' tha American Phil'sophical Association—a bunch o' Jefferson's pointy headed pals from tha old days wuz in that an' ney finally made 'im president 'cause zey liked havin' 'is name on tha stationery. But that wuz somethin' else. Tha point is that back in them days, it wuz OK fer pointy heads ta believe in God like Rush did. He wuz allez tryin' ta convert fokes to his religion. O' course, ez soon ez 'e hears that Jefferson wants ta be President, 'e starts pokin' 'round ta find out 'bout what kind o' religion 'e's got.

"Jefferson don't want no part o' that 'cause 'e don't want Rush blabbin' ta tha voters 'bout what 'e's up to b'fore tha election since 'e knows ain't none of 'em wanna president who's workin' on some strange new scheme.

335

So 'e's bobbin' an' weavin' like Mohammad Ali an' Rush cain't getta glove on 'im fer two years while tha campaign's goin' on.

"Finally, Jefferson gits 'lected president an' 'e's suckin' on a moufful o' leaves an' spinnin' round in nis char in na oval office when this ahdea pops inta 'is head 'bout how tha pagan ritual sacrifice tha Baron wuz talkin' 'bout wuz tha same thin' ez tha sin-redemption thin' Rush wuz allez carpin' on, an' that both o' 'em wuz in tha frieze. That's when 'e finally seen tha big picture."

"What was in it, Honey?" Suzie asks, blowing a bubble at Paige.

"It's like ... all tha shit people 're doin' is really tha same shit," Paige explained. "Ya know, like we're all in it t'gether ... "

Suzie stopped chewing her gum and reflected for a moment. "Does that make sense?"

"I cain't see it," Paige admitted. "Anyhow, that's when ol' Tom figgered out that tha frieze wuz really 'bout what's gonna happen at tha end time."

"What's gonna happen then?" Suzie asked, watching the weeds go by.

"Tha way Jefferson figgered it, ever'body wuz gonna git together an' be happy."

"That's nice ... "

"Yea, but whall 'e wuz cookin' up this picture down nar in tha basement o' tha White House, tha French got this new gener'l named Napoleon an' 'e's kickin' tha Germans' butts an' tha Baron's hollerin' fer Jefferson ta send 'im 'is leaves. Jefferson went on down ta Monticello an' packed a chest up an' shipped it off ta Germany. But by tha time it gets thar, tha leaves 're stale er sompin so none o' tha Germans get high, an' na French continue whippin' 'em. That done it fer tha leaf deal."

"Aww ... "

"Jefferson ain't got time ta worry 'bout that 'cause 'e's got 'imsef on nis secret mission ta get ever'body together. Prob'em is, thar ain't no way fer 'im ta do it 'cause all tha newspapers 're full o' stories 'bout how 'e's been screwin' a slave chick who's livin' with 'im at Monticello. O' course this's got ever'body riled up 'cause it's agains' thur religion. Finally, one day 'e gits some books by another guy in Philadelphia named Joseph Priestly who's Rush's buddy. Priestly's another one o' them pointy headed sorts in tha American Phil'sophical Association. Jefferson s'posed 'e's tha smartes' guy 'round 'cause 'e discovered oxygen. Anyhow, 'e wrote these books 'bout how Jesus Christ ain't really God. Jefferson thought that all 'long 'cause 'e wuz inta that natur'l religion shit, but Priestly's a guy with a lotta clout 'cause 'e discovered oxygen an' 'e ain't got Jefferson's slave problem. Jefferson figgers he'll git Priestly ta tell ever'body how they ken git t'gether an' have utopia like at tha end times in na Bible if they'll just quit worryin' 'bout God an' take up suckin' on 'is leaves instead. With that, 'e starts cutting up a par o' Bibles an' patching 'em t'gether ta show how fokes ken b'have like Price said without havin' God sendin' 'em ta hell.

"When 'e's finally done, 'e sends tha Baron this letter 'bout how 'e's got tha big picture in focus an' how if men git with 'is natur'l religion they won't need no God, ner good shepherd, ner none o' that shit 'cause they'll have somebody that ever'body ken hate. An' 'e tells tha Baron that Aaron Burr's tha right guy fer tha job."

"Now I see," Suzie exclaimed. "He was like Richard Nixon."

"Yea. It's kind o' like that," Paige agreed. "Fer a while 'e thought John Adams wuz gonna be tha guy 'cause Adams wuz wreckin' na country with tha Alien Seditions Act. Then, when Hamilton come out as tha head o' tha Monarchist party, he thought it might oughta be him. An' thar wuz a bunch o' others, but 'e finally settled on Burr 'cause tha House of Representatives almos' made 'im President an' that would o' screwed up Jefferson's plan ta fulfill tha prophecy 'bout tha end times. That pissed him off so bad that 'e made Burr tha Annny-Christ. That's when Jefferson tole tha Baron that 'e'd put tha Vespasian frieze on nis parlor mantle 'cause it helped 'im d'feat tha great Satan an' tha rest of them devils. An' since tha whole bidness wuz 'bout gettin' t'gether an' bein' happy, 'e wuz gonna sell people all tha leaves they'd buy so they could be natur'l like him . . . and he could finely be rich!"

"And that's why the frieze on the mantle is the center of everything," Suzie said admiringly. "You know," she cooed, snuggling up against him. "You remind me a lot of Thomas Jefferson—except you're not a wimpy fag." She sat there contentedly for a moment when a troubling thought dawned on her. "Honey, tell me again—if Madam Marja took Ried's money, and your Daddy's bull's gone, how are we going to get rich?"

"When ah have them seeds, ahl run tha bidness tha same way Ried done."

"YEAAAAAA . . . . . ." Suzie cheered, waving her hands in a wild celebration. "That's your best idea ever!" She leaned over and gave him a big kiss on the cheek. As she was settled back in her seat, something else occurred to her. "Does Madam Marja have them too?"

"Naa," Paige answered casually. "Thar in 'is green house." Just then the pick-up emerged from the wooded trail into the lower corner of a sloping meadow. At the top of the meadow was a low stone retainer wall. Above the wall they could see the dilapidated buildings in Rieds' compound. It was dominated by a 1950's-era white cinder block split level that looked like it had crashed into the hillside at a high rate of speed. Along its lower level, spilling carelessly onto the patio, was a greenhouse with several panes of glass missing. Across the patio, enclosing the compound, was the shell of Ried's studio. "Here we are," Paige said, pulling to stop beside the retainer wall. "Let's see what we got . . ."

"I'm turning into just another stupid female," Marjean groused. "It must be something in the air down here. When I got here, I was fine. I didn't have any conflicts. I was fierce and focused . . . But now, I feel . . . I feel like doing things for me. You know what I mean?"

Gerta was too busy clutching the steering wheel of her silver Mercedes to hear what Marjean was saying.

"It's hard serving two masters—I mean mistresses," Marjean corrected herself. "I'm not sure how much longer I can keep sacrificing my personal life for this idiotic movement. Don't get me wrong," she added. "I feel good about what we've accomplished. All we need to do is to take a couple more bold steps, then everything will be set."

"Ah-huh," Gerta grunted, as though she agreed.

Aster, who was sitting in the back seat, said nothing.

"This is what we're going to do," Marjean continued. "You're going to leave Tim a message that Claire wants to meet him at Tilghman's cottage—he's so vain he'll think it's true. When he gets there, we'll finish him off with the shotgun Tilghman keeps in his library. We'll toss the gun under the house so it looks like Tilghman panicked after shooting him. You'll come forward as the heartbroken sweetheart and sob your way through how Tilghman beat Tim up when he came onto Claire in your hotel room. That will establish Tilghman as predator with violent and jealous tendencies. Then I'll tell about what Aster and I found at the lake after

Roberta was murdered . . . That should be enough to hang Tilghman," she concluded. "When can we get it done?" She suddenly wondered. "Tomorrow's Sunday . . . Tilghman's likely to be home. We'll shoot for Monday," she announced. "He won't be around Monday."

"Are you sure this is safe?" Gerta asked, as though the weed-choked fire trail she was following might suddenly yawn open and swallow them up.

"What do you mean?" Marjean snapped, glancing at her companion for the first time since they had started up Wolfpit Mountain. Gerta's face was filled with the kind of anxiety city people feel when they encounter things in the wild.

Marjean stared at her companion for a long pitiless moment. "Pull over there," she said at last, pointing to a wide spot up ahead of them. Gerta peered at the sloping shoulder as though it were the edge of the Grand Canyon. "Just park the goddam car!" Marjean ordered impatiently.

Gerta did as she was told. "I'm not used to driving on unpaved roads," she explained with a relieved sigh. The explanation came too late. Marjean had already climbed out and was scanning the woods in front of the car. Aster was standing ghostly-like beside her.

"There it is," Aster said, pointing to a worn line that receded inconspicuously into the woods

"That's it," Marjean confirmed. Her bearings established, she marched forward. Aster followed close behind. A moment later they were out of sight. Gerta locked the car and stumbled through a tangle of branches and cobwebs, desperate not to be left behind.

"I'm going nuts," Marjean announced as she advanced down the narrow trail. "There must be something in Charlottesville that f__ks people up!" She grumbled. "Everybody here goes nuts—it's just a matter of time. The father's paranoid and has an army of drones spying on me. The brother's psychotic and wants to kill me. Ried's a schizoid who thinks he's still in Vietnam. Her boyfriend's got everybody hating him in less than a week. And the bimbo from *The Post*! She's a looney from the Mad Hatter's tea party. I gave her the story about how Tilghman murdered Roberta—God knows what she did with it. Aster here's a certified basket case—doesn't have a dime to her name . . . " That clearly bothered her. "If I weren't showing her how to cope with the macrocosm, they'd have to put her away . . .

"And don't get me started about Thomas Jefferson!" she swore. "That racist, sexist bigot . . . Did you know that he wrote a plan to revise the laws of Virginia?" Silence . . . "Well he did—right after he wrote the Declaration of Independence. One of the things he said in his plan—which he never did—was that slaves should be free! Wasn't that nice of him? He wanted to send them back to Africa! Swell huh? And why did he want to do that? Because his pals had 'deep-rooted prejudices' against their slaves and because the slaves would never forgive their masters for owning them . . . Jefferson said this would produce 'convulsions' that would end in the extermination of one race by the other. I suppose he was right about that," she observed, after considering the idea. "He wrote a book called *Notes on the State of Virginia*," she continued. "In it, he said—Shoate' would love this—'the improvement of blacks in body and mind, in the first instance of their mixture with whites, has been observed by everyone, and proves that their inferiority is not the effect merely of their condition of life.' Does that sound like a guy who thinks that *all men are created equal*?" She sneered. "He owned his wife's half-sister—just like Shoate' said. I guess it was Ok back then to rape your sister-in-law—at least if she was black and you were massa and needed to get your rocks off. God! He makes me want to puke. You know what we should do before we leave this pest hole—level that place up there on his mountaintop. That would be a fitting tribute to that self-serving blowhard."

She looked back at Gerta who was panting along a few paces behind her. "As soon as we've taken care of Tim, we're going back to New York. Everything'll be fine up there," she said confidently. "They're too busy keeping the peace to care about what we were doing three years ago. I'm taking over Ried's business," she added. "It's perfect for me. I know who his customers are. And we'll be in a good location," she said, referring to Gerta's loft. "Everybody loves Ried's dope—especially his Albemarle Green hash! All you need to do is give me the seed money so I can buy Ried's crop.

"If he gives me any trouble," she continued, "I'll just remind him that I found a little device that the FBI would love to see—you mean he was making bombs in his studio!" she exclaimed with rhetorical surprise. "Anyway, it's not safe down here with her crazy brother stalking me. He's such a pig!" she added contemptuously. "No wonder he's broke." She walked on a few paces in silence. "Say! Something just occurred to me." She turned again towards Gerta. "Ried must have gotten more than one letter from

Douglas. Don't you think?" She didn't wait for Gerta to answer. "I bet he's got them stashed somewhere in his house. If I had those letters," she calculated, "I'd have them both by the balls. Then I could keep the bomb. You never know when something like that might come in handy!"

"I've been wondering about this Roberta woman you keep talking about," Gerta finally managed to ask. "Who was she anyway?"

"You know," Marjean said, responding to a different question. "If I can't get Claire to put that story out, I should give it to somebody else! Why don't you mention to Tim that you've heard Paige is colluding with Henry Tilghman to suppress information about the murder of Paige's mistress. That'll get the wheels turning. I'll bet Tim's on the phone to Ogden before you can say 'I cannot tell a lie.' Marjean laughed with satisfaction. "There's more than one way to skin a cat . . . What were you saying?"

"I was wondering who this Roberta person is . . ." Gerta said.

"She was just one of Paige's flunkies," Marjean answered. "I had her pegged right from the start—Paige sent her down to get the goods on me. The next thing you know, she was up there doodling with Ried and he was blabbing all about what we'd been doing in New York. That synched it. I brought her in like she was a big deal, and we liked her and everything. Then we got rid of her . . . Actually, it was kind of neat. I designed an ideogram that showed . . . " She stopped suddenly. "I never did find out what happened to Ried. He was supposed to be the Prince of Darkness at our initiation. Men are such idiots," she growled, resuming her march. "The fact that Paige has kept his mouth shut shows that I was right about her," she repeated. "He's going to do whatever it takes to protect his little cupcake," she laughed, plucking Aster's cheek. "That means he'll go along with the lynching party when it gets around to hanging Tilghman. It's all written in the stars," she added, dismissing the matter.

Marjean marched on with new energy. "And I'm getting pretty tired of this thing with Rank," she repeated after another half dozen paces. "I think we should dump her once we're rid of Tonto." She considered the idea again. "I mean, what can she do for us? Tim's cultural revolution is going to stall out once we get him out of the way—Douglas sure isn't going to draw flower children to Washington! So we don't need her to wreck that train. And Daddy's plan to rejuvenate his paleo-phallic system is going to self-destruct as soon as Roberta's story hits the front page of *The Post*, which is going to

341

happen the next time Goldilocks gets Mr. Kiss-My-Ass-I'm-The-Boss between the sheets. It's like I said, everything's lining up.

"Rank's irrelevant—just like her side-kick from safari country . . . All we need to do is keep the sisters talking—how hard is that?" She called back over her shoulder. "The more they talk, the sooner this f__ked up system will collapse. That cultural castration stuff Rank was talking about is going to happen whoever becomes the czarina of Femistan. It's the nature of the thing—women hate men. If it weren't for sex, they'd never stop fighting. It'd be like cats and dogs. The good news is that cats are smarter and meaner than dogs. That's why we're gonna win. Have you noticed how fast public discourse is filling up with psychobabble? Like I said, it's inevitable!

"I've got the hook into Rank with that shit about the woman clothed in the raiment of the sun," Marjean gloated. "I found it in the Book of Revelation the other night—it's kinda catchy, don't you think? It creates all kinds of possibilities, you know . . . *who has Gaia called to rule over women people?*" She sang in an off chord. "We're going to have to find some good-looking chick and get her pregnant—Ried would like that . . . ." She paused. "I'm going to have to think some more about that . . . it's not like I have to have an answer tomorrow. The way the stars work, things come out a little at a time. So I can wait and see what happens. If somebody comes along, Woman Spirit can come out with a prophecy. In the meantime, I think Woman Spirit will just keep her mouth shut and make like she's guarding the secrets of the womb! That's the best way to stay out of trouble . . . " She laughed with self-satisfaction. "You know what the secret really is? *Tertium Datur!* Ried explained it to me while we were putting together the Prince of Darkness stunt. I hate to say it, but that's why it works so well for women people," she admitted. "They never think about anything except how they feel. You know that, right? That's the one thing men can't handle. So we're going to eradicate rational discourse—because it's sexist! And then we'll make them listen to how women feel about things . . . all . . . day . . . long! You know like at the club, and in the gym, and on TV. We'll have women sports casters in their locker rooms. God!" She cackled. "That would even drive me nuts!" She punched her fist into the air. "TERTIUM DATUR!"

She walked on a few paces more, then signaled for the column to stop.

"Here we are," she said in a hoarse whisper, peering through a curtain of leaves. Ried's rundown split level was below them halfway down a grassy slope. There was a rutted turnaround in front of it. "It looks like he's here," she said, pointing at the rusty green Jaguar parked near the front door. Marjean skipped down the slope and glided around the car. When she reached the door, she turned to confirm that no one else was coming own his crater-filled drive. Satisfied, she tried the knob. "It's unlocked," she whispered again. She pushed it open just enough to pass through. Aster followed her in. A second later Gerta joined them on the flagstone landing. To the right was a five-step flight that led to the upper floor. To the left were stairs that led down to the greenhouse.

"Fred," Marjean called out cautiously. There was no answer. She sniffed the air. "No fumes either," she said, starting down the stairs. "If he isn't passed out in the greenhouse, he's probably working in his studio. Sometimes he makes medals," she explained. "Sometimes he makes bombs. It depends on what kind of dope he's doing." At the bottom of the stairs, she called his name again. "He gets a little funky if you surprise him," she said. "Most of the time he thinks he's in Vietnam." It was easy to see why. The greenhouse was a jungle of overgrown plants. "Look at this place," Marjean said, shaking her head in disgust. "He must have gone on another one of his shooting binges." She tiptoed across a shattered pane of glass to a leafy grove in the center the greenhouse. "This is his famous Albemarle Green marijuana," she said, pulling off a leaf. "This is his seed stock. He'd kill you if he caught you taking any . . ."

She started for the door on the far side of Ried's marijuana patch but drew back in alarm. "It's Paige," she hissed, clapping her hand over Aster's mouth. "Quick . . . upstairs!" Marjean led Aster back up the stairs. Gerta scrambled after them. Marjean paused on the landing. Gerta raced past her and started out the door. "No," she said, grabbing her from behind. "We need to hear what they're talking about." With that, she turned and raced up the second flight of stairs. It led to a large, cluttered space with a wall of glass windows that faced in the direction of Belmont Farm. The view was spectacular! A telescope on a tripod was stationed in front of the middle window. Marjean glanced left toward the kitchen. To her right was a hall, which led to another pair of rooms. The one in the front was Ried's library. Marjean turned to the other. It was Ried's bedroom. She hurried her companions into it. "Gerta," she said, pointing to the rumpled bed, "you get under there. Aster and I will be in the closet." They concealed themselves as the greenhouse door opened.

There was a moment of breathless silence. Then Gerta whispered emphatically. "Marjean, I've found the letters!"

"Holy Moly!" Suzie exclaimed when she saw the marijuana trees. "Is that what I think it is?"

"Yea," Paige said. "It's 'is seed stock. He cross-breeds 'is plants with stuff that ta makes 'em more potent—er sompin." Paige was pointing to a row of bushes behind the marijuana patch. "It's another one o' them thangs 'e learned in Nam. Ah never touch tha stuff mahsef, but fokes tell me its strong . . . like it's laced with acid."

"Well keep it away from me," Suzie said, stepping behind him. "Where are the seeds?" She continued, looking around.

"This is them," Paige said, staring at the green tangle. "We gotta pick 'em . . ."

"O . . . M . . . G!" Suzie wailed. "That'll take months."

"We'll cut 'em down an' take 'em back ta tha barn. We ken work on 'em thar. Help me git 'em bundled up so we'll haul 'em out ta tha truck."

"Well . . . Ok," Suzie agreed reluctantly. "But first I'm going to see if I can find that address." She looked around. "Where's the phone?"

"Thar's one over on tha counter," he answered, starting to harvest the plants with a pair of shears he'd found leaning against the wall. "Thar's another one upstairs in na kitchen."

Suzie tiptoed across the glass-strewn floor and went over to the counter. "I found it," she said. "And here's a pad!" she exclaimed, her voice filling with excitement. "Oh drat! There's nothing on it. Wait a minute . . ," She began shading the top sheet with a pencil she picked up from the counter. "I saw the Man from Uncle do this once on TV . . ." Look! There's something here . . . It says . . . deer blood . . . chicken wire . . . stakes . . . Aww . . . " She groaned, her spirits plunging. "I'm going to check the phone upstairs," she announced in a burst of optimism. With that, she turned and disappeared through the door into the stairwell. "Honey, the front door's open!" She called out in alarm.

"That don't mean nuffin," Paige yelled back. "Ried allez lef' it open.

Shut it an' lock it," he instructed. "We don't need nobody droppin' in whal we're workin'."

Suzie did as he said, then mounted the second flight of stairs. "Holy Moly! What a view!" She exclaimed, looking across the cluttered room toward the wall of glass. "And he's got a telescope!" She went over to it and placed her eye on the observer's lens. "Honey," she yelled, "you better come look at this!"

"Ahm busy," he shouted back at her.

"Seriously," she yelled again. "Come up here and look at this."

"Oh fer Chrise sake," he swore, stomping up the stairs. A moment later he appeared in the living. "This better be good . . . "

"Look in there," Suzie said, pointing at the telescope.

Paige crossed the room and squinted into the eyepiece. "Holy shit!" he roared. "Looks like ya hit tha bulls eye, Baby Doll!" He checked it again to be sure. "Them's tha biggest marijuana plants ah ever seen!" He stood up and looked out the window in the direction the telescope was pointing. "It's over thar b'hind Jefferson's Pond—by that ol' greenhouse." He looked admiringly at Suzie. "That's beautiful Baby! Ya found us a grubstake!"

"Yippee!" She trilled as Paige trotted back down to his work in the greenhouse. "We're going to be RICH! . . . Now where's that phone?" She wandered down the hall into the bedroom. "What a mess. No human being could live five minutes in here," she murmured. "He's even worse than you, Honey," she called out.

"Hurry up," Paige called back. "Ah wanna git this shit loaded an' git out o' here."

"That's right," Suzie muttered to herself. "He said it was in the kitchen. She turned around and started off in the other direction. "I see it," she called, scurrying through the living room and into the kitchen. ". . . but there's no pad!" She moaned, looking around beside the phone. She about to leave when she noticed the bulletin board beside the refrigerator. "Honey!" She screamed, tearing out of the kitchen and down the stairs. "Look what I found!" In her hand was a piece of paper. Written on it were the words: Thomas Jefferson. Monticello. Charlottesville, VA 22902.

"What the hell are they doing?" Marjean cursed, peering cautiously through the crack closet door.

"I think he cut down those marijuana plants," Gerta whispered.

"That's impossible," Marjean said, creeping out of the closet with a box of shotgun shells in her hand. "Ried would kill him," she said, slapping the cartridges angrily. She inched over to the window and peered out. "Oh my God!" She gasped. "What happened to the studio?" She stared for a moment in disbelief. "He blew himself up!" she gasped. "That stupid ass . . . " Her body suddenly stiffened. "And they're taking his seeds! OH MY GOD!" Gerta joined her at the window in time to see two huge bundles of marijuana bobbing toward a black pick-up truck parked beside the retainer wall. "I'll kill him myself," she howled, rushing back into the closest to find Ried's shotgun. As she did, the engine started, and the pickup rolled off down the hill. "Oh! JESUS CHRIST!" Marjean screamed, stumbling out of the closet with Ried's shotgun in her hand. Aster followed her to the window and stared out at the wreckage of Ried's studio. Just then, Marjean whirled around and slammed into her. "You idiot!" She roared, shoving her out of the way. "Why didn't you tell me he was dead!" She threw the weapon down and stormed down the stairs to the front door.

"Marjean!" Gerta called after her. "What should I do with the letters?"

"Bring 'em!" she called back, ". . . and bring the gun and the shells . . . "

The cottage seemed to be empty when Henry returned from his run. He therefore assumed that she had gone for a walk. He went up to his room and shed his clothes, then stepped into the bathroom and turned on the shower.

Through the drum of the streaming water Henry heard the sound of footsteps on the stairs. Then he heard the door latch click. "I'll be through in a minute," he called through the shower curtain. The door latch clicked again. Now he thought he heard a rustling sound somewhere in the room. He stopped to listen. In the next instance Claire pulled the curtain back.

"Would it be too inconvenient if I joined you?" She asked, stepping in next to him.

He found himself staring into her dangerous blue eyes. The spell they cast was mesmerizing. He stood frozen in their thrall as she leaned forward and brushed his lips with hers. As she did, his mooring lines snapped, and his psyche swirled away in a dream-like rapture. All that was left were her entrancing blue eyes. He wrapped his arms around her and drew her to him in the cascading water.

It was too late now. He took her hand and led her into his room. When she had stretched her shimmering body on the bed in front of him, he leaned over and kissed her again. His hand glided silently over her thigh. As he caressed her, her breathing became heavy. "Oh! Henry!" She groaned at last, her body trembling. Gripping him with fierce passion, she swallowed him into her sanctuary. He gazed down at her. As the waves of pleasure radiated through him, the last barrier washed away, and the lovers merged into a single being.

Gently. Then forcefully. She parried his thrusts. Sometimes daring him with flashing eyes. Sometimes, with closed eyes, looking inward and exalting in her labor. Suddenly her eyes opened, and she peered up anxiously at him, fearful that he might leave some part of her longing unfulfilled. A fiery chord sounding deep within him ignited a climactic explosion. She groaned with pleasure and pulled him down to her. Covering his mouth with hers, she held him tightly and caressed him with her tongue.

Then there was stillness, neither partner daring to move lest they break the spell.

At last, they separated.

Henry lay staring into the afternoon light. "Tell me something, will you," he asked, breaking the silence.

"What?" She stretched out her hand and touched him without opening her eyes.

"Am I dreaming?"

She rolled over and planted a silent kiss on his lips.

"What a relief," Henry sighed, taking her into his arms. "I was afraid it was real."

"What are you talking about," Claire giggled, smiling down at him.

Henry gazed up into her smiling face. "We don't even like each other..."

"You don't like me?" She pouted, her face wrinkling into a frown.

"We haven't exactly..." Henry searched for the word, "meshed."

"I think that's changed now," she answered, gazing at him thoughtfully. "What do you think?"

"I think..." Henry paused to think. "I think you're right..."

"Good!" She teased. "You *are* capable of human feelings." She leaned down and kissed him again, then rolled back onto her pillow and closed her eyes. "I liked your poem, Henry," she said in a contented voice. "Would you like to hear mine?"

Henry turned toward her. "Yes," he said, waiting as she composed herself.

"The golden sun beckons me," she began,
Come, I hear him say.
Lie down in the lush green grass
And I will judge your fate . . ." She paused.
Will you lose your way?
Or does love await?"

She paused again.
"Send a boyish lover into my arms.
Let him fill me with forgotten joy
And touch me with his magic wand,
So I may be the new day's dawn."

She waited for him to speak. He remained silent for a long time. "I hear different things in it," he said finally

"Do you?" she said, turning to see his face.

"Am I right to say it's self-referencing?"

"Yes," she said, watching him closely.

"Well, first," he said, glancing over at her. "It's very sensual.

"You think so?"

"Yes, in a poignant way," he continued. "It speaks to an emptiness yearning to be filled."

"Um-hmm . . . "

"When did you write it?" He asked.

"I just made it up," she said, giggling again.

"No!" You didn't," Henry stammered. "It's too good."

She laughed in delight. "You think so?"

They gazed into each other's eyes.

"Yes," Henry said to himself. "Things have changed . . . "

Henry lay quietly for a while savoring the experience. "Claire," he said turning toward her.

"Yes," she answered.

"What are we supposed to do now?"

"Don't you know?" She asked without moving.

"No."

"We're going to..." suddenly she bounced up and landed on him. "...finish our shower."

"The shower!" The water was still drumming in the bathroom. "We've probably run out of hot water," he cursed.

"Good," she cried, jumping out of the bed. "We'll be safer in cold water." She was out the door before Henry's feet hit the floor.

Henry found her standing beneath the spout with the soap in her hand. "Here," she said, handing it him. "Make yourself useful... wash my back." As she turned to face the water, she clasped her hair in a fold on top of her head.

"Hold still," Henry instructed her. "This could be tricky." He started at her neck and carefully soaped his way down her back.

She hummed gayly as he worked.

"What's that tune?" he asked.

"You don't recognize it? Thanks a lot!" She butted him to punish his bad manners. "Haven't you ever heard *Swan Lake*?"

"I was just about to say that."

"You were not, you liar," she huffed.

"Say, did I mention that I loved your poem?"

Claire started a little chugging motion like a mechanical toy rotating on its pedestal. She gave his cheek a peck as she passed by in her circuit. "You're cute."

Henry guided the soap over the curve of her rump. He felt her shiver as he slipped the bar between her legs. "Henry!" she protested. "If you don't behave yourself, we're never going to get out of here."

"I'm just doing my job, lady," he replied, pressing his body against hers.

"Any chance the weird sisters have bugged this room?" Claire wondered, pressing into him.

"I'll check it out as soon as I finish up here," he volunteered. His hands migrated over her slender hips and up to her breasts. The soap clattered on the shower floor as his fingers reached her nipples. She arched her shoulders and took a deep breathe, then laid her head on his shoulder and opened herself to his exploration. His hands swept down over her ribs and joined in an apron across the plain of her stomach. Her body tensed as his fingers spilled over her crown and touched the soft fold of her maidenhead.

"OHHH!" she gasped, pulling away suddenly. Henry felt it too. The hot water had finally given out.

"That was a message from Woman Spirit," Claire declared from her refuge on the far side of the shower curtain.

Henry braced himself long enough to wash off, then closed the spigot and grabbed his towel. The familiar strains of *Swan Lake* met him as he stepped into the hall at the top of the stairwell.

Henry threw his blazer over his shoulder and stepped into the hall at top of the stairway. The door to the bathroom was still closed. He tilted his head and heard her humming. He skipped on down the stairs. In the kitchen he poured two glasses of wine and placed them on a tray. He took the tray with him out onto the porch and set it down on the table. He gazed out over the valley. It was going to be another beautiful evening.

"Henry?" Claire called his name.

"I'm out here."

A moment later she stepped through the door. "I have another job for you," she said smiling.

"Anything like the last one?" he asked.

"Not quite." She held up a gold chain. Stepping forward she placed it in his hand. Then she turned and bowed her head. He laid the necklace on her breast and locked the clasp. "There," he said.

She turned back and poured herself into his eyes. "I'm happy," she announced. "Are you?"

"Yes," he said. Then he stood back and whistled. "You're stunning!"

She twirled around playfully. Henry nodded his approval. She was casually elegant in a white sleeveless blouse and pleated black linen pants. She had a black ribbon in her hair that made it gleam. The low-cut neckline of her blouse highlighted the strands of woven gold that lay brazenly on her bosom. The hem of her blouse hung loose at her waist in a way that accentuated her athletic figure. Her black slippers mounted on two-inch heels. One strap crossed her foot below her arch. Another looped behind her heel. Henry watched her graceful movements and remembered how she moved while they made love.

"Would you like a glass of wine?"

"Yes," she answered, her eyes sparkling.

He lifted the second glass and handed it to her.

"Here's to the evening," she said, raising a toast.

"To the evening," Henry repeated, clinking her glass.

They stood for a moment absorbed in the view. "Claire," Henry said, breaking the silence.

"Yes Henry?" she answered expectantly.

"I need . . . I mean . . . there's something I want to ask you . . . "

She smiled coyly.

He took another sip of wine and cleared his throat. "How is someone like me . . . " he started, turning to face her, "supposed to deal with someone like you?"

She looked into his eyes. "I don't understand," she answered cautiously.

"I mean . . . What are we going to do with each other?"

"I'm a little nervous myself," she confessed. "Is that what you mean?"

"Maybe we're climbing the stairway to heaven," he answered, turning toward the valley. "But what if we just jumped a rail?" He turned back toward her. "Where are we going to land when we come down?"

She watched him without answering.

"Look," he tried to smile, "we live in different worlds. Is there some place where they intersect?"

"I don't know, Henry," she answered with a puzzled laugh. "Life's funny, isn't it? Haven't you ever taken a chance? Haven't you ever dared to do something that changed your life? What are you afraid of?"

He shrugged. "You?"

"Honestly!" She exclaimed. "Men are such wimps. You act like you're so brave, but you're frightened to death—of WOMEN!"

"How come all of a sudden I'm so swell?

Claire stared into her wine. "I promised myself that I wouldn't cry anymore, but you're making it tough." She took an anxious sip. "I tried to say it in my poem. I thought you heard it." She looked up. "People need to be part of something, Henry. You are. You're part of Raymond Paige and

Oscar Denker's mission. You have your work at the Jefferson Academy. Those things define you and give your life meaning . . . don't they?"

"I suppose they do," Henry conceded.

She tried to settle herself, but the edge remained. "I need to be part of something too!" He saw the tears welling up in her eyes.

"You are!" He protested.

"I'm not," she said, taking a quivering breath. "It was all a facade. You thought that all along—didn't you." She looked across the valley. "You know what's so special about you, Henry? I'll tell you—you're real. Simple, huh?" She laughed as her eyes filled with tears. "I bet you would have never guessed."

Henry felt a sudden pang. Did he really want to know this? Wasn't it better just to make love? Did it really matter what she thought so long as they both enjoyed the sex? He swallowed the last of his wine and set his glass down on the tray.

"Do you understand what I'm telling you?" she asked, her voice wavering.

This was it. The moment of truth. She waited as he came up to her. He put his arms around her and pressed her head to his shoulder. "Yes," he said as he stroked her hair. "I understand."

Henry guided his car down the driveway. "There are some things going on here that you don't know about . . ." He glanced at her to emphasize his warning.

"I know about Roberta," she answered. "Is that what you are going to tell me?"

Henry looked startled, then alarmed. He stopped the car and looked at her. "What do you know about Roberta?" He finally managed to ask.

She put her hand on his arm. "You're going to have to trust me, Henry."

He searched her eyes without speaking, then nodded. "I trust you, Claire."

"We're two of a kind," she said, with a hollow laugh. "Two castaways clinging to the wreckage."

"That bad huh . . ." Henry said, glancing over at his companion.

"Maybe worse." She settled back in her seat. "Roberta was murdered," she said, thinking out loud, "and Marjean says you killed her." She reached over and patted his knee. "Don't worry—I know she's lying."

Henry shook his head in admiration. "You're amazing."

"I am amazing!" She agreed. "It's nice to meet a man who realizes it."

"You're amazing," Henry repeated, "but I think I deserve some credit for penetrating your chrome-plate know-it-all Washington exterior."

"You certainly do!" she said, pinching his cheek playfully.

"So you met Marjean . . ." Henry observed.

"And Aster . . . they paid me a visit this morning while you were gone."

"Really!" He wasn't surprised. "And she told you that I killed Roberta . . ."

"Yes. And to prove it she showed me a medallion with her initials on it and a pair of tennis shorts." She eyed him suspiciously. "Where they yours?"

"Could have been," Henry replied dryly. "So she had the medallion . . ." Henry remembered the empty lanyard around Roberta's neck. "Why don't you believe her?"

"Two reasons," Claire explained. "First, she's a schemer."

"What's she up to?"

"I don't know yet."

"What's the other reason?" Henry asked.

Claire deliberated for a moment. "I've seen your diagram . . ."

"God!" He swore helplessly. "Nothing is safe from you . . ."

"You should be glad I'm here," she said, looking over at him. "In case you don't know it, you're in **big** trouble."

"That's what George said," Henry acknowledged.

"George?"

"A friend of mine who's a lawyer in Atlanta—I've retained him to give me counsel."

"What did he say?"

"He said to keep my mouth shut until he looks over the papers I sent him."

"When are you going to talk with him again?"

"Probably in a couple of days." Henry answered. "Now . . . tell me how you happened to find the drawing . . ."

"I wasn't snooping!" She said self-consciously.

"Of course not! It never crossed my mind."

"I was thumbing through that mutilated copy of Schumpeter's book in your library," she explained, "and I spilled my lemonade."

"The drawing wasn't in that book," he noted.

"It was under your desk blotter—along with the remnants of my lemonade. I found it while I was cleaning it up."

Henry stared at her for a long moment. "Huh . . . well . . . I guess that's possible," he shrugged, stepping on the accelerator.

"What are you going to do?" Claire asked, as they sped past the Shadwell historical marker and onto Route 250.

"Maybe it'll blow over," he answered without conviction.

"Roberta's dead. That's not going to blow over. Not as long as Marjean is willing to tell people that you killed her."

"Yea . . I know."

"What happened?"

"Marjean told me they were having a gathering in the barn. I wanted to know what they were doing so I went over. They were doing their usual weird stuff. I drank something Marjean gave and started to float away. That's about the time I realized that Roberta was the centerpiece in this Zodiac circle hanging from the rafters—she must have been drugged too. Anyway, I remember Marjean handing me all these implements and seeing marks appearing on Roberta's body. After that everything went blank. I woke up the next morning in my living room."

"The diagram shows where the different symbols were on Roberta's body—is that right?"

"Yea . . ."

"When did you create the diagram?"

"I found her the next morning . . . She was on the dock at the lake. I didn't know she was dead until I touched her. Her body tipped into the lake . . . I pulled her out and made the drawing."

"What happened to the body?"

"I think I better wait to hear from George before I get into that."

Claire looked worried, but accepted the answer "You know what I think?" She continued.

"What?"

"I think we should decipher the diagram."

"You do?" He sounded surprised.

"Yes," she answered firmly.

"That could take a while," Henry warned.

"I have some time," Claire replied.

"Good," Henry smiled. "When can you start?"

"I've already started . . ."

Henry nodded. "You know about sun signs and birth charts and that sort of stuff?" he asked.

"Of course! That's how people in Washington plan their lives."

"You might just come in handy," Henry conceded.

"You never know . . . "

———————

Henry pulled the ticket from the machine at the far end of Pool Hall Alley and proceeded into the parking lot.

The lot was bordered on the back by the C & O's railroad tracks. Several spots were open along the tracks. Henry parked his Comet in the one next to the black stretch limo. "I used to leave my keys in this car," he announced, recalling the time his car was stolen. "Everybody here is supposed to be honest, so I figured it was Ok. Well actually, it wasn't here," he corrected himself. "It was over at the Architecture School—I used to study in the library there. The chairs were comfortable and the women in the Art History Department were all tomatoes."

"It's my fault," Claire sniffed, setting off across the parking lot. "I should have known you were a skirt chaser—most men are."

"No. It's my fault," Henry objected, trotting up beside her. "I should have known that you were the jealous type and showered at the gym."

"And if I were?"

"I'd stop going to the Architecture School Library . . . ."

"You're cute," she snapped, pinching his cheek again.

Two figures approached them from the other end of the alley. "That's T.P. Wells," Henry whispered. "He's the greatest IM basketball player who ever lived. That's how he got his name. T.P. stands for Two Points. His real name is Walter. I may be the only living soul still Charlottesville who knows that."

"Who's the woman?" Claire wondered, referring to the tomato walking beside him.

"That's Hunt Fisher," Henry answered. "She's Trip's Dudley's landlord—he's Oscar's doctor."

"Hunt?" Claire repeated, questioning the name.

"It's short for Huntley—her mother's family had some connection with George Mason," Henry explained. "Her late father was Washburn Fisher. His grandfather founded the Washburne Military School shortly over in Waynesboro—sometime after 'the recent unpleasantness.' He died last year, and she took over running the farm. I've been over there a few times. It's got a lot of out-of-the-way places that would be good for growing dope. That probably has something to do with T.P. being with her."

"Do you know her?" Claire asked.

"Not really. She and Aster are friends . . ."

"I see," Claire said, studying Wells' features as they came together. He was a few inches over six feet and thin to the point of emaciation. His hair was long and matted and his beard was full. His eyebrows dominated his face. They knitted together over the bridge of his nose in a way that gave him an air of mystery. He was wearing a loose T-shirt, a pair of baggy gym shorts, and high-top Converse All Star sneakers. When he was near enough, Claire read the words printed on his T-shirt: *Get High - Smoke Albemarle Green.*

"T.P.," Henry greeted his friend. "I almost didn't recognize you with the beard!"

"I am Raja Veda now," he answered with a transcendental nod.

"My apologies. How are things?"

"Cool," Raja Veda nodded again.

"And business?" Henry asked

"I heard Roberta Wiley drowned out on Belmont Farm?" He said, ignoring Henry's question. "You live out there, don't you?"

"Who told you that?" He asked, glancing at Fisher.

"People tell me things," he said, shifting his gaze to Claire.

"This is Claire Fox," Henry said, introducing his companion.

"How," he nodded mysteriously. That was all Hunt Fisher had time for. She stepped over to the pool hall door and signaled to Wells. "Gotta go," he said, nodding again to Claire. When he reached the door, he pulled it open. The unsociable heiress disappeared inside. Raja Veda disappeared a second later.

"What does Mr. Raja Vada do?" Claire asks, as they passed through the alley onto the Corner.

"He's a very savvy guy," Henry replied. "When we were undergraduates, he paid his bills playing high-stakes poker. He never went for the big pots, but he never held losing hands. Hustlers liked having him in their games because he kept things going while they fleeced the suckers. I heard about one game where some guy lost his Jag." Henry took Claire's hand and led her across the busy street.

"Those kinds of things died out after the women arrived," Henry replied. "Women don't play poker..."

"Sounds like the University needs more women," Claire observed.

"This is the Medical School," Henry said, gesturing to the collection of buildings on their left. "Oscar is in there," he added as passed by. Henry spoke again after a few quiet steps. "Tell me something..."

"What?"

"What did you meant on the porch when you said it was 'all a facade'?"

Claire looked away. "I can't talk about that now..."

"What happened between you and Ogden?"

Claire bit her lip. She meant to tell him... but not now.

Henry stopped and looked at her. "I have to know."

"Martin didn't like my story," she said at last.

"No?"

"It didn't follow the party line..."

"I see..."

"...I expected to straighten things out during our meeting this afternoon..."

"How were you going to do that?" Henry asked.

"You're going to hate me," she said, her face reflecting her deepening inner turmoil.

"Try me."

"I was going to tell him about..." The word stuck in her throat. "I was going to tell him about Roberta..."

"You were going to tell Martin Ogden about Roberta..." Henry

357

conjured a picture of his diagram. "That would have wrecked us," he said, looking at her in stunned disbelief.

She knew that already.

"What happened then?" Henry asked, looking off.

"...he called me a whore and told me to get out," she said, shortening the story.

"And that's when you came down into the bar..." Henry said, finishing it.

"Yes," she whispered.

"He hit you too, didn't he," Henry added. For a moment, he contemplated the empty feeling that was forming in the pit of his stomach then walked on.

Claire called after him. "Henry...wait! I want to see Oscar."

"We're kind of short on time," Henry snapped.

"I don't care," Claire said.

Henry stepped up to the desk at the far end of the entry hall. "Can I help you," the receptionist asked.

"We'd like to see Oscar Denker," Henry answered.

The receptionist checked her records and looked up. "He's on the fifth floor," she said, pointing to the elevator behind her desk. "Check in with the duty station when you get there...Visiting hours are over at 7:00," she called after them as they walked to the elevator.

Neither spoke as the cab ascended. When the door finally opened, they saw Nurse Davis standing at the duty station. "Well! Look who's back!" she said, as they approached. "And this time you've brought your wife..." She glanced at Claire's left hand and saw that she wasn't wearing a wedding ring. "Oops. I guess not."

"We're just friends," Claire said, glancing tentatively at Henry. "Is Dr. Denker still receiving visitors?"

"Dr. Dudley is with him now." She leaned over the desk and looked down the hall. "He should be through shortly."

"Is everything all right," Claire asked.

"Ah! There he is now," Nurse Davis announced cheerfully.

Henry turned to see the lanky doctor striding toward them. "Yo!

Bro!" He called out "That's how the brothers here greet each other," he added when he reached them. He looked at Claire. "Have we met?"

"Yes . . . I know Bill Hughes," she said, with a relieved smile. "Bill was Trip's roommate at Harvard," she explained to Henry.

"Claire Fox!" The surgeon suddenly remembered. "You see everybody you ever knew in Charlottesville—that's what the natives say . . . Of course, everybody they know is from Charlottesville!" He looked at Claire then at Henry. "What are you doing with this guy?"

"We're here to see Dr. Denker," she said. "How's he doing?"

"He's coming along fine. In fact," Dudley reached into his coat pocket and pulled out a set of keys, "he asked me to give you these. That's a good sign," he explained. "It shows his head injuries haven't impaired his ability to process information." He handed the keys to Henry. "You can say hello, but don't stay too long—he needs to rest. Say," he added, addressing Claire, "why don't we get together for a game of bridge while you're here. My friend Helen plays, Henry plays . . . and you play!"

Claire looked at Henry who stared back at her without speaking. "I'd like that," she said, stilling looking at him.

"I'm off tomorrow evening," the doctor informed her. "Come over around six . . . I'll make dinner." He saluted and marched off down the next hall. A moment later he was gone.

"You know Trip . . ." Henry said, as they walked toward Denker's room.

"Slightly," Claire answered. "He was very entertaining . . . It'll be fun catching up with him . . ."

"Here we are . . ." Henry pushed the door open and held it as Claire entered Denker's room.

"Well!" Denker exclaimed with a frail smile. "What a pleasant surprise."

Claire hurried over to him and took his hand. "I've been looking forward to this all day," she said, smiling down at him. "How do you feel?"

His face was badly swollen, and his scalp was crisscrossed with stitches. A couple of containers with clear liquid hung from a stand beside his bed. Tubes from these pouches ran under the sheets. "I'm pretty sore," he answered, squeezing her hand. "But I feel better now that you're here. And Henry! I didn't mean to exclude you . . ."

"Sounds like you had a close call last night," Henry said, approaching the bed.

"They say I have a couple broken ribs," he replied. "It's painful if I move—so I try not to. Otherwise, I think I'm all right . . . the old head's so hard it can take almost anything." He paused to catch his breath. "Did Dr. Dudley give you the keys?"

"Yes," Henry said, extracting them from his pocket and holding them up so Denker could see them. "We saw him on our way in."

"Good! Would you mind giving them back to Fenton," Denker asked. "He was kind enough to give me a set so we could get into the house while we were preparing the program. I meant to return them last night, but it slipped my mind."

"What are they for?" Henry asked, inspecting them.

"The mansion . . . the silver key opens the grate at the southeastern end of the central passage. The gold key opens the entrance door on the southeast wall of the basement display area. That's the staff entrance to the mansion," he explained.

"I'll see that he gets them," Henry promised. "We're on our way to the dinner at the Colonnade Club now. Maybe we'll see him there."

"I hate to miss it," Denker sighed.

"We're going to miss you too," Claire said, consoling him. "But the important thing is for you to heal up."

"Did Raymond speak with you?" Denker asked, shifting his gaze to Claire.

"Yes. We had an interesting conversation."

"He was going to offer you a position . . ."

"He did," she smiled.

"Will you take it?" Denker asked hopefully.

"I'm considering it," Claire smiled. "It has a number of attractive aspects," she added. "Like working with you . . ."

Denker blushed. "Well, I hope it works out. You would be a wonderful addition to our staff." He focused then on Henry. "There is something I would like you to do," he said, lifting his hand. Henry stepped forward and took it. "I spoke the other day with Emerson Spies at the Law School— brilliant man! He was praising a faculty member he brought in last year. Do you know Delilah Wanamaker?"

"Prout mentioned her while we were with him this afternoon," Henry said, "but I haven't met her."

"Emerson thought it was time to incorporate some humanist material into the curriculum over of there so he recruited Ms. Wanamaker—from UPenn I think."

"Prout said she teaches Legal Ethics," Henry observed. "He's working on a book about rhetoric in contemporary politics," Henry added. "John Rawls factors into it somewhere . . . you know, Justice as Fairness. I gather he's been picking her brain."

"Good . . ." Denker sighed. "Do a little spade work for me, will you. See if Ms. Wanamaker has anything we might use." He thought a moment. "I'm not sure about Justice as Fairness."

"I'll look into it," Henry said. "You'd better rest now . . ."

"Yes," Denker said, closing his eyes. "Now go and enjoy yourselves . . ."

They crossed the East Range and entered a lane that led up the hill to Mr. Jefferson's Lawn.

The lane was lined on both sides by serpentine walls. Behind the wall to their right was the garden of Pavilion IV. Behind the wall to their left was the garden of Pavilion VI. At the head of the lane was a parking area that was bounded by the brick foundation wall of the colonnade. A white-washed stairwell rose from the parking area to the Lawn. In the opening at its top, Claire could see a single white column silhouetted against the pale blue sky.

"You're awfully quiet," Claire noted as they approached the stairs.

"I'm thinking . . ." Henry answered without looking at her.

"What are you thinking about?" She asked.

"What am I thinking about?" Henry repeated. ". . . I'm thinking about . . . the keys."

They mounted the stairs and crossed under the colonnade onto the Lawn.

"What are you telling me?" She asked again.

Henry stopped and looked at her. "What do you want me to say? That I still trust you? Or maybe you'd like me to tell you how much I enjoyed reflating your crushed Washington-insider ego . . ." He walked on. "Well thanks," he called back over his shoulder, "but I've got better ways to stay busy."

"Henry," she called after him. "Wait!"

He stopped.

"It isn't supposed to be like this," she said, as though it made any difference.

"I suppose not," he nodded and started to walk on.

"Henry," she called after him.

"What?" He snapped, turning back toward her.

"Can we just stand here a minute?"

Henry stopped again.

Claire gazed up the tree-lined lawn toward the Rotunda. The moon had risen and was hovering on the shoulder of its charred shell. "It was perfect," he said, voicing the emptiness he felt.

"I see that," she observed wistfully.

"A fire gutted it in 1895," he volunteered. "When Sanford White rebuilt it, he eliminated the upper room, which was the library in Jefferson's original plan. Since then, it's been a single cavernous chamber." Claire listened quietly. "White put a star in the floor directly under the center of the dome," he continued. "If you tap it with your foot, the sound bounces off the inner surface of the dome back into your ears. It's a huge amplifier," he added, "almost enough to deafen you."

"The University sponsors a gala here every year," Henry continued, afraid she would say something if he stopped. "It's called the Beaux Arts Ball . . . The men wear evening cloths, and the women get dolled up . . . They dance all night and drink to Mr. Jefferson's health. They've raised enough money to restore the interior the way it was in Jefferson's original plan. They were going to start work next year. I guess they'll start a sooner now . . ."

Clusters of students were celebrating Openings Weekend along the colonnades. Music from their stereos rippled past Claire like an evening tide. It was Motown! That's the way they partied at UVA. It seemed to fit. Her gaze settled on the statue at the far end of the Lawn. "Who's that?" she wondered.

"The Blind Poet—Homer," Henry answered, conjuring up his mythical gifts . . . voice of the Gods . . . seer of Truths . . . font of Wisdom . . ."

"Poet," Claire cried out. "Tell me the secret of life . . . Miracles happen, don't they?" She asked no one in particular. She waited for a moment then settled back into her place on the Lawn. "We can go now," she said.

Mr. Paige had planned to end the conference with an event in the Rotunda. After the bombing, Dr. Denker suggested they hold it in the Colonnade Club, which occupies Pavilion VII on the West Lawn. It had been the first building constructed in Mr. Jefferson's academic village. Paige liked the idea and had enough clout to make the last-minute arrangements.

Henry guided Claire through the entry hall and across the corridor, which held the stairway to the second floor. They continued through the North Parlor and across the second corridor that connected the club's north and south wings. The north doors to the Solarium were open, and when they entered it, they found it was already full. Mr. Paige was standing on a platform at the far end of the room. "Ladies and gentlemen," he said, speaking into the microphone in front of him. "Could I have your attention please." He waited, smiling as the room gradually quieted. During this interval, Henry and Claire inched their way to a place by the terrace door where their view was unobstructed.

"Thank you," he said. "Just a few quick announcements before I introduce our speaker. First, I want to thank all of you joining us this evening. You're helping to start a tradition that is going to continue far beyond next year's Bicentennial celebration." The audience congratulated itself with a brief round of applause.

"I would also like to express our gratitude to the faculty of the University of Virginia for allowing us to use their beautiful facility this evening." The audience echoed his thanks with another peel of applause. "We had planned to hold this event in the Rotunda. But I'm sure you know that it was damaged during a fire that took place last week. The authorities now tell me that it is being investigated as arson," he added. A murmur rippled through the room. "I'm sure I speak for all of us when I urge that no effort be spared in bringing the guilty parties to justice." There was another brief round of applause. "I would also like to thank the Monticello Foundation and specifically Fenton Somerville, head curator of its museum, for his contributions to last night's program and for many other considerations." There was more applause.

"Let also recognize the immense contributions of the Jefferson Academy's director, my friend and colleague, Dr. Oscar Denker. Without his dedicated assistance, this program would not have been possible." There was another round of applause. "I'm sorry to tell you," he continued, "that Dr. Denker could not be with us this evening because he was in an accident on his way home last night." A hush settled over the hall. "Fortunately," Paige informed them, "his doctors assure us that he is going to be all right." The news was met with a collective sigh of relief.

"Finally, I want to thank the members of the Jefferson Academy's staff." He stepped back and led the assembly in another brief round of applause. "Before turning the podium over to tonight's keynote speaker," he said, stepping back to the microphone, "I would like to remind you that next year marks the two-hundredth anniversary of the signing of the Declaration of Independence. The Jefferson Academy will lead the celebration with its own bicentennial program. With your continued support, it will be another great success.

"Thomas Jefferson warned us two hundred years ago that people cannot be ignorant and remain free," Paige informed them. "That's why we're going to focus on education. The Jefferson Academy is going to make 1976 a year for learning about America's heritage," he announced. "We want to help Americans to understand that political freedom is this country's most precious asset.

"After two-hundred years, and in spite our of status as a super-power," he continued, "the world remains a dangerous place. The future is as uncertain today as it was then. As troubling is the fact that we're facing it as a nation divided. Our political freedoms are more vulnerable in these circumstances. That's why we're going to re-focus public attention on the principles that have made America great.

"Our forefathers were on to something when they framed our national motto—E Pluribus Unum," he declared. "My grandfather understood what it meant. He led the Union charge that broke the Confederate line at Petersburg, Virginia in 1865. 'Rally round the flag!' That's the way he put it. Now it's our turn. Let's make sure that today's Americans understand what it means to be united!" The audience applauded again.

"Now without further ado, I would like to introduce a man whom you all know. He has distinguished himself as an educator and public servant. His most recent service to our country has been as special prosecutor for the Watergate investigation. Our guest currently holds the Carl M. Loeb University Professorship at the Harvard University School of Law. Ladies and gentlemen, please welcome a man who I greatly admire, Archibald Cox."

The room filled with enthusiastic applause as the bow-tied celebrity joined Mr. Paige on the podium. Mr. Paige shook his hand, then stepped aside.

Cox waited for the applause to subside. "Thank you," he said. "Thank you," he repeated, gesturing for the crowd to be quiet. "I appreciate your warm welcome. And I want to thank you, Ray . . . " he looked around to locate his host. "I want to thank you on behalf of all of us here for organizing this forum. Gatherings like this are essential if government of the People, by the People, and for the People is to be perpetuated." He stepped away from the mike and led the assembly in a round of applause to honor their host.

"When Ray asked me to make this address," Cox told his audience, "I drew up a list of possible topics. As I reviewed it, however, I realized that one stood out above all the others—the issue of *public trust*." There was a spontaneous burst of applause. "Ladies and gentlemen, it is safe to say that we have just passed through one of the most serious political storms in our nation's history. Now that it's behind us, we must address the underlying issue. How can we preserve our political system if our elected officials treat their offices as vehicles to promote their private interests?"

Claire stood next to Henry, quietly searching the crowd for her friend. As she scanned the sea of faces, someone spoke her name.

"Miss Fox . . . "

She turned to see Fenton Somerville. "Oh! Fenton!" She grasped his hands impulsively. "We were hoping you'd be here . . . "

"And Mr. Tilghman is here too?" Somerville asked. "Why," he exclaimed, prying his eyes off Claire, "he's right beside you!"

"Dr. Somerville!" Henry said, springing to life. "We were just over with Oscar. In fact, he asked me to . . . "

Claire stepped in front of him so he could not complete his sentence. "Dr. Denker wanted us to tell you how much he . . . enjoyed the program last night."

"It was my pleasure," the curator replied. "But did I hear Raymond say that Oscar was in an automobile accident?"

"Yes," Henry answered, scowling at Claire. "His car went off the road on his way down Monticello Mountain."

"He's going to be all right though," Claire assured the scholar.

"Thank Goodness!" Somerville said with a relieved sigh. Then straightening up into his most formal pose, he addressed Henry. "Mr. Tilghman," he said. "Did you not tell me that you speak German?"

"Yes . . . I believe I did," Henry said.

"Well, a funny thing has happened," Somerville announced. "Perhaps you remember that we were taking about Baron de Riedesel yesterday."

"Yes. I recall . . . "

"I received a package in the mail this morning, which contains letters written by the Baron and Thomas Jefferson! And they're in German!" He raised his eyebrows to express his astonishment. "Jefferson isn't supposed to have known German," the curator informed Claire.

"Really!" She replied, digesting the mystery.

"I'm wondering," the curator continued, addressing Henry again. "Would you be willing to translate them for me?"

"I'll be glad to help . . . if I can."

"Wonderful!" Somerville exclaimed. He thought for a moment. "I know tomorrow is Sunday, but if you were able to come over in the morning . . . the Museum will be closed . . ."

"What time," Claire asked, accepting for both of them.

"Would 7:00 be too early?"

"That will be fine," Claire confirmed, placing her hand on Henry's arm.

"Excellent," Somerville said, clapping his hands. "I'll tell the grounds people to unlock the lower gate. Just drive up and park in the lot beside the gift store. I'll be watching for you . . . Yippee! T.P. Wells

"There's nothing that troubles me more than an unrepentant non-juror who's happy!"

Somerville turned. "Why, if it isn't the conniving king of Whiggery!" Somerville jested in a low voice and extended his hand to William O. Douglas, the Monticello Foundation's longest serving board member. "My favorite inquisitor! He doesn't understand a thing Thomas Jefferson said," Somerville pretended to whisper to Claire and Henry.

"If you boys aren't polite to each other," Barbara Tuchman warned, joining the circle, "you can't go out at recess."

"Barbara!" Claire cried, hugging her friend and mentor. "I've been looking everywhere for you." She pulled the older woman aside. "I need to talk with you . . ."

"By all means," the other answered, sensing a problem. "Let's go into the garden. It will be quiet there. Will you excuse us," Tuchman said to the others before leading Claire off through the crowd.

Douglas took the curator by the arm, he led him into the hall. "What was that you said about Jefferson speaking German?"

"Isn't that amazing? Somerville exclaimed. "I just received a collection of letters written by Baron de Riedesel and Thomas Jefferson–and they're all in GERMAN!"

"German!" Douglas repeated darkly.

"I know," Somerville answered. "Isn't that bizarre?"

"Where did they come from?" Douglas wondered, watching Somerville.

"It seems they were sent to us by a fellow in the town. What's strange is that he addressed the package to Thomas Jefferson . . . He wanted Jefferson's legal opinion about some land he seems to think still belongs to the Baron!"

"It's obviously a prank," Douglas announced. "I have no doubt that the documents are forgeries."

"Oh no," Somerville assured him. "They're real! There's no question about that!"

"Where are they now?"

"In my office . . ." Somerville replied.

"You're sure they're safe . . . " The ancient Justice asked anxiously.

"Absolutely!" the curator assured him. "The building's impregnable, and the grounds are guarded twenty-four hours a day."

"Tell me again how that works?"

"We have a cruiser that completes a circuit around the mountain every fifteen minutes. It's very secure."

"That's comforting to know," Douglas smiled. "So when can I see them?"

"Mr. Tilghman has agreed to come over tomorrow morning..."

"Good! I'll be there first thing," Douglas replied, eying Henry suspiciously. Having settled the matter, Douglas seemed to relax. "You want to test me again on Jefferson—is that your game?"

Henry listened for a minute then drifted out of Somerville's debate with Douglas.

For a moment he joined Professor Cox's audience. "Let's not kid ourselves," Cox was telling them. "Men like Nixon have been in the government since the dawn of the republic. Lyndon Johnson is another example," he added, illustrating his point. "He came to Washington with ten dollars in his pocket. Forty years later, he was President of the United States with a net worth of twenty-million dollars. Where did that money came from?" No one answered. "I don't mean to imply that the two men are alike," Cox added. "Johnson at least gave his constituents their money's worth." Laughter rippled through the audience.

"I guess it's easier to do that when you have friends in the Congress... Nixon didn't have any," the prosecutor added. "When his enemies came after him, he couldn't fend them off. Our watchdogs in the press, who managed to sleep through all four of Johnson's decades, woke up in time to get the Watergate story. During the feeding frenzy," the Harvard Professor observed, "they finally pulled the curtain off Washington's dirty little secret... There are some corrupt people in public service!" He gave his audience a minute to digest his words. "It's no good pretending this is a 'Nixon problem.' Watergate has undermined public trust in <u>all</u> branches of our government!" The special prosecutor's expression became still more grave. "I'm sure you all understand that if we allow this to take root, the consequences will be disastrous. We have no alternative," he informed them. "We must clean our house! Fortunately, we have the tools—the ballot box and the *Court*!"

Henry made his way across the room and stepped out onto the porch. What a night, he thought, taking a deep breath. As he revived, someone touched him on the shoulder.

Turning, he saw Prout. It hit him when he shifted his gaze to Prout's companion. Moses had brought the burning bush! It took Henry a moment to adjust mentally. Prout's companion was a Hollywood sizzler! She was as tall Prout. Her short dark hair was a tangle of curls that may have come from neglect or an expensive stylist. He could not see her eyes because she was wearing oversized Jackie Onassis dark glasses. From her ears dangled a pair of golden discs that matched the 3-inch gold Mayan calendar pendant that lay on her breast. She was wearing a bright orange blazer, which only partially concealed her tight blue bodystocking. She was standing on a pair of 4-inch blue spike heels.

Henry was still synthesizing the lady's fearless ensemble when Prout cleared his throat. "Henry, I would like you to meet Delilah Wanamaker." As he spoke, she removed her dark glasses and revealed her mesmerizing green eyes. They were fixed on him! "Professor Wanamaker, this is my friend Henry Tilghman," Prout continued with his introduction. "He's at the Jefferson Academy."

Wanamaker studied him for another moment then offered her hand. "It's nice to meet you, Henry.".

"It's always a pleasure to meet a fellow Wahoo fan," Henry said, complimenting her display of UVA's colors. He gave her hand a firm shake. "I was just talking with Oscar Denker about you," he continued.

"Oscar Denker is the director of the Jefferson Academy," Prout informed her.

Wanamaker smiled and nodded then took over. "You and I have something in common, Henry . . ."

"We do?" Henry sounded surprised.

"You're one of Jim's sounding boards," the ethicist announced. "So am I!"

This wasn't quite true, but it pleased Henry to hear her say it. "I'm interested in what Jim is doing," he explained, "but I mostly listen . . . It's pretty sophisticated stuff—Wittgenstein's poker, I mean . . . you probably know all about it . . ."

"It's what Jim's doing with it that interests me," the Law Professor announced. "It's original—and timely . . ."

"I'm very glad you're here," Henry repeated. "Professor Spies recently mentioned to Dr. Denker how impressed he is with your work. Dr. Denker therefore asked me to learn about what you are doing . . . and whether it might fit into the programs we're planning to present at the Jefferson Academy . . ."

Wanamaker smiled. "Emerson is a dear—and a visionary! He big took a chance," she added, "when he hired me . . ."

"How so?" Henry was surprise.

"I don't teach money courses," she replied. "That's what draws the top people and gives the school its ranking."

"What do you do then?" Henry asked.

"I give the Law social context," she said, ". . . so tomorrow's legal sharks can improve society while making their fortunes!" She watched Henry to see he was surprised.

"Good!" Henry said, trying to picture George Edmund sitting in Wanamaker's class. "How do you attract students?" he wondered. "So far as I am aware, legal sharks aren't interested in legal ethics!"

"It's mostly posturing," Wanamaker conceded, "but the material is substantive . . . and it improves conversation at gatherings like this . . ."

"I suppose it does," Henry agreed. "Do you have a couple minutes to tell me about it?"

"Sure . . ." Looking around, she spotted three chairs at the north end of the balcony. "Save those chairs, and we'll get some wine . . . Red or White?"

"Whatever you can find," Henry said, turning toward the chairs.

Prout and Wanamaker were back a couple minutes later. He was carrying two bottles of wine, red in one hand, white in the other. She was carrying three glasses. Taking the seats beside Henry, the Legal Ethicist distributed the glasses, and the bartending Wittgensteinian filled them.

"Delilah is more than a conversation piece," Prout teased. Wanamaker rolled her eyes. "She's brilliant! Her first course at the Law School traces the history of Justice," Prout continued. "In the second, she examines the relationship between Justice and the Law, which is where we connect."

"It has changed so much in the past one-hundred years," Wanamaker said, taking over, "that the men who framed the concept wouldn't recognize it."

"I'm not surprised," Henry said after a swallow of wine.

"Dalilah knows more about this than anybody I know of," Prout added with an approving nod. "Her insights have helped me crystalize my thesis."

"Diversity is changing the nature of politics," she announced. "Instead of providing a means for achieving consensus, framing policy, and promoting the common good, as John Locke envisioned, it's becoming a tool for organizing factions, inciting opposition, and suppressing public discourse about policy and the common good. It's now a tool for inciting social conflict, and in this form, it is undermining the willingness of people to promote the well-being of their communities and of society in general."

"That's right!" Prout agreed. "Delilah can tell you how Justice has become a rhetorical weapon that ideologues are now using to destroy modern political society . . . People like Ray Paige—and Delilah—are its last hope!"

As Prout refilled the three glasses, Wanamaker began to sketch out her work.

"Samuel and John Adams wrote relevant patriotic texts during the years leading up to the American Revolution," she explained. "They more or less followed John Locke in respect to the role Justice plays in political society . . . They did this by referencing Justice in its legal model and by implying that it was essential for social harmony. But neither cousin defined what he meant by "justice" or otherwise discussed the concept apart from confirming that just laws must be universally applied.

"The flaws in political society became increasingly conspicuous with industrialization. New forms of corruption materialized as capitalists, with help from their partners in government, built complex commercial combinations and accumulated vast fortunes. The booming economy produced a thriving new American middle class and general improvements in the public well-being. But it did not prevent the formation of a new tier at the bottom of society. By the beginning of the 20th century, the sufferings of these unfortunate people, together with the abusive behavior of the moguls who were blamed for causing it, became concerns for reform-minded activists who launched the movement we know today as progressivism.

"Vernon Parrington was an outspoken progressive academic. I give him credit for framing the concept of Justice that energized the progressive movement. What Parrington characterized as "Social Justice" later became known as Distributive Justice. Social Justice doesn't fit within either the Ethical Model or the Legal Model. I characterize it as the *Economic Model*.

"By the time this new concept of Justice formed, expectations that social harmony could be achieved by being well-mannered and by settling property disputes with traditional legal methods had all but disappeared. Economic and cultural disparities between society's members had grown so large that there were no longer prospects for bridging them. Progressives responded to these disparities by devising plans to re-allocate the nation's wealth in ways they characterized as "fair."

"This utopian enterprise soon encountered problems, however. In the first place, wealth does not simply exist. Some combination of capitalists and workers have to create it before it can be confiscated and redistributed. Unfortunately, capitalists weren't particularly interested in risking their fortunes so progressives could take what they made and give it to those less fortunate. A second problem had political and ethical aspects, being that the reformers who were inventing and administering this benevolence were neither good as managers nor immune to corruption.

"The social logic that underpins 20th century progressivism was framed two decades before the French Revolution by Jean-Jacque Rousseau. Rousseau sowed the seeds for that upheaval by arguing that 'man is free, but everywhere in chains.' This idea found an enthusiastic audience among France's educated bourgeoisie, whose prospects were limited by France's tightly closed hereditary hierarchy. What appealed to France's untitled technocrats was Rousseau's reassuring premise that before being corrupted by the acquisition of private property, men lived together in peace in a natural state of equality. Rousseau's political theory inspired the revolutionaries who overthrew France's bankrupt monarchy because it stressed the need for a political system based on social equality.

"The synergies between Rousseau's back-to-nature political theory and progressivism stops there, however. Rousseau condemned social inequality, but he did not blame capitalistic "plutocrats" for causing it. It was caused, Rousseau explained, by disparity in the abilities of men.

"This empirically verifiable fact did not keep Marx from designing a social system to eliminate the disparities in wealth. His theory of man in society—Historical Materialism—centers on the perennial conflict between owners (his Bourgeoisie) and those who work for them (his Proletariat). To make it more inhuman, Marx staged his "class struggle" in a netherworld void of both Justice and Happiness.

"Progressives like Vernon Parrington, whose masterwork, *Main Currents in American Thought,* won a Pulitzer Prize in 1928, praised Marx's communist system even though "wage slaves" who worked in the capitalist systems he despised were far better off than those who answered to the brutal ideologues who ran worker communes in Soviet Russia. The fact that Parrington and his progressive successors thought—and still think—that the best way to manage the unfair distribution of private wealth is to enslave the people in a totalitarian system where there is no wealth, no justice, and no pursuit of happiness, is almost as awful to contemplate as the horrifying record of communism.

"This brings us to Rawls," the intellectual historian announced after finishing her second glass of wine. "You may remember that Professor Rawls unveiled his master-of-the-universe moral system as the cultural revolution was experiencing its climactic moment. I don't think it was a coincidence," Wanamaker added, looking at Prout, "that Rawls's unveiled his plan as Woodstock Nation was conducting its people's congress—do you?"

Prout answered with a laugh. "I warned you, Henry. She's as fearless as she is brilliant!"

The legal scholar shot a cool glance at her companion then refocused on Henry. "Do you remember the closing number in *Godspell?*" she asked. "It captures the pomposity of Woodstock's world builders." Henry listened attentively. "As the curtain falls, Jesus Christ's disciple are singing, *'we can build a beautiful city, not a city of angels but finally a city of man.'* It's a moving scene, but the people who sang about building that city never built it—or anything else! Neither did the citizens of Woodstock Nation. They're daydreamers not world builders! But the reason the city they were singing about does not exist is that the world does not work the way their rhetoric suggests. The real world is an infinity of undetectable and unmanageable aspirations and an offsetting number of contradicting obstacles! These perpetually conflicting forces have worked against every well-intentioned plan human beings have concocted to improve their condition. And because they do, they usually fail.

"Take Woodstock," Wanamaker continued, illustrating her point. "It burst into existence, glowed brilliantly for a few soggy days, then fizzled away into a cloud of rhetorical hot air. Rhetoric transformed Woodstock into a cult utopia. It's still wafting through the atmosphere. But Woodstock stopped being *real* when Krishna's naked worshipers got dressed and went back to school.

"Here's my point: the master-of-the-universe system Professor Rawls devised to manage wayfarers who are inherently unequal—and naturally suspicious of each other—is just as much of a fantasy as Woodstock Nation. Woodstock Nation rested on the obsessions of a few with propping up 'multi-cultural' society. Justice as Fairness rests on the obsessions of a few elitist social engineers with propping up "multi-cultural" society. The two phenomena came in hand in hand, and because neither of them works in the real world, they are going out hand in hand. Neither provides a way to improve the condition of men in society. Only sharing values and uniting in pursuit of common goods can do that."

"Bravo!" Prout applauded, his eyes fixed on the legal scholar. "Clear, simple, and real! To Delilah Wanamaker!" he declared, raising his glass. "May she live forever." Henry watched the scholarly realist as the Wittgensteinian proposed his toast. When he was done, she pursed her lips and blew him a kiss.

"To Delilah Wanamaker!" Henry repeated and swallowed the rest of his wine. Suddenly an image of Claire appeared in his mind's eye. He was wrong, and suddenly he knew it.

Barbara Tuchman settled Claire on a bench in a shadowy corner of the outer garden and took a seat beside her. "What is it that's bothering you?"

"Everything is going wrong," Claire whispered. The words dislodged the last measure of her resolve, and tears began to stream down her cheeks.

"Oh Claire!" The older woman said gently, wrapping her in a motherly embrace. "What's happened?"

"I've had the most awful encounter with Martin," Claire sobbed through her tears.

"There, there . . ." Tuchman said, stroking her hair. "I know he can be sharp . . ."

"You don't understand," Claire said. "He hit me!"

"Martin struck you?" Tuchman exclaimed. "Why that's outrageous! Whatever could have possessed him?" She pulled back and looked at Claire sternly. "I think you should tell me about your relationship with Martin. Have you . . ."

"Yes," Claire confessed timidly. "We've become . . . intimate."

The other woman shook her head. "That was a mistake . . ."

"I know," Claire whispered. "But it happened so . . . suddenly."

"Martin is a very persuasive man," Tuchman conceded, picturing him in her mind's eye.

"There's more," Claire said.

"Something beyond your . . ." Tuchman searched for the right word, ". . . relationship?"

"Yes," Claire said. "He's taken me off the Jefferson Academy assignment and gave it to Jack Rhoades."

"You showed him your story?" Tuchman asked, frowning.

"Yes," Claire said, catching her breath. "Everything was all right when I went over it with him before publication. But this afternoon, he told me that I had made mistakes and that I was making the paper look bad."

"Claire," she said, stiffening. "You must tell him immediately that you're finished with him! That's all there is to it!"

"I guess I thought . . ."

"You have no choice," Tuchman repeated more forcefully.

"You're right," Claire sighed. "There's no way I can work with him now . . ."

"Power corrupts people," the older woman observed, shaking her head. "History is full of stories like this." She studied Claire with an inquisitive gaze. "And sex . . . It destroys working relationships . . ."

"I know . . ." Claire whispered, burying her face in hands. "There's something else," she said, peering up.

"What's that?" the older woman asked sympathetically.

"Raymond Paige."

"What about him," Tuchman wondered, her voice sounding a new alarm

"He wants me to join his staff . . ."

"Really?" Tuchman's seemed relieved. "That's interesting . . ."

"What do you think?" Claire waited as the other woman considered the idea.

"Raymond is a fascinating person," Tuchman replied. "He's a visionary. But he is also a man of action. Not many men would dare to do what he has done. You understand, of course, that he and Martin are rivals. Martin thinks that whatever success Raymond achieves will come at his expense. Therefore, he is searching for a way to discredit him. Nothing would please him more, I'm sorry to say, than to destroy the Jefferson Academy."

"Then why didn't he object to my story when I showed it to him?" Claire wondered.

"Perhaps he misjudged how able Raymond actually is," Tuchman speculated. "Martin tends to dismiss people he doesn't like. But when he got here and saw what Raymond was actually doing, and the people who were helping him . . . it was a stroke of genius, for example, to have Archie Cox speak this evening, he finally realized how dangerous Raymond is. Archie is one of Martin's most trusted personal advisors!" Tuchman explained. "Having him speak tonight has given Raymond instant credibility."

"No more than you!" Claire protested.

"Thank you, Claire. You're sweet," Tuchman smiled, reaching over and taking Claire's hand. "Now tell me what I can do for you?"

"Tell me what I should do," Claire implored, pressing Tuchman's hand.

"If you accept Raymond's offer," the older woman advised, "the circles you are traveling in with Martin will close to you. People you think are your friends will turn their backs . . ."

"Will you?" Claire asked, staring into her friend's eyes.

"No, of course not," she answered, smiling. "You're much too important . . . But you haven't told me what Raymond wants you to do," she added with a refreshing laugh.

"I think he wants me to insulate him from the Martins of the world," Claire replied with a self-effacing smile. "He'll probably withdraw the offer if he finds out what's happened . . ."

"That's not how Raymond operates," Tuchman observed confidently. They sat for a moment in silence. "With your help," Tuchman added, "Raymond could very well become our next President."

The audience listened in riveted silence as Cox built his case for Court action. "Chief Justice Marshall created this extraordinary power with his Marbury vs. Madison ruling."

"Perhaps you remember the situation. Jefferson had directed his Secretary of State, James Madison, not to deliver a commission that Madison's predecessor had prepared for William Marbury. Marbury responded by suing Madison in the Supreme Court. In his opinion, Chief Justice John Marshall stated, 'It is emphatically the province and duty of the judicial department to say what the law is. Those who apply the law in particular cases must necessarily expound and interpret that rule. If two laws conflict with each other, the courts must decide on the operation of each.' With these words," Cox announced, "Marshall established the supremacy of the Court under the principle of Judicial Review.

"Jefferson opposed Marshall on this. He endorsed the ancient tradition exemplified in the Anglo-American common law. This heritage imposes on judges the obligation to decide 'according to the law'. This refers to the ideal of a coherent and continuing body of principles formed in the statutes, judicial precedents, writings of legal scholars, traditions approved by historic practice, and the like . . .

"Fortunately," Cox concluded, "Marshall prevailed. Under his method of interpretation, the Court validates its decisions by the authority of our Constitution *and* the law it has already made. Yet it still has the flexibility to shape the law to fit the changing circumstance of our changing society! Thanks to Marshall, the law became dynamic. This has allowed our great country to evolve and grow.

"Marshall's finding has given the Court the power to respond to minority demands for social justice and to the demands of the disadvantaged for economic justice. Imagine the distrust that would exist today if the Court had turned its back on their appeals!"

Cox scanned the room. "I understand that Justice Douglas is with us this evening." A murmur of excitement rippled through the room as Douglas waved from the back of the room.

"Come up here, Bill," Cox said into the microphone.

"Excuse me, Fenton," he said, starting toward the podium. "Let me take care of this, then I want to respond to your challenge . . ."

Cox proceeded with his introduction as Douglas he made his way to the speaker's platform. "The genius of the Court," Cox explained, "is reflected in the creative ways it has applied the power of judicial review. Indeed, during Justice Douglas's forty-year tenure, it completed one of its most important philosophical restructurings. When Douglas took his seat, the Court's emphasis was on preserving a small central government and protecting open markets. Behind Justice Douglas's leadership, the Court has come to accept the idea that it must shape the Constitution in response to the changing needs of our society."

Douglas stepped onto the speaker's platform and received another warm round of applause. "You were there," Cox said, shaking his hand. "Why don't you tell us how it happened."

"You probably think I put him up to this," Douglas responded as the crowd clapped and laughed. "Just for the record," he added, "I didn't!" He turned then to the speaker. "Thank you Archie for the great service you have provided the country through the Watergate proceedings." The crowd clapped again. "Professor Cox is right," Douglas announced. "The Court *has* grown since I arrived in Roosevelt's first administration—and that's not Teddy's administration," he quipped as the audience applauded. "The dominant philosophy then was a theory called 'dual federalism'. It was an idea that originated with James Madison in Federalist Paper #51. It didn't take hold in the Court until the latter part of the last century. Under this theory, the country was divided into two mutually exclusive realms. Specific limited areas of human activity were assigned to the federal government. There, the federal government was sovereign, and no State might intrude. Whatever was left was assigned to the States. There, the States were sovereign, and the federal government might not intrude. During Roosevelt's administration, a majority finally formed in support of a theory that is now referred to as 'judicial activism'.

"Of course, we had the little tiff with Roosevelt that led to his Court-packing challenge. That resulted in the brief ascendency of 'judicial restraint', which allowed Roosevelt to push his Depression-era social programs through the Congress. But the Depression—and then the War—solidified our belief that it was not enough for the Court to keep markets operating freely and to guard citizens against the excessive use of government power. We realized that one part of society often needs to be protected against injustices perpetrated against it by another. We therefore began searching for a legal or logical connection important enough in itself and in the eyes of the law to establish this new legal principle..."

Prout stepped back out onto the terrace and rejoined Henry and Delilah. "When you get to that point," he said, tuning the speaker out, "it's not a society anymore. I can't tell you how pissed it makes me to hear this kind of twaddle after risking my hide in Vietnam."

The silver shadow floated up the darkened slope. It stopped at the crest of the hill and hovered there like a ghost in the night. "Good!" Marjean said, gazing over the steering wheel toward Henry's cottage. The house was dark, and Henry's car was gone. "The coast is clear!"

"What if he comes back while we're inside?" Gerta worried.

Marjean ignored the question and guided the Mercedes down the slope to the parking area. She pulled to a stop beside Claire's MG.

"What if the door's locked," Gerta asked, in a timorous voice.

"Oh, for Christ sake!" Marjean swore. "Will you shut up!" She shoved open the car door and climbed out.

"You stay here and keep watch," Marjean instructed Aster, who was sitting in the back seat.

"Come on," she said to Gerta. Gerta followed her fearless leader across the lawn and up onto the porch. Marjean stepped to the door and placed her hand on the knob. She looked back at Gerta as she turned it. "There!" She exclaimed triumphantly. "You can relax now!" Before Gerta could imagine another danger, Marjean charged into the house. She moved quickly through the living room and into Henry's study. "Give me the towel," she commanded, reaching back toward Gerta.

"I left it in the car," her accomplice admitted stupidly.

"Well go get it!" Marjean bellowed angrily. "We can't leave any prints on the gun."

Marjean watched through the window as Gerta scurried back across the lawn and opened the car door. A moment later she was back with one of the motel's white bath towels. Marjean snatched it from her and carefully draped it over Henry's shotgun. Then she lifted it from its resting place and marched out of the Henry's study.

"You've got the shells—right?" She snapped.

"Yes. I put them in the trunk."

"Good. Let's get out of here."

"I assume you got my letter," Paige said, leading Martin Ogden out onto the terrace.

"I did," Ogden replied. "Frankly, it caught me off guard," he added, revealing his irritation.

"I like to follow protocol on matters like this," Paige continued, ignoring Ogden's rebuke. "Claire's going to play an important part in our program next year."

"I appreciate your candor, Ray," Ogden answered disingenuously. "But to be perfectly honest, I don't see how it can work. We've been bringing Claire along for three years, and she's finally hitting her stride. I'll be very surprised if her story on the Jefferson Academy isn't nominated for a Pulitzer—which is, of course, a testament to the exciting things you're doing here," Ogden added gratuitously. "We'll hear about that after the first of the year. By then, of course, the Presidential campaign will be heating up . . . I don't see her leaving before that's finished . . . By the way, has she spoken with you about your plans?"

"No," Paige replied, as if the question surprised him. "I've been so darn busy with the program I haven't had time to think about it. In fact," he laughed as a waiter approached with a tray of glasses, "I was hoping to get your perspective while you were down here . . . "Bring me a scotch," he whispered in the waiter's ear." "Would you like something?" he continued, gesturing to Ogden.

Ogden waved him off. "Nothing for me, thank you . . . I'd be more than happy to get together with you for a conversation," he added.

"Let's do it then," Paige said. "How long are you going to be in town?"

"I have a few things wrap up, so I may stay through Monday."

"Good!" Paige said. "I'll have my lieutenant call you tomorrow and set something up." Just then Paige noticed Henry's group at the far end of the porch. "Whoa!" he said, jabbing Ogden. "How about that young lady! Not like the gals we used to know—huh!" Paige laughed harmlessly.

"Henry," he called out. "Bring your friends over and meet Martin Ogden." They all rose and made their way to where the two men were standing. "This Henry Tilghman," Paige said, introducing his assistant.

"We met last night before dinner," Henry said, stepping toward Ogden and extending his hand. "Nice to see you again, sir."

"I remember," Ogden said, studying him as he shook his hand. "You were with Claire Fox . . . "

"This is James Prout," Paige proceeded. "We're trying to pry him away from the Hoover Institute—he's got a new way for evaluating social policies. Isn't that right James?"

"That's a good way to put it," Prout nodded, and shook hands with Ogden.

"And this is . . . ," Paige paused, focusing on Delilah.

"Delilah Wanamaker," she said, extending her hand. "It's nice to meet you, Mr. Ogden. I'm on the Law faculty," she added.

"Yes, of course," Ogden said. "Very nice to meet you, too, Professor Wanamaker."

"Glad you could join us this evening," Paige nodded to her, completing the introductions.

Before he could continue, Barbara Tuchman mounted the porch steps. Claire was beside her.

"Good evening Raymond . . ." Tuchman said, joining the group. ". . . Martin."

Martin bowed gallantly then focused on Claire. "Claire," he commanded like an emperor. "I have dinner reservations for the two of us at the Boar's Head. Are you ready to go?"

All eyes fixed on the young woman. "As a matter of fact," she answered, glancing at Henry, "I have other plans." Ogden watched impassively as she came up to him. "But I want you to have this." With that, she raised her hand and slapped his face.

The muscles in his cheeks tightened as he clenched his teeth. "I see we all make mistakes," he said, somehow bridling his anger. He nodded to Mr. Paige, then marched down the steps. A moment later he disappeared through the garden gate.

Tuchman immediately grabbed Claire's hand. "Will you excuse us, Raymond. I promised Claire that I would introduce her to some of your guests."

"By all means," Paige replied with unflappable poise.

Claire touched Henry's arm as she passed by. "I'll be inside."

"What did you think of our speaker, Mr. Prout?" Paige asked, taking a sip from his scotch.

"Jefferson was an implacable anti-hierarch," Prout replied, "and he was highly suspicious of the jurists on the Supreme Court. In fact, he called them '*a subtle corps of sappers and miners constantly working under ground to undermine the foundations of our confederated fabric.*' I agree with Jefferson on this point—we have to be on perpetual guard . . ."

"Do you agree with that, Ms. Wanamaker?"

"I'm a Lockean, Mr. Paige. I believe that communities have to be unified in pursuit of common goods if they are to perpetuate. I think Jim agrees with me that hierarchies of better men cannot decide for the people what ends they should pursue. For one thing, history shows that when such cadres form, they pursue their own interests . . . and in this process, they are prone to trample on the rights of those whose destinies they undertake to improve—if that is what they are trying to do. Locke conceived of society as a unity of its members. This was fundamental to the majoritarianism he claimed is the only legitimate form of government. The well-being of individuals in society depends on their pursuit of their common good, not on the enlighten vision of jurists in their courts."

"Well said!" Paige nodded. "We're on that line ourselves, aren't we Hank?"

"We were just talking about that," Henry informed his boss.

"I think Jefferson was right in what he wrote shortly before he died," Prout continued. "*They are construing our constitution from a co-ordination of a general and special government to a general and supreme one alone. This will lay all things at their feet . . . I say that against this every man should raise his voice, and more, should up lift his arm!*"

"Hold on now!" Paige objected. "It might come to that, but we're not there yet."

"Based on what Cox and Douglas are telling us," Prout observed. "I'd say we're pretty damned close."

"That's why we're going back to the basics," Paige announced. "Like my grandfather used to say: Rally 'round the flag boys! Before you form a citizen's militia, let's give it one more shot. The people might just get the message."

"Nobody's going to fix the Court problem," Prout announced ruefully. "Douglas's crowd has been re-wiring the country's circuitry for forty years! Everyone younger than me has lived their whole life under the watchful eye of what Madison called 'a will in the community independent of the majority.' They go to Washington and stroll through that marble rotunda on the Tidal Basin. They read 'all men are created equal'. They hear smart little men in bow ties tell them how benevolent their institutions are and how proud they should be that their Supreme Court has the courage to promote such utilitarian principles. Douglas's ruling class has turned America into a nation of simpletons! Boobus Americana is never going to understand that they have made Thomas Jefferson the spokesman for something he hated!"

"Merrill Peterson has been helping me put together some things on Jefferson," Paige replied, taking over of the conversation. "He showed me the letter Jefferson wrote to Abigail Adams where he argued that 'a little rebellion now and then' was a good thing. This is where we come in... About the time he wrote that letter, he also wrote one to a man named Edward Carrington. He said there that since the basis of our government is the *opinion* of the people, our first objective must be to keep them informed. If people become inattentive, he warned, our congresses and assemblies, our judges and governors would become 'wolves'.

"But Douglas and his cronies have made a big mistake," Paige announced. "They've fooled themselves into thinking that they're the only ones who can conduct a revolution! The thing you have to remember James, is that it's a lot harder getting people to accept a screwball idea like Douglas's social justice than it is to persuade them that they have the right to pursue their own happiness."

"That's assuming they can think," Prout murmured under his breath.

"In that letter to Abigail Adams, Jefferson said, 'the spirit of resistance to government is so valuable ... that I wish it to be always kept alive.' That's our job," Paige balled his fist and punched his hand. "Good men have to step forward and do their duty! Mark my words!" he swore, "Once the people express their will, the Court will change its tune."

Nelson Rockefeller stepped out onto the terrace in time to hear the final words of Paige's pep talk. "I wish you'd told me that before I ran for President," he grinned.

"You would have won! No question." Paige laughed, shaking his hand.

"Seriously . . ." Rockefeller said, "what do you think?"

"It's going to take three things to save the country," Paige answered firmly. "First: Christian faith! Faithful people are unselfish," Paige announced. "More than that, they believe that events follow a divine purpose, which is inherently good. This endows them with common understandings of Law, Justice, Moral Responsibility, Public Service, and Private Duty. Second: familiarity with the Classics. When people are acquainted with their heritage in Reason, they understand that they will achieve their personal fulfillment by living virtuously. Third: the Common Law. Common Law obliges government to protect the rights of its people by enacting laws to which they consent. Taken together, these three conditions create a social fabric in which men of good will can co-exist and prosper. If you eliminate any one of them, freedom and prosperity will eventually disappear." Paige glanced at his watch. "Speaking of disappearing, are you ready, Nelson?" Rockefeller nodded. "Well then gentlemen," he bowed. "Ms. Wanamaker, I like the cut of your jib!" He said, bowing again. "I'm sure Dr. Denker will be contacting you."

The Vice President winked at Henry as he passed by. "Don't forget about that political career . . ."

"I won't," Henry assured him.

Barbara Tuchman guided Claire into the front parlor. Archibald Cox was greeting well-wishers there so the room was crowded. As they picked their way toward him, they bumped into Frances Rank. She and Professor Shoate' were having an animated conversation with Merrill Peterson, who had become the Thomas Jefferson Foundation Professor of History at the University when Dumas Malone retired in 1962. Tuchman braced herself and stepped into the conversation. "Hello Frances, how nice to see you again . . ."

Rank stopped talking and looked at the tall slender woman. Recognizing Mrs. Tuchman, she formed a pained smile and nodded. She brightened, however, when she recognized Claire. "Any luck with the search?" Rank asked, without mentioned its object.

Claire smiled awkwardly. "I'm making some progress . . . How about if I call you tomorrow afternoon. Do you have a number?" Rank looked at Professor Shoate' who pulled a business card out of her sack.

"I take it that you've already met Frances Rank and Professor Shoate," Tuchman said, expressing surprise.

"Yes," Claire answered meekly, "I attended one of their planning sessions this morning . . . They want me to help them find a civil rights lawyer," she imagined, "to sue men people for the abuses they have inflicted on women people . . . since the beginning of time . . ."

"Yes," Rank confirmed fiercely. "We deserve reparations for the discrimination and economic injustice we have suffered since the founding of this sexist regime. Men people have been violating our civil rights since day one!"

"Da's da *white* men people," Shoate' said, correcting her feisty companion. "Dey's da one's dat come off wif all da money! And Jussice Douglas is tha Anna-Chris!

Tuchman back looked at Rank.

"Damned straight," Rank snapped. "And we're calling his bluff! All his BS about social justice is nothing but a smoke screen so he can gather more power into his own clammy hands. You're part of his elitist network," she said, shaking a finger at Tuchman, "so it doesn't matter to you . . ."

"Das tellin' it da way it is," Professor Shoate' swore.

"As an historian," Tuchman answered thoughtfully. "I'm not aware of any precedents for such a suit . . . Actually, I think history is running the other direction."

"Wuss zat?" Shoate' snapped.

"One of the most consistent efforts underlying the women's movement has been the elevation of heroines," she explained. "This has always been important because women's expectations for independence, fortitude, and valor are below that of males. But still, there have been women in history, Queen Boadicea in first century Britain, for instance, and Joan of Arc in France, and Catherine the Great in Russia, who have led tribes, armies, and nations. Why has this been so rare?" Tuchman wondered rhetorically. "If we're talking about the great sweep of history—thousands of years—then it may be appropriate to say that it reflects the practical wisdom of nature. In a world defined by conflict," she said qualifying her answer, "men, who are physically more powerful than women, are better suited for these tasks! I guess what I'm saying," she added with a polite laugh, "is that if women are going to rise up, we should do it as women with our own power and virtue—not because we win a court judgement."

"That's the kind of speech you'd expect from someone who's not stuck below decks," Rank sneered.

"Well, consider it this way, Frances," Tuchman countered. "Technology is advancing, and warfare is becoming less and less useful as a political policy. Consequently, male warrior aggressiveness is diminishing as a societal asset. As this pattern has formed, more and more opportunities have opened for women to lead as *women*. I wonder?" she continued, "How beneficial would it be for women to win a class action suit for discrimination that transforms the imperative of this inevitable social transition into another legalistic ruling that places the natural process under the authority of a male-dominated Court?"

Ogden stormed through the garden's outer gate. In his haste he failed to notice that someone was entering.

"Hey! Watch where you're going," Tim Hardin shouted, fending off the human projectile. "Martin!" He exclaimed, his voice warming when he identified the UFO. "You're just the guy I'm looking for. If you'll slow down for a minute, I'll give you a piece of news that'll blow you away..."

Ogden sensed from the tone of his voice that it was something he should hear so he stopped and focused on the other man. "What is it?"

"I have this from a very reliable source," Hardin announced, inflating the suspense.

"Ok..." Ogden deadpanned.

"Paige is covering up a murder!" Hardin announced, watching as Ogden's expression transformed. "His mistress..." he added, further dramatizing his news. "Tilghman drowned her in one of the lakes out there on his estate!"

"Well now!" Ogden exclaimed, breaking into a smile. "That *is* interesting! How did you hear about it?" he wondered.

"I have a reliable source," Harding repeated with a toothy grin.

"I suppose it's too much to ask for the name your source," he observed.

"Let's just say it's a friend of the deceased," Hardin replied evasively.

"Fine. We don't need to get into details—yet," Ogden agreed. "Has the body been recovered?" He asked like the reporter he had once been.

"That information has not been provided . . ."

"It's simple enough to find out," Ogden announced. "I'll have somebody call the coroner's office first thing Monday morning. In fact, I'll do it myself—nothing would please me more than to confirm what you've just said!"

"You're not leaving, are you?" Hardin asked suspiciously.

Ogden did not respond.

"I hope you're not rushing off because your girlfriend smacked you or something corny like that," Hardin teased.

Ogden stiffened. "I'll call you tomorrow," he said and marched on to the limousine that was parked in the alley.

―――――――――

Somerville balanced his plate with a juggler's skill and followed Douglas into the south parlor. Douglas directed him to one of the two chairs in front of the hearth. Both men sat down.

"You have a set of letters Jefferson wrote to Baron de Riedesel," Douglas began.

"Yes." Somerville replied. "It's an unprecedented find!"

"I'm curious to know when they were written," the Supreme Court Justice continued.

"Jefferson' wrote his first letter in December 1784," Somerville replied.

"That means he was in France!" Douglas announced.

"Yes," Somerville agreed. "These letters could very well settle the question of his supposed epiphany . . . "

"They'll prove I'm right once and for all," Douglas asserted, throwing down the gauntlet.

"You're so tediously predictable, Bill," Somerville sighed as he polished his fork with his napkin. "You'll say the salon cognoscenti transformed him into a utopian whatever the letters contain . . ."

"You're never going to see the light are you Fenton . . ."

"Tell me your thesis again," Somerville requested as he tucked his napkin under his chin.

"In Jefferson's concept of human rights, individual prerogative is subject to the general interest of society."

"Stop!" Somerville ordered, pressing his temples to assuage an unseen pain. "Jefferson never spoke of individual prerogatives."

"Come on, Fenton," Douglas pleaded, dipping a shrimp into his cocktail sauce. "You have to *interpret* the record . . . "

"Shame on you!" Somerville said, shaking his fork at Douglas. "You sound like a reporter who bends the facts to make the story work."

"Someday you're going to have to deal with the fact that Jefferson did not recognize property as a natural right," Douglas responded, breaking his roll.

"Someday you're going to have to admit that Jefferson wrote the Declaration of Independence to bolster his argument for the sovereignty of the American people," Somerville objected as he consumed a forkful of his stuffed chicken.

"That's a dodge, and you know it," Douglas protested, herding some Maryland crab onto a corner of toast. "The reason he omitted property as a natural right is that he was opposed to the exploitation of small farmers by land barons. Do you deny that?"

"It never ceases to amaze me how much of Jefferson you're willing to chop off to make him fit into your Procrustean bed," Somerville observed, plucking a ripe tomato from his salad.

"He opposed the capitalistic system Madison and Hamilton foisted on the American people while he was in France," Douglas continued, as he crunched a crab hors d'oeuvre.

"Now you're going to cite his letter to Madison," Somerville smiled, wiping his fingers on his pants.

"What did he mean when he said that the earth belongs to the living?" Douglas countered, cleansing his pallet with a sip Chardonnay. "And let's not forget his assertion that the earth is given as a common stock for man to labor and live on, which he said in his October 1785 letter to Madison."

"I'm glad you asked," Somerville replied as he sliced another corner off his chicken. "Perhaps we can settle this dispute after all."

"The earth belongs in usufruct to the living," Douglas continued, preparing another crab toast. "Individuals, being part only of a society, are subject to the laws of the whole—Jefferson said that in his September 1788 letter to Madison."

"Ok . . ." Somerville nodded as he filled his fork with potato salad.

"And every society has the right to establish the fundamental principles of its association," Douglas continued, after swallowing his crab. "That was in his letter to Crawford in June of 1818."

"You're not convincing me, Bill," Somerville mumbled through a mouthful of potato salad. "It's like I told you the last time we had this conversation. You simply have to get straight about what Jefferson was doing in the Declaration. There's no disputing it—he was committed to inalienable rights for *individuals*! Individual rights are the building blocks of a free society. 'The rights of the whole can be no more than the sum of the rights of individuals.' That's what he said in the letter he sent Madison in September of 1789.

"When you get home, read what Jefferson said in his *Summary View of the Rights of British America*," the curator instructed. "Not only does it contain all the offenses he listed in the body of the Declaration, it contains the first formulation of his argument for American sovereignty," Somerville paused to smear some salad dressing on a cucumber. "In his autobiography, he described the *Summary* as a discussion of the 'political relation between us and England' and claimed that he was inspired to write it by the 'many unwarranted encroachments' of the Crown on the rights of the colonials. Now pay attention Bill—this is where you're going off the tract. Foremost among these was the introduction of *feudal tenures* into the colonial land law. According to Jefferson, it was a 'fictitious' principle that all land belonged originally to the King. I quote:

From the nature and purposes of civil institutions, all the lands within the limits which any particular society has circumscribed around itself are assumed by that society... This may be done by themselves collectively, or by their legislature... and if they are allotted in neither of these ways, each individual of the society may appropriate to himself such land as he finds vacant.

"In making this argument," Somerville continued, after finishing his cucumber and locating the heel of his roll, "Jefferson was not only disavowing the King's right to the virgin lands of the new world, he was also rejecting the right of all Kings to make hereditary land claims! This was an argument on behalf of America's colonial settlers, not an argument against the private ownership of property.

"Now here's the point," Somerville said, gazing at the remnants of his dinner. "His proximity to France's profligate aristocracy rekindled his natural antipathy toward hereditary government. When Jefferson saw the destitution of the French peasantry against the backdrop of the nobles' lush private parks and wasteful game preserves, he became patriotic all over again. Thus aroused, he began his correspondence with Madison—and de Riedesel. Jefferson said, for example 'hereditary branches of modern governments are the patrons of privilege & prerogative & not of natural rights of the people whose oppressors they generally are ....'" Somerville laid his fork down. "You're confusing his hatred for hereditary government as support for the utopian social doctrine of France's most extreme radicals. If our best minds make this kind of mistake," he added gloomily, "what kind of future is there for our Jeffersonian republic?"

"I hate to be a party pooper, Fenton," the Supreme Court Justice replied, "but chickens come home to roost. The issues that concerned Jefferson have taken on some new shapes, but they're essentially the same. French Physiocrats supported Turgot during his twenty-month tenure as Louis XVI's Comptroller General. What they wanted to do was institute a land tax to pay restitutions to individuals who had been driven off their piece of the earth's common stock ... "

"Hold on," Somerville objected. "It's true that Jefferson was concerned about the aggregation of land in the hands of the privileged few. But he was never opposed to private property. I grant that he intended to use the power of government to redistribute it to create a yeoman class in his new country. But apart from this little sleight of hand, his main interest was to protect individuals from the impositions of *government*! He was constitutionally opposed to authority at every level whether it was an overbearing federal bureaucracy or a council of tribal elders—anything that deprived individuals of their right to pursue their private happiness.

"And besides," he added, "the idea of some communitarian agency holding property in 'common stock' is exactly opposite to what our societal covenant guarantees. According to Locke, 'the condition of human life, which requires labor and materials to work on, necessarily introduces private possessions.' Jefferson only added to it the general observation that inheritance laws are social conventions, not 'natural' laws."

"Let's suppose you're right," Douglas posited. "The practical fact is that the needs of society are elastic. Jefferson understood that when he said, 'every Constitution and every law naturally expires at the end of nineteen years. If it be enforced longer, it is an act of force and not of right." Do you remember that one—to Madison in September of '88 . . ."

"Our laws rest on principles that have been validated by the judgement of time," Somerville replied. "Heaven help us if we become clever enough to circumvent them."

"That's bullshit!" Tim Hardin informed Barry Commoner. "The issue isn't public trust. It's that government can't deliver the services people want and need. You talk about the environment. How is government supposed to clean it up when the means of production are controlled by greedy capitalists who don't give a shit about anything beyond their profits? If they're ever called on the carpet, they pay off a few of our cracker-jack public servants and—presto—the problem goes away!"

"What's your solution?" Commoner asked, lifting his wine glass.

"Jefferson talked about the science of government. Let's create one that follows the principles of science and management. Look at the one we have now," he sneered. "You know where it came from? The dark ages! The white men who settled here arrived with the idea that they would make themselves rich. The systems they set up served the interests of the rich. In the south, it was the big landowners. In the north it was the wealthy merchants and factory owners. Wherever you went, the legislatures and the executive branches of their governments were controlled by small cadres of wealthy men.

"Then Madison and Hamilton came along with their federalist scheme. They asked the same men who controlled the local legislatures and executive offices to implement an overarching central government. At first, they recoiled at the idea because it would have encroached on their authority. But then it dawned on them that they could make themselves even richer in a national government where they would control the public treasury... and dispense government patronage... and administer an expanding bureaucracy. Opportunities for graft came rolling down the pike right on schedule. You remember the assumption issue? That was Hamilton's idea. Jefferson vigorously opposed it. When it was adopted, the bastards who were privy to the plan set about scalping profits from their uninformed neighbors. This produced huge windfalls for some and impoverished others. Other disputes followed the same course–locating the capital, chartering the national bank. You get the picture?"

"Yea..."

"Sectional interests divided the country on the issue of the nation's executive officer. Parties formed. The northern party was led by Alexander Hamilton. The southern party was let by Jefferson. Both were run by scoundrels and liars who were out for nobody but themselves. Jefferson was smart enough to parley the animosity of his supporters into a political movement that got him elected President in 1800. Of course, he won because the stupid Federalists pissed everybody off with their Aliens and Sedition Acts. Jefferson called the election 'the Revolution of 1800.' Ever since then it's been ongoing gang warfare between men who, as Richard Henry Lee once said, 'construed the law most favorably for increasing their own power.' That's democracy in America! Nothing gets done— aside from padding the pockets of the rich. I say it's time to dump the whole damned system. And the people are ready!"

"Ready to do what?" Commoner asked, coyly.

"They're ready to institute Jefferson's original plan!" Hardin announced.

"I haven't heard about that," Walter Cronkite announced, joining the conversation.

"When he got back from France, Jefferson designed a system based on the idea that the way to improve people's lives is to take care of them better. I call it 'prislegeism'!" Hardin explained with growing enthusiasm.

"It's a communitarian idea that merges the welfare that is available in most colleges today with the organizational discipline that you have in a . . ." he cleared his throat, "prisons."

"That's fascinating . . ." Commoner conceded. "This could be an intellectual break through—Jefferson would certainly have appreciated it . . . "

"Exactly," Hardin agreed. "We're standing in one right now!"

"If I'm following you," Cronkite interjected, "it would be like Plato's Republic only its guardians would distribute social services."

"That's how we as social scientists are going to achieve the common good," Hardin declared.

Claire was standing near the door listening as Hardin described Jefferson's communitarian system. Across the room she saw Henry. She drifted around Hardin's circle and came over to him. "I'm ready to go. Are you?"

"Yes," he replied. "It's been a long day."

He followed her into the entrance hall and opened the door.

The parties were still going, and their music was still rolling down Mr. Jefferson's Lawn. They listened for a moment, glad to be somewhere where people were actually enjoying themselves.

"Claire," Henry said.

"What?" She answered, turning reluctantly.

"I want to apologize for being such an ass."

Claire smiled. "Let's just say we're even."

The moon had risen over the Rotunda. "Do you have a minute?" Henry asked.

"What?"

"I thought we could walk a little."

"Let's," she agreed.

They started down the colonnade toward Homer.

"I'm worried," Henry confessed as they strolled along the white columns.

"I know," Claire answered, taking his hand.

"It feels like a freight train's coming, and we're stuck on the tracks," he said, looking off. "It's not just me—it's Mr. Paige, and Oscar, and the Jefferson Academy. Everything's on the line."

"Henry," Claire said, pulling him to a stop. "I'm going to be here . . ."

"You are?" he said, pulling up and looking into her eyes. Claire nodded.

They descended the stairs by Pavilion IX. "Barbara thinks I should take to take the job," Claire said, changing the subject. "What do you think?" She asked.

"I . . . don't know . . ."

"Don't you want me to . . ."

"That's not it," Henry interrupted. "It's . . . Life isn't something you can plot on a chart . . . at least it isn't for me. You're called to do things because you know they're right for you—they resonate. At least that's the way it is here. Is the Jefferson Academy important to you?"

Claire pondered the question. "That's what you were asking me on the porch, wasn't it." she said.

"Yea, I suppose so," he agreed, glancing at her.

"Is this my calling?" She rephrased it.

"I remember once in Professor Home's Wittgenstein class," Henry remembered. "We were discussing theories of knowledge . . . somebody asked him if dogs could talk."

"Funny question," Claire observed.

"Philosophy's like that," Henry agreed.

"What did he say?"

"No . . ."

"How did he know that?"

"That's what my classmate wanted to know," Henry replied. "Home said that if a dog could talk it would!"

Claire laughed. "You're saying that if I were the Jefferson Academy sort, I'd be at the Jefferson Academy . . ."

"Something like that . . ."

"Things happen, and people respond," Claire answered. "Mr. Paige said he *might* run for President," she added, illustrating her point.

"He's a great man," Henry agreed. He paused and looked at her. "Is that what you want?"

"Barbara thought he could win," she said, avoiding the question.

"Is that what you want?"

"That's one of the things I want," Claire admitted.

"It's going to be tough . . ."

"I'm pretty tough," Claire replied.

"You proved that on the terrace," Henry laughed. "That took a lot of guts..."

"It was the right thing for me to do," Claire repeated.

"Good," Henry said. "Then I'll be your friend forever." He leaned over and kissed her cheek.

Claire squeezed his hand. "You know what concerns me," she said, changing the subject. "Roberta—nothing's safe as long as she's haunting Jefferson Country. We need to find out who killed her. Once we've done that..." she stopped, and looked at Henry, "...I'll take the job!"

"Ok! I'm with you." Henry nodded.

They were standing in front of Homer. "But come," Claire recited, "let us talk no more of this, for you and I both know sharp practice, since you are far the best of all mortal men for counsel and stories, and I among all the divinities am famous for wit and sharpness; and yet you never recognized Pallas Athene, daughter of Zeus, the one who is always standing beside you and guarding you in every endeavor..."

Henry stood transfixed as Claire repeated one of his favorite passages from Homer's Odyssey. "Surely," he replied "I was on the point of perishing by an evil fate in my palace, like Atreus' son Agamemnon, unless you had told me, goddess, the very truth of all that has happened. Come then, weave the design, the way I shall take my vengeance upon them; stand beside me, inspire me with strength and courage, as when together we brought down Troy's shining coronal."

Douglas stepped forward to intercept Hardin.

"I told you to stay away," Hardin snapped.

"Tim, we have to talk." Douglas took his protégé by the arm and guided him to the side of the room. "You and Fred must stop this terrorist campaign," Douglas whispered urgently. "Promise me..."

"You're through giving orders," Hardin sneered. "I'm running things now." He started to leave.

"I'm not going to let you destroy what I've spent forty years building," Douglas vowed.

Hardin turned back to him, his face red with anger. "You hide-bound old goat! All you're concerned about is your damned place in history. You're through. Do you hear me! Now stay the hell out of my way or I'll wreck you too." A twisted smile spread across his face. "And I have just the way to do it . . ."

≋

PART III

Henry guided his Comet across the Rivanna River bridge and started up Pantops Mountain. "The Albemarle Lounge is just over the crest of the hill," he said. "That's where Bart Paige hangs out. He's got a booth in the back where does whatever business he does."

"I think we should pay him a visit," Claire announced.

"Oh?"

"He's got some kind of issue with Marjean," she added. "I bet it has something to do with Roberta."

"Could be," Henry allowed, "but I don't think it's a good idea to go in there."

"Why not?"

"For one thing," Henry said, "Paige is a creep."

"Anything else?"

"The Albemarle Lounge serves some pretty tough customers."

"Let's see," Claire replied.

"Are you sure?"

"Nothing ventured, nothing gained," Claire announced, closing the discussion.

"Ok," Henry sighed. "Get ready—there it is." He pointed toward a one-story brick building in a bulldozed clearing on his left. "And there's Paige's truck," he added.

"We have to talk with him," Claire said, ignoring the cold shiver that was running down her spine.

Henry steered into the unpaved parking lot. "This isn't one of your DC networking cafes," Henry repeated as he turned off his engine. "People in there can be pretty unfriendly if they don't like you . . ."

"I can handle it," Claire answered defiantly.

Henry led the way to the door. "Don't forget to smile," he said, opening it.

They stepped into a dark cloud of cigarette smoke and beer seasoned with country music. *Today I started lovin' you again,* a voice warbled through the smoke.

"Merle Haggard," Henry said.

"I'm right back where I've really always been . . . I got over you just long enough to let my heartache mend, but today I started lovin' you again . . ."

"What?" Claire yelled over the noise.

"Never mind . . ."

It took a minute for Claire's eyes to adjust to the dim light. When she could see, she scanned the room. The wall to her left was covered with pictures of hunters standing beside dead deer. In the center was the trophy head of a twelve-point buck. Its antlers grazed the room's suspension ceiling, which was badly stained. The light fixtures were covered with multi-colored cellophane patches like ones she'd seen in store front churches. Glancing down, Claire noticed that she was standing in saw dust.

"It absorbs the beer," Henry explained.

The bar ran the length of the wall opposite the door. Behind the bar, a mirror ran between two stacks of shelves filled with whiskey. The front of the bar was lined with chrome-legged stools. Seated on them were rednecks and sidewinders dressed in country garb. The women with them wore tight jeans and tank tops. To the right of the bar, Claire saw a dance floor. Beyond it was a stage. Beyond that, along the room's back wall, were the booths Henry had mentioned.

Claire focused on the faces reflecting in the mirror. That's when she realized that the men on the stools were all staring at *her*! Just keep smiling, she told herself as Henry led her to the bar. "Name your poison," he said as the bartender approached.

She looked at the bottles that cluttered the boards on either side of her. "I guess I should have a Miller Draft," she answered.

"Smart," Henry whispered out of the side of his mouth. "Make that two Miller Drafts," he told the bartender.

Just then somebody with a deep voice yelled out from the far end of the bar. "Hey dandy, whar'd ya find that perdy gal?"

The blood drained out of Claire's face as the bar crowd jockeyed to get a clear view of her. *Oh Lord!* She prayed. *Get me out of here* ... She held her breath as Henry took a steadying swallow of beer and turned toward the voice. She was about to faint when she saw a smile spread on his face.

"Moose!" Henry hollered back, unable to disguise his relief. "Come on," he said, grabbing his beer. "It's Moose Shifflett!"

Claire followed him down a line of Saturday night women with honky-tonk faces. "Talk about good luck," Henry called over his shoulder.

Claire was too busy avoiding eye contact with the lounge queens to appreciate it—or to hear Ernest Tubbs: *ah'm walkin' tha floor over yooooo ...*"

Moose Shifflett reminded Claire of the Daniel Chester French statue of War she'd seen at Chesterwood during her visit there the previous summer. He was at least six feet six inches tall and about two hundred and eighty pounds. He had close-cropped hair, high cheek bones and small squinty eyes. *Thank God he likes Henry!* Claire rejoiced silently, pressing closer to him.

"You're a long way from Shifflett's Hollow," Henry said, shaking the giant's giant hand. "What brings you down here?"

"Cousin Billy," Moose Shifflett said, nodding toward the bartender. "I hep 'im out Sadurd'y nights—thangs git a little rowdy sometimes." That reminded him, and he scanned the lounge for signs of trouble.

"That's what I hear," Henry observed. "What are you doing the rest of the time?"

"Mosely haul' cattle fer Albemarle Livestock," Moose said, taking a pull on his beer. "Fac dis, ah jes' dropped off a load o' heifers over yonder." He tilted his head toward Belmont Farm.

"At the breeding station?" Henry asked.

"Yup," he answered, staring at Claire.

Henry got the message. "Moose, I'd like to you to meet my friend Claire Fox."

"Hello darlin'," Shifflett said, imitating Conway Twitty. "You an' Henry 're friends, huh? Ah guess that means ah kin dance wif 'er—right, dandy?" He said, throwing an elbow into Henry's ribs.

"Don't let the sun set on you in Tulsa ..." Waylon Jennings warned.

"You won't believe this, Moose," Henry wheezed, holding his side, "but Claire here doesn't know to dance."

"Aw hell!" he said, clapping Henry on the shoulder. "Ah's jus' foolin' with ya. Ah seen ya come in," he said confidentially, "Ah figger'd ya might jes' stay out tha way—tha boys has gotten kina touchy since them strangers come in."

"Thanks for the tip," Henry replied, looking at the crew of long hairs at the far end of the bar. "How about if I buy you a beer," he asked, laying a twenty on the bar.

"Hey Billy," Moose called to his cousin. "Three more." Then he looked at Claire. "Don't many classy gals like you fine ner way in here..."

"I bet there aren't many moose either," she flirted back with an arresting smile.

"Yea," he laughed, "ahm it!"

"Hold on," Henry said, raising his finger. "This's my all-time favorite song!" They listened to Marty Robbins' opening guitar riff for *El Paso*. "Say," he asked. "Is Alton still playing? His cousin Alton and I worked on the same construction crew for a couple summers," Henry explained to Claire. "That's where I met Moose."

"Yea," Moose nodded. "He's got ta doin' gospel music. He's thankin' 'bout startin' a church," Moose added.

"Does that mean he's gonna quit running moonshine?" Henry wondered.

"Ah don't know nuffin 'bout that," Moose grinned.

"I used to buy a pint a week," Henry told Claire.

"Yea," Moose reminisced. "He has tha bes'—no buddy ever went bline..."

"He's just kidding," Henry assured Claire.

"You bin huntin'?" Moose asked, moving on.

"No. I've been too busy. How about you?"

"Naw," he said, "but Alton had himself a time tha other naght..."

"Yea?"

"He was up thar in na park," Moose said, like everybody poached game in the Shenandoah National Park. "He got a young buck raght off. Since it wuz early, 'e kicked some leaves on it an' wen' lookin' fer a'nother..."

"It's a crime to hunt in a national park," Henry explained to Claire. "If they catch you, they take your gun and your car, and put you in jail."

"Really! What happened?" Claire asked, looking back at the moose.

"Cousin Alton's a charmer—ain't 'e Henry," Moose said, glancing down at Henry.

"The sweetest guy I ever met," Henry affirmed to Claire.

"Anyhow, he wen' over tha nex' hill an' in no time he's got himself a big doe. Alton ain't that big, but 'e's strong as 'n ox, so 'e hoists 'er up on nis shoulders an' starts back tha way 'e come. Up 'e comes over tha hill whar 'e lef' 'is buck an' whose stannin' nar but tha game warden!"

"Oh no!" Claire gasped.

"Like ah sed, ain't nothin' ol' Alton caint handle . . . So 'e mosies on down ta whar tha warden's standin' an' looks at tha buck like it's tha firs' tom 'e ever seen it. The warden's givin' 'im this dark look—ya know what ah mean. 'Well how 'bout that!' Alton sez, ignoring it. 'Yoe got one too!'" Moose smacked Henry on the shoulder. "Ain't that jes' like Alton!" he roared.

Before Henry could respond, there was a streak of loud cursing and the crash of furniture and breaking glass. Henry looked over to see an irate redneck pummeling the pinball machine in the corner. "Ho thar!" Shifflett roared, rising off his barstool. "Whadda ya thank yer doin'?"

Henry and Claire watched as he pushed his way through a circle of spectators that had gathered around the miscreant. They were shouting encouragement as he battered the machine into a pile of rubble. Moose stepped up behind him and grabbed his collar. As he pulled him away from the machine, the drunk took a wild swing. Dodging the blow, Moose responded with a quick left to the other's chin that knocked him senseless. "Ah tole you already," he said, dragging the groggy troublemaker to the front door. "Don't be comin' 'roun' here when yer drunk!" With that he lifted him up and threw him out.

Having restored the peace, Moose returned to his place. "Alton wants me ta git inta perfession'l rasslin," Moose said, taking another pull from his beer. "He wance ta be mah manager."

"I hear that there's big money in it," Henry observed.

"Yea," Moose answered with a hungry smile. "Say, did ah tell ya that ah hauled that bull fer Mr. Paige?"

"No," Henry replied.

"Yea—ah picked 'im up a couple days ago."

"Oh yea? Nobody told me about that," Henry confessed. "Which one?"

"The big one . . ."

"You mean Aberon of Belmont?"

"Yea! Him."

"I didn't know he was going anywhere," Henry admitted. "Where'd you take him?"

"Up ta Monticello," Moose answered, swallowing the rest of his beer.

"What's over there?" Henry wondered.

"They got some kina thang goin' on," Shifflett shrugged.

"Who's running it?" Henry asked.

"A German guy–de-sompin er other," Shifflett replied.

"De Riedesel?" Henry and Claire guessed simultaneously.

"That's him . . ."

"Did you meet him?" Claire added.

"Yea."

"What did he look like?" Henry asked.

"Medium size, dark wavy hahr. Had one o' them moustaches—ya know what ah mean?" He said, stroking the corners of his mouth so Henry would get the picture. "Looked lock tha devil's own cousin."

"A rakish looking guy with a Poncho Villa moustache—that's Ried!" Henry announced to Claire. "I wonder what he's doing with Mr. Paige's bull?"

"Dint say . . ."

"I'll have to ask Mr. Paige about that," Henry said, making a mental note. Then he looked at Claire. "We should talk with Bart."

She nodded.

"Is he still back there?" Henry asked, looking at Moose

"Yea . . . ef you'da been here earlier ya coulda heard 'im sang!"

"I didn't know he could sing?" Henry said, showing his surprise.

"He can! He wuz up thar with the ban'. Fokes seemed ta like 'im—he sounds kina lack George Jones!"

"Huh!" Henry shrugged. "Anybody with him back there?"

"A crowd come in a whal ago, an' they wuz talkin', but they moved to thur own booth. Two o' 'em 're reguller guys," he said. "They brung a scarecrow with 'em," he added, referring to Wells. "Tha one that come in after that—with tha injun braids—he like ta set tha place off. An' that bunch at tha end o' tha bar's got ever'body feelin' a little edgy. . . Somebody's gonna do sompin," Moose warned, "an' na shit's gonna hit tha fan."

Henry eyed the strangers at the end of the bar. They were wearing tight leather pants, tye-died T-shirts, and long Rolling Stone hairdos. "Do me a favor Moose," Henry said, sliding a twenty along the bar. "Don't leave 'til we're gone . . ."

"If sompin starts," Shifflett added, slipping the bill into his shirt pocket, "go out tha back door."

"Ok," Henry said, shaking Moose's hand. "See ya' around."

Claire followed him toward the dance floor, which was now full of two-steppers. A rangy female vocalist dressed in a sequin blouse with a red kerchief tied around her neck was singing Loretta Lynn's popular girl song: *If you don't wanna go to Fist City, better detour 'round my town.*"

Paige's eyes brightened when he noticed the blond standing at the end of this table. They dimmed again when he realized it was Claire.

"Hello," Claire said with her most disarming smile. "Mind if we sat down?"

Paige grunted something that Claire interpreted in the affirmative. She slipped on into the seat beside Suzie. Henry slid in beside Paige.

"What kin ah do for ya," Paige asked, eyeing them suspiciously.

"I was hoping to get some information from you."

Henry glanced at Suzie. If looks could kill, Claire would have been dead.

"Like what?" Paige asked, refilling his empty glass of tequila.

"I saw you get hit at the conference yesterday," Claire replied solicitously. "Are you all right?"

"Yep," he said, patting his head. "Ah survived. Now whadda really wanna know?"

"I'm trying to find out about Roberta Wiley," Claire confessed.

"What about 'er," Paige asked, his expression darkened further.

"I'm doing a story on the Jefferson Academy, and I wanted some background information on her."

"Why don't ask him," Paige said, gesturing toward Henry.

"I understand that you introduced her to your father," Claire said, ignoring his question.

"Did he tell you that?" Paige asked, eyeing Henry suspiciously

"Actually no," Claire dissembled. "It was your father."

"Yea," Paige admitted reluctantly. "Ah met 'er raght here! She wuz a real go getter—that's how come Daddy liked 'er." He smiled at Suzie. "Ah din't see 're after that."

"Did she have much contact with your sister and her friend?" Claire continued.

"Ah ain't got no ahdea," he said after swallowing his tequila.

"How about you," Claire asked. "Do you have much interaction with your sister or Marjean?"

"Ah thought you wuz askin' 'bout Roberta," Paige answered, suspicion coming into his voice.

"I'm curious about the Belmont community," Claire explained. "It's uniquely . . . diverse. Don't you think?"

"Ah s'pose," he said without having the slightest idea what she was talking about.

"I understand, for example, that your sister's dome is the only structure Buckminster Fuller ever built in Virginia."

"He kin take tha damn thang back—an' them with it," Paige said. "Ah don't want nuffin ta do with any of 'em."

"If that's the case," Claire observed, "what were you doing spying on them this morning?"

"Whadda ya mean?" He asked, glancing at Suzie.

"Your truck was parked on the hill above the dome while I was visiting with them this morning," Claire replied. "Are you denying you were there?"

"Ah mighta been over thar . . ." he allowed. ". . . checking mah cattle. Ain't that right, Baby Doll."

She nodded. "Some people *work* down here," Suzie announced haughtily.

"I hear you sent Aberon of Belmont over to Monticello," Henry observed.

"Whud you say?" Paige snapped.

"I said I heard that you sent Aberon of Belmont over to Monticello."

"Well . . . uh . . . yea, we done . . ." Paige mumbled, glancing again at Suzie.

"My friend said he delivered it to a guy named de Riedesel . . ."

Paige squinted like he was thinking."

"You know him?" Henry asked.

"Sure ... ah mean ... 'e's doin' a program up thar," Paige lied, "It's ...
ah ..."

"It's a secret!" Suzie announced.

"Thomas Jefferson had a friend name de Riedesel," Henry observed.

"Yea!" Paige nodded, happy to change the subject. "Ried tole me
that ..."

"Ried knows about Baron de Riedesel? Henry responded, knitting his
eyebrows.

"Sure," Paige boasted, taking over the conversation. "He had a book
with 'is letters in it! Din't you know that?"

"No."

"Ah'll tell ya sompin else ah betcha don't know ..."

"What's that?" Henry asked.

"That de Riedesel feller got Jefferson ta put that frieze on nis mantle—
it's got the secret of the universe in it!"

"Really!" Henry marveled. "Did Ried tell you that too?"

"Yep—he tole me it wuz in nis book."

"Maybe that's where Hardin saw Jefferson's constitution," Claire observed, looking at Henry.

"Sounds likely," Henry agreed. "Now let me tell you something,"
Henry said, leaning forward toward Paige.

"Yea?" Paige said suspiciously.

"De Riedesel's the guy whose got your father's bull up at Monticello,
and he's Fred Ried!"

"It ain't Ried," Paige said, setting his glass down slowly.

"How do you know that," Claire asked.

"'Cause Ried's <u>dead</u>—blew himself to kingdom come!"

Henry and Claire walked past the corner booth on their way to the exit
Moose mentioned.

Henry's eyes landed on Wells. He also recognized Tad McCray who
was seated next to him. They were huddled with someone Henry did not
know. He wasn't a Charlottesville softy. He looked like a killer. Henry hurried Claire past the booth and out the door.

Two vehicles were parked behind the bar. One was a VW van painted to look like a Greyhound bus with the words 'Country Dog' printed in large black letters on its side panels. Beside it was a limo with tinted windows and government plates.

"You know anybody who drives a limousine in DC?" Henry asked as they made their way to the front parking lot?

"That looks like the one I saw at the Boar's Head Inn this afternoon," Claire said, climbing into the passenger's seat of Henry's bronze Comet.

"And the one I parked next to in the lot on the Corner. . ." Henry added.

Who could this be, Ogden wondered as he lifted the receiver beside his bed.

"Martin? Is that you?"

Ogden recognized Douglas's gravelly voice. "Yes Bill!" He said, still feeling tense.

"I looked for you at dinner, but Barbara told me that you'd left. Are you all right?"

"Ahh . . . yes . . . ahh . . . something unexpected came up," he answered cryptically.

"You'll never guess what I discovered," Douglas continued, excitement coming into his voice.

"What?"

"Somerville has the journal!"

"The missing journal?" Ogden echoed.

"Somerville has it in his desk at Monticello!"

"You've found Burr's Unicorn!" Ogden exclaimed with a triumphant laugh.

"Yes . . . and more importantly, I've located my letter!"

"What a stroke of good fortune," Ogden murmured, picturing the story on *The Post's* front page. "We've got to get it. Where did you say it is?"

"In Somerville's office on the second floor of the mansion," Douglas repeated. "That's why I'm calling. I'm going over there first thing in the morning. I'll call you when I get back—are you going to be there?"

"I'll wait . . ."

"The God's are smiling on us once more, Martin," Douglas announced.

Henry pulled to a stop in front of his cottage and gazed out across the moonlit valley. "It's nice to be home," he said, taking a deep breath. It was another sultry night, and the moon was near full.

"Yes," Claire agreed, sharing the moment. "There's something about the evenings here..."

They climbed out of the car and passed through the gate into the yard. As they approached the steps to the porch, Henry reached out and touched Claire's hand. "I want to make love to you in the moonlight."

Claire turned back and looked into his eyes. Then, without speaking, she led him to a place in the lawn where the moon was full in view. Henry pulled back. "I have something for you," he said.

"What is it?" She asked smiling expectantly.

"A poem..."

She giggled in delight. "Tell me."

"It goes like this: *Slip off your cloak the moon whispered glowing...*" As he spoke, he unbuttoned her blouse. She moved her arms and let it fall to the ground behind her. He set his hands on her hips and kissed her. She gazed receptively into his eyes as his fingers released the clasp on her trousers. "*...And I'll gild your body with silvery light...*" He said as he slipped his thumbs over the waistbands of her panties and easing them down. She waited as he finished undressing her, then stepped away and stood naked before him. Her body glowed in the shimmering light. Henry lowered himself onto the grass and clasped his hands behind his head, never taking his eyes off her. *"Now charm the stars that hold your fate..."* She smiled down at him, then raised her arms toward the sky, commanding the heavens to behold her. "*...And make them court you through the night.*" She sank down beside him and opened his tie. "*...They'll guide you safely through the dawn,*" he said as she undressed him. *"To greet the new day full and strong."* When she had finished her chore, she settled on top of him, like a cat in his lap.

She perched on her elbows and looked down into his face, her fingers outlining aimless circles on his temples. "Full and strong..." she mused. "I like that." She lowered her head and kissed him. "You get an A-plus in poetry."

"Am I right?" He asked looking up into her eyes.

"Sometimes," she smiled. "Like now . . ." She rolled onto her back and pulled him on top of her.

—————

Claire woke to the sound of water drumming in the shower. She was in Henry's bed. She looked out the window across the field into the new day. She turned back to see Henry coming through the door. He wore a towel around his waist. He was drying his hair with another one. "Good morning," he said cheerfully. "How are you?"

"I'm *strong*—and hungry!" she announced.

"I have just the thing . . . black coffee."

"With toast and marmalade?"

"With toast and marmalade."

She sprang naked from the bed and came toward him. "Good!" She said, brushing catlike against him.

—————

They crossed the Rivanna at Randolph's Mill. It was 6:50.

"Look in the back there," Henry said, gesturing with his thumb toward the back seat. "See if you can find my small crowbar."

Claire climbed up and leaned over the seat. She rummaged for a moment in the well behind the seat then held up a fifteen-inch metal rod with curved beveled ends. "Is this it?" She asked.

"Yea . . ."

"What are you going to do with it?" She asked, settling back into her seat. "

"I'm going to steal the journal," Henry announced.

"You're going to *steal* the journal!" Claire repeated, staring at him in surprise.

"Well," Henry said, correcting himself. "I'm going to borrow it . . ."

"You think it has the key to the diagram," Claire surmised, guessing his motive.

"Yea," Henry nodded. "I have a lot riding on it . . ."

He was right. "That was interesting what Paige said," she observed.

"I'd like to know why Ried sent the journal to Somerville," Henry added.

"Do you think Roberta's murder could be connected to Hardin's conspiracy?" Claire asked, looking at Henry.

"There's something strange about that skull," he answered, meeting Claire's eyes.

"You have a plan!" She exclaimed, poking him in the ribs.

"Remember when Fenton described how Jefferson expanded the house?"

"Yes."

"He said there was a sealed door in Jefferson's closet."

"Yea!" Claire said, picturing the door at the head of Jefferson's pass-through bed.

"How about this?" Henry proposed. "When we're finished our work, you tell Fenton that you'd like to see the Tea Room again."

"Why the Tea Room," she asked.

"Because it's at the other end of the house," Henry explained. "Tell him you want to see the busts or something. He'll be eager to accommodate you! Get him to take you across the balcony. On the way, I'll excuse myself to visit the head. Then I'll duck down the south stairs . . ."

"But instead of going to the restroom, you'll sneak into Jefferson's closet, climb the ladder to the storage room, and poke through the wall into his office!"

Claire re-examined the crowbar. "Why not just use the door?" She wondered, glancing at Henry. "That would be easier—wouldn't it?"

"That would mean I'd have to carry the journal a lot farther."

"Why? What are you going to do with it?"

"You're going to love this," he said, laughing.

"What?"

"I'm going to hide it in the commode!"

A look of admiration spread on Claire's face. "Henry! You're brilliant!"

"Thank you," he agreed. "Then we'll sneak over and get it tonight."

". . . with the keys Oscar gave you," Claire added. She considered the plan. "It might just work."

"Once I've stashed the journal, I'll join you in the Tea Room. Just keep asking him questions until I get there."

"I can do that," Claire announced.

"What a team!" Henry beamed.

Henry turned into the entrance and followed the second roundabout to the pedestrian crossing. The gate beyond it was open.

He proceeded through it and continued up the mountain. A moment later, they emerged from the woods. Above them was the sun-bathed orchard, its dew-covered grass sparkling like diamonds in the morning light. They drove past the dogwood field to the mountain's north face. This brought them to an intersection. The staff parking lot rose on their left. On their right, a spur led down the hill to the groundskeeper's sheds and the lower gardens. Further on was the third roundabout. Some way below it was the Rivanna River. Just ahead of them, near the crest of the hill, was the jitney stop at the front of the mansion.

Henry entered the parking area and guided the car to a space near the gift shop. Fenton Somerville was waiting for them on the balcony. "You're right on time," he called down as they mounted the stairs to Mulberry Row.

He met them at the top of the stairs. "Good morning Miss Fox," he beamed. "Mr. Tilghman," he said, extending his hand. "Good of you to come! Are you ready to go to work?"

"I'm ready." Henry said, showing the curator his Cassall's German/English dictionary.

Somerville led them across Mulberry Row to a set of brick steps. They mounted to the first landing. Somerville turned left there and stepped onto the brick terrace. Angling to the right, he led them past the kitchen and into the south passage. "Bill Douglas will be joining us," he explained as they proceeded toward the cellar's south entrance. "He has his own keys so we can go ahead and get started."

They were in the ninety-foot passage that ran beneath the south promenade. One like it also entered the cellar from the north side of the house. Both had worn stone floors and white-washed stone walls. They were illuminated by seven semi-circular windows mounted shoulder-level in the western wall. Claire and Henry followed the curator to the heavy metal grate that served as the cellar's exterior door. Somerville opened it with a large silver key like the one Trip had given Henry the previous afternoon. He then guided them forward into the lower level of the mansion. They passed under Jefferson's bedroom and into a gallery that filled the space below the entrance hall. The doors along the west wall of the cellar opened into storage rooms. Ignoring these, Somerville turned into the exhibit area and approached a door in the gallery's south wall. Unlocking it, he pushed it open and gestured for his companions to enter.

Claire and Henry stepped into a small windowless anti-room with modern lightening and a polished tile floor. "This is the guide's lobby," Somerville informed them. Through the door to their left was a modern kitchen. Ahead of them were the stairs up to the residence. Beyond the stairway was a security station. A passage led from the security area to the front corner of the house. Along the way were a restroom and the guide's dining area. Somerville identified them as they approached the stairs.

Two circuits around the closet-sized stairway brought them to the second floor. Somerville led them across the windowless hall to a door with his name on it. "Here we are," Somerville said, unlocking it and pushing it open. Henry followed Claire into a room the size of Jefferson's cabinet, which was directly below. "This is my nest," Somerville announced, joining them.

The room was packed with books and papers. It therefore seemed much smaller than Jefferson's. Its only window was below the chair rail in the south wall. Although it faced the light, it was obscured by Somerville's cluttered desk. The room therefore had, as he suggested, a dark nest-like atmosphere.

Henry eyed the north wall. "Is that the door to Jefferson's closet," he asked pointing to a faint recess in the wall.

Somerville stepped forward and drew an outline on the wall above an overloaded side table. "It is right here, in the center of the room," he said.

"So that part of the wall is just plaster over lath," he observed, studying the position of the partition blocking the doorway.

"That's right," Somerville nodded. With that he returned to his desk. He fumbled a moment with his keys. Finding the right one, he opened the top drawer. "And here is the manuscript," he announced, extracting a thick manila envelope."

Henry stepped forward to see as Somerville unsheathed it. Done, the curator placed it ceremoniously on the desk and stepped back like the Archbishop of Canterbury after crowning a monarch. "Behold!" He intoned. "Baron de Riedesel's gift to posterity!"

"Can we touch it?" Claire asked sheepishly.

"I should think so," Somerville replied. "We have to comb out its secrets, don't we?"

Claire lifted it off the table and studied the ox skull on its cover. "This is the same as the frieze on the mantle," she observed.

"I noticed that," Somerville confirmed. "I'd say it portends some interesting reading . . ." With that he turned to Henry. "Now young man, the spotlight rests on you!"

Henry took the portfolio into his hands and began to leaf through it. As he did, he considered how best to proceed with the work. "Dr. Somerville," he said, "I think it would be more productive if I translate and Claire transcribes."

"Is that agreeable to you, Miss Fox?" Somerville inquired.

"Yes," she replied. "That's a good idea."

Henry continued to thumb through the book's uneven pages as Claire scanned the apartment for a suitable place to work.

"Here," Somerville said, reading her thoughts. "Let me clean this up." He shuffled the papers on his desk into a pile, then set them on a shelf beside his desk.

"We're going to need another chair," Claire said, looking about the room.

Somerville straightened up. "You're absolutely right!" He exclaimed. "Let me see . . . I'll just borrow one from the guide's library across the hall." With that he turned and marched out of the room.

"Claire!" Henry whispered urgently. He was holding a twice-creased piece of stationery. "This is from the United States Supreme Court!" He mouthed the words in amazement. Before he could say more, he was interrupted by the sound of Somerville returning with the chair. Henry refolded the letter and slipped it into his coat pocket.

In the next instant Somerville appeared. "Here you are," he said, sliding the chair up to his desk. "How's that?"

"Perfect!" Claire smiled, settling herself on the borrowed chair and pulling out the writing panel above the desk's left-hand drawers. "Now all I need is some paper—and a pen."

Somerville turned back to the shelf beside his desk and lifted a legal pad from the top of a stack. "And there are your pens," he added, setting a box of Bics down in front of her.

Henry laid the journal down in the space Somerville had just cleared and took the seat beside Claire. The book was opened to the page where

Henry found the letter. "Now let me see," he said, cracking his knuckles like Victor Borge warming up for a concert. "This document was written in Washington on June 12, 1801."

"So far so good!" Somerville cheered.

"Dear Sir—I hope it pleases you to hear that I have at long last decided to implement your recommendation for the molding in the parlor! You thought I would never make up my mind. But as the poet said, alleum res tempus!" Henry paused. "What does that mean Dr. Somerville?"

"Things take time," he replied.

"Huh ... where was I? *"... In the end, oddly enough, it was not the Palladian form that decided the matter—though God knows how many sleepless nights that caused me! I chose it because it fit as a memorial to my victory over the monarchists! Name if you can a more fitting place to celebrate the triumph of light over darkness. Isn't it ironic that I alone will see it for what it is! I have taken a liberty and introduced a minor alternation to the panel over the hearth,"* Henry looked at Claire. "Are you getting this?"

"Yes! It's fascinating. You were just discussing it the other evening, remember Fenton."

"Certainly. What does he say about it?"

"You recall, of course, the words of Pallas Athene—behind the mask of him whom the gods love is the secret of the house. That sounds like some kind of clue doesn't it?" Henry observed, looking at the curator.

"Ha," Somerville cried. "I know that passage. "It's from *The Odyssey*. She had taken the form of Eumaios—Odysseus' 'faithful swineherd,' and in that form she was revealing to Telemachus that his father had returned to Ithaka to re-claim his estate."

Just then, they heard the footsteps of someone coming up the stairs.

"That will be Bill," Somerville announced.

"Fenton?" A voice called. "Are you there?"

"In the office, Bill. Come on back..."

A second later, the longest serving member of the United States Supreme Court appeared in the doorway. Behind him in the shadows Henry recognized the man in the booth with Wells and McCray.

Douglas's eyes landed immediately on the journal. Like an iron filing drawn by a magnet, he was pulled to the desk. "Do you mind?" He said, nudging Henry aside.

"No not at all," Henry replied, marking the tension in the jurist's face.

Somerville, Claire, and Henry watched in silence as the wizened Justice seated himself and began paging through the document. He became increasingly agitated as his search advanced. "It's not here!" He exclaimed, turning to Somerville.

Somerville smiled back at him benignly. "What's that Bill?"

Douglas glared at the curator, then caught himself. "Why... er ... Jefferson's constitution."

"That's in here?" Somerville exclaimed. "How ingenious of you to know it. Is it in one of his letters? See if they're listed chronologically..."

Douglas flipped through a few more pages, then he stood up. "I'm going to take a closer look at this at my office," he said, gathering the journal under his arm. "I'll send it down when I'm finished."

A perplexed look appeared on Somerville's face. "You're welcome to look at it here," he said, "but I would violate my fiduciary responsibility if I allowed it to leave the premises. I'm sure you understand..."

"I see," Douglas snapped, setting the book back on the desk. "Thank you for your time." With that, he turned and stormed out of the room.

"I'll send you a copy when we've finished translating it," Somerville called after him.

"Woooh!" Claire exclaimed as though she had touched something hot. "Is he always like that in the morning?"

"Let's see if there is an index," Henry said, taking back his seat. He turned to the front of the journal. "Yes. This looks like it." He was staring at a page with a numbered list. "Are you ready Claire?"

"Ready," she answered.

"The first item is entitled a *Certificate of Initiation to Der Konigs Kameraderiegesellschaft der Wachtkorp*–I guess that could be translated as the Company of the King's Guardians."

"Interesting," Somerville responded.

"The second is a *Report on the Formation of the General Staff of the Army*... am I going too fast?"

"No—you're fine," Claire replied without looking up.

"Good... The third is a *Notification of Appointment* – to the *Planning Board of the Prussian Army*. The fourth is the Baron's *Appointment* as *Commissioner of Manpower and Training*—wow he was really up the ladder wasn't he!" Henry exclaimed, looking at the curator.

"Oh! This is fun," Somerville shivered with excitement.

"The fifth item," Henry continued, "seems to be a report from the Commission of Manpower and Training. The title is *A Summary of Military Requirements.*" He paused so Claire could catch up. "The sixth is entitled *A Proposal for Enhancing the Fitness and Endurance of Conscripts.* There's a sub-entry here which says *Practical Applications for Organic Stimulants to Promote the Endurance and Physical Prowess of the Common Soldier.* I bet that's interesting reading," Henry mused, looking at Somerville.

"I'm sure it will be," Somerville concurred with academic intensity.

"The seventh looks like a draft for a *Plan to Unify the German States,*" Henry announced, returning to the list.

"We must remember that the German states were evolving into a nation at that time," Somerville noted.

Henry nodded as if it had been on his mind. "The eighth is: *Death-notice for His Royal Highness Frederick II King of Prussia,*" he reported, glancing at Claire. He waited a moment for her to complete the record, then continued. "The ninth is a report titled *How to Win the Coming War with France.* Ahh!" He exclaimed with sudden interest. "The tenth item is a header–*Letters: Summer 1785 – Fall 1789.* Here is another header for *Letters: Winter – 1790.*"

"Those would have been written after Jefferson returned from France!" Somerville observed enthusiastically. "That means we'll learn about the conflicts in Washington's cabinet."

"Do you see a reference to Burr's Unicorn" Claire asked.

"Not in the Index," Henry replied, reviewing the list. "Shall we begin with the letters," he asked, turning to that section. "I expect they will be more interesting than the Baron's reports."

"That's fine," Somerville replied. "I'll sit and listen. If anything comes to mind, I'll just pipe up."

"Please do," Henry nodded. He then returned to his work. "The first letter is from Jefferson to de Riedesel. It's dated *Paris, December 14, 1784.* Ready Claire?"

"Ready," she saluted with a wave of her pen.

"'*Sir*,' it begins, '*what an unexpected pleasure to find that you are stationed in Paris! And that you attend Madame Helvetius's celebrated salon! I know from Dr. Franklin that the elegant lady is carrying on a tradition established by her late husband.*'"

"By the way," Somerville interjected, "Claude Helvetius was a wealthy financier who transformed himself into a philosophe by eavesdropping on conversations that took place at the salon of Baron Holbach. The Baron was also known to Jefferson, who owned several copies of his great work, *The System of Nature*. Holbach embraced the materialistic philosophy of Descartes and wrote several anti-religious tracts, all of which influenced Helvetius. Helvetius had become a Freemason in 1747, and 'fellowcraft' colored his interpretation of the Baron's sweeping critiques. In Helvetius's hands, genius owed to the excellence of one's education, and social virtues reduced to utilitarian standards based on the needs of society . . . All the best people, the Dauphin, Rousseau, and Voltaire, for example, condemned his great work, *De l'esprit*," Somerville continued, "and it was publicly burned . . . Now that I think of it," the scholar added, "Helvetius visited Frederick the Great in Berlin in 1765—I wonder if he met the Baron there?"

"Perhaps he tells us," Henry replied, returning to the letter. ". . . Madame Helvetius carried on the tradition established by her . . . Ah! Here we are . . . "*I am anxious to attend one of her gatherings to see what they are. But alas! The good Doctor has told me nothing of how men who commune there conduct themselves . . . Without some schooling, I fear I should violate some common protocol and ruin myself in their eyes. This would be a disaster since I have come to France join their society. I would therefore welcome the opportunity to draw on your familiarity with the social and political terrain in order to tailor my manners and speech to succeed in my 'secret' mission. Thus far, my diplomatic career has been singularly unspectacular as there is nothing for me to do but to pretend industry. I take pleasure in this, I must confess, as it affords me time to assemble my notes on Virginia for publication. I see this as the means to establish myself in the estimation of Chastellux's enlightened peers. Perhaps you are familiar with a reliable printer who can be trusted with such a personally important job.* It's signed *TH. Jefferson*

"Excellent Mr. Tilghman. Excellent!" the curator exclaimed. "Your translation is clean and true to his voice.

"Thank you, Dr. Somerville. I appreciate the compliment."

"Shall we try another?" Somerville suggested.

"This next one is <u>to</u> Jefferson," Henry continued. "It's dated *Paris—January 3, 1785: My dear friend, permit me to share a few facts about the society you have decided to join so it does not disappoint you. In the first place, for all its cultural glitter and presumption, it has <u>two</u> generic classes. That which is called the 'Public' is the literate upper crust of the Gaulish leviathan. The other is known as the 'Populace'. This is a sump of ignorant, low, and unhealthy scum. The philosophes who seem so charming from a distance are of course among the former. In time, I have no doubt that they will demonstrate to you what a disreputable lot they are. They are for most part treacherous and clever to the degree they are able to veil their seditions in a miasma of philosophic gas. By order, these are either nobles with private grievances against the Court (because they have not been appropriately favored), or lawyers, bureaucrats, and clerics (who resent the anonymous living they receive at the King's pleasure). What I find most disturbing is their enthusiasm for an ideology that rests on the ridiculous proposition that a horde, which is by nature violent, ignorant, and base, can govern itself! Read Plato's* Republic *and tell me what has changed in two thousand years! All you need do is go among the common people. The truth is plain to see. You will find in their collective mind not a candle's worth of enlightened reason. There is no Metaphysics beyond pre-historic superstition; no method beyond self-interest; no mathematics at all. What then is this social revolution Madame's salon is promoting? Imagine if you can the character of the society this rabble would create if—God help us—it ever acquires the power rule. The mind numbs! How would it maintain itself other than through murder and robbery—it knows nothing more! Fortunately, the liberal cabal that has set itself to undermine the authority of the government is an insignificant minority. The Populace, for all its poverty and misery, shares none of its revolutionary zeal. They want only cheap bread and wine to wash it down. No indeed! Injustice and oppression, which are the natural order of things, are not causing the rabble to organize? That is the handiwork of the King's own cousin. The Duc d'Orleans and his friends are deliberately undermining the King's sovereignty and the authority of his government through misapplication of the Duc's wealth. And for what purpose? Power! He seeks the scepter for himself. Unless you have been totally disoriented by the salon fumes, you still understand the facts of nature. Despite the rantings of the salon cognoscenti, men are savages. Even fools know that* *the state of nature is a __dangerous__ place! I assure you that if the Duc succeeds in undercutting the King, there will be blood in the streets—not the empire of enlightened reason heralded by the philosophes. There are enough thugs and murderers in the slums of Paris alone to snuff out the light in every salon in the world. One day a madman will emerge from his garret and persuade them that lunatics like M. Rousseau and cynics like his nemesis M. Voltaire make sense. If you want an honest picture of the perfect society they will form, go listen to that mongrel Marat in the Cordeliers and imagine what it would be like answering to a legislature filled with men of his ilk! It is interesting to contrast the orgy of enlightened pretentiousness that takes place in Madame's salon with the movement that is bringing the German-speaking peoples toward nationhood. I look forward to talking with you about this. In the meantime, I will send you a copy of the report that I prepared for His Highness the King of Prussia. Let me say that I found the services of Philippe-Denis Pierres on Rue Saint-Jacques most satisfactory in producing this small edition of my study on German Unification. It is signed: F. de.R.*

"It sounds like he is writing about us," Claire groaned.

"Yes," Somerville agreed. "There are many parallels between his society and times and ours."

"Shall we do another," Henry asked.

"By all mean," the curator agreed. "Are you able to continue Miss Fox?"

"Absolutely!" Claire replied firmly.

"This is from Jefferson. It is dated Paris March 12, 1785: *Meine liebe Herrn–I am delighted to see that time has not dulled your Teutonic edge. Your assessment of the political situation here might provoke another man. But I, well-remembering your military prowess, will not be goaded into a frontal assault. I do not dispute your observations, but I contend that the corruptions of hereditary government are legitimate grounds for rebellion and that those who seek to apply methods of science to improve society should be commended. To those who gather in the name of reason at Vore' I say Bravo! You are too quick in dismissing the evils against which the liberal spirit rebels. Being now a diplomat in service to my country, it is my profession to accept your views with equanimity. However, in respect to the efforts of France's progressives, I perceive them to be in the same heroic service as the patriots who brought political freedom to America. Contrary to your thesis, that did not lead to anarchy. The fruit of that conflict was the establishment of the rights of man as the basis for government. Indeed, it is the motto of my country—Opposition to tyranny is service to God! The first duty of our citizens is to put an end to despotism. I do not yet know the character of France's "populace", but I cannot imagine that, should it rise up against tyranny, it would accept anything less than a government formed in the light of Reason. This is the passion of the leading reformers—Rochefoucauld, Lafayette, Condorcet and their circle. In this opinion, I have been much persuaded by the work of M. Cabanis who has substantially codified human behavior into a new branch science. I know of no enlightened person who finds fault in applying the scientific methods of Bacon and Newton to the study of man himself. So what if political considerations underlie this research? Surely they do not outweigh the benefits science will bring to man in society! In this light, I turn to your penetrating report on the unification of the Germans. Is it not ironic that you judge the Offenlichkeit of the 'literarische Kultur' to be the essential power in the advance toward German nationhood? Why should it be an uplifting force east of the Rhine and a danger to society west of it? I will have my own manuscript published in two months. When I took up the project shortly after your arrival in Charlottesville, my purpose was to defend the New World against the arrogance of the old. Is it not ironic—that the silent object of my labor is now to achieve the recognition among its cognoscente! To accomplish this, I am expanding my first printing by a factor of ten. (Let it not be said that the glory of enlightened acclaim is not a potent narcotic.) The list of recipients grows daily. As many copies are now destined for scholarly readers in England and the rest of the continent as here. I hope you will not be offended to hear that I have reserved the first copy for Chastellux. His perfect character and intellect represent my greatest source of inspiration. And of course, there are the political considerations. It is my hope that he will agree to deliver copies to Buffon and Daubenton whose theories I have conclusively refuted. Among the 'philosophes', I have included the Marquis de Condorcet (who I'm told is the youngest to gain membership to the Academie de Science), and the Abbe Morellet (who is soon to be inducted into the Academie Francaise). I have already shown the Abbe the manuscript at the request of Chastullux and he has expressed delight) Then, of course there is yourself, Lafayette, Diderot, duPort, St Etienne, Corney, and my American colleagues. Hearing your views in respect to the character of these men would be most interesting to me. I close with the news that I have found a residence that completes the picture I have of myself as a renaissance man. They tell me that the Hotel de Langeac was built to house the mistress of the King. It is indeed lovely. It will cost more than I can afford, but I am compelled to implement certain alterations to make it suitable for a gentleman's household. I expect to take up residence in the fall.* This is also signed *TH. Jefferson.*

"Is it not interesting that three-hundred years after Newton re-defined the conflict between reason and nature that it continues to bedevil us," Somerville observed. "I suppose it always will . . ."

"Let's do one more," Claire said, "then I'm going to need a break."

"Ok," Henry agreed. "The next one is to Jefferson and dated Potsdam June 5, 1785: *Liebe Freunde–accept my apologies for the delay in this answer to your last letter. I know you will excuse me because I have been laboring strenuously on your behalf. As you know, the King does not actively embrace the idea of a commercial treaty with the United States. His Majesty's indifference owes little to his official friendship with the Court in London. Rather it is a part of his characteristic reluctance to make agreements that do not enhance his strategic position. I am happy to report that the issue has at last been resolved in your favor. The persuading factor was the King's decision to endorse my recommendation concerning the proposal for the treatment of noncombatants and prisoners of war. This is what you would call a trial balloon. Dr. Franklin's draft appears to be acceptable to His Majesty and I expect that an authorization to sign it will be issued shortly. I am most anxious to counsel you privately before you become completely disoriented by narcotic vapors of the salons. Clearly you do not appreciate the danger in opening the floodgates of disorder. Your faith in the progressive thinkers who are certainly the most unproductive members of this debauched society causes me grave concern. Europe is not an empty space like the new world. If a revolution were to start here, it could spread anarchy across the entire continent. Your rebellion did not produce a republican government because propagandists incited the people to overthrow what you characterize as 'despotism.' It formed because your wilderness empire is populated by Englishmen who understand what liberty is. If it were filled with men who think like peasants and slaves, do you think the result would have been the same! Do not confuse rationalist visions of perfection with the common good. In the real world, the common good rests on social order, which is rooted in force! Mark my words, one good regiment can do more good in this ungodly world than all the nagging prattlers in all of its universities. As for your book, I have no doubt that it will be a success. Schemers like Robespierre, Mirabeau, St Etienne, and Sieyes are always hoping to prove that the unperfectable can be perfected. Perhaps you have discovered the secret of Paracelsus? Or located DeSoto's fountain of youth? Of the men you name, I know a few things. To understand them you must first know something about Mme Helvetius' departed spouse, Claude-Adrien. He is the yeast that makes the loaf rise. It takes but a glance to see that he is another one of Frances's greatest hot air balloons—a paragon of self-indulgence and false logic. I shall send you shortly a paper documenting these observations. For your own sake, my friend beware! F. deR.*"

"Do you suppose he said anything about Sally Hemings!" Claire wondered.

"That's a good question," Henry agreed.

"It's just 10:00," Somerville said, looking at his watch. "We have plenty of time."

"When did she arrive in France?" Henry asked, turning the pages forward.

"In June of 1787," Somerville replied.

"Here's a letter Jefferson wrote in April from <u>Nice</u>," Henry observed, looking at the curator. "What was he doing in Nice?"

"He took a number of trips while he was in France," the curator explained. "The one to the south of France is perhaps the most interesting..."

"Why is that?" Claire asked.

"Because he was clearing his mind after encountering Maria Cosway," Somerville replied. "Poor devil—he was as unsuited for love as he was for war."

"How so," Claire wondered.

"Do you know anything about Maria Cosway?" he asked.

"No..."

"Well then!" Somerville announced. "I will give you a sketch... If you don't understand Maria Cosway, you can't possibly understand Sally Hemings. Let me see," he said reflectively. "Maria Cosway was one of several women with whom Jefferson socialized during his tenure in France. The others were arguably more eminent," he observed. "Three were American," he added. "These were Abigail Adams, Angelica Schuyler Church, and Anne Willing Bingham. Five were French. Madame de

Tesse was Lafayette's aunt. Madame d'Houdetot had once been the apple of Rousseau's eye. Madame de Tott was a friend of Madame de Tesse and an Homeric scholar. Madame de Corney was the wife of Ethis de Corney. Corney had been Lafayette's aide during the American Revolution. In 1784, he was at the center of a formidable network of revolutionary operatives in Paris. Madame de Brehan was the sister-in-law of Count de Moustier—there was rascal!" Somerville added.

"Maria was of English stock," he continued. "She was described by a contemporary as a 'golden-haired Anglo-Saxon, graceful to affectation and highly accomplished in music.'

"Her maiden name was Maria Hadfield," Somerville continued. "She was born in Leghorn, Italy in 1759, to a successful English hotelier and his Italian wife. Tragically, a deranged nurse murdered six of her brothers and sisters while she was a child. This frightening experience seems to have inspired in her the deep-seated religious faith that eventually called her to take the holy orders. Her father was moderately well-off and provided her with a liberal education in her home city of Florence. She studied music and painting. We can see that she was gifted by her election to the Florentine Academia del Designo. She went on to study in Rome with Pompeo Batoni who some considered the greatest artist of his day.

"When her father died in 1781, the family went to London where Angelica Kauffman took Maria under her wing. A painter herself, Kauffman introduced Maria to her circle of connections including the antiquarian/collector Charles Townley whom Maria had known in Florence. One of the painters in Townley's entourage was a man named Richard Cosway. This chameleon-like fellow was just beginning to flourish as the court painter for George III's debauched son.

"A year in London depleted the Hadfield inheritance," Somerville explained. "Maria's mother therefore began searching for a suitable match for her charming daughter. Richard Cosway appears to have been the high bidder.

"Maria's marriage to Richard was thus one of mutual convenience. He was able to provide for her material needs. In return, she was an attractive companion who promoted his career by charming his patrons. They entertained lavishly at Schomberg House, their home on Pall Mall. Maria soon acquired the reputation as an international hostess whom envious gossip linked romantically with the Prince of Wales, the Italian castrato Luigi Marchesi, and the Corsican general Pasquale Paoli among others.

"Cosway encouraged her flirtations but thwarted her artistic development. This pattern of behavior evidently reflected his concern over his own position, which was a distinguishing characteristic.

"Apart from these practical matters, Maria seemed to have no relationship with Richard. In modern parlance, I suppose it would be said that the marriage was stifling to her. On the other hand, Cosway made few demands upon her, and he did provide her with an interesting, comfortable life. Under the circumstances, it is easy to see how Maria would have retreated into herself," Somerville confided. "In this process, she must have become increasingly coy. Here was a highly intelligent, talented, and complex woman, trained by necessity in the art of guile. It would have been difficult to draw her out from behind her defenses—don't you think?" He asked.

"I suppose so," Claire said, nodding.

"John Trumbull, the great interpreter of the American Revolution, was responsible for introducing her to Jefferson. He arrived in Paris in early August of 1786. The purpose of his visit was to capture the likenesses of the French officers who had been present at the Yorktown surrender. During this visit, he was Jefferson's house guest at the Hotel de Langeac. In the course of his work, Trumbull met the Cosways and joined them on a tour to see the artistic treasures of the French capital. At some point, Jefferson joined them. When Richard and John returned to their work, the American diplomat took over as Maria's escort. Together they visited the Palais Royal to see the duc d'Orlean's heralded collection. They also went to the Louvre and the royal chateaus at Fontainebleau, St. Germain, and Versailles. On one memorable occasion they toured the park at Marly. This was one of the country estates built by Louis XIV. It was famous for its gardens, which featured magnificent statutes of Numidian Horses by Guillaume Coustou. Sending his coach on to the village, Jefferson and Maria shared a quiet picnic 'under the Bowers of Marly.' This was the moment their friendship might have blossomed into a romance," Somerville observed. "But it came and went!"

"What happened," Claire wondered.

"Consider who Jefferson was," Somerville replied. "This was a man who lived with his mother until he was twenty-seven. When the muse finally called him—arguably the most eligible bachelor in Virginia—he pursued his best friend's wife. He eventually courted and married a 'spinster' with a young child. It is reported that he pledged to her as she lay dying that he would never marry again. These are not the characteristics of the blooded colts who attended his university after his death—or today!" he said, winking at Henry. "Indeed, it appears there was something in his composition that made him uncomfortable as a suitor—just as he was uneasy speaking in public.

"He was sorely challenged by the glamourous libidinous society he encountered in France. On the one hand, he was excited by the *beau monde* and its *femmes dangereuses*. At the same time, however, he objected to it for violating the republican vision he had cultivated of women carrying the family. He imagined the modesty and domestic virtue of women to be the ultimate foundation of social harmony. Do you see the conflict?" He asked, looking at Claire.

"Mmmm..."

"At one point, he observed that the Jews, the Greeks, the Romans, the Swiss, and the Dutch had lost their Republican principles and habits—and their Republican governments—because their women became liberated."

"Oh my," Claire worried. "That *is* deeply ingrained!"

"Yes," Somerville agreed. "Such views made it difficult for him to sustain relationships with his American female friends. Indeed, his friendships with Angelica Church, Anne Willing Bingham, and Abigail Adams all eventually dissolved."

"How sad," she sighed.

"Yes," Somerville agreed. "Anyway, imagine them together on that afternoon at Marly... Cupid poised with his bowstring drawn... muses playing bewitching melodies on the wings of the breeze and coaxing Thomas to gaze into Maria's goddess eyes... Everything was set... except the suitor's psyche! Within it, there raged a turmoil that Calliope herself could not calm. Jefferson took pleasure in forming liaisons with courtesans who shared his passion for music, literature, and the arts. I assume he was intrigued by the thrilling, dangerous possibilities. But he was also on a ceaseless vigil against *demimondes* who might undo the holy cause of Liberty. Add to this his uncertainty in his ability to court, which he masked with his deathbed vow to his wife. How would these conflicts be resolved?" Somerville wondered.

"How were they resolved?" Henry asked.

"Until now," Somerville said, eyeing the volume on his desk, "We have had only a few clues. The most telling are in his famous Head and Heart letter.

"What were they?" Claire asked.

"First, let me finish the story," Somerville said. "In mid-September, about a month after their interlude at Marly, they were strolling together along the Champs Elysees when something possessed him to vault over a low fence. This has always called to mind the German Professor Malone describes, who, to give himself the air of lightness, jumped out the window."

Claire laughed the imagery.

"Is this the behavior of a man who is comfortable courting worldly women?" Somerville asked Claire.

"He sounds more like a teenager with a crush," she answered.

"Precisely!" Somerville agreed. "This woman perplexed him. She probably frightened him. She had drawn him out of his sanctuary into a world beyond his control. He didn't know what to do!" Somerville surmised.

"You make him sound like a geek," Henry observed.

"A geek?" Somerville repeated obtusely.

"A geek would be like someone in the engineering school who wears three different plaids and has a shirt pocket filled with colored pens," Henry explained.

"He certainly had the mentality of an engineer," the curator conceded. "We can see that in his preference for Architecture over the Fine Arts . . . But to complete the story," he said, interrupting himself. "He tripped and fell and broke his wrist. He finished the walk holding his injured wrist. When he reached home, he sent for a surgeon. By then, of course, it was severely swollen and difficult to treat. Under the circumstances, it's not surprising that the attending physician set it improperly. Maria tried to see the convalescent the next day, but her husband thwarted her plan. Two weeks passed . . .

"It was the day before she was to leave Paris. Jefferson was still in great pain but dragged himself out of bed to attend a farewell dinner. The next day he again abandoned his convalescence, this time to accompany her and her husband to their departure. A week later he wrote his famous letter. And look what he said. Head and Heart talk of Mr. & Mrs. Cosway! Heart proceeds to announce that 'morals were too essential to the happiness of man to be risked on the uncertain combinations of the head.' Later Heart says, 'fill papers as you please with triangles and squares: try how many ways you can hang and combine them together. I shall never envy nor control your sublime delights.' How would you react to such a letter, Miss Fox?"

"I wouldn't be swept off my feet," she observed.

"The parts don't seem to fit together," Henry agreed.

"Indeed!" Somerville nodded.

"What happened?" Claire asked.

"Maria went back to England. Shortly after her departure, Jefferson set off for the south of France."

"To clear his mind?" Henry interrupted.

"That's what I think!" Somerville agreed.

"What does Jefferson say?" Claire asked.

"Go ahead," Somerville gestured to Henry. "Read us the letter."

"Ok ... *Nice April 11, 1787: I have now been away from Paris three weeks and know nothing of what has transpired since my departure. My last undertaking was to attend the Assembly of Notables. My journey has given me leisure to reflect on its proceedings. I wrote encouragingly to Lafayette who was seated there. I told him that if the King acts responsibly, good could come it. In the first place, I said, he should commit himself to recalling the Assembly when this session adjourns. In turn, the delegates should organize themselves into two chambers instead of their current seven—the Lords and the Commons as it is in England. Then they should persuade the King to call the deputies to the Commons who are chosen by the people for the Provincial administrations. Finally, the Nobles should be allowed to choose their own deputies. This would create a truly representative legislature. The King might then preside as the executive officer, albeit with an hereditary tenure.*

"*I further averred that the first order of business of the new government should be to develop a constitution and a bill of rights. (I have been speaking privately with Lafayette and Rabout de St. Etienne about drafting such a charter when the time is right. Of course, I must be careful lest I appear to be using my diplomatic office to undermine the government.) That is what I said to Lafayette, but I say in confidence to you that the most remarkable effect of this convention is the number of bon mots it has generated. I think that were they collected it would make a more voluminous work than the Encyclopedia. This occasion, more than anything I have seen, convinces me that this nation is incapable of serious effort but under the word of command. The people at large view every object only as it may furnish puns and bon mots; and I pronounce that a good punster would disarm the whole nation were they ever seriously disposed to revolt. In this regard—as in so many others—you have proven to be right! When a measure so capable of doing good as the calling the Notable is treated with so much ridicule, we may conclude the nation desperate, and pray to God that we are gone when it receives its justice. I am glad therefore to be away. Since leaving the Capital, my mind has been fixed on less-intriguing subjects. For example, while in Nimes I was seduced by a new mistress! Do you know the Maison quarree? The stocking weavers and silk spinners around it consider me as a hypochondriac Englishman set to write with a pistol his final chapter. How cruel life is to me! I flee Paris to escape ensnarlment with one morsel only to be smitten by another. The trial has convinced me that I am at bottom an Epicurean. Like that ancient hedonist, I seek only tranquility. As he says, the summum bonum is not to be pained in the body, nor troubled in mind! Yet try to follow this simple principle in the company of women! Every moment is a hazard. Diderot argued that women's apparent inferiority is due to their legal subordination and poor education rather than any innate difference between the sexes. But he should consult Lavoisier on the science of chemistry. Place a charming femme in the proximity of any man and a dangerous reaction will follow: badinage, intrigue, seduction. I hold hereditary government responsible for the depravity of this culture. Marital infidelity is a natural consequence of material excess. It has corrupted the whole society. Who here can resist an evening's engagement with a woman skilled in the social arts. The greater her skill, the more dangerous she is. As I stand on guard against these tender assaults, I am struck by the empty bustle that occupies the daily life of French women. How different they are from the chaste republican women of America. They spend their days like mill-horses treading the same circle round and round. One by one they pass without a destination beyond the present moment. Insert an un-inoculated American male in this setting and he will soon cultivate a taste for European luxury and dissipation. He will contract partiality for aristocracy and monarchy. He will follow his new friends into the strongest of all human passions. He will be beguiled, not suspecting that the playful intrigues he shares will ultimately undermine his happiness. Before the gates of truth open to him, he will learn that infidelity to the marriage bed is an ungentlemanly sin. As I contemplate these things, I consider myself lucky to have escaped. It was only by a hair's breadth. I shall not allow myself to stumble back into that pit—I assure you of that. I gazed into siren eyes and listened as Psyche whispered in my ear. My blood ran hot. She, sensing my condition, smiled still more alluringly, beckoning me like ripe fruit to be plucked. But in the clutch, I was saved by something Lafayette told me. It seems a funny thing to remember at that moment—that the husband of his mistress committed suicide! It was as though old Epicurus himself interrupted me. Do you want such a thing on our conscience, he demanded? Will you have more after your conquest than you have now—answer me? There must be something, I said. But it will not be tranquility, he replied from beyond the veil.* It's signed *TH. Jefferson*

"The final pronouncement!" Somerville intoned. And it's just as I thought. Poor Maria! She was merely a spectator to a contest between Jefferson and himself." Somerville gazed abstractly at Claire. "He couldn't cope with her as a mere companion, nor surrender his peace for a mistress..."

"You said something about knowing Maria before we could understand Sally," Claire reminded him.

"Yes," Somerville said, settling back into the moment. "This psychology guided Jefferson's interactions with *all* women," the scholar observed, "even Sally Hemings! But she, unfortunate girl, had another problem..."

"What was that?" Claire asked.

"She was neither a femme dangereuse, nor a salon habitué, nor a paradigm of republican virtue. That wasn't her fault mind you—she was a fourteen-year-old slave girl born and raised on the James River."

"So how did Jefferson connect with her?" Claire asked.

"I've never found an answer," Somerville replied.

"Wait," Henry said. "Here's a letter that may provide it!"

"Really!" Somerville exclaimed.

"It's dated "Paris, May 10, 1788.""

"Go on," the scholar urged.

"Sir—you will be interested to know that the gay and thoughtless Paris

that greeted me three years ago has now become a furnace of Politics. Men, women, and children talk of nothing else. Society is spoilt by it for no two agree. It is like the Babylon of Genesis. All tongues in Paris (and in all France it is said) have been let loose, and never was a license for speaking against the government exercised more freely or more universally. Caricatures, placards, and bon mots, have been indulged in by all ranks of people. The Count Arois, sent to hold a bed of justice in the Cour de Aides, was hissed and hooted without reserve by the populace. The papers are full of such stories whether or not they are true. The sport is so good that even the British Ministry has joined in. The true ideologue still thinks that we are on the road to the rule of right reason. But from my perspective, it has veered into the darkness you anticipated. Let us hope that it does not end there! As I watch the crisis unfold, I wonder at how the new world order flaunts the immutable law of reason. Perhaps its motto should be <u>tertium datur</u>! This, they say, is the principle of irrationality. I suggest that we call it the Paradox of the Middle Term. What do you think? The King greets each new reversal with a new bumper of wine. Against this depressing backdrop, I have been studying the new American Constitution I received from Mr. Adams. There are many things in it which weaken my disposition to support it. For one, the American Presidency is structured like a bad edition of a Polish King. What we have lately read in the history of Holland, in the chapter on the Stadtholder, would have sufficed to set me against a chief magistrate whose tenure has no limit—had I not opposed that from the beginning along with the judiciary. As for the house of federal representatives, I do not consider it adequate to the management of affairs either foreign or federal. And in the Senate, I wager it will take no more than a generation before its offices provide life tenures too. Once this has been established, every succession will be a study in intrigue and bribery. Nor will it be possible to turn the rascals out for they shall surely have mastered the art of marshaling the energies of the government to their own advantage. Once they have perfected their methods, the new American republic will become just another in history's long list of hierarchical tyrannies. The flimsiness of the logic underlying the entire enterprise displays itself in the three-fifths provision for counting southern Negroes. I grant you that we have trapped ourselves in this non sequitur. But how can we rest a government on it? Is this not what I said? Tertium Datur! What are we to do with them, I wonder? It is the nature of civil society to be closed for it is common custom not positive *law that insures social order. Where are these alien creatures to fit? They are as foreign to us as the Jews were to the Babylonians. They are destined by providence to dwell forever in the wilderness. Even if we devoted every bit of our fortune to the enterprise, we would never succeed in incorporating them into our society. Their animosities will become the more acute to the degree we succeed in raising their self-awareness. There is a young girl here who attends my daughter. She is, truth be known, a half-sister of my departed wife. In-deed, there is a resemblance since they shared the same sire. Her mother had a white father as well, which is apparent in her own bright complexion and the aptitude of her siblings. The entire family came into my possession upon my father-in-law's death thirteen years ago. Since then, I have been at a loss what to do with them. It has been an unending headache. I should like to manumit them, but what would they do? Where would they go? Who would speak for them? You understand, sir, that when I cease to be their lord and master, I must become their defender and advocate. There are many whites in the south who would gladly trade places with them for there is no living to be made in agriculture and there is no manufacturing! I have noticed that the French tutor has taken an interest in young Sally. She is coming of age so perhaps I should just close my eyes and allow her to disappear. Then I would have one less care gnawing at me. She is learning the language and is light enough to pass as an interbred moor. I am sure she would do fine as a citizen of France. While I am speaking of the ruinous state of southern agriculture, let me point out the cruel irony in it for our only hope of preserving a republican govern-ment in America is to remain an agricultural society. If poverty forces the people from the land into large cites, they will become as depraved as the mobs who fill the streets of Paris. I am thankful at least that our ladies have been too wise to wrinkle their foreheads with politics. They are the true foundation of virtuous society. It shall flourish only so long as they have the good sense to value domestic happiness and to continue to cultivate it. There is no part of the earth where domestic happiness is so much enjoyed as in America. We owe this to our women. And fortunate we are. Look at the situation here. Everyone, men and women alike, stalks pleasure. I find it revolting. That reminds me, I have begun browsing through the work of your German metaphysician in the light of your endorsement, but I must respectfully decline my support for his system. Since I have read "Candide" by Voltaire, I shall never be able to consider his work in a serious light. And besides, I reject all metaphysics. My*

philosophy can be summarized in two simple sentences: Ignorance is prefera-
ble to error; and, He is less remote from the truth who believes nothing than
he who believes what is wrong. Metaphysics is nothing more than a chain that
binds the minds of modern men to the dark ages and its lunatics. I am a nat-
uralist trained in the Law and must adhere to the path of reason such as it is.
I cannot rationalize a God that floods his creation with chaos and calamity as
Herr Leibniz appears to do. Why should we not follow Candide and cultivate
our own gardens? In this vein I am writing a new constitution—I shall send
a copy to you when I am finished. In the meantime, expect the worst! Tertuim
datur!' It's signed TH. Jefferson."

"One of them removed the letter," Douglas growled.

"Which one?" Bildner asked.

"I couldn't tell," Douglas replied. "I guess the safest thing to do would be to take care of all of them."

"Ok."

"Here's what I want you to do," Douglas explained as his chauffeur opened the door of the limousine and guided him in. "On the way out, pull into the parking area at the bottom of the hill and take a look at the ticket office building."

Bildner allowed a white Jeep Cherokee to pass before he pulled out of the parking area. Written in large black letters on the vehicle's door were the words 'Monticello Security.' The uniformed driver waved as he passed by. Bildner waved back.

"I want you to set it on fire," Douglas announced. "I want a big fire! Do you follow what I'm saying? The kind that will get the security people down there. Once they're there, neutralize them."

"Ok," he answered without emotion.

"While you're doing that, I'll retrieve the journal and see if I can find the letter. If I can't," he said, "we'll have to take care of the house too." Douglas waited as Bildner confirmed his instructions. "When I'm done, I'll meet you down on the third roundabout below the cattle pen. We'll follow that on around and go out on the river—have a boat waiting there for us and stash a car out of sight on the other side. We'll go up the river to 250, pick up the car, and disappear . . . One more thing," Douglas added after reflecting

433

for a moment. "I need to get my other letters back—you understand?"

"Yea . . . what about the girl and her friend?"

"Arrange an accident."

"Wonderful!" Somerville crooned. "I dare say these are the most revealing things Jefferson ever wrote. And you've done a marvelous job with your translations—both of you."

"Thank you, Dr. Somerville," Henry smiled. "It's a great privilege to have the opportunity."

"I feel the same way," Claire assured him. "When do you want to resume the work?"

"Let me see," Somerville thought. "We have the system. What we need to do next is to catalogue the journal's content. Could we meet again tomorrow morning?"

"I need to check with Mr. Paige," Henry said, glancing at Claire.

"Of course," the curator nodded.

"Fenton," Claire asked, following her cue. "Before we go, would you have time to show me the Tea Room again?"

"Why certainly," he beamed. "We did rather rush through it the other day . . . Let me put this away," he said, taking the journal from Henry, ". . . then we'll go down and have another look at it—it's a treasure trove!"

Henry watched the curator slide the binder back into its sheaf and place it in his desk.

"Shall we go?" the curator said when he had locked it.

"Would it be all right if I detour down to the rest room?" Henry asked as they stepped out of Somerville's office.

"By all means," he answered. "You know where it is—at the bottom of the stairs and to your left. You can meet us in the Tea Room . . ." With that, he opened his office door. "Come along, Miss Fox," he said, beckoning her with his outstretched hand. "We'll take the shortcut across the balcony."

Henry watched them go, then darted down the stairs to Jefferson's apartment. The door to the entrance hall was open and he could hear Somerville chatting with Claire as they crossed the balcony. He glanced across the foyer and confirmed that the door into the north passage was closed. Good! That would muffle the noise he was about to make. He reached into the sleeve of his jacket and extracted the crowbar from his pant leg.

Henry waited as the voices of the other two died away. Then he tiptoed through the door into the library annex. He paused again. It was still quiet. Suddenly something moved beyond the glass door to the conservatory! Henry pressed against the wall as a uniformed guard crossed the promenade going in the direction of the west lawn. Henry stepped quickly into Jefferson's cabinet. The guard, who was visible through the south window, proceeded around the ancient poplar in the direction of the back portico. When he was gone, Henry slipped into the passageway at the foot of Jefferson's bed. The door to the privy was ajar. He pushed it open and stepped it. It was illuminated by a dim light from the vent in the mansion's roof. Jefferson's chamber pot was there—waiting to be filled.

Henry poked his head out of the privy and peered cautiously through the window in the west wall. Satisfied that the guard had passed on, he crept along the edge of the bed to the closet door. He pulled it back enough to squeeze through, then disappeared inside.

Henry stepped through the archway into the Tea Room and joined Claire who was listening to Somerville describe one of the busts. She gave him and anxious look but relaxed when she saw him nod. "Fenton was just telling me about George Washington," she said, casually brushing plaster chips off his jacket.

"It is, of course, the work of Houdon. He was by far the most notable artist Jefferson patronized. In fact, he purchased seven of Houdon's works," the curator continued. "In addition to the bust of himself, there was Captain John Paul Jones," Somerville saluted the captain, "Franklin, Lafayette, and Washington here. This set constituted what he called his 'most honorable suite.' It was not enough, however, He also acquired busts of Turgot and Voltaire which you've seen the entrance hall.

"One of his first official duties upon his arrival in France," the curator explained, "had been to commission Houdon to create a statue of Washington for the Capital of Virginia in Richmond. Houdon accepted the commission and left a few months after that with Franklin, who was returning to America after completing his diplomatic service in France.

Houdon modeled this bust while staying with Washington at Mount Vernon. He then returned to France and completed it, mounting the head on a body he created using Governor Morris as his model. All the busts are plaster reproductions of the original works," Somerville noted. "Jefferson purchased them shortly before his own departure—no doubt with the idea that he would display them here!"

"Oh Fenton!" Claire exclaimed. "You're such a fountain of knowledge. Is there anything you don't know about Thomas Jefferson?" She gave him an admiring hug.

"Yes," he blushed. "But you and Mr. Tilghman are going to fix that."

"By the way Dr. Somerville," Henry interrupted. "Did you receive a bull up here the other day?"

"A bull!" He seemed puzzled. "What would we do with a bull?"

"Aren't you having some kind of livestock exhibit," Claire asked.

"Maybe you're breeding some cows . . ." Henry suggested.

"Check with Peter down at the shed."

"Martin . . ."

"Yes! Bill!" The publisher replied into the receiver. "Did everything go smoothly?"

"No," the Supreme Court Justice snapped.

"What happened?" Ogden asked, gazing at the mountains in the distance.

"The letter was missing," Douglas announced.

"What about the journal?" Ogden said, pressing him for that information. "Did you get that?"

"No," Douglas snapped again. "I tried to cow him, but Somerville didn't buckle."

"Damn!" Ogden swore. "I'll guess we'll have to try something else." He thought about Hardin. "Let me think about it and get back to you . . ." He hung up the phone before Douglas could respond. No reason to let him cloud your thinking, Ogden said to himself.

Hardin didn't like morning meetings, but under the circumstances he was glad to make this exception. Bildner and his two partners were waiting for him at the Albemarle Lounge. *This is the perfect place to meet Charlottesville's low life,* Hardin mused as he opened its front door. He found them in one of the booths in the back.

Hardin had a knack for engaging people, but he was having trouble interpreting Bildner's stony expression. McCray and Wells were equally inscrutable. "It seems Marjean has gotten hold of the money Ried said he would lend Paige," Hardin continued. "She must have grabbed it while he was stoned."

Bildner's expression didn't change. "Shit happens . . ."

"Yea, but he'll kill her if you sell her the crop."

"The world'l be a better place," Bildner replied humorlessly.

"The problem with that," Hardin observed, bending the issue to his purpose, "is that he's threatening to expose the operation."

Bildner glanced at his colleagues. "What are you saying?" he asked, cutting Hardin off.

"Give me until Monday to get things straightened out. I'll settle things between Paige and Marjean. If I have to, I'll buy the crop myself. Things will go much smoother . . ."

Bildner looked at his partners. Neither moved.

"It can't hurt to wait a couple days," Hardin pleaded. "Look at the hassles we'll avoid."

"Ok," Bildner nodded.

"Good. I'll have it all straightened out by then," Hardin smiled unctuously. "Say," he added looking around, "is there a phone in here?"

Bildner gestured toward a door behind him. "On the wall next to the men's room."

Hardin glanced in the direction of the phone. "If you will excuse me . . ." he said climbing out of the booth.

McCray watched him disappear into the back hall. "Where did Ried get a hundred grand?" he asked.

"There is no hundred grand," Bildner said.

"How is Paige going to pay us then?" Wells asked.

"That's not the plan . . ."

Hardin unlocked the door. As he entered the room, Gerta stepped out of the bathroom. She was wearing her robe and drying her hair. Hardin ignored her and went to the phone. Lifting the receiver, he dialed Ogden's number.

Ogden answered on the first ring. "Yes."

"Martin . . ."

"Tim!" Ogden said, recognizing Hardin's voice. "I've got great news! Douglas has located the manuscript. He tells me that it's at Monticello. The curator has it in his office. Have you met Fenton Somerville?"

"Yea, I know Somerville," Hardin answered, picturing an over-weight goofball in a ruffled blouse and knee britches. "Where's his office?"

"Douglas said it's on the second floor of the mansion."

"Somerville's office is on the second floor of the mansion?"

"Yes—Douglas was there earlier this morning. He tried to commandeer the folder, but Somerville made a fuss . . ."

"What did you expect?" Hardin sneered. "Somerville wasn't going to let Douglas walk off with a precious collection of Jefferson's documents! We're going to have to pinch it—I've already made the arrangements."

Martin smiled. "Maybe you're right," he agreed.

"You bet I am," Hardin snapped, "and I am going to need a hundred grand . . ."

"What!"

"Don't give me any shit, Martin. I'm getting you one of the most important document in American history—Burr's Unicorn! Viva la Revolution!" Hardin cackled into the phone. "A hundred grand is cheap!"

"You're right," Ogden said, acquiescing. "It's a bargain at that."

"I need it by tomorrow afternoon," he said. "Deliver it to me here at the Holiday Inn." He stroked his forehead, "Put my room number on it—219—but keep my name off it. Have it marked to the attention of . . . Fred Ried."

———————

Henry looked both ways, then accelerated onto the state road that ran past Monticello's entrance.

"You know something?" Claire said, extending a finger and twirling his hair, "You're brilliant."

"Why thank you," he smiled. "I consider that a real compliment coming from a *lumière* like yourself."

"What a team," she laughed, looking down the road.

"We still have to get the journal out of the house," Henry cautioned.

"Yes," Claire agreed, "but at least it's safe." That reminded her. "Where are we going now?"

"I was going back to the cottage..."

"I don't think that's a good idea," Claire said, suddenly serious. "You saw the look on Douglas's face."

"You're right! He's onto us..." Henry reached into his jacket and pulled out the letter. "What's in this?" he asked, handing it to Claire.

She unfolded the paper and inspected the heading: "*The Supreme Court of the United State of America.* Beneath the heading was the Court's official emblem. She focused on the text of letter. "*Fred,*" she began, "*I have warned Tim in the most explicit terms <u>not</u> to proceed with his preposterous plan to bomb the Rotunda. I am extending the same warning to you! The very idea is an affront to me. There is no way that I am going to allow a cabal of deranged adolescents to undermine forty years of painstaking work with an 'Aquarian Revolution', whatever that might be! Given the short distance we have left to travel, I should think you would understand the advantage of our alliance. I say again that the best way to accomplish our common objective is to pacify the opposition! We must not give the public a reason to focus on the systems we are instituting. The worst thing we can do is wake the sleeping giant—dumb as it is. Tim and I will both be in Charlottesville on the 9th for the Jefferson Academy's issues conference. Let's meet then and get things back on track!' It's signed W.O.D.*"

"William O. Douglas," Henry intoned.

"Yes..."

"There's no telling what he'd do to get this back," Henry observed. "I know! Let's go over to Trip's—we'll be safe there... and we can work on the diagram!"

"Before we do that, I think we should find out what happened to Ried," Claire replied.

"You're right," Henry nodded. "We can take the Unimog up to his place and have a look around."

Henry picked up the receiver in the shed and dialed Mr. Paige's private number.

"Hank!" Paige said when he heard Henry's voice. "I've been waiting for your call. Is Miss Fox still with us?"

Yes," Henry replied.

"Good," Paige commended. "She's Ok?

"She seems to be," Henry said, eyeing her.

"Good . . . that episode last night had me worried," Paige confessed. "You've been with Somerville?" he continued.

"Yes . . . We helped him translate a few of the letters Thomas Jefferson wrote in German . . . You're not going to believe this . . "

"What?"

"In the binder that held them—I found a letter written by William O. Douglas . . . to Fred Ried."

"Wait a minute!" Paige seemed confused. "Did you say that you found a letter written by our illustrious Supreme Court Justice?"

"I know it sounds strange . . ."

"Jesus Christ!" Paige swore. That's big—real big!"

"And it looks like Fred Ried was the guy who sent the documents to Monticello," Henry continued.

"Is that what Hardin was grilling me about—Jefferson's Constitution?"

"I expect that's part of the collection . . ."

". . . So Ried had it. That snake! He probably stuck Douglas's letter in there—sounds like a set up," Paige observed. "Do you have it?"

"Yes . . ."

"What's it say?"

"Douglas warned Ried not to bomb the Rotunda. . ."

"Douglas warned Ried not to bomb the Rotunda—is that what you just said?" Paige repeated in disbelief.

"Yes . . . and he came up to Monticello this morning looking for the letter."

"He must know you have it," Paige observed. "Douglas would probably kill you to keep that kind of story out of the papers. Where are you now?"

"At the Unimog shed—Claire and I are going up to Ried's place and see if we can find out what happened to him."

"Something happened to him?" Paige was again surprised.

"Bart told us that he blew himself up."

"How the hell would he know that?"

"I don't know. It has something to do with your bull," Henry explained.

"Aberon of Belmont?"

"Yes . . ."

"What about him?" Paige demanded.

"A friend of mine said he hauled him to Monticello the other day," Henry explained.

"The hell you say!" Paige swore." I never authorized that. Where the hell's Bart?"

"I haven't seen him . . ." Henry was relieved to say.

"I'm going over to the barn right now," Paige announced. "Meet me there. I'll wring his goddam neck!" Paige swore as he set the receiver down.

———————

"Take a look at this," the District Attorney said, stepping away from the telescope in Fred Ried's living room.

"What?" The sheriff asked, leaning over and placing his eye on the viewing lens. "Hell! That's Bart Paige," he exclaimed. "What's 'e doin' over there?"

"Looks to me like he's cutting marijuana . . ." the DA replied, gazing off in the line of the of telescope.

"Oh yea?" Bailey said, putting his eye back on the lens. "That son-of-a-bitch," he hissed through his teeth. "An' tha girl's there with 'im." He stood up. "I'll get Troupe on the radio an' have 'im arrest them . . ." He turned and started toward the stairs.

"Hold on," Hoagland said, catching the sheriff's arm. "Let's let him finish what's he's doing."

A confused look appeared on the lawman's face. Then he grinned as a thought of convicts doing hard labor in the hot sum formed in his mind.

"If we're lucky, maybe he'll introduce us to the people on the other end of the pipeline," the DA observed, peeping again at Paige.

———————

"Why do you suppose Ried sent the journal to Monticello?" Claire asked, returning to what Henry had said to Paige.

Henry leaned over so he could hear her over the roar of the Unimog's diesel. "What's that?"

"Why would Ried send the journal to Monticello?" she shouted into his ear.

Henry shrugged. "Maybe he was trying to create a diversion..."

"But why would he use Douglas? And why would he pick Monticello?" Claire countered. "...unless..." it suddenly occurred to her.

"Unless what?" Henry repeated.

"Unless he was trying to lure Douglas to Monticello!"

Henry considered the possibility. "What would he gain by doing that?"

"He has a grudge against Douglas," the former reported answered. "Douglas threatened him. Ried got angry. Now he's getting even."

"Huh!" Henry shrugged. "I suppose that could be..."

"Do you think it's just a co-incidence that the insignia on the Baron's manuscript is the same as the figure on Jefferson's mantle?" Claire asked, shifting to another matter.

"Don't forget about 'the secrets of the house' Jefferson mentioned in his letter," Henry added.

"Something's definitely going on with that frieze," Claire observed.

"Where do you suppose Ried got the journal to begin with?" Henry wondered.

"Maybe he stole it..."

"Who from?"

"I don't know," Claire answered. "...maybe be it was in his family."

"Do you think <u>Fred</u> <u>Ried</u> is related to Baron <u>Fred</u>erick de <u>Ried</u>esel?"

"Bingo!" Claire exclaimed.

———————

Bart Paige heaved another armful of marijuana onto the pile in the back of his pickup truck. "Les' take this back ta tha barn and stow it with tha seeds," he panted.

"Yea," Suzie moaned, mopping her sweat-soaked brow. "I'm hot!"

They climbed into the truck and started down the hill toward Jefferson's lake.

442

"How come you're so sure Ried's dead," Suzie wondered. "The guy at the lounge last night said he was up at Monticello."

"He don't know shit about shit!" Paige sneered.

"What if he faked blowing himself up," Suzie persisted. "I saw an episode on Hawaii 5-0 once where this guy . . ."

"Ain't no way he'd let somebody snitch 'is seeds if 'e wuz alive," Paige interrupted. "Anyway, Bildner's guy's 're takin' in the crop an' Hardin's gonna git me mah hunnerd gran'—so it don't make no dif'rence which he is . . ."

"How is Hardin going to get the money back from Marjean?" she asked.

"Long es ah git my money, ah don't give ah shit!" Paige swore.

"What if he kills her?" She exclaimed. "And takes the money? And buys the crop himself!"

"He'd do it too . . ." Paige sneered. "Cep' fer one thing."

` "He might have been working a deal for himself with those guys!" Suzie continued, worrying.

"Yer fergittin' 'bout the ace ah got up mah sleeve, Baby Doll." Paige laughed. "If 'e wants tha journal bad 'nough to giv' me a hunnerd gran', 'e ain't gonna snitch mah crop!"

"And it's up there at Jefferson's mansion," Suzie said, comforting herself.

"Tha guy that runs tha place's got it," Paige added. "Hardin sez it's in nis office."

"Why doesn't he get it himself?" Suzie wondered.

"B'cause he's a longhair'd pussy," Paige snorted. "We'll git up thar t'naght and grab it. Then we'll be set ta roll."

"What about the bull?"

"Ahl leave a note and Daddy ken get 'im after we're gone." Paige answered.

"And we're gonna be rich, rich, RICH!" Suzie trilled, snuggling up to her hero.

Mr. Paige's field green Mercedes was parked in front of the Belmont breeding station when Henry and Claire arrived in the Unimog. Henry shut off the engine and climbed down as Mr. Paige stepped through the barn door.

"Come on inside," he said, scanning the surrounding fields.

They entered the building and went into its office. "Sounds like you've stepped into something," Paige observed.

"Yea—Douglas is probably gunning for us," Henry half-joked.

"Let's see the letter," Paige said as seated himself behind the desk.

Henry pulled it out of his coat and handed it to the former naval intelligence officer.

Paige scanned it and looked up. "This is an outrage!" He growled. "Douglas is one of our nation's highest-ranking public servants . . . How can he be involved in something like this! You see what we're up against, Miss Fox?" he asked, looking at Claire. "Termites—big ones—are in the crossbeams. If we don't get rid of them, they'll destroy the country."

"I think you're right," she nodded somberly.

"You want to go up to Ried's place—is that right?" He said, looking at Henry. "Is it safe?"

"Ried hasn't been around for several days," Henry explained. "Maybe we can find out what happened to him."

Paige nodded. "What about Hardin. Where's he?"

"I saw him at the dinner last night," Claire responded. "He's staying at the Holiday Inn."

"And Douglas is staying at the guest quarters at the Colonnade Club," Paige added. "He's got a driver named Bildner—he's worth keeping an eye on. Do you know him, Hank?"

"No."

"I had to arrange a parking permit for him—Douglas rides around in a stretch limousine these days. How's that for a utopian leveler?"

"That must have been him last night," Claire observed, looking at Henry.

"Yea," Henry agreed. "And he was with Douglas this morning!"

"Let me keep this," Paige said, waving the letter. "If you're going to be out there running around, you don't want this in your pocket."

"Right . . ." Henry agreed.

"Looks like we're going to have to fight for you too, Miss Fox," Paige added, addressing Claire.

"What you mean?" She asked, smiling uncertainly.

"I spoke with Martin Ogden last night," Paige replied. "He doesn't want to let you go."

"Really!" Claire laughed. "That skunk—as if he has anything to say about it."

"Check in with me when you've finished at Ried's," Paige said, moving toward the door.

"By the way," Henry said to his employer. "Dr. Somerville has asked us to meet again tomorrow morning."

"By all means, Hank. Do us proud!"

The senior Paige was standing in front of the barn's open doors as his son's black pickup swerved into the parking lot. "Oh God!" Bart Paige wailed. "It's Daddy!"

Henry steered the Unimog along the edge of the field, but his eyes were fixed on Ried's compound.

"Looks like something happened up there," Henry said.

"I'll say," Claire agreed, staring at the ruins on the left end of the retainer wall.

Henry pulled up beside it and turned the engine off. Before he climbed out, he looked over at Claire. "Ready Comrade?"

"Yep."

They hit the ground in synch and scrambled up onto the flagstone patio. As they did, Ted Hoagland emerged from the ruins of Ried's studio. "Well! Look who's here!" he announced.

Claire looked at Henry, alarm spreading on her face.

"It's all right," Henry assured her. "This is our District Attorney. Ted Hoagland, I would like you to meet Claire Fox, who's here on assignment from *The Washington Post*."

"How do you do Miss Fox," he said in his most congenial suspicious voice. "What brings you up here on such a fine afternoon?" As he spoke, Sheriff Bailey appeared in the door of the greenhouse.

"We heard Ried was dead," Henry reported. "Claire wanted to see if it was true."

"Who told you that?" Hoagland asked.

"Bart Paige," Claire replied.

"Oh yea!" Hoagland said, filing the information in his memory bank. "What else did he say?"

"He said that Ried was an expert on Thomas Jefferson," she answered. "Is that why you're here?" she asked, turning the tables.

The DA studied her for a moment. "I guess it can't hurt to tell you," he said. "Mr. Ried has been operating a drug factory up here."

"Really?" Claire looked around. "Right here—under your nose?"

Hoagland frowned. "We've known about it for some time," he said. "But we've been hoping to meet his friends."

"Lookie here Ted," Sheriff Bailey interrupted from the doorway.

Hoagland led the way into the greenhouse where Bailey was standing next to a bed of stumps. "Looks like he cleared out."

The DA stooped down and picked a marijuana leaf up off the floor. "Yea..."

"You know what this is?" Claire asked, pulling a leaf from a line of bushes on the back row. "No," the District Attorney replied, shifting his focus to the plant behind Claire. "Can't say as I do."

"It's coca," Claire said. "It's the source of the alkaloid people use to make cocaine!"

Hoagland looked at Claire, then at Bailey. "He was manufacturing cocaine too?"

"Huh," the Sheriff grunted.

"Have you found his body?" Claire asked, gesturing toward the rubble at the far end of the terrace.

"Don't expect to," Hoagland answered, glancing at the remains of Ried's workshop. "We think he blew it up to throw us off his trail."

"It's Gerta..." Frances Rank announced, unchaining the door.

Gerta Biederman clambered into Professor Shoate' Elliewood Avenue apartment.

"I thought you and Woman Spirit were doing the people's justice," Rank snapped, re-locking the door behind her.

Shoate' peered at her through the kitchen door.

"I've been raped!" Gerta announced mechanically. "...a man dressed in black..."

446

"You don't look no dif'rent?" Shoate' said, stepping into the front room.

"Where did it happen?" Rank interceded.

"At the dome . . ." the shaking victim groaned.

"Did you recognize him?" Rank asked, pressing on with her investigation.

"It was a devil . . . with a skull . . ."

"Wha'd he do?" Shoate's asked.

"He made me strip naked," she said.

"You?" Shoate' exclaimed.

"Then he forced me to . . ."

"What?" Rank demanded impatiently.

"Go outside . . ." Gerta sobbed.

"What happened then?" Ranked continued.

"He ransacked Aster's house!"

"Sounds like 'e raped the house," Shoate' said, looking at Rank.

"Did he say anything?" Rank asked, focusing again on Biederman.

"Yea—whud 'e say?" Shoate' repeated.

"Something about 'standing before the sea of glass,'" Gerta moaned.

Rank grabbed her bag. "It's him!' She roared heading out the door.

"Whoz' zat? The Professor asked, falling in step.

"The anti-Christ!"

"Here we are," Henry said, as he approached a grove of towering old oaks. Claire read the sign at the edge of the grove: *Rose Hill Farm.* Below the name was the address: *Ivy, Virginia.*

"You wouldn't know it from the sign and the driveway," Henry volunteered, "but this is one of the most beautiful farms in Albemarle County."

Henry turned in and drove slowly through the grove. A moment later, they emerged from the woods onto the farm. Handsome pastures with whitewashed fences lined the rest of the drive, which continued about a quarter of miles to a stately manor house. Its second story was visible above the antient boxwood hedge that separated the mansion's grounds from the farm. Claire could see the roof of its portico in the center of the building and pairs of chimneys on both of its ends. Henry turned onto the farm road that crossed the drive on the farm-side of the hedge. He followed it around the house. Behind the house was a long sloping meadow. Beside it was weather-beaten brick cabin with a decrepit front porch that ran the cabin's length. Henry pulled to stop in a parking area next to it.

"Trip won't mind if we make ourselves at home," Henry said. "Not that he'd know the difference . . ." Henry climbed out of the car and walked around the cabin to its front steps. He then mounted the steps and crossed the porch to the cabin's door. "This damned door," he cursed. "It was Duncan White's idea," he grumbled as he bent down and grabbed the handle on the door's bottom cross-plate. "The porch is slanted so he decided this was the only way to hang a screen."

"Very creative," Claire said, sliding under Henry's arm.

She entered a dark room permeated with the smell of charred wood. As her eye became accustomed to the lack of light, she saw the hearth that filled the wall to the right of the door. It looked like it had never been emptied. "Is this where Uncle Remus lives?" Claire asked.

"Probably once upon a time," Henry replied.

"Don't you think it would be more pleasant on the porch?" Claire asked. Without waiting for Henry's reply, she turned and marched back to the door. "Oh!" She said when the door didn't open.

"On the bottom," Henry reminded her.

"Bizarre," she muttered.

There were two green director chairs on the porch. Claire took the one nearest the end-rail. "Did you learn anything from your astrology books?" She asked, opening the diagram.

"A little," Henry replied. "I learned that astrology connects certain celestial bodies with what happens on earth . . . I learned that the circle in which these bodies move is the Zodiac . . . I also learned that the Zodiac is divided into twelve sections known as . . ."

"I get the picture," Claire snapped, cutting him off. She smoothed the page and began studying the figures on it.

"One thing I was trying to figure out," Henry explained, "is whether the sun signs were connected to the areas of the body they rule."

"Never mind that," Claire snapped. "Let's start with this one . . ." She pointed to the circular emblem on the right side of the page.

"That was on her stomach," Henry volunteered. "I enlarged it so I could display all its component symbols."

"It looks like it expresses something meaningful." Claire observed. "The ox skull is in the center. The signs of the Zodiac form its outer perimeter. At the top of the circle, directly above the crown of the skull, is Aquarius, and between the skull and Aquarius is the earth . . ."

"That's the earth?" Henry repeated, taking a closer look at the glyph above the skull.

"The three small figures below the skull are Mars, Venus, and Uranus," Claire continued. "I'd say it's a pictogram." Claire concluded.

"You may be right," Henry agreed. "It must mean something . . ."

"Let's suppose," Claire continued, "that together these figures form a system . . . and that each symbol identifies a particular function within the system."

"That would simplify the analysis . . ." Henry agreed.

"Since the signs of the Zodiac form the outer boundary of the pictogram," Claire continued, "let's suppose that the system is the physical/spiritual universe."

"Ok," Henry agreed.

"That puts the skull in the center of the universe . . . like a controlling force!" Claire exclaimed.

"Exactly!" Henry agreed.

"In the vastness of the universe," Claire mused, massaging her forehead, "only four objects are identified."

"That must mean they have special significance," Henry added, following her line of thought.

"The earth is larger than the other three," Claire observed, "and it's located directly between the force and Aquarius."

"So maybe it's the object of an Aquarian force!" Henry venture, completing Claire's thought.

"That's my guess," Claire agreed.

"And since the other symbols are smaller and beneath the skull . . ." Henry continued.

". . . they signify characteristics of the force . . ." Claire said, completing Henry's thought.

"What are they?" he wondered, leaning forward to see them more clearly.

"Symbols of planets . . . Mars, Venus, and Uranus."

Henry sat back and waited for her to define them.

"Mars is the red planet," Claire began. "In Roman mythology, Mars was the God of War. Between campaigns . . . he impregnated a young woman named Rhea Silvia. Rhea Silvia was the daughter of Numitor, King of Alta Longa east of Rome, and a vestal virgin. In due course, she gave birth to Romulus and Remus, who were the twins who founded the city of Rome. According to the Romans, Mars had a violent, combative nature to which they attributed the success of their conquering armies. In 500 BC, Rome was a city-state on the Italian peninsula. But by 200 BC, the Roman Republic had conquered all the kingdoms in the peninsula, and over the next two centuries it conquered Greece and Spain. In the process of integrating Greece into the empire, the Romans adopted key elements of Greek culture, like, for example, its dedication to Philosophy and Literature. Ares is an example of this," Claire continued. "In Greek mythology, Ares is the God of War. The Romans borrowed their idea that he was a destructive force. But they also gave him positive attributes in the sense that he guided the creation of their empire."

"Interesting," Henry observed. "One positive force. One negative force. Mars is obviously a fitting influence on an Aquarian revolution . . . What about Venus and Uranus?"

"Let's see," Claire began. "Venus is our nearest planetary neighbor and is sometimes characterized as Earth's twin because of its similar size and orbital location. In terms of mythology, Venus was part of the cultural absorption that took place as the Romans integrated Greece into their growing empire. In Greek mythology, Aphrodite was the Goddess of beauty and sexual love. In Roman mythology, she became the Goddess of love, erotic passion, maternal care, sexual reproduction . . . She was also the mother of Aeneas, who was an ancestor of Romulus, and in the first century BC, Julius Caesar claimed he was descended from Venus, which made her a progenitor of the imperial dynasty. Her importance diminished as an object of worship with the rise of Christianity.

"So she had sexual and political dimensions," Henry summarized. "Those are characteristics of the Aquarian Revolution!"

"As for Uranus," Claire continued, "in Greek mythology, Uranus is the son and husband of Gaia."

"Who?"

"Gaia is the daughter of Chaos," Claire explained. "She is also the mother of the titans who fought against the Gods of Olympus."

"You know some shit!" Henry said, looking with amazement at his companion.

"Gaia is also the Goddess of the Earth—and the guiding spirit of the Women People!" Claire exclaimed as an image of Marjean formed in her mind.

"So ... Gaia is the guiding spirit of Women People, and her sons are warriors who are fighting to overthrow the rulers of the universe ... Wow!" Henry intoned as he studied the drawing. "What are Uranus's characteristics?"

"Self-expression, intuition, imagination—things like that," Claire replied.

"If the symbols on Roberta' body represent people," Henry observed, "I'd say that Mars represents Tim Hardin, that Venus/Gaia represents Marjean and her feminist cult, and that Uranus represents Fred Ried. He has all sorts of spooky connections with the Aquarian revolution."

"That sounds about right," Claire agreed, standing up. "Maybe the force is the revolutionary impulse," she added as she stood up and stretched her back. Somewhat revived, she drifted to the end of the porch and gazed out. "Henry!" she said, edging back from the rail.

"What?" He asked, noticing her alarm.

"That Country Dog van is over there by that barn."

Henry came up behind her and peered at the barn. "That's it all right," he said. "And there's Wells. He's unloading something."

"And there's the guy who was sitting beside him in the booth last night," she said, referring to McCray. "You know what!" she exclaimed. "That's marijuana!"

"Come on," Henry said, guiding her into the room at the end of the house—it was the only window that faced the barn. As they watched, Hunt Fisher stepped out. "Looks like they are moving bundles from the van and storing them in the barn," Henry whispered.

After completing the transfer, the three porters remained in the barn for some time. Wells and McCray finally emerged and climbed into the van. Fisher was the last to come out. She slid the two barn doors shut and locked them. She climbed into the van's cargo hold and pulled its door shut behind her. Claire and Henry listened as the engine wheezed and watched the van rumble off. The cloud of dust pluming up in its wake allowed them to track it to the main house.

The antient boxwood hedge that surrounded the house formed the upper boundary of the meadow. An overgrown fence line separated Trip's cabin from the meadow, but a rusty gate in front of the cabin gave its occupants access to it. The barn was across the meadow beyond another rusty gate. Henry peered at the mansion from his perch at the window. Near its veranda, he could see the top of a sculpture. As he studied it, he realized he was staring at the head of a bull on the shoulders of a man. He was staring at a Minotaur! It suddenly occurred to him that Hunt and her accomplices were part of Ried's Aquarian Revolution.

"Let's go see what's in the barn," Claire said, drawing him out of his revelation.

"Ok," Henry said. She was already at Duncan White's screen door. He opened it and followed her out.

Before approaching the gate, Henry detoured to his car and collected his crowbar. After a sweeping security check, He pulled the gate back. "Ready?" He asked.

"Ready," she answered.

In the next instant, the two sleuths were galloping across the pasture toward the barn. It took a second for Henry to unlatch the barn gate, then another mad dash to barn's front doors. They were secured with a strong lock, so Henry, followed by his comrade, crept around the barn's corner and down a slope where they found a side door. It was also locked, but the latch plate was attached to a worm-eaten door jamb that Henry easily pried off. They entered an undercroft with two rows of stalls. Near the door was a musty old staircase. Claire led Henry up the stairs and into a dirty, cobweb filled room filled with old tools and other assorted junk. The door on its far side opened into the barn's central hall. A tractor with a farm wagon was parked in the middle of this hall. The wagon was piled high with stalks. Behind it was an old door resting on a pair of sawhorses. On one end of this makeshift table, overhanging its sides, were marijuana plants waiting to be stripped. Beside them, in the middle of the table, was a mound of stripped leaves. Beside the leaves was a stack of white plastic garbage bags waiting to be filled. Beneath the table and on the floor around it were empty apple crates.

"Phhfffwww," Henry whistled, gazing at the wall of stacked crates on the far side of the workbench. "Looks like they're just finishing up."

Turning toward the wall behind them, Claire spied the bundles that Wells and his comrades had just unloaded. These fresh-cut plants were hanging upside down on pegs so the resin in the stems could drain into the leaves.

"That must be the last of it," Claire said, looking at Henry.

"We'd better get out of here before they come back," Henry observed, starting for the tool room door.

They retraced their steps down the stairs through the stable to the side door. Henry peered out, then stepped out of the barn. He made another scan there, signaled to Claire to join him, then pulled the barn door shut and reset the lock plate. The two trespassers sped back to the gate where they took one more look around. "Are you ready?" Henry asked. When Claire nodded, they took off across the meadow and disappeared through the opened gate in front of Trip's cabin.

"Some safe-house . . ." Claire panted as they crept up its porch stairs.

"I don't claim to be infallible," Henry protested as he lifted Duncan White's door.

"Do you think this has something to do with that gathering last night?" Claire asked, leading him into the dark cabin.

"Looks like part of the drug deal I was telling you about," Henry agreed, collapsing on the couch in front of the hearth.

"What are you going to do?" Claire inquired as Henry lifted the phone on the table beside the couch.

"I'm calling Prout," he replied. "Something tells me we're going to need him before we're through."

He dialed information and got the number for the Boar's Head Inn. "I'd like to speak with the bartender in the Hunt Room," he said when the Inn's operator answered. A moment later Prout's voice came on the line.

"Hey boy!" He exclaimed. "You comin' over—with your ritzy blonde?"

"No," Henry answered. "We want you to come over here."

"Where are you?"

"At Trip's. You know—where you get your vegetables."

"Is the squash ripe?" Prout wondered.

"Forget the squash," Henry snapped. "Looks like the back end of a drug deal's sitting in the barn across the way . . ."

"Call the cops!" Prout suggested.

"We can't have them mucking around right now," Henry explained.

"Why not?"

"Because we've got some business to take care of . . ."

"What might that be?" Prout wondered.

"We're going to sneak into Monticello tonight to retrieve a journal, and we need you to take us up there . . ."

"Prout laughed. "You'd better call James <u>Bond</u>!"

"If we don't get it," Henry warned, "Douglas will . . ."

"William O.?" Prout hissed.

"Yes."

"We don't want that," Prout agreed without waiting to find out what it was.

"You're a good man, James!" Henry announced.

"There're still a few of us," Prout agreed. "I don't get out of here until eight . . ."

"Get your gear and meet us here at 8:45."

"You mean my . . ."

"Yea—fully loaded . . and bring the jeep—we'll be going up the side of the mountain."

———————

Hunt Fisher checked her watch. It was exactly 4:30. The phone rang right on schedule. "Fisher," she snapped, as she brought the receiver to her ear.

"Everything cool?" Hardin asked.

"Yea," she replied. "We cut the last of the crop and put in it the barn. We'll have it all picked and bagged this evening."

"Good! We're just about done here . . ." Hardin blew a marijuana smoke ring toward Monticello Mountain.

"Are you coming over?"

"No. I'm going to snitch the seeds from Barty boy . . ."

"You want me to meet you?"

"Yea . . . Meet me in the back parking lot of the Holiday Inn. I'll be there by six—I'll give you the seeds. Then I'm going to see the weird sisters . . ."

"Over at Belmont?"

"Yea . . . they want to meet at Henry's cottage. I gather they've arranged some fireworks." The idea made him laugh. "I'll connect with you after that."

"I'm meeting Bildner at the groundskeeper's shed at Farmington." Fisher reminded him.

"What time is that?"

"8:45—is that too early for you?"

"Yea. Let's meet at University Hall . . . say 10PM."

"We'll be in the limo," Fisher said.

Hardin laughed. "Yea . . . brilliant!"

"Good luck!" Fisher said before setting the receiver down.

"It'll be a blast!" Hardin answered as the line went dead.

———————

Frances Rank was the first to reach the lake. She paused to catch her breath, then stomped out onto the dock. "This is the sea of glass—right?" she growled, looking back at Gerta.

"That's what Marjean said," Gerta answered apologetically.

"Well where the hell is she?" Now Rank was pissed. "We're here," she growled, reddening, "on the cusp of the next great transit . . . the dawn of a new cosmic age . . . ready to fulfill the ancient prophecy . . . set to cleanse Gaia of male tyranny . . . poised to restore Women People as the rulers of the world!" Her temperature rose with each syllable. ". . . and the star sisters have something better to do!" Just before exploding, she glanced down into the water. "Uhhhh . . ." she grunted.

"Wha'?" Shoate' asked, coming up beside her and looking down. There in the water below, gazing up with bulging, sightless eyes, were the earthly remains of Woman Spirit. "Sister Broomstick!" she exclaimed. "Wha's she doin' in nar?"

Gerta joined them at the end of the dock. "Ahhhhhh!" she screamed when she saw Marjean. "Ahhhh . . ." she screamed again for good measure.

"For Christ's sake!" Rank bellowed. "Will you shut up!"

"It's the end!" Gerta wailed.

Rank glanced at Shoate'. "She's got a point." She closed her eyes and pinched the bridge of her nose. "What are we going to do . . . you remember the rest of her prophesy?" she asked, peering sideways at the UVA professor.

"Sompin 'bout goin' up on na mountain," Shoate' remembered, ". . . an' purgin' tha temple—ba fahr."

Rank took a deep breath and gazed off into the distance. Suddenly her face brightened. "There's the damned mountain right in front of us!" she bellowed, pointing triumphantly at Monticello Mountain. "And there's a temple on the top of it!" She began to shake. "It's all coming together—just like Woman Spirit said!"

"Sister . . ." Gerta's whining voice brought Rank's celebration to a sudden end. "I meant to tell you . . ."

Rank eyed her doleful companion. "What?"

"Martin Ogden told Tim that the constitution you're looking for is up there . . ."

"Eureka!" Rank roared, throwing her arms around Gerta and leading her through a gleeful jig. "That settles it! All we have to do now is get rid of it!" She released her befuddled partner and thrust her hand into her bag. "Then Gaia can bless the law of the Women People . . . and the new age will begin!" She began to dance again, this time waving her charter triumphantly in the air.

"What's this Hank tells me about Ried being dead?" Mr. Paige demanded.

"Yea," the younger Paige grunted, spitting in the dust. "Ain't nobody seen 'im fer a week, so ah went up thar yasterday ta see what wuz goin' on. All that's left of 'is workshop is a pahl o' rubble. Looks like he blew himself up."

"Did you find any body parts?" the older man asked.

"No," the younger man conceded.

"Did you call the police?"

"Jest az ah wuz doin' nat," the younger Paige explained, "ah seen that he had a bunch a marijuana in nis greenhouse! When ah went to see what wuz goin' on, ah foun' a telescope in nis livin' room pointed at a grove o' dope on na hill above Jefferson's pond." He gestured to the cargo in the back of his truck. "He wuz growin' dope raght here on na farm!"

"Marijuana?" His father asked, focusing on the green mountain in the back of his son's pickup truck.

"Raght here under our very nose!" Bart Paige announced indignantly. "Ahm jes' glad ah got to it 'fore somebody got hurt . . ."

"Get rid of it," Mr. Paige ordered.

"Tha's jes' what ahm fixin' ta do," Paige assured his father.

"What about the bull?" Mr. Paige continued, "Hank said you sent him up to Monticello."

"Tha's right," Paige boasted. "An' happy ta do it!" He added. "They wuz so nice in what they did fer you, ah figgered we might help 'em out with thar breedin'." He watched as his father digested his story. "As a madder o' fact," he added, "ahm goin' up thar soon's ah git this dope into tha trash pit."

Paige nodded, still staring at the marijuana. "Why do I worry so much about you?" he asked himself.

———————

"What do you suppose happened to Aster?" Rank wondered, picking her way through the debris-strewn dome.

"That monster probably carried her off," Gerta volunteered.

"Something's not right," Rank agreed. "She and Marjean were inseparable."

"Look here," Shoate' said. "If we're gonna lif' tha const'tution we gotta have a plan. Ya see what ahm sayin'?"

"That's right," Rank agreed, banishing Aster from her mind.

"An' ah got jes' tha one!"

"Oh yea?" Rank said, focusing again on business. "What is it?"

"Ah spent mos' o' tha summer diggin' 'roun' Betty Hemin's cabin. Right! So ah know 'bout tha paf that runs up fom 'er cabin ta tha big house. See what ahm sayin'? We kin park by tha slave buryin' groun' off tha main road an' go on na 'roun'-about ta Betty's place. Fom thar, we kin take tha paf up ta tha garden, hop inta tha tunnel by tha kichen, an' slip on inta tha house."

"What about tha door?" Rank asked, weighing the feasibility of Shoate's plan.

"Ah got tha key raght here," Shoate' announced reaching into her bag. The other two women watched as she pulled out a snub-nosed 38. "Here,"

457

she said screwing a cylinder onto the barrel. "Jes' so we don't d'sterb da neighb'rs..."

"Good!" Rank grunted. "Now where'd you say the constitution is?" she asked looking at Gerta.

"Tim said it's in the curator's office on the second floor," Gerta peeped.

"Let Gaia's will be done!" Rank crowed. "We'll go up there as soon as it's dark."

Suzie watched as Paige pulled the last few plants out of his truck bed. "Can we go now?" she called out of the passenger's window.

"Yea," Paige replied, coming around to the driver's door and climbing in. "Let's git tha hell outta here b'fore Daddy comes back." He started the engine and threw it in reverse.

"Where're we going now?" Suzie asked, pulling a stick of gum out of its wrapper.

"Up ta tha lounge ta see Arty," he said. "When it's dark, we'll go git tha book..."

"Are you really going to join Arty's band?" she asked as they sped up the highway towards Pantops Mountain.

"Shit yea!" he said. "Ah ken sing ez good ez him... an' b'sides, ah gotta keep mah eye on mah merchandise!"

"Here comes a green station wagon," Claire called into the house.

Henry stepped to the railing on Trip's porch and watched his rusty green Plymouth pull to a stop.

"You're early," the doctor called up to them as he lowered his tailgate. He pulled out a bag, shoved the tailgate up and walked around to the front steps. Behind him was his bridge partner. "Helen, introduce yourself to my old shipmate," he said as he passed under the door Henry had lifted open.

"You must be Claire," she said with a warm southern smile. She extended her hand as she arrived on the porch. "I'm Helen Ford. Trip said you've sailed together..."

Claire laughed, taking Helen's outstretched hand. "Four of us spent a week cruising in the Penobscot Bay a few years ago."

"That sounds like fun!" Helen nodded. "Did the weather cooperate?"

"It was beautiful . . ."

"Trip also says that you play bridge," Helen continued.

"I'm not particularly good," Claire warned.

"Neither am I," Helen whispered, patting Claire's arm. "Hello Henry," she said as she passed under the door he was still holding up.

Before Henry could decide what he should do next, Dudley reappeared and ducked under his arm. In each hand, he held a bucket. "I understand somebody's been complaining about the door," he said, handing one of the buckets to Claire. "Come on. Let's go pick some corn."

"You have corn here?" She asked, looking around.

"In the garden," the doctor said, trotting down the steps.

Claire followed him down the steps and together they disappeared around the corner of the cabin.

"She's a peach!" Helen said, poking Henry's arm. "Does she work with you at the Academy?"

"When she got here the other day," he explained, "she was a reporter for *The Post*. But now she's considering an offer from Mr. Paige."

"Ooh!" Helen laughed, raising her eyebrows, "That would be good for you . . . By the way, how did your program go?"

"You should have come . . ."

"Susan Davis told me it was *smashing* success," she said with a mischievous smile.

"You know Nurse Davis?"

"We're old friends . . . everybody at the medical school knows everybody in the hospital." Then she remembered. "Susan said one of your guests needed stitches to close a scalp wound?"

"That was Bart Paige," Henry laughed. "He started a riot during the panel discussion . . . That was the low point," he added

"What was the high point?"

"When Claire belted her boss on the Colonnade Club's terrace last night."

"Oh my," Helen scowled. "Won't that hurt your press coverage?"

"I hadn't thought of that," Henry confessed. "Did you know that Claire wrote the article in Friday's paper?"

"I saw that!" she said, admiringly.

"Something interesting came up during dinner last night," Henry confided.

"What was that?"

"The curator at Monticello asked Claire and me to help him translate a collection of letters Thomas Jefferson exchanged with Baron Friedrich de Riedesel."

"Why would he do that?" she wondered.

"Because they are in German!" Henry announced.

"I didn't know Jefferson spoke German?" she replied.

"Nobody knows that!" Henry answered. "That's one of the things that makes it interesting."

"You speak German, don't you Henry!" The medical school professor exclaimed.

"Ein bisschen," Henry said, qualifying his skill. "Claire and I spent the morning translating letters Jefferson wrote two hundred years ago!"

"I bet that was interesting," Helen imagined. "What did they say?"

"Jefferson and de Riedesel seem to have been confidants," Henry replied.

"No kidding—who would have thought!" Helen marveled. "No one I know—other than you, Henry—has even heard of Baron de Riedesel!"

"Their letters contain a lot of behind-the-veil stuff," Henry continued. "In one, for example, Jefferson explained how he was trying to finagle his way into Madame Helvetius's salon. In another, he told de Riedesel how he escaped from the clutches of Maria Cosway."

"Did he reveal the steamy truth about his relationship with Sally Hemings?" the doctor wondered.

"Yes," Henry replied. "Only it wasn't so steamy."

"Darn it!" Helen laughed.

"How can I say this?" Henry wondered, searching for the right words. "She wasn't the kind of person he noticed . . ."

"I've wondered about that," Helen agreed. "What could they have had in common? A visionary patrician and an uneducated farm girl . . . He was thirty years older than she was, wasn't he?"

"Not only that," Henry explained, "somewhere along the way, Jefferson got the idea that the most perfect women embrace 'republican' values, which meant that they derived their happiness from pursuing 'domestic virtues.'"

"I see!" She didn't see. "Sally wasn't in that mold either . . ."

"Well," Henry reflected, "according to accepted history, she bore children from multiple fathers . . ."

"When do you think that Jefferson learned German?" Helen wondered, redirecting the conversation.

"While he was in France, I suppose . . ."

"Why do you think he wrote in German rather than English?" she wondered.

"Smart!" Henry said, pointing a knowing figure at his inquisitive companion. "Only you would ask a question like that." He thought a moment. "It may have been that he felt more comfortable revealing his deepest secrets in German . . ."

"Yo! Bro!" Dudley called from the corner of the cabin. He was carrying a giant squash in each hand. "When the corn is in the bin," he announced, raising the one in his right hand, "the gourds are on the vine!"

Claire appeared next. She was carrying both buckets—filled with corn. "He insisted on serving two vegetables," she explained, answering Helen's quizzical look. "Now that I know all about gardening," she announced as she came up onto the porch, "Trip has offered to get me a job at a roadside stand . . ."

"Now we're going to have a shucking party," Dudley announced. "Get the door, will you Henry . . ." He passed under it and disappeared into the cabin. A moment later the voice of Mother Maybelle Carter rolled out of the cabin door, across the porch, and into the heavens beyond: *Will the circle be unbroken / Bye and bye Lord, bye and bye / There's a better home a waiting / In the sky, Lord in the sky . . .*"

The doctor reappeared with two more chairs. He arranged them with the other two in a circle. "This is how folks do things in Virginia," he said, handing everyone a bag. "When in Rome," he said, taking an empty seat, "do as the Romanians!"

"I see he hasn't changed much," Claire said, exchanging a smile with Helen.

Ogden was on the line. "Yes Martin," the Supreme Court Justice answered sourly.

"We need to talk about your plan . . ."

"The plan's set," Douglas snapped. "And you're part of it so get ready. Bildner will pick you up at the front entrance at 8:45 . . . And Martin, remember . . . If you're not with me, you're against me!"

"Calm down!" Ogden said with a conciliatory laugh. "It's just that Tim has made arrangements . . ."

"I forbid you to bring him into this!" Douglas swore, his voice trembling.

"Bill," Ogden protested, doing all he could to avoid being roped into the dangerous escapade the old Justice had planned. "You're not the only one here who has an interest in Jefferson's Constitution."

"Who else knows about it?" Douglas demanded, as though he were interrogating a pleader across the bar.

"Well . . . er . . . I don't know . . ."

"I'll see you at 8:45," Douglas repeated and slammed down the receiver.

"How's Oscar doing?" Henry asked.

"Fine," Dudley replied. "He should be able to go home tomorrow . . . He said you were going to an event at the Colonnade Club."

"Have you met Fenton Somerville in your far-flung travels?" Henry wondered.

"Does he ride with the Keswick Hunt?" Dudley asked, starting on another ear of corn.

"I don't think so . . . Anyway, I was telling Helen that Claire and I were at Monticello this morning helping him translate a journal that arrived in the mail the other day."

"Henry and Claire were translating letters Jefferson wrote in German!" Helen said, clarifying the project.

"Wahrlick!" The doctor exclaimed. "Er spricht Dutch?"

"Yes," Henry replied. "By the way," he added, "we've got to go over there later this evening."

"Why's that?" the surgeon wondered.

"There's been a bomb threat against the mansion . . . and they've asked the Academy to hold the journal until the situation is resolved," Henry lied.

"When do you have to leave?"

"Jim Prout is picking us up here at 8:45 . . ."

"In that case, we'd better eat so we have time for some bridge," Dudley observed, gathering up the corn.

Henry stepped ahead of his friend and raised the door. "Say," he said, following Dudley into the galley, "I don't want to alarm you, but there's something going on here you should know about . . ."

"What's that?" Dudley asked as he filled his biggest pot with water.

"The barn is full of marijuana—looks like Hunt and her pals have been growing it."

Dudley stopped what he was doing and considered Henry's news. "Now that you mention it," he said, "some strange people have been floating around here lately. One guy looks like a scarecrow and drives a van that looks like a greyhound bus—I was beginning to think I was in Kansas . . ."

Leroy led Fenton Somerville down the steps to the patio. Mr. Paige was having a cocktail there with his wife. "Fenton!" he cried, welcoming his guest. "Wonderful of you to join us!"

"You're too kind," the curator blushed, shaking his hand. "Good evening Mrs. Paige," he said with a deferential bow."

"Good evening Dr. Somerville," she replied formally. "We're both delighted with the program—and the way you've handled it." An envelope appeared in her hand. "Here is a small token of our appreciation."

Somerville shuffled over and took it. "How kind of you," he smiled. He opened it and extracted a check with five digits. "Your generosity is overwhelming . . ."

"It's our pleasure!" Paige announced, patting his guest on the back. "Now that we're finished with the conference, we need to get moving on the bi-centennial program."

"I am at your disposal," the curator bowed.

"Good," Paige beamed. "Can I offer you something? A glass of wine perhaps?"

"A glass of Madeira would be nice," the curator agreed.

"Leroy, get Dr. Somerville some Madeira."

"Has Henry spoken with you about our project?" Somerville wondered.

"Yes, fascinating," Paige exclaimed. "I told him to proceed. And if there's anything you need," he added, "anything at all, feel free to call on me . . ."

"Wonderful! Henry's such a talented young man . . ."

"Yes . . ." Paige agreed, "and we hope that Miss Fox will soon be part of the organization."

"Splendid," Somerville concurred, lifting the glass of Madeira off Leroy's tray. "To Thomas Jefferson and the pursuit of knowledge," he said, raising a toast.

"And to the principles he bequeathed us!" Paige added. His wife joined them as they clinked their glasses.

"Do you have any idea what the letters contain?" Mrs. Paige asked.

"The correspondence appears to run from Jefferson's arrival in France into his first term as President," the scholar replied. "Judging from the ones Mr. Tilghman translated this morning, we are going to learn about a lot of things Mr. Jefferson has managed to keep hidden for the past two hundred years."

"Might that include things valuable to our program?" Paige wondered.

"Absolutely!" Somerville declared. "For example, he might provide insights into Jefferson's mature views on Natural Law and Natural Right. And the status of Property—he was very coy about that in his early writings. Then, of course, there's the issue of judicial encroachment. And I am personally curious to know whether he actually believed that public virtue could be sustained among the masses in the absence of organized religion . . ."

"I'm sure you'll keep me informed," Paige observed.

"By all means!" the Jefferson scholar replied.

"How's the security up there?" Paige asked.

"It's interesting you would mention that," Somerville replied.

"Why?" Paige wondered.

"Well, . . . Bill Douglas asked me the same question last night!"

"Really!" Paige raised his eyebrows.

"He was concerned about the manuscript,"

"Was he!" Paige exclaimed.

"You can rest at ease . . ." the curator responded, as if to put his host's mind at ease. "The property is patrolled twenty-four hours a day seven days a week."

Paige nodded. "By the way," he added, changing the subject, "I was speaking with my son this afternoon, and he told me that he'd sent our prize bull up your way."

"Mr. Tilghman mentioned that last night," the curator replied. "But as I told him, that's out of my department. You need to speak with the property manager."

Just then Leroy appeared. "You have a call from a Mr. Ted Hoagland," he informed Mr. Paige.

"Would you excuse me, Fenton," Paige said, raising and stepping to the table on the side of the patio.

"Yes Ted . . ."

"I'm sorry to bother you, Mr. Paige," the DA said, "but I thought you should know that Sheriff Bailey found Tim Hardin's body at Henry Tilghman's cottage a little while ago. It was riddled with buckshot . . . from Tilghman's shotgun."

"Any tattoos on it?" Paige asked.

"Not this time . . . But he did have that medallion around his neck."

"Hmmm," Paige murmured, digesting the news. "How did you happen to find him?"

"We got a tip from an anonymous caller," the DA replied.

"That sounds suspicious," Paige observed. "What did he say?"

"It was a woman," Hoagland said, correcting him. "She said that Tilghman had been fighting with Hardin over the girl."

"Miss Fox?"

"I guess . . ."

"That doesn't sound like Hank," Paige observed. "When did the murder take place?"

"Sometime within the last twelve hours."

"Hank was up at Monticello this morning—isn't that right, Fenton?" Paige called over to his guest.

"What's that?" Somerville responded.

"Wasn't Tilghman with you this morning?"

"Yes," the curator nodded. "From 7:00 until about noon."

465

"Did you hear that?" Paige repeated into the receiver. "Tilghman was with Fenton Somerville from 7:00 this morning until noon."

"I still need to talk with him," the DA announced.

"That's your call," Paige shrugged. "Where are you now?"

"I'm getting set to do a flyover in the chopper," the DA replied. "By the way," he added. "Do you know what kind of car Tilghman drives?"

Tilghman drives some old bronze thing," Paige answered.

Before he could set the receiver down, the DA spoke again. "One more thing," Hoagland added in a tense voice.

"Yea?" Paige snapped.

"It appears that your son is involved in Fred Ried's drug operation..."

"He told me Ried is dead!" Paige retorted.

"I don't think so," the DA responded.

"You think Ried is alive?"

"Yes," Hoagland affirmed. "In fact, we have a warrant out for his arrest."

"On what charge?"

"Cultivating illegal crops."

"Marijuana?"

"It's more complicated than that," Hoagland replied. "Ried was growing coca and marijuana in his greenhouse... We think he crossed them and that he's growing a new species of marijuana... on your farm!"

"What do you mean?" Paige demanded.

"Looks like he's hybridized an Asian stock with coca plants. If we don't find it," the DA warned, "it could begin to seed naturally. If that happens, we'll have a *real* problem!"

"That son of a bitch!" Paige swore. "I should have run him off after that gem scam—him and that creature down there with my daughter!"

"We'd like to talk to your son," The DA continued. "Do you know where we can find him?"

"I saw him a couple hours ago at the breeding barn," Paige responded. "He said he was going up to Monticello to pick up the bull."

"I'll give you a call if I spot him."

"I'll be here," Paige snapped and hung up the phone.

"I was just telling your lovely wife how much I love your view of Monticello," Somerville crooned. "It's so peaceful!"

Trip was about to deal a new hand when Prout appeared in the door.

"Oh dear!" Helen exclaimed when she saw his jungle fatigues.

"Head for the hills!" Dudley called out. "The revolution's begun . . ."

"I hope this is the right place," Prout said, flashing his signature grin.

"James," Henry called out, stepping around the card table to the door. "You're right on time." As he approached the door, Delilah Wanamaker stepped into view. The law school's first female faculty member was wearing the same camo gear as Prout down to the combat boots and the charcoal smears on her cheeks.

Henry pushed the door up so the two ninjas could enter. "Helen, remember Jim Prout," the doctor said just to be sure.

"Yes, I do!" she smiled. "But I haven't met his comrade."

"Delilah Wanamaker," Prout said, stepping to one side, "meet Helen Ford, radiologist at the UVA hospital."

"I don't like being home alone," she said by way of an introduction. "It's nice to meet you, Helen."

Henry studied the legal scholar for a long moment. "You may not be the stay-at-home sort," he agreed, "but this is different . . ."

"You don't expect me to go into action without my lawyer," Prout joked.

"You're not going to ask Delilah to do this, I hope," Henry protested.

"Of course I am!" Prout answered without hesitating. "There's nobody I'd rather have with me in a tight spot."

"But it may be dangerous . . ." Henry protested.

"Delilah's a crack shot and a master of the martial arts," Prout snapped. "She could break me into pieces if she wanted to."

Wanamaker put her arm over Prout's shoulders and gave him a peck on the cheek. "Fortunately," she said, addressing Henry, "I haven't had to—yet . . ."

"Ok," he said, giving in. "It's your call . . ."

Claire watched the exchange. Now she stepped in front of Wanamaker and took her hands. "I'm glad you're here . . . we're a team."

"I'm in," Wanamaker said with a resolute nod. "We're going to take care of this business," she announced, closing the discussion.

"I guess this means we're going," Claire said. "Thank you, Trip, for a fun evening! And it was so nice to meet you, Helen."

"Yes—I hope we can do it again soon," she said, staring at Claire with an anxious expression. "Take care of them, Delilah," she added, placing her hand on Delilah's arm.

"Would you like to take some squash?" Dudley asked as they file past him out the door.

"Another time," Prout said with a wave of his hand.

"If you don't mind, I'll leave my car here," Henry said, patting Trip's shoulder.

"Leave the keys," he added. "I'm having some problems with the Plymouth . . ."

Claire took the seat in the back next to Prout's duffle bag. As she settled herself, she noticed a gun barrel protruding through its drawn neck. On the floor, a couple flashlights were lying next to a webbed gun belt with a holstered 45 and some ammunition clips. Delilah took the place on the other side of the gear. "You never know," she shrugged, giving Claire a reassuring look.

Henry climbed into the passenger's seat next to Prout. "Ready?" he said.

"Which way?"

"Go over to 64," Henry answered. "We'll take the Shadwell exit at 250. Go east past the store then take the left at Randolph's Mill. Right after you across the Rivanna bridge, cut down to the river, and I'll show you Jack Jouett's trail—we'll follow that over to the foot of the mountain."

"How far is that?" Prout asked.

"About two miles from the bridge," Henry guessed. "When we get to the Monticello property, we'll take one of the trails through the woods up to the second roundabout. We'll leave the jeep there and go the last couple hundred yards on foot . . ."

"That brings me to my next question," Prout continued. "Why are we doing this?"

"We're going to retrieve a collection of letters from Thomas Jefferson's privy," Henry replied.

"Jefferson's privy," Prout snorted. "I didn't know he needed a privy!"

"I can explain," Claire interrupted.

"Good," the ex-marine grunted.

"There are two things going on . . ." she continued.

"First," Prout ordered.

"There's been a murder . . ."

"A murder . .," Prout repeated, glancing at Henry. "Are you listening to this Professor?" he called over his shoulder.

"Yep," Wanamaker shot back.

"Keep this quiet . . ." Henry continued.

"Ok," Prout agreed.

"Two days ago," Henry began, "I found Roberta Wiley's body at the lake above my cottage."

"Ok," Prout nodded. "What was the other thing?" Prout asked, throwing the jeep into first gear.

"Tim Hardin has fired the opening shot in the Aquarian Revolution." Claire responded.

"Would that have anything to do with the explosion at the Rotunda?" Wanamaker wondered.

"Yes," Claire replied.

"You're coming into this kind of late," Henry observed, "so there are things you don't know—yet. First," he continued, "everything seems to be connected to an ox skull icon in the frieze on Jefferson's mantle."

"Sounds mysterious," Wanamaker said.

"It really is," Claire agreed. "The victim's body was covered with hiero-glyphics, and one was that ox skull symbol."

"It's also on the cover of de Riedesel's journal, which is part of the collection we're going to Monticello to pick up," Henry added.

"And it's on the medallions that our prime suspects are all wearing," Claire continued.

"Who are we talking about," Wanamaker wondered.

"Tim Hardin, who you know, Aster Paige, who is Raymond Paige's daughter, and Aster's companion, whose name is Marjean. A guy named Fred Ried made the medallions, and I suppose he is also wearing one."

"I knew a guy named Fred Ried in Vietnam," Prout announced. "He was in special ops—flew cover for us a bunch of times. He was good at smoking out gooks . . ."

"What did he look like?" Henry asked.

"He was about six feet tall. Dark wavy hair . . . looked like the devil's handyman . . . women loved him."

"Did he have a moustache?"

"Like Poncho Villa."

"That's him!" Henry said.

"Have you met Bildner?" Prout asked.

"I've seen him," Henry replied.

"He and Ried were buddies—they did everything together . . ."

"Mr. Paige mentioned his name," Claire added.

"That's right," Henry nodded." He's Douglas's chauffeur."

"That's bad," Prout scowled. "Ried's wild. Bildner's psychotic . . ."

Henry swallowed.

"So Roberta may have been murdered by a gang of Aquarian revolutionaries," Wanamaker summarized. "Where does Douglas fit in?"

"He has some kind of relationship with Hardin and Ried," Henry explained. "And it sounds like they masterminded the attack on the Rotunda."

"And it sounds like Jefferson is an unnamed co-conspirator," Prout ventured.

"There's some kind of connection," Henry agreed.

"At this point," Claire announced, "the DA considers Henry the prime suspect in Roberta's murder."

"Now I'm getting the picture," Wanamaker nodded. "You need to unravel the mystery so you're not hung for a murder you did not commit!"

"Yes!" Claire agreed. "We think the key to the mystery is the ox skull on Jefferson's mantle. We think Jefferson revealed why he put it there in his correspondence with de Riedesel . . ."

"And if you can find that out, you think you will be able to decipher the diagram!" the legal scholar surmised, "and save Henry from . . ."

"That's right," Henry confirmed.

"You've seen de Riedesel's journal," Prout supposed.

"Yes," Claire replied. "We were with Fenton Somerville this morning interpreting letters written by Jefferson and the Baron . . . As we were starting, Henry found a letter that Douglas had written to Fred Ried."

"What did the letter say?" Wanamaker asked.

"Douglas warned Ried not to blow up the Rotunda."

"Obviously Douglas has to get the letter back," the law school Professor concluded. "Does he know you have it?"

"Yes," Claire said. "He showed up in Fenton's office right after Henry found it—and put it in his jacket pocket! Douglas immediately pushed Henry out of the way and started paging through the journal. When he didn't find his letter, he gave Henry a withering look."

"Douglas knows you have his letter," Wanamaker repeated, ". . . and he has Bildner on your trail . . . and if Bildner doesn't get you, then the long arm of the law will."

"Yep . . ." Henry gulped.

"That's all of it," McCray said, pulling the van's cargo door shut.

Hunt Fisher looked at her watch. It was 8:15. "Right on schedule," she said. "Help me lock up, then we'll go." They pulled the sliding doors together. Fisher flipped the metal latch across the lock plate and snapped the lock through the loop. She followed McCray back to the passenger's door and squeezed in beside him. "Ok," she said, pulling the door.

"Where to?" Wells asked, stepping on the accelerator.

"We're going to make the switch at Farmington," she answered. "Go in 250 and I'll show you where to turn."

The light was fading, but Trip could still see the van in front of the barn. "It looks like they're wrapping up," he said, glancing at Helen. A moment later the engine whined and the van started off.

"I really think you should call the police," Helen said.

"You're probably right." He picked up the phone, put it to his ear, and dialed '0'.

"Number please," said an operator.

"I'd like to speak to the sheriff," the surgeon said.

"I'll connect you now," the operator responded in a mechanical voice.

"Albemarle County Sheriff's Office," another voice announced.

"This is Dr. Dudley at Rose Hill Farm in Ivy. I want to report some suspicious activity on the premises."

"Is this a domestic issue?" The sheriff's dispatcher asked.

"It's more like a drug issue," the doctor replied.

"Hold the line please . . ."

"This is Officer Troupe," the next voice announced. "Can I help you?"

"It looks like some people out here are moving a van-load of marijuana," Dudley said.

"Are they there now?" Officer Troupe asked.

"They just left . . ."

"Do you have the license number for their vehicle?"

"No, but it shouldn't be too hard to spot them," the doctor supposed. "They're driving a VW bus with the words 'Country Dog' painted in bold letters on its sides."

"Could you spell that," the Sheriff's deputy asked.

"C-o-u-n-t-r-y D-o-g."

"And you're Dr. Dudley at Rose Hill Farm in Ivy."

"Correct," Dudley responded.

"I'll pass this information on to Sheriff Bailey. Give me your telephone number in case he needs to contact you . . ."

"The number here is 6-5-4-7-7-3-4."

"Thank you Mr. Dudley. You'll be hearing from us."

The surgeon hung up the phone. "This would be a good time to go over to your place," he said, looking at his guest.

"Do you think we should try to warn Henry and Claire," Helen wondered.

The jeep crossed the Rivanna at Randolph's Mill. At the end of the bridge, Prout turned off the state road and jostled down the embankment to the narrow flood plain beside the river.

"Jack Jouett made this trail famous on June 4, 1781," Henry informed them as they turned onto a rutted path at the river's edge. "Now that I think about it," he continued, "we're on the same kind of mission."

"What's that?" Prout asked as the jeep bounced along tree-lined trail.

". . . risking our lives to rescue Jefferson from a nefarious invader!"

"We're much better armed," Prout said, looking at Delilah in his rear-view mirror.

"Jouett was taking his ease in a tavern called The Cuckoo about forty miles east of here," Henry remembered, diverting the conversation. "As luck would have it, Colonel Tarleton stopped at the same tavern to have dinner. Jouett hung around long enough to discover that Tarleton and a couple hundred British dragoons were on their way to Charlottesville to round up Governor Jefferson and the members of the Virginia legislature, which was meeting in Charlottesville. Jouett mounted his horse and set out in the moonlight. He rode through the night, following back roads and trails, which he knew because he lived in the area. He crossed this ground on the last leg of his ride, suffering the lashes of thorns and low-hanging branches to warn Jefferson. He reached Monticello in time to have breakfast with Jefferson. Then he rode on to the town and warned the legislature. Jefferson got away," Henry added. "But Tarleton nabbed seven law makers."

"How much farther is it?" Prout asked.

"About a mile—we've got to be careful," Henry warned. "There are a couple deep gorges between here and Monticello. We'll have to cut into the woods to get around them."

"You'll have to show me," Prout replied, slowing his speed.

"Did you bring the keys?" Claire asked, tapping Henry on the shoulder.

"Yes," Henry nodded, pulling them out of his pocket and holding them up."

"Good boy," she said, patting him on the head.

"When we get up to the first roundabout below Mulberry Lane," Henry said, finalizing his plan, "we'll lay low until the security patrol goes by. Then we'll duck into the magnolia tree on the left side of the front lawn. You all can wait there while I sneak across to the south terrace and into the cellar. When I get inside, I'm going to see if there's something in the mantle, then I'll grab the journal out of the privy and join you back at the tree."

"Ok, " Prout nodded. "Sounds simple enough."

"If you see something while I'm inside," Henry continued, "flash your light in the library window."

Ogden checked his watch when he saw the headlights appear on the access road. It was 8:44. He stepped to the end of the Boar's Head's entrance awning and waited as the vehicle turned into the inn's driveway.

473

He could see it then. It was a VW bus, not Douglas's stretch limousine. It rattled into the circle and came toward him. Ogden spun around to avoid contact with the debris it carried. The van screeched to a stop behind him. Then he heard a gravelly voice. "Get in!" it said.

Glancing back over his shoulder, Ogden saw the wizened face of Justice Douglas peering at him through a half-opened passenger window. "Hurry up," he snapped, pointing with his thumb to the cargo bay. "We're on a tight schedule."

Ogden flushed but did as he was told. "What the hell is this?" he complained from his seat on an empty apple crate.

"What do you want?" Douglas responded. "A police escort!"

"Well ... er ..." Ogden stammered, considering for the first time the security aspect of their mission.

"Relax," Douglas said in a cool voice. "We've got the whole thing laid out."

"You're sure it's safe ..."

"Yea—as long as you follow instructions," Douglas warned. "We're going up Rte. 53 past the Michie Tavern. Before we reach the entrance to the mansion, Bo's going to let us out. He'll go on past the front gate and stash the van. Then he'll go into the parking area and create a diversion to draw the security people away from the house. In the meantime, we'll hike through the woods to the third roundabout. What is it Bo, about two hundred yards?" The aged jurist asked.

"Yea," Bildner nodded.

"Bo has a golf cart waiting for us there," Douglas continued. "We'll take that through the cattle pen up to the haha wall on the west lawn and wait there for Bo's signal. When the security crew's gone, we'll drive into the north passage. I'll unlock the exterior door, and you'll take the cart right into the cellar. Once we're inside, we'll go up to Fenton's office on the second floor, force the lock, and get the journal out of his desk. In five minutes, we'll be rolling back down the mountain!"

"What about the exit plan?" Ogden demanded.

"Bo will meet us at the third roundabout and take us down the trail to the river. He's got a boat down there to take us up to the 250 bridge. We've got a car there to take you back to the Boar's Head. You'll be in your bed by 10:30—with the journal!"

The Silver Mercedes crossed the Rivanna at Randolph's Mill. Gerta was driving. Shoate' was giving her directions from the passenger's seat. "Take a right at tha stop sign."

"How much further is it?" Rank asked from the back seat.

"A mahl or so," Shoate' answered.

"Let me see," Rank mused. "The kingdom is going to fill with darkness, and the men people are going to gnash their teeth—I like that . . . Then there's going to be thunder and lighting and the earth is going to quake. Then a princess in the raiment of the sun is going come forth . . . and the dragon, which is the anti-Christ, is going to devour her . . . Of course, she'll already be on the mountain so that part of the Prophesy has already been fulfilled," she recounted. "Gaia's going to strike the temple and purge it with flames . . . Then the temple is going to collapse, the minions of the anti-Christ are going to be slaughtered . . . and the anti-Christ is going to flee into the wilderness. When he's gone, Gaia's going to bless our new charter . . ." Rank's voice rose, "and Women People will rule the world again!"

"Hallay-loo-ya!" Shoate' sang out.

"Who's the dame dressed in the raiment of the sun?" Rank asked, suddenly anxious.

"It ain't Sister Broomstick . . ." Shoate' laughed. Then she too became serious. "Ah see tha temple thin'," she said. "But who's gonna be fightin' wif Gaia? Tha's wha's got me stumped."

"Whoever it is, he's a cooked goose," Rank snapped. "And we'll be there with the scroll!" she added, leaning forward and waving it in Shoate's face.

"Slow down now," Shoate' cautioned Gerta. "We jes' 'bout thar," she said, pointing toward a wide shoulder ahead on the right. "Tha's tha trail," she said as Gerta eased her gray Mercedes off the state road into a makeshift parking area. "Tha's whar Tom Jefferson buried 'is slaves," Shoate' said, gesturing to an open space among the trees.

"Ok," Arty said, staring into his beer. "You can come along, but we're not doin' any of the shit they play in here—you understand?"

"Don't make no dif'rence ta me," Paige smiled. "Ah ken sing anythin' . . ."

"Honey," Suzie interrupted. "Shouldn't we be going?"

Paige looked at his watch. It was a few minutes before nine. "Yea!" He said, downing one last tequila shooter. "We're gonna run a little erran'," he told Arty. "Ahl have tha money t'marra mornin' an' ahl have tha crop bah t'morra evenin'. Soon's ah git it, we kin git tha hell outta here!"

"Good," the rock star grunted.

They lay on their stomachs in the tall grass and watched the security vehicle come up the south drive. The beam of its headlights shown into the darkness above them for a long moment then swung to the east as the white jeep crossed Mulberry Lane. After pausing in front of the house, it continued around the circle and passed out of sight.

"Come on!" Henry commanded, scrambling to his feet.

Claire, Delilah, and Prout raced after him across the dappled lawn. A second later the intruders disappeared into the leafy apron of the magnolia that filled the lawn in front of the mansion's south wing. Its leaves enclosed a skeleton of branches that extended in a Fibonacci series around the tree's bulky trunk. Picking their way through them, they reached the opposite side of the shelter.

Looking out, Henry studied the mansion's south terrace, which was directly in front of him. Down the slope on the left was Mulberry Lane. About the same distance to their right was the east portico. A brick walk extended from Mulberry Lane along the mansion's eastern perimeter. It proceeded past the portico and along the north terrace. A second walk, which crossed in front of the chambers beneath the mansion's south promenade, intersected the first at the corner of the terrace. At this corner was the entrance to the mansion's south passage. The only obstacle between the magnolia tree and this entrance to the building was the low hedge that lined the walkway along the front of the house.

Henry hunched down next to Prout. Claire and Delilah hovered over them like guardian angels. "I'll flash a light when I get inside," Henry whispered.

Claire leaned down and kissed his cheek. "Good luck!" Wanamaker added, patting him on the back. "We're with you . . ."

Henry jumped through the leaves, darted across the lawn, and burst through the hedge. His companions watched as he bounded across the landing and spun sharply to his right. In the next instant, he disappeared into the south passage.

Claire knelt down beside Prout. "I suppose you're used to this," she whispered anxiously.

Prout was holding his Stoner M63 carbine in his right hand. He raised his free hand and gave Claire a reassuring pat. "Don't worry. This is a piece of cake . . ."

Claire took a deep nervous breath and glanced at the weapon. "I hope you're right!"

"He's in," Wanamaker whispered, pointing to the flashlight beam shining out of the piazza window.

"Good, "Claire said, squeezing her arm.

Prout suddenly tensed. Turning in the direction of his gaze, Claire saw three shadowy figures crossing Mulberry Row. She watched them float up the slope in bat-like silence. A second later, they disappeared into the passage Henry had entered a few moments before.

"Oh Jim!" Claire gasped, grabbing his arm.

"Stay calm," he said, flashing his light into the library window.

As they waited for Henry's response, they heard an explosion somewhere on the far side of the mountain.

"What was that?" Wanamaker said, pushing to the edge of the canopy.

"Sounds like incoming," the former marine answered, rising to his feet and flicking his carbine's safety off. He then stepped forward and joined his comrade. The two warriors were now ready for action. As they gauged the situation, a siren began to scream. It seemed to be coming from the vicinity of the explosion. As they listened to this new disturbance, they heard something puttering beyond the west end of the house. Prout stepped out from the refuge to get a better look. Wanamaker followed him. "It sounds like . . . a golf cart!" she whispered, straining to see through curve of the hill.

"I'm scared," Claire said, joining them on the edge of the lawn. She pressed against Wanamaker as Prout shined his light again into the library window. Suddenly, there was a loud rumbling noise.

"Jim!" Wanamaker shouted, "behind you!"

He turned in time to see the headlight beams rising out of the orchard on the mountain's northeastern slope. A second later a black pickup surged into view. It swerved across the dappled lawn and accelerated up the walk. The three vigilantes watched in stunned silence as it rocketed up the steps and sliced between the giant columns. Then, with a teeth-jarring crash, it pierced the double glass doors and disappeared into Thomas Jefferson's majestic entrance hall.

"I'm going in," Prout roared, snapping an ammunition clip into his carbine's magazine. Claire held her breath as he sprinted toward the portico steps. Before he'd covered half the distance, the house lit up and the ground shook. The noise of the explosion was deafening. A fusillade of glass and shattered wood sprayed out across the lawn. The two women watch helplessly as Prout flew toward them through the air. He hit the ground hard and rolled to a stop at their feet.

"Jim!" Delilah screamed, kneeling down.

"Is he breathing?" Claire gasped, leaning down beside her.

Wanamaker placed her fingers on her friend's neck. "He has a pulse," she announced. "He's out cold!" she announced, rising up. "Look after him . . . I'm going to find out what's going on." She stepped over this Prout's motionless body, picked up his rifle, and headed toward the corner of the burning house.

"Oh God!" Claire screamed, focusing on the flames jumping through the mansion's gaping windows. "Henry's in there!"

Prout grunted and moved slightly. "Jim," she cried, collapsing beside him. "Are you Ok?"

"Just barely," he said, touching his bloodied forehead. "Where's Delilah?"

"She's gone," Claire managed to say. "She took your rifle." Her voice was drowned by a cracking noise that sounded like a million bones breaking. As they watched, the east portico collapsed, sending Jefferson's stone sentries tumbling into the yard. A great cloud of smoke and ash followed them out to where Claire and Prout were huddled.

Somerville watched in stunned horror as the volcano-like eruption lifted the crest off Monticello Mountain.

Leroy appeared at the top of the steps and hurried down to the terrace where the trio were standing.

"Mr. Hoagland is on the line," he whispered to Mr. Paige

Mr. Paige reluctantly shifted his attention from the horrifying spectacle and stepped to the phone. Ted!" he said with a commander's voice. "Do you see what's going on up on Monticello Mountain?"

"Yes," the DA shouted over the roar of his helicopter's engine. "I'm coming across 64 now."

"Somerville's with me," Paige announced. "Swing over and pick us up—we need to get up there right away."

The sound of the rotor grew louder until it was right over their heads. Looking up, Claire saw a police helicopter skirting the edge of the billowing smoke cloud.

"Let's go," she said, putting her hands under Prout's arm and helping him to his feet.

"You go ahead," Prout said, pulling back. "I'm going to find Delilah."

Claire eyed his jungle fatigues and the 45 on his hip. "I understand..." she nodded. "Be careful..."

The marine squeezed her hand. "You too..."

Claire turned and started off across the lawn. When she reached the terrace, she looked back. Prout was gone. She gritted her teeth and set off toward the Bachelor Cottage. Rounding the corner, she hastened up the slope toward the helicopter.

As she approached it, the cab door opened. Mr. Paige was the first to climb out. Then Fenton Somerville appeared. The District Attorney appeared next followed by the pilot.

"Miss Fox!" Mr. Paige exclaimed when he saw her. "What on earth are you doing here? Is Henry with you?" He looked around, but she was alone.

Claire stumbled toward him. "He's in there," she whispered, tears streaming down her cheeks."Good God!" Paige exclaimed, staring at the inferno.

There was another sharp crack. Then another and another. They watched the dome shiver. Then came the sound of shattering glass as the oculus fell from its mounting. Flames shot like a roman candle through the hole it left in the dome's crown. A moment later, the dome gave way, dropping like a dead man into the fire. A wave of smoke and ash washed out toward them.

"Oh Lord," Somerville gasped with Biblical anguish, "The fire of God hath fallen from heaven!"

As if on cue, the roof gave out with an exhausted groan, then it too dropped into the flames. Another cloud belched out across the lawn, this one enveloping them. Gradually the rotor dispersed it and the remains of the house came back into view.

"What's that," Claire asked, pointing to the base of the great poplar in front of the south promenade. "There's something's moving over there."

All eyes focused on the form that had appeared below the window of Jefferson's study.

"IT'S HENRY!" Claire screamed. "Henry!" she cried, racing to him. "You're alive! You're alive!"

Henry rose to his hands and knees. He hovered there as he gulped down several mouthfuls of air. As he did, Claire hurled herself on top of him and smothered him with kisses.

"Oh Henry!" She panted, looking down through her tears. "You're alive..."

"You mean this isn't heaven?" He smiled, stroking her hair.

"Here," Claire said, pulling his arm over her shoulder. "Let's get you to the fresh air." Together they staggered out into the lawn. "Get some water!" she ordered as they approached the helicopter's startled passengers. "Somebody! Bring water!" she cried again as she released him onto the grass.

Somerville hurried to the reflecting pool and grabbed the bucket that was next to the spigot. He plunged it into the pool and shuffled back to where Henry lay.

"Here Henry," Claire said, cradling him in her arms, "Drink this."

Henry raised up on his elbow and drank. Then he pulled the lip of the bucket down so the water poured over his head and face. "Ahhh!" He groaned, settling back.

"By God Hank!" Paige bellowed, bending over his tattered aide. "How the devil did you get out of there?"

"Don't talk," Claire said gently.

"I found it," he croaked, gesturing to something lying in the grass beside him.

"What's that?" Paige asked, noticing the object for the first time.

"Jefferson's chamber pot," Somerville announced, stepping forward and peering into it. "What is this?" He said, lifting a metal box into view. Beneath it, was the journal. "You saved the journal!"

"The secrets of the house," Henry rasped.

"You pierced the frieze!" Somerville surmised.

"It was the only way..."

"What the hell's going on here?" The District Attorney demanded irritably.

"I was going to get the journal," Henry explained, laboring to pronounce each word.

"Dr. Denker gave him your keys," Claire told the stunned curator.

"But first I went into the parlor... I had to know..."

"Of course," Somerville repeated solemnly.

"I pried the molding off the front of the mantle," Henry wheezed. "There was an alcove in the brick work. That's where I found the box..."

"What about the fire?" Hoagland demanded.

"I took it with me into Jefferson's bedroom..."

"Henry hid the journal in the privy after we finished translating it this morning," Claire explained to the astonished curator. "We were afraid Douglas would steal it..."

"Why would he do that?" The curator wondered in amazement.

"Just as I stepped into the privy to retrieve the journal," Henry continued, "there was a violent explosion. It knocked me to the back of the closet and sucked the door shut behind me."

"It's like a bomb shelter," Somerville told the others, "with its own ventilation system," he added.

"I wouldn't have made it otherwise," Henry rasped.

"Amazing!" Paige exclaimed, gazing at the ruins of the house.

"How did you get out?" Hoagland wondered.

"I stood on the seat of the commode and pressed up against the wall—that was the safest place," Henry explained. "I could hear things crashing down and figured the building was beginning to disintegrate. After a while, the door began to burn. About that time, the roof caved in. That sent a cloud of smoke into the privy, and I thought that was the end, but the vent cleared it. That's when I saw that the debris from the roof had suppressed the flames in Jefferson's study. I put the box in the chamber pot with the journal and scrambled out into the passage. It was just a step from there into Jefferson's study. I couldn't tell what the fire was doing because there was too much smoke, so I just plunged through it and dove out where I thought the window was. I must have hit the desk," he said, revealing a nasty bruise on his ribs. ". . . Fortunately the sash was gone . . ."

Fenton had continued to clutch the box and the journal as Henry related the harrowing details of his escape.

"Open the box, Fenton," Claire urged, when he was done.

"Yes . . ." the curator agreed eagerly.

Everyone stepped forward as he pried open the lid. In the fire's flickering light, they saw a set of handwritten pages. Somerville carefully lifted them out of the strongbox. "I expect that the last hand to touch this document," he announced, examining the script, "was Thomas Jefferson's!"

"Read it," Claire said.

Somerville set the box on the grass and adjusted his glasses. Then, in the glow of the burning mansion, he read the first page"

Dear friend, whoever you are, I salute you! You have discovered my secret. I wonder how long it has taken. But never mind . . . It pleases me to speak to you from the land of the shades. For here a long night—an endless night—is before us. Read on and I shall reveal to you things I was careful to conceal during my life.

First, let me say that I never tired of looking at the frieze you have, I presume, destroyed! Truth be known, it was a memorial I created for myself—my self-commemoration for winning Reason's victory over Nature! The strange-seeming ornament told the epic tale. In the beginning is Chaos. Then there is Progress, which is the overcoming of the Endarkenment. Lastly, there is light. The force in this Enlightenment is Reason!

I won this millennial war in my Revolution of 1800. So proud was I of my role in the victory that I placed my celebratory memorial at the center of my universe. I won Man's ultimate triumph! With all due humility, I tell you that I shall surpass all those who have merely claimed a scepter. Where are they now? All gone—conquerors and their empires—into the mists of time! But my victory will endure! Of this, I have no doubt.

Baron de Riedesel, who opened my eyes to many things, brought Vespasian to my attention during his residence in Charlottesville. We spoke many times after that about his temple and its frieze. Tacitus has remained much on my mind since then. Since you have unraveled the secret of Vespasian's frieze, I have no doubt that you know his story. You will therefore understand when I say that the truth begins with this distant Roman. Tacitus says this of him: he alone—unlike the emperors before him—changed for the better. Uncorrupted rulers are rare indeed! This is how I wish to be remembered.

Next are the secrets what I want to reveal:

"This seems to be an introduction," Somerville said, shuffling the page to the back of the set. "It ends with Jefferson's signature. Below it, he wrote the year—1801. The accompanying text apparently reveals his inner most secrets. Shall we see what they are?" He turned back to the papers in his hand and began to read:

I developed a close friendship with Baran De Riedesel. But in spite of our extensive correspondence relating to matters of architecture and design, he seems to have accepted that my sole interest was to highlight my own enlightenment by building a villa in the mode of Andreas Palladio.

It is true that my designs are substantially "Palladian". For example, I followed him in the proportions of the great columns on the east and west porticos. These were in the Doric order. In the interior of the house, I made certain small modifications to Palladio's rules. The dining room was decorated in the Doric order according to his instructions. In the tearoom, I followed Albano placing rosettes in the soffit and in the metope. In the north piazza, I followed the Doric order as it is found in the Baths of Diocletian. I used Palladio's Ionic version in the modillions in the entrance hall, and in my bed chamber, I copied his illustration of the entablature in the temple Fortune Virilis in Rome. In the parlor, I followed Palladio's Corinthian order in the design of the moldings and decorative elements. But the frieze on the mantle and the entablature above it are much more than rote reproductions of a Corinthian decoration. The Baron, it seems, never grasped this.

Palladio knew the frieze as an ornament in the Temple of Jupiter the Thunderer. Desgodetz duplicated this misnomer. Their error was finally exposed when the ruins of the temple were excavated two decades ago. It was then determined that Vespasian's son Titus laid its foundations and that his brother completed the structure a decade after Titus's death. The true meaning of the frieze then became apparent. It ceased to be merely a Corinthian adornment and became instead a rendering of Vespasian's great victory in the Year of the Four Caesars.

On one level, the frieze illustrates a sequence that has been repeated again and again. The skull has special significance in this repetitive process. It illustrates Disorder and Ignorance. In Nature, it represents Chaos. In human society, it represents Corruption and Incompetence. Altogether, it portrays the absence of Reason—Irrationality. As for a name, I call it Tertium Datur, which describes the natural—benighted—condition of Man.

On another level, as I say, the frieze is a fitting tribute to my success because I prevailed against three corrupt rivals just as Vespasian did during the Year of the Four Caesars.

Tacitus described the natural order in The Histories. (I know it by heart.) He said this:

> "From time immemorial, man has had an instinctive love of power. With the growth of our empire, this instinct has become a dominant and uncontrollable force. It was easy to maintain equality when Rome was weak. World-wide conquest and the destruction of all rival communities or potentates opened the way to the secure enjoyment of wealth and an overriding appetite for it. This was how the smouldering rivalry between the senate and people was first fanned into a blaze. Unruly tribunes alternated with powerful consuls. Rome and the Roman forum had a foretaste of what civil war means."

Plato told us that the story of man in society is a tale of degeneration.

We know now that instead of a single epic decline, the decline is repetitive. If the Bible is to be believed, as Paine claimed, the Jews formed the first democracy. A millennium passed before the Golden Age of Greece dawned. The Romans duplicated the feat of the virtuous Athenians. But as with Pericles's masterpiece, theirs was overwhelmed by scoundrels who robbed their comrades of their freedom. Even the heirs of the liberty-loving Anglo-Saxons proved unworthy, snuffing out their republican light before a decade passed. In my time, we have had a leader, General of the Army in time of war, Executive Officer of the Government in peace, who was a shining symbol for a promising new order. In him, Reason attempted to establish her empire. How quickly he was carried out of his element! How foolish—flawed—he was in trusting the counsel of men who shared tyrants' cravings for power. Before my very eyes he delivered our fledgling republic into the hands of predators. No less frightening, I confess, was the sheep-like willingness of the people to accept them as their rulers.

> *"A sudden lightening flash from the clouds lit up the sky. The doors of the high place abruptly opened, a superhuman voice was heard to declare the gods were leaving it, and in the same instant came the rushing tumult of their departing . . ."*

What is Tacitus telling us here? It sounds like the Apostle harkening the end time. In fact, it is a living part of human history. It came and the effects were cataclysmic. Then it came again! And again. And again. But the world did not end. It merely darkened. And in the darkness, new seeds germinated. When my time came, I toppled another generation of tyrants and uprooted their system. Yet, so mild were the tremors of <u>my</u> revolution that not a drop of blood was shed. This is the legacy I leave my fellow men. It is not a <u>government</u> founded on laws that make society perfect. It is a <u>method</u> of change, facilitated by the authority of Reason and good will, that protects men against the corruptions of men.

I laugh at how de Riedesel and Rush harangued me with their mystical doctrines. Grace! Forgiveness! Redemption! These notions are repugnant to thinking men. The idea that the dead live in Paradise is nothing more than a deception despots use to perpetuate their corruptions. I totally reject these dogmas. Nor do I understand how reasonable men can rest their world on such an odious concept! Had they placed their faith as I do in Reason instead of ghost-filled theologies, they would know that the chaos that is waiting to swallow their souls resides in the shadows of benighted minds.

History proves to reasonable men that the author of Nature created his work to destroy it. I laugh even now to repeat its fundamental principle. Tertium Datur! Disorder is an integral part of creation. Paradise, transient as it is, is produced by human industry alone!

"You are called to be the ruler of men who can tolerate neither slavery nor liberty."

Who indeed can rule when the people themselves are the foremost enemies of the state? Was it the fault of Pericles that his followers were unworthy of their inheritance? Or Cato. And what of poor Cromwell? Is he to be blamed because Englishmen preferred monarchy to republican government? The truth is plain enough for those willing to see it. Nobility is not a quality of common men. Look at France! There will never be a finer opportunity for social science. It was a Lazarusian corpse waiting dutifully for a life-giving touch. Yet instead of utopia, its deliverers created the Terror! Yes, they erased the vestiges of the Ancien' Regime. But apart from that, they accomplished nothing! They merely prepared the way for Napoleon to seat himself on an emperor's throne. What happened to the egalitarian society the philosophe promised?

I will not be goaded by millennial visions. My purpose is to raise up an honest yeomanry. They are the good in society. I shall plant the power in them so they can create an Arcadia within our boarders. When one generation passes away, its youthful successors will renew the covenant and start again. This, I say, is the only way to preserve freedom. It is entirely beyond backward-looking self-servers.

"In the pursuit of an empire there is no mean between the summit and the abyss."

I experienced many anxious moments watching as the revolution in France unraveled. And as it did, monarchists here launched a calculated assault on our republic. But I never lost the faith that inspired me as a young man. In the years since, however, I have come to understand the baseness of "the people." Ideologues spill far too much bile pillorying society's leaders. (My turn will come no doubt.) In truth, the Achilles heel in the body politic is the venality of their followers. How many 'good' men condone tyranny? As I witnessed the betrayal of those who died creating democracy in America, it occurred to me that my own fate lay in their hands! This has remained my most enduring revelation.

Thus I, a private citizen of contemplative nature, dared to resist. My purpose at the outset of my project was to protect my own liberty against the depredations of mindless people and their tyrannical leaders. As I proceeded, I grasped the true purpose of my revolution: unless I controlled my own destiny, I would be trampled by a credulous mob!

The revelation was entirely sound, but impractical to present as a general rule. I therefore built my campaign not on the light that guides the best men, but by stirring the dark passions that guide lesser men. In the end, the victory was as sweet. My enemies were vanquished by weight of numbers—at the ballot box no less! Despite the corruptions beneath the laureled helmet, it was a victory for Reason. I, at long last, established a system that could perpetuate through the generations. Others have described an army of elks led by lions. I prefer an army drone led by reliable partisans.

The illuminati in the Parisian salons imagined that perfection in society could be produced by common people freely exercising their inherent wisdom. At one time, I accepted this. But I now know this is not the case. The first societies were natural organisms that lived and died in spite of their people. When people in those communities were hungry, their pressing concern was food. When they were not hungry, few of them cared at all about food. Condorcet, a lamented friend, taught me this lesson with his life. Prior to the rise of Reason, societies perpetuated not because their members exercised inherent wisdom. They survived as long as they did because they faced common perils. When this bonding agent weakened sufficiently, their society dissolved, and they disappeared.

The truth is revealed in the histories of the Greek and Roman republics, and in the failure of the revolution in England. And in the

French Terror! The truth is this: there is no inherent wisdom in the people. When they have had the power, they have chosen to be led by tyrants. Corrupt leaders produce corrupt societies. In my time, I have had to deal with Hamilton, Adams, and Burr. The American people would have followed each them had I not prevented them.

To defeat my enemies, I took a great chance. Now that I sit in the ruler's chair, I can say how much I abhorred the conflict. In fact, by defeating my enemies, I gained the power to define the common good and how the people would achieve it! It was more than a fair trade off!

In Plato's civil society, every man has his place and guardians to rule him in the name of the common good. Plato's utopia became a prison, however, because the people are not allowed to pursue their happiness. It is different in our modern political society. Everyone there is in perpetual pursuit of Happiness. The primary occupation of guardians in political society is, therefore, to shape the perception of it in the minds of the people. To succeed, as I demonstrated in my last rebellion, better men must organize, and when they are organized, they must take perpetual care to teach those beneath them what makes them happy and how to acquire it. Unless these men—I call them nature's aristoi—manage the herd, our modern political society must also fail.

"Oh my!" Somerville stammered. "Something isn't right here . . ." He turned again to the text in his hands.

Politics is war. One must win to have the wherewithal to make and implement policy. Therefore, victory is the entire good in political society. Nor is there a place in the system for those who fall short. Those whom I vanquished—Hamilton, Burr, Adams—prove my point. Prominence did not save them. It only lengthened their fall. In candor, I hate them all. Not only did they betray the revolution of enlightened Reason, they betrayed <u>me</u>! Did they think I would not understand the game they were playing? Read Tacitus! Is not Perfidy his story? I know it chapter and verse.

Mr. Adams, the boiling kettle, was ever the plotter. I should have known from his methods that he was not to be trusted. I know what happened—he remained too long in England and became blinded by the glitter of his aristocratic hosts. Thus was he persuaded to think that a monarch is necessary for stable government. His book on the American constitution revealed his political innocence—or should I call it stupidity! And so he was wooed by stealth monarchists. I blame him, though, for believing his countrymen were favorable to monarchy. Thus beguiled, he abandoned his republican sentiments and became the calculating shill for a counterfeit movement. He sealed his political fate by turning his back on the light. In doing so, he led his own faction into oblivion. It is all there in the frieze.

Having studied the matter in detail then and since, I am certain when I say that there is nothing to natural law and natural right apart from Hobbes's claim that every creature in nature is at liberty to preserve himself. I condemn Locke's formulation of it because he has reduced it to mere artifice. Moral Law revealed by Reason! He never revealed it. Without proof, I can claim as a natural law whatever is in my power to enforce!

What then is the well-spring of right in society? It is in the common law, which develops organically as primitive societies develop their social institutions. Nature allows primitive societies to configure themselves. It blesses those that are well-formed and buries the rest. Adams understood these things as well as I, but it suited him to rely on Locke's concoctions rather than organization and management.

Even in defeat Mr. Adams held the power to sway the federalist vote in a way that could easily have squelched Burr's rebellion against me. I approached him as a friend and longtime colleague and implored him to do this. My appeal was entirely warranted as a matter of national interest, but he steadfastly refused. Instead, he took it as an opportunity to embarrass me. He proclaimed that no honorable man would undertake to cheat the people of their will by dealing behind their backs. "In public affairs," he said haughtily, quoting Thucydides's Funeral Oration of Pericles (which we both knew well), "we keep to the law. This is because it commands our deep respect." Because it pleased him to injure me, he went on. "We do not rely on secret weapons, but on our own courage and loyalty." I recall his every word: "What I would prefer is that you should fix your eyes every day on the greatness of Athens as she is and should fall in love with her. When you realize her greatness, then reflect that what made her great was men with a spirit of adventure, men who knew their duty, men who were ashamed to fall below a certain standard." So ended our interview and our relationship.

"Do you imagine that Nero will be the last of the tyrants?"

Adams would not have arrived at his pathetic end had he not been by nature vain, irritable, and a bad calculator of the force and probable effects of the motives which govern men. For then he would doubtless have recognized that he was nothing but an instrument discarded by Hamilton.

I became aware of Hamilton when my source reported to me in Paris the content of his lengthy oration on the floor the Constitutional Convention in June of 1787. In that speech, he revealed his monarchical leanings by arguing for life tenures for the President and the Senate. I had long known such sympathies were prevalent among the Cincinnati but had assumed Knox to be their source. (Being not in their membership, I have always remained on my guard against them.) From that moment, I had my eye on Hamilton. Indeed, though it has always been my purpose to conceal the fact, my anxiety over his influence on the fledgling republic induced me to take a counter-balancing position in the first cabinet.

For sheer magnitude, nothing could exceed my differences with Hamilton in placing a Bill of Rights in Madison's imperfect Constitution. He stated his position for all to see in No. 84 of the Federalist Papers where he offered this specious analysis: 'Bills of Rights' are not only unnecessary in the proposed Constitution but would ever be dangerous. They would contain various exceptions to powers which are not granted and, in their very account, would afford a colorable pretext to claim more than were granted . . . Why, for instance, should it be said that liberty of the press shall not be restrained, when no power is given by which restriction may be enforced?"

As you doubtlessly understand, this is the kernel of the issue. Hamilton displayed his ultimate cynicism in obstructing the Bill of Rights for he knew the government would fill with wolves like himself who would pursue every opportunity to expand their power. Where an end is prescribed, are not the means also implied? This is a mandate

490

for government by fiat. And it was for just this reason that Hamilton wanted his way forward to be clear.

I recognized this immediately, but I resolved to test him before openly engaging him. As it happened, I had to wait some time after I arrived in New York on March 21, 1790. The opportunity finally arose in early-June. I was on my way to see the President when Hamilton accosted me on the street. For half an hour he walked me back and forth in front of the President's door. In this time, he reconstructed the conflict in the legislature, described the temper of its members from the Creditor states, advised me as to the danger of a northern succession, and swore that the government would collapse unless an agreement were reached forthwith. I, having been warned by Madison and Rush as to the poisons associated the Assumption issue, saw in Hamilton's pathetic behavior my opportunity to take charge. Accordingly, I proposed that he dine with me the next day and promised to arrange for certain of his public opponents to join us. This, I suggested, would provide an opportunity in which reasonable men could consult together coolly, and with some mutual sacrifice, they might reach a union-saving compromise. Thus, I laid my trap for the crooked little man.

To my chagrin, he proved to be cleverer than I. He dominated the negotiation, which I allowed, and with my help, he came away with a deal that nearly ruined me politically. Not only did it soil my reputation among my southern friends, it reduced my influence with the President. In truth, my plan to allow Hamilton to nationalize the debt in return for putting the Capital on the banks of the Potomac has been one of my greatest political blunders. As the dimensions of this blunder became clear to me, I realized that I was dealing with a malignant genius and that the only way to clear him and his followers from the government would be by force de main. It was then that I formed my alliance with Burr. Would that I had never met either of them.

As for Burr, I shall never cease to be outraged by his betrayal. He violated our covenant and locked me in a near hopeless position, having persuaded the federalists in Congress that less injury would befall their crippled cause with him seated in the office of the Chief Executive. Indeed, I shall find ways to hound him to the end of time.

These conflicts and personalities are all illustrated in the memorial

I have created in honor of my final victory. Since I no longer reside at my monument to liberty, feel free to share the details I have provided here with my countrymen.

One more point before I stop: I have written many constitutions. The last one, which is here below, has never been made public. I wrote it for Mr. Burr, who at that time I admired. Indeed, it was my intention for him to lead an expedition in the West.

The political situation deteriorating as it was in Washington's court, all options required consideration. One solution lay in an alliance with my French connections (with whom I refused to break in spite of the Terror). They could hardly be ignored since they held on our border an endless wilderness in which there is ample room for a vigorous people to establish a more perfect state. Burr, however, declined to lead the enterprise as opportunities were opening to him for political advancement in New York. I was therefore obliged to abandon the project. When Burr defeated Clinton in the New York Senate race, I took up the novel idea of organizing a faction with him at my shoulder and defeating my adversaries in open election.

The Constitution I drafted for the aborted venture with Burr— some call it Burr's Unicorn—reflected a good deal of immature thinking in regard the social principles that were in vogue in France prior to the fall of the Monarchy. These included the rule of the majority based on universal civil and political rights and various other provisions to insure social equality and equal justice. Having now gained the supreme power, I repudiate them all. Indeed, as my thinking matured in respect to the qualities and abilities of the common people, I gradually abandoned my attachment to the idea that society can be perfected through the science of government. My focus now, as I said above, is to suppress the common man's periodic (and predictable) romance with tyrants.

My original optic was based on ideas shared with me by Doctor Richard Gem and others in pre-revolutionary Paris. My service in Washington's first administration taught me, however, that it is not just the laws of property that must be rewritten at the beginning of each new generation. The social contract (which I despised when we were under hereditary government, but which I now vigorously endorse to counterbalance the mongrelization that accompanies open society) must be renewed to establish rightful claims to government services. The issue is still preventing the dead hand of the past from holding that which it has no right to hold. The way to do this, I am convinced, is to require that the entire society re-organize itself every nineteen and a half years. Then tyranny will have no chance to root itself. Let free, able-bodied men re-form into a body politic and begin each new cycle with fifty acres and their debts cleared. And let women hold dominion in their homes and guard the virtue of the new society with each generational transition. The earth must always belong to the living for the dead have no right to control it.

Somerville lowered the pages and allowed his audience to see the stunned look on his face. "There you have it," he said in bewilderment. "Everything we thought we knew about Thomas Jefferson appears to be wrong... The house is gone," he sobbed, "and so it the mystique!"

———————

"Here's yours Tad," Fisher said, handing him a brown package. "And here's yours T.P..."

"It's been a pleasure," Wells assured her, stuffing the bundle into his sack.

"You got the seeds—right?" McCray asked, climbing out of the limo.

"Yea... I got them from Fred when I picked up the money."

"What are all these medallions for?" Wells wondered, peering into the box at his feet.

"Fred's preparing for his next mission..."

"Where's it gonna be this time?" Wells asked.

"We're going big time," Fisher announced.

"Hollywood!" McCray exclaimed.

"We're going to Washington," Fisher laughed. "Capitol Hill!"

"The nipple of democracy," Wells sneered.

"That's it," Fisher nodded. "Fred's planning to take over the place."

"How are you going to do that?" McCray asked.

"He's gonna make a Bible-thumping cracker from Georgia the next President."

———————

The Sheriff walked onto the lawn from the direction of the cemetery. "Ho thar!" He called to the DA.

"Where the hell have you been?" Hoagland called back angrily.

"Ah guess you ain't seen tha mess down b'low," Bailey answered, coming over to the DA.

"No," Hoagland said. "We've had our hands full up here . . ."

"Well tha road's completely gone," Bailey announced. "Got a ten-foot hole in it—clean across . . . Ain't no way ta git up here cep' on foot!"

"You're shittin' me!" the District Attorney swore.

"Ah swar!" Bailey pledged.

"Any sign of Paige?" Hoagland asked, seeking better news.

"Naw, but Troupe pulled Tilghman over by Farmington," he announced.

"What the hell 're you talkin' about?" The DA snapped. "Tilghman's right over there!"

Bailey ignored the rebuke. "An' he said a shipment o' dope's movin' in a van with 'C-o-u-n-t-r-y- D-o-g' written on its sides."

"Now you're talking," Hoagland exclaimed, slapping the Sheriff on the back. "I'll bet that's Ried! Have you got the roads blocked?"

"Yea—ah got the whole force out lookin' fer it," the Sheriff crowed.

"Good!" Hoagland cheered.

Hoagland's celebration was cut short by a voice from the shadows. "Drop your gun Sheriff," Bildner ordered, stepping out of the darkness. His Uzi was pointed at the lawman's head. "Everybody put your hands up!"

Bailey did as he was told.

"Now," Bildner said, waving his weapon at the others, "all of you get over there," he pointed to a place near the reflecting pool, "and sit down . . ."

A drum began to beat in the darkness beyond the north pavilion. Turning toward the sound, the prisoners saw a form emerge from the shadows.

Claire recognized Astor. She was wearing the black bodystocking like the one she had been wearing during their first encounter. Resting on her breast was a medallion with the skull of an ox. A shimmering gold cape hung from her shoulders and trailed on the ground behind her. On her head she wore a crown with twelve stars. Across her left shoulder was the strap for the drum she was beating. Across her right shoulder was the strap of a pouch. She marched forward solemnly toward the group seated in the lawn. On one step, she beat the drum. On the next, she reached into her pouch and dropped a handful of meal on the ground. On she came in this manner until she reached the center of the sward. She turned there and beat the drum again.

On this cue, another figure stepped out of the shadows. This was a male, also clothed in black. On his head he wore a black turban with a gold disk mounted on its face. Henry recognized the ox skull symbol—and Fred Ried! Ried held in his hand, in ceremonial formality, a long-bladed slaughter knife. As he marched forward, he chanted devoutly. *Om . . . Om . . . Om . . .* Behind him, completing the procession, sauntered Mr. Paige's prize Angus bull, Aberon of Belmont. Every step brought the massive creature to another deposit of meal, which he devoured before continuing on.

"*Om . . .*" Ried chanted as he marched past Aster, *Om . . . Om . . .* he chanted as he approached the crowd seated by the reflecting pool. He halted in front of Somerville and his companions. There he dropped the point of his sword into the ground. "*Om . . . Om . . . Om . . .*" he intoned, completing the chant. "Can you believe it?" He said, smiling at his audience, "The bull likes that!"

No one moved.

"Everybody doin' ok?" Ried asked, coming up to Somerville. "I don't reckon you'll be needin' this," he said, lifting the journal off the grass beside him.

"What the hell do you think you're doing?" Paige bellowed, rising.

Bildner stepped forward with his gun leveled at the former naval commander.

"Shhhh!" Ried signaled with his forefinger to his lips. "You'll upset the bull." He paused for a moment and thumbed through the journal. "The letter's gone . . ." he laughed, looking back at Bildner. "It's like feeding the pigeons . . . anybody seen old sourpuss?" he asked, looking around. "No, I didn't think so . . ."

Then he straightened up and tried to look serious. "The time has come," he announced, "to bring this little ceremony to a close. I want to thank each of you gremlins for the professional way that you have done your jobs. I'm speaking to you here today because each of you has done your *duty*!

Servants, well done!" he trumpeted, starting down the line. "Raymond here waved the flag so we'd all have something to shoot at. The District Attorney—and the Sheriff," he laughed and shook his head, "made the law look bad while we wrapped things up! Claire and her boyfriend got things coming together prying the secret out of the skull. Ol' Fenton Somerville here minded the temple so it would be ready for the grand finale. And let's not forget the rest of the cast," he said gazing off into the billowing smoke. "Uncle Billy started the ball rolling with his utopian scheming. Timbo made an army of new age Luddites believe that virtue is to hate material well-being. Martin Ogden fogged up the news so normal people wouldn't understand what was really happening. Professor Shoate' toppled the pillar of enlightened society. Frances Rank turned rational discourse into a symbol of oppression. Marjean made doodlin' in the darkness sound like a higher order of thinking. Gerta went along . . . None of this was easy, ya' know," Ried smiled. "And dear little Aster . . . she provided us with a terrific stage here in the heart of Jefferson Country. Thank you, Aster, sweetheart," he said, blowing her a kiss. "Roberta set it up for the final scene. Bart Paige and Suzie—bless their hearts wherever they are, kept me up on the local news. And I . . ." Ried laughed, ". . . I got all this done in time for the next show to start! Isn't that right?" he said, looking at Aster.

She beat the drum in response . . .

"In that case . . ." he said, signaling for a fanfare.

Aster beat the drum twice . . .

"I hereby declare the beginning of the Age of Aquarius! The world is now officially new again—and open for business!" As if to confirm it, the bull bellowed.

"I have just enough time," Ried continued, looking at his watch, "to tell ya' all the secret of the universe!"

No one responded.

"Chaos passes the time!" He announced.

"Rubbish," Somerville snorted.

"Oh?" Ried replied, fixing his gaze on the obstreperous curator. "We've got a troublemaker in our midst!" With that, he lifted off his turban. 'I have got just the thing for people like you," he said, reaching inside. He pulled out several fat joints and handed them to Somerville. 'Take one of these every three hours—it'll help you to loosen up. Remember! You can't see the big picture unless you expand your mind!"

Somerville took the joints and looked perplexed.

"I guess you didn't get to that *tertium datur* thing that Jefferson cooked up," Ried observed, continuing on.

No one spoke.

"Well, here's how it works," Ried explained. "The Baron was a Leibnizian, so he knew that there are an infinite number of possible worlds. But when he finally started expanding his mind, like I'm saying, he realized that if everything possible doesn't happen sometime, then God would violate the Principle of Plentitude. That would make his creation <u>imperfect</u>! See what I'm saying? If what God created was imperfect, then he wouldn't be perfect, and . . ."

"Stop!" Somerville ordered. "Leibniz said *this* is the <u>best</u> of all possible worlds!"

"Yea," Ried nodded. "He never got past the Tertium non datur part—you know, where it's either A or ~A . . ."

"What else is there?" Somerville wondered, eyeing the joints he was holding.

"The part where A or ~A *and* A and ~A."

"That's a self-contradiction," Somerville thundered.

"It's no big deal!" Ried shrugged. "There's order *and* disorder! Right! So there's a principle of order, which is the Law of the Excluded Middle. But there's also a principle of chaos. That's what the Baron discovered. Jefferson called it the Paradox of the Middle Term, but the Baron always referred to it as Jefferson's Paradox!"

"What's that again?" the scholar asked skeptically.

"When people like *you* apply the Law of the Excluded Middle," Ried continued, "there's order and light. When people like *me* apply the Paradox of the Middle Term, there's disorder and darkness. See how it works?"

"That's nonsense!" The scholar objected defiantly.

"Welcome to *Tertium Datur!*" Ried laughed. "Say! Did you get to the part about the Baron's revelation?"

"No," Somerville replied.

"That explains it," Ried announced. "That's the key to the whole thing.

Now listen," he said. "As a good Leibnizian, the Baron knew that all things are possible with God. Right! One day, while he was thinking about what that meant, something prompted him to draw two lines—a short one and long one—right next to each other. All things are possible for God, he figured, so let him make these unequal lines equal. Right! Just then, something caused him to make a point next to the shorter of two lines so he could draw a third line from the point across the tops of the two unequal lines, and a fourth line from the point across the bottoms of the two unequal lines. Are you with me?

"Yes, Somerville, replied sullenly.

"Suddenly it occurred to the Baron that lines with the same number of points are the same length. Right? Then he drew a line from the point across the two unequal lines. And he drew another. And another. And lo and behold, for every point on the longer line, there was a corresponding point on the shorter line.

"When he saw that, he prostrated himself on the ground and praised the Lord for making two unequal lines equal. But when he was done, some weird impulse caused him to mark a point in a different place. And when he did, lo and behold, he found he could draw lines through the long line and not transect the short line. You see! Depending on your point of reference, the same lines are either equal or unequal! When the Baron saw that, he stuck some leaves in his cheek and started sucking. That's when the light came on—just because unequal lines are equal, it doesn't mean they aren't unequal! And even though unequal lines are unequal, that doesn't mean they're not equal! See the paradox? When it's light it's dark and when it's dark it's light! There's disorder in the order and order in the disorder! The tertium's in the datur and the tertium's *not* in the datur. That's the kind of world God made!" Ried announced with a triumphant smile.

"What purpose is chaos if the world is a string of infinite possibilities?" Somerville demanded, renewing his objection.

"Imagine what it would be like," Ried observed reflectively, "having to watch an endless string of grade-B movies without a reject button . . ."

Just then Aster beat the drum.

"Right!" Ried nodded, checking his watch. "Now it's time . . ." he said, pulling the sword out of the ground and turning toward the bull, "to sacrifice the bull."

"Keep your hands off my bull!" Paige roared, leaping up and charging toward Ried.

As he did, Bildner raised his gun and fired.

"Daddy," Aster screamed as she watched her father stumble and fall.

Then there was click somewhere in the darkness.

The assassin instinctively turned toward the sound.

"Over here," a voice said.

Bildner sprayed the area with a burst of fire. As he did, a bullet slammed into the disk that hung from his neck. He ripped off several shots, but these were into the ground. His body then crumpled on top of them and was still.

Delilah Wanamaker stepped forward, her Stoner M63 trained on Ried. Prout followed her out of the darkness and hobbled up beside her. "The party's over, Ried," he said. "Put the sword down."

As he spoke, a gust of wind swept across the mountain top and filled the plain with smoke. Through the dense shroud came the bull's terrified bellowing.

"Run for your lives!" a voice commanded through the thickening chaos. "The bull's loose!"

The freed captives groped frantically for safety as the wind thundered about them. The sense of impending disaster increased with every breath. Somewhere out of the dim came a high-pitched whine and the breathless beating of the helicopter's whirling rotor. There was no time to consider its significance in the chaos. Survival was the only thing that mattered.

As the fearful beating faded into silence, the wind subsided. Now there was no panic, only an anxious band of survivors peering from their shelters and wondering what had happened, wondering anxiously whether the end had come or gone. As they watched, the smoke dispersed, and the place became orderly again. Only now, where the helicopter had been, there was a golden disc.

Hoagland was the first to move, being drawn like a magnet to the spot. "What the hell is this?" The District Attorney swore, snatching the medallion off the grass.

As Hoagland inspected the strange object, Somerville asked an even more pressing question. "Is he . . . dead?" he asked, bending over and looking into Mr. Paige's chiseled face.

"Daddy!" Aster cried, dropping the drum and rushing to her father's side.

"Hell no! I'm not dead!" Paige snapped, squinting at the startled curator. "I've got too much to do to die! Don't worry, Sweetie Pie," he said, taking his daughter's hand. "Daddy's not going to leave you." Then he craned around. "What happened to the bull?"

"He's over there," Somerville reported, pointing to the meal pouch next to Ried's abandoned sword.

"Good!" Paige nodded, settling back. "As least he made it through Ok..."

"Dr. Somerville," the DA called. "Is there a phone that works somewhere on this infernal mountain?"

"There's one in the gift shop," the curator answered with a forlorn sigh.

"Sheriff, get Somerville to show you where that phone is and have a medivac chopper dispatched on the double... Then find somebody to patch that crater. We've got work to do!"

"What about my chopper?" The pilot demanded.

"Scramble the Air National Guard!" He ordered. "I'll get that son-of-a-bitch if it's the last thing I do!"

"Come on Mr. Somerville," the Sheriff said, patting him on the back. "Les' go fine that phone..."

"Woe and alack!" The curator wailed hopelessly. "What am I going to do?"

"Sompin alles turns up," the Sheriff said, ignoring the other man's anguish.

"You think you can catch him?" Paige asked, peering up at Hoagland.

"He can't beat the system," the DA said as he scrutinized Ried's medallion.

"Good," Paige nodded, his mind moving on to the next issue. "Miss Fox," he called.

"Yes," Claire answered, appearing at his side.

"I think Fenton's going to need your help..."

"Don't you worry," she said, resting her hand on his arm. "We're all going to rally 'round the flag!"

Paige squeezed her hand. "I knew I could count on you," he said.

"And Professor Wanamaker!" he added, looking up at the gun-toting legal scholar.

"I'll tell you what concerns me," the DA continued. "...all that gobble-de-gook about the light and the dark—looks like we've got some kind of cult thing going on here!"

"Yea..." Paige said, gritting his teeth. "There's no telling what Ried'll do if we don't stop him!"

"What about this thing?" Hoagland asked again, contemplating the skull. "Ya suppose it has some special meaning?"

The tattered marine limped forward and scrutinized the object in the DA's hand. "You know what Wittgenstein said," Prout volunteered philosophically.

"What's that?" the DA snapped.

"Was jenseits der Grenze liegt, wird einfact Unsinn sein."

"What the hell 're you talking about," the DA swore disgustedly as he shoved the medal into his pocket.

"I'll tell you what it means," Henry said, staring blankly into the smoldering center of Jefferson's universe.

"Ok," the DA said. "What?"

"Tertium Datur..."